An Armada Three-i

*Three Great
Chalet School Stories*

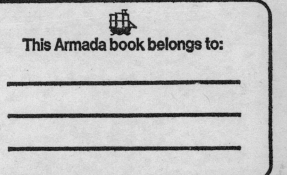

...da *Chalet School Three-in-One* was
...shed in the U.K. in Armada in
...Fontana Paperbacks,
... ames's Place, London SW1A 1PS.

Published pursuant to agreement with
W. & R. Chambers Ltd., London and
Edinburgh.

Printed in Great Britain by
Love & Malcomson Ltd., Brighton Road,
Redhill, Surrey.

CONDITIONS OF SALE:
This book is sold subject to the condition that
it shall not, by way of trade or otherwise, be lent,
re-sold, hired out or otherwise circulated without
the publisher's prior consent in any form of
binding or cover other than that in which it is
published and without a similar condition
including this condition being imposed on the
subsequent purchaser.

The Head Girl of the Chalet School
Jo Returns to the Chalet School
Carola Storms the Chalet School

Elinor M. Brent-Dyer

Chalet School Stories in Armada

The School at the Chalet
Jo of the Chalet School
The Princess of the Chalet School
The Head Girl of the Chalet School
Rivals of the Chalet School
Eustacia Goes to the Chalet School
The Chalet School and Jo
The Chalet Girls in Camp
Exploits of the Chalet Girls
The Chalet School and the Lintons
A Rebel at the Chalet School
The New House at the Chalet School
Jo Returns to the Chalet School
The New Chalet School
The Chalet School in Exile
Three Go to the Chalet School
The Chalet School and the Island
Peggy of the Chalet School
Carola Storms the Chalet School
The Wrong Chalet School
Shocks for the Chalet School
The Chalet School and Barbara
Mary-Lou at the Chalet School
A Genius at the Chalet School
Chalet School Fête
A Problem for the Chalet School
The New Mistress at the Chalet School
Excitements at the Chalet School
The Coming of Age of the Chalet School
The Chalet School and Richenda

1
The Head Girl of the Chalet School

The Head Girl of the Chalet School was first published in the U.K. in a single volume in hardback in 1928 by W. & R. Chambers Ltd., London and Edinburgh. This revised edition was first published in Armada in 1970 by Fontana Paperbacks.

© W. & R. Chambers 1928.

CHAPTER I

THE COMING TERM

TWO girls were walking down Palmerston Road, Portsmouth, with a graceful swing which drew the eyes of the passers-by to them. The elder of the two, slender and pretty, with an unusual amount of brown curling hair tied loosely back from a vivid face, was holding forth to the other, a much smaller girl, with black eyes shining out of a pale pointed face, which looked the paler for the straight black hair cut round it, page's fashion.

"It's going to be difficult, you see, Joey," said the older girl as they paused before a café, where they evidently expected to meet someone. "If only Madame hadn't gone and got married this year!" she added.

Joey pulled her brown cap more firmly on to her head before she replied. "I think you are a bit selfish about that, Grizel," she said mildly. "After all, she did wait a whole year before she did it, and it's worse for Robin and me than for you."

"I do wish Bette had stayed on till the end of the year," said Grizel! "After all, she's only just eighteen, and heaps of girls go to school long after that. Why, the Head of the High was nearly nineteen!"

"Yes; and now she's at Oxford," said Joey. "Bette is only going to be at home. I'm sorry if you feel like that about it, old thing, but it can't be helped! — And there's Maynie and the Robin *at last*!"

The two girls turned to look down the road to where a tall, graceful girl of twenty-two or three was coming along, holding the hand of a small girl of eight, whose lovely little face was lifted to her companion's as she talked rapidly and eagerly, with gesticulations which, in Robin Humphries, were not surprising, as she was half Polish.

As they saw the two girls awaiting them, the pair hurried their steps, and presently they were all seated round a table, chattering away, while Miss Maynard, who was maths mistress at the Chalet School to which they belonged, gave her orders to the waitress.

"Didn't know you were coming, Robin," said Joey, as she helped the small girl to unfasten her coat and hang up her hat. "Thought you were going to stay with Mrs. Maynard this morning."

"It was such a fine day," said the mistress, "that I thought she might as well come. She loves Portsmouth—don't you, *mein Vöglein*? And we go back to-morrow."

"Isn't it joyous?" said Joey eagerly. "I love England, of course; but the Tyrol is home now, and I'm dying to see my sister again! How she *could* be so stupid as to get mumps at Christmas is more than I can think! It's messed up her holidays, anyway!"

"Poor Tante Marguérite!" said the Robin pensively. "Will she be quite well now, Joey? Shall we go to see her when we get home?"

"Sure of it," said Joey. "Shouldn't wonder if she wasn't at Innsbruck waiting to welcome us."

"I wish Madame was back at the chalet!" sighed Grizel, her mind reverting to her own particular problems once more. "It won't be easy this term—Easter term never is!"

"But you've been games prefect long enough to be able to carry responsibility," said Miss Maynard bracingly. "Why are you so upset about being head girl?"

"Games give you a certain hold," explained Grizel. "Gertrud will do well as games pre, she'd have done just as well as head girl. I wish I hadn't been chosen. Of course, I shall do my best, Miss Maynard; but it *won't* be easy."

"Nothing worth while ever is," replied the mistress. Then she changed the conversation. It was true that the Robin never repeated things; still, it was better that she should not hear Grizel's woes voiced quite as plainly as this. Therefore Miss Maynard turned to Joey and asked her some question about the books she had come to buy.

"Got three of them," replied the girl. "The Francis Thompson was five bob, but worth it! The Green's history was five too. The other thing was sixpence."

"I can't understand *how* you can read those awful goody-good books," interposed Grizel. "It isn't you a bit, really!"

"I think they're so priceless," said Joey, with a grin. "And, anyway, they do teach you a lot of history."

"But they're so biased," objected Grizel. "The one you lent me seemed to be fairly reeking with hate for the English and George III and his ministers. It's so silly, too, when it all happened more than a hundred years ago."

"Well, they had a lot to put up with," said Joey broadmindedly. "After all, Grenville and his idiotic Stamp Act was enough to drive anyone mad, especially when they hadn't a chance of saying anything one way or another. And Miss Annersley says that it was a very good thing for us that the American colonies *did* break away. So it was all for the best."

Grizel shrugged her shoulders. She was not historically inclined, and, to her way of thinking, it didn't really matter whether the Americans had remained part of the empire, or whether they broke away from it. She simply could not understand Joey Bettany's interest in people long since dead and gone. They finished their lunch with an amiable discussion of books for the school library, in which even the Robin joined, for she read a good deal for her eight years, and had her own views on the subject of stories.

"We've got plenty to take with us," said Miss Maynard at last. "That case will be full now; and I won't have any more to look after than I can help. Your three must go in your suitcase, Jo. As it is, we shall have a good deal of luggage."

"That's the only bother about bringing books from England," said Grizel. "I've got one to put in *my* case too."

"Well, we can't help it," said Jo philosophically. "After all, we can't expect to get books there in English—at least, not all the books we want.—Yes, thank you, Miss Maynard, I've quite finished. Shall we get ready to go now?"

"Yes, I think so. Fasten up your coat collars, and collect your possessions, girls.—Jo, see to the Robin.—I want to go to the china shop to get one or two things, so we must hurry, as we ought to catch the early train if we possibly can. I don't like motoring through the forest after dark in this weather."

Miss Maynard made all the haste she could, and an hour later saw them in the train for Southampton, the girls glancing at their books while the mistress made up her accounts and the Robin peered out at the fast falling dusk. "Me, I do not like the English winter," she announced suddenly.

"Don't you, darling?" asked Miss Maynard absently, as she tried to balance her account. "Never mind; we'll soon be back at the Tiern See. You like winter there.—Girls, we are nearly at Southampton; close your books and pack up, or we may miss the train. We shall have a rush as it is."

They got ready once more, and in the scurry for the little local train that took them to Lyndhurst, they forgot what they had been talking about. Once in the Lyndhurst train, they began discussing school once more, for all of them loved their school in the lovely, picturesque Tyrol.

It had been run by Joey Bettany's sister, Madge, until the previous summer, when she had married Dr James Russell, head of the big new sanatorium on an alp high up the Sonnenscheinspitze, a mountain on the opposite side of the lake. The present head was Mademoiselle Lapâttre, who had been joint-head with Miss Bettany until her marriage. Miss Maynard was senior and mathematical mistress, and four other English girls formed the rest of the resident staff. An excellent matron ran the domestic side of the school, and Herr Anserl from Spärtz, the little market-town at the foot of the mountains where the Tiern See lies, three thousand feet above sea-level, came twice a week to give piano-lessons to the most promising of the girls. Singing was taught by Mr Denny, who was obliged for the sake of his health to remain in the district, and whom the girls privately thought rather mad. Masters came from Innsbruck for the violin, cello, and harp; and young Mrs Russell had, for the last term, come down from the Sonnalpe twice a week to give lessons in English literature. This term, however, the state of the roads would make such a thing an impossibility. When March should come, bringing with it the rapid thaw, the paths would be well-night impassable on the lake side of the mountain, and Dr Jem, as all the girls called him, had vetoed the idea for that term, at any rate. Consequently, when Miss Maynard had informed her ex-head that she intended to spend the Christmas holidays at home, and had begged leave to take Joey and the Robin with her that they might have a really English Christmas, Mrs Russell had agreed. It suited her better, for her husband had been summoned to a medical conference at Vienna for the week between Christmas and New Year, and she naturally wanted to go with him. So Joey and Robin had come to England, and Grizel Cochrane had come with them to spend her Christmas at her own home in Devonshire. A week ago she had joined the others in the New Forest, and was to travel back with them to Austria. This would be her last year at the Chalet School, for she would be eighteen in May, and then she was to go to Florence to study music in earnest under one of the best masters there.

It cannot be said that Grizel looked forward to her future with much enjoyment. She was not really musical, though hours of practice rigorously enforced by her stepmother while she had been in England, and then carried on under Herr Anserl in Briesau, had made her a brilliant instrumentalist. What was to happen after Florence no one seemed to know—Grizel and her step-mother were not in sympathy with each other, and her father was too much immersed in his profession—he was a barrister with a wide practice—to care overmuch about the daughter he had seen comparatively rarely. Since she was ten, Grizel had been very much a lonely child, and to her the Chalet School was the only real home she had ever known.

It was home to Joey Bettany too, though she knew that her sister and brother-in-law wanted her to feel that the pretty chalet outside the Sonnalpe stood for that now. She liked Jem very well, and she adored her sister, but Briesau, where she knew everyone and everyone knew her, was far dearer to her than the Sonnalpe with the big sanatorium and its sad community of people who had come there in search of health.

As for the Robin, she had been left motherless two years before this story opens, and had been sent to the school while her father was in Russia on business. The business had long since been finished, and Captain Humphries was secretary to Dr Jem. The little girl was a frail little creature, so, since she was happy at school, it was deemed better to keep her there, away from the sorrow of the Sonnalpe except at holiday times, when she and Joey would generally be at the chalet, where her father lived with the doctor, "Uncle Jem," and his pretty wife.

So for all the girls, and also for Miss Maynard, whose

eldest brother was assistant at the Sonnalpe, Briesau and the Chalet School meant far more than school ordinarily does. They had all enjoyed their stay in England, but they were all very glad to be returning to Austria, and they talked about it as they were trundled along to Lyndhurst, where the Maynards' car would meet them, and whirl them through the forest for seven miles to Pretty Maids, the Maynards' big house.

"What I think is so topping," said Jo, as she accepted a lump of toffee from the sticky packet Grizel was offering her, "is the idea of seeing Basle. We've only rushed through in the train before, and I *do* like seeing new places. It's got heaps of history, too. All sorts of jolly interesting things happened there, and I'm simply yearning to see it!"

"You and history!" jeered Grizel, who was mathematically inclined, and regarded her history lessons as evils to be avoided.

"It's so jolly interesting! I like to know what people did and how they lived, and so on. It's heaps better than horrid old geometry and algebra, anyway!" retortetd Joey, whose views on mathematics were revolutionary in the extreme.

At this point Miss Maynard thought it best to interfere. Jo and Grizel were ordinarily good friends, but both had fiery tempers, and neither fully understood the other, so that battles between them were apt to be fierce if short-lived.

"There is plenty to see in Basle," she said. "I know Robin will love the Zoo—won't you, baby? And there is a very interesting museum and a good picture gallery."

"Topping!" approved Jo. "I love animals, and pictures are awfully interesting. What's in the museum, Maynie?"

Out of term, the girls were allowed to use this nickname of a popular mistress since they had stayed at her home more than once, and were very welcome visitors there.

"A good part of it is devoted to natural history," said Miss Maynard.

"Butterflies and things?" said Grizel.

"I suppose so. Then there is the picture gallery with some very famous pictures—one or two by Hans Holbein the Younger, I believe. There is a special history museum in the Barfüsser Kirche, which is famous. You will like the armoury collection and the treasury, I know, even if the historical side of them doesn't interest you. And you will want to see Father Rhine, of course."

"I love the Rhine, ever since I read *The First Violin*," agreed Grizel. "Of course, I'd rather see it at Cologne with the Bridge of Boats. Shall we have time to go to Schaffhausen to see the Falls?"

Miss Maynard shook her head. "I'm afraid not, Grizel. We are spending one day in Paris, and three in Basle, and Schaffhausen is a good four hours or so from Basle. You'll have to wait for that till the summer. Then, if we do as we have planned, I will take you there for a few days on our way to Cologne and the Rhine cities."

"But Joey and Robin won't be with us," objected Grizel. "I know it's awfully decent of you to say you'll take me to the Rhine cities before I go to Florence, but Jo is going to spend the summer hols with Elisaveta in Belsornia, and the Robin is to go to Paris with the Lecoutiers. Even Juliet won't be there, as she is going to the Sonnalpe to be with Madame." She referred to Mrs Russell's ward, Juliet Carrick, who was at present at London University, reading for a mathematical degree.

"I'm sorry, Grizel," said Miss Maynard. "If we could do it, I should say 'yes' at once. But there will be a good deal to get through before term begins, and we shall have none too much time as it is. Later on we may be able to arrange for the four of you to go together."

Grizel gave up worrying, and as they were nearing Lyndhurst, they all gathered up their parcels and prepared to leave the train. But she had by no means given up the idea as yet. That was not Grizel Cochrane's way. It had led to trouble in the past, and was to do so again before she learned her lesson.

CHAPTER II

BASLE

"NOW, have we got everything? Four cases—two bundles of rugs—your attaché cases—Grizel's music case—the picnic basket? Is that all? Then come along, girls, or we shall miss the train, and I don't want to do *that*!—Come, Robin! Keep close to me."

Followed closely by the Robin and at a little distance by Grizel, Joey, and a burdened porter, Miss Maynard walked down the long platform of the Gare de l'Est, where the Paris-Wien express was standing, and quickly found the carriage reserved for them. It was nearly nine at night, and they would reach Basle round about five the next morning; but all four were accustomed travellers, and Miss Maynard much preferred to do the travelling at night when the girls would be sleeping, than through the day, when active Grizel and Robin would find the time pass slowly. Joey was less of a trial on long train journeys, for she was always happy as long as she had a book.

The mistress quickly made a nest for the Robin in one corner with rugs and an air-pillow, pulled off the sturdy little boots, and tucked her up comfortably. Tired from a long day in Paris, she fell asleep almost at once, heedless of the bright lights, the hoarse shouts of the busy porters. Miss Maynard then turned her attention to the girls.

Since they had been in Paris all day, and had been talking French, which came as naturally to them as their own tongue—all four were trilingual as a result of being in a school where English, French, and German were all spoken freely—she fell into French in bidding them prepare for the night.

Joey and Grizel did as they were told to the extent of rolling themselves in rugs, and curling up on the seats which had been widened by the pulling out of a kind of underseat. Experienced travellers, they slipped off their boots, exchanged their brown velour hats for tams, and in ten minutes were ready. The mistress herself did not attempt her preparations yet. She knew that she would read for an hour or two as soon as they got off. The children were different, and all were accustomed to early hours.

Then silence settled down over them all, and Miss Maynard presently fell asleep till a quarter to five when an attendant came along announcing that they were nearly into Basle, and would arrive there in ten minutes' time. Moving as quietly as she could, Miss Maynard woke up Joey and Grizel, and bade them get ready to leave the train. The Robin she left. The elder girls quickly and deftly put their things together, rolling up rugs, and strapping them with a neatness and precision which told of experience in journeys.

At this point the train slackened speed, and ran into the deserted station, where only the flaring lights and a few sleepy-eyed porters spoke of the life that thronged it through the day. Miss Maynard leaned out of the window, and summoned one to come and get their things, while she herself picked up the Robin, who slept on serenely through it all, and Joey and Grizel took their rugs.

Soon they were on their way to their pension, where a drowsy night-porter let them in. They all went straight to bed, and slept till noon.

* * * *

Joey was the first to wake. She sat up in bed, wide awake in a moment. Then she looked across to where Grizel lay, still fast asleep in the bed in the corner.

She looked very pretty as she lay there, her cheeks rose-flushed with sleep, and her long brown curls scattered over the pillow. But æsthetic sights were not in Miss Bettany's mind at the moment. Moving quietly, she lifted her pillow, stood up in bed to get a surer aim, and then hurled it well on to Grizel's face.

That young lady sat up with a muffled howl, wildly clearing curls and sleep-mists out of her eyes while the pillow fell to the floor. "Joey Bettany! You little brute! And I was having such a gorgeous dream!"

"Time you were beyond dreams, my dear!' retorted Joey, curling herself up on the bed, and hauling the *plameau* round her shoulders. "It's midday! Nearly time for *Mittagessen*! Get up, you lazy object!"

"Lazy object yourself!" said Grizel indignantly. "You've only just wakened yourself! I know you, Jo Bettany! And if you hurl any more things at me I'll yell the house down.—I say! there's someone coming—chambermaid or something! Cave!"

Joey made a wild dive, and when the round-cheeked Gretchen came in bearing rolls and honey and coffee on a tray for the two, she found them both lying very properly in bed, though the younger fräulein did not seem to have any pillow, and the other one had two!

When she had gone, Joey sat up, and demanded her pillow back again.

"No fear!" retorted Grizel. "You chucked it at me

most brutally, so now you may do without! It's no good coming and scrapping for it, for you'll only upset the coffee if you do, and then there'll be a row!—Stop it, Joey! You'll have the tray all over the bed if you go on like this!"

"Give me my pillow, then!" retorted Jo, hauling away at it with such goodwill that she finally succeeded in getting it out from under Grizel's shoulders, nearly upsetting the tray and its contents as she did so. With a cry of triumph she darted back to her own bed and *Frühstück*.

"Pig!" said Grizel indignantly. "You *are* a little horror, Joey!"

"Hurry up and get on," was the only answer Joey vouchsafed as she devoured her rolls and honey, and drank the bowl of milky coffee which she appreciated far more than the tea she had in England.

Seeing nothing else to do, Grizel did as Joey suggested, and presently they were dressed in their pretty frocks, so that when Miss Maynard came, as she imagined, to waken them, they were standing at the window, looking out at the quiet street below, ready dressed. They turned as she entered.

"*Grüss Got*," said Joey, with the charming Tyrolean greeting which she loved so. "Oh, Maynie! Just look at those darling dogs!'

Miss Maynard laughed as she crossed the room, and looked out of the window at the sight she had expected to see—a low-wheeled cart with big milk-can slung across it, and drawn by two big dogs, who were padding sedately along as if they knew how important was their charge. The whole equipage was guarded by a small boy of about ten, who bore a long whip, which he cracked continually to encourage his steeds, not that they took any notice of either it or him.

"Jo! You baby!" laughed Miss Maynard. "You must have seen the same thing dozens of times before this! They do it in practically every European country! I'm sure you saw it when you were in Munich!"

"Yes; I know," agreed Joey. "But those are such *dear* dogs—nearly as nice as my Rufus!"

"They aren't the same breed," said Grizel critically. "Rufus is a St Bernard, and I don't know what you would call those!"

"Just plain dog, I should think," said Miss Maynard as she turned from the window. "Well, I came to call you two; but as you are ready, I will go back to Robin. *Mittagessen* is at one, but I didn't think we should want any so soon after *Früstück*. What do you say to going out now? We can get *Kaffee* at a *pâtisserie*, and you can make up for it at our evening meal. Do you agree?"

"Oh, rather!" cried Jo. "Where are we going first? I want to see that history museum you told us about. Can we go there?"

"If you like. I believe the Robin is longing for the Zoo. What would you like, Grizel?"

"I'd like to look at the shops and the town," said Grizel.

"Well, we can't do everything," said Miss Maynard, with a little inward smile for the difference between the two girls shown in their replies to her question. "We might look at the shops, and also see the Barfüsser Kirche to-day, if you like. Then to-morrow we must give the Robin her turn, and go to the Zoo. In the afternoon I should like to see the museum in the Augustinergasse—that's where the picture gallery is, Grizel. Then on Thursday we might explore the town, and see some of the old university buildings. Basle is one of the oldest university towns in Europe, you know, and any number of famous men came here during the Renaissance. Does that programme meet with your approval?"

"Yes, rather," said Joey emphatically.

But Grizel shook her head. "I do so want to go to Schaffhausen and see the Falls. Couldn't we possibly?"

"No, Grizel," said Miss Maynard. "I've already said we can't. In any case, this is not the weather to go and see waterfalls. I have told you I will take you in the summer; please let that be sufficient."

"What on earth makes you so mad on the Rhine Falls, Grizel?" Joey asked curiously when Miss Maynard had gone off to help the Robin to dress. "You are an ass to fuss like this. Maynie won't go, and you ought to know it by this time. She always means what she says."

But Grizel was a determined young lady, and when she took an idea into her head it required a good deal of dislodging. She had by no means put Schaffhausen out of her thoughts, as Joey was to find later on. Now, she merely requested the younger girl not to bother, and began to get into her hat and coat.

It was a cold day, colder than it had been in Portsmouth, but it was a dry, bracing cold, and as they were warmly wrapped up, they looked forward to their walk. At Briesau it had to be very bad weather for the girls to be kept indoors. So Joey and Grizel put on stout boots, and tied big scarves across their chests, and turned up the fur collars on their coats, and when they had wriggled into their warm woollen mitts, felt ready for anything. Miss Maynard and the Robin, similarly attired, met them at their door, and they all trooped downstairs, laughing and chattering.

The first thing to do was to get to the shops, for Grizel was anxious to see them and to buy some ribbons to send to "Cooky" in her far-away Devonshire home. Cooky had always been a great ally of hers, and Grizel remembered many a kindness the big sonsy woman had shown her, and always did her best to repay. Ribbon from Basle to trim her new spring hat would be greatly appreciated. It was a good point in a character that was inclined to be hard, and the Chalet School people had always encouraged it. The discipline Grizel had undergone at the hands of her step-mother for four and a half years had been very bad for the girl. As a consequence of it, she fought for her own hand first, and was very selfish, only trying to get what *she* wanted, without much regard for other people. It was, as Mrs Russell had said at the end of the previous term, when she was discussing the point with Mademoiselle, a big experiment putting Grizel into the position as head girl. "She will either do magnificently—or she will fail badly," she had said. "But, Elise, I feel sure that Grizel will try to make a success of it. It may make all the difference to her in after life. And we have only these two last terms to influence her. After that she goes to Florence, and it is out of our hands."

Mademoiselle had agreed, and so they had sent for Grizel, and had informed her of their decision. As has been seen, she had been disturbed by it. She knew, for Mrs Russell had told her, that to be successful she must set the school first; herself last. Grizel hated to do anything and fail; but she did not like the sound of that "School first; self last." It looked as if things would not be too comfortable. She had tried to get out of it; had pointed out that Gertrud Steinbrücke was her age, and as old a Chaletian as she was; that she was Captain of the Games, and had her music to work at. It had all been of no avail.

"I want you to take it, and to do your best with it, Grizel," Mrs Russell had said, holding the girl's grey eyes with her own steady gaze as she spoke. "Come, dear! You say you have been happy here. It isn't asking much to ask you to give us your best work for the last two terms you will spend with us. I know you will come back to see us, Grizel, but it's not the same.

And, drawn to it by the appeal in those deep brown eyes fronting her, Grizel had agreed. But she had made a proviso to herself. She would accept, and would do her level best. School should come first all the time, and self should have a poor chance, so far as she could manage it; *but*—she would have her own way during the holidays.

They went gaily down the street. It was a glorious day for a walk, sharp and crisp, with a snap of frost in the air and frozen snow on the pavements crunching under their tread. The Robin danced along, clinging to Joey's hand, while Grizel herself walked demurely by the side of Miss Maynard, chattering to her in German. She had been far slower than Jo to pick up languages, but they had come at last through ceaseless practice. As for Jo, English, French, or German, it was all one to her. She knew a certain amount of Italian too, and had a slender portion of Russian, a fact which had proved of great use to her during the summer term, and which had been the means of rescuing her friend, Elisaveta, Crown Princess of Belsornia, from the hands of her father's cousin, a half-mad man, who had tried to kidnap and hold her as a hostage against her father, now King of Belsornia, and her grandfather, who had been the reigning king at that time. Elisaveta was now Crown Princess, and too important a personage to finish her education in any school, so she had had to go back to governesses in Belsornia. But the friendship between her and Jo was not likely to die, even though they could not meet, and Joey got letters every week from "Your loving Veta."

As in Portsmouth, people turned to look at them. All four were so graceful, moving with a free, easy grace that had its roots in constant practice of the old English folk-dances. Miss Maynard smiled as she noted how elderly men looked at the Robin with her almost angelic loveliness, and how they smiled to receive one of her fearless beams at them.

In the shops she still attracted attention, and while Grizel was debating whether Cooky would like vivid purple or lurid green for her hat, the assistants were murmuring among themselves about "*das Engelkind.*" The marvel was that the child was not made conceited by all the petting she received. It never seemed to affect her in the least, however.

When, finally, Grizel had fixed on a green ribbon, which was bright enough to please Cooky, and yet did not scream at one, they went out and visited the toy-shops, where the baby bought two little wooden bears, one for Inga Eriksen, and the other for Amy Stevens, these two people being her greatest friends. "And Tante Marguérite," she pleaded. "I have two francs left. What can I buy for Tante Marguérite?"

It was while Miss Maynard was helping her to choose a little wooden chalet that Grizel drew Jo to one side and said, "Joey, are you game for a rag?"

"Rather; what is it?" demanded Jo.

"You know I want to go to Schaffhausen and see the Rhine there? Well, let's go to-morrow when Maynie takes the Robin to the Zoo. We don't want to see it—there's only chamois and bears and things like that. We'll leave a note saying where we've gone, and slip off about eight in the morning. Then we can go there and see the Falls, and get back in the afternoon. Like the idea?"

"I think you must be mad," said Jo, staring at her. Quite mad! There'd be a fiendish row, and we'd jolly well deserve it after doing down Maynie like that when she's been so decent stopping here for three days to let us see the place! I knew you went off it sometimes, but I never thought you did it to that extent! It's one of the rottenest things I've ever heard of!"

Grizel was furious. It was bad enough to have a mere kid like Jo Bettany say such things to her; but what hurt most was the look in Joey's eyes. There was scorn there, and disgust. There was also that which reminded the elder girl of the time when she had run away in a fit of rage to climb the Tiernjock, a dangerous mountain, perilling both her own life and Joey's in the attempt. Jo had followed her to fetch her back, and the pair had been caught in a mist on the verge of a dangerous precipice, where they had had to wait till help came. Jo had not meant to remind the elder girl of this, but Grizel remembered all the same. It added to her fury, and she flung herself away with a low "Little *prig!*" which brought the angry colour to Jo's face. Happily, before anything further could happen, the Robin appealed to them for assistance in making up her mind which of two chalet models she should choose, and by the time this knotty point was settled both looked more or less normal again. They were far enough from feeling it though.

From the shops they went to the Barfüsser Kirche, a church dating from the fourteenth century, but now used as the historical museum. There the Lallenkönig attracted the Robin, and she insisted on standing to watch the head stick out its tongue and roll its eyes at her, they could scarcely get her away. However, Miss Maynard finally got them to the great collection of arms, where Joey revelled to her heart's content in the curious weapons of the ages, weaving stories about them in her head, while Grizel wandered round, interested in the growth and development of warfare. From the armoury they went to the series of rooms intended to show the development in the furnishing and arranging of rooms from the fifteenth century onwards, and here Jo was in her element indeed. She invented stories for the Robin about the people who had lived in the different rooms, and gave them the most astonishing adventures. The Robin was entranced. Miss Maynard had to cut them short, or they would never have seen the rest of the building.

The Treasury, containing relics of the days when Basle had been one of the foremost of the Catholic sees, didn't interest them half so much, though Joey looked at the beautiful altar vessels with awe, and was specially pleased with the reminders of Erasmus, the great Renaissance scholar, who became the friend of Sir Thomas More, one of her heroes. She was rather disappointed to find no relics of her favourite Napoleon, but the rooms containing the musical instruments, quaint old citherns and citoles, lutes and harps, and the beautiful specimens of stained glass delighted her.

"Only think," said Jo, pausing before one beautiful example of a cithern; "Laura may have played to Petrarca on that!"

"What on earth do you know about Laura and

Petrarca?" demanded Miss Maynard in astonishment.

"Oh, only that they were lovers, and he wrote sonnets to her, and invented a type of sonnet," returned Jo.

After that Miss Maynard decreed that it was time for *Kaffee*, and hustled them all out and to a *pâtisserie*, where they had milky coffee and delicious cakes all honey and nuts and cream. If Grizel was a little quiet, no one noticed it, and the other two made up for her silence. They had to hurry back to the pension in the end, for it was getting late, and *Abendessen* was at seven. The Robin had rolls and butter and milk in bed, but the others went down and made a good meal, after which they went out for a walk along the lighted streets, where sleighs were dashing along the snowy roads, and the night was gay with the jangling of sleigh-bells.

When they came in it was after nine, so Miss Maynard decreed that they should all go to bed. She saw the other two to their room, made sure they had everything they wanted, and then left them, bidding Grizel see that the light was switched off at ten.

As soon as she had gone, Joey dropped the frock she had just taken off on to a chair, and turned to Grizel. "Now," she said.

CHAPTER III

THE FALLS OF RHINE

GRIZEL turned sharply at the word, and looked at the other girl. "What do you mean?" she asked coldly.

"I'm going to have it out with you—that's all!" Joey sat down on the edge of her bed and looked Grizel squarely in the face.

'Have what out? And I do wish, Jo, you would try to remember, occasionally, that I am nearly three years older than you are. You speak sometimes as if you thought I were as old as—as—the Robin."

"I don't think you're as old, sometimes," retorted Joey. "You don't behave like it."

'That will do! Even if we do go away together for

holidays, that's no reason why you should cheek me like this. I'm head girl, remember!"

"I wish *you* would try to remember it!" said Joey fervently. Then her tone changed. "Grizel, don't go to Schaffhausen! It isn't playing the game by Maynie! If you want us with you, I'll ask if I can go in the summer before I go to Belsornia to Elisaveta." But her first words had done the mischief, and even this sacrifice had no effect on Grizel, who could be thoroughly wrong-headed on occasion. She now looked at the younger girl with an expression of scorn, and said, "Mind your own business!"

"But, Grizel——" began Jo.

"That will do! I'm not going to be spoken to like that by a mere junior. If you can't talk about anything else, you'd better be silent. Anyway, I don't want to talk to you. You're a bit swelled-headed, Jo. I suppose it's because Madame is your sister. It's a pity, because you *could* be quite a nice child, if it weren't for that."

Jo went white with anger at this unpleasant speech, but she said nothing. She got up from the bed, and went on with her undressing. Grizel followed her example, and they went to bed in utter silence. Joey had a hot temper, and Grizel had said an unforgivable thing just now. Things were at a deadlock.

Grizel soon fell asleep, for she was not imaginative, and, angry as she was, her emotions were little likely to disturb her rest. Joey, sensitive and temperamental, tossed about restlessly in her bed for two hours or more before she finally dropped off.

Grizel woke up at six o'clock in the morning, and, as soon as she was sufficiently wide awake to realise what had occurred the night before, slipped out of bed, and, with a cautious glance at the bed in the opposite corner, switched on the little reading-lamp over her own. Then she dressed herself swiftly and warmly, putting on her thickest things. She had determined to get to the Falls of Rhine somehow, and knew that to do so she must make an early start. She wasn't sure how far Joey's sense of duty might carry her, either. That young lady scorned to tell tales, but no one knew better than Grizel that this was a case when she might rightfully feel that she was reporting, and not "sneaking."

Jo slept on soundly, and never stirred when the door

opened and her companion slipped out and shut it carefully after her. She slept on till long after her usual time for waking, and, indeed, until Miss Maynard, wondering at the unusual quiet in their room, came along to see that they were all right.

In the meantime Grizel, her head held very high, ordered hot coffee and rolls for herself at the bureau, and consumed them when they came in as airy a fashion as if she were not doing things she knew very well to be wrong. To the *Kellnerin* who served her she said that she was going on to Schaffhausen by the early train, and the others would join her later. She felt pretty safe in saying that last, for she knew that Miss Maynard, at any rate, would come to seek her, and she had no intention of hiding from her once she had got her own way. She had made inquiries the night before, and had found that there was two hours between the train by which she intended travelling and the next one. By that time, as she reckoned, she would have seen all she wanted to see, and would be quite content to come home. She finished her meal, and then set off for the Bahnhof.

Basle is a very old and picturesque city, and the long streets, with their quaintly gilded and frescoed houses, had reminders at every corner of the time when Basle was one of the great university towns of Europe. When Grizel reached the Badenischbahnhof, she found that she had just time to get her ticket for Schaffhausen.

It was still dusk, and mists lay low over everything; Grizel felt in her satchel for her book, and settled down for a good read. People passing the compartment in which she was looked curiously at her. In Switzerland the young girl of the upper classes no more roves about by herself than her sister in other European countries does. There is a great deal of freedom, it is true, but *la jeune fille* is well chaperoned for all that. To see a girl of seventeen quite without any relative or maid to look after her was unusual. When the daylight finally came, with bright wintry sunshine, Grizel put aside her book to look at the view, without any idea that she had aroused such interest.

She found the landscape uninspiring on this cold morning, when everything was covered with snow, and there were no mountains such as she loved. The railway here runs through the Rhine valley, which is low-lying, and only shows gentle undulations till it nears the environs of

Zurich. It is a fairly populous valley, but Grizel was bored with the towns—and she soon lost interest in them and returned to her book. But this, too, seemed to have become dull, and so she took refuge in her thoughts. She wondered what they were saying at Basle. She could imagine Joey's indignation when she woke up and found herself alone. Miss Maynard would be furious, of course, and the Robin would be full of wonder. It wouldn't be a pleasant journey back to Innsbruck.

For the first time, Grizel began to repent her daring. After all, her idea at the first had been to have Joey with her, and here she was—alone. If Jo hadn't been so emphatic she would have left it alone. Then she pulled herself up short. It wasn't playing the game to blame Joey—Grizel rather prided herself on being fair. It was rather unfortunate that she had got on to that tack, for now a doubt came into her mind as to whether she was playing fair anyhow. Miss Maynard would be worried she knew, and, after all, she *was* head girl. Suddenly she sat bolt upright. An awful thought had struck her. What if Madame, who still had a good deal to do with the school, should think that, since she had gone off in this mad way, therefore she wasn't fit to be head girl?

Grizel's eyes widened in horror at the idea. If it were so, she could never stay on at the school. Everyone knew that she had been chosen, and the disgrace of being degraded would be more than she could endure.

The slowing-down of the train warned her at this point that they were nearing a station. She would get out and go back at once. With Grizel, to think was to act. She collected her things in double quick time, and when they drew up by the platform at Waldshut, went along the corridor, and descended the little steps, and made for the barrier. There she had no easy time of it in explaining to the ticket-collector why she had got out at a place twenty-four miles before the destination marked on her ticket. At first he thought that she had made a mistake, and got out, thinking she was already at Schaffhausen. Her bungling explanation that she had forgotten something—so she had!—roused deep suspicion in his mind. However, he could see nothing for it but to let her go, and told her when the next train back to Basle was. She found she had forty minutes' wait before her, and the snow had begun to fall again. She decided to go out and

25

find a *pâtisserie*, and see if she could get chocolate and cakes. She went out into the street, feeling rather forlorn, and, after losing herself twice, managed to find a shop. She had spent so long over finding it that she had to hurry, and scalded her mouth with the hot chocolate.

Then it was helter-skelter back to the station, where she only just caught her train, and had to find a seat in a crowded compartment with two or three voluble Swiss ladies who talked the whole time, an old curé, who read his breviary industriously, and two youths of school age who were obviously German, and who stared at her unceasingly, and made remarks about her and giggled to each other. Of all the uncomfortable journeys she had ever taken, that struck Grizel as the worst. It seemed a never-ending age before she saw that they were nearing Basle, and then she could have cried with relief. As soon as the train drew up inside the station she was out of it and off through the streets, where the snow was now whirling down, as hard as she could go. At length she turned into the Sternen Gasse, where their pension was, and made her best pace along it. The doors were shut, of course, and she had to wait while the porter came to open them. When he saw her he exclaimed in surprise, but Grizel was past minding that. She pushed past him and along to the stairs, where she was met by the manageress, who was coming down. At sight of the English girl she stopped with uplifted hands. "Fräulein Cochrane! But *das Fräulein* has gone to seek thee at Schaffhausen!"

"Well, I'm here," said Grizel. "Where are the other two?"

Frau Betts looked at her severely. "Fräulein Bettany and *das Liebling* have gone too. Fräulein Maynard said that they would go straight to Innsbruck from Schaffhausen once they had found you. They have taken the luggage—all. Fräulein Maynard was very angry—as in truth she had right to be! She said she would not feel happy till she had you all safely with your relatives. They have been gone these two hours!"

Grizel sat down limply on the stairs. She had got herself into a nice mess! If she had had any sense she would have wired them from Waldshut, and then no one would have gone chasing off after her. As it was, she had no idea what to do or where to go.

She did the best thing she could have done for herself.

Worn-out, remorseful, and hungry, she forgot her pride and burst into tears.

At the sight Frau Betts, who was a good-natured soul, forgot her indignation, and hastened to apply comfort. "Hush, *mein Kind*! You are wearied, and must rest. Fritzi shall hasten to the post-office and send a telegram to the station at Schaffhausen to say that you are here. You shall have a meal, and we will send you to them there. Come to my room."

She led the wearied girl to her own little sitting-room, and made her lie down on a sofa. Then she came with a tempting little meal on a tray, and after the girl had eaten all she could, sent the long-suffering Fritzi out once more to seek a *droschke*. Into this she packed Grizel, seeing that she was warm and comfortable. Then she bade her *Auf wiedersehn* and went back into the pension, shutting the door firmly behind her.

Oh, that weary journey! Grizel couldn't fix her mind on her book, for she was too worried over what Frau Betts had said about Miss Maynard's anger. She positively shivered when she learned that they were nearing Neuhausen, the station for the Falls, and for a moment she felt as if she would have preferred to stay where she was. However, cowardice was not one of Grizel's faults, so she pulled herself together and left the train as bravely as she could. At the other side of the barrier she saw Miss Maynard waiting for her—a very grave Miss Maynard, who made no comments, good, bad, or indifferent, on her behaviour, but simply bade her hurry up and get into the sleigh that she had hired.

Grizel did as she was told in a dreary silence, and no word was spoken till they reached the hotel. There she was bidden to get out, and go in at once. In the vestibule she waited till Miss Maynard joined and, still in that terrifying silence, led her to the room where Joey and the Robin awaited them.

At sight of Grizel the Robin ran forward, but Miss Maynard stopped her.

"No, Robin; not yet.—Take off your things, Grizel. Put them on that sofa for the time being. Now I want an explanation of your conduct."

Grizel stood there, twisting her fingers together. "I— I'm very sorry," she said.

"I hope you are," said Miss Maynard, still in that grave,

cold voice. "You have given us all, Frau Betts, Joey, and myself, a very anxious time. You have given us needless trouble, and added to our length of journey. If there is anything that will serve as an excuse for your conduct, I want to hear it."

Grizel stood there, fighting desperately with her tears.

Joey saw it, and braved the mistress's wrath. "Grizel," she said, "I honestly didn't mean to put your back up. If it was what I said made you do it, it's my fault as much as yours. I *am* a tactless ass!"

It was a way out; but Grizel had her code, and she stuck to it. "It was my own idiocy, Joey," she said.

"But I expect it was my being so beastly about it made you go on and do it," urged Joey, whose soft heart couldn't bear to see Grizel look so unhappy. "Word of honour, Miss Maynard, I'll bet it was me as much as anything! You know what I am!"

Miss Maynard looked at her. "Yes, Joey, I know. But Grizel——"

She got no further, for Grizel interrupted her. "It wasn't really Joey at all! I wanted to go, so I just—went. It's like that time I went off to climb the Tiernjoch. You'd think I'd have learnt a little sense from that, but I haven't! I'm awfully sorry, Miss Maynard. I simply didn't think. I know I'm not fit to be head girl now."

"Oh, tosh!" said Jo easily. "Of course you are. Maynie will forgive you 'cos you are sorry—won't you, Maynie?"

Miss Maynard shook her head. "It's not so easy as all that, Jo. As Grizel herself says, if she can go off like this for a mere whim, then she *isn't* fit to be Head at the Chalet School. We've got to feel we can depend on our head girl."

"Well, you will on Grizel after this," declared Joey. "Anyhow, this isn't schooltime—it's hols! So do let it go at that, won't you? I'm sure Madge would."

"Do you think so?" asked Miss Maynard, with a smile.

"Yes. She always trusts us to carry on and do our best. Look at the times she's forgiven *me* for doing mad things!"

"I shall have to tell her," said Miss Maynard, taking a sudden decision. "It will lie in her hands, Grizel. Meanwhile, we had better go and have *Kaffee*. Our train goes at six, and I want to see about one or two things. As far as I am concerned, the thing is shelved for the moment.

Luckily the Robin created a diversion by flinging herself on the girl. "*Pauv'* Grizel," she murmured.

Grizel picked her up and hugged her, thankful to hide her face among the black curls for a minute or two. When she looked up again Miss Maynard had gone off to see the manager about *Kaffee* and a picnic basket, for they would not get into Innsbruck till the next day. Nothing further was said, and they embarked on the last part of their journey very peacefully.

CHAPTER IV

HOME AGAIN

"INNSBRUCK at last! What ages it has seemed since the tunnel! Buck up, Robinette! We're nearly in! Pack up, Grizel! We're almost there! Oh, hurrah for dear little Innsbruck and Madge."

It was Joey, of course. The rest of the party got their things together in more orderly fashion, while she hung out of the window, talking and gesticulating wildly as the great train swept through the suburbs of Innsbruck, and finally slowed down by the platform. Standing waiting on it was a slight, graceful girl—she looked no more—clad in long green coat with big fur collar turned up, and a soft green hat. Her face was flushed with excitement, and as her dark eyes encountered the wildly waving Jo at the window they glowed with welcome. As the train stopped, Joey made a wild dive along the corridor and nearly fell down the steps into her sister's arms. "Madge—Madge, old thing! It's topping to see you again!"

"It's splendid to see you, Joey," replied the voice she loved better than any other sound in the world. "You've grown again, you monkey! You're as tall as I am now!" Madge Russell looked with a smile at the clever, sensitive face on a level with her own, and then turned to greet the others. "Robin! My little Cecilia Marya! Have you had a good time, *mein Vöglein*?"

The Robin, clasped tightly in the arms that had come to take the place of her mother's, tucked her curly head into "Tante Marguérite's" neck, and squeezed her rapturously. "Oh, so nice! Tante Marguérite, *bien aimée*, I do so *love* you!"

"Well, leave a little of me for the others, my pet!" laughed Mrs. Russell as she set the little girl down and turned to greet Miss Maynard and Grizel.

The latter flushed under the welcoming kiss, but her ex-Head didn't notice it, for she was shaking hands with Miss Maynard, and asking questions as to their journey. "Did you have a good time, Mollie? Decent fellow-travellers? We just got back from Vienna two days ago. It was so jolly. We stayed with the von Eschenaus—they are back again. And I've got some news for you all. Wanda is betrothed."

"Who to?" demanded Joey as they all moved to the barrier.

"A young officer in her father's regiment."

"Gee! How priceless! Fancy Wanda engaged! That makes two of our old girls! First Gisela, and now Wanda! When's she to be married?"

"In the summer. I met him while we were there, and he is a charming young man. He adores Wanda, and she him, so I think they will be very happy." Madge Russell, happily married herself, smiled reminiscently. "You will hear all about it from Maria when term begins. She was wildly excited about it. Wanda is very sweet, and is longing for the spring to come. They mean to pay us a visit at Briesau then. She wants to show him her English school."

Joey sighed. "It's awfully nice for them, of course—I mean Gisela and Wanda. But it does seem as though we were all growing up frightfully quickly! Don't you think they are too young, Madge?"

"Gisela is twenty and Wanda is nineteen. And at least we shall have Gisela fairly near us. I am so glad Gottfried Mensch decided to join Jem at the Sonnalpe. I shall like to have my first head girl living next door, so to speak." She smiled at the new head girl as she spoke, but Grizel looked very grave. She was wondering whether she would be allowed to follow in the footsteps of Gisela Marani now. Luckily the Robin tugged at Mrs Russell at that moment, so the girl's expression passed without comment for the moment, though Madge Russell had noticed it, and wondered what it meant.

"Tante Guito"—the Robin sometimes abbreviated the

longer name this way—"are we to stay with Onkel Riese and Tante Gretchen?"

Madge laughed at the "Uncle Giant," a name of Joey's bestowing on the kindly father of two of the Chalet School girls, who had been a great friend of theirs ever since the school had been opened. Then she nodded, "Yes, littlest and best! They would have come to meet us, but they thought I should like you to myself at first."

"Where's Jem?" asked Joey.

"He had to go back to the Sonnalpe at once," explained his wife as she tucked the Robin into the big sleigh which was awaiting them in the Bahnhof Platz, and which they had reached by this time. "He is looking forward to seeing you all to-morrow. You are to come to us for the rest of the week, you know."

"Good!" Joey heaved a rapturous sigh, and then sank down into her corner on the other side of her sister.

"Has Mademoiselle come back yet?" asked Miss Maynard as she took her seat facing them, with Grizel by her side.

"Yes; she arrived yesterday. Simone is with her, but Renée has a sprained ankle, so Madame Lecoutier is keeping her at home till half-term. Then she will bring her, and see the school for herself. Cosy, Robin?"

"Yes, thank you," replied the Robin, slipping her hand into the slender one at her side. "Tante Marguérite, have Gisela and Gottfried arranged for their wedding yet?"

"Yes; that's another piece of news for you. But Gisela was to be at Maria Hilfe, so I am going to leave her to tell you all about it. She wants you three to be her bridesmaids, with Frieda and Maria, I know. Wanda is to be married in August too."

"Shall we go to Wien for that?" asked Joey anxiously. "I hope it won't be late, or it will cut up my time with Elisaveta. Have you any idea of the date, Madge?"

"It will be during the first week," said Mrs Russell. "As for cutting up your visit to Belsornia, Elisaveta will be there too, and I expect you will go back with her. At least the King said so when he wrote to tell me about it."

"That's good; I suppose Wanda will have a very swish wedding. Where will Gisela be married, do you think? In the Hof-Kirche?"

Madge refused to commit herself.

By this time they were driving down the Friedrich-

Hertzog Strasse, making for the bridge, for the Maria Hilfe is a suburb across the river. Joey looked out at the busy streets, where sleighs were going about crunching the crisp snow under their shining runners and filling the air with the silvery jangle of bells. The celebrations of Christmas and New Year were over, but the shops still had a gay appearance. The snow lay thick on the ground and the steep roofs, and gave what the English girls were wont to call a "Christmas card" air to the town. It was early afternoon, but some of the shop windows were already lighted up. They turned down the Markt-Platz, and in a few minutes they were going smoothly along by the side of the Inn, which lay still and black under its coating of ice. Across the fine stone bridge they turned, and then they drove up the long Mariahilf Strasse to the door, where two tall, pretty girls of twenty or thereabouts were standing, eagerly awaiting them.

"Here at last!" exclaimed the taller and fairer of the two as the sleigh stopped, and Joey scrambled out to be seized and kissed warmly by both. "And our little bird! How well thou art, *mein Blümchen*!"

The Robin, well accustomed to endearments, held up her face for a kiss before she ran into the house, and began to skip up the stairs. It was a long way up, for the Mensches' flat was on the third floor. At length she was there, and springing into the arms of a slight girl of fifteen. Frieda Mensch was much smaller than the rest of her family, typically German, with long flaxen plaits on her shoulders, blue eyes, and an apple-blossom skin. She was very pretty, though by no means as attractive looking as her elder sister. Bernhilda, with her corn-coloured hair in a coronal of plaits round her head, was charming enough to have stood for one of the princesses in *Grimm's Tales*. A door opened at Frieda's joyful exclamations, and Frau Mensch, very fat, very fair like her daughters, rolled out and caught the visitors in a close embrace. "But how we have missed you, my children! There seemed to be something lacking in our joy this Christmas. *Die Grossmutter* has wearied for your return; she is in the salon now. Come, my children, and greet her."

She led the way to the long narrow salon where a tiny old woman, Herr Mensch's mother, was sitting by the big white porcelain stove. Old Frau Mensch was only two years short of her century, and she was very frail, but her eyes still snapped vividly, and she made herself felt in the little household. Joey went up to her, curtseying first in the pretty, old-fashioned way the old dame liked, and then offering her hand. The Robin followed her example, but she was kissed and crooned over.

Then Frau Mensch the younger—Tante Gretchen, as the girls had learned to call her—swept them all off for a meal, which she was sure they needed after their journey.

Joey heaved a sigh of joy as she settled down to a bowl of soup and a big slice of rye bread. "English food's all very well," she said, "but I love what we have here. I used to get so bored with the white bread. I *love* this!" She took a large bite out of her slice, and beamed on them all.

"Joey, you needn't act so like a little pig," said her sister severely. "Even if you *are* glad to get back, I think you might have a little less to say about your food! Was she like this in England, Grizel?"

She purposely included the elder girl in the conversation. That there was something wrong with Grizel was patent to anyone. Now, as the girl shook her head, she bit her lips. What *could* be the matter? However, it was no time to ask questions now, so she turned to Miss Maynard with some idle remark about the journey.

"Quite simple," was the answer. "Paris was delightful, and we had a good time seeing the shops at Basle."

"I thought you meant to stay longer," said Mrs. Russell. "Why did you leave it so soon?"

"It was pouring with snow," said Joey hastily. "You never saw anything like it! If it's going to be bad weather, it's best to be at home, *I* think!"

Madge frowned. Then she decided to say nothing, though Jo's rudeness in bursting in like this on her conversation with Miss Maynard was both unusual in her and outrageous. As for Grizel, she had no more to say, but ate her soup and bread, and drank the coffee which Bernhilda set before her. When the meal was over, the girls went off together for a chat, and the Robin, who was sleepy, was tucked up on the sofa to take a nap. Frau Mensch had some household tasks to see to, so she went out, leaving the other two together after excusing herself. She had barely closed the door behind her when Madge Russell turned eagerly to the other. "Molly! What is the matter? What happened at Basle? I'm sure something did, or you would never have come off so suddenly. Why on earth did you go to Schaffhausen at this time of year? I got the shock of my life when I got your wire from there saying you were coming back at once. And what is wrong with Grizel?"

Miss Maynard frowned. "It's difficult to tell you, my dear. Yes, Grizel has been as mad as usual. I thought she was cured of wanting to go off on expeditions of her own, but evidently she isn't. As for Schaffhausen, it was her doing we went there. She ran away to see the Falls of Rhine yesterday morning without saying anything about where she was going, though she and Joey had had a battle royal over it the night before. Jo seems to think that it was partly her fault that Grizel went off as she did. There may be some truth in it. It's quite possible she did say things that put Grizel's back up. At the same time, Grizel has no excuse for going off as she did. If it hadn't been for what Jo was able to tell me, I shouldn't have known where she had gone. Then, when she was half-way there, the silly child seems to have repented, and turned back—without wiring to let us know that she was returning. The result was that I packed up and took the other two off to Schaffhausen to seek her, and was met on the platform by a wire from Frau Betts saying that Grizel was there, and asking what they were to do. I wired them to send her on by the next train. She was very penitent, I must say, and has behaved very well since then. But honestly, my dear, I think we shall have to reconsider making her head girl. It seems to be impossible to place the smallest reliance on her."

Madge sighed. "Poor child! That's what's wrong with her, of course. She's dreading being degraded. I can't decide yet, Mollie; it's altogether too big a thing. And it's quite true that Jo can be horribly tactless when she is roused. I wish I knew what to do!" She got up, and began to pace backwards and forwards.

Miss Maynard watched her. She saw the difficulties, but she was not blessed with much imagination, and she did not know Grizel as well as the ex-Head did. To her way of thinking, it would be very unwise to risk having such a girl as head girl of the school. "It's hard luck on Grizel," she agreed; "but what else are you to do?"

"I can try her again," said Mrs Russell.

"My dear, how often have we done that already? Grizel has always been a problem."

"The trouble with Grizel is that she had far too much authority over her for four years. The second Mrs Cochrane has always resented her existence, you know, and she scarcely allowed the child to call her soul her own. I think it's that which makes her difficult at times now; and when I'm tempted to be angry with her, and deal strictly with her, I remember that."

"But other children are made to be obedient," Miss Maynard reminded her. "Where would you find parents expect more unquestioning obedience than with the Maranis? The Mensches are pretty strict, but Gisela and Maria have been taught the most unquestioning and absolute obedience. And it's the same with most of our girls—the continental ones, at any rate. I like it better than the calm disregarding of orders that one gets nowadays from children."

"So do I," returned her friend. "The trouble is that Grizel was thoroughly spoilt by her grandmother for five years before her father's second marriage. Then, though our girls have been taught to obey on the word, they aren't nagged at. That's bad for anyone, and it is Mrs Cochrane's chief failing."

"Well, what are we to do? I know that she expects to be degraded. If you think we ought to try her again, I am quite willing. Only I do hope she's learnt her lesson *this* time, and will play no more such wild pranks. I *cannot* see how any girl of nearly eighteen can be so mad!"

Mrs Russell nodded. "I know. But it's just Grizel. I will have a talk with her, and see what she says, and, of course, we must consult Mademoiselle. Then, if you and she agree, I think we must give the child a last chance, I *don't* want to degrade her. That sort of thing sticks, and it might harm her more than it would do her good."

The door opened at that moment, and Grizel came in. She had slipped away from the others, and had come to learn her fate. "Has Miss Maynard told you, Madame?" she faltered.

"Told me what?" asked Mrs Russell.

"About my running away to Schaffhausen? I know it was a mad thing to do, but I wanted to see the Falls of Rhine so much, and I didn't think."

Miss Maynard got up and left the room. She felt that it

would be easier for Grizel to make her confession if she were alone with the Head—for so they all thought of Mrs Russell.

"Yes, Grizel. She has told me. I am very disappointed in you."

Grizel's lips quivered. "I'm awfully sorry, Madame. I just didn't think."

"That is the trouble with you, Grizel," said Madge gravely as she drew the girl down on a chair beside her. "You *don't* think; and so you give everyone endless trouble. Do you think that a girl like that ought to be our head girl?"

Grizel shook her head. She couldn't speak, for she was fighting desperately for self-control.

"I want you to have another chance," said Mrs Russell quietly. "Miss Maynard and I are going to talk it over with Mademoiselle. If she agrees, we will try you for this term. But remember, Grizel, if we do, it will really be your last chance this time. I dare not hurt the school for the sake of one girl."

She dismissed the girl after that, but Grizel went away happier than she had come. She knew that kind-hearted Mademoiselle Lapâttre would agree to giving her this chance.

CHAPTER V

THE PREFECTS' MEETING

IN the prefects' room, Grizel sat alone. It was the first Saturday of term, and she was to hold her first prefects' meeting. She had been looking forward to it, but now that it was here she felt sudden doubts as to whether she would be able to manage as well as her predecessors had done. Sitting there by herself, she went over them in her own mind. Tall, graceful Gisela, with her wide commonsense and her quiet tact, which had helped to bring her through that first test year; big, steady Juliet, who had been the Head's right hand, and the beloved of all the juniors; pretty Bette, who had had only one term of office, but had proved in that term that she, too, possessed the something which goes to make leaders. Yes; they were a fine trio to follow, and she must work hard if she meant to rise to their level.

For once in her life Grizel saw herself with open eyes; saw how her actions really looked. She did not like it. Something foreign to it came into her face as she sat there, looking unseeingly out of the window that gave on to the long narrow valley which runs into the mountains from the shores of the Tiern See. She vowed to herself that she would make good in this term of trial. She would *not* let Mrs Russell, Miss Maynard, or Mademoiselle down, come what might. In her grim determination she clenched her hands and squared her jaw, robbing her face of half its beauty, but giving it an added character.

Well might Rosalie Dene, the second prefect, who entered the room just then, exclaim, "Grizel! What in the world has happened?"

Grizel's face resumed its normal appearance as she said hastily, "Nothing! What should have happened?"

"I don't know, I'm sure," said Rosalie, pulling up a chair to the table and sitting down. "You looked as if—as if—oh, I don't know! As if you were declaring war on someone."

"What nonsense!" Grizel laughed.

Rosalie shot a quick glance at her, then she decided to change the subject. "Where do you think the others are? They're late!"

"Here they are," said Grizel, whose quick ear had heard the sound of light footsteps. "Come along, you people! I was beginning to think you'd forgotten all about it!"

"I am sorry," said Gertrud Steinbrücke, "I was talking with Mademoiselle about the library, and had not noticed how late it was."

"And we were getting the middles and juniors started with their hobbies," added Mary Burnett, a sturdy English girl, with a pleasant face and downright manner. "Jo, Paula, and Marie are looking after the little ones, and the middles are with Eva and Dorota. Jo says, Grizel, do you want to discuss the magazine? If so she'll come. But if you don't she'll stay where she is."

Grizel thought. "No; I don't think we shall need her this afternoon," she said slowly. "We must have a meeting of the committee soon, though. Do you mind running down and telling her, Mary, old thing? Ask her to find out from the others if they can have a meeting after tea, will you?"

"Righto!" Mary went off on her errand, and the rest of the prefects and sub-prefects settled down.

They made an attractive group as they sat there. There were eight of them. Grizel was in her place at the head of the table. Next her was Rosalie, fair, quiet, and very English-looking. On her other hand was Gertrud, who had taken her place as games captain, and below her, Luigia di Ferara, an Italian girl, who was the eldest of them all, since she would be eighteen in three weeks' time. Below these grandees sat the sub-prefects—Vanna di Ricci, another Italian girl, and a great favourite with everybody; Lisa Bernaldi, the only day-girl to be a prefect; Mary Burnett, when she should come; and Deira O'Hagan, a wild Irish girl from County Cork, whose glowing, dark prettiness told of her Spanish grandmother. Deira was something of a firebrand in the school, for she was hot-tempered, haughty, and very nearly as strong-headed as Grizel herself. The two always sparred when together. They were too much alike in character to get on well.

Mary came back presently and took her seat, and Grizel stood up to open proceedings. "This is the new term," she said slowly. "We have, unfortunately, lost Bette Rincini, who made such a splendid head girl last term, and I've got to do my best to carry on the tradition she has left. I hope you'll all help me." She paused and looked round at them all, but even Deira was smiling and nodding approval. She went on: "We had better have the report of last term now, I think, and then we can decide what we are to do this term. Rosalie, will you please read it."

She sat down, and Rosalie stood up and read out the following report. "'Last term was a good term. The snow did not come till half-way through November, so we were able to have hockey and netball nearly the whole of the term. Inter-form matches were played, and the Sixth Form came first, with the Fourth second, the Fifth third in hockey. In netball, the Lower Fourth were first, the Second second, and the Third third. During October a party of English schoolgirls were staying at the Stephanie, and they made up a team and challenged us. The game was won by the Chalet School by three goals to one.'—

That was in hockey," she added, turning to the others for a minute. "They also challenged us at netball, and won by seventeen goals to twelve. 'In the Hobbies Club good work was done in handicrafts, and an exhibition was held on the last Saturday of term. The cup offered by the staff to the form that did the best and most original work went to the Fifth Form, who gained it through Frieda Mensch's dolls of all nations, and Josephine Bettany's marionette theatre which she had made herself. In the Guides, two girls, Grizel Cochrane and Mary Burnett, won the all-round cord, and Gertrud Steinbrücke, Deira O'Hagan, Josephine Bettany, Paula von Rothenfels, and Marie von Eschenau passed the First Class test. Other Guides did well in the tests exams held at the end of term, ninety-two per cent passing in these for which they had entered. In folk-dancing we all worked hard, and we learned several new dances, and also began sword-dancing. We did Flamborough, and hope to do Kirkby this term. The eighth number of our magazine, the *Chaletian*, appeared, and was better than ever. It has been decided to have a copy of each number bound and placed in the school library so that girls may always see how we have progressed since we began it. It was also decided to hold an Old Girls' Day once a year, and this was fixed to come in the summer term, and, if possible, on Madame's birthday, the fourth of July. Our annual Nativity play was given in the new hall, which Herr Braun had built for us during the last summer holidays, and was a great success.' That's all," went on Rosalie, closing the exercise book. "It was a fairly full term, though nothing like *some* we've had!"

"No floods," added Grizel; "nor any fires or raging thunderstorms. It was a dull term on the whole, wasn't it? I can't think of a single thing you've left out, Rosalie. Shall we sign it, you people?"

They all agreed, so the book was passed round, and the eight people signed the report.

The next thing was to decide what they were going to do about games for that term. Easter was always rather a difficulty for them. The first few weeks gave them ice sport, but March generally brought the spring thaw with it, and everything was muddy, and skating, ski-ing, and snowball fights had to be taken off the programme. On the other hand, neither netball nor hockey was possible, as the field was more or less a swamp. This meant that something else had to be provided, and it was the prefects' duty to make suggestions.

"What about tracking games?" suggested Gertrud.

"All right if the thaw is quick. If it isn't, well, it's all wrong," replied Grizel. "You know what it's like then—knee-deep in mud! Matey would have a fit if we brought the youngsters into anything of the kind. As far as that goes, she'd have a fit over any of us. The cleanest person can't help looking like a tramp after tracking through mud and puddles."

"What about rounders?" suggested Mary.

"Where's the use? If we could have rounders, we could have hockey and netball—netball, anyhow."

"I suppose it'll resolve itself into our usual walks," said Rosalie. "The middles hate them, but it can't be helped, I suppose. That's the only drawback to living here."

"Well, it's a jolly small drawback!" declared Deira. "I'd a million times rather be at school here and put up with the thaw than be in a town—even Innsbruck!"

"All the same, I think we ought to try to think of *something* fresh," insisted Grizel. "As Rosalie says, the middles hate walks, even when they can break rank and wander. Can't anyone think of something?"

"I have thought of something," said Lisa shyly, "but I do not know if we may do it."

"Well, let's have it, anyway," said Grizel.

"It is that perhaps we might make expeditions for geography and history at the week-end. Do you think it would be possible? We could not go every week-end, of course, but if the middles knew that they would have a trip to Hall one Saturday to see it, and to learn all they could from it of history, do you not think they would make fewer objections to a walk the other Saturdays?"

"It's an idea," said Grizel slowly. "There's a good deal we could see. We ought to do Innsbruck thoroughly, you know. And then there's Salzburg. And the Stubai glacier. The only thing is, it would cost rather a lot, wouldn't it?"

"Not if we made a large party," said Vanna, joining in for the first time. "Surely we could manage it then. The big difficulty to me is how we should get to Spärtz. The railway does not open till May. We should have to walk down the mountain-side, and in thaw time that would not be pleasant. Also, we could not take the juniors."

"No, there's that to think of too. If expeditions can be

arranged for the rest of the school, we must manage something for the babes," said Grizel slowly. "They could manage Innsbruck, perhaps—even Hall, they might do. But Salzsburg is a longish train journey, and would tire them; and the Stubai is out of the question, of course. But it *is* an idea, and a jolly fine one. We'll see what the staff say, anyway."

"Then what can we arrange for the little ones?" asked Rosalie. "We must have something ready for them, you know, or the other idea will be squashed at once."

There was truth in what she said, and the eight girlish faces wore heavy frowns in their endeavours to settle this difficulty. One or two suggestions were made, but all had to be rejected. Some of the little ones were very little—no older than the Robin. One or two were delicate; and there was always Matron, who was a good sort but waged war on mud and dirt of all kinds. It was Mary who made the best suggestion.

"Couldn't they have little expeditions of their own? They love Spärtz. If we could get them down there they could have a good time in the gardens, and there is a good *conditorei* where they could have cakes and coffee. Then they couldn't do as much as we could in one day, so they might take two or even three over Innsbruck."

"It isn't so much the getting them there as getting them back," said Grizel thoughtfully. "It's a long pull up the mountain, and they would be tired to begin with. Even if two of the staff and a pre and a sub-pre were with them it would be a business getting them home again. People like the Robin and Paulo's little sister would be done, and the staff won't agree to anything that's going to keep them in bed all next day."

Things were at an impasse, so they decided to leave the question alone and get on to the next business, which was settling duties for the term. Here the first dispute arose. Grizel as head girl had so much on her hands that she could take on nothing beyond her turn at prep and cloakroom duty. Gertrud was Captain of the Games, and that would keep her occupied. Rosalie Dene agreed to undertake stationery, a task which just suited her, for she was orderly and methodical—two very necessary qualities for the work.

"Then, if I may, I will see to break, Grizel," said Lisa.

"As I am here during school hours only, it will be as well for me to do that."

"It's a good deal of work," said Grizel doubtfully. "Oughtn't you to take turns with someone?"

But Lisa refused to hear of it. She had no evening duties, she said, and no morning work. She would rather do the break duties herself.

"Then Luigia, will you do library?" asked Grizel. "Joey will help you as usual, I suppose. And Vanna, you had better be music prefect again. You learn with Herr Anserl, and know just how he likes things. Plato needs looking after too," she went on, referring to their eccentric singing-master. "Mary, you had better see to the form-rooms, and also the staff-room, if you don't mind. That leaves hobbies for you, Deira."

Mary and Vanna had agreed with nods to the duties she assigned them, but Deira was not pleased, and took pains to let them all know at once.

"I don't want to be hobbies prefect," she said. "It's the most tiresome job of the lot, and you never get a chance to get on with your own work. I don't like it at all, at all!" The others stared at her in undisguised amazement. So far, no one had ever objected to any duty given her by the head girl. You simply accepted what was given you, and did your best with it. When Grizel had recovered her breath she said so.

"I don't care what you've always done," said Deira calmly. "A change is a good thing sometimes, and I'm not liking the work. Why shouldn't I be music pre?"

"'Cos Vanna is," Grizel told her. "She knows Herr Anserl, and you don't even have lessons with him. If you did you'd not be talking rubbish about wanting to have more to do with him than you could help!"

"Deira can have form-rooms if she likes, and I'll do hobbies," said Mary, who was by way of being a peacemaker, and who saw that both Deira and Grizel were likely to have a quarrel if left long to themselves. "I don't mind. I'm not doing anything special this term—only going on with my stamps. You know the babes take a lot of time sometimes, and if Deira has anything extra she wants to do it would be rather a trial."

"Have you?" asked Grizel of Deira.

"No; I haven't," said Deira sulkily.

"Then you can't change, Mary.—I'm sorry you don't

like being hobbies pre, Deira, but all the other jobs are settled. Besides, anyhow, I don't see why you want to argue about it. The rule here is that the head girl settles the work."

" 'Tis a rotten rule, it is, then!" responded Deira with spirit. "I'm not agreeing with it at all, at all, Grizel Cochrane! Why should you choose, as if we were kids?'

"Because I happen to be head girl," Grizel told her firmly.

"Don't be silly, Deira," said Rosalie. "We've always settled things this way, and no one ever made a fuss about it before? You didn't object last term yourself."

"Ah, Bette was head girl then," said Deira.

"So you're making this fuss just because *I'm* head girl now?" said Grizel. "Well, you can go on making a fuss, but you'll be hobbies pre till the end of term. And so I tell you!"

"And I won't do it! And so I tell *you*!" retorted Deira. "'Tis a tyrant you are, Grizel Cochrane! I'm not going to put my neck under your heel!"

"Nobody asked you! Don't be so absurd!" said Grizel crossly. "And if you won't be hobbies pre, then you won't have any job at all!"

Fire flashed in Deira's grey eyes, and her face was flushed with passion. What might have happened next there is no saying, but just then the Robin knocked at the door. "Please, it is *Kaffee*, and Miss Durrant says will you have it up here, or will you come downstairs?"

"We'll have it up here, Robin," said Grizel. "Will two of you go and fetch it, please? Now, Deira," she went on, turning to the girl as Mary and Vanna followed the Robin out of the room, "I'm sorry I didn't know before you disliked being hobbies pre, but it can't be helped now. Next term, if you *still* want it, you can have a shot at Music; for this term the duties are arranged, and will have to stay put. I showed the list to Mademoiselle last night when Madame was down, and they both saw it, and said it was all right. Of course, they couldn't know you would object. If they had, they might have asked me to alter it! As it is, they didn't, and it's signed. Madame won't be down for a fortnight now, so it will have to stay. *Don't* do your duty if you feel all that bad about it. I dare say we can manage. But it'll be rotten of you if you don't!"

Deira turned white, and her eyes gleamed black with rage. She knew that the head girl had the whip hand. Mrs Russell was no longer working Head of the school, but she still took part in it; all lists were signed by her, and all big arrangements had to be discussed with her. Mademoiselle Lapâttre had insisted on that before she had agreed to become the nominal Head. If Madame, as they still loved to call her, were not coming from the Sonnalpe for a fortnight, then the lists must remain as she had passed them. All the same, Deira was very angry. She had protested, not so much because she disliked the work, as because she objected to Grizel's rather dictatorial manner. Her protest had not worked, but she loved Grizel none the better for that.

"If I must, I must," she choked out at length. "All the same, Grizel Cochrane, I'll be even with you yet!"

"Rats!" said Grizel briefly, and began to discuss other duties with them as if nothing had happened.

Mary and Vanna brought in *Kaffee und Kuchen*, their afternoon meal, and they were all too busy settling days and work to notice how silently the Irish girl sat through their discussion. She drank her coffee and ate the cakes they passed her without realising what she was eating or drinking. Her temper was aroused, and she was resolved to make Grizel Cochrane smart for what she had said.

When the meeting had ended, and Lisa had gone home with her father, most of the prefects went off to their dormitories to change into light frocks, as they were going to dance that evening. Grizel was left behind, and Gertrud stayed with her.

"I wish you had not spoken to Deira quite as you did, Grizel," said the Austrian girl rather nervously, for she did *not* like speaking about it at all to Grizel, who was quite likely to turn on her.

Grizel looked at her frowningly. "I rather wish I hadn't myself," she owned; but she does rile me so! After all, Gertrud, I couldn't have given in. It isn't the way we do."

"No; but you were very sarcastic,' said Gertrud bravely. "She is angry, Grizel."

"Well, let's hope she gets over it quickly," said Grizel. "Oh, Gertrud, I wish Bette had stayed on! I didn't want to be head girl one bit! But if I'm it, I'll *be* it!"

Gertrud said nothing. There seemed to be nothing to say.

Grizel slipped an arm through hers. "Gertrud, I couldn't alter things like that! You *do* agree with me there, don't you?"

"Oh, yes; I agree with that," said Gertrud readily. "But Grizel, Deira is very angry, and she does bad things when she is angry. She is sorry after, I know; but it never stops her from doing them the next time she is—how do you call it?—upset."

Grizel stood still, a funny look on her face. This description might have fitted her. "Well," she said finally. "I will try to keep out of her way and not make things worse."

She wished she had kept her temper, and *not* been sarcastic about those lists.

CHAPTER VI

DEIRA GETS HER OWN BACK

"HAS anyone seen my manuscript book?" asked Grizel Cochrane abruptly, coming into the big form-room on Sunday afternoon.

The middles, who were all there, stared.

"Your manuscript book, Grizel? No, I haven't," said Margia Stevens at length. "When did you have it last?"

"It was in my music locker on Friday," replied Grizel. "I put it away just before afternoon school, and I slipped a letter from home into it. Now I can't find it, and I want it—at least I want that letter."

"Did you have a letter? Lucky you!" said Margia.

"It was an old one," said Grizel briefly. "Haven't any of you seen the wretched thing?"

They all assured her that they did not, so she went off to hunt through all the lockers in case she had slipped her book into the wrong one. Mademoiselle came along and stopped in astonishment at the sight. "Grizel!" she cried in her own language, "what are you doing here?"

"I am looking for my manuscript book, Mademoiselle," explained Grizel, lifting a flushed face.

"But this is Sunday! You cannot do harmony on Sunday!" protested Mademoiselle.

"Oh, it wasn't for that I wanted it," said Grizel, rising from her knees to stand before the nominal Head of the school. "I left a letter in it, and I want the letter. I thought I had put the book into my locker, but it isn't there, so I was looking to see if I had made a mistake and put it into someone else's, as I was in a rather a hurry."

"Yes, *ma petite*; in that case you may look for the book," said Mademoiselle, passing on and leaving Grizel to go on with her hunt—a fruitless hunt, as it proved to be.

Wherever that book was, it wasn't in the music lockers. Finally Grizel gave it up and went to turn out her desk, though she was certain she had not carried her harmony into form with her.

Gertrud came in as she was busy, and opened her eyes widely.

"It's my wretched manuscript book," explained Grizel once more as she ran through a pile of exercise books. "I simply can't find the thing! It seems to have vanished off the face of the earth!"

"But harmony!" protested Gertrud.

The rule about work on Sunday was strictly kept at the Chalet School. No lessons at all might be done then. In the mornings the girls went to the little Roman Catholic chapel if there was a service—all of them that were Catholics, that is. The rest had a service of their own in one of the form-rooms. In the afternoon they were free to amuse themselves with books, puzzles, or painting. The little ones had to lie down for an hour. After *Kaffee und Kuchen* Mademoiselle took the Catholics, and Miss Maynard the English Church girls for an hour, and they had quiet talks together. After that they were free once more till bedtime. Margia Stevens in her first term at the school had told her mother that they had "such gentle Sundays." The girls were never likely to forget their Sundays at the Chalet School. Hence Gertrud's surprise at Grizel's statement.

The head girl knew what was passing in her mind. "Oh, it isn't harmony; only I left a letter of Grannie's—the last she ever wrote me—in it, and I want that letter."

Gertrud's pretty face softened. Everyone knew that Grizel had loved her grandmother, who had died two years previously, and who had adored and petted her. She kept that particular letter because in it was a good deal of gentle, loving advice which she very seldom followed, it is true, but which she liked nevertheless.

"Perhaps the book has been taken to our room," suggested Gertrud practically, that being the only sort of sympathy Grizel would permit. "Shall I go and see?"

"It's awfully good of you, but I think I'll go myself. Come, though, if you like."

Gertrud slipped an arm through her friend's, and they went upstairs together. In the prefects' room they found Vanna, who was writing letters, and Deira, who was reading. The Irish girl scowled as the two came in, and turned her back on them. Vanna, deep in her home letter, took no notice of them as they hunted through the cupboard and then went through the long, low book-shelves that ran along the wall at one side.

"It isn't here," said Gertrud at length, when the most consistent search had proved that, wherever the missing book was, it wasn't in the room.

"Where on earth can it be?" said Grizel, a puzzled frown on her face. "I'm *sure* I put it into my locker, because I remember I had finished all my harmony for Herr Anserl, and I put it there to be ready for Monday. If I bring it up here, I nearly always forget to take it to my lesson, and nothing makes him madder than to wait while I go and fetch it. I *know* I put it there with my music; and now it's gone!"

"Perhaps it has fallen out and been put into lost property" suggested Gertrud.

"It might. I'll go and see. Who has the key? Whose week is it?"

"Deira's," said Gertrud, after a glance at the neatly written list on the notice board.

Grizel turned to Deira. "Deira, may I have the key to lost property?" she said.

"It's hanging up beside the board there," mumbled Deira, not looking up from her book.

Grizel, thinking that Deira was still angry over yesterday, took no notice of her manner, but got the key and went off. Gertrud did, however, and remained where she was, looking at the Irish girl with a frown. Grizel came back in five minutes' time, empty-handed, and hung up the key on its nail. "No; it wasn't there," she said. "I can't imagine where it can have got to."

"What are you looking for?" asked Vanna, who had

roused out of her letter by this time, and was taking an interest in proceedings.

"My harmony book. You haven't seen it, by any chance?"

"No; not since you had it on Friday," said Vanna. "But harmony, Grizel?"

"It's the book I want. There's an old letter in it—that's all."

At this Deira started and went white.

Gertrud noticed it. "Deira, have you seen Grizel's book?" she asked.

Deira faced her and remained silent. She hardly dared tell the truth, and she could not lie over the matter.

Grizel's attention was now attracted. "Deira! Do you know where it is?" she asked.

"Not now," said Deira, almost inaudibly.

"Not now? What on earth d'you mean?" demanded Grizel impatiently.

Her impatience had one good effect. It made Deira speak up. "I meant what I said. I haven't the least idea where it is at this moment. On the ash-heap, I should think."

"The ash-heap? What on earth are you talking about?" Grizel had gone paler, and her eyes were beginning to look steely.

"Well, isn't that where the ashes are thrown?" Deira spoke defiantly but inwardly she was feeling anything but defiant.

"Ashes? D'you mean you've *burnt* it?" Grizel was white now, and her lips were set in a thin straight line. Deira felt frightened; however, she wasn't going to let Grizel Cochrane know it, so she shrugged her shoulders.

"If you know, why ask?"

"You've *burnt* it?" repeated Grizel, as if she could scarcely believe her ears.

"Yes, I've burnt it! I vowed I'd make you pay for your sarcasm yesterday, and I have! It's fine and early you'll have to be getting up to-morrow, if you want to get that harmony done again before your lesson!"

"Deira! But how *could* you?" cried Gertrud. "It was a wicked thing to do! And you have burnt Grizel's letter too! Her letter that she cherished!"

"Oh, dry up!" said Grizel impatiently. "What does it matter about the letter now it's gone? As for the book,

Deira O'Hagan, what right had you to burn school property to satisfy your silly temper? Of all childish things to do, I must say that strikes me as *the* most childish I've ever heard of! The Robin wouldn't do a mad thing like that! Oh, I shan't tell!" with unutterable scorn in her voice. "You needn't be afraid of *that*——"

"I'm not afraid!" retorted Deira. "If it comes to that, I'll tell myself!"

"Yes; I can see you!" Grizel was realising her loss, and her hot temper boiled up. "Dash off to Mademoiselle's room now, and tell her that you lost your temper, and did a thoroughly childish, spiteful thing like that just to work it off! I can see you!"

"I will! Do you suppose I care for you, Grizel Cochrane?" raged Deira.

"Girls! What does this mean?" Miss Maynard had come into the room after vainly rapping for admittance, since everyone was too much interested in what was going on to heed anything else.

At the mistress's words Gertrud looked distressed, and Vanna frightened. Grizel uttered a scornful laugh and turned away. Deira, stung to utter fury by that laugh, sprang forward. "I have been after telling Grizel Cochrane what I think of her, Miss Maynard," she exploded, becoming more and more Irish as she went on. " 'Tis not meself would be afraid of her, for all the haughty airs of her. And, since actions spake louder than words, I been telling her 'tis I have burnt her harmony book!"

"You've—*what*?" exclaimed Miss Maynard, startled out of her usual self-possession.

"I've burnt her harmony book," repeated Deira, still too angry to care what happened.

"*Deira!* Are you mad?"

Deira treated this as if it had never been uttered and swept on, " 'Tis not meself'll be submitting to the tyranny of her, be she fifty times head girl here. She may be English—the curse of Cromwell on thim all!" (this last with a sudden hazy remembrance of her old nurse)—"but I'm Irish, and there's niver a one of us fears the tyrant——"

But by this time Miss Maynard had recovered herself, and she interrupted what promised to be a long harangue on the wrongs of Ireland. "Deira, leave the room at once

—at once! Go to your dormitory, and don't leave it till I give you permission."

Deira glared at her, but Miss Maynard was to be obeyed, and the look the excited girl received from the mistress helped to cool her down considerably. She turned and went without another word. Miss Maynard waited till she had gone, and then attended to Grizel. "Grizel, will you kindly explain to me the meaning of this *disgraceful* scene? What has happened between you and Deira?"

Grizel shook her head. Tell tales she would not; also, she was too angry to speak.

Seeing how matters stood, Miss Maynard turned to Gertrud. "Gertrud, you seem to have kept your head. Will you please tell me what all this is about?"

"Grizel and Deira had quarrelled," said Gertrud, after a moment's pause. "Deira has burnt Grizel's harmony."

"Is it really true? She really has done such a childish thing?"

"Yes." Poor Gertrud felt miserable over the whole thing.

Miss Maynard stood in silence for a moment. "Why has she done this, Grizel?"

"Deira didn't like all the arrangements yesterday," mumbled Grizel at last, when she had kept the mistress waiting as long as she dared. "I made her angry, and this is to pay me out, I suppose."

"How did you make her angry?"

"I—said things."

Miss Maynard forbore to question further. She sent Grizel off downstairs to the others, and managed to get a more detailed account from Vanna and Gertrud. She got more than she had bargained for; for Vanna, thoroughly frightened, told about the precious letter that must have gone, too, and this helped to explain Grizel's attitude. When the young mistress had finally got everything there was to get she went off to Mademoiselle to report to her.

"And now, what are we to do?" she asked when she had finished.

Poor Mademoiselle put her hand to her head. "I cannot think. I only wish our dear Marguérite had never left us and got married. How to deal with this extraordinary happening I do not know. Deira must be punished, of course, but I fear that will do little good. It will not make her really repentant for what she had done, nor will it return the letter. As for what Herr Anserl will say when he hears about the harmony, I shudder to think!"

"He'll roar, I suppose," agreed Miss Maynard. "He always is noisy over things like that. But Grizel certainly can't get all that work done over again in time."

"Doubtless, my dear Molly," replied Mademoiselle dryly; "but that will not help us in dealing with the matter. Here comes Marie with the coffee. We had better try to forget it for the time being, and take our rest while we can. As for Deira, she had better stay by herself. Will you go and ask Matron to put her in the sick-room for the rest of to-day. She will be better left alone, I think, till she has had time to realise what she has done."

CHAPTER VII

A DEADLOCK

"HERE'S Madame at last!" The cry came from Grizel, who had been anxiously watching the mountain path along which their ex-headmistress must come to reach the school. Things were uncomfortable, and had been since that memorable Sunday. Deira had been allowed to join the rest of the school the next day, but she kept by herself, speaking to no one.

"What to do, I know not," said Mademoiselle, speaking to a conclave of Miss Maynard, Miss Durrant, who was the junior mistress, and Miss Wilson, who taught general subjects.

"We had better send for Madame, I think," said Miss Wilson thoughtfully.

Miss Maynard shook her head. "I don't think we ought to bother her, if we can help it. The Sonnalpe is a good way away for a tramp in this weather"—it was snowing heavily, and threatening to become a blizzard before long—"the paths won't be safe. Also, I do think we ought to settle our own difficulties."

Luckily for them all, Mrs Russell sent a message to say that she was coming down to see Joey, so the matter had been shelved for the time being. Deira found herself left severely alone by the others, and Grizel, anxious to do her best to prove to "Madame" that she had been justified in her forgiveness by being an excellent head girl, had worried from morning till night about the trouble in the school.

She had done what she could to set matters right. She spoke to the Irish girl as nicely as if she had done nothing —which further enraged Deira, who was under the impression that Grizel's attitude meant that she didn't care— and fulfilled all her duties as carefully as she could. Joey even accused her of becoming old-maidish.

When at length the day Mrs Russell had fixed for her coming arrived, Grizel spent all her spare time at the window, watching. Joey and the Robin joined her halfway through break, and the three of them were in the prefects' room, staring up the valley, when the head girl's joyful exclamation told them that their expected visitor was coming. Joey promptly made for the door, closely followed by the Robin. Grizel waited by herself. Slowly, very slowly, she was beginning to see things from other people's point of view, and she knew that the three would prefer to have their first meeting in privacy.

As it happened, they were all doomed to disappointment, for the bell rang just then, and all three had to go to classes. The Robin heaved a sigh, and trotted off to her own quarters at Le Petit Chalet, the junior house. Joey turned aside from the passage, and went to her formroom, where she proceeded to display the most remarkable ignorance of the doings of Louis the Ninth and his Crusaders; and Grizel went down to the Sixth, and tried to forget her troubles in German literature and *Wilhelm Meister*.

Meantime the person so eagerly looked for went quietly up the snowy path to the house, where she was welcomed by Mademoiselle, who drew her into the little room still known as "Madame's study," and rang the bell for Luise, the maid, to bring *Kaffee und Brödchen*.

"Oh, but it's good to be back, Elise!" sighed Mrs. Russell, leaning back in her chair and looking round the familiar room with tender eyes. "I am as happy as can be at the Sonnalpe, but I do miss my girls at times."

"But you are happy, *ma Mie*?" queried Mademoiselle. "You would not be without *Monsieur le Docteur*?"

Madge shook her head. "Oh, no! But the Chalet

School is part of me still. You don't know how much I sometimes wish I could be in both places at once! If only Jem could have built his sanatorium down here it would have been ideal. But the Sonnalpe is better for his work, and—and I wouldn't really change, even to be Madge Bettany of the Chalet School again."

Luise entered at this moment with the little meal, and the two joined in it and more school gossip till the bell rang for the end of morning school. Then Mademoiselle rose, "You will excuse that I run away, *ma petite*. There are one or two little things to which I must attend before *Mittagessen*. I will send Jo to you."

She went off, and three minutes later Joey appeared and hugged her sister tempestuously. "Madge! It's just like old times seeing you here! It was rotten of the bell to ring just when we saw you coming! How long are you going to stay?"

"Three days," replied her sister. "Jem has had to go off to Vienna again, so I said I'd rather come here till he comes back. Now, tell me your news."

"Except for this idiotic fuss with Deira and Grizel, I don't think there *is* any," replied Jo, rumpling up her hair with her hand.

"Fuss with Deira and Grizel? *What* fuss?" asked her sister sharply.

"Oh, it isn't Grizel's fault," declared Joey. "She's been jolly decent about it all. Only Deira went mad and burned her harmony, and her grannie's last letter with it!"

"*What?* Sit down, and tell me what it all means!" commanded Madge.

"I can't tell you much more. Deira had a row of sorts with Grizel—don't know what about, though. You know what Deira is. She lost her temper, and tried to pay Grizel out by burning her things. *I* think it was an utterly mad thing to do and she doesn't seem to care, either! Grizel has been jolly nice about it, and I know she was upset about the letter. No one can do anything with Deira, and she mopes about all day by herself. None of us want to talk to her, though we're polite, of course. Deira won't say she's sorry, and it's been jolly unpleasant!"

Madge Russell turned matters over in her own mind. She felt glad, on the whole, that she had decided against accompanying her husband to Vienna. During the three days she would be at the school surely she could clear up this trouble. Not unnaturally, she felt inclined to blame Grizel herself in the first instance. It seemed almost certain that she had brought this trouble on herself.

Joey, watching her sister's face, guessed what was passing through her mind, and tried to put matters as straight as she could. "Madge, I don't think this is Grizel's fault. In fact, the other prees practically say it isn't, though they won't tell *us* what's happened. Grizel has been awfully upset about it all, and she's done her best to straighten it up—honour bright, she has. Only, Deira doesn't seem to want it straightened."

Madge frowned. "Sure of this, Joey?"

"Positive certain,". declared Joey. "Do believe that it isn't her fault, Madge."

"Do you think I'm condemning her unheard?" asked her sister dryly. "You've never called me unfair before, Joey."

Joey crimsoned. "No; but I think—things—make you feel that—that—that——"

"That—what?" demanded Mrs Russell, as the orator came to a distressed halt.

"Well, that it is more likely to be her fault than Deira's."

Madge Russell looked at her sister again. Then she nodded. "You're right, Joey—and it *is* unfair!"

"I didn't say so!"

"Not exactly. But you *meant* it, didn't you?"

Jo fidgetted. Then she looked up. "Yes; I think I did. I can't bear you to be wrong in anything!"

"I'm often wrong, Jocy-baba," sighed her sister, an arm round the slender shoulders. "I certainly was there! Listen! Here comes the Robin!"

Joey wriggled away, and stood up as the Robin came racing into the room and flung herself on "Tante Marguérite" with cries of joy. "Tante Guito! How lovely to have you again! School isn't so nice without you!"

Mrs Russell kissed the rosy face upturned to hers, and ruffled the short curls as she said, "You have me in the holidays, *Bübchen*."

"That's not the same," said the Robin sagely. "We want you all the time—Joey an' me!"

"And I want you! Are you being a very good girl, sweetheart?"

"I was second—but *second* in my form last week," said

54

the Robin impressively. "And I have no order marks all this term!"

"Papa will be pleased to hear that. He sent his love to you, my pet, and when Uncle Jem comes home again he will come down for a weekend at the Post, and you and Joey are to stay with him."

The Robin squeezed her hands together in her joy. "But that will be *jolly*!" she said emphatically.

"Topping!" Jo added her comment. "Will it be next week-end, Madge?"

"Yes, I think so. And I am here for three days this time, Robin; and I am going to ask Mademoiselle if I may take my classes again. She tells me that Miss Annersley has a bad cold, so we will send her to sick-room, and give her a rest while I am here."

The Robin hugged her again as the only possible means of expressing her joy, and the bell rang for *Mittagessen* just when everyone was nicely tousled, for Joey had joined in the hug. They made a frantic rush for the "splasheries" on that, and the two children had to run, while Mrs. Russell followed more soberly to the staff-room, where she was greeted with acclamations as the staff filed out to go to the *Speisesaal*.

"You will take your own seat, Madame?" said Mademoiselle, who was already in her old place, leaving the head of the staff table to the younger woman. Mrs Russell nodded, and went there. Then she said grace, and they all sat down.

It was like old times to sit there, looking down the room at the long tables with the fresh girl-faces turning to her; and yet there were differences. Gisela, Bernhilda, Juliet, Wanda, and Bette were no longer there. Grizel Cochrane sat in the head girl's seat, dispensing the soup to the little ones, and Joey was no longer a child. Others had grown up, too, and there were new faces among the little ones. Particularly, Mrs Russell noticed Grizel and Deira. The former looked grave and preoccupied, and the latter was plainly miserable. She merely played with her food, and made no attempt to join in the merry chattering in which even Frölich Amundsen, a new little Norwegian, was managing to take part, though it was French day, and till she came to the school she had never heard a word of French.

Mademoiselle's eyes followed the girl's, and she looked

very serious, though she said nothing. When the meal was over, however, she caught Deira outside, and brought her back to insist on her eating some of the soup which Luise had kept warm. "You must eat, Deira," she said firmly. "You will make yourself ill if you do not, and that I cannot permit."

Deira took it then, but with a very ill-used air. She escaped as soon as she could, and went off to her own quarters, feeling that the whole world was against her.

Madge Russell had gone up to the prefects' room, meanwhile, and was having a chat with her girls, who rejoiced loudly when she told them that she was going to teach during her visit.

"Oh, Madame! But that will be so nice!" cried Luigia. "It will be as it was before."

"I am so glad," said Rosalie. "We do miss you, Madame."

"What books shall we need?" asked Mary Burnett. "It's literature for us first lesson this afternoon?"

A shout of laughter rose at this; even Grizel joining in.

"But how like Mary!" chuckled Gertrud. "You are in haste to begin, my dear."

"Well, it's better not to waste any time," said Mary in her matter-of-fact way.

"Shall it be Shakespeare?" asked Vanna. "It is so long since we had a Shakespeare lesson with you, Madame."

"Yes; if you like," said Madge. "What are you doing this term?"

"*The Tempest*," said Rosalie. "We're just finishing the first act."

"Very well, then. Bring your *Tempests*."

Grizel produced hers from the shelf, and the others made haste to find theirs. While they were busy, the head girl turned to the ex-Head of the school. "Madame, may I speak to you after school? I do want a talk."

Mrs Russell looked at her thoughtfully. "Yes, Grizel. Come to my study and have *Kaffee* with me, will you? I shall be alone."

"Thank you," murmured Grizel. "It is good of you. I do want a talk with you."

Madge looked at her anxiously. The girl was paler than usual, and there were shadows under her eyes. She had been taking this thing hardly.

"I am sure you are working well in all ways this term,

Grizel," said Mrs Russell gently. "I can see that for myself."

The colour touched Grizel's face, but she said nothing more, and the return of the others waving their books put an end to the conversation for the time.

From the Sixth, which numbered six girls only, Mrs Russell went on to the Fourth, which was the largest form in the school, and there she received a rapturous welcome. The afternoon finished up in the First, where the babies, as the older girls called them, were having "At the Back of the North Wind" read to them, with explanations where they were needed.

When the last school-bell rang the few day-girls went off to get ready for their walk to the various chalets round the lake where they lived; and Mrs Russell retired to her old bedroom, changed her frock and brushed out her pretty curly hair. Then she went down to the study, where she was waylaid by Jo, who wanted to know if she and the Robin might come to *Kaffee*.

Madge shook her head. "I'm sorry, Joey, but Grizel is coming, and I want to see her alone."

Joey's face fell grievously. "Oh, Madge! We do so want to be with you!"

"I shall go over to put the Robin to bed," said her sister quietly. "You may come to my room early to-morrow morning."

"Righto, then," said Jo reluctantly. "But it's rotten luck all the same!"

"Can't help that," said Madge austerely. "Grizel needs me more than you do just now. Run along! You shall have your innings to-morrow morning."

Joey went off, fairly contented with this promise, and her sister went into the study. Grizel put in an appearance three minutes later, and then Luise arrived with *Kaffee und Kuchen*, and they were left alone.

Grizel started the ball. She took her coffee from the Head, accepted a cake, and then said nervously, "Have you heard of what has happened, Madame?"

"Do you mean between you and Deira? Yes; Jo told me."

A silence followed. Then the girl set down her coffee and turned to the Head. "Madame, on my honour as a Guide, I *have* tried!"

Madge looked her full in the face, but the grey eyes

never dropped beneath hers, so she said, "Give me your version of the story, Grizel. I want to know everyone's side before I say anything."

Grizel told her story, and told it very fairly. She admitted that Deira had "made her wild," and she had been sarcastic about it. "But I never meant to make her as mad as this," she concluded. "I'm sorry, Madame."

Madge looked at her thoughtfully. "You don't realise what a bitter tongue you have when you are roused, Grizel," she said. "I am not excusing Deira's action. It was a piece of most unpleasant revenge, and thoroughly childish into the bargain. But what I want you to realise is that you are by no means blameless. I shall not say any more. I think you have suffered over this, and there is no need for anything else. I want to tell you now that if you only go on as you have been doing lately, I shall be quite satisfied to have you as head girl. As for Deira, I will see her presently, and try to put this right. Now, tell me what you have been doing in games so far."

After that she kept the talk to the games till it was time for Grizel to take prep. She sent the girl off, a different being from the one who had come in at half-past four, and asked her to tell one of the middles to send Deira to her.

Grizel went, happier than she had been since the beginning of term, and for a few minutes Mrs Russell was alone. She got up and wandered round the room, examining her old treasures, till a tap sounded at the door. In answer to her call it opened, and Deira came in.

It was easy to see that the girl was in a bad mood. She dropped her regulation curtsey, and then stood with a defiant air.

"Come and sit down, Deira," said Mrs Russell cheerily, though she was far from feeling it.

Deira sat down on the edge of a chair, and waited for what was to come.

Madge Russell promptly tackled her with, "Well, are you happy this term?"

"I'm all right," said Deira sulkily.

"Are you *really* happy, Deira?" repeated the low, musical voice.

Deira sat struggling hard for self-control. She won it, and as her eyes hardened, Madge realised that it was going to be no easy matter to put things right.

"I'm as happy as I want to be," she said.

"You are easily satisfied," said the Head. Then leaning forward, "Deira, you are *not* happy. No girl could be after doing what you have done. Why did you do it, child? What has Grizel done to you to make you feel like this towards her?"

Deira shut her lips firmly, and sat in stolid silence. Mrs Russell tried every means in her power to get her to talk, but she obstinately refused to say a word. Finally, the Head had to give it up. But she had learnt enough to know that in this instance Grizel was comparatively blameless, and she wondered that the English girl had managed to show such patience and forbearance.

"You may go, Deira," she said at length. "I am disappointed in you."

Deira went—and stood not upon the order of her going. She just managed to get up to her cubicle before her self-control vanished, and, lying on her bed, she cried heart-brokenly. That last sentence of the Head's had cut home. She would have given anything to have been able to go back to the study and say she was sorry for it all. But she felt she could not do that—yet.

The devil of pride was having it all his own way with poor Deira.

CHAPTER VIII

THE SNOW-FIGHT

THE wind, which had been heavy, died down during the night, and frost set in. Joey Bettany, waking at the unearthly hour of five, tumbled out of bed to look out at the starry sky, and saw the white and silver tracery on the windows, which told that the earth was in an iron grip which was likely to continue for the next few weeks. By dint of breathing hard on the panes and rubbing the place with the corner of her dressing-gown, she managed to make a peep-hole for herself, and to view the landscape. The snow lay white and sparkling under the light of the dying moon, and the brilliance of the stars was a good augury. "Thanks be!" she breathed, as she got back into bed after a look at her watch to reassure herself that it was much too early to go to Madge. "Now we'll get out for a bit!"

She lay awake, for she dared not switch on the light, or she would have awakened the others. However, she had plenty to think about. She was in the middle of writing an exciting story about the Napoleonic wars, and she wanted to think out her next chapter. For the first time in her life she was finding her work difficult. The characters would not do as she wanted. They insisted on going their own sweet way, and the story was developing on quite other lines than she had intended. "I can't think what's wrong with the silly things!" she grumbled under her breath. "Why can't they do as I want? They seem to go in all directions!"

It was, had she but known it, a very promising sign. Her paper children were becoming real. It is only when a story tells itself that it is worth much.

Jo lay quite happily planning the deeds of her hero, little realising that when it came to writing them down they would work out differently, and cause her endless trouble and annoyance. The minute she heard the clock chime six she scrambled out of bed again, and struggled into her dressing-gown. Then, with her electric torch to light the way, she tiptoed out of the room and up the stairs to the room where her sister lay, dreaming happily of her absent husband.

Madge was rudely awakened by cold feet wriggling down beside her, and she sat upright in the shock of the moment.

"All right; it's only me," said Joey in carefully guarded tones. "Lie down again, old thing. I've come for a chat."

"Did you put on your bedroom slippers?" demanded Madge, as she lay down with a caution justified by the narrowness of the bed, and put an arm round her sister.

"I did; but it's freezing like everything. Shouldn't wonder if the wolves don't come out on the plains again. They did that first winter we were here. 'Member?"

"Yes, I do! For goodness' sake keep your feet to yourself, and get them warm! They're like lumps of ice! And so are your hands!" as she encountered one of them.

"All right! I'll warm up soon. Have you got enough bed?"

"Yes; heaps! Have you? For any sake, don't fall out, and waken everyone."

Jo chuckled as she snuggled closer to her sister. "They'd get a shock! Maynie's beneath. She'd think it was a young earthquake!"

Madge gurgled in company as she wriggled herself comfortable. "That's better! You're still on the bony side, Jo! I wish you'd fatten up a little!"

"Oh, I'm as fat as I want to be," returned Joey easily. "I should hate to be square—like Mary, fr'instance!"

"Mary's not *fat*. She's built that way."

"Well, *I'm* not fat cos I'm built *that* way—sort of sylph-like, you know!"

Madge buried her face in the pillow to stifle her laughter. Joey was straight and thin. "Sylph-like" was the last expression one would have used to describe her. She was much too bony.

"Well, I'd rather be scraggy than tubby!" declared the insulted lady. "And *you* can't talk, anyway! There's nothing chubby about *you*, my lamb."

"Chubby? Well, I should think not!" Madge, whose round slenderness certainly gave no evidence of fat, sounded indignant.

"Keep your hair on! I said you aren't!"

"Jo, do you think we could manage a snow-fight this morning?"

"Rather!" Jo was wide-awake in a minute. "What a topping idea! D'you really think we could?"

"Well, I don't see why not. You people have been shut up closely since term began. It will be as well to make the most of the fine weather, for one never knows how soon it may begin to snow again. I think we'll cut lessons, and stay out most of the morning. Skating will be out of the question, I'm afraid, as the ice will be too rough for it yet. A snow-fight seems the best thing. You'll have to keep moving, you know."

"Righto! The others'll love it, of course!"

They discussed the idea for a short while, then Joey drifted off into other things, and they talked till the rising-bell went.

At *Frühstück* it required no penetration for her to know that Joey had already passed on her idea of the snow-fight to as many of her friends as possible. There was an air of excitement about the middles, and they giggled and murmured together as much as they dared or were able.

When all conversation has to be in a language foreign to some, at least, views are apt to remain rather limited in expression. Still, they made quite noise enough, and Mrs Russell rather wished that she had warned Jo to say nothing till the whole school was told. It was too late now, however, and the table was lively, to say the least of it.

None of the seniors knew, for Jo had not mentioned it to them. They looked mildly surprised at the animation of their juniors, and Grizel began to wear a worried air. She knew that this sort of thing generally preceded a piece of outrageous naughtiness. The Head decided to keep them all in suspense no longer, so when grace had been said she checked them as they were about to leave the room, and told them what she proposed. Everyone was delighted, of course, and they raced away to make their beds, chattering gaily, while the staff congregated round the empty tables and discussed the affair a little further. It was decided that the babies were to have their own snow-fight in front of Le Petit Chalet, as the older ones might be unintentionally rough. The others were to divide into two camps, one captained by Grizel, the other by Gertrud.

"Let them stay out as long as they want—or can," said Mrs Russell, with a glance at the barometer, which was very low. "We must be about to send in anyone who gets tired, of course. Some of them can't stand as much as the others. Mademoiselle and Miss Durrant will look after the juniors, and they can all have a good time. I believe our trouble with Deira will be straightened after she has had a good two hours or so of exercise in the open air. The confinement of the last few weeks has probably helped to upset her."

"Quite likely," said Miss Maynard. "I only hope it is so. Well, shall we go and do what we have to do? The girls won't be long now."

Half an hour later the whole party was ready to go out. Everyone was well wrapped up, and everyone wore stout boots, with heavily nailed soles. They rushed out, shouting and laughing.

It was very silent outside, and a heavy grey sky showed that the snow would soon be falling again. From Le Petit Chalet there came the sound of the juniors' voices as they tumbled about, laughing and dancing, and making snowballs. Mrs Russell left the girls, to go and see that they were all right, and Miss Maynard and Miss Wilson set to work to get the sides organised. Grizel and Gertrud had "picked up" in the house, so the two parties separated, and were each given a part of what was the flower garden in summer. They were to settle their own tactics, and the one that was driven from its own part was to be accounted the vanquished side. Several of the youngest girls were busy making snowballs, piling them up ready, while the seniors directed their movements. Gertrud, anxious to keep the peace as far as possible, had chosen Deira for her own side, and now set her to over-seeing the efforts of the middles, while she herself posted various people at different places along her front. Then the battle began, and raged furiously. The mistresses had their work cut out to keep out of the line of fire, and yet be on the spot to see that no accidents happened.

Joey Bettany, fighting for Grizel, slipped in the snow, and went down with a wild yell, which was echoed by two of the enemy, who promptly bombarded her, so that it was some time before she was able to struggle to her feet again. Frieda Mensch, caught by Paula von Rothenfels of the other side, had her face well scrubbed with snow before she managed to retaliate in the same way. The shouting became more and more breathless, and the laughter shriller, as the excited girls rushed and swooped, and flung handfuls of snow at each other. The dry powder could hurt no one, and the balls were not hard, so it was all very good fun. Even Deira lost her sullen air, and dashed about and shouted as hard as anyone.

Grizel, leading her side, and gradually forcing the other from its place, seemed to be everywhere at once. Now she was driving one of the enemy away; now she was rescuing one of her own followers; now she was hurling snowballs as hard as she could go at her foes. One struck Deira in the face, though, as a matter of fact, it had been aimed at Gertrud. Gertrud, however, had dodged, and the snow passed by her, and caught Deira. The girl was already excited by the exercise. She scarcely knew what she was doing. To her eyes it looked as though Grizel had taken deliberate aim at her. She stooped, and grabbed at something which was lying on the ground and had been turned up in the scrimmage. Without hesitating one second, giving herself no time to realise what it was or what she was doing, she flung it with a sure aim, and caught the other side's leader full on the temple.

Grizel flung up her hands, gave a little cry, and went down.

At first it was looked on as a joke. It was only when Grizel lay there horribly still and silent that they realised that something had happened. The fight stopped at once. Gertrud dropped the ball she had poised to hurl at Jo, and hurried to the other girl's side. Miss Maynard raced across the garden and dropped on her knees. Grizel lay quite still, her face as white as the snow, and a thin trickle of blood showing where the missile, whatever it was, had struck her. The mistress wiped it gently away, and her lips tightened as she saw the nasty cut.

"Go and get one of your mattresses, girls," she said quietly.—"Joey, go and ask Madame to come here; she is over at Le Petit Chalet.—Gertrud, bring me the brandy from Matron, and ask her to get a bed ready at once.—The rest of you go in, all except Mary Burnett, Rosalie Dene, Deira O'Hagan, and Eva von Heiling—Luigia, will you please take charge till someone comes?"

They did as they were told at once. Joey shot off like an arrow to fetch her sister; Gertrud went to tell Matron; and two more of the seniors rushed up to the nearest dormitory to get a mattress. Mrs Russell had come by the time they returned with it, and was kneeling by the side of the unconscious girl. Except for the little group round Grizel, the garden was deserted now. By Grizel's side lay what had caused the accident—a sharp piece of stone, which Deira in her blind fury had flung without noticing what it was. She stood amongst the others, very white and frightened. No one, of course, had any idea that she had done it. In the heat of the battle her action had passed unnoticed. But she knew herself, and was already in an agony of remorse. They got Grizel on to the mattress, and then the girls named by Miss Maynard, helped by the staff who were there, slowly lifted it, and the girl was borne off to the sick-room, where Matron, calm and capable, already had a bed opened for her, and dressing ready for the wounds. Miss Wilson went off to ring up Dr. Jem to bring him post-haste, while Mrs Russell and Miss Maynard did what they could for the girl.

They had got her undressed and into bed, when she began to moan, and Madge Russell turned to her colleague. "Mollie, go and tell the girls that she is alive. I dare do nothing more till Jem comes—I don't know enough about it. It has been a near thing though, and I'm afraid of concussion."

Miss Maynard went off to relieve the anxious girls, who were in the big class-room, talking in subdued tones. Deira was there too. She heard what the mistress said, and her white face became whiter. Miss Maynard, preoccupied and worried, never noticed her. She gave Mrs Russell's message, and left the room. Outside, in the passage, she was startled to feel a tense, nervous grip on her arm. Turning round, she saw Deira, and, eager to return to the sick-room as she was, she felt that she must stop. "Deira, my dear, don't look like that. Grizel is alive; we hope she will soon be all right again."

"You don't understand," said Deira in husky tones. "It's my fault—if Grizel dies, I am a murderess! I did it!"

CHAPTER IX

THE FEUD ENDS

"IF Grizel dies, I am a murderess," repeated Deira tremblingly.

Miss Maynard looked at her keenly. She realised that the girl was on the verge of hysterics, so she pushed open the door of the study, and drew her in. "Now, Deira, sit down and tell me what you mean," she said quietly, as she closed the door and switched on the lights, for the sky had darkened ominously, and the little room was dusky.

"It was my fault," said Deira. "I was angry with Grizel. She threw a snowball at me, and it hit me. Sure, I thought 'twas on purpose she'd done it, and out of spite, so I picked up what was handy, and threw it. 'Deed, Miss Maynard, I never saw what it was. I didn't think at all, at all! Oh, Miss Maynard, will she die?"

"Nonsense," said Miss Maynard briskly. "She's alive, and she may be ill; I can't tell you that she won't be. But we hope it won't be very bad. Only, Deira, think what your temper has done, and might have done. If Grizel had been killed you would never have forgiven yourself, I think. Now I must go. Mrs Russell may be wanting me." Deira nodded. She was putting a tremendous restraint on herself at the moment. Actually she wanted to scream and cry, she realised.

Miss Maynard knew what was passing in her mind, and guessed that, for the present, the girl was best left to herself. "You may stay here, Deira," she said gently. "I think you would rather do that than go back to the others. If anything happens with Grizel, you shall be told at once."

Then she left the room, and Deira, settling back in her chair, tried to recover herself.

The house was very silent now. The girls had gone to their form-rooms, and were trying to fix their minds on their work. Mademoiselle had come over from Le Petit Chalet, and was giving the Fourth their lesson in French literature. The Sixth were working at maths by themselves, since Miss Maynard was still upstairs in the sickroom. The Fifth were doing geography with Miss Wilson; and Miss Durrant was busy with the babies in their own house. As for the Third, Gertrud had come to them, and was giving them German *Dictat*. Outside, the snow had begun to drift down again, and in the study the only sound was the crackling of the wood in the stove. The quiet soothed Deira. She got up from the chair, and moved over to the stove to feed it, and to warm herself. Now that her excitement was gone, she felt cold.

She had been alone for more than an hour, when the door opened, and the Robin peeped in. "I want Tante Marguérite," she said.

"Madame is with Grizel," said Deira.

The Robin shut the door, and came up to her. "Is Grizel then sick?" she asked, lifting big dark eyes to the elder girl's face.

"She—is not well," stammered Deira. It was plain that the school baby knew nothing of what had happened. Could she tell her?

The Robin was full of sympathy. "*Pauvre* Grizel!" she said. "Has she eaten too much of chocolate?"

"She—has had—an accident. Madame and Miss Maynard are with her," said Deira.

"You are sorry 'cos you were cross with her? Never mind, *pauvre* Deira. She will soon be well," replied the Robin comfortingly. "Don't look so sad. Me, I will stay with you."

She slipped a chubby hand into Deira's, and snuggled

up. The Irish girl sank on to the sofa, and lifted the baby on to her knee. The Robin put warm arms round her neck, and hugged her.

"Oh, but 'tis the darlin' you are!" murmured Deira, returning the hug. The Robin took it quite calmly as her due.

"How did Grizel hurt herself?" she asked suddenly, when she had bestowed a few more hugs on the elder girl.

Deira did not dare to tell her of what had happened. For all she knew, it might be Mrs Russell's wish that the juniors should know nothing of what had happened. So she temporised. "She got hit with a stone which was flung by mistake," she said, going as near the truth as she could.

"Oh!" The Robin drew in her breath in a long-drawn sigh. Then she turned and looked at Deira. "How dreadful!"

"It's—awful!" said Deira unsteadily.

"An' it's dreadfuller for the one who threw the stone," went on the Robin, pondering things out in her baby way. She looked up, and caught sight of Deira's face. "Deira! was it *you*?"

There was a moment's silence. Then, "Yes," said Deira.

She half-expected the child to draw away in horror, but the Robin simply snuggled closer. "Oh, *pauvre* Deira!" she said, lapsing into the French.

Deira had heard the others say more than once that the Robin was the best comforter to have when you were in trouble, but she had never felt it before. Now, as the baby's arm encircled her neck, and the warm, soft weight tumbled into her lap, she felt the truth of it. "The stone —was—a mistake, Robin," she said unevenly. "I—I didn't know what it was."

" 'Course you didn't! Never mind, Deira. Tante Marguérite will understand—she always does! She'll know you're sorry, and she'll forgive you. So will Grizel. Don't cry, poor Deira!" For Deira had begun to cry, softly and bitterly, but in a very different way from what she had wished an hour ago. Unfortunately, once she had begun, she found it hard to stop; and when Mrs Russell, leaving Grizel for a few minutes to find the girl whom she had just been told was the cause of all the mischief, she came on a Niobe-like scene, for by this time the Robin was crying too, out of sympathy for a grief she could feel, even if she couldn't understand it.

"Girls! Why are you crying like this?" asked the Head quietly. "Robin, you must stop at once."

The Robin had been trained to obedience, so she choked back her sobs and said brokenly, "Tante Guito, Deira is *so* sorry."

"I am sure she is," said Mrs Russell. "Crying won't help matters, though. So you must both stop at once, and you can run over to Le Petit Chalet, Robin. I will come to you at bedtime, but I can't come before. You will be good, *mein Vöglein*?—Yes, you may kiss Deira, and then run away. Joey shall come presently. Ask Gertrud to take you across—she is in the prefects' room. And be sure you are well wrapped up."

The Robin kissed Deira, and then trotted off to seek Gertrud, and give her Madame's message. Deira still sobbed on, though she was making heroic efforts to check her sobs.

The Head gave her a minute or two. Then she stooped over her. "Deira, I want you to control yourself. I cannot stay here long, for I must go back to Grizel. But I can't leave you like this. Come!"

Deira fumbled for her handkerchief, and the Head put her own into the hot hands. Then, while the girl dried her eyes, Madge Russell made up the fire in the stove again. When she thought that Deira had herself in hand, she spoke again. "Deira, Miss Maynard tells me that you say that you are to blame for what happened."

"Yes, Madame."

"I am very sorry for you, dear. And yet, I am glad in this. I think you will learn a very terrible lesson from this —how far your temper can take you when you give way to it. Will you try to think about it? I don't think you will ever again let yourself bear malice or carry on a feud with anyone as you have done this time. But remember that the girls are not to know if we can help it. It must lie between Grizel and yourself, and me. Miss Maynard knows, and I think we must tell Mademoiselle. But no one else is to learn it if we can manage it. Do you understand, dear?"

"The—the Robin knows," said Deira with a catch in her voice.

"Yes; but I shall tell her she is to say nothing. I am

68

sorry she does know, but I suppose you couldn't help it. I don't believe, in the excitement of the moment, that they knew who threw the stone. I am going to ask you to be as much your usual self as possible. That will keep them from guessing. If they have missed you, they will only think that you were upset because you and Grizel had been on bad terms, and you were sorry you hadn't made it up. You are very tired now, so I am going to send you to bed. Go and undress yourself, and lie down. Try to sleep, and when you join the others, remember I have forbidden you to tell them anything."

Deira nodded and got up. She was worn out with the force of her emotions. She got to bed, and was there for the rest of the day. No one came near her, for they were still very anxious about Grizel, who had never recovered consciousness, but still lay in a state of coma. The others decided, as Mrs Russell had said, that Deira was upset by the thought that she had refused to make friends, and now she couldn't.

"Poor old thing! I bet she feels rotten!" said Jo Bettany to her own particular clan.

"I guess she's mad with herself all right," agreed Evadne Lannis, an American child famed in the school for her extensive slang vocabulary, which after three years was as unique as ever it had been, though she managed to curb her tongue a little during term-time. "I'd feel a skunk if I were her!"

"She must be very unhappy," sighed Frieda Mensch.

"Is—is Grizel going to *die*?" asked Simone in awed tones. The next minute she was sorry she had spoken, for Joey rounded on her with startling vehemence.

"For pity's sake, Simone, dry up! Of course she isn't! If you can't be more cheerful, just be quiet! You're a regular Job's comforter!"

What Simone might have replied to this tirade nobody ever knew, for just then Paula von Rothenfels announced that Dr Jem was coming up the path, and Jo darted out of the room to welcome him. She got little satisfaction, for Madge had been watching the path eagerly for the last hour, and was already in the passage, and sent her young sister back to the form-room post haste.

It was after seven that evening before the doctor left Grizel's bedside, and then he went to see Deira. Mrs Russell, however, came down to tell the anxious girls that it was all right. Grizel had come to herself, and had murmured something about a "rotten head" before she dropped off into natural sleep. She would be in bed for the next few days, but she would soon be herself again.

The girls were overjoyed at this news. It had seemed such a terrible thing that their jolly snow-fight should have ended in this way. The older ones, at any rate, realised that there might have been a tragedy, though no one knew what had caused it. The general idea was that the ball which it was supposed had been flung at Grizel had got frozen—this was Joey's ingenious idea—and had been harder than the others.

The school went to bed that night happy once more, and Vanna even took the trouble to peep into Deira's cubicle to see if she were awake, so that she might hear the good news. Deira, however, was asleep, exhausted by repentance and excitement, so the Italian girl went on to her own domain, and the dormitory undressed in silence.

Grizel slept for most of the next two days, sleeping herself well again, as Dr Jem had prophesied. He went off to the Sonnalpe the next day, leaving his wife behind, for the path would be difficult, since the snow was still falling, and also she was anxious to see Grizel out of bed before she left her.

It was not till four days after the affair that Grizel asked anything about the other girls. Then, one afternoon, when Madge was sitting knitting by her side, she spoke. "Madame, will Deira come and see me, do you think?"

"I'll send her up after *Kaffee*," answered Mrs Russell, without any further comment. She had wondered how much Grizel knew of the accident, and if she was aware that the Irish girl was to blame for it. It was impossible to tell from the head girl's manner, but it looked rather like it. She had lain back on her pillows with a satisfied air, and said no more on the subject. Instead, she demanded to know when she might get up.

"I *loathe* bed!" she remarked. "It's all very well at the proper time, but I hate it when you've got to stay there!"

The Head laughed. "Bed in the early mornings is desirable, I suppose," she said.

"Rather! But I've had enough of it now. Can I get up to-morrow, Madame?"

"We'll wait till Dr Jem comes and sees you again," said Madge cautiously.

Grizel heaved a deep sigh, but the bell ringing for *Kaffee* precluded what she might have had to say, and Mrs Russell went off to join the others, leaving her in Matron's charge with a mischievous smile.

Five o'clock brought Deira to the room. A shame-faced Deira she was, with a scared look in her eyes, for she guessed that Grizel knew all there was to know about the accident.

Matron tucked some more wood into the stove, warned the visitor against exciting the invalid, and then went out, leaving them alone.

When she had gone Grizel held out her hand. "Will you shake now?" she asked.

Deira took it. "Do you know?" she said.

"Know what? About that stone? Yes; but you never meant it."

"I didn't," said Deira. "It was—temper. I'd have chucked a—a *log* at your head just then."

"Let's be thankful there wasn't one handy!" said Grizel with a grin. "Half a brick's good enough for me, thank you!" She gave Deira's hand a friendly grip.

"I'm sorry," said Deira.

"Righto! It was my own fault as much as yours! I've a beastly tongue, and you've a beastly temper, so we'd better cry quits!"

Deira suddenly bent down and kissed Grizel. "You're jolly forgiving," she said; "'tis meself will remember that."

And so the feud was ended, and when Matron came half an hour later they were discussing the absolute awfulness of their last French translation-book.

CHAPTER X

MARIE'S NEWS

MARIE VON ESCHENAU went home for a weekend to be present at Wanda's betrothal party. That was the beginning of it all, as was proved later. Joey had been invited to go too, but she had started a cold. So she was relegated to the sick-room while Marie went off with the aunt who came to bring her. It is a thirteen hours' run from Innsbruck to Vienna where Marie lived, so they had to start on the Thursday night, as the feast was on the Friday. Sunday would see her on the return journey, so that she might miss as little of school as possible.

"Lucky wench!" grumbled Joey when Marie came to say good-bye and tell her how sorry she was that they couldn't both be there as they had hoped. "I say, you might bring me something from the show—a sprig of myrtle, or something."

"I will bring all I can," replied Marie, who was very fond of Joey in a quiet fashion, totally unlike Simone's rather hectic adoration. "I will also bring some cakes from that pastry-cook's you so much like."

"Marie, you *gem*! And some of those honey and nut things with cream in them! I love them!"

"Also a large piece of Wanda's betrothal cake," added Marie. "I must go now, *Hertzliebchen. Auf Wiedersehen.*"

She went off, and Jo burrowed under her blankets and growled to herself about her ill-luck. Grizel, coming to sit with her later on, found her thoroughly disgruntled. Frieda had no better luck; and Simone left the room in tears!

On the Sunday Jo was pronounced to be all right again, and was allowed to join the rest of them in the house. There was to be no going out for her for another day or two. The snow had ceased, but it was freezing hard, and there was a bitter wind. As it was, she was too thankful to get away from the sick-room and Matron, who was kind but dull, and be with all her friends again. So she made the best of things, though it was very tantalising to see the pale winter sunshine turning the frozen snow into a thousand sparkling diamonds, and not go out in it. The Robin stayed with her while the others went for a long walk in the morning. When they had returned, Miss Durrant took the school-baby for a brisk run to Seespitz, the tiny hamlet at the end of the lake.

As it was Sunday, the juniors came over to the Chalet to spend the day as usual, and there was enough noise made to justify Miss Maynard's remarks about "monkey-houses". This was the one day in the week when the girls might speak their own language all the time without let or hindrance, and they made the most of it. French,

German, and Italian were the chief languages, but there was English, of course, and some Norwegian, for there were four Norwegian girls in the school now; and a little Hungarian. As Miss Wilson had once said when they all got started, the Tower of Babel wasn't in it!

In the afternoon they passed the time in the usual way, and *Kaffee* was taken by themselves, the staff having a much-deserved rest over at Le Petit Chalet. The prefects were in charge, and Luise was in the kitchen with Rosa, the sister next in age to her—a treat always allowed the maid on Sundays.

After a while the talk turned on to the legends which surrounded the place. The Tyrol is full of stories, and Jo Bettany had learnt as many of them as possible, with an eye to the future, when she meant to use them in the books she was going to write. Frieda's father had been born and brought up by the Tiern See, and he had told the future novelist many tales, rejoicing in the deep interest she showed in them.

This afternoon, when they had finished their *Kaffee und Kuchen*, and had carried the china back to the kitchen as was the rule, the little ones insisted that Jo should tell them some of the stories.

"Tell how the Tiern See became a lake, Joey," pleaded Margia Stevens's little sister Amy. "I love that story. I'm going to make a ballad of it some day."

Like Jo, Amy had resolved to be a writer when she grew up, but her bent was for verse, and she had written some very pretty things already. Their father was foreign correspondent to one of the big London dailies, and the two girls had lived in many places, leading a gipsy life till they had been sent to the school four years before this. Both were clever children, and their wandering years had given them a wide knowledge, as well as a fairly full vocabulary in more languages than little girls generally attain. Amy was a great favourite at school, so when she clamoured for the tale, the rest joined in, and Joey, nothing loth, began at once.

"Once upon a time," she said, dropping her voice to a mysterious undertone, "there was a great city where the lake now is. Its streets were thronged with citizens; beautiful houses rose on either hand; and in the centre was a magnificent church. Every week-day the streets rang with the cries of the merchants and pedlars; the clinking of the hammers on the beaten gold and silver work, which was the chief industry of the town; the shrill voices of chaffering women, buying for the needs of their households; and the clatter of wooden shoon on the wide pavements. On Sundays the golden bells in the church steeple called folk to prayer, and the songs of sweet-voiced choristers rose to heaven from the heart of these mountains, where men lived in such wonderful surroundings. But the day came when the great prosperity of the people made them careless of what they owed to God. They forgot Him in their eager seeking after wealth and pleasure. Sunday by Sunday the bells called them to come to worship Him in vain, and things got to such a pass that the young lads used to play skittles in the aisles of the church even while divine service was going on, and the very priests themselves never said them nay.

"A good old hermit who lived near warned them that a judgment must fall on them as it did on Sodom and Gomorrah if they continued in their evil course, but they only mocked at him and paid no heed to his warnings. There came a Sunday when the sun shone down brightly on the city, with its ways thronged with people—men, women, and children all going off on pleasure bent. Save for the priests who droned out the Mass so carelessly and badly that it was an insult to God, none had been near the church except the skittles-players. All seemed well, and they thought they had nothing to fear. Then, even while the streets rang with careless laughter, a terrible thing happened." Jo dropped her voice a full tone, and some of the little ones crept nearer together. "Water began to rise above the paving-stones of the church, and to wash about the feet of the false priests. The skittles were overthrown, and the players scattered in terror. But still the water kept on rising. It flowed out of the church now, and the houses were soon awash to the sills of the windows. Terrified, the people tried to flee, but there was no safety for them. The water rose and rose with appalling rapidity, and, ere the sun had sunk to his rest in the flaming west, there was no city left. Where it had been was a still blue lake, cradled amongst the mountains, and nevermore did anyone see the wicked people who had forgotten God in the days of their prosperity. Only on fine moonlight nights, when the summer stars are glowing in the skies, if you row across the Tiern See in a boat, you may see, if you look down through the water, the gilded spire of the church gleaming up from the depths; and if you listen, you may catch faintly the chime of its golden bells, rocked to and fro by the current."

Jo told the story well—it was one that appealed to her. When she had finished a deep sigh arose from the listening throng of girls, and there were cries for more. So she told them the story of the Bärenkopf mountain, which was rather similar, and which taught the same lesson; only, in this case, it was a wicked baron who was punished by the earth on which his castle was built being raised up so that castle, baron, and all were flung down into the valley, and some of the earth with them, till they were covered from sight.

It was very dark in the room, for someone had switched off the lights to give the tales more dramatic value, and the fire in the stove had sunk to a red glow, which made the shadows very big and fearsome. In their interest in Jo's narrative, no one noticed that the door had opened and shut again, and it came as a terrific shock to everyone when someone came across the room asking in astonished tones, "What do you do, then?"

Wild screams arose at the shock, and Gertrud made a mad dive to switch on the electric light. When they could see once more, Marie von Eschenau stood before them, her eyes like saucers with astonishment. Never had she been welcomed like this!

"Marie!" cried Margia, characteristically the first to recover herself; "when did you come?"

"Just now—with papa," replied Marie. "What is the matter with you all?"

"It's Jo's fault," returned Evadne. "She was telling us bogey-tales of round here, and we never heard you till we did."

Marie laughed at this Irish speech, and kissed Jo, who was standing looking rather pale. She had succeeded in frightening herself as well as her audience, and was slow to recover. "*Marie?*" she said. I thought—I thought it was the wicked Baron Rheinhardt."

"Me, I thought it was the Devil," remarked the Robin, who was still standing clutching Grizel, on whose lap she had been sitting.

"Well, it is me only," returned Marie. "Papa has to go to München, and he said that he would bring me with him to-day instead of waiting till to-morrow, as Tante Sofie does not wish to go home yet.—Paula, I have here a box of bonbons for you from mamma, and some confitures from Tante Sofie." She held them out to her cousin, who took them rather dazedly. "Also, Wanda had two betrothal cakes, and I have one for us. It is outside in the auto."

"Was it a decent show?" asked Jo, who was recovering from her shock rapidly now.

"But yes; it was very nice, and Wanda had on a new gown of white satin. There was a great feast and many speeches, and Wanda's *Brautigam* has sent chocolate for us all. I had a new frock, too—blue silk, and we were very merry. Wandy had many betrothal gifts, and she is very happy. They will be wedded in July, and Paula and I are to be her maids. Wanda wants as many of us to be there as possible. She and Frieda will come to see us next term."

Having scattered this information on them, she sat down by the stove and warmed her hands at the blaze which Grizel had just made. The others now came round her and poured out questions, demanding details.

Wanda would be like a princess from Madame d'Aulnoy," murmured Simone sentimentally.

"Well, that's nothing fresh for her," said Jo amiably.

The rest agreed with her. Marie von Eschenau occupied the place of school beauty now, but everyone who had known her sister was agreed that Wanda far outdid the younger girl. She had passed into a sort of legend as far as the school was concerned. The picture of her in her white frock with her wreath of myrtle, and the string of pearls her uncle, the Graf von Rothenhels, Paul's father, had given her, was lovely enough to please the severest critic.

Herr Hauptmann Friedel von Glück came in for a very second share of the interest, though Marie had assured the girls that he was very amiable, and handsome as a prince out of the *Märchen*.

"Friedel's father is very kind," said Marie presently. "He asked many questions of me about us here, and says he thinks it is a very good school. Oh, and Joey, he knows all this part, for he used to climb the mountains round here when he was a boy, and he says he knows there are some wonderful caves near. He says you reach them through a narrow opening in the mountains, and you go down and down till you come to them, and they are all glittering inside as if they are made of diamonds. He thinks they must be under the lake, for he says they pass on to another cave, where there are stalactites, very beautiful. But no one knows about them, for people are afraid to venture, lest the water should break through."

"I say! How interesting!" Jo's fancy was enchained at once. "What else did he say about them, Marie?"

But the others were not very enthusiastic, and refused to listen to chatter about caves. What they wanted was to hear more of the betrothal feast. Herr Rittmeister von Eschenau came to say good-bye to his daughter before they were satisfied, and Marie had to stop her tale, to kiss him, and listen to his commands for good work and behaviour. Then he had to say a few words to Jo and Grizel, whom he knew quite well, and pat Maria Marani on the head. When he went out some of them went with him to rescue the spoils of the feast from the car, and then the bell for *Abendessen* rang, and after that the juniors were packed off to bed, and the middles had to follow half an hour later.

However, once they were undressed and in their pyjamas and dressing-gowns, Jo went through to Marie's cubicle, and, sitting on the bed with the *plumeau* tucked round her, proceeded to extract all that had been said about the caves. It was not much, but it was quite sufficient to excite Jo's imagination. "I wonder where the opening is," she remarked, sitting with her knees hunched up, and her hair all on end as usual. "Wouldn't it be topping if some of *us* could find it? Just think! They might make a show place of it, and then they would need guides, and ever so many people would come, and the peasants would be able to make lots more money in the summer, so that they wouldn't be so poor!"

She spoke with fervour, for four years in the Tiern valley had taught her how pitiably poor the peasantry were. They had only the summer in which to garner their harvest. In the winter they had to live on their summer earnings, and often that meant hard living and being on the verge of starvation for most of them. In the mountainous regions the Tyrolese pray for a short winter, and a mild one. Otherwise, life is a bitter thing for them. In the summer most of the men are cowherds, taking the cows up to the pastures on the grassy alms which run like shelves along the lower slopes of the mountains, and live up there with them, many never coming down till the cows come down in the autumn. When winter comes they have to return to their homes in the villages, while the cattle are safely housed in sheds and byres, where one man can do the work that three or four do from May to September or thereabouts. They have no other means of livelihood, and in their homes, tragedy stalks near during a long or hard season.

Jo knew this. She had come near it herself one year, when a poor family had been obliged to drown the pups of their great St Bernard, Zita, and had even spoken of shooting Zita herself. Joey had managed to rescue one of the puppies, and Madge had bought him for her. He was now a magnificent fellow, living up on the Sonnalpe, where he had more freedom than at school. The young headmistress had also taken care of Zita for the winter months, thus relieving the family of a heavy charge. After that, she had told them that if ever they were in such straits again, the big dog might winter at school. Since Zita's pups, when they arrived in the summer, were a source of income, the offer was gladly accepted and Zita had been at the school part of the previous winter. So far, she had not come this year, for the snow had come late, but if it continued for long the girls knew they might expect their great guest. Hence Jo's eagerness over the caves.

Marie, however, was a girl of very different kind. She was by no means adventurous, and rather shrank from the idea of going down into the bowels of the earth to hunt for caves. "I would rather not, Jo," she said. "But perhaps some of the men might go."

"Oh, but it would be gorgeous if our girls did it!" declared Joey. "It—it would be like saying 'thank you' for all they have done for us here."

"Well, I don't suppose we should be let," said Margia, who had strayed into the cubicle to listen to the conversation. "Think of the fuss they made when Grizel went off up the Tiernjoch, and that wasn't half so dangerous!"

"It was jolly dangerous," said Jo. "That beastly mist came down, and she was caught on that precipice place! It was ghastly!"

"Well, I don't see us getting permission to go hunting

for caves in the mountains," insisted Margia. "Madame would have a fit!"

"She mightn't know till we'd found it."

"Don't be an ass! The very first thing they'd do if any of us went missing like that would be to ring them up at the Sonnalpe to see if we'd gone there!"

There was a good deal of truth in this, but what further Jo might have said on the subject was prevented by the ringing of the silence bell, and Miss Maynard came along five minutes later to switch their lights off.

CHAPTER XI

HALF-TERM

THE days passed quickly after this. Too quickly, Grizel thought, as she counted the weeks of school-life left her, and felt how the time was going. She was devoted to her school, and she dreaded the break that the summer would bring. Always energetic, she devoted herself to doing all she could for the school, and, amongst other things, worked hard for the sale of work.

"I'm sick of fretsawing," grumbled Joey one Wednesday afternoon as she sat down to her treadle machine, and proceeded to adjust a fresh saw-blade. "As for the sale, I never want to hear of it again!"

"But there's so little time," said Grizel. "It will be half-term in three days' time, and after that we shall be in the thick of it before we know where we are."

"Thank goodness it *is* half-term!" said Jo vigorously. "And thank goodness the snow's stopped falling at last. Luise says that she thinks there will be no more now till the thaw. We always get a little then. I say, Grizel, d'you think we'll have a flood this year?"

"Shouldn't think so. Not since they deepened the bed of the stream again. We shall be safe enough. With that ditch round the place, I should think any flood there was would be drained off completely."

"You never know! Look at the Mississippi floods! They seem to get those every year, whatever they do."

"Oh, talk sense! This isn't the Mississippi, or anything

like it! It's a different kind of soil, for one thing!"

Jo cut a piece of her new puzzle, and then sat back. "We aren't having any excitements this term. We generally have something thrilling at least once in the term. I don't count your accident, 'cos it didn't affect all of us, except that we all had fits about you. I mean like the flood we had two years ago. Or the fire last summer term, when the fireball dropped during the thunder storm. *That's* what I call an excitement!"

"I dare say you do!" retorted Grizel. "Personally, I prefer a quiet life. There's the sale at the end of term if you want any excitement. And we are going up to the Sonnalpe for half-term. You be contented with that, and get on with your puzzles. I want twenty, if you can manage them."

"I've got nine done," said Jo. "This is the tenth. I don't believe you'll sell more than fifteen, anyway, even if I can get them done. I wish Friday was here."

"It'll come jolly soon. You'd better wish for decent weather while you *are* about it! I know that it's unlikely to snow again, but if a howling wind gets up, we shan't be allowed to go. That path is fairly well exposed to a west wind, and it's not too nice in a north gale."

"Oh, the wind's going to stay put," declared Jo. "It *couldn't* be so maddening as to rise when we want it to be calm!"

"The wind never does do what you want," said Grizel. "I say, Joey, *do* get on. It will be time for singing soon, and you could get a lot done now if you chose."

Joey grunted, but made her treadle go as fast as she could, cutting the puzzle carefully, but at such a speed that it was small wonder that her saw suddenly broke off. "That settles it! I'm not going to fuss to stick another in!" she announced. "Plato's arrived already, and the bell will go in a minute. I've cut a third of this beastly thing, and I've only three saws left. Someone going to Innsbruck on Saturday will have to fetch me some more."

"I will buy them, Joey," said Frieda.

"Thanks awfully. I'm going to give it a rest till after the exeat. There's the bell!"

She finished putting her work away, and then dashed off to the singing class, where Mr Denny—Plato, to the girls—proceeded to be more eccentric than usual. He always spoke in the language of Tudor times, and, since his one idea was his art, he made many and startling statements. From his point of view, all education should be based on music, and he quoted from Plato's *Republic* in season and out—Hence his name. The rest of the week was full of hard work, though Jo obstinately refused to touch her fretwork again, in spite of all Grizel could say!

It was a beautiful day, with a nip of frost in the air, just enough to make brisk walking enjoyable, and the climb up to the Sonnalpe a real treat. The Robin was to be carried up the path on her father's back—he having come over to Briesau to fetch the three girls—and the others would scramble and climb as best they could. They started off about eleven o'clock, for it would take them four hours, and the daylight would be fading by two, since the mountains cut it off.

Well wrapped up, they tramped down to the lakeside, and there Captain Humphries strapped on their skates for them, and they set off across the frozen lake. They were all expert skaters now, even the Robin managing well on her small blades, and they were soon at Seespitz, the nearest point to the foot of the Sonnenscheinspitze, the mountain of the Sonnalpe. There they took off their skates and left them with Frau Hamel, mother of two of the girls, Sophie and Gretel, who were still in school, before they set off along the narrow path till they came to the foot of the mountain.

"Gorgeous day!" said Joey, stopping to sniff the fresh, bracing air. "I do love a sharp, clear day like this! Think what it'll be like in England now!"

Captain Humphries smiled as he lifted the Robin, preparatory to beginning the climb. "I have not been in England for a good many years now, but I can imagine it!"

"Wet—cold—*slushy*!" said Jo, with a pause between each of the words. "I love England, of course, but oh, I loathe her winters!"

"Me, I do not like them at all," said the Robin from her perch on her father's shoulder. "I like the Tiern See, though, and I *love* going to see Tante Marguérite!"

"We all do," said Grizel as she struggled up the rocky path. "Come on, Jo! Don't lag, old thing!"

"It's so slippery," complained Joey as she scrambled breathlessly after the others.

"Never mind; we shall soon be there," said the captain, who was swinging over the ground as if he had no burden at all. Then he set his little girl down, and went back to help the older girls.

It took three hours' hard scrambling to bring them to the easier path which led finally to the Sonnalpe, and the sun had disappeared by that time. Joey stood and looked down at the valley below. The lake was black with its ice, and the snow lay white all round it. Immediately beneath them was Seespitz, with its Gasthaus and villas. Farther along was Buchau, where there were two or three farm-houses, and the ferry-landing. Beyond lay the pine-woods, black against the snow, and beyond them the great limestone crags and peaks of the mountains.

In the west the sun was sinking in a glory of saffron light, which told of high winds for the morrow, but Jo paid no heed to this at the moment. She stood there, her little pointed face glowing with the beauty of it all, her black eyes soft and unfathomable.

"Come on!" said matter-of-fact Grizel at last when her patience was worn out. "It's after three, and we've got half an hour's walk yet before we reach the Sonnalpe."

With a deep sigh Jo turned her back on the glory, and they set off on the last part of the way. It was very easy now, so the Robin was walking, her hand in her father's, her tongue going at a great rate. Jo and Grizel came behind them, arm in arm, for the path was fairly broad hereabouts, and saying little. Jo was still entranced by the memory of the loveliness she had witnessed, and Grizel was tired and out of breath. They reached the alpe itself at last, and here they found Dr Jem waiting for them. "Hullo!" he said. "I saw you people from the sanatorium, so I waited for you. I've got the runabout here, so I'll take you all along to Die Blumen in it. Come along! You'll be at home in ten minutes, or less, now!"

"Thank goodness!" sighed Grizel as she fell into step between them. "I'm pumped!"

"You're like Hamlet, my child—fat and scant of breath," he said teasingly.

"I'm *not* fat!" returned Grizel indignantly. "I'm out of training, if you like. We've had no chance of it this term with such awful weather. But fat I am *not*!"

"You ass, Grizel!" said Joey. "You always rise to Jem. I can't think why you do it!"

Grizel laughed, her momentary indignation forgotten as they rounded a curve and saw the doctor's little runabout standing before the steps that led up to the great sanatorium. "Well, I'm tired, anyway! I'm jolly glad you saw us and waited, Dr Jem!"

"You're late, aren't you?" he said. "I know Madge expected you earlier than this!"

"It was such a pull up," explained Joey. "It's beastly slippery too."

"We're here now, anyway, and that's all that matters," laughed Grizel as she slipped into her seat and held out her arms for the Robin. "Can you squeeze in, Jo?"

"Rather! How's Uncle Ted going to manage though?"

"I'm going to walk," said the captain.—"I have a call to make at Wald Villa before I come up to Die Blumen. Tell Mrs Russell I'll be along presently, will you?"

"Very well," said the doctor. "All safe, you people? All right! So-long, Humphries!" He pressed the starter, and they were off and bowling jerkily over the snowy ground.

"I don't think much of your roads," chuckled Joey. "A bit on the bumpy side, aren't they?"

"A bit," agreed the doctor. "We are going to have them seen to during the spring. Here we are! Tumble out, and run along in. Madge will be waiting for you."

They scrambled out and ran up the long path which led to the door, where Madge, wrapped in a shawl, was waiting to welcome them. In the summer the ground on either side would be a beautiful flower-garden; but now it was white and bare, with a few miserable-looking bushes here and there. They raced to the door where their hostess was standing, and were all caught in a clump as she pulled them in. "How late you people are! I was beginning to think something had happened and you weren't coming! Come along in! Straight upstairs, and get your things off and change your shoes! You know your rooms, don't you? Joey's next to ours, and Grizel on the other side of her. Robin, you are to sleep in papa's dressing-room, just opposite. See to her, Joey; I'm busy cooking."

Joey nodded, and they ran upstairs and along the passage till they came to their rooms. They were very dainty, furnished in the fashion of the country, with panelled walls and high white-washed ceilings. The beds had white, tent-like curtains, and one or two copies of famous pictures hung on the walls. Jo's room communicated with her sister's, and the Robin's with her father's. None of them had brought any clothes, for they kept some there in case of need. They got out of their outdoor things, changed their sturdy boots and stockings for silk and dancing sandals, brushed their hair—a very necessary thing in Joey's case—and finally ran downstairs again.

"I am hungry," observed the Robin.

"Are you, dearie? Well, Marie is bringing *Kaffee und Kuchen* now, so you won't be hungry long," replied Madge, lifting the small girl on to her knee.

"That's a mercy!" declared Joey. I'd have had to tighten my girdle or something if you had wanted us to wait much longer. Here's Jem again. I say, Jem, I've nearly finished my story! The only thing I can't decide is what to do about marrying them."

"Aren't you going to marry them?" asked Madge, who had been privileged to read the first part of this tale. "I think I should, Joey. What else can you do with them?"

"I could kill 'Raymonde' off," said Jo. "Then 'Adelaide' could—could——"

"Well? Could—what?" demanded Jem.

"Go into a convent?" suggested Grizel.

"Of course not, idiot! She's not a Catholic!"

"Marry them, of course," said Madge. "Don't make them unhappy, Jo! Even if it's only a story, let them end up all right."

"Lots of stories don't," argued Jo as well as she could for a mouthful of cake. "Look at *A Tale of Two Cities*, and *The Old Curiosity Shop*, and *The Mill on the Floss*."

"It requires genius to write a tragedy, Jo," said her brother-in-law. "I grant you that Dickens and George Eliot got away with it; but nothing is worse than the mawkish rot that some people write."

"Well, there's *Comin' through the Rye*, an' *Trilby*."

"I've never read the first, but Du Maurier was as much a genius as Dickens," said Jem.

Jo had just remembered that Madge would know nothing about the caves, and she promptly poured out all she had gleaned from Marie, together with her own theories on the subject. The doctor was interested at once. "I say, that's interesting!" he said. "When I was last in Vienna I met that open-air fiend, Professor von der Witt—you remember, Madge? He said he thought there ought to be something of the kind hereabouts, but I don't think he knew anything definitely. I must write and let him know about this!"

A ring at the telephone put a stop to their chatter just then, and Jem went to answer it. He came back looking serious. "It's the sanatorium. That poor fellow is worse again—Maynard thinks he can't last many hours now. I must go, dear."

Madge rose at once. Seven months as a doctor's wife had taught her many things. Her face was very grave as she followed her husband from the room. The girls looked at each other miserably.

Only the Robin seemed untouched. "Papa, is it someone going to Paradise?" she asked.

"Yes, my pet," he replied quietly.

"Let's go and see Rufus," suggested Grizel, shying away from the subject. "He's in the shed, Captain Humphries, isn't he?"

"Yes," said the captain. "Go through the kitchen, children, and don't stay long. Perhaps you had better go and bring him here."

They went off to call Joey's best-loved possession, a magnificent specimen of a magnificent breed, and presently returned with him, just as Madge entered. The Robin's father had gone, but she joined in the romping of the others. Six o'clock brought the baby's bedtime, and she was whisked off, Rufus following, to have her bath, while the elder girls settled themselves with books.

There was a long silence in the pretty room, then Jo put her book down. "Grizel!"

"Yes?"

"Grizel, isn't it awful? Just when we are having a jolly time, that poor man over there is—dying."

Grizel nodded. She was older than Jo, but she had not thought as deeply as the younger girl. Her mind had been running on the same subject while she had been pretending to be buried in her book. She had neither the Robin's baby faith, nor Jo's contemplative nature, and she shied away from her thoughts. "You'd better go on with your book," she said. "It's nearly time for *Abendessen*."

Jo returned to the pages, but she was not following them. Her thoughts were all on that mysterious thing that was happening at the sanatorium.

Madge divined it as soon as she entered the room after tucking up the Robin, and she crossed over to her sister.

"Joey, you need not be sorry for this poor fellow. He will be joining those he loved best to-night. The priest was here this morning, and he is prepared."

The two girls came and sat on the floor beside her.

"Madame, what is death?" asked Grizel.

"Just falling asleep with God—to awake in His presence—that's all," said Madge Russell.

"Then why are we afraid of it?"

"Because it means a change, and most of us are afraid of changes that we don't understand. But, Grizel, there is nothing to fear, really, any more than there is anything to fear when we fall asleep at night."

Grizel sat silent, thinking this over.

"God is with us through it all?" asked Joey.

"Yes, Jo. He never leaves us if we have faith in Him."

It was not many weeks later that this came back to both girls in another and very different place, and those quiet sentences helped them to face what looked like certain death with courage and calm.

Now, as they sat there, the telephone bell shrilled. Madge rose and answered it.

Presently she came back. The two faces turned to her with questioning in their eyes.

She nodded. "Yes; he has fallen asleep, and will waken in Paradise."

They said no more, but the rest of the evening was a quiet one. Their week-end had begun sadly, but, somehow, they were not as sad as they had thought they would be, and the event cast no gloom over their holiday.

Jem had not returned by nine o'clock, when Madge insisted on Joey and Grizel going to bed, since they were tired from their scramble.

"I'd like to go on with my book,' Joey protested.

"You may do that tomorrow," said her sister serenely. "Bedtime for you now. Your eyes are like saucers, and Grizel's aren't much better. Off you go, both of you! I'll come round and put the lights out presently."

Grizel was already asleep when she went to them, but Joey was lying awake. That's all it is?" she asked, apropos of nothing, as her sister bent to kiss her.

Madge understood. "Yes, Jo; that's all."

"I shan't forget," said Joey. "O-o-ow! How tired I am! G'night, Madge!"

CHAPTER XII

THE ROBIN IS LOST

"GIRLS, have you seen the Robin?"

The prefects looked up as Miss Maynard came into their room, this question on her lips.

"But no, Madame," said Vanna. "I have not seen her all day."

"Nor I," added Rosalie. "When did anyone last see her?"

"Nobody seems to know," replied the mistress with a worried look. "Amy says she went off for her afternoon nap as usual, and Klara saw she was tucked up. Since then, no one knows anything about her."

"Is she with Joey?" asked Grizel.

"Jo has been working all the afternoon, and knows nothing about her. She was never missed till half an hour ago. Girls, are you *sure* you haven't seen her anywhere?"

They shook their heads.

"We had German literature at two," said Grizel, "and at three we came up here. I had my lesson with Herr Anserl at half past, but I saw nothing of her then."

"Well it's very mysterious," said Miss Maynard. "Where *can* she have got to?"

"Could she have gone to talk to Luise?" suggested Gertrud. "She is very fond of her, and Luise loves our baby."

"That's an idea. She may be in the kitchen."

"I'll run down and see, shall I?" proposed Mary, getting to her feet. "I won't be a second, Miss Maynard."

She tore off downstairs, but returned to say that Luise had seen nothing of the Robin that day. "And please, Miss Maynard, she thinks she may be in the shed with Rufus."

Rufus had come back from the Sonnalpe with his mistress, who had declared that she simply *must* have him with her for the rest of the term. As there were only five weeks left, Madge had agreed, and the big dog had been duly installed in the shed when the girls came down with him. Miss Maynard promptly went off to see if she could find Robin there, and the prefects returned to their various pursuits without thinking any more about it. It was something of a shock to them, therefore, when the mistress returned ten minutes later to say that only Joey was with the big dog, and she had declared that the Robin had not been there when she had come.

The seniors dropped their work, and at once Grizel began an organised search party, and sent them over to Le Petit Chalet, forming another with which she hunted through the chalet till there was not a hole nor a corner which they had not investigated. It was in vain. The Robin had vanished.

"It's as strange as it was the day that you and Eigen rescued Rufus, Joey," said Simone, referring to one of Jo's exploits of two years before; "we couldn't find you then, and we can't find the Robin now."

At the reminder, Jo had rushed out of the room.

"Where has she gone?" demanded Marie von Eschenau.

They were answered by the return of Jo, leading Rufus, and Grizel behind her.

"Rufus can track her!" cried his owner. "He helped me to find Elisaveta in the summer, and this is snowtime. St Bernards are always able to do things in the snow! Hang on to him, someone, while Grizel and I get our coats and tammies!"

Evadne obligingly caught the dog's harness—and the pair vanished, to reappear wearing their outdoor things, while Grizel had the Robin's rolled up into a bundle under her arm. Jo was waving a vacuum flask which Luise had filled with hot coffee, and they looked well equipped for their expedition.

There was no staff to stop them, for all the staff were busy hunting through the grounds in case the little girl had got lost there. Grizel gave her orders. "Gertrud, go over and tell Klara to have the Robin's bed warmed for her.—Rosalie, see that there is a hot bath ready.—Vanna and Luiga, you might go and look after the babies.—Deira, you and Mary must see to the middles.—Eva, go and tell Mademoiselle that we have gone with Rufus to see if he can track her. Ask Matey to ring up the Sonnalpe, and ask if Doctor Jem can come down *without alarming Madame*! The rest of you, for any sake, be good! There's enough trouble as it is. Come on, Jo!"

They dashed off, and presently the girls saw them at the gate of the fence, showing the dog something small, which Evadne pronounced to be one of the Robin's gloves.

Evidently Rufus found the scent at once, for he dashed forward at a pace that made the girls pant breathlessly after him. Jo had hold of his chain, but he towed her along. Grizel running hard to keep up with them. Right round the fence he led them, and up to the pine-woods that covered the slopes of the Bärenbad Alpe. There he began to lead them through the trees, keeping far from the path which they usually followed.

"Help!" thought Grizel. "How on earth has she got this far?"

On went Rufus, never slackening his pace for a moment, and on went the girls. They were now reaching a part of the mountain that they did not know. How the Robin's baby feet had carried their owner this distance was a question neither Grizel nor Jo could settle.

Just as both of them were beginning to feel that they could not go on any longer, and Joey was starting a stitch in her side, the dog suddenly stopped, circled round restlessly once or twice, and then, sitting down on his haunches, threw up his nose and bayed loudly. The melancholy sound nearly finished Jo, who was tired, and Grizel felt suddenly helpless and despairing. "What *has* happened to her," cried the head girl. "Oh, Rufus, do stop that awful noise! Make him dry up, Joey!"

Joey put her arms round his neck, and kissed him on his cold nose. Then she turned to Grizel. "Grizel, where has she gone to? Do you think Rufus means that she's buried in the snow?"

"Nonsense! How could she? It's as hard as iron!" Grizel stamped on the ground to give emphasis to her words, and the ringing sound of her nail-studded boots on the frozen snow gave point to her rejoinder.

"Then what has happened?"

"Someone may have found her, and carried her," suggested Grizel.

"But who?"

"That's more than I can tell you. I didn't think anyone came here. It's supposed to be haunted, you know. Look here, Jo, suppose we go on a little farther and try him again. He might be able to pick up the scent. I don't think she's been carried off, if that's what you are thinking. There's no one—*what's that?*"

Jo turned, and looked fearfully in the direction in which she was pointing. What she expected to see, neither she nor anyone else could have told at the moment. What she actually did see was a deep cleft in the rock wall not far from where they were standing, and asleep in it was a strange old man with long white beard and hair, and in his arms, warmly wrapped up in an old deerskin, was the Robin. Both recognised her black curls at once, and both made for the group immediately. Rufus followed them, barking vociferously.

The noise woke the strange bedfellows, and the Robin sat up, holding out her arms to the girls, while the man lay where he was, gazing at them with wild blue eyes in which there was something which Grizel mentally described as "uncanny".

"*Herzliebchen!*" Jo had caught the baby to her. "Little beloved! How could you run away like this and leave us? Are you cold, *Bübchen*?"

"But no, Joey, I am very warm," replied the Robin, rubbing her curls well into Jo's mouth as she snuggled to her. "This gentleman, Herr Arnolfi he is, and he has kept me so warm. He was taking me to see where the fairies live, and we got tired, so we sat down to rest."

Grizel turned to the old man, seeing that Joey was too busy hugging the fond lamb to trouble with him. "Why did you take her off?" she demanded in German.

He chuckled in a meaningless manner, rising slowly to his feet. "It is the queen of the fairies, my little lady. I was but taking her back to her own realms."

With a little gasp of horror Grizel realised that they had to do with a madman. He might be harmless, but none the less he was insane. If he chose to resist them they were only two girls, and she had read stories which told her of the strength of insanity. Somehow they must get the baby home without frightening her. Choosing her words carefully, she answered, "It is the wrong time of year, Herr Arnolfi. Now, the fairies are all asleep till the spring shall come. Then she may go back, but now, she would be alone without attendants to wait on her. You would not be so cruel as to condemn a queen to that, would you?"

He looked at her, a madman's cunning in his eyes, that

wandered restlessly over them. "How do I know that you mortals will let her go? I am of the fairy-folk myself. Give me the little queen, and I will be her faithful attendant until the spring shall come."

"But it is not fitting that she should go thus," persisted Grizel, all her wits bent on getting them away before his insane anger should break out. "She is not robed as befits a queen. Neither has she jewels." In English she added, "Joey! Get her wrapped up, and away! Put her on Rufus's back."

Jo at once lifted the child on to the back of the great dog, who was well able to take the light weight, and had often acted the part of horse before. But she made no attempt to move. She had grasped what was the matter, and she had no intention of leaving Grizel to face the maniac by herself. The Robin, not realising, simply took the dog's fur in her hands, prepared for a merry ride on his back.

"Get off with her," said Grizel urgently. *"Quick,* Joey!"

"And leave you to this lunatic? It's likely, isn't it?" remarked Jo scornfully.

"Then tie her on, and send Rufus home. He can carry her easily. But get her away!"

Joey obeyed promptly, tying the Robin as well as she could with gym girdle and scarf. "Hold tight, darling," she murmured. "Tell them to let Rufus bring them here when you get home."

The lunatic had watched their movements with increasing suspicion. Now he turned to Grizel. "The queen has her steed. But you must go. It is not fitting that mortals should behold the court of the fairies. Go, I tell you! Go!"

He was plainly becoming excited. Grizel nodded to Jo, who guessed what it meant. Flinging out her arm in the direction in which they had come, the younger girl cried, "Home, Rufus! Home, boy!"

The gallant animal at once set off, loping along easily. As he sped off the madman gave vent to such an eldritch yell as terrified the two girls left behind, and he made off after the great dog, tearing over the snow with gigantic bounds, that, it seemed, must bring him up to Rufus in no time. But Rufus was alarmed, and he quickened his pace, the Robin clinging with terrified grip to him.

"Come on, Jo!" shrieked Grizel, catching Joey's hand. *"Run!"*

They set off at their best pace, running down the slope away from the cleft. The lunatic was still pursuing Rufus and his precious burden, but even his insane strength was running out, and already he was losing ground. Grizel realised that as soon as he saw this he would probably make for them, to wreak his vengeance on them, and she made no attempt to follow the dog's tracks. Instead, she ran steadily out from them, trusting that the shape of the valley would bring them to some well-known path sooner or later. As for Jo, she couldn't even think. She simply ran blindly on, clinging to Grizel in a blind faith which was their salvation, for had she known that they were not following Rufus, the chances are that she would have argued the point. As it was they tore on, breathless, terrified, and well-nigh blind with fear. Finally, Jo tripped up over a buried tree-trunk and fell headlong, dragging Grizel after her.

They were up in a moment and dashing on with bursting lungs, but the fall had broken their headlong flight, and in less than three minutes they knew that they could not go on. Their run fell to a walk, and, finally, Joey sank down on the ground, her hand at her side where the cruel stitch was catching, and fighting for breath. Grizel was not in much better case, but she was able to realise that they must not stay there. The cold was cruel, and already the stars were beginning to show in the skies, and they had no means as yet of knowing where they were.

The head girl bent and pulled Jo to her feet. "Come on, Joey! We can't stop here. Hang on to me, and I'll haul you along."

"I can't!" gasped Jo. "Grizel, I can't! Let me alone! Let me alone!"

But Grizel persisted. In spite of her own weariness she managed to drag Jo along with her, though it was a slow progress, and she was terrified in case they were going round in a circle, and should come up with the old madman again. Joey was becoming a dead weight and was ceasing to protest against being made to walk. Grizel knew that she herself could not go on much longer, and she shuddered inwardly as she thought of what might happen if they had to go much farther.

Mercifully, help was nearer at hand than she had supposed. Just as she was beginning to decide that she could not move another foot, the sound of voices came to them from amongst the trees, and there were lights to be seen moving in their direction. With a final effort the head girl let go her hold of Joey and called as loudly as she could. Then she, too, sank down on the ground, utterly exhausted. Three men who had come over the great Tiern Pass from Germany found them there two minutes later, and had to carry them to Lauterbach, the little hamlet at the Austrian end of the pass. Neither of them recovered consciousness till they were safely in one of the chalets, where the rescuers dosed them with brandy, to bring them to. It was some time before they could recover their wits sufficiently to say where they came from, and by that time the Chalet people, led by Dr Jem and Rufus, had succeeded in tracking them to the hamlet.

Both were so completely done that they had to stay where they were for the night, and when they were brought home next day they were put straight to bed and kept there. Joey was in the worse case. Grizel was strong as a young pony, and, except for a stiffness which soon wore off, she recovered from her fright and exertion rapidly.

Jo, on the other hand, was so worn-out that it was decided to separate her from everyone, and she was taken to her sister's bedroom, where she stayed for ten days, finally coming downstairs looking white and big-eyed, and inclined to be easily upset. Of the three the Robin came off best. She had been frightened by the old man's chasing of her and Rufus, but they had soon got away from him, and they had not gone far before meeting the search party from the Chalet, which had set out as soon as Eva had given Mademoiselle Grizel's message. It had been by accident that they had gone in that direction at all, but the baby was quickly taken from her perch and carried home in Miss Durrant's arms.

Her story, when they got it from her, was that she had finished her afternoon nap, and had got up, dressed herself, and gone out into the playing-field, as she was permitted to do on fine days. She had been running along by the fence when the old man had suddenly appeared at the other side, and had called to her and told her to come with him, for he would take her to Fairyland. She had never thought of its being naughty, but had gone off quite happily, and he had been very good to her. When she had grown tired he had offered to carry her, but she had refused, for she wanted to be a real school-girl, and she was a Brownie, anyway, and Brownies don't fuss over trifles. At last, when they had reached the cleft, he had picked her up, and told her that now he was going to take her through it to Fairyland, where she would be queen. Only he was tired and must rest. So he had sat down and taken her in his arms.

The next thing she knew, Joey and Grizel and Rufus were there, and then they had put her on Rufus's back, and sent him home with her, and the old man had been *very* angry. He had run after them, but Rufus had run faster, and then Miss Maynard and Miss Durrant and Miss Wilson had come, and Miss Durrant had carried her home. And she was very sorry. Please would they forgive her?

"You were very naughty, my child," said Mademoiselle, You are not permitted to leave the school by yourself. Poor Joey and Grizel had a terrible time, and now they are ill in bed because you were so naughty."

The Robin wept bitterly. She adored Joey, who was her ideal in everything, and she was not allowed to go near her beloved. Grizel, too, had been very kind to her. They could have inflicted no worse punishment on her than she had brought on herself, and after a little more talk Mademoiselle consented to forgive her, and kissed her.

However, that escapade of the Robin's was to have much farther reaching results than they yet realized, but after Grizel had been gently told that she should never have gone off as she did, nothing more was said. In Jo's case, scolding had to be put on one side. Her nerves had received a severe shock, and she was not herself all the rest of the term.

As for the old man, he had vanished as completely as if he had never existed. If it had not been that all three girls told the same story, and told it independently, those in authority would have decided that he had been a figment of imagination.

The Briesau people had another explanation of him. *They* said that he was a devil who had vanished by the aid of Satan, and that the children had had a narrow escape from being carried off to hell!

CHAPTER XIII

THE HOLIDAYS

THE rest of that term passed quietly and quickly. The girls busied themselves with their preparations for the sale, and Joey managed to content herself with her fretwork. She remained very quiet, and was still easily upset, even when the end of term came, so that the staff were thankful that in a few days she would be safely in her sister's care.

Rufus, who had proved himself such a hero, was well on the way to being spoiled, for everyone petted him, and he was rewarded with tit-bits dear to his doggish heart, and some of the middles nearly came to blows over the question of who was to look after him while his mistress was absent from him. It was finally settled by the prefects themselves, who undertook to see to his grooming and baths, and so saved the school from what looked like some promising feuds.

"For goodness sake, try to behave as though you *were* middles, and not juniors!" said Grizel, whose first act on leaving the sick-room had been the settlement of this affair. "*None* of you will have anything to do with him, because *we* will do all he needs."

The sale was a huge success. By the time the girls had laid out all they had made themselves, and added to it all the contributions from other people, they found that they had enough for two needlework stalls, one handwork stall, a sweet stall, a toy stall, and the little ones' lucky dip. When it was all over they counted their takings, and there was wild rejoicing when they found that they had made enough to keep one of the free beds filled for a whole year.

"I vote we do this every year," said Grizel, as she locked her cash-box; "then it could be the Chalet School bed, and Doctor Jem would always feel sure of *that*, anyway."

"Good idea," said Mary. "I vote we do. What do you others think?"

They all agreed, and Grizel was made to sit down then

and there and write to Doctor Jem, telling him what they intended doing.

The result of this was that when Grizel, Joey, and the Robin put in an appearance at the Sonnalpe on the first day of their holidays, they were escorted ceremoniously to the sanatorium, and taken to the big free ward for children. There were no patients there yet, though some would be arriving shortly. It was a sunny room, with picture-flowers, and a glorious view from the windows. But the girls paid no heed to all this. One thing only caught their eyes. The middle cot had a brass plate over it, and on this was engraved "The Chalet School Bed."

"Jem! You *ripper!*" gasped Jo. "Oh, how decent of you to get it done before we came up!"

"It's topping!" said Grizel. "Ever so nice, Doctor Jem."

"I like the shiny thing," remarked the Robin gravely. "Why has it our name up, Oncle Jem?"

They explained it to her carefully, and she listened with a beaming face. When they had finished, she heaved a deep sigh. "I will save all my *Schillings*," she said.

Doctor Jem stooped and kissed her. "You are a darling," he said.

The Robin kissed him back, and then turned to Mrs Russell. "Will it please you, Tante Guito?"

"Very much, my pet."

The next few days were spent in taking walks in the neighbourhood, but they soon exhausted all the possibilities, and by the time they had climbed the mountain twice they were ready for something fresh.

"That's the only drawback to here," said Grizel, as they sat in the salon after *Kaffee* one day. "There aren't many places you can go to, and now it's thawing, the whole place is ankle-deep in mud! This is the second time today I've had to change my stockings!"

"Well, I had to change every solitary thing," declared Jo between two bites of *apfeltorte*. "You'll have fits when you see my laundry, Madge!"

Madge Russell laughed. "I don't doubt it for one moment. If there *is* any mud you can get into, you seem to make for it headlong, Jo. I never knew anyone like you for it! You're worse than Dick used to be!"

"Has the Indian mail come today?" asked Jem.

"Yes; but I haven't opened it yet. It's a thick package this time, so I expect Mollie managed to get time to put in a decent letter for once," said his wife, as she produced the letter from her twin brother, who was in the forest service in the Dekkan. "Yes; there's something from her."

"Goodness! What a screed!" ejaculated Jo. "Read us what she says, Madge."

Madge nodded and began:

DEAR PEOPLE,—It is such ages since I wrote you a decent letter, that I thought I'd take this opportunity, while mother is with us and looking after the twins and baby, to let you know what we are doing. I should say, what we are going to do, I suppose. Because this is to warn you that we are coming home in June, and hope to be with you in August. Dick gets leave early in May, and it's a six months' furlough this time. We are coming straight to you, so I hope you can have us. If you can't, we'll go to one of the hotels by the lake-side.

If you're not all dying to see your nephew and nieces, you ought to be! Rix and Peggy are imps of wickedness. Where they get it from I can't imagine! Not from me, that's certain. I suppose it must be Jo, for Dick says you were never as sinful as our twins are. As for Babs, she's still at the stage when she sleeps most of the time, and is a good little thing. She is like Dick—the image of him, I think! He, of course, says he doesn't know where I see it. The first time I told him he had the cheek to go off to the nearest mirror and examine himself carefully, murmuring all the time, "I *may* be plain, but I'm not as bad as all that!" As I told him, he doesn't deserve a daughter at all!

Rix is like that photo of Madge she sent us on her wedding-day. Peggy is dark like me, and Dick says, like Joey too. Can you picture them *my* children? Dick and me with three kiddies. Of course, Babs is only three weeks old yet, but still it does make us seem *old*! After all, the twins are thirteen months now; they can walk and talk, though a lot of their conversation is absolutely unintelligible.

Babs is to be christened next Sunday. We are going to call her Mary—after me; and Bridget after my little sister, who died before I was born. I suppose she will be Biddy as soon as she is old enough for a name. That won't be for ages yet.

What is happening at school? Have you had any more excitements this term? I am longing to see it, and to get to know all the girls. You've written so much about them that I feel as if I knew them all. We want to stay till term begins again—I suppose you'll have broken up by the time we arrive? Still, I shall hope to see the Robin and Juliet and Grizel, if she hasn't left you by then.

Babs is howling for me, so ayah will be fetching her. Therefore, my dear relations, I must wind up this epistle. You can't say I haven't done you proud this time!— Much love to all, from MOLLIE.

"Isn't she a sport?" said Jo enthusiastically. "Fancy me with three nieces and nephews!"

"You've only one nephew and two nieces," Grizel pointed out to her.

"Oh, well, you know what I mean. What does Dick say, Madge?"

"Mainly full of his furlough," replied her sister. "I'm glad they're coming. I've been wanting to know Mollie ever since I first heard of her. From her letters, she's a dear. Also, I *am* longing to see the babies. How nice of Rix to be like me!"

"He must be a discerning youth," laughed the doctor, with an admiring glance at his charming wife. "Mollie will have her hands full with those three kiddies!"

"Oh, she'll have an ayah for them," said Madge easily. "Well, what are we going to do with ourselves now?"

"Let's play at something," suggested Joey. "The Robin will have to go to bed soon."

"There are yet two hours," protested the Robin.

"Well, two hours goes jolly fast when it's near bedtime," declared Joey. "What would you like to play at?"

" 'Walking Up the Hill-side'," decided the Robin. "Oh! Here comes papa!" She ran to meet her father, who picked her up, and came into the room with her on his shoulder. He was smiling as he came, and Joey thought, not for the first time, that "Uncle Ted" was a dear when he looked like that.

"I've some news for you all," he said as he sat down, transferring his little daughter to his knee. "You may have three guesses among you."

"An expedition to-morrow," said Jo instantly.

"That's right as far as it goes. But you must get nearer than that, Joey."

"We are going to Salzburg," said Grizel instantly. It

was a long-desired trip, and had been promised to them for some time.

"Clever girl! Yes; I saw the Lannisses to-day, and Mr Lannis has to go over on business. He offers to take you three and Mrs Russell if she can come."

"The children may go," replied Madge. "I'm afraid I can't."

"Oh, Madge! Why not?" Jo's voice was full of disappointment.

"I'm sorry, Jo, but I haven't the time. What arrangements did you make with Mr Lannis, Captain Humphries?"

"I said we would ring them up and let them know," replied the captain. "He is going by car, and is taking Evadne. If the children may go, he will meet us at the foot of the mountain at nine o'clock. They must bring things for the night, as he thinks it is too far to go and come in one day, and his business may take a little time. Mrs Lannis is not going, but her French maid will be there, so that the girls won't be left alone while he is at his meeting. He hoped you would go, Mrs Russell; but if you couldn't, he says Suzette is quite capable of looking after them. They will, of course, promise to do as she says." He glanced down at his own little girl, who nodded her curly head. "Me, I will be very good, papa; I will do all Suzette tells me."

"And you others?" He looked across at Joey and Grizel.

"Oh, rather!" said Jo. "I'll be an angel without wings if you let us go, Madge."

Madge laughed. "If you are, it'll be the first time, and I can *not* imagine you being angelic on any occasion, Jo. Still, I feel sure you will do as you are told, and not give Mr Lannis any trouble."

"I'll look after them," promised Grizel, and Madge was satisfied. She knew that if Grizel kept the other two out of mischief, she would necessarily keep out of mischief herself.

So it was arranged, and as soon as Captain Humphries had had his coffee, he went off to ring up the hotel where the Lannisses were staying and tell them that the girls would come.

As for those young ladies themselves, they rushed upstairs to pack a small case with their belongings as soon as the meal was over. Madge followed to suggest early bed, since they would have to be up by five the next morning, and would have a full day. She drew Grizel to one side while the other two were joyfully arguing about their trip.

"Grizel, I want you to promise me that you will try to see that the Robin is in bed by eight o'clock at latest. I know that Evadne sits up to all hours at home, and I expect you and Jo will not get off before ten. But the Robin *must* go as near her usual time as possible. It won't hurt Jo to sit up for once, and, of course, you are much older, and ten is not too late in holiday times when you are not working, and can sleep later the next morning. But the Robin would be worn out for the rest of the week if it was permitted her. Will you see to it, dear?"

Grizel nodded. "Yes, of course I will, Madame."

"I'm sorry to burden you with all this responsibility, Grizel; but after all, if I can't trust my head girl, whom can I trust?"

"I'll do my honest best," promised Grizel, a little more colour than usual touching her pretty face. "I can't do more."

"Then I can let you all go quite happily," said her Head with a smile. "You are a great comfort to me, Grizel. I feel I can trust you with them anywhere."

The commendation was deserved, for that term had shown that Grizel, when she put her mind to it, could be as trustworthy and as steady as ever Gisela or Juliet had been. Jo had taken good care that everyone should know how the head girl had tried to send her off with the Robin, and faced the maniac alone, and it had been Grizel's doing that they had got off as they had. Madge felt that the turning-point in the girl's career had come when they had resolved to give her one more chance, and was glad that she had done so; and though she had had a good many qualms at first, she was proud of Grizel now.

There was no chance of saying anything more, for Joey and the Robin came racing up at that minute to demand if it was really necessary to take an extra pair of stockings, as Marie Pfeiffen, who had come to help them, insisted.

"It'll be such a bore carting all that along!" said Jo.

"Well, if you don't take the stockings, it will mean that you'll have to stay at the hotel if you get your feet wet. Of course, if you like that idea, you can leave the extra pair behind. But you may please yourself about it." Eventually the stockings went in, though it entailed twenty minutes spent with a darning-needle, which had been her reason for objecting. Jo loathed mending, but she had no intention of spending the precious hours in Salzburg shut up in a hotel.

CHAPTER XIV

SALZBURG

GETTING up early in the morning was not a favourite pastime of Grizel's, though Joey was usually an early riser. On this morning, however, the head girl was first out of bed, and was nearly dressed before Jo made any move. Madge was dressing the Robin, who was wild with excitement at the prospect of seeing Salzburg, and it was the faithful Marie who woke up Miss Joey.

They were to go down as quickly as possible, for Mr Lannis had said he could not afford to wait, as his business appointment must be punctually kept, and he wanted to have lunch first. In the afternoon, while he was away, Suzette would take the girls to see the house where Mozart was born, now the Mozart Museum.

From there, they would go on to the cathedral, though Joey refused to be very much interested in it. Her favourite period of architecture was the Gothic, and the Salzburg Cathedral was built in the early part of the seventeenth century in the Italian baroque style, which she disliked. The Robin was anxious to see the famous fountain, the Hof-Brunnen in the Residencz-Platz, of which Amy Stevens had often told her. The Stevens had spent more than one winter in this beautiful town, and the great fountain had been Amy's favourite spot in it. Grizel had no special desires, and Evadne only wanted to go for the sake of the trip.

She greeted them joyfully when they arrived at the foot of the mountain, escorted by the doctor. "Say! Isn't this real nice?" she inquired, as she made room in the car.

"Gorgeous!" replied Jo ecstatically. "I'm dying to see Salzburg!"

"Your old Nap had a lot to do with it, I suppose?

That's why you want to see it all so much, I guess. What I want is to hear that weird music thing at the Franciscan Church, and they don't let females in—mean skunks!"

"*What* weird music thing?" demanded Grizel.

"Don't remember its name, but I'm real mad to see it!"

"Well, if they don't let women in, I don't see you doing so," grinned Joey unsympathetically. After a pause she continued, "I say, isn't this positively gorgeous? I love mountain scenery!"

Evadne looked out of the window casually. "It's not so dusty. I say, Joey, what d'you bet I get in and hear it, after all?"

"Nothing! You jolly well won't! Talk sense, Evadne, and let it alone! You'll only get run in if you try it on! They'd be safe to send for the *gendarmerie*. Don't make such an ass of yourself!"

Grizel, who had been staring out of the window, roused up to what was going at this point, and demanded to know what they were talking about. Jo enlightened her, and she promptly squashed her hostess. "Don't be mad, Evadne! Do you want to let your father in for paying a big fine? For that's what it would come to."

Evadne murmured something about "Poppa could afford it all right," but she ceased to discuss it, and the four returned to their gazing out of the window at the scenery.

It was very wonderful. At this point the road runs through mountains—the junction of the Tyrolean and Bavarian Alps, though they never crossed the frontier. Then it turns down into the Salzach valley, and follows the silver Salzach along till it reaches the suburbs of Salzburg. The suburbs are no more interesting than those of any other city, but in the great Mercedes-Benz they were soon left behind, and they came to old Salzburg, the great ecclesiastical city that generations of archbishops have built up on either side of the stream. On the east rises the great Kapuzinerberg hill, and on the west the city is flanked by the Mönschberg, both with wooded slopes, and houses nestling among the pines, larches, and silver birches.

The old houses, with their deep-red tiles and steeply sloping roofs, make one think of fairy-tales; and the glimpses of the silver river, the old cobbled streets, and the views of the grim castle of Hohen-Salzburg, which can be caught now and then, all go to add to the impression.

Joey was wild with delight, and the Robin shared her joy, though the other two unromantically declared that they were hungry, and wanted lunch!

Their wishes were fulfilled almost immediately, for Mr Lannis drew up outside a restaurant on the far side of the river, and told them all to "come out, and get a hustle on about it."

Joey looked about her with a dissatisfied air, for they were now in modern surroundings, and there was nothing in her eyes that was interesting. The others pressed after the busy American into the restaurant, where they were served with a delicious meal.

"Well, Miss Joey, how do you like this place?" queried their host, as they ate soup full of macaroni and very delicious.

"It's awfully pretty, of course," said Joey, "but I love the old town that we came through to get here."

"Joey's mad on history, poppa," said Evadne. "I guess she doesn't think much to *this!*"

Mr Lannis laughed. "Why, we're right next door to the Schloss"—he pronounced it "slosh"—"Mirabell, which they reckon to be a fine sight, and chock-full of history."

"Oh, can we see it?" begged Jo eagerly.

"Why, I guess so. You'll like the gardens, anyway, and they have a wonderful aviary here. I ken't take you myself, but Susie will look after you all, and to-morrow we'll go and visit the castle—if it's open on the Sabbath, which I guess it is in these parts.—See here, Grizel, I'll give you the money now, and you all meet me at our hotel at Six. You're to get your *Kaffee* at four as usual, and you ken go shopping, for I want you should all take back a little gift to remember this visit. I guess there's enough there to give you each some spending-money, and the rest will pay for your sight-seeing and *Kaffee und Kuchen*. Finished your soup? Hi, *Kellner!*"

The waiter came to change their plates, and serve them with tiny trout-like fish which were cooked in some wonderful sauce. It was followed by a fricassee of chicken and a pudding that made Evadne regret aloud that she had eaten so much of the other courses. They had coffee, and then Mr Lannis rose, paid the bill, and delivered them over to Suzette, whom he charged to take good care of them.

Suzette, taking the Robin's hand firmly, sent the other three on in front of her where she could keep an eye on them all the time, and they made their way to the entrance to the beautiful gardens of the Schloss, which the Archbishop Wolf Dietrich von Raitenau had had built for the lovely daughter of a Salzburg merchant in 1606. Grizel paid the small fee demanded, and they entered the grounds, where they were soon gasping with admiration. Here, in this sheltered part, the flowers bloom nearly all the year round, and at the end of March, when their own part of the country was just beginning to wake up, the beds were showing daffodils, narcissi, snowdrops, hyacinths, and many other spring flowers, while the velvety turf of the fine lawns was as green as if winter were not just ended. The place is almost a miracle of beauty, with long avenues, bordered by fine trees; ponds, fountains—at which the Robin cried delightedly—mazes, and beautiful groups of statuary. High above this, across the river, towers the huge fortress of the Hohen-Salzburg, like a grim sentinel keeping watch over a Sleeping Beauty.

"It's gorgeous!" cried Jo. "Fancy living here, and being able to come into this whenever you wanted to! What was the name of the lady? Anyone know?"

Nobody did, and she had to wait till they saw Mr Lannis again to learn that the lady's name had been Salome Alt, and that she had been a great friend of the archbishop's, who also had the credit of the great cathedral to his name.

At the aviary the Robin went nearly wild with delight, and insisted on staying there so long that it was nearly four before they could persuade her to leave it, and come to the town for *Kaffee und Kuchen*.

The town pleased them, though Joey declared that the shops were "rotten" compared with those of Vienna, which she knew well. Still, they got an excellent meal in a pretty Café Corso on the Gisela Kai, where they looked on to the silver river winding its way through the heart of the city, and feasted on wonderful cakes, with Suzette keeping a watchful eye on them all to see that they did not overdo it. She was very proud of her four charges, for Grizel, Evadne, and the Robin were pretty children, and Joey made up in distinction of appearance what she lacked in beauty.

When their appetites were satisfied they went shopping,

and in the shops they found many charming things. Grizel bought "Cookie" a view of the cathedral, and also provided herself with some handkerchiefs embroidered with peasant embroidery for Mrs Russell. Evadne invested in a paper-knife adorned with a head of the great archbishop for her father, and presented Jo with a pen-holder wonderfully and weirdly carved. Jo bought post-cards, a tiny ashtray for Jem, a doll for the Robin, and a collar for her sister; and the Robin, after many confabulations with all of them, spent her money on—a pencil-case for the doctor, a brooch for his wife, handkerchiefs for the three girls, a collar for Suzette, a match-box for Mr Lannis, and a new tie for her father.

"Papa will like it, *n'est-ce pas?*" she said to Joey, displaying its glories of blue dashes on a mauve ground to them all.

"He'll be overcome," vowed Joey, when she had recovered her breath.

"You see," explained the small girl, "papa always wears such sad colours, so I thought he might like this. It is so pretty."

The thought of what Captain Humphries, who was always clad in dark things, and whose ties certainly bore no affinity to the lurid thing exposed to their view, would say on being informed that he was expected to wear it nearly convulsed Grizel and Jo, though Evadne, not knowing him as they did, saw nothing to laugh at, and opened her eyes when Joey, with a feeble excuse about "something awfully funny in that policeman," gurgled wildly, and Grizel joined her.

He's just like all of them, I guess," she said, after a prolonged scrutiny of the unconscious gendarme. "I don't see anything to laugh at about him."

"And it is not *comme il faut*," added Suzette severely. "Young ladies should not thus laugh in the street. They should be calm and well-behaved. Permit that I wrap up the cravat, *ma Petite*, and let us now return to our hotel."

The Robin gave up the tie, and she folded it up inside its paper, and, with a final look of reproach, sent Evadne and Grizel on in front, keeping Jo and the Robin with her.

As the Robin was not permitted to sit up for dinner, they showed Mr Lannis their purchases before that, and he was highly gratified at their gifts. He was in a fine good humour, for his business had gone well. He told them that he was going to take them all to the theatre except the baby, and on the next day he would take them to the Mozart Museum and the cathedral, as well as the castle. Then the gong sounded for dinner, and the Robin trotted off to bed cheerfully, for Suzette had promised to sit beside her and tell her fairy-tales before she went to sleep, and Evadne had said that Suzette was a "ripper at stories! Guess she makes 'em up half the time, but they're *pie*!"

A pretty musical comedy from Vienna was under way when they reached the theatre, and the three girls enjoyed it immensely.

"One of the very nicest times I've ever known," said Jo, as she shook hands with Mr Lannis. "If to-morrow's like today's been, this will be a topping visit!"

However, much was to happen before then.

It was half-past two in the morning, and Jo was having wild dreams in which Archbishop Wolf Dietrich, Salome Alt, the play they had seen that night, and the Robin's gift to her father were all thoroughly mixed up, when a bell suddenly clanged out sharply, startling her awake at once. At the same time, there was a wild shriek of "Fire!" through the building, and a noise of people hastily and horrifyingly awakened from sleep. She started to her feet at once, grabbing the first garments that came handy, and struggling into them at top speed, while she shrieked to Grizel, who was sleeping in a bed in the opposite corner. Grizel tumbled out, and made for the electric switch, but in vain. She, too, grabbed her clothes, and got into them in hot haste, while Jo made for the door to get to the Robin. It was opened as she reached it, and Mr Lannnis came in, the baby in his arms, Evadne following him, and Suzette, completely unnerved, and in wild hysterics, clinging to his arm. His face brightened as he saw, by the light of his electric torch, that the girls were awake and quite self-controlled. A wave of smoke came in with him too, and they could hear the dull roaring of the fire, though, as yet, they could see no flames.

"Here, Grizel," he said sharply; "take the baby! There's a fire-escape at the end of this corridor. Come along, all of you!"

He hustled them out, flinging an arm round Suzette, who screamed incessantly, and literally carrying her along the corridor, down which he ran, the children after him.

They found the window to the escape blocked with people, many of them frantic with terror; and the noise of their cries, the agony in their faces, made the two English girls sick with horror. Evadne was crying quietly with fright, though she made no scene, only clung to Joey. The American realised that it would be dangerous to take the girls into that panic-stricken crowd, and turned back. He remembered having seen another escape at a window on the storey above them. Without a word he dragged Suzette along, the girls following him. Up the stairs they went, and came into a much narrower corridor. Here there was only one man, who was wrestling with the fastening of the window that gave on to the escape, and a fat, elderly woman. Awful as was their peril, Jo suddenly gave vent to a little giggle as she recognised her. "It's Frau Berlin!" she said to Grizel. "We're always running over her at times like this."

Grizel, the Robin close in her arms, looked, and remembered the woman they had met during their first term at the chalet who had treated them so rudely, and whom Madge had later saved from a burning train when they were coming from the Dolomite district. Mr Lannis had dropped Suzette, who sank on the ground, moaning in terror, and made for the window, which he broke open with the first thing that came handy. Then he lifted Evadne out, and bade her go down as quickly as she could. Grizel put the Robin out next, and Jo followed. The American directed her to go on, and was turning back to pull Suzette up, when Frau Berlin made a dash, and clambered through the space, rushing down at a pace that was likely to endanger the lives of the children who were in front.

"Go on and stop her," said the strange man. "I will see to the woman."

Mr Lannis obeyed—there was no time for argument, for already the flames were beginning to lick through from the lower windows, and the girls were in fearful peril. He reached the frenzied woman just in time to stop her from trying to thrust Grizel aside, and, holding her in a grasp that bruised her, shouted to the girl to go on steadily, and keep to the outside hand-rail. Frau Berlin writhed and struggled in his grip, but he was a big man, luckily, and the thought of the harm she might do to the children gave him the strength to hold her, while his unknown friend got through with Suzette, and joined him.

None of them was likely to forget that journey down the iron stairs. By the time the two men with their charges had reached the first floor of the hotel the escape was almost wrapped in flames, and it was a miracle that they got through alive. Mr Lannis's first thought was for the girls. They were all standing at the bottom, in charge of one of the firemen, who was trying to get them away. The Robin had been thrust by Jo to the outside of the escape, and, with the elder child's skirt flung round her, was unhurt. Evadne and Jo were sights to behold, with their grimed faces and singed hair, but, save for one or two superficial burns, they were not damaged. Grizel was much worse off, though they did not know this till later on, when they were all retiring to bed in another hotel where they had taken refuge. She had been scorched by the flames, but not badly. The burns smarted, but she had reassured her host that she was all right; then when she put up her hands to tie back her hair, she gave a shriek, for a long curl came off in her fingers. Her cry was echoed by the other children, and Mr Lannis, very much bandaged, and still red-eyed from the smoke, came in to see what had happened. In the centre of the big room where the four were to sleep stood Grizel, holding her severed lock, while Jo and Evadne were standing aghast, and the Robin, from the bed where she had been tucked in by a now steadied and remorseful Suzette, was eyeing them with deep interest.

"What's got you all?" asked the big man.

For reply Grizel dropped her curl, put her hands to her head again, and literally ran off the lengthy locks. Then she stood there, denuded of her long hair, and looking scared. It had all been scorched in the flames as she had torn through them, and so had come off at the first tug.

Mr Lannis was horrified. At first he was afraid that her neck was burned, but the hair had saved it. Only— Grizel was fated not to put up her curls for some time to come. There was nothing to be done. Once he realised that the girls were really all right, Mr Lannis ordered them off to bed, and stayed there till they were safely between the sheets. In the morning he took Grizel to a hairdresser's and had her cropped, as that was the only thing to do. The hair had been scorched pretty close to her head, and was all uneven.

"What *will* Madge say when she sees you?" said Joey. "She'll have a fit, I should think!"

"She'll be so glad that we are all alive she will say nothing," replied Grizel soberly. "If I hadn't shaken my hair over my face, *it* would have been burned, and I'd rather lose my hair than that."

"Oh, well, it'll be a saving of time in the morning," said her friend comfortingly. "But *oh*, Grizel, you do look so different with it all gone!" She gave a hysterical little giggle.

Grizel shook her slightly. "Jo, shut up, you ass! Suzette's bad enough without *you* starting! You're to come and see if your new things will fit."

She and Mr Lannis had been shopping, for all their clothes had gone in the fire which had left their hotel completely gutted. He had insisted on refitting them, and, what was more, had bought their gifts over again, though the head girl had tried to stop him. Several coats and hats had been brought to their present resting-place for them to try on, and they were soon all fitted out, even down to underclothes, for they had all put on very little in their escape, and the Robin had had nothing but her pyjamas and dressing-gown.

When that business had been done, Mr. Lannis marched them off to the station. He was not fit to drive the car, which had to be left in the garage till someone could bring it home. They were to be met at Spärtz by Dr Jem, to whom he had phoned, with the runabout, for the railway was not yet opened.

"What happened to Frau Berlin?" asked Joey as she sat down in her corner, the Robin cuddled close to her.

"Hanged if I know," replied Mr. Lannis forcefully. "That woman should be shut up! She might have——" He paused and looked at them. He was doubtful how much they realised of the danger from the frantic woman.

Joey answered this unconsciously. "She might have fallen down and killed herself. I don't like her, but it would have been horrid if that had happened, and it might have done."

"She's a pie-faced, rubber-necked four-flusher," said Evadne. "Those railings were as open as anything. She'd have gone *some* crash if she *had* gone."

Grizel shivered slightly. She knew what danger had threatened them all, if the others didn't. It wouldn't have been Frau Berlin who would have fallen through the railings. Mr Lannis noticed it, and promptly began to talk about the history of Salzburg to divert her mind from the memory. He was so successful that twenty minutes later Jo and the head girl were well away with their old argument as to whether Napoleon was a great man or not, and they kept off dangerous topics for the rest of the journey, much to the American's relief.

CHAPTER XV

THE NEW TERM

"MATRON, can I unpack now, please?"

"Please, Matron, which is to be the new girl's cubey in our dorm?"

"Matron, may I have the window cubey this term? *Do* say I may!"

"Please, Matron, Miss Maynard says if the new girl, Cornelia Flower, is unpacked, can she go to the study? If she isn't, can she go as soon as she *is*?"

Matron sat back on her heels and glared round the importunate throng. "If you don't all stop talking for five minutes," she remarked, "you'll drive me into the nearest lunatic asylum. Now, Jo, give me Miss Maynard's message again, please."

Like a parrot Jo repeated her message gravely, and the harassed lady who saw to the physical welfare of the Chalet School nodded. "Cornelia Flower is unpacked, and may go with you now. Her cubicle is Number Five; can you remember that, Cornelia?"

"Ya-as," drawled Cornelia, a fair, sturdy girl with enormous blue eyes.

"Then trot along with Jo. She can look after you for the present.—No, Evadne; you may *not* have a window cubicle. I know what that would mean! You will sleep in Number Seven, as you did last term.—Yes, Ilonka; I am ready to unpack you now, so come along, and don't waste time.—Paula and Frieda, you may be getting your cases opened; and, Simone, you can help to carry Ilonka's things to her cubicle."

Having thus disposed of her charges, Matron turned

back to her work, and Jo walked off with Cornelia to the study, where Miss Maynard was waiting to interview her before deciding into which form to put her.

It was the last week of April, and the weather was gloriously fine, so when Joey had seen Cornelia close the study door after her, she wandered out into the flower garden, where she found her own special gang, with the exception of the people who were unpacking, all congregated together, and discussing the new term. Her appearance was hailed with cries of delight.

"Here comes Jo! Now she will tell us everything!" The speaker, Bianca di Ferrara, ran forward and linked her arm in her leader's. "Jo, we wish to know if it is true that Madame is not coming down to school at all this term? Luigia says that Grizel has said so."

"Yes; quite true," replied Jo. "Jem thinks the walk will be too much for her in the hot weather. So she's going to stay up at the Sonnalpe, where it will be cooler than down here."

"But, Jo, what happens about her birthday, then?" demanded Margia Stevens.

"Don't know, I'm sure! We'll have to have the 'do' without her, I suppose."

The girls looked at each other in dismay. Ever since Mrs Russell had come to the Tyrol and established her school on the shores of the Tiern See, they had kept her birthday as a festival, and the idea of not having her with them for it was one they did not relish.

"How very—not nice!" said Klara Melnarti at length, after a blank silence.

"Can't be helped! P'r'aps they'll have us up there for it," suggested Jo. "Jem said he would think of it. It all depends."

"Oh, but that would be ravishing!" declared Bianca, beginning to smile. "Jo, Grizel said that we were to have some new girls this term. Do you know anything about them?"

"I've just carted Cornelia Flower off to Maynie," said Jo cheerfully.

"What is she like?" asked Klara. "She has a pretty name."

"Well, she doesn't live up to it—as far as looks go," said Jo. "She's nearly square, and she has a jaw like—like—well, like a ramrod! About fourteen, I think, and she's in the Yellow dorm. Who's Head there this term? Anyone know?"

"Mary is, I think," said Bianca.

"Well, she's got a handful in Cornelia, or I'm blind! What possessed Matey to put two Americans in one dorm?

No one felt able to reply to this question, so they passed it over, and asked if Jo knew anything about the other new girls.

"Two more middles—but they're to be day," was the response. "Sisters, who are at the Post with their people. And I believe the babes are getting one."

"Then we are more than sixty this term," remarked Bianca with satisfaction. "That goes well! Of what nationality are the new girls, my Jo?"

"Bavarian," replied Jo. "They come from München, I think. Oh, and I've got some topping news for you all! Remember Marie Pfeiffen? Well, she's to be married next week, and we're all to go to the wedding! There's richness for you!"

A hurricane of exclamations of joy greeted this announcement. Many of the girls knew Marie very well, for she had been maid at the school for three years, only leaving it when her young mistress went to the Sonnalpe.

"Are we going to the dancing as well?" demanded Margia, when they had calmed down a little.

"*Rather!* What do *you* think? That's the best part of it. We're to go for three hours, and I've promised to have a dance with Andreas!"

"Rot! How can you? You don't know the *Schuhplattler*!" retorted Margia.

"I do! He and Marie taught us one during the hols. Grizel and I are going to teach you people, so that you can all do it. Besides, they are going to have some waltzes as well."

"Mean to say we're going to lift great men off the ground like they do?" asked Margia incredulously.

"Talk sense! This is one of the milder ones. Even the babes are to go for a while! There'll be some excitement, won't there?"

Bianca laughed. "There won't be any work done next week," she said. "When does the wedding take place?"

"On Thursday—a week to-day. Marie was awfully bucked with her present, by the way. She's hung it in her kitchen, and she's going to stick a table underneath, and keep flowers on it as long as she can. Isn't it topping of her?"

"Very nice indeed," said Bianca.

The Chalet School's gift had been a large group of the whole school, which they had had framed, and had sent up at the end of the previous term. Marie had been overjoyed at it—partly because one exactly the same hung in Madame's salon.

The group broke up after that, Jo going back to the study to see if Miss Maynard had finished with Cornelia, and the others scattering to various parts of the school ground.

At the study door Jo encountered Grizel, who was coming in search of her, to tell her that Cornelia was waiting for her, and grinned at the head girl cheerfully. "Hello, old thing! Haven't seen you since *Mittagessen*! What have you been doing?"

"A million things, I should think," said Grizel, running her fingers through her neatly-cropped hair—this departure had created quite a sensation already!—and heaving a sigh. "Miss Maynard has finished with Cornelia, Jo, and sent me to find you."

"Righto! I was just going to fetch her. Wonder where Maynie's put her."

"You'll know pretty soon, I expect. *Not* with Evadne, I hope, or prep *will* be gorgeous!" declared Grizel, who had suffered many things from Evadne during prep.

"Oh, Evvy's an ass," said Jo cheerfully. "Well, I'd better be pushing off, I s'pose."

"Yes; and while you're about it, I should advise a little less slang! Where you pick it all up, I can't think!"

"It must be in the atmosphere," returned Jo, as she tapped at the door.

Grizel went on, and left her to take charge of the new girl once more, which she did with the utmost cheerfulness.

"I have put Cornelia in the Lower Fourth for the present, Jo," said Miss Maynard. "Will you show her her form-room, and introduce her to some of the other girls. —You must make haste and learn some German and French, Cornelia, or you may not be able to talk at all meal-times."

"Ya-as," drawled Cornelia again. Then they went out, Jo dropping the little regulation curtsey, while the new girl stared at her, and walked soberly down the narrow passage to the big form-room where two or three of the Lower Fourth were busily putting their desks in order for the morrow.

"D'you always do that?" asked Cornelia, as they went in.

"Do what?"

"Duck like that."

"Rather! It's manners all the time here, and so you'll jolly well find out."

Cornelia looked at her with limpid eyes that said nothing, and then followed her up to a little group where Evadne Lannis was holding forth about the hotel fire.

"Hi, Evvy! This is Cornelia Flower," said Jo, interrupting ruthlessly. "She's to be in your form, so you can look after her.—These other people are Cyrilla Maurus, Giovanna Donati, Selma Khrakhovska, and Signa Johansen, Cornelia. They're all about your age, I think. Thirteen, aren't you?"

"Most fourteen," said Cornelia.

"Oh, then, that's all right.—Which desk can she have, Giovanna?" She turned to Giovanna, the form-prefect the term before.

"That one by the window, Joey," said Giovanna in her soft, un-English voice. "We will all look after Cornelia."

"Thanks!" Joey turned on her heel, and left the room. She had a rooted objection to "doing sheep-dog," and her theory was that new girls got on best if left to find their own feet. Perhaps if Cornelia had shown any signs of being nervous she would have stayed, but that was the last thing the new girl was. So Jo went off on some quest of her own.

Meanwhile, the Lower Fourth found to their joy that they had welcomed a genius into their midst. Cornelia was original when it came to sin, and she soon showed that she had no intention of being the form's conscience, or anything like that. On the contrary, she brightened them all up by her exploits, and they soon followed in her lead. Even Evadne, the self-sufficient, had to admit that the new girl could outdo them all in wickedness.

It was Cornelia who introduced into prep one of the harmless little green snakes they sometimes found outside, sending half the girls screaming on to the tops of their desks while Grizel, who was in charge, gingerly lifted the creature with a shovel borrowed from the kitchen for the purpose, and carried it off to the fence, over which she dropped it with a little suppressed scream.

She also suggested vaselining the blackboards, but Margia squelched that idea by the crushing remark, "We did that *ages* ago! You *are* behind the times!"

But it was she who mixed salt with the tooth-powder used by some of the seniors, and it was this prank that brought about her own undoing. Grizel, on being informed by Dorota Heilinge and Eva von Heiling of what had occurred, held an inquiry, and found out the author of the misdeed, with the result that Cornelia went before a prefects' meeting, and startled them all into notice of herself by her calm impudence. As it was a first offence—so far as they knew—they let her off with a reprimand, and she went, not noticeably quenched at all.

"We must keep an eye on that kid," said Grizel when she had gone. "There's more in her than meets the eye!"

She fell foul of Jo Bettany on the third day of term, when she had a battle royal with Simone, and reduced that young lady to such a fury of weeping as drew even unsentimental Jo's attention. After sundry inquiries as to the cause of the squabble, Miss Jo told Cornelia what she thought of her; and as Jo's tongue could, on occasion, outdo anything even Grizel could produce, she got home more than once, and left the new girl mentally writhing. Not that Simone received much consolation from her friend. She was ordered "to stop being a sponge!" and taken off to play a slashing set of tennis which left her no time to brood over her wrongs. All the same, Jo was not going to have one of her special friends tormented by a "cheeky brat of a new girl." Cornelia, on her side, resolved to get even with Jo. But just then Marie's wedding intervened, and hostilities were postponed.

CHAPTER XVI

MARIE'S WEDDING

THE Thursday morning of Marie Pfeiffen's weddingday dawned bright and clear. Usually, the Tyrolean peasant prefers to hold his wedding during the Carnival time—that is, in the winter. But Marie had been impressed by her young mistress's happy wedding-day in the previous July, and had refused to be married at the usual time. Her bridegroom had backed her up in her request to hold their festival when the days were sunny, so they had braved local custom, and chosen May for their wedding-day. In any case, Marie meant to have all the other details of her great day in accordance with the best traditions of the valley, and the girls knew, for they had been told, that there would be all the usual dancing, shooting matches, sports, and feasts that had from time immemorial been the leading features of a Tiernthal wedding.

Their invitations had duly come to them in envelopes tied with red and green ribbons, which they had all put away to keep as mementoes of the occasion. There would be no school, for the marriage service would take place at half-past nine. So at ten past they all walked down to the little white-washed chapel, clad in their white frocks, big white hats, and white shoes and stockings. They were solemnly escorted to seats near the front, and at half-past nine punctually the wedding party appeared.

Marie was attired in the dress of the valley—a short, full, red skirt, a black velvet bodice with full sleeves of white linen, and a lace kerchief knotted over the bodice. On her head was the wreath of rosemary which is worn in many of the Tyrol valleys by brides, and called by them "Mary's Flowers," in honour of the Virgin. Her bridegroom also wore his national costume, and they made a striking pair as they stood before the old white-haired priest who served all the churches round the Tiern See.

The service was not a long one, and presently they moved out to the fresh sunshine. At the door of the church stood two of the bride's brothers with huge bunches of artificial gold and silver flowers with which they presented those guests who were expected to come to the feast. The girls were all presented with one of those posies, and followed the bridal procession across the grass to the Kron Prinz Karl, where the feasting was to be. Herr Braun acted as host, for, in this valley, as in many others, the parents have as little to do with the actual arrangements as possible. A table had been set aside for the school-girls, and here they sat, and were feasted on strange foods. One dish consisted of pork, boiled in fat; another was of veal, cooked in some strange way, and adorned with slices of potatoes and cabbage; yet another was of bacon, cooked in butter, and served with spoonfuls of the butter poured over it. These were followed by dishes of dried figs, oranges, pears, and grapes, and the whole was—literally, as far as the peasants were concerned—washed down with huge mugs of beer. The girls were given tiny glasses of wine to drink, and then milky coffee.

The staff kept an anxious eye on their charges, for there was no saying how this unusual food would agree with them. Luckily, they were able to serve themselves by Herr Braun's special arrangement, so no one got more than a taste of any of the queer dishes. Joey, who hated fat, solaced herself on fruit, and several of the others did the same.

The peasants, meanwhile, ate steadily through enormous servings of the same things, and seemed no worse for it. Merry shoutings and laughter kept the whole room in an uproar, and it went on for two hours!

By this time most of the little ones were drowsy, but when a move was made to go into the other room where the musicians could be already heard playing softly, they roused up and followed with the rest.

The first business to attend to was the giving of the money gifts. Marie's godmother sat before a table on which stood a large dish, covered by a napkin. Her Uncle Gustav sat at one side, with a big sheet of paper, a pen, and a bottle of ink before him. The guests advanced, one by one, and slipped into the old dame's hand a small sum of money which she hid under the napkin, while the uncle wrote down the sum on the paper.

"What on earth is that for?" murmured Mary to Grizel.

"So that when there are any weddings in the guests' families, Marie and Andreas will know how much to give," replied Grizel cautiously. "Don't stare so, Mary! Your eyes look as if they were going to drop out!"

"Well, it's so weird!" retorted Mary. "Of all the business-like ways of doing things! I don't think I quite like it."

"I think it's rather a good idea," said Deira, joining in the conversation. "You get what you give. Jolly neat, I think!"

Mary shook her head. She didn't approve, in spite of Grizel's murmured, "It's the custom, you ass! They've always done it!"

The girls had all been warned to bring money, so when

the other guests had put in their contributions, they advanced and slipped their *Schillings* into the old lady's hand.

"She might look a bit more cheerful over it," murmured Jo to the faithful Simone, who was standing beside her. "It might be her own funeral she was attending!"

As the commentator was standing very near the lady, it was just as well that the latter had very little English, and didn't understand the remark, otherwise she would have been hurt. It is no part of the *Ehrenganger* to show gratification at the gifts. They are not for her, but for the wedded pair, and they must thank their friends—not she. When the giving was over, they passed on to where Marie and Andreas stood side by side, she with a glass of wine in her hand, he with a huge bun, both greasy and solid, with which the guests were presented as they left the "pay-table." The wine had to be drunk to the health of the newly wedded pair, and the bun was taken away to be eaten later.

Then the dancing began. And how those peasants did dance! Some of them were content with merely waltzing round and round; but some of the young men went in for far more spectacular doings. Jo was spinning round the room in the arms of good Herr Braun when one of Marie's younger uncles suddenly fell on his knees with a resounding bang, and, folding his arms across his breast, bent backwards till his head touched the ground, when he kept up a rhythmic tap-tapping with it, while his partner continued dancing round him. As suddenly as he had gone down, he sprang to his feet, his arms still folded, and, catching the pretty girl with whom he had been dancing, went on as if nothing had occurred.

Two or three athletic youths fell on their knees, and moved round and round on them, beating the floor in a way that made the girls ache for very sympathy, though these hardy young fellows made nothing of it, and after a minute or two of it would spring up, and go on waltzing as if they had never stopped.

"Goodness!" gasped Rosalie to Gertrud, with whom she was dancing. "Have they *any* skin left on their knees?"

The Tyrolean girl laughed. "Oh yes! They are accustomed to doing this, and they don't mind it. What you ought to see—only we cannot have it here, as the ceiling is so high—is the figure where the girl swings up her man and then goes on revolving, while he dances with his feet on the ceiling and his hands on her shoulders."

Rosalie stopped dead. "Are you pulling my leg?" she demanded.

Gertrud shook her pretty head. "No. It is really so. I have heard my father speak of it. I do not know if it is done in this valley; but I know it is in some. My father says that he has seen a couple dance like this for six minutes without stopping."

After about an hour of this kind of entertainment the musicians stopped playing, and one of the young men sprang up and sang a couple of lines, his partner standing beside him, her eyes modestly on the floor. Miss Maynard, who knew that sometimes these *Schnadahüpfler*, as they are called, are inclined to be questionable, was rather worried, but there was nothing to trouble her, and presently the orchestra went on. Jo, who had given the bridegroom his promised dance, and was rather weary now, slipped aside, and watched the trio with deep interest. There was a pipe, a zither, and a *Hackbrettel*. This last is a weird arrangement of bits of wood of various lengths and shapes, fixed on plaits of straw, and struck with a wooden mallet. Each gives out a different sound according to its size or form, and the result is not so bad as might be expected.

Finally, there was a little silence, in which people crowded back to the dining-room to quench their thirst, and then began the *Ehrentanz*, which is danced by the bridal couple, the nearest of her relations, and any guests whom the bridegroom specially wishes to honour. The rest of the dancers crowd round the walls and watch it in silence, while the host and his wife stand near the musicians. As the couples waltz slowly round the room, these two present each with a full glass of wine, of which the lady sips a little. She then hands the rest over to her partner, who drains it. While this is going on, the brother of the bride sings a short rhyme in praise of his new brother-in-law as that worthy passes him every time he goes the round of the room. Sometimes this is turned into rather a rowdy affair, but on this occasion everyone liked the groom, so no one rose to challenge all that Fritzel Pfeiffen sang about Andreas.

Naturally Jo, Grizel, and the Robin were requested to join in the dancing, and so were Mademoiselle, Miss Maynard, and Miss Carthew. It is impossible to refuse without giving hurt to the feelings of the happy pair, so they joined in. When it was over, Marie and Andreas set out for their home, and the guests prepared to give themselves full swing. The girls also left the dancing-room at the suggestion of Herr August, and went to watch the shooting-matches, of which they soon tired. It was two o'clock by this time, and the sun was growing hot. Several of the little ones were tired out, and were inclined to be fractious, so Miss Carthew and Mademoiselle took them off home, where they were sent to bed, and left to have a quiet nap till four o'clock. The others stayed where they were or wandered about on the grass, where several couples, temporarily tired of the dancing, were doing likewise.

Among them was Herr August, as they all called him, to distinguish him from his brother, Herr Pfeiffen. He was one of the men on the little steamboats which run on the Tiern See in the summer, and the girls knew him well, and like him immensely. Evadne, Jo, Margia, Simone, Paula, Frieda, and Cornelia, who had patched up a temporary peace with Jo, ran up to him when they saw him by himself, and demanded accounts of other weddings which he had attended. He was very willing to accede to their requests, and sat down with them round him, and told them stories of shooting-matches and *Schuhplattler* exhibitions, in which the most marvellous feats had been performed.

When he had exhausted his repertoire, he sat silent for a minute. Then he turned to Jo. "Fräulein Joey, I have heard that the demon who tried to bear away the little Fräulein Robin has been seen again of late."

Jo sat up—she had been lounging against Frieda—and demanded, "Where?"

"Up on the haunted glen. He is as you say—tall, and with white hair and very blue eyes. He wears deerskins, and has neither hat nor shoes, and he dances and sings all the while."

"Horrid old thing!" said Jo, with an involuntary shudder.

"Who is it?" asked Cornelia, who had not heard of this before.

They nearly fell over themselves to tell her, till Joey, shrieking above the others, induced them to be quiet and let her tell it. She told it as well as she had told those legends during the previous term, and, hot day as it was,

Margia averred that her blood ran cold at Jo's description of the maniac's anger when they had sent Rufus off with the Robin.

Cornelia listened with bated breath. "What an adventure," she said.

"It was indeed a terrible happening," said Herr August. "Luckily Our Blessed Lady was watching over *das Engelkind*, and so saved her from being dragged down to the demon's lair."

"It wasn't!" cried Frieda indignantly. "I mean, it was Grizel and Joey who saved her! Our Lady helped them, but they were there!"

"Ah, but it was our dear Lord and His Holy Mother who prompted the thought to take the dog," said Herr August, who possessed the simple, unquestioning faith of his race. "I think, too, that They watched over *die Fräulein* in their hour of peril, and saved them from the wrath of the demon."

"I'm jolly *sure* it was God," said Jo in her own language. "If He hadn't been with us all the time, goodness only knows *what* would have happened!"

"Joey," said Margia abruptly, "what do you think that cleft was?"

"A hole in the mountains," responded Jo promptly.

"Yes; but *what* hole?"

"Why, just any hole! What d'you mean? Are you driving at something?"

"Well, I don't *know*, of course, but——" Margia paused.

"But—what? Oh, get on," cried Jo impatiently. "What's your idea—if you've *got* one, that is!"

Margia looked at them all. Herr August had got up, and sauntered off, seeing that the little ladies were well occupied. They were all literally hanging on her words.

"Get on!" said Jo again. "What is it?"

"Well," began Margia, "do you remember what Marie said Wanda's fiancé's father said about our lake?"

Jo shook her head. "No—oh yes, though, I do! He said that there were some wonderful caves either near it or under it. D'you mean, Margia, that you think that hole was the way in?"

"Well, it looks rather like it, doesn't it? It's in the part they all swear is haunted. None of the lake folk will go near it. You heard what Herr August thought of that old looney? I'll bet you what you like that's the way into the caves, and he lives there."

There was a thrilled silence after she had finished speaking. Then Jo spoke slowly. "I see what you mean. If one of them is all glittering and crystally, he might think it was Fairyland. That's why he's got that crack-brained notion about taking our Robin there. Oh, Margia! Supposing he had! Supposing we *hadn't* got there in time?"

"Well, you did," said Margia, in matter-of-fact tones, for Jo looked rather as if she might cry. "The thing is: If that's the way, then the caves can be found; and if they're safe, they can be used as you said."

"Oh!" Jo sat up again, her face blazing at the thought. "And it's *us*—it's the school that will have helped to discover them! Oh, Margia! You brain!"

"Come along, you people! I've been yelling at you till I'm hoarse! Why on earth can't you listen, you little nuisances?" It was Grizel, of course, and an irritated Grizel, who had to walk across from the other side of the pasture under the blazing sun.

They got meekly to their feet, but, just as Jo was about to announce their glorious idea, the head girl cut in with, "Now don't talk! Come along! It's nearly four o'clock, and we have to get *Kaffee und Kuchen* for ourselves today."

When they reached the chalet they found the rest bringing their afternoon meal into the flower garden, and setting the tables in the shade of the two big trees that grew at one end of it.

"Come, children!" cried Miss Maynard, as she saw them. "Run along and change your frocks, and then come and help. What *has* made you so long in coming?"

She did not pause for an answer, and they went off to change before they came downstairs to help bring out the china and cakes. Then the little ones came racing across from Le Petit Chalet, and since mention of the Robin's adventure before any of them had been banned, they were obliged to be silent.

The chances are, however, that they would have discussed it some time during the evening, and the seniors would have heard of it, in which case much might have been saved. But just as Mademoiselle was marshalling the little ones off to bed, Miss Maynard's brother appeared on the scene. He came straight across to Jo. "Go and get

"Very little indeed. So now, you've got to forget about the whole thing and set your energies to getting better. You break up on Tuesday and we set off to Canada in just over a fortnight's time. I want you with us *part* of the time, anyhow."

"Has anyone told Dad and Mother?" Carola asked.

"Not yet; that's *my* job and I wanted to see you first. Any message for them?"

"My love. And please tell them I simply love the Chalet School and I'm awfully glad I'm here, if—if I did——"

"Storm it in the most outrageous manner," Jo finished for her. "By the way, if ever you are moved to put out a fire again, you might look round for something of a thick cloth nature and not use your poor hands. Not much sense in that!" quoth Jo. "There's quite a good cloth on the table. Why didn't you use that?"

Nurse, coming to send Jo away, reflected the grin that overspread that lady's face as Carola made her usual excuse.

"I—I didn't think!"

say that's untrue, Grizel. I'm not going to lie about it. But you get it into that thick head of yours that it's over—finished! After today, I shall never speak of it to you again. Understand?"

"If—oh, I'd never have forgiven myself if—if——"

"Ah," said Jo with unusual gentleness of tone, "we can all say that about lots of things. I'll only say this and then you and I are going to forget. When things go wrong, it's just as well to learn to hold your horses a little. Count a hundred, Grizel—count a hundred before you fly off the handle. That's all. Now, my dear, I want to wish you every happiness and every success in your new life when it begins. You've got to write frequently and let us know all about it, mind. Oh, and, by the way, Mollie's out there. Oh, don't be an ass! Jack's sister—our Miss Maynard. She lives outside of Auckland. I'll write and tell her to look out for you as soon as you sail. You'll go by boat, I suppose?"

"Of course I shall! Where's the money coming from to fly?"

"Anyway, you'll love the voyage. I know how I loved the voyages to and from India. Now I'm off to San. Goodbye; be good!"

She was off, but what she had said sank deep into Grizel Cochrane's mind. The whole affair was to make a very big difference in her character, and the Grizel who returned to England on a visit five years later was a very different woman from the one who had so nearly caused a tragedy in the Chalet School.

Jo ran lightly down the corridors, and presently was tapping at the door of San. Nurse came to answer it, and agreed to let Mrs. Maynard visit her patient for ten minutes. Jo had to rub it in very hard that she was, as she had said, *in loco parentis* before Nurse would grant even this grace. However, she got her way and Carola, opening languid eyes, saw the clever, sensitive face with its beautiful eyes bent over her.

"Mrs. Maynard!" she whispered. "How is Len?"

"Sitting up and taking notice," Jo told her, sitting down beside her. She stooped and kissed the girl. "Thank you, Carola, from the bottom of my heart, for what you've done. We owe Len's life to your quickness. I'm certain of that."

The languid eyes brightened and Carola smiled a little. "I'm glad she's not much the worse."

up like billy-oh and then my coat caught and I thought I was going to be burnt to death, only Carola knocked me down and sat on me and hit me and the fire went out."

"A good time was had by all, in fact," her mother chuckled again.

"Mamma."

"Yes? What is it, sugarpie?"

"I shall never be a martyr."

Jo sat down limply on the bed and regarded her eldest girl with startled eyes. "Who wants it? And what on earth makes you think that? What *is* all this in aid of?"

"Well, I couldn't," Len said defensively. "Not if I had to be burnt to death, anyhow. It hurts too jolly much."

"Well, there's no need for you to think of it at present, anyhow. And if God meant you to be a martyr, He would give you the courage, so you needn't worry about that any more. I've something to tell you about Auntie Daisy. What do you think? When we come home from Canada in the summer she is going to be married, and you three and Primula are to be her bridesmaids! How's that for news?"

Just as Jo had meant, the pair forgot about being martyrs and beset her with questions about "Auntie Daisy" and her wedding. When she finally left them, they were considering with great solemnity just what would be the best thing to give her for a wedding-present.

"Well, that's so much done!" she thought as she closed the door behind her after assuring them that she would be on time to take them home for the holidays next Tuesday. "The next thing is Carola, poor kiddy! Oh, no; the next thing is obviously Grizel!"

The little room was at the farther end of the corridor where Grizel's music room was, and just as Jo turned to head for the San the music room door opened and Grizel emerged. She went white when she saw Jo and her eyes fell. Not quickly enough, though, for Jo to have missed the look of apprehension in them. She swept forward, crying, "Oh, Grizel! My poor lamb! *Don't* look like that at me! It was an accident, and anyway, I shan't eat you!"

"An accident that should never have happened!" Grizel spoke almost harshly. "Whatever I might have been feeling, I'd no right to go chucking matches around like that. If—if anything had happened, Jo, I should have been to blame."

Jo pulled her into the room and shut the door. "I can't

As for Jo, Miss Annersley had gone down to the ferry to meet her, and after reporting on Len who was very sorry for herself and inclined to be very cross, she told Grizel's story as eloquently as she could. Jo was inclined to "flare up" as Biddy had said; but by the time the Head had walked the pair of them right past the Big House and nearly to the other end of the islet, not to speak of talking herself nearly hoarse, that lady had calmed down.

"It's Grizel," she said finally, "just Grizel! All right, Hilda; I'll say nothing—or very little, anyhow. And now, what about Carola? Jack and I are *in loco parentis* at present. Is she really ill?"

"Her one hand is in a bad state, but it *will* heal in time. She is inclined to be feverish, too, but that will pass off. Don't worry, Joey. By the time you sail for Canada, I expect she'll be on the high road to recovery. As for your *in loco parentis*, Nell and I are taking that on while you're away, so suppose you leave her to us and concentrate on your own affairs."

Jo had three interviews before she went home again. The first was with her daughters. Len had been moved into a little spare room so that Carola might be kept quite quiet. The two small girls were together and Miss Wilson had had the wonderful house moved up so that they could play with it. Therefore, Len's first greeting to her mother referred to that.

"Look, Mamma! Isn't it lovely? And Con says we three are to share it. Isn't it super of her?"

Jo grinned. "Only what I should have expected. I never knew you three when you *didn't* insist on sharing. Well, Con, my lamb, you're a clever child and you beat your mother hollow. *I* only thought of thirty-one materials."

Con surveyed her mother with solemn brown eyes. "I just thought and thought about all the things in La Maison des Poupées and what they were made of, and I seemed to remember dozens. *Only*, Miss Alton saw my list after and she said I must have extra spelling next term if I couldn't spell better than that."

Jo chuckled heartlessly. "I suppose you were in such a hurry you just went by the sound. That sort of thing won't pan out where the English language is concerned, my lamb. Well, and what have you been doing to yourself, young Len?"

"It wasn't me—'twas the basket," Len cried. "It blazed

476

"Daisy? No! What about Daisy?" the Head asked quickly.

"Didn't Jo tell you?"

"My dear girl, I never saw Jo to speak to after the opening."

"Oh, I see. As Mary-Lou said, you had to spend time being polite to people. Well, Daisy's engaged, too—to a doctor at her hospital. Jo's very bucked about it, because, as she says, it'll mean that Daisy has a home of her own now. I know she's had one with Madame and then with Jo, but it's not quite the same thing."

Miss Annersley nodded. "I'm very glad for Daisy. And now, Biddy, it's after eleven and time that both of us were in bed. Good-night, and sleep well. Carola's life is in no danger, though she will have a good deal of pain to endure for the next few days, poor child. We have a great deal to be thankful for."

"We have that!" Biddy stood up. "Good-night, Miss Annersley, and thank you very much."

Grizel had her interview with Miss Annersley next day after Dr. Peters had been to see the patients and been able to assure the anxious Heads that Len would soon be well again and Carola was going on as well as possible. What was said, neither ever told, except that Grizel hunted Biddy out and told her briefly that Miss Annersley had offered to back her in the new business until she could use her own money. She was leaving at the end of the summer term and would sail for New Zealand almost at once.

"Well, I wish you all the luck in the world," Biddy said.

"Thanks, Biddy. You've been a real stand-by. Thank you for telling the Head—everything. I knew I had to, but I didn't see how I was ever going to do it."

"Oh, well, maybe I'm inheriting Jo's mantle. You know Dr. Jem always did say she was a champion butter-in. I thought, maybe, I was taking too much on myself, but I knew 'twould be a hard thing for you to do. And isn't it grand about Hilary?"

"*Hilary?*" Grizel eyed Biddy as if she thought she were mildly insane.

"Haven't you heard? Hilary's engaged—and so is Daisy Venables!"

Biddy ran off after that, for she was due to take duty with the Juniors, so she was unable to watch Grizel's reactions to the news.

"so I hope her nerves won't suffer too badly. But I'm afraid this will put an end to her music. The doctor is afraid that there is damage done to one finger which will weaken it seriously."

"Oh, well, 'tisn't as if she meant to go in for it for a career," Biddy said consolingly. "And isn't it the good news about Len! Does Jo know, Miss Annersley?"

"Not yet. Dr. Peters will go over first boat tomorrow and tell her himself when he has seen Len. She couldn't come here even if she knew, and there was no sense in giving her a bad night on Len's account. Thank God it *was* Len and not Con! Len is a matter-of-fact little person and Dr. Peters thinks she will be over the shock very quickly. We're keeping her in San for a day or two to keep her quiet; but he expects she will be fit enough by Tuesday and then we break up. They have the trip to Canada in a couple of weeks' time, and that will be enough to take her mind off the whole thing."

Biddy nodded. Then she knelt down beside the Head and looked up at her. "I want to tell ye how it happened," she said, becoming richly Irish in her earnestness.

"Do you know? We have all been so anxious about Carola I'm afraid I never thought of it till you spoke."

"I do so," Biddy nodded. Then, still kneeling, she told the story she had heard from Grizel.

Miss Annersley heard her in silence—a silence which lasted for some minutes after Biddy had stopped speaking. That young lady took alarm.

"Ah, now, ye won't be angry with Grizel," she coaxed.

"No," Miss Annersley said. "I am not angry. I am too sorry for her to be angry. Say nothing to her, Biddy, tomorrow. I must see her myself. I'm glad you told me, child."

"And you'll speak to Jo, the way she won't be flaring out at Grizel over it?" Biddy wheedled.

Anxious as she was, Miss Annersley began to laugh. "Oh, Biddy, Biddy! What a born wheedler you are! You must leave it to me to say what I think to Jo," she went on seriously. "And now, I have a piece of news for you that I *think* will be no real surprise to you after all."

"If it's that Hilary Burn is going to marry that nice Dr. Graves, 'tis no news at all, at all," Biddy told her calmly. "We've all been expecting it this last fortnight. And did ye hear about Daisy?"

said. "Now, my dear, I see you've had a very bad shock, but you mustn't give way. We have our hands full as it is. Biddy, go and ask Karen for some strong coffee for her and see that she takes it. Then, if you feel that you can't help with the rest, go to bed. I'll come along some time and let you know the latest news. Cheer up! 'All is not lost that is in danger,' you know."

She gave them a nod and went out again. Biddy stood up.

"I'm going to get that coffee. You stay quiet till I come back. Try not to worry, Grizel. It won't help anyone and will only make you unfit to help out." She slipped away to return presently with coffee and the news that Miss Wilson had told the girls what had happened and they were having supper now and then the prefects would see the little ones to bed.

"So there's nothing we can do at present," she concluded. "You drink this and then go to bed and try to sleep."

Once more Grizel shuddered. "*Sleep*! I don't feel as if I could ever sleep again!"

"Oh yes, you will. Sure, it's nonsense to talk like that." Biddy held the cup to Grizel's lips. "Drink this and you'll feel better. Drink it, Grizel."

Grizel drank, and when the cup was empty, Biddy sat back watching her colleague with wary eyes. What she did not tell Grizel was the fact that she had gone to San and told Matron the outline of the story. Matron had given her a sedative to put in the coffee, and before long Biddy saw that it was taking effect. Grizel's eyes were growing drowsy, and she nodded.

"Come along, now," Biddy coaxed. "It's worn out ye are, ye poor creature. I'll help you to bed."

She succeeded in getting Grizel to bed and before long was able to leave the room, sure that the other mistress was sleeping quietly. She went along to San again, but saw no one and dared not go in. However, before they finally went to bed after one of the most eventful days in the Chalet School's history, Miss Annersley sent for her and told her that the doctor said that Len would probably sleep herself all right, though she would have a very sore arm for the next few days. As for Carola, one hand was so badly burned they had had to put her to sleep before they dressed it and she was still sleeping.

"Mercifully, she is a sturdy, healthy girl," the Head said,

"Yes; well, Deira and I became good friends after we'd both left. She married a New Zealander and went out there to live with him. Last year he died and she found that he'd muddled away a good deal of his money and Deira was none too well off. She has one little girl who was born a cripple, so she has to do something about it. There was a business going—books and music—quite a good thing. She hadn't enough capital to buy it herself and she thought of me. She always knew I hated teaching. She wrote and asked if I'd come in with her and I leapt at the idea. I saw Mr. Sothern, the lawyer, and he quite agreed it would be a good thing. Deira had sent over books and papers for him to vet it. He would agree to my having the money. It all depended on my stepmother. He wrote to her and so did I. I had a letter this afternoon saying that she wouldn't agree to letting me have a penny until I was thirty-five. I was to go on as my father had wished. She never liked me, you know."

Biddy said nothing for the very good reason that she could think of nothing to say; but her heart ached for Grizel.

"Well," went on Grizel dreamily, "I read that letter after I'd told Len and Carola to bring my buys to the music room. I'd just finished it when they arrived. I was raging. I got up and went to the cupboard. I was lighting a cigarette and I threw the match away. It landed on the reed basket Len was carrying. Those things are like tinder. It flared up at once and caught her sleeve. I only waited to throw a rug on the basket—no use letting the whole house go up. That's the story."

There was a silence, broken by Matron who came to fetch some things she wanted. She only shook her head when Biddy eagerly demanded to know how the patients were.

"Len is only slightly scorched, but she's suffering from shock," she said. "Carola's hands are in a bad state. Dr. Peters was still here, luckily. He's spending the night at the Christys'. He's in San with Carola now. Poor, plucky child! I'm afraid she'll pay heavily for her courage. By the way, Grizel, were you hurt at all?"

"No, Matron. Carola had most of the flames out before I reached them. I stopped to throw a mat on the basket. It was flaring badly."

"The most sensible thing you could have done," Matron

At length Grizel looked up, and Biddy's heart stood still at what she saw in the dark grey eyes.

"Oh, Grizel, whatever *is* it?" she faltered.

"I set Len Maynard on fire," Grizel replied dully. "Carola tried to save her and—and I'm afraid she's very badly injured."

"Len?" Biddy could scarcely whisper it.

"I don't know. She screamed dreadfully, so she's alive. Carola——" Her voice died away. She was unable to say any more.

Biddy was silent, too. She longed to go and help to see to Carola, for the girl had won herself a warm place in the Irish heart; but Matron had told her to stay with Grizel and Biddy knew that the music mistress should not be left alone yet.

Suddenly Grizel looked up again. "It was an accident, Biddy."

"I know that," Biddy said brusquely. "Don't be silly, Grizel. No one's going to think you deliberately set Jo's girl on fire."

Grizel shuddered. "That—that's almost the worst of it— Jo's girl. And Jo and Madame were both so good to me years ago!"

Biddy was not sure what to say or do, but she must try to get that look out of Grizel's eyes. Grizel was years older than herself. She had been teaching up at the Sonnalpe when Biddy first came to the School. The Irish girl had never liked Grizel Cochrane very much, but it was not in her to ignore the anguish she saw before her.

"Tell me, Grizel," she said. "Maybe 'twill make it a little better. We can't do anything for Len or Carola just now. You tell me."

Grizel turned her eyes on the flickering of the cheery little fire and she shuddered again. "It was my step-mother," she said. "You know I never wanted to go in for music, but my father insisted. I wanted to take up P.T., but he wouldn't hear of it, and I hadn't enough of my own to do it off my own bat. When he died he left me some money outright. More he put into a fund in charge of two trustees—his lawyer and my stepmother. I'm not supposed to have it till I'm thirty-five. All the same, if the trustees would agree, I could draw part of it. You never knew Deira O'Hagen, did you? She left before you came to School."

"I've heard of her, though," Biddy said.

fireplace. She threw short, and it fell, still burning, into the reed basket Len was holding. The tinder stuff caught fire at once and flared up. The flame caught the flimsy material of Len's Chinese dress and in an instant the sleeve was a mass of flames.

Len screamed and so did Carola, who tossed down the things she was holding and was on to the terrified child, beating out the flames with her bare hands while Grizel, with an exclamation of horror, snatched up a rug and flung it on the blazing basket before going to Carola's help. The Big House was an old one with any amount of wood about it and there was a fresh breeze blowing.

The fire, smothered beneath the heavy rug, went out almost at once, but a good part of Len's coat was burnt before the flames there were subdued. Mercifully, she had stout underclothes and, as they discovered later, beyond a long scorch on one arm, she had come to little harm. It was a different matter with Carola. When the mistresses within hearing came tearing to the spot they were just in time to see her swaying and falling if Grizel had not caught her.

Miss Annersley took the unconscious girl from the arms of the music mistress, who stooped over with a face as white as chalk.

"Go and fetch Matron, Grizel," the Head said; and Grizel, shaking and terrified, went.

Miss Burn, who had been telling Miss Annersley some news and come racing with her to the music room, picked up Len and carried her away to be soothed and have her burn dressed at once. Oddly enough, no one else had heard the cries, but Biddy O'Ryan met Grizel and, struck by her face, ran after her to Matron's room to find out what was wrong.

Matron, taking a much-needed rest in a chair by the fire, looked up in amazement when the pair entered. What she saw in Grizel Cochrane's face made her leap to her feet at once.

"Where is it?" she demanded, going straight to the point.

"My music room," Grizel gasped.

Matron made for the door. "Sit down at once," she said curtly. "Biddy, you look after Grizel." Then she was off.

Biddy obeyed her. Taking Grizel by the shoulders, she made her sit down in Matron's chair, brought her a glass of water and then stood waiting till the elder chose to speak.

join the others. The doctor held up his hand for silence again.

"I think you will all like to know that the dolls' house has netted twenty-five pounds five shillings," he said. "And now we have four more raffles for which to draw, so, if you please, we will continue."

Chapter XIX

CAROLA TO THE RESCUE!

IT was seven o'clock. The last of the visitors had gone and the girls were busy dismantling the stalls. Miss Cochrane came into Hall to collect her purchases which she had left at the tepee until now. She looked at the small pile of articles she had bought and laughed.

"I certainly can't carry all that myself," she said. She looked round. "Here, Len! Pile those small things into one of those reed baskets; and you bring the larger ones, will you, Carola? Bring them to my music room. I'll have them there. I'll go ahead and clear a shelf for them. Mind you don't break anything."

She departed on this and Carola and Len set to work to gather her possessions together. The small things were put into one of the reed baskets and Carola loaded herself with the three scrapbooks, teapot, small stool with its seat of woven sea-grass, and hand-painted tea-tray. Then they set off, to find Grizel Cochrane in her music room standing by the table reading a letter which had come for her during the afternoon. Her pleasant smile had vanished and she was frowning blackly.

As the pair entered, she crumpled up the sheet and thrust it into the pocket of her cardigan. "Put the things on the table," she said shortly as she went over to the mantelpiece and took a cigarette from her case lying there. She struck a match and lit up as she went to a cupboard.

"Can we help you to put them away, Miss Cochrane?" Carola asked.

"No, thanks," Grizel spoke shortly. "Put them down and then run off."

As she spoke, she tossed the match in the direction of the

They poured out of the little room into Hall where Dr. Peters was busy announcing the results of the various raffles. The Heads were standing beside him and the girls hurried up to the group.

"Dolls' house result," Tom said, handing the slip of paper with the name of the successful winner on it to the doctor.

"Who is it?" he demanded as he took it. "Anyone I know?"

"Look and see," Tom grinned. "You'll get a shock!"

He opened it and read. His eyebrows nearly disappeared into his hair and he whistled softly. "Not really? I say! What an excitement! Phoebe will be thrilled to hear this." He spoke of his crippled wife whom all the girls knew well.

"Announce it—announce it!" Carola was nearly dancing with excitement.

He turned to show the Heads the name before he did so, however. Then he rang his bell for attention, and when there was silence, he said: "I have just been given the result of the dolls' house competition. I congratulate the winner most heartily on her success." He paused. Then he went on: "The house has been won by—Con Maynard, with thirty-seven materials!"

Con, standing with her sister by the stall, stared at him. The rest of the gang shoved her forward.

"Go on—go on!" they urged. "You've got to go and take it."

Still in a maze, Con went forward, looking very small and childish in her Chinese dress. Someone helped her up to the dais and Miss Burn took her hand and led her forward.

Everyone began to clap and then someone started to cheer. Con stood clinging tightly to Hilary Burn, half-scared at her triumph.

Dr. Peters smiled down at her. "Congratulations, Con," he said, "and now I must give you your prize."

The cheering and clapping died down, to be succeeded by an outburst of laughter as Con said seriously, "Thank you very much, Uncle Frank, but please can't someone else take it for me. I couldn't possible hold it, you know," she wound up.

There was more clapping and cheering, under cover of which Hilary Burn released her hand and sent Con back to

a picturesque affair, whereat Bride pretended to swoon with horror, but was jerked to her feet by Tom, who had no patience with such antics; said a few earnest words about the crying need for the Sanatorium and the great work it was doing; then she declared the Sale open and set an example to everyone by hurrying off the platform, without even waiting for the vote of thanks due to her, and demanding three separate dips for her three little girls at home.

After that, it was a case of business first, and everyone was kept hard at it. Matron's jam vanished "like snow on a dyke," to quote Jean Ackroyd's aunt who had turned up. The toys sold well, too, and before the afternoon was half over practically all the sets of bedding and every carpet, too. The people in charge of the competition for the house had scarcely time to breathe, as Nancy Chester said when she handed over to Audrey Simpson. So far, no one had come anywhere near the number of materials used, either.

"So there's a chance for you, Auntie Jo," Bride said when her aunt appeared shortly after the country-dancing display and demanded to be told what she had to do.

She groaned loudly when she heard, but sat down and began to write with grim determination. As no one was allowed more than ten minutes for a list, some of them were scribbled in a manner that made the inspectors groan loudly.

"Anyway," Bride said during a short pause, "we've made twelve pounds ten with it already, so it's jolly well worth it. No, Mary; I simply can't make head or tail of that word. You'll just have to let it go."

At long last, when most of the stalls had been pretty well cleared and people were packing up to go home, intending competitors ceased to come and the girls settled down to go through all lists which had reached thirty or over. Biddy O'Ryan and Hilary Burn joined them to help and they scanned those lists carefully. Then Hilary looked up at Biddy, who nodded.

"Yes; she's got it after all! So sucks to you, Bride Bettany," she added, completely forgetting in her excitement that this was *not* the way for a mistress to speak to a pupil.

Bride grinned. "I'm jolly glad. Good for her! But however she got so many is beyond me. Come on and let's tell the world."

know it isn't choosing the name this time. What have you got in store for us?"

Tom grinned. "Wouldn't you like to know?"

"Yes, I should," Jo said frankly. "What ghastly effort have you provided for us?"

"You'll find out presently," Bride said soothingly. "I say, Auntie Jo, if by chance you should win it you'll keep it, won't you? I mean, I know the Trips have La Maison des Poupées, but they've been completely goggle-eyed over this. They're even having a shot at it for themselves. They haven't a chance, of course. I don't know that *you* have, for that matter. But *if* you should get it, do stick to it for them."

"O.K." Jo agreed.

She was hailed at that moment by Biddy O'Ryan who wanted the latest news of Daisy Venables. Jo, cocking an eye at the Fifths, decided to remove Biddy to a less public spot before she gave it, and escorted Biddy to a far corner where she broke to her the news of Daisy's engagement to a young doctor at her hospital. She was puzzled, however, by Biddy's method of taking it.

"That's *one*!" Biddy said mysteriously. "When are the rest to know?"

"One what?" Jo demanded; but Biddy refused to answer this.

"Sure, you needn't be minding me. Oh, look! Here comes the Opener!" Biddy hurriedly disappeared, and Jo, replying to the beckoning she was receiving from Miss Annersley, joined the opening party to be introduced, much to her wrath, as "Mrs. Maynard, Lady Russell's younger sister. We can't have Lady Russell with us today—I expect you know that she and Sir James are in Canada at the moment. Mrs. Maynard is representing her, however."

The Viscountess who was the Opener replied charmingly and Jo had to swallow her wrath and answer in kind. Then they mounted the dais, and a tiny Eskimo, the School "baby," presented her with a bouquet.

Jack Maynard had been unable to represent the Sanatorium, so his place was taken by Dr. Peters, another of the doctors there and an old friend of the School. He spoke briefly, explaining the object of the Sale; introduced the Viscountess, and then sat down. The Viscountess, with a smiling look round at the eager young faces of the stall-holders, was very merciful. She congratulated them on such

see," Peggy retorted. "You hop back to your tepee, and watch your language or fined you'll be! Trot!"

Peggy was Peggy, so Mary-Lou departed, not noticeably crushed, and the Head Girl went on her lawful occasions while the others moved on to admire the Second Form's Chinese stall which was in charge of Miss Edwards, their form mistress. "Teddy," as she was known to the School, was a good sort, but she possessed a tongue which kept them in awe, so this part of the room was fairly peaceful.

"You'll come and buy from us, won't you?" Len Maynard implored.

"I will," Carola said. "I want that little ware stand with the tapers in it. I say, I do like your kit, you two!"

"Mamma made it," Con explained, standing beside her sister. "It was an old frock she had in a play when *she* was at school. It's awfully gay, isn't it?" She held out the skirt or her coat, and extended one leg to show off the beflowered and betinselled cotton of which their Chinese coats and trousers were made.

"Jolly!" Clem said appreciatively. "It's a lovely yellow."

Betsy Lucy of the Fourth had been keeping an eye on the window. Now she suddenly squeaked, "They're coming! I can see them!"

"Cripes! We'd best get back!" And Clem headed the rush back to their stall.

Then the doors opened and the visitors poured in. No selling was allowed until the Sale had been declared open, but they thronged round the stalls, admiring and exclaiming at the work the girls had produced. The dolls' house, needless to state, came in for any number of congratulatory remarks, and the Fifths were smirking with complacency by the time Jo Maynard, who had made a bee-line for the Chinese stall first, had reached them. She surveyed them with a frown.

"Take those self-satisfied grins off your faces!" she ordered. "If you're going to be as swelled-headed as that over the thing, I shall strongly advise the Heads to give you the plain needlework stall next time, and see how you like *that*!"

The smirks hastily vanished. Then Bride said anxiously: "You're having a shot at the competition, aren't you, Auntie Jo?"

Her aunt nodded. "Have I ever once failed to do it? I

from the Sale. How do I manage if I'm stuck in the little room all the time?"

"You won't be needed for the first twenty minutes or so," Clem said. "You'll have to rush round and get what you can then."

However, when they reached the Hall, they discovered that this point had already struck their elders and betters, and Tom Gay, who was responsible for all arrangements connected with the house, called them together and informed them that it had been decided that there should be relays of them. The four already chosen would be "on" for the first half-hour and then four others would relieve them, and they could do their buying before coming to help at the stall.

There was half an hour left now before any visitors would come, so they strolled round Hall, admiring the efforts of the rest of the School and marking various things they hoped to be able to buy.

"Those kids are nearly crackers with excitement," Clem remarked, nodding towards the igloo where the Eskimos, clad in woolly garments of the appropriate fashion, were buzzing about like a swarm of hysterical bees. "I wouldn't be their mistresses for something!"

Mary-Lou, looking most unlike a Red Indian with her yellow plaits and wide blue eyes, was near enough to hear this and giggled. "I heard Miss Phipps telling them if they couldn't be quieter she'd pack half of them off to bed. I say, Clem, can I have a go for your dolls' house? I've never bothered with one before, but I do think it's a simply wizard effort."

"Why not?" Clem demanded. "You haven't the foggiest notion what the comp. is—no one has but ourselves and the Heads. You have a go if you want one. It'll give you something to think about."

"That means it's something beastly," her small friend said shrewdly. "Oh, well, it'll be fun, anyhow."

"You'll be fined if you use language like that," Peggy Bettany, who had overheard her, observed. "I suppose you'll think that fun, too?"

Mary-Lou's eyes widened with horror. "This is the *Sale* day, Peggy," she reminded the Head Girl severely. "You couldn't do that today!"

"Just you go on using forbidden slang like that and you'll

notices, 'No Smoking,' and have them put up round Hall. Then you needn't fear even matches or lighters. And talking of no smoking, I haven't had a cigarette today. Join me in one now." Miss Wilson held out her case.

"That's an excellent idea," Miss Annersley helped herself and lit up. "People are so careless about matches." She turned to the house telephone and called up her secretary, Miss Dene, and gave her the instructions. "There!" she said, coming back to sit by the open window through which the March sun was pouring a glorious blaze of light. "I think it'll be quite safe now."

"Then sit down and get your breath. It's nearly time for Mittagessen, and after that we shan't be able to call our souls our own much before seven o'clock."

Mittagessen was ended by half-past twelve, the School cleared the tables at top-speed and then streamed off upstairs to deck themselves for the afternoon. This took a little time, for the Maories had to be painted with tatoo marks and so had the Red Indians. The Indian ladies contented themselves with washing their faces in strong coffee and the Persians reddened their lips and left it at that.

"Thank goodness *we* don't have to bother with make-up muck," Clem remarked as she struggled with her plaid which would *not* fold neatly across her. "Now, all of you, you know exactly what you have to do, don't you? Carola, you and Jean go with Rosalie and Vanna to the little room by the door to give out paper and pencils. Rosalie will be at the door, but if she's called off, you'd better do that, Carola. Don't let anyone in who hasn't a ticket to show. Be sure you see that they put their names on the papers. When you've got two dozen, hand them over to Nancy Chester or Primrose Day to correct."

"Let's hope they all write so that we can make it out!" Jean said darkly. "You know how some grown-ups scrawl. We'd get our work returned if we dared show up such scribbles as *I've* seen—our doctor's prescriptions, for instance."

"Oh, that's part of a doctor's job," Clem told her airily. "If they wrote too clearly, people would know what they were having and it might put them off! There! I've got this thing fixed at last! Ready, you folk? Then come on!"

"Just a tick!" Jean said. "I want to buy some things

Miss Annersley burst into laughter. "They certainly will! I only hope you have packers who know how to make up parcels securely. If not, I'm afraid all your pretty paper will be wasted." She turned to her colleague. "Do you remember our Fairy-tale Sale in Tirol? The Bishop wandered round with all sorts of oddments drooping sadly out of the very inadequate parcelling that was all some people had thought necessary to provide. Joey had to take pity on him and *she* provided him with an old fish-basket into which she packed everything. He told me later that his parcels were all quite safe when he got them home, but some of them had a distinctly fishy odour at first!"

The pair broke into peals of laughter at this reminiscence. Gillian Moggeridge, standing near, opened her eyes widely.

"Do they have *bishops* in Tirol?" she exclaimed.

"My good child, what else did you suppose?" Miss Wilson demanded. "Really, Gillian!"

"Well, I didn't know. Somehow I thought it was only *us* had them—and the R.C.s too, of course," Gillian explained.

"All Tiroleans are Catholics—or most of them, anyhow," Miss Wilson told her. "He was a Catholic bishop, naturally. Frieda Mensch's great-uncle, as a matter of fact—Oh, don't be silly! Frieda von Ahlen, Mrs. Maynard's great friend."

"Oh, I see," Gillian murmured as the mistresses went on to admire the bric-à-brac stall of the little girls and congratulate their form mistress on the truly Chinese effect she had contrived with paper lanterns, imitation peach-blossom, and cardboard gables of enormous curves fastened to the top of the stall.

"Really, the girls have done better than ever," Miss Wilson said when, their inspection over, they retired to their study.

"Yes; I think they have." But Miss Annersley seemed dissatisfied about something.

"What's wrong?" her friend demanded.

"It's only that I wish we could have used something else for the Dip. I'm always afraid of cotton-wool; it *is* so inflammable!"

"Oh, nonsense, Hilda! In any case, none of the children are in it. Besides, there isn't an open fire anywhere about. But if you feel nervous, I'll tell Rosalie to print some big of fudge for Miss Annersley and Miss Wilson. That'll be all right!" She beamed at the two Heads, who retired feeling mentally breathless, a state of mind to which she often reduced her elders.

"It isn't that she's cheeky—though I admit she can be when she chooses," Miss Wilson said to her friend as they made for the toy stall. "It's simply the calm way she has of treating the most grown-up of grown-ups as dear friends."

Meanwhile, the Fourths were all engaged in giving Mary-Lou their opinion of her behaviour.

"Though, goodness knows, we ought to be used to you now," Cherry Christy added.

"Really, Mary-Lou, you are the limit," one of her chosen friends, Viola Lucy, chimed in.

Verity-Anne Carey smiled at them all. "Don't worry. The Heads will only say, 'It's just Mary-Lou!' and that will be that," she said.

This was so true that the Fourths left it at that. In any case, they had plenty to do, and they knew well enough by this time that they could, as Viola said graphically, talk themselves black in the face and Mary-Lou would never turn a hair.

Having seen the Fifth Forms' show a fortnight before, the mistresses imagined that a mere cursory glance and a few words of praise would be all that was needed from them. When they reached the stall, however, they felt impelled to do more than that, for the girls had exerted themselves to the utmost, and the piles of toys laid out among thistles and gorse were really remarkable. Moreover, as Polly Winterton pointed out with some pride, they had gone one better than everyone else in the matter of wrapping paper. The School always bought two or three reams of white kitchen paper for these occasions and practically every girl in the three forms had spent her spare time for the past three days in painting their share of the paper with tartan patterns. Carola had a book of all the tartans, and they had passed it round and copied them, each girl taking one tartan and concentrating on that.

"That's a good idea," Miss Wilson said, gazing at the wrapping paper admiringly. "Whose idea was it?"

"Carola's," Clem said. She giggled as she added, "We had a go at painting the string, but it just didn't work. However, the paper won't look so dusty and *our* parcels will have quite a cachet!"

want it pushed over. I'll do it myself. As for you, Signa, let me catch you doing one wicked thing again today, and you'll go to bed at once and stay there till tomorrow."

The Staff moved on to admire the Persian effort where the girls had hung up draperies, and disposed fruit and vegetables in as artistic heaps as they could manage on their stall, while great jamjars begged from Karen had been roughly enamelled in what purported to be Persian designs, and were crammed with daffodils, tulips, early wallflowers, and narcissi. The big tin bowl from the School's "Dommy Sci." kitchen was a mass of violets, and they had filled one Dickie Christy had brought from home with primroses.

"A very artistic stall," Miss Annersley commented to Peggy Bettany. "Who gave all the jam? Matron again? How *does* she do it? She always gives us dozens of jars for the Sale, but I can't say that I've ever noticed the School going short at any time."

Peggy grinned ruefully. "We've been allowed one dessertspoonful each for the last fortnight," she said. "We knew Matey was giving jam when *that* happened."

The Heads laughed, and went on to admire the Red Indian tepee which was draped with travelling-rugs of every lurid colour they could contrive and was decorated with "Indian" drawings pinned up everywhere. Mary-Lou and Verity-Anne had written excitedly home for sundry curios, and these had been sent, and adorned the inside where the objects for sale were hanging from strings, or piled into big reed-woven baskets.

The Maories showed piles of sweets made by the Dommy Sci. classes as well as cakes from the same source. Jo Maynard had sent a large contribution which her Anna had made, and various other nearby friends had also rallied round.

"Have a jam tart or a piece of fudge, do," Mary-Lou pressed them.

"No, thank you, Mary-Lou. A jam tart would be twopence lost, and even a piece of fudge can count," her Head Mistress told her. "I'll buy some fudge this afternoon, though, if there's any left by the time I manage to come round."

"I s'pose you have to spend ages being polite to everyone," Mary-Lou said sympathetically. "I'll tell you what, though: I'll save you each a quarter, shall I, before it all goes? O.K. Vi—Doris! You are to keep two quarters

head of Special Sixth this year, those very superior damsels who were having an extra year's school and specialising.

Anthea counted the cups and saucers. "Well, that gives us sixty, so surely we'll have enough."

She began placing the cups down the long trestle-table commandeered from the dining-room.

It was the morning of the Sale, and everyone was scampering everywhere, the whole place filled with noise and chatter, since rules were in abeyance for the time being. In Hall, the forms in charge of stalls were very busy setting out their wares. A concert was to take place in the Kindergarten, which was an army hut set to one side of the Big House, and a country-dancing display was billed for half-past three in the gym. In the prefects' room the Mr. Young who had married Miss Linton in the summer, thereby leaving the School lamenting a very favourite mistress, had undertaken to do lightning portraits at half a crown a time. Altogether, the girls had decided that this ought to be the best effort they had ever managed.

The two Heads, who had been hard at it all the morning, strolled into Hall after elevenses to admire the general effect, and really, it was worth admiring. At the top of the room was the dais on which the opening ceremony would take place. It was banked up with pots of ferns and flowering bulbs, and great jars of pussy willows had been disposed across the back on stands. To one side stood the "igloo" of the Ekimos, constructed of bamboos with sheets spread over, and the outlines of the snow "bricks" marked with black tacking. The "dip" consisted of snowballs made of cotton-wool, each containing some prize. Miss Norman had wisely insisted that those for boys must stand at one side of the igloo, and those for girls at the other. The small folk were very busy making neat piles and as excited as was good for them.

"I shan't be surprised if we have tears before the day is over," Miss Wilson observed as she surveyed them. Then she made a dive forward. "Signa! You bad child! What do you think you're doing?"

Signa went red and she dropped the red blackboard chalk with which she had been chalking at one side. "Eskermo igloo for dips."

Miss Norman looked at it with resigned horror. "I might have known! Get a cloth, one of you others, and let me wipe it off. *No*—not you! It's only a frail affair and I don't

bit off my loofah and put *that* in the bathroom, and that'll make one more."

"Then you'll have to gum it round the edges or something, or it'll fray out," Clem told her. "I've got a sliver of soap left. I'll wet it and try to shape it into a little tablet. We could dye it pink with red ink. I don't suppose the *dolls* 'ud mind if it came off on them!"

In the end, however, they had to give up with just forty-eight materials. However, they felt they had done really well, and when the Heads finally passed the scheme, Bride awarded the accolade to the genius who had thought up the scheme before the assembled members of all three forms.

"It really is a wizard idea. I was beginning to think we'd never solve that problem, but Carola's done it for us. I vote we cheer her!"

This was not allowed for a moment. They had no wish to be called to order for making a noise. But the happy Carola was delighted to take the will for the deed when Tom said, "Cheer be sugared! D'you *want* to lose us all order marks, Bride? What an ass you are sometimes! All the same, Carola's done us proud, and I move a hearty vote of thanks to her for a really super idea!" This last with a sudden memory of the many church bazaars and meetings she had had to attend. "All in favour hands up—and *don't make more row than you can help!*" A forest of waving hands assured everyone how the girls felt, and Carola went to bed that night as happy a girl as you could have found anywhere.

Chapter XVIII

"A-SELLING WE WILL GO!"

"HERE you are, Natalie. Cook says that's the very last cup she can spare. How many does that make?" Jean Mackay set down a laden tray on the table in the Seniors' common-room as she spoke and looked anxiously at tall, stately Anthea Barnett—yes; she was the "young monkey" Mrs. Barnett had spoken of when she met Cousin Maud at Southampton!—who was

"Me." Primrose took a hand. "They're cork. I cut them out of medicine-bottle corks."

"And what about the chandeliers in the sitting-rooms? Tom, you made those, didn't you? What are they made of?"

"Copper wire and gilding. The candles are wax tapers I found in a box at home."

"*They* look wizard," Polly replied. "And those wee shades Primrose made for them are smashing! What are they made of, Prim?"

"Cellophane in the dining-room, so you can't use *that* again," Primrose said. "The drawing-room ones are parchment I pinched from home."

"This form seems to have gone in for a lot of pinching altogether," Bride said austerely. Then she chuckled. "I did a bit myself. Those inner curtains in the drawing-room are a bit of silk brocade Mummy had in an old bag of Grannie's. I saw it one day and I thought it was just exactly what we wanted, so I—er—*lifted* it."

They giggled appreciatively at this. Carola wrote down "brocade" and then looked round for the next thing.

Jean supplied it. "What about the paste we used for the papering? That's made of flour, isn't it? Put it down, Carola."

So it went on, one after another remembering something, until Carola's list reached the bottom of the page twice over and she had to turn over and write on the back. At last no one could think of another thing, so they told her to count up what they had remembered and waited breathlessly while she did so.

"Thirty-nine!" she said when she had gone over the columns three times. "Oh, can't we possibly get it to fifty? Oh, wait! The sponge in the bathroom! That's forty, anyhow."

"The sawdust in the seats of the chairs! I got it from the sawmill near us at home!" Vanna Ozanne cried excitedly. "Then that makes forty-one. Can't we *possibly* get nine more?"

"The leatherette on top of the writing-desk in the morning-room," Nancy Chester said instantly. "Oh, and brass! The door-knocker! It's a tiny brass ring, isn't it, Tom?"

Tom nodded. "It is. And I've got an idea. I'll cut a tiny

dozens of different kinds of material in it. Let's count them up and make a list. Then we can tell people there are so many and ask them to name them, and the one that gets the fullest list gets the house! *Now* do you see?"

There was silence for a moment as they took it in. Then they saw and the noise they made was enough to have brought someone in authority down on them if everyone had not been so busily occupied that they had no time to bother about the Fifth Forms.

"It's a smashing idea!" bubbled Primrose, using forbidden slang in the excitement of the moment. "We ought to be able to get quite a long list. There's the cotton for the bedding——"

"*And* linen," Sybil supplemented this. "I bagged three of Uncle Jack's best linen hankies for the best sheets and pillow-cases."

"Whatman paper for the pictures and water-colour paint." This was Polly. "And then there's the cellophane over them and passe-partout for the frames!"

"There's the paint for the outside, if you come to that," Bride put in. "It's oil-paint, so it's another material. Carola, it's a super idea! Come on, all of you! Get a pencil and paper. Carola—you're doing nothing—and we'll remember while you write the things down."

At first it was easy enough. They could think of all the obvious things. When she had scribbled them down, she shook her head, however. It was not nearly enough—only twenty-two articles.

"We've got to have at least double this." she said definitely. "It won't be any real competition if this is all. I'm sure there's crowds more if we can only think of them. What did you stuff the mattresses with, for instance?"

"Cotton-wool," Sybil replied at once. "And I took some kapok from one of Auntie Jo's cushions that was leaking a bit for the little pillows and cushions."

Carola looked up. "How d'you spell 'kapok'?" she asked.

"'K-a-p-o-c-k'," Clem obligingly spelt. "At least, I think so."

Carola wrote it down and then asked, "What about those nifty little dinner mats in the sideboard drawer? Who made those?"

Carola slowly closed the sides of the house. Then she went over to where Tom was waiting. She held the pieces of wood which Tom put into her fingers without saying a word. Tom paused to look at her.

"I say, you're not stuffy about what I said, are you?" she asked doubtfully. "I didn't mean anything."

Carola started awake and shook her head. "Of course I'm not stuffy, I was just thinking. Tom! You've used lots of different kinds of stuff in it, haven't you?"

Tom stared at her. "I should just think we had! What do you call the furnishings? Are you crackers?"

Carola looked at her and then gave a chuckle. "It sounds rather like it, I suppose. No, I'm not. It's only—I've got the ghost of a germ of an idea for the comp. Don't talk to me, Tom. I want to work it out."

Carola went back to her seat, set her elbows on the table, buried her chin in her hands, and stared thoughtfully at nothing. The others were too busy to notice her, so everyone jumped violently when she suddenly bounced up, exclaiming, "Eureka! I've got it, I do believe!"

"Got what?" Bride demanded crossly as she sucked the finger Carola's outburst had caused her to prick with her needle. "What's biting you?"

"The comp.! I believe I've got a real idea at last!"

With one accord they dropped their work. "You've got an idea? What is it?" Tom wanted to know.

"Let's have it," Clem ordered. "Is it any good?"

"It had better be!" Polly Winterton spoke darkly. "You made me jump so. I've smudged green right across my sky."

Carola paid no heed to them. She turned to Tom eagerly. "Tell me, Tom, what did you use to make the house— materials, I mean?"

Tom reached out and felt her head. Carola shied away.

"I'm *not* crackers! Don't be such an ass, Tom! Answer my question and tell me what materials you used."

Tom gave it up and condescended to reply. "Wood— and glue—and raffia—and glass for the window-panes. What are you getting at?"

"And there's the canvas and wool for the mats—and the muslin for the curtains—and the silk for the inner ones in the drawing-room—and—oh, heaps of things!" The words came tumbling out. Carola was almost incoherent with excitement. "Oh, don't you *see*, all of you? There must be to be one from each form. Here, Prim, you can represent Lower Five A, and—and—you can take Lower Five B, young Clem. Come on!"

"We'll go on with our work while you're gone," Elfie Woodward, an ornament of the Upper Fifth, said. "We're out to make the biggest sum, aren't we? Then let's stop huddling up like this and get cracking."

There was common sense in what she said. The Fifths had plenty of work to finish, so they went to the cupboards, fished it out, and when the three delegates returned a quarter of an hour later, they came in to a busy room. Everyone dropped what she was doing, however, and a chorus of eager voices demanded, "Well? What do they say?"

"Well, it's not washed out altogether," Bride told them. "They say we can keep it in mind, and if we really *can't* do any better, we can use it—*may*, I mean—but they don't think much of it. It was Bill who said that, by the way," she added with a grin.

"As if we needed anyone to tell us that!" Tom said with scorn.

"Well, there's one thing," Nancy Chester remarked decidedly. "We fix it for ourselves. No going outside the Fifths for an idea! Don't you go and ask Auntie Jo, Bride, d'ye hear?"

"As if I should!" Bride cried indignantly.

Carola, who had been wondering if it would be any use to suggest doing that very thing, went scarlet, but no one was noticing her at the moment, so she was not called on to explain her sudden blush. She finished off her thread, broke it, and held up the little knitted frock on which she had been busy to shake it out.

"Finished?" Clem asked. "It's sma—er—wizard. You really are a decent knitter, Carola. Look, you folk!"

Carola folded up her frock and laid it in her workbox until she could press the seams. She had nothing else on hand at the moment, so she strolled over to the house, opened the sides, and stood gazing in admiration at the contents. Tom looked up and saw her.

"Hey!" she called across the room. "The house isn't likely to give you any ideas, no matter how much you stand there trying to mesmerise it! If you've finished your own job, come here and hold these bits while I glue them together, will you?"

charge far more for an entrance fee. What do you say, Miss Annersley?"

"I agree," Miss Annersley said promptly. "You can't make it less than five shillings. What ideas have you about the competition, by the way?"

There was an awful pause. The girls had all racked their brains to solve this problem, but so far no one had done it. Nancy Chester of Upper Fifth had suggested that intending competitors should guess the complete cubic content of each room and then of the house itself, and had been howled down for such an appalling suggestion.

Rosalie Browne had proposed that the competitors should be asked to choose a name, and then the School could vote on the list and the winner would get the house, but that, too, had been vetoed. There was good reason, therefore, for their stricken silence at Miss Annersley's bland question.

She surveyed their crestfallen faces with laughing eyes. "Not found anything *yet*? Oh, you'll have to do better than this. There's only a fortnight left, you know. Put your brains in steep and see if you can evolve something worth while. The house deserves it, you know."

The Staff left shortly after that, having seen everything and complimented the Fifth Forms on their industry and ingenuity, and those young ladies instantly went into a huddle, to quote Bride, on the subject of the competition.

Bride, sitting on the corner of a table, swinging long, brown-stockinged legs, mused a moment. Then she looked up. "We mayn't have guessing the name of the house, but do you think they'd let us name the family and make them guess *that*?" she asked hopefully.

"We can *try* it, I suppose," Tom said gloomily. "What d'you think of calling 'em?"

"Something appropriate, anyhow," Gillian said. "We can't pitch on anything like Smith, or Jones, or Brown. They're too ordinary."

Sybil Russell grinned. "Before we start working our poor brains too hard, what about going and seeing if the Heads will pass that?" she suggested.

"Good idea!" Tom looked round. "Here, Bride, you beetle off to the study and put it up to them and see what they say."

"O.K.; but I'm not going alone, so don't you think it," Bride responded, sliding down from her table. "There's got

Tom had given her house lattice windows which swung open delightfully, and the front and back doors also opened and shut.

The furnishings were as delightful as the house. Nella Ozanne, who was amazingly clever at both fretwork and wood-carving, had produced a stately set of dining-room furniture in simple Chippendale style with padded chair-seats and a little sideboard whose one drawer really pulled in and out. She had also made chairs and tables for the drawing-room and a delightful little china cabinet into which the girls had put tiny papier-mâché vases, painted and decorated by the artistic members of the form. Jean Acheson, another fretwork enthusiast, had contributed the morning-room furniture and someone else had attended to the kitchen, which had an imitation range made of wood and painted black. The fireplaces were of copper wire, also painted, with little wooden mantelshelves over them. Polly Winterton had drawn and painted the pictures that were glued to the walls, Tom refused flatly to have her work marred by tacks.

The best needlewomen in the forms had made the curtains, table-covers, and wee cushions that gave the place such a well-finished appearance. They had also made the bed-linen for the little four-posters Nella had managed for two of the bedrooms. The other two bedrooms had beds made of matchboxes, and matchboxes glued together, framed in stout pasteboard and painted, provided tallboys and low chests of drawers. Audrey's carpets were laid on the floors except in the kitchen, bathroom, and nursery, and for these they had used American cloth which they had painted in tiny squares, or, in the case of the nursery, with sprays of flowers. The dressing-tables and wardrobes had slips of looking-glass framed so that the dolls' family might look at themselves. As for the dolls, they had been provided by an artistic member of Special Sixth who had been interested in puppetry and had contrived a very pleasant-looking family which the Fifths had supplied with extensive wardrobes.

The Staff simply gasped when they had taken it all in. They knew the girls had set out to outdo anything they had done before, but this excelled their imaginings.

"Well," Miss Wilson said when at last she stood back, "I haven't the least idea what you propose to do in the way of a competition, girls, but I honestly think you must

They agreed to this with acclamations. It was decided to ask leave to use Upper Fifth, which was a large room, for the show and certain of the mistresses were to be invited to come and pronounce on it.

After tea and prep, the girls sped off to bring their collection from its cupboards and drawers and then set it out. Abendessen came all too soon for them, but when it ended, they had twenty minutes or so before Prayers in which to finish and select the Staff who were to be privileged to see their show. Finally, it was ready, and Clem and Bride went off to invite the mistresses.

The two Heads, Mademoiselle, Miss Burn (now quite recovered from her accident), Biddy O'Ryan, Miss Norman, and Miss Dene (the school secretary) were all summoned and came agog to see what the girls had been doing.

They exclaimed with surprise as they saw the quantity and variety laid out. There were cuddly toys made of material or knitted rag dolls, beautifully dressed; piles of dolls' clothes of all sorts and sizes; a heap of little carpets made by Audrey Simpson, a very quiet member of Lower Fifth A, with canvas and wool; boxes of bedding and bed-linen; sets of toy furniture and separate items as well; in short, everything they could think of and make. But the gem of the whole collection was undoubtedly the dolls' house.

Tom Gay had been responsible for the house itself. She had made it out of tea-chests which she had taken to pieces, cut to the sizes she wanted, and put together to form a veritable mansion. There were four rooms on the ground floor as well as the hall, from which rose a staircase with a landing half-way up and a turn in the stairs: and only Tom knew how much labour and temper had been spent on this last item! Over the door was a bathroom, fitted up with a tin bath and all the other etceteras, which were the only articles of furnishing the girls had bought. Four bedrooms were over the sitting-rooms and kitchen and in the roof were two more rooms. All the sides were on hinges and opened. The roof was a thatched one, the thatch being of yellow raffia. The house had been painted outside to imitate the old black-and-white houses, and inside, every room was properly papered with the exception of the kitchen and bathroom. They had been painted.

your own crew!" before she flung off, leaving the Junior Middle feeling that it might be as well to leave Carola alone, as well as very indignant as the shaking which had been thorough.

Luckily for all concerned, Mary-Lou was an honest young thing and she owned to herself that *perhaps* she had deserved Carola's fury. Anyhow, she wasn't going to tell any tales and no one but their two selves ever knew anything about it. Even more luckily, the very next morning Miss Annersley reminded them after Prayers that there was only a fortnight left before their Sale, and thereafter Carola's exploit sank into the background. Lessons had to go on as usual, but apart from them and their games periods, the girls talked, thought, and *dreamed* Sale.

It was always an important event in the Easter term. Nor was the School ever satisfied with just a "plain" Sale. One year they had used fairy-tales. Another time it had been a Willow Pattern Sale, when the girls all turned Chinese overnight and the stall-frames were transformed into quite good likenesses of pagodas and Chinese houses. This year, they were to represent many nations. Special Sixth, who had charge of the tea-room, would be Indian ladies and had already been practising the art of wearing a saree. The two Fourth were to be Red Indians and had charge of the needlework stall which was to be turned into a tepee—or as nearly one as possible. The Thirds had pleaded to be allowed to be Maories and were to make of their sweets and cakes a Maori "Pah." The Sixth, who were to have fruit and vegetables and flowers, had insisted on being Persians, and devoted a good part of their spare time to manufacturing for themselves slippers with turned-up toes and the round, fez-like caps Persians are supposed to wear. The bric-à-brac stall with fretwork, pottery, shell-covered boxes and photograph-frames and other oddments had been given to the Second Forms who were to be Chinese, and the Kindergarten had charge of the lucky dip as usual and were to be Eskimos. The two Fifths had undertaken the toy stall and, at Clem Barrass's suggestion, were to be Scots in kilts, bonnets, and plaids.

"We'd best see just what we've got," Bride Bettany said to the others. "I vote we have a show tonight and see what's finished and what's still left to be done. Then we'll know where we are."

Suddenly Matron's stern face creased. Her eyes twinkled, and she had to bite her lips to steady them. "I see. Well, girls, I'm afraid you won't enjoy your doughnuts this time. I advise you to let them severely alone."

"But—*why*?" Clem demanded, wide-eyed.

"Because Carola took the wrong bottle." Matron paused again. Then she flung her final bombshell among them. "Those doughnuts of yours were fried in *cod-liver oil*!"

Then she departed, leaving the entire School staring at each other and the unhappy Lower Fifths with startled eyes and dropping jaws.

Chapter XVII

CAROLA SOLVES A PROBLEM

NEEDLESS to state, once the School had got over its first shock it revelled in the latest "yarn." Carola was assured that no one would ever forget it. She was asked with mock sympathy if her sense of smell had returned yet; requested for other new recipes; told that she really ought to write a cookery book as it was bound to be original if nothing else!

She bore the teasing very well at first. Then she lost her temper one day when Mary-Lou, all innocence, pressed a note into her hand—a note that purported to come from Karen the cook, begging her to say if she would advise using Epsom salts or salts of lemon in place of the proper article for flavouring the soup?

Carola read this effusion and then went in search of Mary-Lou, who had meant to join her own gang for safety but had delayed as she had just thought of a delightful joke she wanted to play on Polly Winterton. She was leaving the bathroom when Carola ran her to earth and there was no one near. Mary-Lou, looking up, felt rather apprehensive as she saw the angry blue eyes looking down at her and the flushed face. She gave a little giggle from sheer nervousness and that was oil on the fire. Carola said nothing. She simply took the younger girl by the shoulders and gave her a good shaking, finally shoving her away with the remark: "Perhaps that will teach you to keep your silly tricks for

She might have had more to say, but Vanna Ozanne and Tom Gay had both helped themselves and bit into their doughnuts with every anticipation of a treat. Vanna followed Mary-Lou from the room at even greater speed. Tom hurriedly removed *her* mouthful with more haste than elegance, and exclaimed, "Cripes! What *have* you kids put into the things? They're ghastly—frightful!"

"They're *not*!" exclaimed half a dozen indignant voices.

"But they *are*!" Tom maintained, hurriedly picking up her cup. She gulped down her tea and then went to the urn for more. "*Urrh*! Of all the beastly tastes!"

Peggy rapped on the table with the handle of her knife. "Less noise, please," she ordered. "Tom, stop making those awful faces. You aren't poisoned, anyhow."

"I'm not so sure of that," Tom retorted, swallowing down her tea. "What on *earth* have you kids been doing? The thing just reeks of bad fish!"

"*Bad fish*!" The Lower Fifths were nearly speechless at this. Clem managed to collect herself, however.

"That, I'm certain, they don't! We had a clean fish-kettle that Frau Mieders took off the shelf and the frying fat had never been *near* fish of any kind. It came straight from the bottle!"

By this time, various of the cooks had helped themselves and were tasting gingerly. It was plain, even to them, that Mary-Lou, Vanna, and Tom had real reason for their behaviour. Peggy Bettany took one, and lifted it to her mouth. Before she could bite into it, however, the door opened, and Matron appeared on the scene.

"Who got the oil for frying from my room?" she demanded.

Carola stood up. "I did, Matron. I couldn't find you, and Frau Mieders was waiting, so I—I just took some."

"Indeed?" Matron glared at her and Carola wilted visibly. "Can't you read, eh, child?"

By this time, Carola was convinced she had come near poisoning everyone, and her voice was shaky as she replied, "Yes—oh, yes!"

"Didn't you read the label on the bottle?"

"I—I couldn't. It—it was so oily," Carola stammered, nearly in tears now.

There was an electric pause while the girls wondered wildly what was coming next. *Had* Carola got hold of something that would make them sick?

doughnuts," Rosalie Browne remarked with conviction as Frau Mieders pronounced the first boiling "done," and lifted the basket to let it drip before turning the doughnuts out on to the sugar-covered papers.

By four o'clock there were four large heaps of nicely-browned and sugared doughnuts, and the kitchen had been restored to the perfect neatness about which the mistress was always most particular. The hot oil had been set aside in the scullery to cool sufficiently to allow it to be poured off into the flagon, and all the windows opened to get rid of the fish-and-chips smell which still hung round.

When the last utensil had been washed and wiped and put away in its proper place and every vestige of mess dealt with, they were dismissed just as the bell rang, to get ready for tea. They bestirred themselves, and were down first, eagerly watching the faces of the rest as they saw the treat in store for them.

The Sixth came in shortly after the cooks and the rest were not far behind. The exclamations at sight of the platefuls of swollen brown and white beauties on the tables made the Lower Fifths preen themselves more than ever.

"I hope you had the decency to send samples to the Staff," Peggy Bettany remarked to Clem Barrass as she sat down.

"Frau Mieders took a plateful for them," Clem replied. "Bread-and-butter, please."

The School had an unwritten rule that no girl was to eat cake or buns until she had eaten at least two pieces of bread-and-butter. Mary-Lou who, like *Amy* of "Little Women" fame, was fond of delicacies, hurriedly choked down her two pieces and then, with a smug smile at the rest who were still busy with bread-and-butter, took a doughnut and bit a huge chunk out of it. The Lower Fifths watched her eagerly, prepared for an exclamation of delight. They, by the way, had been eating in a much more ladylike manner.

Mary-Lou's reaction was anything but what they had expected. She solemnly chewed her mouthful, gave a gasp, jumped to her feet, upsetting her chair in her hurry, and vanished incontinently from the room, regardless of Peggy's stern command: "Mary-Lou! Where are you going? Come back at once and ask for leave!"

"Choked," Dickie Christy said. "That's what comes of trying to hog your food instead of eating it decently."

had to look for her. What she did *not* say was that Matron proved quite unfindable, so she had simply looked round the tiny room where all medicants were kept, found the big jar of yellowish oil, and calmly helped herself—Frau Mieders had given her a large container as she went out of the kitchen.

She set the thing down in a corner after emptying the contents into the big fish-kettle the misress pointed out to her. Frau Mieders herself set it on top of the cooker. Carola went to collect her materials, and silence fell on the kitchen while the girls set to work to mix their dough.

"What about jam?" someone asked when most of the dough was out of the mixing-bowls and on the floured boards. "Do we put it in to cook or after they come out?"

None of the recipes in Frau Mieders' book told this— never mentioned jam, so far as that went; but when the girls assured her that doughnuts must *always* have jam in them, she decided that it should be put into a pocket in each little ball before the said balls were dropped into the fat which was beginning to boil. She produced a great jar of rhubarb jam and the girls delightedly inserted spoonfuls into their balls.

At length they were ready, and while four of the cooks collected the dough balls, some of the others were set to cut out large squares of brown paper to hold the sugar in which the doughnuts must be rolled when they came out of the oil.

"Funny how the smell of fish and chips always hangs about," said Jean Ackroyd as she rolled a ball between her hands to get it round. "I can smell ours yet!"

"Yes, it's what you might call a penetrating smell, isn't it?" Clem agreed. "When I was at school in York I sat next a girl whose people kept a fish-and-chip shop and she always reeked of it, poor kid."

Frau Mieders laughed. "I do not notice it—but then I have a catarrh of the nasal passages and can smell nothing these five days."

The girls murmured sympathy and she turned to the business in hand, the wire frying basket was half-filled with doughnuts and carefully lowered into the boiling oil, and the girls came in turn to stand and exclaim as the small balls they had produced swelled to proper doughnut size, which was almost twice as large as they had been.

"If they liked our fish and chips, I'll bet they *love* our

Clem Barrass, who had recovered from her German measles and was back in school again.

Frau Mieders, who had planned a programme of various scones, looked doubtful. "Doughnuts?" she queried. "But why doughnuts, Clemency?"

"Well, they're done in deep fat—I remember that from the time we were in the Rockies," Clem, who had travelled widely with her parents at one time and another, explained.

Frau Mieders had found a recipe. "I see it says they must be fried in lard. Now, of this I have but little—certainly none for frying."

"*Couldn't* we use vegetable oil?" Clem asked. "It didn't make any difference to the fish, did it? I should think it would be O.K.—I—I mean quite all right—for doughnuts."

Frau Mieders nodded slowly. "I think it might do. At any rate we will try it. *One* doughnut to be made for each girl and one over for a friend. We cannot waste materials," she added firmly.

"What do we need?" Vanna Ozanne asked briskly.

Frau Mieders read out the recipe for them to write into their recipe books and then sent Rosalie Browne to the store cupboard to find the big flagon of vegetable oil kept there. Alas! When Rosalie produced it, it was only about a third full. The faces of the girls fell considerably at this. They were all agog to try their hands at doughnuts, but now it looked as if that were out of the question. It was left to the ever-fertile Clem to solve the difficulty.

"Couldn't we use *olive* oil?" she queried. "That's vegetable oil, all right, and Matron has a *huge* jar of it. I'm sure she'd lend us some if we asked her."

"Shall I go and see?" asked Carola, who was nearest the door. She loved her cookery lessons, never before having had the chance to compound much beyond toffee and fudge, and very rarely even that. Doughnuts promised to be really interesting, and she was quite as keen as anyone to try her hand at them.

Frau Mieders was a kindly soul who rarely said "No" if she could manage "Yes." She nodded, and Carola shot off at once. The rest were told to read over their recipes, see what they needed, and begin to collect the ingredients.

Carola was away a little while, but explained it by saying that she had not found Matron in her room and had

and put a stop to all such stories, even when they're playing."

Next day he bore his girls off for a long walk in the afternoon, and they returned rosy and fresh and with enormous appetites. What was more, greatly to the relief of everyone, Con stopped sleep-walking and had no more nightmares, so that episode ended after Signa had been interviewed and told she was to tell no more frightening tales to the others.

In any case, the weather was fine enough for the Juniors to be out most afternoons, playing rounders, which gave them little time for stories, frightening or otherwise.

And then Carola, just to keep things from becoming monotonous—or so Jo said when she heard the tale—produced a new legend to add to the many the School cherished.

Long before this, when the School was in Tirol in fact, a domestic science class had been introduced as part of the curriculum. Every girl as soon as she reached Lower Fourth attended for the whole of one day in the week and was instructed in all kinds of housework, including mending of linen and, best of all, cooking.

This class had, in its time, made School history. No one was ever likely to forget what happened when Cornelia Flower had given out garlic cloves instead of the more usual variety to flavour the apple pies her form was making. Another time, Joyce Linton, sister of Miss Linton who had taught in the School until the previous summer when she had married, had set out to make saffron cakes and used flowers of sulphur instead of saffron. There were other episodes quite as startling, and now Carola added one that took the fancy of everyone who heard of it— including Lady Russell in Canada.

On a certain day towards the middle of March it seemed good to Frau Mieders, who had been domestic science mistress from the beginning of the class, to teach the two Lower Fifths the art of deep-frying. They began with fish coated with thick batter before it was fried, and potato chips, all of which were devoured with much enjoyment at Mittagessen. The Lower Fifths smirked complacently at the compliments they received on all sides on the delicious first course they had provided, and certainly their heads were all a little swollen by their success.

"Please may we make doughnuts for tea?" suggested

Then she sat up with a little scream of rapture. "Papa! Oh, how lovely? When did you come? Is Mamma here, too?"

"Not this time. What were you dreaming about, Con?"

Still drowsy and therefore not on her guard, Con replied at once. "It—it was the big horse." She gave a shudder.

"What horse, pet?"

"The one that lives at the bottom of waterfalls and comes up and takes little girls away to live with it until it eats them. Oh, Papa, it isn't *really* true, is it?" She clung to him, her eyes dilated with fear, and he held her in a safe, warm clasp.

"True? Of course it isn't! How on earth could the poor thing breathe at the bottom of a waterfall?" he demanded, with such an air of plain common sense that she relaxed with a long breath.

"O-oh! I hadn't thought of that. Of course it couldn't. Then it is only a kind of fairy-tale? Oh, I'm so *glad*! That's super!"

"And anyway," he went on, "where's your waterfall in this part of the world? Honestly, Con, what *has* become of your wits? But you needn't worry, even if you live with fifty waterfalls round you! No horse of any kind whatsoever could be stabled under a waterfall, so you can be very sure there isn't any such beasty. Now lie down again and go to sleep. Your guardian angel is always beside you, and you needn't be afraid of anything. Got that?"

She nodded as he put her back into bed and tucked her up. "It's all right. I'm not afraid—no-ow." She ended on a little yawn, and fell asleep again.

"Who's been telling the poor bairn about kelpies?" Jack demanded when at length they left the room. "That bad Clem?"

Miss Annersley shook her head. "That's no kelpie! It's a Norse superstition and I can guess who was at the bottom of it."

"So can I—young Signa or that sister of hers. Well, I'm glad to know what's caused all the fuss. I don't suppose you'll have any more trouble with her now. Keep her quiet for a day or two with plenty of milk and eggs and early bed. Keep her in the fresh air as much as you can. That's all. Is she having her tonic?"

The Head nodded. "Trust Matey to see to that!" She drew a long breath. "Thank goodness we've got to the bottom of it! Well, tomorrow I shall interview Miss Signa

Chapter XVI

CAROLA DOES A LITTLE COOKING

JACK MAYNARD arrived that evening in answer to a somewhat agitated telephone call from Miss Annersley. He still insisted that Jo must know nothing of Con's exploits. All three of the little boys had had German measles, and though none of them had been more than poorly and peevish for a day or two, he felt she had had enough. In the meantime, he proposed to find out what was at the bottom of Con's nightmares and sleep-walking.

Jo was not to know of his visit to St. Briavel's.

The pair were in bed and asleep when he arrived. Miss Annersley still had Con in her own room and was sitting there doing her work in the evenings.

"I thought it wiser for the next week or two," she explained as she took the doctor up. "I hope to heaven, Jack, you can find out what has upset Con like this. They stick to it that they aren't eating anything but what the rest have, nor is anyone telling stories at unlawful hours, which was the other thing I thought of."

"Well, I'm here till the day after tomorrow, so I'll do my best." They were in the room by this time and he bent over the camp-bed where Con lay sleeping profoundly, her long black lashes making little fans on her pink cheeks. "Looks fit enough," He straightened up and they went to the desk at the far side of the room. "I'm inclined to think you may be right and someone has told them stories. Con's an imaginative little person—much more so than the other two. What wouldn't affect them might upset her."

A murmuring from the camp-bed reached them and both turned in time to see Con throw back the clothes though still fast asleep. Her father went quickly across, laid her back and tucked her in.

"No, Con," he said firmly. "Lie still, my pet."

A minute or two later he gently roused her. "What were you dreaming, Con? Tell Papa."

Con opened her brown eyes and stared at him sleepily.

lumps! And so—something went tick-tick, and it wasn't a clock!" Con wailed.

"The electric light meter," Miss Annersley said at once. "I'll take you and Len down in the morning and show you the little wheel that keeps turning all the time. Biddy, is that milk ready yet?"

"Just!" Miss O'Ryan poured it into a cup and brought it, and the Head held the cup to Con's lips.

"Drink it up, Con, and stop crying," she said briskly. "You're quite safe now, and you'll wake up everyone else if you howl like that. Nine is much too big to be a baby. What would Mamma say?"

If the Head had petted her there is no doubt that Con would have kept up her wails. This matter-of-fact way of dealing with things reassured Con as nothing else could have done. She stopped howling, though her chest still heaved with sobs and she choked over her milk. She was calmer when it was finished.

"I'm taking Con to have a bath," Miss Annersley said quietly. "Carola, go and seek some clean pyjamas for her and bring them to my room. Miss O'Ryan, you might just go the rounds with Peggy and see if Con's yells have roused anyone. If they have, just say that one of the Juniors has been upset and I'm dealing with it. Thanks for your offer, Carola, but I think Con had better spend what's left of the night with me."

Con put up a filthy arm and embraced her Head with it. "I was *so* frightened, Auntie Hilda," she said with a hiccup.

"Never mind. It's over now and you're going to sleep with me for a treat," Miss Annersley said cheerfully. "Switch the light off, Peggy, and shut the door after us, please."

She bore Con off to be undressed, sponged down, and her grazed arm and knee bathed and bound up. By the time this was done, Con was asleep again and never knew when she was snugly in bed, Miss Annersley's arms round her so that she could not walk off again in her sleep. By this time, Peggy and Carola were also asleep. Only Biddy O'Ryan was left to finish her round and then climb wearily into bed with a deep sigh and a hope, voiced aloud, that no one would disturb the School for what remained of the night.

"And that's only four hours," she said as she switched off her light and lay down. "What a life!"

"I don't know," Carola said. She shivered. "If—if she's outside in her pyjamas——"

"Go and dress, you three," Miss Annersley said sharply. "Then come——"

Her words were cut short by a sudden fearful bellow from just under their feet. They all jumped, and Peggy cried, "That's Con! Where on earth can she be? Not outside, surely!"

She dashed at the door and began tugging at the heavy bolts, but Miss Annersley stopped her. "No; she must have got into the cellars somehow. I don't know how. I always understood that Karen kept that door locked. It's all right, Peggy. Come quickly, girls! Biddy, give me that torch, please."

Biddy handed it over, and the four made for the kitchens. Miss Annersley led the way to a small entry behind the kitchen door, and pulled open the door within. She flashed the torch down the stairs whence was coming a series of howls.

"Con!" she called. "It's Auntie Hilda. Don't yell like that or you'll wake the entire School. I'm coming!"

The howls softened though they did not cease. The Head ran lightly down the stairs, and presently reappeared with the queerest little object in her arms.

"Shut the door," she said as she came into the blessed glow of the kitchen light. "Biddy, go and hunt in the pantry for milk, will you? Con, stop that howling at once. It's all right. Auntie Hilda has you and you're quite safe."

Carola came and knelt by her side as she sat in the big chair that belonged to Karen the cook. She kissed what she could see of a black-smeared pink cheek. Con was a most appalling-looking little object. She must have been in the coal cellar, for she was black from head to foot. A spider's web, thick with coal dust, adorned her black curls, and she must have stumbled over something, for one sleeve was torn, and a long graze was reddening on her arm.

"Don't cry, Con," Carola said. "It's quite all right." She looked shyly at the Head. "I know she can't go into San, Miss Annersley, but could she share my bed?"

"Or let me have her," her cousin said, coming with a duster from Karen's drawer and removing the cobweb. "It's all right, precious."

"I was alone—and in the dark—and it was full of

necessary if we can find the imp and put her to bed again. I'll go this way and you go that. Try every bathroom."

But though they conscientiously tried every bathroom and then every dormitory on the corridor just in case, as Biddy said, they drew blank everywhere.

Thoroughly roused by this time, Biddy led the way to the other corridors, but they had no better luck. However, they did wake up Peggy Bettany who, as Head Girl, had the privilege of sleeping by herself in a tiny room, and when she heard that her small cousin was missing, she came out to help with the search.

High and low they sought, but no Con was to be found anywhere. By the time they had been over the whole house, not omitting the kitchen regions, and only leaving the infected part alone, Biddy was seriously alarmed.

"We'll have to get Miss Annersley," she said when they came out of the Junior common-room, which was the last. "This is beyond me. You two go into Senior common-room. It's still pretty warm there. I'll go and get Miss Annersley."

The Head Girl looked very grave and Carola took fright.

"Peggy, you—you don't think she—well—could she get out of a window?" she asked timidly. They knew Con could not have escaped by a door, for the outer doors were all locked and bolted.

"It looks like the only solution," Peggy said, "but I don't see how she could possibly. The windows down here are all latched and those in the dormies can only be opened so far—and that's not far enough for even a kid like Con to squeeze through. I just don't understand *where* she can have got to!"

Nor could Miss Annersley when she arrived with Biddy. She questioned Carola closely, and then told her not to be so upset. She had done the best thing she could. All the same, she could not disguise the fact that she was very anxious. She refrained from sending Carola to bed, for she saw that the girl was working herself up to such a pitch that she would never sleep.

"You and Peggy had better dress," she said. "Miss O'Ryan, too. In the meantime, I'll call Mademoiselle and we two will go over the house again. If we can't find Con, then I'm afraid it means that she has got out somehow. Carola, was she dressed or in her pyjamas?"

soundly asleep that Carola had to shake her before she could rouse her.

Biddy sat up, her masses of long black hair showering round her, and turned sleepy eyes on the intruder.

"Well, and what are *you* wanting, may I ask?" she demanded.

"Oh, Miss O'Ryan, would you come to Con Maynard?" Carola begged.

"Con?" Biddy was still rather foggy.

"Yes; she woke me up with crying out and I found her trying to get out of bed——"

"Walking in her sleep again?" Biddy was out of bed in a moment and pulling on her dressing-gown. "Fish my slippers out from under the bed, Carola. Why on earth did you leave her, anyhow?"

"I got her back into bed and sat with her a while—*ages*, in fact," Carola explained. She did not mean to exaggerate, but those ten minutes of sitting in the dark beside Con had seemed hours. "She was sleeping all right, so I tucked her in tightly and then came to find someone, only no one seems to be in their rooms. You're the first I've found."

Biddy nodded and picked up her torch from the bedside table. "I see. Well, come along, though if you sat with her so long and she stayed put, I expect she's all right."

The two ran softly upstairs to the dormitory, and Biddy made straight for the cubicle. Switching on her torch, but careful to keep the light lowered, Biddy drew aside the curtain and the pair peered in. The bed-clothes were lying in a heap on the floor, and Con had vanished!

Carola's face was horrified. She was about to exclaim, but Biddy kept her head and set a firm hand across her mouth.

"Hush, will ye?" she said in an undertone. "No need to wake the rest. She can't have gone far, anyway. We'd best search here first."

Tiptoeing from cubicle to cubicle, they made the rounds. All the beds except Carola's own were occupied and no Con was to be found. She had evidently roused up after Carola left the room and gone out. Biddy dropped the last curtain and led Carola out into the corridor.

"Now," she said, "let's think. She hasn't gone to another dormy or someone would have waked up and we'd have known about it by this. We'd best try the bathrooms. I don't want to bother the Heads yet, as it may not be

School had to face the fact that they had German measles in their midst.

Next day Verity-Anne joined Mary-Lou before breakfast, and by midday seventeen Middles and five Juniors were keeping them company. Len Maynard was among them, but not Con, who remained splendidly well the whole time. Jo, on being told, laughed and said that, after all, it was a mild affair. Stephen was up and about again, and Charles, who had begun two days after his brother, was demanding lots to eat. In the end, out of the whole School, thirty-seven went down. The rest escaped. Three dormitories were turned into sick-wards and the people turned out had to go where they could. Matron had her hands full, and so had Nurse. The prefects were turned on to more dormitory duty and some of the Senior Middles were also pressed into service, among them Carola. Clem had been one of the first to succumb, along with three more from the same dormitory.

Carola was sent to sleep in the end cubicle of the Junior dormitory of which Con Maynard was an ornament. She took a special interest in that young person, having been attracted to her from the first. Consequently, when one night she was roused by a cry from Con's cubicle, she slipped in and found the child trying to get out of bed, still fast asleep.

Carola was in a quandary. She knew that someone in authority ought to be fetched, but she did not like to leave Con alone in case of what she might do. Neither did she want the other small girls to know of it. She got the sleeping Con back into bed and tucked her in firmly. Then she sat down beside her for a little. Con seemed to have settled down again, so after ten minutes of this, Carola made sure that the bed-clothes were securely tucked round her and slipped out to go in quest of someone.

Matron was sleeping in the wing where the patients were, so she could be of no help. Carola went down to the next corridor and tapped on Miss Wilson's door. There was no answer, so, greatly daring, she opened the door. The light was on and the bed was empty. No help to be found here. Carola withdrew, and tried the next room. Here, too, she drew a blank.

Eventually she found Biddy O'Ryan's room and that young lady was in bed and asleep. In fact, she was so

had expected, this brought him over on the Tuesday after a week-end in which Con had behaved as any normal little girl ought. Con was thrilled to see her father, and he begged leave for her and Len, took them off home for the afternoon and returned them about six. Then he demanded an interview with Matron and the Heads.

"Well?" Miss Annersley demanded when they were comfortably settled in the sitting-room the two Heads shared.

"Nothing to account for it. They stick to it that they haven't been eating anything but what the rest have and they don't lie awake telling hair-raising tales to each other. She's growing very quickly just now, and I'm inclined to set it down to that. I've had a tonic made up for her—here it is, Matey. See she takes it and keep her quiet. She ought to be all right soon. Don't say anything to Joey. She's been very good about it, but I know that she has fretted over Margot, and just at present I'd rather she was spared anything more. You know what an excitable creature she is and there's nothing really wrong with Con that I can see."

"All very well, so long as Jo doesn't come haring over to see the girls," Miss Wilson told him.

However, a week later Jo rang up agitatedly to say that Stephen, who had been poorly and fretful lately, had come out with a rash and she feared measles.

"Heavens!" Miss Wilson, who had taken the call, was thoroughly upset. "And Jack had the girls over to see you last week!"

"It *may* be just German measles," Jo said. "Stephen isn't really ill—just poorly, and as cross as a bear with a sore paw. The girls didn't see him, either, as he and Charles were at a birthday party that day. I should stick 'em into quarantine and hope for the best."

This optimistic point of view robbed Miss Wilson of her breath for the moment, and Jo had rung off before she recovered sufficiently to tell that lady her views. "Bill" left the telephone and went off to Matron, who declared that as the children had not met she didn't think it likely the little girl would take it. She agreed, however, that it would be best to quarantine them, and not only them, but the entire form.

And then Mary-Lou complained a week later of feeling headachy. Matron whisked her off to San, but by the next morning she was a lovely shade of rose-pink, and the

They were shooed back to bed, and Miss Wilson took the sobbing Con off to her own room where she was speedily soothed back into calmness. Matron administered a cup of hot milk when the storm was over, and a pacified and sleepy small girl was finally tucked back into bed and thereafter slept peacefully till next morning.

"I think I'll have her in San if this sort of thing occurs again," Matron said next day when severe questioning of the entire dormitory had elicited the facts that no one had smuggled food in, nor had they been telling stories after lights-out. In fact, all they had done was to go blamelessly to sleep until Con's yells woke them. "What about letting Jo know?"

Miss Annersley shook her head. Before she had left, Jo had confided a secret to her friend, and that lady was determined not to worry Mrs. Maynard if it could be avoided. "I'll write to Jack at San," she said. "By all means take Con if you think it wiser, Matey. In that case, though, Len must be warned to hold her tongue. Jo was really anxious about the little monkey when she was here on Wednesday."

Matron raised her brows. "Oh, like that, is it? Well, it's only what we could expect, Jo being Jo. Will she go to Toronto at Easter, then?"

"Oh, yes. Plenty of time before October. They're returning at the end of June. It will probably do Madam all the good in the world. She's missed her Margot very badly, and as she's taking her entire family with her, she'll be happy again."

Matron nodded. Jo was her darling, though wild horses wouldn't have dragged it from her. She quite agreed that if the Maynard family was to have an addition in the autumn it would be just as well for their mother not to have anything to worry her. Her hands would be full enough without that.

"We'll tell Len that Con's tummy seems to be upset as she's having bad dreams and we don't want to bother her mother about it," the Head decided. "That will keep her quiet. In the meantime, I'll write to Jack as I said and I expect he'll come over to see his daughter for himself at the first opportunity."

So it was left. Con was sent to the School San for the week-end, and Miss Annersley wrote to Dr. Maynard giving him a full account of what had happened. As she

Jo nodded. "It isn't like her, is it? Thanks, Hilda; I think that's a good idea. Are you busy?"

Miss Annersley nodded. "I go to the Sixth for poetry when the bell rings. And there it is. You must look after yourself until tea-time. Why don't you invade the Staff-room and see who's there?"

"Excellent idea! So I will! By the way, what's the news about Hilary?"

"Recovering steadily now the temp. has gone down. Matron was on to Dr. Graves this morning and he said there was no reason why she shouldn't return next Monday, though she must be careful for the next few weeks of course. Thank heaven neither Signa nor Carola seems to have been affected by it. We were a little anxious about Signa, but she's eating well and sleeping well. By the way, Thora may be coming across next week if she can get away. She can't come before as she isn't out of quarantine till then."

"Out of quarantine? What on earth do you mean?"

"Oh, I forgot, you wouldn't know. She's had all three of the boys down with chickenpox. Axel was the last and his quarantine ends next Monday. Nothing bad, she says, merely tiresome. Now I *must* go."

Miss Annersley had been collecting her books while she talked, and now she left the room. Jo ranged round it for a minute or two. Then she, too, departed for the Staff-room, where she found Biddy O'Ryan correcting books, and settled down for a good chat.

Len and Con duly came to tea with their Heads and mother and were cautiously sounded. It turned out that Daisy had treated them to nothing more deadly than sugar-topped buns, so Con's somnambulism was not to be explained that way. She looked well enough, and she and her sister brought their usual healthy appetites to the meal, so Jo went home thinking that it must be a final hang-over from the former trouble.

Three nights later, such part of the School as was still up were startled by wild yells proceeding from one of the Junior dormitories. Matron got there first, of course, and found the cause of the trouble. Con had been having nightmares, and had wakened screaming, thereby rousing her whole dormitory. When Matron erupted into the room she found the other little girls all clustered round the now-weeping Con, who wept loudly and noisily for her mother

"That shook Jo," she remarked to Mademoiselle, who had been present and shamelessly listened in. "Well, unless they've had any contraband, which I greatly doubt, it's clear enough that food has nothing to do with Con's attack. I must see Bill about this. I'm having no somnambulism in the School if I know it."

Jo arrived during the afternoon, still indignant that anyone could think that she would allow her children to gormandise, and, secretly, a little anxious. It was Matron's "free" day and she had gone off to Swansea as soon as Mittagessen had ended. Miss Annersley had returned with the noon ferry and she had to listen to Jo's diatribes as Miss Wilson was teaching.

"You must feel a good deal better for having got all that off your mind," the Head observed when Jo ran down at last. "You'd better come across later on and let Matron have the benefit of it. I don't know why *I* should be the only one to be scolded—especially as I had nothing at all to do with it."

Jo laughed shamefacedly. "Sorry, Hilda, but I really can't understand why Matron of all people should accuse me of such doings. She ought to know me better than that," she added in injured tones.

Miss Annersley eyed her thoughtfully. "I should imagine she couldn't resist the temptation," she said. "You nearly always do rise, Jo."

Jo glared at her. Then she giggled like a schoolgirl. "Oh, well, I suppose I'll have to forgive her. All the same," she went on, "I don't like this sleep-walking business coming back. Nor will Jack when he hears of it. But what can possibly have started it is more than I can say. I *know* they had only their usual simple meals, and they didn't have many more sweets than usual. Daisy's gone, or I'd have asked her what they had when she took them out yesterday morning. But even if she treated them to cream cakes with their coffee, *once* of that shouldn't have set Con off again."

"Suppose you stay for tea and see them and find out?" her friend suggested. She patted the parcel of bedroom slippers the pair had left at home and which Jo had made an excuse for coming. "They need know nothing but that you came to bring these. We'll invite them, shall we, and see what we can find out. All the same, if Daisy really did treat them liberally to cream cakes, I'm surprised at her."

Grizel Cochrane nodded good-night and departed. Ten minutes later the room was empty, Mlle. Berné, the last to leave, switching off the lights after a final look round to be sure that everything was as it ought to be. Satisfied, she shut the door and hurried upstairs, meeting Matron in the corridor.

"Con is fast asleep," that lady said. "So is Carola. I shall let Jo know about her daughter, all the same. I would very much like to know what has started the trouble again."

Mademoiselle laughed. "Perhaps she has been eating too many sweets or apples," she suggested. "I know that the dear Jo saves her own sweet ration for her children. So does Daisy Venables, who is at home for the present. And then there is Robin's ration, too. Jo told me that when Robin went to Switzerland she left her sweet coupons behind for the children. It would be possible. After all," Mademoiselle's black eyes twinkled wickedly, "this is just the last day of half-term. If I were you, Matron, I'd ask Jo what she has been giving her children."

Matron chuckled. "How indignant she'll be! Upon my word, I think I'll do it just for the fun of hearing what she has to say."

"Oh, do—and pray let me be present when you do it," Mademoiselle cooed sweetly as she turned to go. "Bonne nuit, chérie."

"Good-night," Matron replied as she turned in at her own door, still chuckling at the thought of Jo's fury when she was called to account for her daughters' diet during half-term.

Chapter XV

ADVENTURE FOR CON

NEXT DAY Matron duly rang up Jo, who protested wildly against the idea that she had allowed her family anything indigestible, half-term or no half-term. Before Matron had finished with her, she was literally squeaking, so indignant was she, and when she finally hung up, the School's domestic tyrant was one broad grin.

growing opaque. Miss Edwards tucked her in, picked up the glass, and departed.

Matron followed Miss Edwards back to the Staff-room. "Tomorrow I'm making inquiries to find out what those monkeys have been eating," she said. "Con's all right now. Carola had tucked her in so tightly she'd have had some difficulty in getting out again, and she was sleeping quite quietly. I'll ring Jo tomorrow, though, and let her know. Con may be the quiet one of those three externally, but her brain is easily excited. Hot milk every night for her for the next few weeks. We can't have that sort of thing going on."

"Con won't love you," Miss Stephens, who was Con's form mistress, observed. "She'll drink any amount of cold milk; but she told me once that she loathed it hot."

"Oh, well, it won't hurt her, and it's soothing," Matron retorted. "Carola all right, Dollie?"

Miss Edwards nodded. "I doubt if she was awake when I closed the dormy door behind me. We don't get much money, but we *do* see life!"

"I believe you," Miss Wilson said drily. "Well, it's growing late and we can't do anything more about anything at the moment. I vote we end this session and seek our beds. I'm tired." She yawned as she spoke. "Thank goodness, Hilda will be back tomorrow, and I can turn the lily-pool business over to her."

"There's one thing," Matron said as she watched the younger mistresses begin to put the room to rights. "Signa's mother is an Old Girl, and she does know what things can be like here. Thora always was a sensible girl and she's not likely to make a great fuss."

"I should imagine," Miss Norman said with some bitterness, "that she knows all to well what her younger daughter is like. Thyra is her mother over again, but that monkey Signa must be a hop-out-o'-kin."

"Oh, I don't think so." Miss Wilson gave a sudden gurgle. "Have you forgotten that awful sister of hers—Astrid? If you ask me, Signa is merely a second Astrid."

"I'd forgotten Astrid." Miss Norman began to laugh. "What a life she led us all! But it was nice naughtiness, Nell. She was bad, but not horribly bad. I suppose you're right, and it's coming out in her young niece. Well, I'm off to bed. Good-night, everyone! Dollie—you coming?"

Miss Edwards nodded. "Just let me gather up my work. You off, Grizel? Good-night, then."

histoire from the girls. La pauvre Carola! I am glad indeed that she is here."

What more might have been said on the subject no one will ever know, for just then there came a hurried bang on the door and Carola herself appeared, with tousled hair and eyes looking as if they would drop out of her head.

Miss Wilson jumped to her feet. "Carola!" she exclaimed.

Matron was there too. "What's wrong? Are you ill?" she demanded.

"It's not me but Con Maynard," Carola replied, looking scared. "I—I think she's been walking in her sleep. I've got her back to bed but I thought someone ought to know and go to her."

Matron was off without more ado. The Head asked quietly, "How do you know Con was sleep-walking? Why weren't you in your own room?"

Carola turned red. "I woke up and felt thirsty, so I was going to the bathroom to get a drink of water," she explained. "Then I saw Con walking along the corridor with her eyes wide open." She gave an irrepressible shudder. "She did look uncanny! They were all staring and I guessed she was walking in her sleep. I've read somewhere that you shouldn't startle sleep-walkers awake, so I just said, 'Why, Con, you come back to bed this minute! You oughtn't to be here now.' Then I took her hand and went with her to her dormy. She didn't wake up, and I got her back into bed all right. Then I thought you ought to know, and Matey—I—I mean Matron—wasn't in her room, so I came here."

"I'm glad you were so sensible about it," Miss Wilson said quietly. "It's all right. Con does walk in her sleep sometimes, but she hasn't done it for more than a year and we all thought she had outgrown it. You had better go back to bed. Miss Edwards, will you take her up, please? You might give her some warm milk once she's in. That will put you to sleep again, Carola, as well as relieving your thirst. Good-night!"

Miss Edwards rose and escorted Carola back to her cubicle, where she gave her a glass of hot milk, and waited until she had finished it.

"Feel you can sleep now?" she asked casually as she took her glass.

"Yes, thank you." Carola's blue eyes were already

queer that any girl's people should be so absorbed in departing on a cruise of the Caribbean that they couldn't even spare the time to have her properly outfitted for school. It also helps to explain how she has heard so many of the really big musical folk. I've wondered about that more than once."

Miss Wilson glanced at her. "You never said anything to us about it."

"Well, to tell you the truth, I rather thought she was drawing the long-bow, and if it had gone on I meant to come to one of you and suggest you talked to her about the beauties of truth," Grizel drawled.

"I wish you'd try to give people credit for decency, Grizel," the Head said impatiently. "Is it necessary for you to look on the worst side? Surely, at your age, you must know that there are thousands of folk in the world who are as nice in these matters as you are!"

Miss Cochrane's pretty face was flooded with crimson. However, she could hardly resent this plain speaking openly, though she felt very indignant about it, and mentally scored a bad mark against Carola for being the cause of her receiving it. Grizel Cochrane had a very hard streak in her character which all the care and training of the Chalet School during her schoolgirl years and, later, when she had returned to teach, had not succeeded in eradicating. Motherless at an early age, she had first been left to the care of her grandmother who had spoilt her outrageously; and later, when her father married again, had been called to order by her stepmother with a sharpness and even unkindness which had strengthened her faults. Finally, she had been disappointed in the choice of a career, her father insisting that she should devote herself to music for which she had a superficial gift, while she herself had longed with her whole soul to be a physical training mistress. As he held the purse-strings, Grizel had been forced to give in, but though she was a brilliant teacher and her girls did well, it was largely through fear of her bitter tongue that they worked so hard for her.

Miss Wilson knew this, and could have bitten her tongue out as she finished her little speech. However, it was too late now. She felt thankful that Mlle. Berné took up the tale.

"Well, ma chére, I agree that it is best to keep cette petite

be thinking Carola was no more than a pet dog or a Persian cat!"

"But why, my dear Nell, does she write in this way about Carola?" Mlle. Lachenais asked placidly. "I like la petite. I find her intelligent, well-mannered, all one could ask in a schoolgirl."

Miss Wilson flushed with annoyance at herself, for she had let slip enough to rouse the suspicions of the entire Staff unless she were very wary. Orders were that no one was to speak of the way Carola had come to school. Then she suddenly remembered Miss Norman's remark about Carola having come irregularly, so it was clear that some of them, at any rate, either knew or suspected. Quickly she made up her mind that the best thing was to make a clean breast of the situation.

"I'll explain," she said, "but first I want to say that what I'm about to tell you must go no further than this room. Agreed, everyone?"

"Naturally," Miss Denny answered for the others. "What's the mystery about this new child? Don't tell me she's another princess on our hands! Elisaveta was enough for any one school."

"Oh, it's nothing like that," Miss Wilson assured her. "I'll just tell you the whole story and then I hope we can bury it decently for the future. But, whatever you do, try to keep it from the girls. Some of the little idiots would think she'd done a marvellous thing in gate-crashing on us the way she did; and the more sensible might be inclined to look down on her for making such a fool of herself."

"Gate-crashing?" Miss Denny pricked up her ears, and Grizel Cochrane, who was sitting near her, dropped the intricate piece of knitting on which she was busy, and turned wide grey eyes on the Head.

Miss Wilson nodded. "Just exactly that. Carola quite literally gate-crashed us. I'll explain and then you'll understand."

In as few words as possible, she told the story. Some of the Staff were inclined to be amused at Carola's calm assurance. Others were rather shocked. Those already in the know helped out now and then, and Biddy O'Ryan, when the Head had finished, added a pithy if uncomplimentary few sentences about Miss Curry.

"So *that* explains why she turned up practically minus proper uniform," Miss Cochrane said. "I *thought* it was

"Temp. down, thank goodness, and the chest trouble clearing up. Miss Graves was on the 'phone to me at seven and she said that her brother thinks all danger of pneumonia is ended. She's very weak, of course, but that's only the high temperature. She ought to be back at school by next Monday unless anything else turns up. He doesn't expect it. Hilary is very strong and sturdy. If she had been able to get out of her wet clothes when Carola did, the worst would have been just a bad cold. It was staying there until they brought Signa round that did the damage."

"Carola behaved jolly well," Miss Norman remarked. "she kept her head amazingly. Dr. Graves said that trying to pull Signa's head above water as she did was the wisest thing she could have done. She may have come here in a very irregular way, but I, for one, am very thankful that she did. The rest of the girls were no good—ran round in circles and howled to high heaven! That wasn't much use to Signa."

Miss Wilson, who had found time to go to her study and glance over the mail which had been awaiting her, suddenly grinned.

"What's the joke?" Miss Slater demanded.

"I have some news for Carola, and I'm wondering just what she will think about it."

"Oh? What's that?" Miss Denny looked inquisitive.

"Well, I see no reason why you shouldn't know. It doesn't affect us, but—well—listen to this." Miss Wilson took a letter from the pocket of her cardigan, opened it, and then read aloud: " 'I am writing to ask you to tell Carola that I am engaged to be married to a Mr. Lucas I met on the boat. He has a sugar plantation out here, and some day, when Carola is a year or two older and, I hope, a very different girl from what she is at present, we intend to invite her to spend her summer holidays with us. Of course, this means that even if she had still been with me I must have asked my cousins to make other arrangements for her, as we are to be married here and my house in Boscombe sold with all its contents'."

At this point, Miss Wilson stopped and cocked an observant eye at the others. They rose just as she had hoped.

"Well, of all the selfish creatures she beats the band!" Biddy O'Ryan exclaimed. "Sure, the way she talks you'd

So the party which had set out so gaily in the morning returned minus three of its members and with the rest in very subdued mood.

"I might have known!" Matron said when she had heard the whole story. "I don't believe we've once had a term since this school began without some sort of sensation. Well, you can all go to bed and to sleep, and tomorrow the girls may satisfy themselves with quiet walks and a party at night. Oh yes, my dear! You'll sleep all right. *I'm* going to make sure of that. You're having a dose, and so is Carola. I don't suppose the rest will need it. Come along and take Prayers, and then bed is the order of the day."

And it was so.

Chapter XIV

MISS WILSON PRONOUNCES

"NEVER again!" Miss Wilson declared. "Never, once again, do both Miss Annersley and I go off and leave the School to its own devices during half-term! There are limits!"

It was Tuesday evening, and the Staff, having seen all but the prefects safely to bed, were relaxing in the Staffroom, drinking coffee, eating chocolate biscuits, smoking, and otherwise refreshing themselves. Most of them had turned up during the afternoon, but Miss Wilson had missed the bus and been obliged to come on by the coastal train which had landed her at Carnbach with barely time to make the last ferry. In winter, this was at six-thirty, so it was not until after Abendessen that she had been informed of Friday's disaster. Miss Annersley was not returning until next day, so her co-Head was left to comment on the affair, which she had done with the full force of her vocabulary.

Matron, who had just joined them, gave her a quick look. "That is an absurd thing to say," she said firmly. "If the entire Staff had been there I doubt if they could have prevented Signa from dashing across that causeway unless someone had been holding her very firmly at the time. That child ought never to be let out without a collar and lead!"

"What's the latest news of Hilary?" the Head asked her anxiously.

was rubbing her hair dry. A fire was burning in the fireplace, and already Signa was looking more like herself. As the mistress came in, she opened her eyes, and gave her a little smile. The man was ready with a cup which he held to her lips.

"Drink this—all of it," he commanded; and Signa obeyed.

When she had finished, she gave a little sigh. Her long lashes fell, and she turned on her side. The girl with the towel took the cup, while the man bent over the child. Presently he stood up.

"Fast asleep, thank God! I don't think she'll take any harm now. Where's Miss Burn and the other child?"

"I don't know. Your—the lady took them away," Miss Norman said. She was stooping over the sleeping Signa, watching her with anxious eyes. The little girl's lips were pink again, but she still looked pale, and her damp hair lay limp about her face.

The stranger smiled a little. "Don't be alarmed. I'm a doctor—Dr. Graves at your service—and my sister here is a nurse. She will stay with the kiddy for the moment. Meantime, I want to see those two. They had both cut their hands on the weed and I want to see to them. You come downstairs and my other sister will give you all some tea. I'm sure you need it after a fright like this."

He took Miss Norman away, despite her murmured protests. He was anxious to dress the cuts of the other two, but to his practised eye the mistress was suffering badly from shock, and he wanted to get her downstairs to his other sister.

In the end, Carola, after a boiling hot bath, fresh clothes, and a good tea, declared that she felt quite fit to go back to school. Signa, of course, must stay where she was, and Miss Graves suggested that her sister should stay with her, and they would keep the pair for the week-end. Miss Burn, too, would remain until the doctor was sure that she had taken no real harm. She had been much longer in her wet clothes than anyone else, and her hands were very badly cut with the weeds. Dr. Graves had insisted on her going to bed as soon as she had had a bath, and he had given her a sedative to allay the shock. She still looked very wan when Miss Norman visited her, and she agreed that she dreaded the drive home. If she were all right by Monday, however, the doctor said he would drive her to Carnbach.

they would succeed in reviving the little girl. Her most present duty was to make as sure as she could that Carola felt no real ill-effects from the adventure. So she coaxed and bullied alternately until at long last she got the girl to the bus, where she made the others stand round while she stripped her of her clothes and rolled her in the rug, scrubbing her over it until the blue look began to leave Carola's face and she was able to drink a mugful of the hot coffee without her teeth chattering too much on the rim of the mug.

By the time this happened, a little procession was coming up the slope, the stranger leading with Signa in his arms, rolled in a rug, and the driver helping Miss Burn who looked almost as blue as Carola had done. Signa's head lay against the man's shoulder and she was very limp but the grey look had left her face, and Miss Norman needed no one to tell her the child was alive.

"She's come round," said the man as the mistress came to them, "but she must be put to bed at once. My house is a little way up this road and I'm taking her there. Your man will bring the bus along and then Miss Burn and that elder girl can come in and have hot baths and fresh clothes, and with luck I think you'll escape even colds. Rough!"

The big dog came up beside them and stood wagging his tail and looking up with intelligent eyes. His owner nodded to the driver, turned off, and marched along the road with long strides, while Miss Norman got the rest of the coffee into the shaking Miss Burn, and then they all piled into the bus and the driver drove them to the house where Rough was waiting at the gate.

A lady was at the door looking for them, and she took Miss Burn and Carola off upstairs at once, only pausing to push open the door of a pleasant sitting-room with a hospitable, "In there and sit down. I'll be with you as soon as I've settled these two."

"Go in and sit down and keep quiet!" Miss Norman told the girls fiercely before she ran upstairs after the others, intent on finding out how Signa was.

The lady saw her, and when they reached the bedroom landing she nodded to a door and said, "In there. My brother is seeing to her. She'll be all right soon, though."

"Thank you!" gasped Miss Norman before she turned into a pretty bedroom where Signa, rolled in a blanket, was already in bed, while a jolly-looking girl in the twenties

had remained on the causeway, stretched forward and gripped her coat with his teeth, taking part of the weight off Carola who was shivering with cold by this time, though she clung to Signa like grim death. A moment or two later, and the man had taken the child and was carrying her to where the white-faced Miss Norman was waiting, while Miss Burn helped Carola to scramble up to the causeway, and then followed herself. By the time they reached the little group, Signa had been laid down on Miss Norman's coat, and the man, kneeling across her, was turning her head to one side and clearing her mouth of mud and weed. Then he set to work with artificial respiration while the terrified girls watched him, too frightened even to cry now. Signa looked as if she were dead.

Miss Norman turned to her colleague. "Take those other children to the bus, please, and dose them with hot coffee. There are two flasks left. I sent Jean for the rugs. Take one, and get Carola out of her wet clothes and roll her in it. Take some coffee yourself.'

"No," Hilary said sturdily. "I know about this and it may take us both. You take the girls, and I'll stay here and help."

There was sense in what she said. Miss Norman knew it and made no attempt to argue. She marched the girls off, including the icy Carola who could scarcely walk, even with the help of the mistress's arm. Her teeth were chattering, for lake water in February is a chilling thing, and she was looking very blue and pinched. Half-way up the steep pitch that leads to the main road they met Jean and the bus driver, both laden with the rugs Miss Norman had insised on bringing in case the evening turned out chilly. She stopped Jean and took one from her. The man went plunging down the slope at top-speed.

"Hurry with those rugs, Jean," was all the mistress said as she turned to Carola once more. "Come along, Carola. We're nearly there, and when you're out of your clothes and have a hot drink you won't feel so bad. Come, dear: you mustn't stand still."

"I—I'm so *tired*," half-sobbed Carola who, between cold and shock and the weight of her streaming clothes, found it very difficult to move at all.

"I know, but you'll feel better once you're in the bus." Miss Norman was inexorable. Signa she had had to leave to Miss Burn and the stranger. She could only hope that

causeway with little heed for its narrowness or where she was going.

Carola had just finished the mugs and stood up. She was nearest, and even as Miss Norman called, "Signa! Come back at *once*!" the elder girl was crossing after naughty Signa with swift, sure steps.

"I *must* see the water-rat!" Signa called back.

Carola had almost reached her. Already her arm was outstretched to catch the little sinner, when Signa made a false step. Her foot slipped and she overbalanced. With a wild cry she splashed into the water, and the next moment Carola was after her.

Mercifully for everyone, the water here is not deep nor are there many weeds, though quite enough to cause alarm. Miss Burn was along the causeway in a flash, while Miss Norman very sensibly kept the other girls from following.

"*No*, girl! Stay where you are! Jean, run quickly to the bus and see if the man is there. He went to have his dinner, but he ought to be back. Bring him and also the rugs from the back of the bus. Thank God we thought of bringing them. Thyra, stand *still*!"

Thyra, frustrated in her effort to dash after Miss Burn, burst into tears and Doris Hill had to go to the rescue. Thyra was only nine, and Doris, four years older, was quite a big girl in her eyes. She clung to Doris, sobbing pitifully, an example suddenly followed by Bridgie, who howled at the top of her voice and occupied her two sisters very completely.

Meanwhile, Signa, in falling, had been caught by the weeds, and Carola and Miss Burn were working frantically to pull her up. Miss Burn wrenched and tore at the things holding the little girl in a vice-like grip, while Carola, who had managed to get her arms round the child, hauled valiantly to bring her head above the water.

Help was close at hand, mercifully. A man and a big retriever dog, attracted by the noise Thyra and Bridgie were making, suddenly appeared at the other end of the causeway. He took in the situation in one glance, snatched a big knife from his pocket, and was by the side of the two rescuers, slashing at the weeds almost before anyone had seen him. The weeds gave under the sharp edge of the knife. Carola contrived to pull Signa's head above the water, and a minute or so later saw Signa's limp little body come up, when the dog who, at a word from his master,

ramparts as far as they could. They peered through the grilles of the water-gate and went up the keep. When they had seen everything and climbed everywhere they were allowed, Carola and Jean took a series of snaps.

Then they entered the bus again and were whisked off to the Bosherston lily pools where they sat on the causeway and ate their lunch, gazing at the great pads of lily leaves that covered the water.

"I'd like to come here in the summer when the lilies are out," Carola said. "It must be marvellous then. It's wonderful now."

"So it is," Hilary Burn agreed. "Mind, Signa! Be careful or you'll tip into the water, and we don't want to have to find somewhere to dry you off! Hold her, Judy."

Little Signa, who had been kicking her heels rapturously against the stonework, desisted, and lunch finished without incident.

"How far do the pools go?" Jean asked.

"Oh, a long way down. You can walk through the woods to either end in summer, but I think we won't just now. It's too muddy, and the paths will be slippery, not to speak of hanging right over the pools in places and the water is deepish. Besides, lilies mean weeds as well. Finish your lunch, and then we must go on to St. Govan's if you want to see it. Come along, girls. Come on to the dry land and help repack the baskets and we'll be off. Careful now, Signa."

One by one they sidled off the causeway to the grassy patch by the side, and Miss Norman heaved a sigh of relief when she saw excitable Signa safe ashore again. The girls set to work to fold paper bags and sheets and tuck them back into the baskets. Hilary Burn carefully settled the emptied flasks into their bag and Jean and Carola counted the mugs before packing them. The two elder O'Connor girls were standing looking at the pools and the two little ones were at the end of the causeway arguing between themselves whether if you stepped on to one of the lily-pad islands, you would go through or not. Signa thought you wouldn't; Bridgie O'Connor thought you would. Suddenly Judy uttered a cry which was echoed by her sister Norah.

"Oh, Miss Burn—Miss Norman! Look! A water-rat—a big one!"

Before anyone could say or do anything, Signa cried, "Oh, where? Oh, let me see him!" and dashed along the

for lunch. The small folk had to content themselves with eyeing the bustling streets wistfully. Then they had passed through the busy area and were running along a broad highway till Judy O'Connor suddenly set up a shout.

"I see the castle! Look! Oh, what a *lovely* castle!"

They all looked eagerly in the direction in which she was pointing, and saw the towers and battlements, with the great keep rising above all, perched on the top of the cliff which had made a natural protection for the place in the Middle Ages. Trees and bushes clung to the cliff, and, as they came nearer, they could see that the castle had been built on a promontory washed on two sides by the river, thus adding to its natural defences.

"It's like a castle in a fairy-tale," Doris said. She turned to Miss Burn who was sharing a seat with her. "Does anyone live there?"

Miss Burn shook her head. "Not now. It looks very complete from here, but when we are inside you will see that it is ruined."

"Oh, what a pity!" Doris cried. "It looks lovely!"

"Why is it a ruin, Miss Burn?" Carola asked. "Who did it—Cromwell?"

"He had a hand in it," Hilary said with a grin. "The weather did a lot more, though. The last owner began to restore it and did a good deal, but it would need a fortune to rebuild it properly. Anyway, who wants that? I'm afraid castles as homes are a thing of the past. You be glad that it's properly looked after nowadays. It's Crown property, by the way, though it was leased to Sir Ivor Phillips. Here we are. Tumble out! No; you can leave the baskets. We aren't going to feed here. Your camera, Carola? Oh, that's another matter."

Miss Norman had been the first to leave the bus and the girls were soon after her, Miss Burn bringing up the rear. They paid their entrance money and were soon through the great arched gateway and standing on the grassy platform which was once the busy courtyard of the castle.

"One moment before you begin to explore," Miss Norman said. "You are to keep together and no one is to try any silly tricks of climbing. A good deal of the castle is unsafe and we don't want any accidents. That's all. If you want to take any snaps, Carola and Jean, wait until we've seen all there is to see. Now come along."

It was a wonderful castle. The girls walked along the

with her jolly laugh. "There's sandwiches, and pies, both meat and fruit, and cakes and biscuits, look you." Then she relented. "There's a bag still with the flasks of coffee and milk, but that's enough for you to carry at once. Gladys will bring the bag to the door. Got your beds to make, haven't you? Best hurry up, then."

Carola thanked her, hurried after Jean to put her baskets on the wide step at the front door, and then raced off upstairs to make her bed and tidy her cubicle before she went down to get into coat and beret and change into stout walking-shoes. They were all quickly ready, and when the two mistresses appeared were already in double file.

"All well wrapped up?" Miss Norman asked. "Yes, I know it's not chilly at the moment, but I expect it'll be dark before we get back to Carnbach and it's never warm on the water at this time of year. Lead on, Carola and Jean. We don't want to miss the ferry."

They set off, the girls carrying the big baskets between them and the mistresses following. The crossing was made as peacefully as usual, and when they marched off the ferry-landing they found a funny little bus awaiting them.

"Oh, I wondered how we were going," observed Judy O'Connor.

"No use having an ordinary coach," Miss Burn explained, "so Miss Annersley ordered this for us. All in? No baskets or anything left behind? Very well, then." She shut the door and the driver, who had kept his motor ticking over, set off.

It was, as Miss Burn had said, a lovely morning. The snow had gone, though traces of it still lingered on the summits of the hills. The February sun shone down on a world that was showing the first faint greening on bushes and tree and the grass was beginning to lose its dead, wintry look. The road ran along valleys where streams chuckled merrily round their stones and small villages were busy and full of life. It was too early for the spring ploughing, but there were signs of new life everywhere. Later, they drove round Milford Haven, making for New Milford, where they crossed in the ferry to Pembroke Docks.

One or two of the younger ones wanted to get out and look at the shops, but the mistresses were adamant. Time was passing, and the castle could not be properly seen in half an hour or so, and they wanted to go to Bosherston

at least it was when St. Govan lived there—and in storms the spray is flung clean over it."

"Who was St. Govan?" Jean demanded.

"A Welsh hermit. Near by is his well, which is a holy well, of course——"

"Can you wish in it?" Barbara Watson interrupted eagerly.

Miss Burn laughed. "I haven't the remotest idea. I suppose you could if you liked, but I don't know that it's a wishing-well. You have a shot, Barbara, and tell us if you get your wish."

"Is there anything else to see there?" Carola asked. She knew the Gower coast, but that is farther west, and Cousin Maud had never gone to Tenby, so it was as new to her as the others.

"The Stack Rocks where thousands of seabirds nest in the season—though I don't think that's now," Miss Burn told her. "We shan't have time to see much more, I'm afraid. Remember, this is only February, and it grows dark early. However, if only the weather holds, I think you people will have a really interesting time of it."

Miss Norman said, "You finished, Carola and Jean? Then we'll excuse you. Pop along to the kitchen for the baskets and set them outside the door. Then you can go upstairs and see to your cubicles. Say your Grace first, Carola!" For that young lady was out of her chair and making for the door.

She came back to stand behind her chair and repeat the School Grace to herself. "I forgot," she explained.

"And take your crocks to the hatch," Miss Burn added. "Be quick!"

Carola did as she was told, and then went racing off after Jean who had remembered everything. She was at the kitchen door when Carola reached her, and Cook was handing over the big basket she had packed overnight, except for the sandwiches.

"Going to Bosherston, are you?" she asked as she gave Carola hers. "My, I wish I was coming with you! My home's not so far from there. There you are, Miss. I hope you have a good time."

"Thank you, Cook. I'm sure we shall," Carola said. "And I hope you can get off some time soon to go home. Is this all?"

"Why, how much more do you want?" Cook demanded

Chapter XIII

UNEXPECTED BATH

WHEN the ten arrived in the dining-room next morning they found only Miss Burn and Miss Norman waiting for them. Matron was nowhere in sight. They sat down after Miss Norman had said Grace to a delicious meal of poached eggs, toast and marmalade, and the milky coffee that was their usual beverage.

"Is Matron not well?" Carola asked Miss Norman as that lady handed her her coffee.

"Quite well; but we need a rest from work as well as you folk," was the brisk reply, "so each of us takes one day off. This is hers. She's celebrating by having her breakfast in bed, and then she's going off somewhere by herself."

"What are we going to do, Miss Norman?" Doris Hill asked eagerly.

"When you've made your beds and tidied up, we're going to Pembroke to see the castle," Miss Norman told her. "We didn't tell you before for it's definitely a fine-day expedition. However, we could hardly ask for a better day at this time of year, so we'll go. Jean and Carola, when you've finished your Frühstück, run along to the kitchen and ask Cook for the picnic baskets."

"Are we picnicking somewhere, then?" Carola asked joyfully.

"We are—at Bosherston lily pools." Miss Norman settled down to her own breakfast and added, "It's Miss Burn's idea. Ask her about it."

Ten pairs of eyes promptly turned on Hilary Burn, who laughed. "I spent part of my summer holidays at Tenby," she explained. "The lily pools are simply lovely, though you really ought to see them in June or July when the lilies are out. It's quite a thrill to see a bud rising out of the water and going 'pop!' as the calyx bursts open. I stood for ages on the causeway which cuts across the pools at one point just to watch them coming up. If there's time and the weather holds, we'll have a look at St. Govan's Chapel. That's built in a fissure of the cliff, miles from any house—

their screeches could have been heard up at the school if anyone had been listening.

Commander Christy and his friend joined in, and Kester Bellever as detective proved himself a most efficient person. By the time he had detected three murderers they had lost any shyness of him they might have felt, and when they had to say goodbye, little Signa Björnessen threw her arms round his neck and kissed him affectionately.

"I think you are so nice," she told him. "I wish you were *my* uncle!"

He laughed. "I think I'd better adopt the entire School as nieces," he said. "Wait till next term, Signa, and you shall come with the others and see my island and my funny little house."

Signa trotted off with the rest, quite satisfied with this. Dickie, who had undertaken to escort them home, chuckled over the little episode.

"Uncle Kester used to be a lonely sort of person," she told the two fifth-formers. "He hasn't any relatives but some distant cousins, and he adopted Gaynor and Cherry and me as nieces. It looks like becoming a habit with him now. Well, here you are! Glad you've all enjoyed it. Carola and Jean, I'm coming over with you on Sunday. Wait for me after church, will you? Bye-bye, everyone."

She turned and ran home while the others went sedately up the holly-hedged path and in at the front door—a half-term privilege.

"Had a good time?" Matron asked as she served their Abendessen.

With one voice the ten replied, "Super!"

"Good! Well, all but Jean and Carola must go to bed after this. Jean and Carola, you can have another hour in the common-room, but mind you're in bed by half-past nine. I'll be up about then to put the lights out."

from school, but you're the first who ever went the other way round. Well, are you coming in? If not——"

"Daisy Venables, do you mean to say—Carola and—let's see—Jean, isn't it? What on earth are you doing in Carnbach? Have you come to visit me?" Jo herself had appeared in the doorway. Now she came swiftly down the path. "Come along in; and Daisy, if you really want to meet Biddy at eleven for coffee, you'd better scram. It's ten-to now."

"Oh lord! And it takes at least a quarter of an hour to reach St. David's Road! O.K., J.O: I'm off! Come on, Rufus!" Daisy gave the lead a gentle tug and set off, accompanied by the big dog, at a great pace.

Jo, left behind, cast a grin after her, and then turned to the abashed pair standing by the gate. "Well, are you coming in?"

"I—I think we'd better not," Carola stammered. "We were just spending the time till eleven and then Matey said we were to go for elevenses and catch the twelve-thirty ferry back. If it's as late as that, we'd better go."

"Just as you like. Anyhow, you two are coming over on Sunday for the day. I was going to write to you this afternoon. That's tuppence saved, anyhow. Come straight over after church. Do you know how to get to the shops from here? No? Well, it's easy enough. Go right down the road, turn right, and carry on, and you'll find yourself in the High Street. You can carry on from there, can't you?"

They thanked her and she waved goodbye to them and returned to the house, while the pair, gradually cooling down from their embarrassment, hurried along the road.

Carola and Jean enjoyed coffee and cream cakes and sat talking over their unexpected meeting with Mrs. Maynard. So long did they gossip that when Carola finally looked at her watch it was to find that they had only ten minutes left in which to catch the ferry. They caught the boat by the skin of their teeth, and spent the whole of the crossing in recovering their breath and tidying themselves after their mad race.

Dickie arrived at two o'clock, and they enjoyed a delightful time at the Christy home, finding Kester Bellever a most interesting person, full of stories about birds both here and abroad. After tea, at which Dickie's cakes figured largely, they all joined in a thrilling game of Murder, and

have said it looked prim, for the spacing at every window varied.

"They've a big family of kids here," Carola said decidedly.

"How do you know that?" Jean demanded.

Her friend pointed to the window over the door where a row of toy animals and dolls were gazing forth. "Look at that! Oh, and there's a big, old-fashioned wooden engine at the far end. They've boys as well as girls."

"You can't be sure. Besides, anyhow, there might be just one of each."

"With all those toys? Talk sense!" Carola said derisively.

In their interest, all thought of manners had been banished and they were leaning against the wall, staring at the house. Suddenly the front door opened and a tall, fair girl in the early twenties came out, accompanied by a huge St. Bernard dog. She raised her eyebrows at the sight of the two schoolgirls. Then she suddenly smiled.

"Hello!" she said amiably while the pair started and went red. "Were you wanting Jo—I mean Mrs. Maynard?"

"Is—is this her house?" Carola cried. "And how did you know——"

"By the uniform, of course." The young lady gave them another smile. "I wore it myself for nine years, so I'd be fairly safe to know it, wouldn't I?"

"You were a Chalet School girl?" This was Jean.

"In Tirol as well as here," the girl replied. "Now tell me your names. Are you coming in?" She opened the gate invitingly.

"Oh, I don't think we'd better. I—we——" Carola ran down.

"Don't be silly!" was the bracing retort. "Come on in and see Jo. I'm Daisy Venables, by the way."

"The *doctor*?" gasped Jean. "The one who's won all the medals and things?" She eyed Miss Venables with awe.

"Primula Venables' sister," Carola supplemented this.

"Yes; that's me," Daisy agreed. "Now tell me who you are."

"I'm Jean Ackroyd and this is Carola Johnstone," Jean explained.

"The girl who ran away to school?" Daisy gave another of those friendly grins. "I've heard all about that, Carola. It was a new one on me. I've heard of girls running away

long as you catch the twelve-thirty ferry back in time for Mittagessen. Have you any money?"

"Yes, we went to Bank with the rest last night," Carola said.

It was rather pleasant to be thought old enough to be trusted like this. Doris Hill was the next eldest of the left-behinds, and she was only thirteen and, incidentally, a chum of Mary-Lou's. Carola and Jean, both fifteen, though Carola was a week older than Jean, felt themselves very grown-up beside Doris.

Once they had seen the happy, jolly crowd into the motor coaches they waved goodbye and then set off to the shops. It was too early for elevenses yet, so they amused themselves by looking at the windows. Then Carola suggested that they should see something more of the little town, so they turned down a broad, hilly road that ended in a pleasant little park through which they wandered.

"Well, we've seen that," Jean said as they came to a gate at the farther end. "Shall we go out this way and see where we get?"

Carola glanced at her watch. "Only ten yet. We don't want elevenses for another hour at least. O.K., Jean. Let's do that."

They left the park and found themselves in a long, tree-lined road with biggish houses standing in their own gardens on either side.

"This looks rather a nice place," Carola said as she led the way.

Jean looked down it wistfully. "It reminds me of home. Our road is just like this."

Carola gave her a quick glance. She was sorry for Jean, so she set to work to distract her mind. "Let's imagine the kind of folk who live in each house," she suggested. "Now this one belongs to two old maids, I think. Did you ever see a primmer place? Even the curtains seem to have been hung with measurements for their apart part all over."

"I think this one belongs to a naval family," Jean indicated the two models of ships standing in either window of the ground-floor.

They went on to the next house which was larger than the first three in the road. It looked strikingly clean and fresh with its brown and cream paintwork. The curtains at the windows were of beflowered silk, and no one could

already showed regiments of green spikes to hint at glories to come when the bulbs were up.

It was not settled quite so easily, but before the three who were, as saucy Jo was fond of reminding them, foundation-stones in the School, had parted, it was agreed that Matron should be in charge and the other two adhere to their original plans.

Thursday morning found the School up and hard at it by seven o'clock. More than half of the girls must be at either Swansea or Cardiff to make train connections. Those who were being fetched by parents expected to be off before eleven, and Frühstück had been ordered for half-past seven.

The ten left behind were inclined to be very doleful about it, with one exception—Carola. She had expected nothing else, so was not upset. Besides, Mrs. Maynard had been over for the previous Saturday evening and had hinted at some plan for herself and Jean.

Dickie Christy, who lived in the island, appeared after breakfast when the two members of Lower Fifth B were lounging in the common-room.

"I say, you two," she began, "you're coming around to us this afternoon. Dad's pal, Kester Bellever, is coming for the night and I thought it 'ud be a good idea if you met him."

"Will they let us come?" Jean asked. "I say, that'll be wizard, Dickie. I've been dying to know him ever since that talk he gave us last term."

"Well, you will after this afternoon," Dickie told her. "Of course they'll let you come. Only too glad, I should think. If it's rotten luck for you to be left, it's just as bad, if not worse, for Matey and the mistresses. Matey simply *bounded* at the suggestion."

"I hadn't thought of that," Jean replied. "Are we the only two, or are the kids coming as well?"

"The whole boiling of you," Dickie replied. "I'm coming for you at two, so mind you're ready. I must fly now. Cakes to make!" She laughed and left them feeling very much happier, and then Carola proposed that they should ask leave to go down to the ferry-landing and see the others off.

Matron was quite agreeable. "You two ought to be old enough to be trusted," she said. "Miss Burn and Miss Norman are taking the others for a walk, but if you two like to go over to Carnbach for the morning, you may—so

Watson—they would have to spend a day and a half getting across to Orkney, and it isn't worth it—the O'Connor girls for the same reason, except that it's Ireland in their case, and Thyra and Signa Björnessen who always have to be arranged for. That's the worst of having foreign children," concluded Matron.

The two Heads thought. Then Miss Wilson spoke. "Well, you're going to Gloucester to stay with your cousins there, aren't you, Hilda? Which of the Staff are off?"

Miss Annersley fished a list out of her desk and looked over it. "Miss Norman is staying and so is Hilary Burn. What are *your* plans, Nell? You haven't said anything yet."

"Because they've been so nebulous. If I wasn't needed here, I thought I'd take advantage of Madge Russell's offer and go to stay at the Round House. Then I could keep an eye on what was going on at Plas Howell. However, it looks as if that must be off, now."

"Rubbish!" Matron said trenchantly. *"I'm* staying. I had word this morning that my sister's two grandchildren have begun with whooping-cough, so I can't go there. I've made no other plans, so I shall stay here. If Ivy Norman and Hilary Burn and myself aren't enough to cope with ten girls we's better give up our jobs at once."

"Well, one of us certainly ought to go and see what's cooking," Miss Wilson said. "Whatever we do finally, there will always be part of the School in England now. Nothing's settled about the Oberland yet, though we can have Frau Hessell's house, Frieda says, and welcome. It's quite a big place and we could build on to it in time. A portion of the School will be here for years to come, though, and now that the Russells have bought Plas Howell from Ernest Howell, the School is definitely fixed there."

"There you are then. You go and I'll stay." Matron scanned her list again. "Carola and Jean are Lower Five B. Doris Hill, Barbara Watson, and Judy O'Connor, are Lower Fourth. Kathleen Watson, Norah O'Connor, and Thyra are Lower Third A; the other two are First Form. Nothing to worry us there. We'll put them all into the big dormitory so that they can be together and no one need worry. Mercifully, the weather has decided to behave itself at last." She glanced out of the window where the garden was glowing under a bright February sun and the borders

Chapter XII

HALF-TERM BEGINS

EASTER fell very early this year, so it had been decided to give the girls a long week-end at half-term and carry on with school until the middle of April. The Easter week-end would be a holiday, but they would have a bare three weeks before the summer term began, and as that was twelve weeks long, things would even themselves out.

"Suits me all right," Jo Maynard had said airily when she heard from Miss Annersley what the arrangements were. "Other things being equal, we sail for Quebec at the end of April, so the girls won't miss any of this term. Also, it will give me time to see about outfits. I must take them looking decent or Madge will say things!"

"It makes a horrid long term," grumbled Bride Bettany in private to her sister Peggy.

"We'll be able to go home for half-term, anyway," replied Peggy.

"We shan't be home for Easter, though, and I do love Easter at home," Bride replied sadly.

"It only happens once in a way. I've looked up Easter in young Len's Missal, and it isn't in March again for eight years."

Half-term began on the Thursday morning and would continue until Tuesday evening. With six days in hand, most of the girls were going home. Sybil Russell would spend the time with her aunt at Cartref. The Ozanne girls, whose home was in Guernsey, were to stay with their relations in Armiford, and so would the Lucy girls. Others were staying with friends, and when Matron had finished her inquiries she found that only ten girls would be left at the school.

"Who are they?" Miss Wilson demanded. "Any prefects among them?"

"No; they are all off this time. Carola Johnstone from Lower Five B is the eldest to stay. Jean Ackroyd from the same form will be here, too. The rest are Doris Hill, whose people are in the south of France, Barbara and Kathleen

of pocket-money each week. However, Miss Annersley had ordered them to do what they could to improve the general usage of English among the younger girls, so they must try. They sat in silence and racked their brains—vainly, at first. Then Nita Eltringham suddenly said she had a germ of an idea.

"What is it?" Peggy demanded. "Trot it out at once."

"Well, you know how they—or the kids, at any rate—hate messing about with dickers? If we catch them using slang let's make them hunt out the proper meaning of the words and write them out so many times. It'll help their spelling as well as their understanding of English, and if we insist it must be in their best handwriting it won't hurt *that*."

"*And* it'll take up their free time, which they'll loathe, so they'll try to reform," Dickie agreed. "I think it's a wizard idea, Nita. What do the rest of you say?"

"Oh, I'm game to try it. I'll try *anything* that'll save us from a lecture like the one we've just had. What do you say, Peg?" Daphne turned to Peggy who nodded.

"We'll try it. It can't hurt them; it *may* do the trick. Anyhow, we've got to do something about it, and no one else seems to have anything to suggest."

"When do we begin?" Frances asked. "Tonight?"

"I think not. Half-term starts the day after tomorrow. We'll hint at awful things if they don't pull up, to give them something to think about over the week-end. When we come back I'll put up a notice about it and we'll start in then," Peggy said.

Daphne nodded. "O.K. That's settled then. Come on! There's the bell for tea. Remember to spread intriguing and ghastly hints about what's going to happen after half-term to anyone who uses outrageous slang, all of you. As Peggy says, we may as well give the little dears something to think about over the week-end."

Laughing, the prefects trooped off downstairs for tea, and before the School broke up for half-term, all the Middles and a good many of the Seniors were being given to wonder what awfulness was in store for them if they didn't reform their mode of language in short order.

was just something Auntie Jo said one day during the hols."

"What was it?" A whole chorus demanded this.

Peggy considered. "Well," she said finally, "it was words to the effect that if Tirol was out of the question for some time to come, there was still Switzerland. Mind, I don't suppose it was anymore than her own ideas," she went on, stemming the tide of exclamations that greeted this with waving hands. "—Be *quiet* and let me finish!—Just the same, it's an idea that *might* come to something."

There was a moment's silence while the prefects digested this.

Dickie was the first to speak. "*Switzerland!*, I hadn't thought of that as a solution. Not that it's likely to affect me," she added. "I'm eighteen in June and leaving school at the end of the year. Cherry would come in for it, of course—and young Gaynor, too, I expect."

"It wouldn't affect a good many of us," Frances Coleman agreed. "You're leaving—I'm leaving—Nita's leaving—so are Mollie and Barbara. Peggy will have another year, I suppose: that's what comes of being an infant prodigy. Daph, what about you?"

"Oh, I'm having another year," Daphne replied. "I shan't be eighteen until next December and I'm to have a year in Special Sixth and go in thoroughly for languages. It would be super if we had a year in Switzerland. Whereabouts would it be, do you think, Peg?"

"Bernese Oberland, I expect." Peggy replied promptly. "They're opening a branch of the San there, and the San and the School have always been part of each other. Mind, girls, I don't know any more about it than I've told you; and please don't go round chattering about it, for it may be only my imagination. Still, I do agree that they seem to be making an extra fuss this year about our German. If we went to the Oberland, German is the native tongue there, I believe."

"Well," Dickie said, "all this is interesting enough, but it isn't deciding how we should deal with slang in the School. That's our present job. Ideas, please, everyone."

Needless to state, this bland request dried up everyone. As pretty Mollie Avery complained, you just can't think when you have a bomb flung at you like that. The girls were fined as a rule for the worse forms of slang, and hitherto it had been quite enough. No one liked to be short

shooting under the guidance of Judy Rose, another of the prefects.

If it had ended there, it might not have mattered so much, but the Staff convened a meeting at which it was decided that the prefects must have been very lax over slang. The two Heads called the grandees of the School to their study and spoke very seriously on the subject and then dismissed them, smarting and indignant.

"When you think," wailed Daphne Russell, "how strict we all were about it last term and how some of those young demons played us up for it!"

Peggy herself spoke. "Of course, most of this comes from the business with Vi Lucy. I must say," she added impartially, "she seems to have excelled herself in the way of language. I had Mary-Lou on the carpet for telling Phil Craven to shut her head, and when I'd finished, she said, 'That's nothing to what Vi Lucy knows. You ought to hear *her* when she gets going—or Clem, either'."

Dickie Christy laughed. "*Or* Mary-Lou herself. Funny kid! She can say things like that, and yet you know that most of the time it isn't sauce. I wouldn't have taken that sort of thing from most of those youngsters, but from Mary-Lou it's something different."

Peggy nodded. "I know. I think it's mainly because she lived entirely with grown-ups all her early years. And though she comes out with statements of that kind, it's neither cheek nor telling tales. As for young Vi, with brothers like John and Barney, what else can you expect? Really," she went on, "I suppose it begins with the German."

"Oh that German!" Judy Rose groaned. "I can manage with French, but German gets me down every time. Why on earth we've got to use it I can't think. Dad says that, so far as he can see, the School won't be going back to Tirol for years to come."

Peggy eyed them all thoughtfully. Daphne, her great friend, saw it, and at once leaped to the conclusion that something was going on in the background and Peggy knew about it.

"*Is* anything likely to happen, Peg?" she asked.

"About Austria? Nothing at all, I should think."

"Then is there an idea of somewhere else?" Daphne insisted.

Peggy shook her head. "I really don't know anything. It

half-term arrived, the Middles were all in a state of revolt, especially the Junior Middles. Even the Seniors were heard to murmur.

The climax came when Vi Lucy, an ornament of Lower Fourth, had to repeat "Ich weiss nicht wirklich was zu sagen" ("I really don't know what to say") seventeen times before Miss Edwards pronounced herself satisfied. Vi was raging by the time she was released. She left the Junior maths mistress with sparkling eyes and flushed cheeks and made a bee-line for her own particular gang, which included Mary-Lou Trelawney and Verity-Anne Carey.

Unfortunately for her, in her anger she let loose in English, and Miss Wilson, coming along, got the full beauty of her tirade. Vi had not spared any slang, and the Head dealt with her faithfully. By the time Miss Wilson had finished, the young lady was realising dazedly that she was docked of a week's pocket-money in the way of fines, never to mention having to learn the whole of "Der Erl-König" by heart, with the prospect of repeating it to Mlle. de Lachenais by the next evening without a mistake.

"And please see that your pronunciation improves, too," "Bill," as she was generally known in the School, wound up. "Now you may go and make the most of what is left of your games time. Explain to whoever takes you that you have been with me."

Vi departed, seething, to explain as best she could to Dickie Christy, who was in charge of their netball that afternoon, and got a very cold reception. As she found it difficult to say all that had to be said in German, and at first gave Dickie the impression that she had gone to Bill of her own accord, this was hardly to be wondered at. When the prefect finally got to the bottom of the affair, she added insult to injury in Vi's estimation by saying, "Well, perhaps that will remind you that slang of the kind you seem to have used is forbidden, anyhow, whatever may be the official language for the day. Now go over to the other court and ask Judy Rose to let you join her team."

It was no use arguing with Dickie, even if Vi could have found the German for it. Dickie was Second Prefect, a very important person, and furthermore, a person who was jolly enough in general, but possessed a gift for sarcasm that made her juniors wary of rousing her anger. Vi, her form's captain, went across to join with the fourteen people who were poor at netball and were practising passing and

Biddy, who had always had a gift for languages, stared. "But it's an easy enough language to learn," she argued. "Look here, what you want is to spend a holiday in Germany or Austria with the natives. You would soon pick it up then. Why don't ye? I can give ye half a dozen addresses if that's all."

Miss Slater looked coldly at her. Biddy O'Ryan might be a mistress at the School now, but the maths mistress still inclined to regard her as one of the girls who had been a regular nuisance in maths lessons. Hilary Burn, who had left the School before Miss Slater had joined it, saw what was in the latter's eye, and came to the rescue.

"Never mind all that now, Biddy," she said. "Tell us what you did about young Carola."

"Well, I was so taken aback ye could have knocked me down with a feather," Biddy explained. "However, I said, 'Hier dürfen Sie nicht englisch sprechen. Versuchen Sie, ich werde Ihnen helfen'."

"And did she understand you?" Mlle. de Lachenais asked.

"Not a word, beyond the fact that she couldn't speak English just then. She stood gaping at me till, as I told you just now, I felt like throwing my book at her."

The Staff laughed, and Miss Wilson coming in just then to make inquiries about Staff evening which was to take place after half-term, the subject dropped.

As for Carola and the rest of Lower Fifth B, apart from three of them, they were all in sympathy with anyone who couldn't speak German. As German had to be their language for the day, and few of them could express their feeling adequately that way, they had to wait until Wednesday, when English was the order of the day. All the same, with two days of German, one after the other, and a rather shocked Staff hounding them on, several people contrived to learn a little more than they had known before. Clem, who had taken the language very lightheartedly up till then, paid a little more attention to her accent, and Polly Winterton knew at least *one* sentence for the rest of her life.

Unfortunately for the School at large, the entire Staff, having had the School's shortcomings brought to their notice so thoroughly by Biddy O'Ryan, considered it their duty to make some improvement. In consequence, German days rapidly became a burden to everyone. By the time

to satisfy Miss O'Ryan. At last, however. that young lady announced herself satisfied, repeated her first question very slowly, and waited for some sort of answer. By this time, however, Polly was so gravelled that she was quite unable to guess at the drift of the German, and Miss O'Ryan had to give it up and pass the question on to Clem, who understood well enough and could even manage an answer, but whose German accent left everything to be desired.

Very patiently the mistress repeated her words and made the fuming Clem go over and over them until they sounded more like German. At last: "Gut. Setzen Sie sich," she said; and turned to Carola who came next.

Carola was all at sea in any case, and had already decided that her best move was to say so at once.

"Please, Miss O'Ryan, I don't know any German." she informed the mistress. "I've never done any till I came here and I haven't learnt much yet. I—I haven't understood a word of the lesson."

A gasp ran round the room at this temerity. As for Biddy, "Sure, I nearly flung my book at her," she told the enthralled Staff later on when she was retailing the story for their delectation. "And will you be telling me why a girl who has been here a whole term can't answer a single simple question in German? What's *happened* to the School?"

"The fact of the matter is," Hilary Burn replied, "that while a few of us do know German and can speak it pretty fluently, we have several folk who either didn't know it, or who had just enough to scrape through their exams. It was different in Tirol where everyone spoke it, and you sort of sucked in with your breath."

"But the French isn't nearly so bad," Biddy persisted. "Why is the German, with extremely few exceptions, so utterly appalling?"

"You can keep the German for all of me," Miss Slater said bluntly. "I'm one of the people who only knew enough to pass exams. When school ended I tossed my German grammar aside with thankfulness. I've always hated it, and I wish to goodness it hadn't occurred to anyone to renew it here. I can tell you, the kids have all my sympathy. It takes me all my time to manage enough to teach anything on German days, and when I *can* manage it I set them tests and exercises to work out."

the girls, she could arrange her lessons to suit herself, and having heard before Frühstück what was to be the order for the day, she had occupied every moment of her spare time in preparing tests for her forms. Meekly they took the paper she had handed out and set to work to do what they could. On the whole, Carola decided, as she wrestled with an intricate decimals of money sum, it was better than having to do arithmetic in German. The room remained silent for the whole of the forty minutes devoted to the lesson. The bell rang and Miss Slater, after collecting her papers, departed for her next form. Miss O'Ryan passed her in the doorway and the girls prayed for another test.

It was not for nothing, however, that Biddy O'Ryan had spent her early years in Tirol. She spoke excellent German and had no idea of forgoing a lesson she considered important just because it had to be given in German. She set to work on the growth of the English colonies in North America and went ahead in great style.

The trouble started when she addressed a question to Polly Winterton, who stared blankly at her. Polly could work when she chose, but she had spent only one term at the School, and had come completely ignorant of any language but her own. One term, even with two days a week of speaking nothing but German, had not taught her nearly enough to follow Miss O'Ryan's fluent remarks, and she had no idea what she was being asked.

The mistress opened her eyes widely as Polly, having risen to her feet, stood silent and crimson and made no effort to answer the question.

"Ich warte,' Miss O'Ryan reminded her after a minute of this.

"Ich ver stehe nicht," Polly stammered—it was one of the few German phrases she really knew.

Miss O'Ryan's blue eyes opened widely. "Wie lang sind Sie hier gewesen?" she demanded.

Polly guessed the meaning of this. "Only since last term," she said, falling back on English in her dismay.

"Sprechen Sie deutsch!" Miss O'Ryan reminded her gently.

"Ich kann nicht. I don't know it," Polly explained.

Still speaking in German, Biddy repeated what the girl had said. "Nun sagen Sie," she said firmly.

Polly knew this and did her best to repeat the German. It took seven repetitions before she said it sufficiently well

fields. She just managed to catch the last ferry that was to run for the next two or three days and landed safely at Cartref where, much to her joy, she found her husband awaiting her, he having run over from the Sanatorium for a few hours, which lengthened to a long week-end. There could be no question of his risking the road through the mountains in such a storm as this was.

Jo set to work on her new book, seeing there was little chance of going out, while he cleared up quite a good amount of clerical work which had had to wait for just such an occasion. In the mornings he escorted their eldest son Stephen, a sturdy youngster of nearly seven, to the Kindergarten school farther along their road and Jo managed to run along at noon to fetch the boy home. That was all the "out" any of them enjoyed during that time.

As for the School, the girls had to content themselves with extra gym and country dancing for exercise. No one was going to allow them to venture out in such a storm. They managed very well on the whole. The Heads promised that when it was fine weather again they should be allowed more time for walks and games practices. Joan Sandys, the Games prefect, grumbled considerably about the time that was being lost, and one or two of the keener folk did their share of grousing, but on the whole the girls behaved very well—for the first few days, at any rate.

Trouble began on the Monday when Miss Annersley announced at Prayers that though French was improving throughout the School, with a few rare exceptions their German conversation was far from being what it ought to be. She therefore desired them to speak nothing but German throughout the day. This was a shock, as Monday was generally devoted to French, Tuesday being the day for German.

Carola, who had been looking dismayed, now turned a horrified look on Clem. "What on earth shall I do? We've had only four German days since I came——"

"We've had more, but you missed them," Clem explained. "Oh, well, we'll just have to manage as best we can. Try your hardest, Carola."

She got no further, for Miss Slater entered at that moment to take them for arithmetic. Now, although they would not have believed it, Miss Slater was no more pleased than they with the Head's edict. She spoke fluent French, but her German was only shaky. However, unlike

"Well, hardly! It doesn't make smooth ice, you know."

"Then if that happens, how are we to get to Carnbach—I say! Was that snow?" Bride broke off to look upward, an example followed by everyone else.

She was quite right. Floating down from the grey skies were one or two flakes, and it was quite clear that there was more to follow, and very quickly. Jo, with years of experience behind her, turned to the girls imperatively.

"It's going to come a young blizzard. We can't be caught in that on an open field. Scram, all of you! Keep to this edge, and stick together! Don't wander, whatever you do! Biddy," in the emergency she forgot the formal title, "you come behind with me and we'll guard the rear. Bride, you, and Primrose, and Tom, and—yes, Nancy Chester, act as whippers-in at the sides. Get cracking, all of you!"

So urgent were both voice and words that the girls took fright and stumbled along at top speed. Jo, however, knew what she was talking about. She and the rest of the Seniors had once been caught in a snowstorm in Tirol. They had been quite near the School at the time, but so bewildering had been the dizzying dance of the fast-falling flakes that they had nearly gone past it. And then they had been on a fenced path with the Tiernsee at the other side. Here, if anyone strayed, it might be some time before she was found, and already the snow was coming faster.

Mercifully, they had not very far to go before they were pushing through the gate leading into the orchard, and before things became too nerve-racking they were streaming along the path two of the men, who saw to the gardens and furnaces, had dug out earlier on, and entering the side-door that led to the Splasheries, followed by a warning from Miss O'Ryan to change at once and go to their common-room.

Chapter XI

A SPOT OF GERMAN CONVERSATION

AS Jo had truly said, they were in for a blizzard. She herself insisted on setting off at once to reach home. Luckily, she had no fear of losing herself as the road down to the ferry-landing ran between fenced

stockings? And Annis Lovell, too? Don't tell me you tried *crawling* down!"

"Sure, that's the very thing they did," Biddy told her. "The rest of us came down on our feet—more or less."

"Carola came *backwards*," bubbled Clem. "I do wish you'd seen it, Mrs. Maynard."

"You can't talk!" cried the justly indignant Carola. "You barged into Bride and the two of you rolled down fighting like a pair of wild cats!"

"Dear me!" Jo looked suitably impressed. "'A good time was had by all,' in fact. We heard wild howls proceeding from this direction, so I volunteered to come and see what all the row was about. Tom and Annis, I'd advise you to enter School in the middle of a *large* crowd, otherwise Matron will tell you *all* about your stockings. Coming, everyone?" She swung round, and strode alongside them, chatting gaily as she went.

"Auntie Jo, how *do* you do it?" Bride demanded with point when they were nearly at the end of the lane.

"Do what?" Jo demanded.

"Walk so easily. The rest of us are sliding——" She did it at that moment and only Jo's hand gripping her arm kept her from going full length again.

"You're as bad as any baby learning to walk," her aunt told her. "As for me, I raked out my old nailed boots. Haven't used them since my last winter in Tirol, but I've kept them well-greased and they've come in very handy today, thank you. I had to come to bring some things to Matron, and the ferries were running at long last. If this frost goes on, however, it wouldn't surprise me if they didn't have to shut down again."

"Shut down again, Jo?" Biddy opened her eyes widely. "Why?"

"The strait looks like freezing over. It's skinned at the edges, anyhow. If that spreads and the ice thickens they wouldn't run the ferries. It wouldn't be safe."

"But I thought the sea *didn't* freeze." Bride protested as they turned into the field.

"Oh, it can. It doesn't often happen in this part of the world, but what about the Baltic? And the sound between Prince Edward Island and the mainland freezes over, too. It takes a pretty hard frost for it to happen, but it has been known, even here."

"Goodness me! Then could we skate on it?"

"*Matey* will have something to say!" She glanced at her thick woollen gloves. "Oh, lord! This means *hours* of darning! I never thought of that."

"In the meantime," Miss O'Ryan said with what severity she could muster, "we had better try to get home before we meet anyone. You two are a pair of ragamuffins."

Miss O'Ryan satisfied herself that there were no injuries and then set to work to get her flock home before anything worse could happen.

"Pair off," she commanded. "Tom and Annis, you go to the middle of the croc. We may not meet anyone; on the other hand, we may, and it's no advertisement for the School you two are."

In the general upheaval, she was forgetting all resolves and becoming richly Irish. Bride Bettany, who had been a very junior junior in the days when Biddy O'Ryan had been a stern but much loved prefect, nudged Primrose Day, another of the same vintage year, and the pair of them chuckled. They remembered what the young mistress had been like in those days, and it was a treat to hear her relapsing from her very beautiful English into the Biddy O'Ryan they had known.

"I always *knew* Biddy would never keep it up all the time," Bride murmured to Primrose.

"Well, could you expect it?" Primrose asked reasonably. "She's always had an Irish accent ever since *I* could remember."

"And before that," Bride informed her. "Come on! She's yelling for us to join up—*Auntie Jo!*"

She made a wild leap forward as a tall, well-known figure suddenly appeared at the end of the lane, and fell full length as a natural result.

Jo gave her a quick look as she struggled to her feet. What she saw was reassuring. "I knew you liked me, Bride," she said sweetly, "but I didn't know your liking was mixed with sufficient awe to make you prostrate yourself at my feet."

Bride greeted this pleasantry with a wild giggle. "Oh, Auntie Jo," she protested. "Anyone would flop with the roads like this. You should just have seen us coming down that slope a few minutes ago!"

Jo looked round the laughing throng. "I did notice you all looked as though you had been in a free-for-all of the most violent kind. Tom Gay! What *have* you done to your

Winterton, screaming the whole time, slid gracefully to the foot of the slope and ended up in a gorse bush. Gillian, with a truly thrilling squall, staggered wildly half-way down, sat down suddenly, and tobogganed on the tail of her coat the rest of the way. Loveday Perowne followed suit and arrived on top of her. It was left to Carola to put the finishing touches to what looked like becoming a regular football scrum. She skidded, swung completely round, and slid *backwards* to the bottom, clutching at all and sundry as she passed them, so that some folk went over at once, while others managed to keep their feet, but had, perforce, to slide the whole way, some ending up like Polly among the gorse bushes which dotted this part of the ground, and others arriving on their backs. All, it is hardly necessary to state, shrieked at the tops of their voices.

Miss O'Ryan, seeing what was happening to her walk, made the fatal mistake of trying to rush to the rescue. For half a dozen paces she kept her footing. Then she, too, slipped, and with arms outstretched like a tight-rope walker, joined the sliders, and brought up with a minor crash against a telegraph pole which she embraced affectionately.

She recovered herself almost at once, and turned round cautiously to see what was happening. The next moment she was on the ground, rocking with laughter. Two girls, Annis Lovell and Tom Gay, who had been last, had gone down on all-fours, and were crawling down the slope with small regard for the knees of their stockings and their gloves, but considerably more safely than most of the rest had done it.

The girls at the bottom, seeing the mistress in convulsions of laughter, turned to look, too, and the sight of Annis and Tom set them off as well, so that by the time the pair joined up, the whole place rang with their mirth.

Tom, having reached the bottom, got cautiously to her feet and looked round with a disgusted air. "What on earth is up with all you idiots?" she demanded.

"You!" Clem choked. "Oh—*o-oh*! I shall be sick if I laugh any more!"

Miss O'Ryan, who was also on her feet by this time, assumed an air of dignity. "Look at your stocking knees!" she said in shocked tones.

The pair hurriedly looked.

"*Crumbs!*" Tom ejaculated when she could speak.

than where I'm standing this minute. Bride, take charge, please."

Bride went forward carefully, and the girls crowded into the space. They were not sorry for the shelter, for the wind came sweeping across the island from the north, chill and cutting, and making eyes and cheeks smart under its lash.

"I'm simply boiling!" Jean observed, "all but the tip of my nose, that is. Gill, you're *scarlet*! You must be cooked alive with all the clothes you've put on!"

"I'm hottish," Gillian agreed, "but it's a nice change after being frozen to death for the last few days. D'you think Miss O'Ryan will let us go down, anyone?"

This question was answered by Miss O'Ryan herself. She appeared, puffing and blowing, round the curve in the path, shaking her head. "Sorry, but I'm afraid 'tis impossible it is. I've done quite a bit of alpine climbing in my time, and I wouldn't try to get down there without an alpenstock for anything you could mention. Besides, it's taken us quite a while to get this far, and we've all the way home to go. We'll have to turn and I'll bring you here another day when it's less of a break-neck business. Back you go, and no grumbling!"

The girls turned and began to go back. The mistress made no attempt to get them into line. She said afterwards that she thought it would be wiser to wait for that until they were safely back in the lane. At a word from her, Bride headed the crowd which crossed the cliff-top path, and began to struggle down the slope. She was a sure-footed creature, and old memories of Tirol were coming back to her legs. Moving carefully, she was soon half-way along to the lane. The rest followed, Biddy O'Ryan bringing up the rear to act as whipper-in.

"This is a lot easier than coming *up* was," Clem said cheerfully.

The next moment her foot slipped, and with a wild yell she slid downwards, crashing into Bride and sending her flying as she grabbed at her, and the pair rolled down to the bottom of the slope, locked in each other's arms, and, as Biddy graphically told the rest of the Staff later on, yelling blue murder the whole way!

It was fatal for most concerned. One or two people began to laugh, and then discovered that they themselves had begun to slide, and once that happened they were fully occupied in trying to keep themselves on their feet. Polly

Miss Bell, Miss Stephens, Miss Edwards, and Miss Burn. The Juniors were kept to the grounds and the Seniors had gone off in little groups, each with a mistress, so the School was widely scattered over the island.

The girls gazed with interest over the well-known scenes, now so different from what they had hitherto known. The field was a wide white plain; the trees, bare and leafless, creaking beneath the weight of frozen snow on their branches; no birds or rabbits were to be seen and the cows were all snug in their byres. Miss O'Ryan glanced at it, and then turned anxious eyes at the sky. However, she felt reassured when she saw it. Snow was certainly there, but it seemed unlikely to come back for a while yet. She led the way out of the field and into the lane where the ruts had filled up, and walking was no more easy than it had been.

"It's warmer here," Gillian said suddenly. "I suppose the hedges act as a kind of protection."

"Some protection!" Clem jeered. "I shouldn't like to be here in a wind. It 'ud be a bit draughty."

"All right, girls? No one feeling cold?" Miss O'Ryan called from the head of the file.

A chorus of protests arose. No one could feel anything but warm, thanks to their wild struggles to keep their feet, and most folk had crimson cheeks, even if they were rather dishevelled by this time.

Miss O'Ryan surveyed them with a hidden smile. She had expected this. "Well, since you're all nice and warm, we'll go on," she said. "Be careful, though. We don't want any broken bones. Besides, I don't see how we could carry any one of you home if you did break a leg or so."

Finally they came out to the common-like space on the cliffs, or the young mistress would certainly never have contemplated bringing her flock. Breathless as the early part of the outing had been, the girls found it even more so as they struggled up the slope, and finally found themselves opposite the opening to the cliff path leading to the Cove.

"I doubt very much if we'll be able to negotiate that at all," Miss O'Ryan remarked, eyeing it thoughtfully. "Sure, it's as slippery as can be." She looked round. "You can come to the head here between the rocks and wait a moment till I see for myself. No one is to come further

"There'll be no need for that today, anyhow." She glanced up at the grey sky. "'There's a lot more to come down yet, or I miss my guess. Pair off, girls, and remember, you must keep moving. This way, all of you. We're going along to Kittiwake Cove first, then right along to the Merry Mermaidens. We'll come back by the high road, by which time I should think you'll all be ready for Mittagessen and a quiet afternoon. Go carefully; it's slippery with this frost."

She was quite right. Slippery it was, and before long the girls were hot and breathless with trying to keep their feet on the frozen surface. Miss O'Ryan revised her first ideas about a walk, and presently announced that they would go to the Cove, but there would be no going along the cliffs. It was much too dangerous with the paths like this. The girls, floundering along, quite agreed with her. Walking properly was impossible. At any moment your partner might utter a wild squawk and grab you, and if you weren't prepared the pair of you might go headlong. Not that anyone wanted to turn back. It was far too good fun for that.

The way to Kittiwake Cove led down the side of a field, through a deep lane, usually full of ruts, and out to the cliff where there was a path cut deep into the rock, leading down to the Cove.

"Can we go down to the shore, Miss O'Ryan?" Bride Bettany coaxed.

"We'll see what the cliff path looks like first," Biddy said cautiously. "I'd like to be taking you all back with unbroken bones. I'll try it first myself, and if it's not too bad I'll let you come."

"I feel like a hen on hot peas," Sybil said presently to Carola whom she was partnering. "We really ought to have nailed boots like we had in Tirol."

"Well, something, anyhow," Carola replied breathlessly. "The backs of my legs are beginning to ache like fun— Ough!" as she just contrived to avoid sitting down violently.

"It may be easier in the lane," Clem said hopefully. "I say! Listen to those kids yelling! I can hear Mary-Lou above everyone else!"

On the sharp, clear air, they could hear faintly wild shrieks coming from the direction of St. Briavel's village whither most of the Junior Middles had gone in charge of

Chapter X

A WINTER'S WALK

FEBRUARY was only a week old when winter suddenly came in earnest. They had great gales of wind which were so violent that no one could go out of doors and the ferries stopped running. Then the wind died down and the calm brought with it snow, and for two days and nights it snowed without ceasing. And, to quote Biddy O'Ryan, as if that were not enough, the snow turned to hail one night and the hail brought with it keen hard frost.

Even in the Big House, with its double windows and central-heating, the girls complained of the cold. Woolly cardigans were dragged over blazers and ankle socks appeared over stockings.

However, the frost proved useful in one way, for on the Friday morning Miss Annersley stopped all lessons, bade the girls wrap up well, and set them all out for walks which had been in abeyance for more than a week now.

"I've put on a jumper, my blazer, a cardigan, and my big coat," Gillian said with a shiver. "I'm wearing two of everything underneath and I can't think of anything else except my scarf."

"I *thought* you looked extra tubby," Jean said amid the yells of laughter that greeted this announcement. "I put it down to having no walks or games, though. Try two pairs of gloves to top off with—do!"

"Well, anyway, I stand some chance of being warm," Gillian told her serenely. "Which way are we going? Anyone know?"

"Ready, you Fifth Forms?" asked Miss O'Ryan's voice. "All got your scarves on? Sure you'll all freeze if you don't wrap up. This is nearly as bad as Tirol."

"Mummy said it was like Tirol in Canada," Sybil remarked as they all trooped out after the young mistress. "I can *just* remember it there, and how white the snow was when the sun shone."

"And we all had to wear dark glasses in case of snow blindness," Biddy supplemented as she led the way.

Gillian began to explain how she had come to the School.

"Our treasured little Jumbo!" Clem murmured. "Tell me one thing, will you, Gill?"

"O.K. What is it?" Gillian demanded.

"Have you *always* been such a curiosity shop?"

"Clem Barrass, you pig!" poor Gillian cried with deep indignation. "And if I *am* curious there are lots of worse faults! You're not an archangel yourself, so just shut up about me!"

Clem chuckled, but subsided. She was quite fond of Gillian, but could not forbear teasing her on occasions. Gillian, who was a sweet-tempered creature on the whole, contented herself with a muttering which died away as the new girl dropped another unexpected brick.

"Why do we have a Sale for that Sanatorium?" she asked.

Everyone within hearing turned and stared at her. The prospectus explained and they were always well aware that School and Sanatorium were very closely linked. The Chalet School undertook delicate girls because the San doctors overlooked the health of the girls, and Matron, who was, as Jo Maynard had once said, one of the foundation-stones of the School, had taken special training in such work. In Tirol, many of the pupils had been at the Chalet because they had relations up at the great sanatorium on the Sonnalpe, which was at the opposite side of the beautiful Tiernsee where the School had first made its home. Since they had been in England, this had not been quite so much the case, but the prospectus laid emphasis on the fact that health was particularly guarded here, together with a brief explanation, and most girls knew about it before they arrived.

"Look here!" Clem exclaimed, "I really think—oh, bother! Grace!"

Peggy Bettany, the Head Girl, had risen at the prefects' table. The talk had to cease for the moment, but Clem resolved to get hold of Carola as soon as she could and find out what she did and didn't know about the School.

"I'm right," she thought as she helped to clear the table. "There is some queer mystery about her coming here. Wonder what it is?" mused Clem. "I don't mind admitting I'd like to know. There's something most frightfully odd about it all!"

across the table at Sybil who was looking flushed. "Was she as bad to you, Sybil?"

"Hair-raising!" Sybil said simply. "I do wish I could learn with good old Sally-go-round-the-moon! *She* never loses her temper, but Cockey seems to keep hers on edge all the time "

"Who on earth is Sally-go-round-the-moon?" Carola demanded.

"Don't you know *that* yet?" Jean queried as she helped herself to a bun. "She's Plato's sister—he takes singing— and she sort of helps out with most things like music and German, and teaches Italian if anyone wants to learn it. About ten people do," she added.

Carola gasped. "We learn French and German and Latin, anyway. Now you say we can do Italian, too, if we like. How many more languages do they teach here?" she asked.

"Only Greek that I've ever heard of," Jean replied. "But it says all about it in the prospectus. We specialise on languages. Didn't your people show you the pros?" she added.

"I've never seen it," Carola returned, quite truthfully.

"How rummy! Before I came here Mummy wrote to about ten different schools, and we had heaps of fun going through all the prospectuses and seeing which we liked best.

Clem, whose school had been chosen much more dramatically, grinned. "Dad chose for me—and nearly had to go on his knees to the Abbess to get her to take me," she said.

"Why on earth?" Gillian demanded, instantly curious. "Had you been so awful at your last school?"

"Not worse than usual," Clem told her placidly. "No; but the School happened to be full up that term before there was any idea of sending me. It must," she added reflectively, "have been quite an experience for Dad. He's accustomed to saying what he wants and getting it."

The others left it at that. Everyone in her School knew that Clem was the daughter of the well-known artist Adrian Barrass, and as his undutiful child had once remarked, a genius thinks the only thing that matters is that he should go the way *he* wants, regardless of other folks and their rights.

"Oh dear!" the distracted Carola thought. "This is simply awful! What ever I say it can't be the truth and I mustn't explain to Clem. If this sort of thing is going on right through the term I shall go crackers!"

Before she had decided what to do, Miss O'Ryan herself unconsciously came to the rescue. "Carola, here's your paintbox," she said, presenting the stunned Carola with the regulation affair that most of the girls had. "Ask Herr Laubach if you can have one of the studio painting jars and get your own from Cook some time before next lesson."

Carola thankfully grabbed the box with a murmured, "Thank you, Miss O'Ryan." She had been saved this time.

In the art room, which was an old army hut attached to the stables, Herr Laubach presented them all with some leafless twigs and set them to making a brushwork study. The others were more or less accustomed to this sort of thing, but to Carola it was quite new. Hitherto, she had done geometrical designs from copies, or freehand work, all of which she had hated. This was rather fun and she settled down to do her best.

Her best was very far from satisfying the art master who was *not* a patient creature, but Herr Laubach somehow seemed to realise that this new girl was at least trying her hardest. On the whole, Carola enjoyed the lesson.

Music came next. She was to learn with Miss Cochrane, who was also an Old Girl and considered a fine teacher.

"Poor you!" was all Clem had said when she heard the news.

By the end of the lesson, Carola felt like saying, "Poor, *poor* me!" If Herr Laubach had very little patience, Miss Cochrane had none at all, and she did have a tongue that could nearly take the skin off you. Finally, she left the music room, running into Sybil Russell who came next, and who was looking apprehensive.

Sybil raised her eyebrows in a mute question and Carola grimaced eloquently. The younger girl's face fell and she went into the room looking very gloomy. Carola went to put away her music and then ran off to make the most of what was left of prep before tea.

"Was it *very* ghastly?" Clem asked pityingly as they sat munching bread-and-butter and plum jam.

"Simply *awful*!" Carola told her feelingly. She glanced

"I—I don't know. I've never thought about it," Carola confessed.

To tell the truth she was utterly taken by surprise at Sybil's words. She knew the girl to be a hard worker. Clem had told her that Sybil's mother, Lady Russell, was the owner of the Chalet School. If anyone had asked her, she would have guessed that Sybil meant to train as a teacher and come to teach at the School as quite a number of the Old Girls had done. Perhaps she meant to take over the needlework.

"Shall you teach when you've had your training?" she asked.

Sybil shook her head. "No jolly fear! I should hate it! Besides," she added honestly, "I haven't enough patience. I'd be throwing things at my pupils in ten minutes. What I want to do is church embroideries, like altar frontals and stoles and copes."

Whereat Carola was once more left gasping, but as they had left the common-room and were now in the corridor she had to be silent.

The next day a further need was shown her. Lower Fifth B had extra art the first part of the afternoon as the weather was so bad there could be no games.

"Take your paintboxes with you, girls," Miss O'Ryan, who had come to tell them, said.

Carola had never thought of a paintbox, and she had never owned such a thing. She turned to Clem who was standing near.

"Clem, what shall I do? I haven't a paintbox."

Clem's red-brown eyes became saucerlike at this. "No paintbox? But it was in the inventory. Oh, my stars and garters! That cousin of yours seems to have made a nice mess of your outfit!"

Carola forgot in her sudden indignation at Clem's remark.

"Well, you can't say it was *her* fault exactly!" she retorted crisply.

"*Not* her fault? Then whose was it?" Clem demanded naturally enough. "Don't tell me she left you to see to your own outfit!"

Carola was in a quandary. If she said Cousin Maud had done so, it certainly wouldn't be the strict truth. She couldn't say she hadn't, Cousin Maud having never seen the thing.

knitter. She was using a pretty basket-stitch, and before the evening ended she had done six inches of her scarf.

"Jolly pretty," Sybil Russell said as she looked at it when they were putting their work away. "All the same, buck up and finish it and then you can start on something for *our* stall. We're doing toys this year, and dolls' things. If you like, I'll ask Dora to let you see what we've done already. Audrey Simpson is making some super carpets to sell separately; and some of the others are doing sets of dolls' bedding and curtains and things like that."

Carola opened wide eyes at this information. "I say! That's a jolly decent idea! But what could I do?" she went on plaintively. "You all know what my sewing's like, and I've never done any woodwork or things like that. You can't when you're for ever moving around."

"I suppose not. But you do knit awfully well. Why don't you knit some sets of dolls' clothes—you know, knickers and frock and vest. P'raps you could do a suit and jumper to match. I'm sure those would sell."

Carola looked at her scarf. "But I wouldn't know how many stitches to cast on. How'd I manage about that?"

"Ask Mademoiselle. I expect she has patterns somewhere."

"Well, it's a wizard idea. I'll think of it."

Sybil nodded. "Yes, do. What do you collect, by the way?"

"Collect?" Again Carola was befogged.

"Yes; we all have some sort of collection. Mine's shells since we came to the island. Clem Barnes collects copies of famous pictures. She's got a super collection. Jean Ackroyd collects models of animals, and so do three or four others. My *real* hobby," Sybil went on as she handed the doll's counterpane she was embroidering to Dora Robson who was responsible for the Hobbies cupboard, "is embroidery. I just love it. When I leave school I'm going to the South Kensington School to be properly trained. They teach you all sorts of stitches, and how to make your own designs, and how to copy ancient ones, and—oh, everything of that kind. Mummy promised me the training if I'd work hard at my lessons till I was seventeen. I'm not a brain like Peggy and Bride," mentioning her two elder cousins, "but I'd work like anything to have my training later. What are you going to do, Carola?"

rising uppermost. "Well, if you can't sew, what *can* you do?"

"I don't know," Carola said truthfully. "Oh, I can knit a little. Would that do?"

"It'll do if that's all," Dickie told her. "You go to Mademoiselle and get wool and needles from her and begin on a scarf for the Sale. That'll keep you going for the moment. Bride, you people shouldn't be hanging about like this. See that everyone has everything she needs and all of you settle to work, please."

She turned on her heel and left the room, and Bride Bettany and Clem Barrass, the two form prefects, set to work to get everyone busy.

"Sybil, you take Carola to Mademoiselle and ask about the wool and needles," Bride ordered her cousin.

Sybil, a really lovely girl of nearly fourteen, turned to the new girl. "Come on, Carola. What colour do you want?"

"I—I don't know," Carola stammered.

"Oh, well, we'll ask Mademoiselle what she's got and then you can choose. She keeps all the wool and needles, you see, because often we can't get what we want at Carnbach," Sybil explained as she led the way to the sewing-room, where Mlle. Berne pulled open a deep drawer filled with skeins of wool in a rainbow variety of colours and told Carola to choose which she liked.

Still rather dazed, Carola pitched on the first she saw—a pretty cherry colour. Mademoiselle asked what she was going to knit, gave her what was needed and provided the needles, and then bade them hurry back or they would have no time to do anything.

"Didn't you really know about the Hobbies Club?" Gillian asked inquisitively when finally they were all settled down and Carola was seated near her. "Why not? It's all in the prospectus."

"I—I don't know," Carola stammered.

"Well," remarked Clem from her treadle fretsaw machine, where she was carefully cutting the backs of some tiny chairs, "all I can say is that your grown-ups must be *most* casual."

Carola, busy casting on stitches, said nothing once more. Some of the girls gave her curious looks. The Chalet School had housed some queer characters in its time, but never anyone quite like Carola Johnstone.

Once she had begun, Carola proved herself a practised

"You just can't account for grown-ups," Polly Winterton put in cheerfully. "I say, Carola, what are you going to do for Hobbies?"

"Hobbies?" Carola asked blankly.

"Didn't you know! We have Hobbies evening twice a week when we all work at our hobbies. This term we have the Sale for the San up in the hills, so we're all hard at it for that," Clem explained. "We had the first evening of the term last Thursday when you were over at Mrs. Maynard's. Our form and Upper Fifth are making a dolls' house and furnishing it. Tom Gay has *made* the house, and the rest of us are doing the furnishings. It's a smashing affair this year——"

"Clem Barrass! What was that you said?" demanded a stern voice.

Clem, looking sheepish, slid down from her perch. "Er —I forgot, Dickie," she said.

"No excuse at all," the big, fair prefect who had spoken told her austerely. "Fine, please. And don't use that ghastly word again. Is Carola Johnstone here?"

"This is her," Polly replied, waving her hand towards Carola.

"Oh, good! Carola, Nita Eltringham who is Hobbies prefect is in bed with a bad cold, so I'm taking it tonight and I've come to ask what you want for your hobby."

Carola gazed at her in silence. Oddly enough, no one had said anything to her about Hobbies until tonight, and she had no idea what to say. Dickie waited a moment or two. Then her patience was exhausted and she said, "Hurry up! What do you go in for—leather-work—basketry— painting? Come *on*! Don't be all night about it!"

"But I don't know what to choose," Carola said at last. "No one ever told me anything about it and I don't know what I ought to do."

"Something for the house, I hope," Clem put in severely.

"But what *can* I do?"

Dickie took the decision out of her hands for the moment. "Can you sew?" she asked.

Giggles arose from those of the girls who had been privileged to hear Mademoiselle on the subject, and Carola went redder than ever. Luckily, Dickie knew the signs.

"Oh, it's like that, is it?" she said, her basic good nature

you should come with me to Armiford where we have an excellent photographer, and have your photo done to send out to Calabar. How's that for an idea?"

"S-super!" Carola gulped hard.

"O.K. That's a date, then. Now scram and wash. The ferry leaves in half an hour, so we'd better think about going. You know the bathroom, don't you?"

Carola nodded and departed, to return looking more like herself. Jo would have kept her for the night, but that might have aroused suspicion at School, apart from which, everyone felt she would be better among her own kind. The best thing was to keep her mind occupied, and all the way over, Jo told tales of her own wicked Middle days until she had the girl laughing despite herself. At the front door of the Big House she stooped and kissed her.

"Your dad has left Jack and me *in loco parentis* for the moment," she said. "If ever you get into a sticky mess, just remember that, Carola, and let me know if things get too much for you." She paused to look steadily at her new charge's face under the porch light. "I don't think I need tell you to stand on your own feet when you can—oh, and try not to stand on other people's! Off you go!"

Carola went off laughing at the conclusion to Mrs. Maynard's speech. At the same time, Jo had awakened a deep devotion to herself in the girl. If ever Carola Johnstone could do anything for Mrs. Maynard she would do it, regardless of any cost to herself.

Chapter IX

COMPLICATIONS!

"WHAT I don't understand," said Clem, balancing on the back of the big settee in the commonroom, "is why on earth your aunt—oh, well, cousin, then!—had to go haring off as she did without seeing that you had everything you needed. After all, the School *does* send out a complete inventory, and all she had to do was to take you round the shops and get all it said."

Carola, very flushed, had nothing to say to this. As she was not, by nature, crooked or untruthful, this part of the affair was almost the worst part of her punishment.

further opportunity for private talk that day. Dr. Johnstone explained that he must return to Calabar as soon as possible, so the Head suggested that Carola should be allowed to spend the next afternoon with him, and then said goodbye after a business talk in Jack Maynard's den.

She took Carola back to school, for that young lady must not miss any lessons; but next day, after rest period, while the others were enjoying their hockey practice, Carola was walking about Carnbach, making the most of her time, for the doctor was returning to Africa next day.

"Cousin Maud said you and Mother were coming back next year," she said to him suddenly as they walked along the coast road in the pale January sunshine.

"Quite true. I shall have a furlough then and we are coming for three months. My work isn't finished out there, though, nor likely to be for a few years yet."

Carola sighed. "Well, you'll be at home then, but I wish you were here always."

"Mrs. Maynard tells me that when she returned home to her house at Howells she will have you for the holidays," he said soothingly. "I understand there is some talk of her going to Canada for a visit at Easter. Miss Annersley will arrange for your holiday then, but Mrs. Maynard has promised to attend to the summer ones. Don't worry; you will have happy holidays, I know."

Carola said no more about it but turned to the exciting subject of the extras she was to take. He had arranged for her to continue with music and to begin verse-speaking. She had wanted singing lessons, but the School music authorities had strongly advised against that for another two years, so she must wait.

Finally, he took her to the best café Carnbach boasted and treated her to a gorgeous tea, after which he took her to Cartref where Jo left them alone to say goodbye. She herself had arranged to return Carola to the Chalet School, for the doctor was off to Cardiff by the evening train as his plane left early next morning.

When he had gone, Jo left Carola to herself for half an hour. Then she went to the drawing-room where she found a very red-eyed girl standing staring unseeingly out of the window.

"It won't seem so long after a week or two," she observed as she shook up cushions and straightened chairs. "In the meantime, I vote that the first opportunity there is

mouth, was a very much older person than he had expected.

"Well, my lassie!" he said, holding out his hand.

Carola gripped it as Jo left them alone, and was drawn close to her father for a warm kiss. Unconsciously, she had been building up a defence against any strictures he might make, but it all melted away at that kiss and she clung to him as if she were the little girl he had been expecting.

"Oh, Dad! Oh, Dad!" was all she said.

"Now I want to hear all about it," the doctor said presently.

Mindful of Jo's words, Carola began and gave him a very fair picture of her life with her cousin.

"I see," he said. "Well, Carola, the first thing you have to do is to apologise to Cousin Maud for all the worry and annoyance you have caused her."

"I've written," Carola said humbly. "Miss Annersley told me to do it on Saturday during letter-writing time."

"Good! Maud won't be unforgiving once she has got over the shock you gave her. Now listen to me. Mother and I have decided to let you stay at the school of your own choice, but you must justify this by your behaviour and your work. Don't give us any reason to regret our decision. I shall say no more about what you did: that is past and done. Only you *must* try to think before you act. You are nearly fifteen, and it's high time you had a little sense. If you go on as you're doing, you may end up by involving not only yourself but other folk in bad trouble."

"I'll try," Carola murmured.

"Mrs. Maynard has very kindly said she will get you what you need. Is there anything else I should know?"

Carola blushed. "There's the bank."

"The bank? What do you mean?"

She explained it to him and he nodded approval. "A very good way of teaching you lassies the value of money. Very well; I'll consult Mrs. Maynard and leave you what she suggests. You are to have a hockey-stick, which she will buy for you. The rest, I think, I must arrange with your Head Mistress."

Carola was almost overcome, and she vowed inwardly to do her best in every way to prove to them that she was really grateful for all they were doing. A ring at the front-door bell announced the arrival of Miss Annersley, Jo ushered her into the drawing-room, and there was no

warm undies, and we hope there'll be time to see about a pair of wellingtons which she definitely needs at this time of year."

Dr. Johnstone thanked Jo gratefully, she refilled his cup, and the conversation passed into a discussion of all Carola would need.

The next afternoon brought her over to Carnbach, escorted by Miss Annersley. Jo met them at the ferry-landing and took charge of the girl while the Head went off on a shopping expedition, promising to appear at Cartref in time for tea. This would give Carola plenty of time to make her peace with her father.

"I—I didn't know you knew Dad, Mrs. Maynard," Carola said as she and Jo walked briskly along the streets shining with wet, for it had rained steadily all night and most of the morning.

"Not me, my child—my husband," Jo informed her. "They were at the Medical together. But enough of that! I've something to say to you, Carola."

Carola turned questioning blue eyes on her at this.

"When you see your father," Jo said gravely, "don't try to hide anything from him. He's had your cousin's side of the story. Now let him hear yours. You're lucky, you know. Your dad's a good chap. He's *not* pleased with what you've done—don't run away with that idea—but he can see *why* you did it. You've got your chance to thrash it all out, and if you don't take it to the absolute limit, you're a most awful flat."

"Yes," Carola meekly agreed. Privately, she was thinking that Mrs. Maynard talked more like one of her own nieces—Sybil Russell, for example, or Bride Bettany —than any other grown-up she had ever met. All the same, Jo's remarks put heart into her, and though she felt anxious to have the first part of her interview over, she was prepared to accept any scolding in store for her with becoming meekness.

As for Dr. Johnstone, when Jo ushered his daughter into the drawing-room where he was waiting, he quite literally gasped, for despite her words of the previous evening he was still not fully prepared for what he saw. In his inmost mind was still a picture of the eleven-year-old he and his wife had left behind them, and this tall, sturdy schoolgirl, with her wavy, light-brown hair drawn back from a centre parting into a long thick tail, her decided chin and firm

who is also Carola's godmother, offered to take the child off our hands, close the house, and see to everything of that sort. I've known Maud all my life, and whatever else she may be, she's conscientious enough. We accepted her offer and let it go at that."

"I see." Jo nodded gently. "There's no doubt that for the first year or two it was quite good for Carola. Now, however, she's been coming up against people of more or less her own age and I expect she felt a lack in her life. The trouble is that the early teens are quite a good age, but fussy. If the little ass had written to you and explained in full, I expect you'd have done something about it. Unfortunately, she seems to have gone off at half-cock and now the washing *is* in the mud."

"Mixed metaphor!" Jack said severely. "You're leaving the kid where she is, aren't you, Andy? Our own two beauties are there, not to speak of Jo's being an Old Girl."

"Oh, yes; Carola can stay there now she's taken things into her own hands. The trouble is I don't want anyone else to know what she's done. At that age there are probably plenty of her friends to think she's been rather clever, and that's the last sort of thing we want."

"You needn't worry about that," Jo told him. "The Head thought of that first go-off. Carola's been forbidden to say anything about it to anyone. I was present at that interview and I can assure you that by the time Hilda and Nell—I—I mean Miss Annersley and Miss Wilson—" she added in some confusion, "well, by the time they'd finished with her you could have put the pieces that were left into a pint pot. She was awfully upset, too, when she was reminded of the anxiety you and her mother must be feeling."

The doctor's eyes lightened. "She's a good enough lassie, but she does go at things bull-headed," he admitted.

"Takes after Pa," Jack Maynard observed detachedly.

Dr. Johnstone suddenly chuckled. "I'll have it out with you later. In the meantime, Mrs. Maynard, thank you for having our meeting here. It may make things a bit easier if I don't turn up at the School this time. When are your Head Mistress and Carola coming?"

"Tomorrow afternoon. Carola hasn't half the things she needs, so we're making that the excuse for bringing her over to Carnbach like this. I don't quite know how much shopping is likely to be done then, but I've got her some

asked. "I'm interested in her. It was a mad thing to do all right, but a jolly plucky one. You're letting her stay with us, aren't you?"

Dr. Johnstone frowned. "Yes; I shall let her stay. My cousin flatly refuses to take any more responsibility for her, and she certainly can't join us. Calabar is no place for small girls."

Jo gave him a startled look. "*Small* girls? What *are* you talking about? Carola's quite a well-grown specimen, and she's nearly fifteen!"

It was Dr. Johnstone's turn to look startled. "Fifteen? Oh, no; she can't be nearly that age," he protested.

"But she *is*. She told the Head that she was born in '36. That makes her fifteen this year."

"She's right about the date, but—good heavens! My wife and I have been visualising her as not much bigger or older than she was when we went away. One forgets how time goes, and I've been so busy."

Dr. Johnstone turned a rueful glance at Jo. "You know, Mrs. Maynard, you've given me a bad shock," he said. "If Carola is nearly fifteen, then she was certainly right in saying she needed school. I wish, though, she had chosen some other method of attaining her wish. This means that so long as we are out of England she has no home, and even at fifteen we can't have her out in Calabar."

"How much longer are you likely to stay?" Jo asked.

"Oh, another three or four years at least. I'm on an official job—don't be afraid: I'm not going to bore you with it."

"Dr. Johnstone, didn't either you or Mrs. Johnstone realise that Carola was growing up very quickly? I've seen her, and she's quite a big girl. It was more than time that she was at a good school. She wants some sort of career, I suppose? Governess training can be good; but when you have it in conjunction with leading a regular nomadic existence I should say it wouldn't be much help."

Dr. Johnstone accepted another scone and bit into it before he replied. "The fact of the matter is this chance came quite suddenly. I had to make up my mind at once—within twenty-four hours, in fact. I had to be on the way within a week. That didn't leave us much time for anything. And—well—my wife has it fixed in her head that I'm not to be trusted alone. She was sure I should get into some sort of sticky mess if she weren't with me. My cousin,

no doubt as to her own tiresomeness in having to be fitted out after school had begun. It took the whole of the games period to supply her, and prep came next, so Carola was left to reflect that it was her own fault that she had been obliged to miss the first hockey practice of the term. She was beginning to realise that by taking the law into her own hands as she had done she had let herself in for all sorts of consequences. Worst of all, at present, was the doubt that filled her as to how her father would look at the whole thing, and whether he would be very angry with her. Well, that was something that could not be decided until he came, and Miss Annersley had said he would arrive early next week. She must just bear it all as patiently as she could until then. All the same, Carola felt that she was being well punished as it was, and she hoped he would not consider it necessary to administer much more.

Chapter VIII

THE DOCTOR ARRIVES

DR. JOHNSTONE arrived on the Wednesday. At the suggestion of Jo Maynard he did not go to the School but stayed at Carnbach with her and her husband, an old friend of his.

"You know, I can't get over Jigger Maynard being the responsible head of a family," he told Jo while they were having tea.

"What's that you called him?" Jo demanded, while Jack Maynard scowled at his friend.

"Hang it, Andy, you needn't have let that slip! Here I've been carefully keeping it hidden from Jo and you must needs go and spill the beans!" he protested. "O.K., Jo—it's 'Jigger.' But let me catch you trying to use it and heaven help you!"

"Shouldn't dream of it," Jo retorted haughtily. "It's a very poor effort when I think of all the things I can call you off my own bat."

The two doctors chuckled, and Jo decided to change the subject.

"What about that girl of yours, Dr. Johnstone?" she

"She runs the School bank." Then, seeing the new girl's bewildered look, Clem explained. "It's this way. We all get weekly pocket money—our crowd have two shillings. You've got to give to the church collections from that, of course. Then you may bring money back with you, but it has to be paid into the bank, and if you want anything for a special reason, like someone's birthday, you go to Teddy on the Saturday before and ask for what you want. And while I think of it, you don't ask for too much or she wants to know why you want it exactly. At the end of term you can either draw out what you have left or else leave it for the next term. Most folk leave it at Easter and summer and draw out for Christmas," Clem added. "You please yourself, of course."

Carola thought with inward dismay of the few shillings she had left. Here was another problem for her until her father came. Would he give her some money for the bank or would he think she didn't deserve any for this term?

"Why can't we just keep what we bring and use it as we like?" she queried.

Clem gave her a grin. "Because we mightn't use it as other people would think right. There was one girl," her grin deepened, "who had got into a frightful row with a Head we had pro tem when Miss Annersley and Miss Wilson were both smashed up in a motor accident. Miss Bubb—that was her name—wouldn't let Gay go home to say goodbye to her brother who was off to China. No one had taken bank—Teddy was mixed up in the accident, too —so Gay had all she had brought, and she was so mad that she got out at night and just went home. She had plenty with her, you see."

"That was ages ago," put in Sybil Russell who was sitting opposite and overheard this. "I remember the fuss there was. Auntie Jo was teaching at the School then and she wrote pronto to Miss Wilson who was less badly hurt than the others, and Bill came haring back to School and Miss Bubb left. You weren't here then, Clem."

"No, but I've heard all about it," Clem retorted. "But you can see, Carola, just why no one wants us to have enough cash to do a mad thing like that again."

For no reason that anyone could see, Carola went pink again. Luckily for her, Mittagessen came to an end just then, and they had to clear the table and then go to rest. After rest she had a session with Matron, who left her in

Clem's brown eyes opened. "Mean to say you haven't got it *yet*? Oh, well, we haven't been back two days yet, and Matey is always up to the eyes at the beginning of term. It's rotten luck, though. That means you'll have to miss hockey—or most of it. You've never played before, have you?" she added.

"No, and I'm dying to begin; but it just can't be helped today. Anyway, I haven't a stick, so it doesn't matter so much."

Clem said nothing but she thought the more. There was some mystery about this new girl. First of all she hadn't been entered on the roll, and that was something that had never happened before so far as anyone could tell. Then she had no uniform. To crown all, it seemed that her folk had let her come without a hockey-stick—and that, to Clem's mind, was the greatest lack of all.

Carola had no idea what she was thinking. She was wondering if her father would be so angry with her that he would refuse to let her play games. She knew from her reading that games were often compulsory at school, but so far she had not heard that they were here.

"Do you know if the Head has told Miss Burn?" Clem asked at this point. "If not, you'll have to see her and explain."

"See who?" Carola demanded.

"Miss Burn, of course. She takes games as well as gym."

"Are games compulsory, then?"

"Why, of course! Oh, folk who aren't frightfully strong don't play hockey or lax——"

"What's lax?" Carola interrupted her.

"Lacrosse; but you don't play that till you're sixteen. As for a stick, you can have my old one until your folk buy you one. Auntie Doris gave me a new one for Christmas because I'd got into the Second Eleven, and my old one is still here, so you can use it."

Carola went pink at this generous offer. "That's super of you, Clem. Thanks a million! I'll take care of it."

"Oh, rot!" Downright Clem looked uncomfortable. "And I say! You watch out for slang. I told you that certain words aren't allowed here, and if you use them you're fined. That reminds me; have you taken your money to Teddy—I mean Miss Edwards?"

"I don't know which she is, and I haven't taken any money to her. *Why* must we?"

"Thank you. And your birthday and the year you were born?"

Carola did some frantic arithmetic on her fingers. "March 10th, and I was born in 1936."

"Then you are nearly fifteen? Now, your father's name, please."

"Andrew Charles Johnstone—that's why I'm 'Carola'," she added. "He's a doctor. Do you want his degrees and things?"

Miss Annersley gave her a look of amusement. "I don't think that's necessary yet. He'll give me those when he arrives. Now, you attended a Kindergarten when you were small, I think? Where was it?"

"In Edinburgh, where we used to live. It was called Monan House. They kept girls up to the age of twelve, but after that we had to leave."

Miss Annersley, who had already had one or two pupils from Monan House and knew their ways, nodded. "Do you remember Kathie Robertson?" she asked.

Carola nodded. "Yes; but she left six years ago, when I was very young," she said; and again amusement lit up the Head's eyes.

"Kathie was here until last summer," she said. "She has gone to Edinburgh University now. She was one of our prefects."

Carola's eyes widened. "Was she really? We all liked Kathie," she added. "She was awfully decent to us little ones."

"I am sure she was. Kathie was a great favourite here, and we were all sorry when she left. Well, Carola, I think that is all at present. You must go back to your lessons now—ah! Too late! There goes the bell for the end of morning school. Don't forget to go to Matron at two o'clock."

"No, Miss Annersley." Carola went to the door, curtsied, and then hurried off to the Splashery, intent on getting there first. One day and a half of school had already taught her that if you loitered you had a struggle to wash before Mittagessen.

"Anything wrong?" Clem asked when they were seated at the table.

Carola shook her head. "Miss Annersley sent for me to tell me to go to Matron for my uniform after rest period," she explained.

days at School going there. She did not need anyone to tell her why Miss Annersley had sent for her. She was certain that at long last the cable had come from West Africa and she was to learn her fate. This thought slowed her steps once she was inside the house, and it was a very anxious young lady who tapped at the door and entered the room in answer to the Head's "Come in!"

Miss Annersley was standing by the window, but she swung round as she heard the door close. "There you are, Carola," she said. "Well, I have had a cable from your father. He is flying home at once to see about you, and expects to be here early next week. In the meantime, you are to go on here."

Carola gulped at this unexpected news. "He's coming home?" she faltered. Then, "Oh, Miss Annersley, do you think he's awfully mad with me?"

Miss Annersley went to her desk and sat down. "Come here," she said.

Carola went. When she was standing before the desk, the Head gave her a sudden unexpected smile. "Why, you silly child, I believe you're afraid!" she exclaimed. "Well, I am going to ease your mind about one thing. Your parents wish you to remain with us." Then, as Carola's whole face lightened, she laughed outright. "That pleases you? I am glad to know it. But, Carola, I want you to remember that, though you are gaining your great wish, you hardly deserve it. You had no possible right to run away as you did. If you wanted school as much as that, your business was to write to your people, telling them so. It was very wrong of you to take the law into your own hands as you did."

"I—I didn't think," Carola faltered.

"That is no real excuse. If you stay here, you must learn to think. However, I am not going to say any more on the subject. Your father will tell you what his opinion of your behaviour is, I don't doubt. We'll turn to a pleasanter subject. You need your uniform. You are to go to Matron after rest this afternoon, and she will fit you out. I'm afraid it will mean missing your games but that can't be helped. Now," she picked up her pen and a printed form, "we have very few of your details. Sit down on that chair and help me to fill this in. What is your full name?"

"Carola Elizabeth Maud Johnstone," the name's owner said.

of the earth's curves. "Very well, Lalla, I will come at once. Go back to your own form quickly."

Lalla Winterton, younger sister of Polly Winterton, made the little curtsy that was considered "good manners" in the School, and withdrew, Miss Wilson hurriedly finished her diagram and then swept the board clean.

"Repeat those from memory in your scribblers. If I have not returned by that time, you may turn to pages 122-124 in your geographies and begin preparing them for next time," she said. "Don't forget to use your atlases while you work. No talking, please."

She dusted the chalk off her hands and departed. Lower Fifth B, left to itself, relaxed the absorbed attention it had been according the mistress, and a distinct groan sounded from one or two people who found the scientific side of geography distinctly hard.

Clem, prefect of the form, uttered a warning, "Hush! Get on with the job and don't yatter!"

As the Chalet School laid great stress on girls having the decency to behave properly whether a mistress was there or not, and Clem was, in any case, a strong prefect, the malcontents subsided and silence reigned as the girls did their best to remember what they had been told.

Polly Winterton was the first to give up. She regarded her page with a long sigh, then took out her geography text-book and atlas, and set to work on the preparation. Carola finished in company with one or two others, and by the time Gillian had given it up as a hopeless job, the entire form was occupied with the description of fruit-farming in Canada.

Miss Wilson returned ten minutes later. Her eyes swept round the room and singled out the new girl. "Carola, go to the study, please," she said. "Now girls, let me see what you have made of the lesson."

Carola rose from her place beside Clem, went to the door where for once she remembered her curtsy, and fled across the stableyard to the house. The geography-room was beside the gymnasium, as well as the laboratories and the domestic science kitchen, and girls who had lessons in one place had lessons in the others on the same morning to save continual passage to and fro.

By this time, the new girl was finding her way about and needed no one to show her how to reach the study. It seemed to her as if she had spent a good part of her first

planned out and there was not a moment to waste over being bored.

As they went upstairs at bedtime after saying goodnight to Miss Wilson who was standing at the foot of the stairs for that purpose, she ventured to ask, "Please, has there been any news from—from Africa yet?"

Miss Wilson shook her head. "There hasn't been time. They would only get the cable today. I don't suppose there will be any reply before noon tomorrow at earliest."

"I see. Thank you very much. Good-night, Miss Wilson."

Miss Wilson's clear-cut, rather stern face softened.

"Good-night, Carola. Don't worry until you must. You go to sleep, and when morning comes remember that it will probably mean waiting only a few hours longer, and those hours will be busy ones for you." She finished up with a smile and Carola went on, somehow cheered.

"What were you saying to Bill?" Gillian Moggeridge asked inquisitively when they were in the dormitory.

The warm colour flooded Carola's face. "It was only about a cable from my people," she said.

"Oh? I hope there's nothing wrong with them?" Gillian asked. She was a kind-hearted girl though she suffered from almost insatiable curiosity which had earned for herself the name of "Elephant's Child," generally shortened to "Jumbo."

"I shan't know until the cable comes," Carola said, vanishing thankfully into her cubicle and pulling down the curtains from the rods.

Gillian gave it up and attended to her own curtains. Half an hour later they were all fast asleep and no one stirred, not even Carola, until the relentless bell called them out of bed next morning.

Chapter VII

THE CABLE ARRIVES

"PLEASE, Miss Wilson, Miss Annersley would like to speak to you."

Miss Wilson—"Bill" to the School—turned round from the board whereon she was illustrating various proofs

neat, soon showed that she was an asset to the form in this way at least, and Miss Burn, with Parents' Day and the gym display given then in mind, decided to keep an eye on this particular new girl.

Gym was followed by an hour's needlework which was taken by Mademoiselle's compatriot, Mlle. Berné, and here, Carola was very much at a disadvantage. She disliked sewing, and did it badly. Mademoiselle had quite a good deal to say to her about her uneven "dog's-tooth" stitches, and made her take out all she had done and begin again. Clem, who after two years at the School had managed to learn to sew really well, smiled sympathetically at her when she set to work to unpick the really appalling sewing she had just shown up.

"Rotten luck!" she remarked in an undertone, with one eye on Mademoiselle.

"Clem, you are talking too much," stated Mademoiselle over her shoulder. "Do more work and less chattering, I beg you."

Clem made a face at Carola and fell silent, and Carola went on picking out her stitches with a long face. She was thankful when the hour came to an end and Clem escorted her to the lab for her botany test with Miss Wilson.

She left it with the satisfaction of knowing that the Second Head, who was also science and geography mistress, thought her quite capable of working with the Fifth Form botany set, and settled down to make the most of the half-hour's "prep" left to her.

Prep was a strenuous time as Carola found. It was strictly limited, but while it lasted the girls were expected to work really hard. Even when they were left without supervision it was the "done" thing to concentrate on your lessons. Carola got down to her French exercise with all her might and by the time the bell rang for the end of afternoon school she had finished it.

Tea was as jolly as all other meals had been, and when it was over they all fled upstairs to change. There was very little time, for evening prep began at half-past five and went on till seven, after which they cleared up and went straight in to Abendessen, as supper was called. That over, their time was their own until Prayers at half-past eight and bed for everyone who was not a Senior. For the first time since her parents left her Carola found her entire day

Latin. Please do your best for her." Then she left the room, the girls rising until the door closed behind her.

"Welcome to Lower Fifth B, Carola," Mademoiselle said kindly. "You speak French, hein?"

"Only a very little," Carola said shyly.

"Eh bien, ça s'arrangera, n'est-ce pas? Eh maintenant, assieds-toi. Ah, Clem! Qu'as-tu, ma petite?"

"There's a spare desk here, Mademoiselle," Clem replied in French with a good British accent.

Mademoiselle waved the dazed Carola towards the seat, and that young person went meekly and sat down thankfully. At least the twenty-two pairs of eyes could hardly fix themselves on her now!

Mademoiselle turned to the board, and soon they were hurled into a brisk oral test on the uses of pouvoir and valoir, in which Carola, who had been thoroughly well-drilled in French irregular verbs by her last governess, acquitted herself fairly well, and merited the "Bien fait!" that Mademoiselle awarded her.

The last lesson of the morning proved to be history, much to Carola's delight, for she had a real affection for Miss O'Ryan. That young lady proved to be an excellent teacher, and the lesson she gave was an eye-opener to the governess-taught girl who had been accustomed to preparing two or three pages from her history book for questioning. Biddy O'Ryan knew what the tradition of the Chalet School history lessons was from experience, and insisted that her pupils should take the facts and reason out the effects for themselves during her energetic lesson on the growth of trade towards the end of the Elizabethan era.

After lunch—which the School, reverting to past custom with an eye to returning to Tirol at some not too distant date, now called "Mittagessen"—they all sought deck-chairs, carried them to the common-rooms, and rested for half an hour, during which time they must be silent, though they might read if they liked. When this was over they marched to the gymnasium, which had once been part of the stables, where they spent an exhilarating forty minutes that Carola enjoyed intensely. She had never done apparatus work before, but she showed an aptitude for it that delighted Miss Burn, who was wont to groan to the rest of the Staff over the plump and lazy Gillian and one or two other young persons in Lower Fifth B who were careless and untidy in their work. Carola, lightly built and

"*Oh!*" Once more Carola forgot she was in disgrace, and her blue eyes sparkled. One more wish fulfilled!

"Then I think it's all settled." Miss Annersley spoke crisply. "I am not going to provide you with any uniform, Carola, until we know that it is necessary. If your parents decide to leave you here, you must have a tunic and blazer and your badges. Matron will provide you with bed-linen and towels for the present. I imagine you have brought none with you."

"I brought three bath towels," Carola said, suddenly flattened out again.

Mrs. Maynard gave her a friendly grin. "*That* won't see you very far; and whatever your folk do they can't settle anything for at least two or three weeks. I'll lend you what you need—table-napkins, too." She turned to the two Heads. "I suppose Bid—Miss O'Ryan, I mean—can't run over this afternoon, can she? If she could, I'd give her what Carola needs. She can? Good! Then I'll be off now, or I'll miss the ferry."

"One moment, please." Miss Annersley held up her hand. "Miss Wilson, would you mind taking Carola to Lower Fifth B? Clem Barrass is being her shepherd just now and will look after her. Carola, tell Clem from me to see that you get your stationery and text-books after Mittagessen and rest, please."

Miss Wilson rose while Carola was saying, "Yes, Miss Annersley."

"Come along," she said. "After you've got your books this afternoon, ask someone to bring you to me in the lab, and I'll see how you shape in botany. Hurry up, or you'll miss the next lesson, and you've missed the whole of this!" as the big bell clanged out.

She led Carola off, and presently that young person found herself standing rather forlornly by the door of a pleasant classroom while Miss Wilson conferred with the little dark lady, obviously French, who was sitting at the mistress's desk. Presently the Second Head turned to the girl standing by the door and waved her forward after a stern look round at the other girls who promptly stopped staring, buried their heads in their books, and looked as studious as they could.

"This is Carola Johnstone, Mademoiselle," Miss Wilson said. "Carola, Mlle. de Lachenais takes you for French and

up as much chemistry as they have; but I'll test her some time before Monday and see."

"Yes; I think that would be best. Very well, then, Carola." The Head turned back to Carola who was listening to all this, wide-eyed. "As you *have* had a year's botany, and seem to have done practically no maths, we had better concentrate on the botany and cut the maths out. No need for you to do both."

"No, Miss Annersley," Carola replied meekly.

"Well, we must see. I think we won't worry too much about coachings, though, until we hear from Dr. Johnstone."

The stranger lady evidently thought it was time she took a hand. "Of course, Mrs. Johnstone may very well decide to come back to England to make a home for Carola and send her to day school," she suggested.

"Oh, I'm sure she won't do that!" Carola cried, forgetting that she was a very naughty girl in deep disgrace, who might be supposed to keep well in the background for the present. "Dad is fearfully absent-minded and he'd never be able to look after himself if she wasn't there to see that he did it. She's told me so often in her letters."

"That may be," Miss Wilson suppressed her. "At the same time, when it comes to choosing between a husband who is absent-minded and a daughter who doesn't take the trouble of thinking before she does mad things, she may decide that her chief duty is to her daughter before she gets herself into really serious trouble, and she must leave him to do the best he can for himself."

Once more Carola's face burned, and she said no more. The stranger lady glanced at her with wicked dancing eyes and then remarked, "Well, we can't say either way until we hear from them. I suppose the only thing we can do is to wait until we do. In the meantime, Carola can't afford to waste time at her age, so she'd better join Lower Fifth B—isn't the redoubtable Clem Barrass a shining light there?—and do her best to show everyone that she repents her insane behaviour up to date by working like a trooper. How about it, Carola?"

Carola looked up. "I'll do my best," she promised. Inwardly she was wondering who on earth the lady was.

Miss Annersley guessed, and proceeded to introduce them. "This is Mrs. Maynard, Carola, though I expect you know of her best as Josephine Bettany."

seems to be nowhere else for you to go, and he will tell us what his wishes concerning you are as soon as possible, I expect."

Carola raised her head, a flash of joy in her eyes at this information, but she encountered Miss Annersley's grimmest glare, and remembered just *why* she was to stay —always supposing the School would keep her. For the first time she began to grasp exactly what she had done, and while she felt no sort of regret for all she had given her cousin in the way of anxiety, she did begin to see that things would have been better all round if she had left some sort of message for Miss Curry. For the first time, too, she began to wonder what her father would have to say about it.

The two Heads, watching her expressive little face, knew very well what she was thinking, but they forbore to say anything. They meant to keep her, of course, unless Dr. Johnstone should propose another plan; but they had talked it over and agreed that she would be none the worse for a few hours of suspense. Nothing could be heard from West Africa until next day at soonest, and Carola could very well wait to know her fate until then. So she sat there feeling rather unhappy and wondering what was going to happen to her, while the three grown-up people in the study watched her.

At lengh Miss Annersley took pity on her. "I have your test papers here," she said, picking up some sheets. "In English subjects, arithmetic, and French, you should be able to work with Lower Fifth B. Your Latin grammar is good; but you construe badly. Still, that is largely a matter of vocabulary and practice. Have you done no algebra and geometry?"

"A little algebra, but no geometry," Carola explained in subdued tones.

"I see. It would mean coaching in those subjects, then. What about science?"

"I did botany about a year with Miss Wilkins, but no chemistry or anything like that. My other governesses weren't interested."

"Then if Miss Wilson thinks you could work with— which set, Miss Wilson?" She turned to that lady questioningly.

"Set V_B," Miss Wilson replied. "They are all Fifth Form girls. If she can work with them, I expect she'll soon pick

that you were nowhere on the liner; and that wasn't until everyone had been searching for you. You seem to have made a complete nuisance of yourself all round."

It was impossible by this time for Carola to go any redder, but she hung her head and regarded the toes of her slippers fixedly and wished that she was anywhere else than here. Miss Annersley's very cool judicial manner made her feel that she had made a complete idiot of herself. Miss Annersley, of course, was quite aware of this, and was satisfied at the impression she was making. The last thing anyone wanted was for Carola to imagine she had done something rather clever, and the Head was well aware that there were plenty of empty-headed girls in the School who would be inclined to make a heroine of the girl who had run away to school like that, if the story ever leaked out.

Miss Annersley went on. "Your cousin—and quite naturally, in my opinion—tells me that she wishes to have nothing more to do with you. She flatly refuses to be responsible for a girl who could treat her in such a cavalier manner."

Not knowing what "cavalier" meant as Miss Annersley had used it, Carola remained dumb. On the whole, she felt she would rather have endured one of Cousin Maud's tirades than this calm, reasonable way of putting her sins before her. Besides, to quote herself much later, the way the Head was eyeing her left her feeling like a downtrodden cockroach!

Miss Wilson suddenly took a hand. "If you felt that you *must* rush off in that way, may I ask why you couldn't leave some message for your unfortunate cousin?" she asked in the blandest tones.

"I—I didn't think," Carola mumbled.

"Then you ought to have done," Miss Annersley told her severely. "A girl of your age—fourteen, aren't you?—should have enough common sense to realise that she can't just disappear in that way without giving a great deal of trouble and worry to all concerned."

Carola had nothing to say. It was by no means the first time she had been told that "didn't think" was no sort of excuse.

"Well," Miss Annersley continued, "your cousin has already cabled to your father since she got my own radio, telling him that he must make other arrangements for you in future. In the meantime you are to stay here, as there

she had never gone further than the second book of "Ora Maritima." She picked out what sentences she could do, but that part of her paper had a markedly blank look when she had finished with it.

Break came next, with milk or cocoa and biscuits. Halfway through, a message came that Miss Annersley would like to see Carola Johnstone when it was over.

"Good! That's to talk over your papers and tell where you're going," Clem remarked. "They never keep you hanging on for very long here."

Carola was still none too sure. It might mean that she was to leave this gorgeous place almost at once. Having tasted its delights, she felt that she just couldn't bear it if it was that and she was sent away, and it was with considerable trepidation that she went to the study for that interview.

Chapter VI

CAROLA GOES ON TASTING

CAROLA tapped at the study door, and Miss Annersley's voice called, "Come in!" She entered, feeling decidedly quaky about the knees. The room seemed to be full of people at first. Then she saw that apart from the two Heads there really was only one lady, a very dark, tall person, who gave her a smile and a quizzical look as she shut the door behind her and stood waiting.

"That's right, Carola," Miss Annersley said briskly. "Come along in, child, and don't stand there by the door. Sit down on that chair. Now," she continued when Carola had seated herself, "we have heard from your cousin, Miss Curry. The boat had to wait a couple of hours at Queenstown, so she was able to make a telephone connection and I have had a long conversation with her." She paused to give full weight to her words, and Carola squirmed uneasily inside her. What had Cousin Maud said?

She was to know almost at once. Miss Annersley decided that her victim had taken the point, and continued. "You have given her a great deal of anxiety, for of course she had no idea what had become of you when she first discovered

she gave that infectious grin which Carola found herself returning.

"How did you manage when you came here first?"

"All right so long as the lessons were in English; but my French was feeble, and my German not there at all. Don't worry, Carola. I expect you'll do all right. Folk are quite patient with you and help you out at first, so long as they see you're trying. If you don't—well, you've had it. That's all."

Carola remembered something. "Who was the mistress who went out after the Heads? She played for Prayers last night."

"That's Miss Cochrane, one of the first of the Chalet School girls. She teaches music. They say she's awfully good, but she's got a tongue that nearly takes the skin off you."

At this point they were halted and turned, and began to walk back again.

"You'll be doing tests after Prayers, I expect, and then we'll know which form you really are in, so you won't have long to wait," said Clem.

Carola thought to herself that if her parents or Cousin Maud should say she must leave this marvellous place she would want to die. She wondered if she would ever be asked to take those tests. However, when they reached the School again and had changed, she was told to go with the others, and after Prayers she was sent to the long, narrow room, usually dedicated to the use of the prefects, and set to working test papers which she did with fair success on the whole. The mathematics, apart from arithmetic, floored her badly, for she had done so little. The English and history, however, just suited her, and she was able to manage most of the French. When the mistress sitting with the girls gave her the German paper, she shook her head.

"It's no use, Miss Bell. I've never done any German at all."

Miss Bell picked up the paper without comment. "What about Latin?" she asked, offering her another.

"Yes; I've done some Latin. May I try it?"

"Please do." Miss Bell gave her an amused look. "Here you are. See what you can do with it."

Carola settled down to the Latin paper, and soon found that though she could manage most of the grammar questions she was all at sea when it came to construing, for

not to go bagging another table's clean one. It's a good scheme, because if a girl is careless, her own table see to it that she doesn't go on. No one wants to sit down to a messy cloth. Now we go upstairs and make our beds and dust. I'll show you your dusters."

She not only did that, but also showed Carola the one and only way Matron passed for bed-making. When that was done, the cubicle spick and span with everything unnecessary out of sight, the cubicle curtains were flung up over their rods to allow the fresh air from the open windows have free passage through the rooms, and the girls streamed off to the Splasheries to get ready for the morning walk. This lasted half an hour, and when they came in, Carola learned that they would have Prayers, and then lessons.

"D'you know which form you're likely to be in?" Clem asked as she strode along beside the new girl.

"No; I didn't do an entrance test," Carola explained, turning very pink as she spoke. She was keeping strictly to the truth, but she felt that she was not being absolutely honest about things, and she hated it. Clem was so straight herself.

Clem gave her a shrewd look. "I rather think you'll be in our form. They don't like infant marvels of learning *or* duds in this place; though I must say the duds are given a real chance. When they can, they put folk of the same age together. You aren't a marvel of learning by any chance, are you?" she added.

"Not very likely! But," Carola said with some bitterness, "it wouldn't surprise me if I didn't turn out a good deal of a dud. You can't work decently when you're for ever on the move and always changing governesses. It just isn't possible."

Clem gave her a grin. "I don't believe *you* are a dud. You don't look it, and you certainly don't talk like it, either. And as for moving about," she added, "I *should* know all about that. My Dad's an artist, and we've always stayed in a place just so long as he could find places to paint. When he'd finished everything he like, we upped stakes and trekked for somewhere else. This is my——" she stopped short to count on her fingers. "Yes; my seventh school. Thank heaven it's to be the last—unless, of course, they get so fed up with me that they turf me out." Again

being responsible for seeing that no one became rowdy. The Heads were seated at a long table running across the head of the room, with the rest of the Staff sitting with them.

"And that's one thing that's so nice here," Clem said. "In crowds of other schools mistresses take the tables, and then you have to be careful what you say. Well, I don't mean the prees don't jump on you if you use certain slang words or make a nuisance of yourself; and on French and German days they jolly well see to it that you talk which ever language it is—or sit silent until you can. They help you out, though, if they see you're trying. Can you, by the way?"

"Can I what?" Carola asked, startled.

"Talk French and German, of course."

"French a bit; German not at all," Carola told her promptly.

"Oh, well, you'll soon pick it up. We all do. I couldn't talk myself when I first came. Sure you won't have any more?"

"Quite sure, thanks. I've had heaps."

"Well, that's just as well, perhaps, 'cos there's the Abbess getting up to say Grace. Up you get! Push your chair right in."

Carola stood up with the rest, and went behind her chair and pushed it close to the table.

Then there was silence, and Miss Annersley said Grace. The Heads left the room at once, and so did a slightly-built, pretty woman in the early thirties, whose brown hair crisped and curled over a beautifully-shaped head. Carola wondered who she was but she had no time for wondering. To her amazement, every girl was piling up her own crockery and cutlery and, beginning with the bottom table, marching to the buttery hatch and handing them through to the maids waiting to take them. Then they marched back, picked up their table napkins, and proceeded with them to a big press, while the prefect folded the cloth after having swept it, and followed to put it in the same drawer. Carola noticed that each of the six tables had its own drawer, and Clem, seeing her surprise, kindly explained it to her.

"Help is short, of course, so we always clear the tables. We each have a drawer, so that if one table has a spill it's got to keep its own messy cloth until they're changed, and

underneath the bureau. You were not allowed to leave anything about. This done, Clem turned to her charge, and gasped when she saw her attire.

"Where on earth is your tunic? Only people above Middle Fifth are allowed to wear blouses and skirts for lessons."

"Cousin Maud didn't get me one," Carola told her truthfully.

"Oh!" Clem seemed rather floored by this. Then she noticed the new girl's woolly cardigan and demanded, "Didn't she get you a blazer either? No? Oh, well, I suppose they'll see about it here."

They left the dormitory, Clem pausing at each cubicle to call the owner's name and make sure that the last girl had gone down before she left the dormitory herself.

"I'm dormy prefect here," she explained, as finally they shut the door behind them. "It's my job to see that the place is clear before I leave. Luckily, most folk are quite good about it, and everyone always is on first mornings." She dived down a narrow flight of stairs, Carola following, and presently the new girl found herself being piloted into a large, pleasant room where little groups of girls of their own age were standing about, laughing and chattering together.

Clem was hailed by half a dozen people as they entered, and Carola guessed that she was a favourite. She was really kind, too, for though she was speedily in one of the groups, she kept the new girl with her, and introduced her all round. Carola was to learn that at the Chalet School it was the tradition to see that new people were made to feel welcome until they had found their feet a little. After that they were expected to fend for themselves. Any girl given charge of a new girl was expected to look after her and tell her anything she ought to know. Everyone did it, but it was a recognised fact that Clem Barrass was one of the best. Not only was she a friendly creature in her own brusque way; she possessed a conscience, and was reliable. Carola had fallen into good hands, and by the time the gong sounded for breakfast she felt that she was fast settling down.

Breakfast, she found, meant porridge, a portion of scrambled eggs on toast, toast and marmalade, and as much milky coffee as she liked. The girls talked quietly among themselves, the prefect at the head of each table

have to scram, or it'll be a cat's lick and a promise for us!"

She hurried Carola out of the dormitory and down the corridor into a short passage whence came sounds of splashing. Before one door she paused.

"Here we are. I take my bath cold, but you *can* have it lukewarm if you like. Shan't be a sec and don't you be, either," she added from the other side of the door to the accompaniment of the sound of running water. "There are two more folk to come after you."

Judging by the sounds, she was in the bath by this time, and three minutes later she was out, still drying her face, and remarking in muffled tones through her towel, "In you go! I've set the tap running, and come straight back to the dormy when you're done."

She raced off, and Carola entered the somewhat messy bathroom and plunged into the cold water once she had tossed off her clothes. She sluiced down as quickly as she could, but with all her haste she could not hope to rival Clem who seemed to have the makings of a quick-change artist about her, and the next girl was thumping impatiently on the door before she had finished her teeth.

"Sorry if I've kept you waiting," she said, recognising Jean.

Jean gave her a nod as she shot in and slammed the door behind her. "O.K., but you can't waste a minute at this time of day. You get back and dress," she called; and Carola scuttled back to her dormitory, aware that she was only half-dried, but glowing from the sting of the cold water. She finished drying, and then hurried into her clothes.

"Tunic, etc., mind," Clem called, still "doing sheep-dog," as the School called it, with all her might. "Don't forget your blazer, and leave your cubey tidy or Matey will have something to say."

Having neither tunic nor blazer, Carola was unable to obey her Mentor, but she put on her brown skirt and cream blouse, and knotted the flame-coloured tie she had coaxed Cousin Maud to buy for her before she pulled on a brown cardigan—the best she could do. Then she hurried to hang up her dressing-gown, place her bedroom slippers neatly together under the bed, and set her brush and comb straight on the little bureau top. Clem arrived before she had done, and demanded her brush and comb bag. Slippers, too, it seemed, were to be put on the shelf

At this point, Carola decided that she had better let them know she was there, so she said with some diffidence, "I say, I'm here, you know."

"*What?*" There was a rush of feet, and then Clem, her red-brown mop tossing wildly about her, pulled the curtains aside. "When did you come up? What was all the fuss in aid of?"

Carola was in a quandary. She had promised to say nothing, and she was not very sure how to parry these questions. Luckily for her, the door at the end of the room opened, and someone came in.

"Clem Barrass!" said a stern voice. "What are you doing there? Why aren't you getting dressed?"

Clem went pink. "Please, Peggy, I was just talking to Carola Johnstone, the new girl," she said.

"Well, be quick, and tell her about the bathroom and so on, and then go and dress at once or you'll be late as usual," Peggy responded briskly.

"Yes, Peggy," Clem said meekly.

"Anyone still in bed?" Peggy demanded.

"I'll just see." Clem whirled round, but Peggy was before her.

"Out, everyone!" she called sharply.

There was an instant rustle, and every girl suddenly appeared round her curtains in various stages of undress. Clem pulled Carola forward and that young lady realised that the fair, very pretty girl standing at the door was the same as the one who had given out the hymn at Prayers, and must be the Head Girl.

"All right," Peggy said briefly. "Be quick and dress, all of you. Carry on, Clem."

She turned and left the room; everyone returned to her cubicle, and Clem, with a hasty "I'll just find out which your bather is," ran off down the dormitory to return with the information that the new girl came after her in bathroom 10. "So you'd best come along with me now," she concluded. "Strip your bed—I'll help you—and then grab your towels and sponge-bag, and come on."

She plunged at the bed, and in two minutes the sheets and blankets were hanging over the chairs; the pillow over the footrail; the mattress had been turned and humped up in the middle.

"Come on, now," the competent Clem ordered, "we'll

Matron arrived, picked up her lamp, and escorted the girl to a bathroom where she bade her wash and be quick about it.

Carola obeyed meekly; but she found time to wonder who had unpacked her cases for her, for she had found everything she needed, even the towels she had taken the precaution of bringing from Cousin Maud's. When she was ready, Matron took her back again to the dormitory, set the lamp down again, told her to say her prayers, and departed once more.

Carola was so nearly asleep that it is to be feared that her prayers were mainly lip-service. She tumbled into bed, where Matron found her when she came back, almost asleep, but wide awake enough to say, "Thank you, Matron. Good-night."

"Good-night," Matron responded after she had tucked the bed-clothes firmly in, and seen that all was as it should be. She picked up her lamp once more and left the cubicle. Before she had reached the dormitory door, Carola was sound asleep.

She was awakened next morning by the switching on of the lights and the sound of a big bell solemnly pealing for the beginning of the day. Still drowsy, she nevertheless threw back the clothes and jumped out of bed. Then she looked round, and triumph swelled her heart, driving away the last remnants of sleepiness. She was at school! Whatever happened now, at least she had had one night of it, and most likely one day to come, too. Then voices rose round her and put an end to her thoughts, and she listened eagerly.

"Oh dear! It simply *can't* be time to get up yet!" came from the cubicle on her right hand.

"Don't you believe it, young Polly!" was the reply from over the way. "It's seven o'clock, so out you get!"

"Oh, how I loathe early rising!" Polly groaned; but a thud told that she was out of bed, and sundry scrabblings probably meant that she was hunting for her slippers. "I say," she went on, "anyone know what's happened to that new girl—the one the Abbess yanked after her Prayers last night, I mean? Clem, weren't you sheep-dogging her? What became of her?"

"Not knowing, can't say," came in Clem's voice.

"I wonder why the Abbess wanted to see her?" This was someone else.

say he's a bit of a psychiatrist. In that case he'll understand the child, I expect. Well, as you say, we can only wait and see."

"I suppose Jo doesn't count?" Hilary asked in a detached manner.

"What *do* you mean?" Miss Annersley demanded, looking at her with the liveliest curiosity. " 'Jo doesn't count'? In what way may I ask?"

"Not telling anyone. Jo isn't any one, is she?"

Miss Annersley looked her up and down and then burst into peals of laughter. "I wish she could hear you! Oh, tell Jo by all means, if you like. Most likely we shall call her into consultation, Madge not being available."

Hilary looked round them all, "Has it dawned on you folk that we've got to do a certain amount of rearranging with this unexpected new kid?"

"I thought of it at once," Miss Annersley said rising. "Therefore, it means early rising tomorrow, so I'm going to bed now. Good-night everyone. Don't be late, please."

Chapter V

THE FIRST TASTE OF SCHOOL

BY the time Carola reached her cubicle, she was too tired to take in much of its details, even if Matron had given her any time to do so. Just outside the door that lady stopped and warned her to be very quiet, as all the rest would be asleep now, or ought to be. Then she opened the door, switching on the little hand-lamp she carried, and lighted Carola down the narrow aisle between cretonne curtains that fluttered in the breeze from the open windows. She stopped before one cubicle where the curtains had not been drawn, a fact she swiftly remedied after she had waved Carola inside. Then she set her lamp down on the bureau.

"Undress as quickly as you can," she said in low tones. "I'll be back in ten minutes to take you to the bathroom."

Carola undressed quickly, being almost morbidly careful about hanging her clothes over the backs of the two chairs to air and setting her shoes side by side in a corner. She untwisted her long pigtail and brushed it out, and then

"I seem to have heard you say that in the dim and distant past," Miss Wilson murmured.

"I seem to have had occasion for saying it most of the time I've been connected with this school," her friend said ruefully. "I said it *about* Joey and *to* her on more than one occasion, and I've gone on saying it about sundry pupils ever since. But I must say we've never been in quite such an awkward position before. Carola wouldn't think of that, however."

"At her age? Is it likely?" Miss Wilson demanded. "What do we do next?"

"I don't see what we can do but wait until we hear from this cousin and the child's parents. If they agree, the best thing will be for her to remain here. Mercifully we have a vacancy. I really feel very much annoyed when I think of our own situation. At the same time, I do sympathise with the girl. She has been very silly, but she had *some* excuse. If this cousin wasn't prepared to stay at home to look after her, she should have let her have her way and go to school. Wrong-headed as Carola has been, I do feel that she is not entirely to blame."

"Rosalie says you cabled that we could keep her here if necessary," said Hilary Burn.

"In the circumstances I don't see what else we could do. And now," she went on, looking round them all, "I want you people and Miss Slater—I must see her before we go to bed, by the way—to promise to say nothing about the thing to anyone else until I give you leave. If Carola stays with us the best thing will be to suppress the definitely irregular way in which she has come to us. If not, then I suppose we must give it out that her people have had to change their plans and she is not coming after all. That will depend, I suppose, on what Dr. Johnstone has to say about it."

"They mightn't want to pay our fees," Rosalie Dene murmured.

"Oh, I don't think there will be much difficulty on that point," Miss Annersley said briskly. "Obviously they are well-to-do people. What I *am* afraid of is that he may think she ought not to be indulged in her wish after the way she has tried to attain it—yes, Nell? What is it?" She looked at Miss Wilson.

"I only want to say that if she is the child of Dr. Andrew Johnstone of Calabar, he isn't very likely to think that way. I know some people who are friends of his and they

"and thanks most frightfully for being so kind to me."

Miss Annersley smiled at her for the first time during that interview. "I'm glad to hear you say that. Now goodnight, and go to sleep as fast as you can."

Carola followed Matron from the room, and once they were gone, Miss Annersley departed for the secretary's office where she found her closeted with Biddy O'Ryan, Miss Burn, and Miss Wilson, all three sitting round the table having coffee.

"Come on, Hilda!" the latter exclaimed. "We've been talking over the School's latest adventure. Did you know that it's all Biddy's fault? I *thought* we should have considered a dozen times before we decided to readmit her to our peaceful fold! Come and tell her what you think of her."

"Sure, how was I to know the little ass would think of such a thing?" protested Biddy O'Ryan indignantly. "I only told her a few stories about Tirol. *I* wasn't to know she'd go off at half-cock like this. Not that I altogether blame her, mind you," she added. "Trailing about from one place to another is no life for a kid of fourteen at all, at all."

"One moment!" Miss Annersley checked the riot. "Rosalie, did you get those two cables off safely?"

"I sent them all right. The post office didn't seem to have much idea when they'd reach their addresses," Miss Dene said doubtfully. Then she added eagerly, "Did you get the whole yarn from her? What had she to say for herself? What on earth is it all about?"

"An overdoing of travel plus a very natural desire to be with girls of her own age," Miss Annersley said as she sat down. "Coffee, Hilary? Oh, thank you. I can do with a cup of coffee, for my head's reeling. That wretched girl had actually disappeared from the *boat* and left her unfortunate cousin to imagine all sorts of ghastly happenings! I only hope my radiogram reaches her quickly before she manages to cable the child's parents. I also think she might have kept a closer watch on the young monkey. She seems to have left her to go by herself to the cabin without bothering to see that she got there. When I taxed Miss Carola with unkindness, she simply said, "I never thought of *that*!" I do wish girls would learn to *think* before they start out to do mad things!"

fighting back her tears with an effort. "It's in Nigeria."

"Thank you, my dear. Oh, Miss Dene, I want you to send another cable—Nigeria, this time." She dictated a reassuring message to Nigeria, and then, as Miss Dene was leaving the room, she added, "When you have sent that off, would you mind asking Matron to come for Carola? It is growing late and I think she had better go to bed at once. We can discuss the whole position tomorrow."

Miss Dene went off, and the Head turned to the pupil who had so calmly foisted herself on to them. "Now, my dear, Matron will come and take you to bed. Tomorrow you will go into School with the rest of the girls, and you must remain here until I can get into proper touch with your people. In the meantime, I am going to ask you to say nothing at all about this very foolish escapade of yours. If, by any chance, your parents should decide to leave you with us, it would do you no good for the girls to know what you have done. All the best of our girls would think you very childish and absurd to have done such a thing, and the sillier ones need no encouragement from such an example as you have set. Promise me, please."

Very red, Carola gave the required promise. It had never dawned on her that there might have to be all sorts of explanations to the School at large; nor that, as Miss Annersley said, the more sensible of the girls would look down on her for carrying out such a wild plan. She knew from her reading that a bad start in school might hang about her for the rest of her school-life, and she realised dimly that the Head was being very generous in trying to prevent that for her.

A knock at the door sounded, and when Matron appeared, the only thing Carola wanted to do was to go to bed and to sleep and forget for the next few hours all about her mad action.

"This is Carola Johnstone, Matron," Miss Annersley said. "She is very tired and should go to bed now. Will you take her up to her dormitory and see to her? We must leave all questions until the morning, I think. I want her to go to sleep as soon as possible."

Matron nodded. "I quite agree. Come along, Carola. It's more than time you were in bed, especially after your journey. Be quick, child!"

Carola turned to say good-night to Miss Annersley. "I'm sorry if—if I'm being an awful nuisance," she said shyly,

"I see. Then please add, 'Can keep if necessary,' Miss Dene. Thank you."

Miss Dene, with a bewildered look at Carola, withdrew, and Miss Annersley turned to the culprit. "And now, child, I think you must tell me the whole story. Of course we must keep you for the night, at any rate. Presently you will go up with Matron, who is putting you into a vacant cubicle in Clem Barrass's dormitory; but I must get this straightened out as far as possible first. I won't keep you long, though. You are too tired for any discussion. Now begin and tell me all about it. You say you hate travelling? Tell me why."

Thus urged, Carola contrived to tell the bare outline of her story, aided here and there by questions from the Head. It took some time, but at last Miss Annersley had a very fair idea of the whole thing. She sat back in her chair as Carola concluded with a final statement of her hatred of travel, and a passionate plea for school, and there was silence in the room for a minute or two, save for the gentle hissing of the flames.

Carola felt better now that she had relieved her mind. She was quite satisfied to sit there, watching the dancing firelight. There was an atmosphere of peace in this room that soothed and calmed her fretted nerves. Presently, however, the Head turned to her.

"Now, Carola, it is much too late for me to talk to you properly. I will see you tomorrow and then we will go into the whole matter thoroughly. In the meantime, please give me your father's full name and address. I must send him a cable at once. Did you ever think that one of the first things your cousin would do when she found you were missing would be to let them know at once? We must relieve their anxiety as soon as we can. I expect your mother is frantic about it."

Carola jumped up with a cry. "*Oh*! I never thought of that! Oh, Miss Annersley, Mother will be nearly crackers! Oh, what *shall* I do?"

She was so nearly on the verge of wild tears that Miss Annersley sprang up, too, and put an arm round her. "Steady, Carola! If I cable at once, I expect it will be all right. Probably the cables will arrive together—or very nearly so." She touched the bell once more. "What is your father's full name and address?"

"Dr. Andrew Johnstone, Calabar," Carola replied,

even staying anywhere for long. I wanted school, but she said she'd promised Mother and Dad she would look after me while they were away, and she couldn't do it properly unless I was with her, and she wasn't going to alter the whole plan of her life just for me, and I ought to be grateful to her for seeing so much of the world. I'm not! I hate the whole thing; and so —I ran away."

Miss Annersley looked a trifle startled. "Do you mean that—my child, where *is* this cousin of yours? She must be told at once where you are. She must be frantic with worry about you!"

"She sailed for Jamaica this morning," Carola said, looking startled in her turn.

This was a jolt for the Head. She had fancied that the girl had slipped off from home or wherever she had been staying with this Cousin Maud, and it would be merely a case of ringing up somewhere—the police, if necessary—to tell the lady where her young cousin was, and returning the child to her in the morning. This news complicated matters horribly. Leaning over, she touched a bell, and there was silence until a tap at the door heralded the entrance of a slight, fair woman in the early thirties, who came quietly in and stood waiting.

"Oh, Miss Dene," the Head said pleasantly, "I want you to send a radiogram for me as soon as possible."

"Certainly, Miss Annersley." Miss Dene went over to a small secretaire in the window, and picked up a pad lying there. "To whom do I address it?"

Miss Annersley looked at Carola. "What is your cousin's full name and the name of the ship in which she has sailed?" she asked.

"Maud Curry—Miss—and the ship is the S.S. *Pantyne*," Carola replied mechanically.

"Thank you. Very well then, Miss Dene. 'To Miss Maud Curry. S.S. *Pantyne*. Carola safe at Chalet School, St. Briavel's Island, South Wales. Please cable instructions.' You had better sign my name and add 'Principal' after it." She paused and looked at Carola. "One moment, Miss Dene. Carola, have you any friends or relations in England to whom you can go?"

Carola shook her head. "No, Miss Annersley. Mother and Dad are in Equatorial Africa, west coast. That's why they couldn't have me with them. I've no uncles or aunts except Uncle Jim in Canada."

354

room, will you come to the study, my dear? Ask someone to bring you, please. I want to see you."

The Head gave the command to stand, and the School rose to its feet while the mistress at the piano turned round and struck a chord. Like one girl, the ranks turned and then, to the tune of a bright quickstep, they filed from the room. Clem had caught Carola's arm and made her stand back so that the rest passed them. When the room was empty, even the mistresses departed, she led her off, down one corridor and along another, where they came to a door before which she paused and tapped. Miss Annersley's voice bade them enter, and the helpful Clem opened the door and shoved Carola through, hissing as she did so, "Go on in, and don't forget to curtsy!"

Chapter IV

CAROLA HAS TO EXPLAIN

CLEM'S last injunction completed Carola's state of confusion, and it was a very discomforted young person who advanced into the room after closing the door behind her and executing a jerky bob of her knees which was intended to be a curtsy. Miss Annersley was alone, seated by the fire in a tall arm-chair, gazing into the heart of the flames. As Carola came towards her, she lifted her head and looked gravely at the girl.

"You are Carola Johnstone?" she said quietly. "Come to the fire and sit down. I want to hear what all this means."

Carola sat down and looked dumbly at the lady.

Miss Annersley had not taught for twenty-seven years for nothing. She knew girls, and she could make a very good guess at what Carola was feeling.

"You know you aren't entered for this school, don't you?" she asked.

"Yes," Carola replied.

"What school *were* you entered for, then?"

"None at all. Cousin Maud wanted to take me to Jamaica with a governess, and I'm so tired of travelling about and never having anywhere for a real home—not

again, welcoming all back to the School for the new term and hoping that the new girls would be happy with them.

"Now it is getting late," she finished, "so I shall say no more tonight. Miss Wilson will call the roll and then you must all go to bed. Tomorrow, those of you who have not yet unpacked will be excused from lessons while Matron wants you. All new girls who have not done our entrance test must go to the prefects' room after Prayers—someone will show you where to go—and a mistress will see to you. Just one piece of news for you. I know that most of you have heard of Biddy O'Ryan and many of the Seniors will remember her from their own Junior days. Miss O'Ryan has come to take the place of Miss Burnett, another old girl, and I am sure you will all want to give her a hearty welcome."

Led by the Head Girl, the School welcomed Miss O'Ryan with a quick outburst of hand-clapping, and Carola, who had already discovered her sitting among the Staff, noted that the charming Irish face went crimson for a moment before the young mistress rose to acknowledge the clapping. Then the girls quieted down as Miss Annersley held up her hand, and Miss Wilson, producing a long roll, began to read the names rapidly, every girl answering "Adsum" as her name came.

On and on she went and naturally no Carola Johnstone was among them. When she closed the roll, saying, "That is all, girls," Clem turned to her new acquaintance, open-mouthed with surprise. Miss Slater, however, had already risen and crossed the dais and was saying something, and before Clem could do more than gasp, "What on earth ——?" the Head had turned to the girls once more.

"Is Carola Johnstone here?" she inquired.

Carola was dumb with shock. In all her planning, she had never bothered to think what must happen once she was safely at school. She remained glued to her seat and never stirred until the watchful Clem poked her.

"Go on, you mutt! Stand up and say it's you!" she muttered.

Thus urged, Carola slowly rose to her feet and faced the gaze of not only the two Heads, but the wildly startled look of Miss O'Ryan.

Miss Annersley had been Head for too long to show much sign of the amazement that was inwardly consuming her. All she said was, "Ah! I see. When you leave the

"Oh, well, that's O.K. then. If you were Catholic you'd have to go with the Catholics for Prayers, you see," Clem explained. "In here!"

She gave Carola a friendly little shove, and the new girl found herself in her first school hall. She looked round eagerly as soon as Clem had steered her to her place. It had originally been a big double drawing-room, but was now cleared, and the walls had been colour-washed a sunshiny yellow with dark green woodwork. Prints of famous pictures hung at intervals round the walls, interspersed with boards of golden oak, bearing names and dates in gilt. Carola knew that these must be Honours Boards, and she simply longed for a chance to go round and read what they said. There was no hope at the moment, for a bell rang and the quiet buzz of chatter that had filled the Hall hushed at once. A minute later the mistresses came through a door at the far end of the room, with Miss Annersley last, and formed into a semi-circle behind the tall reading-desk where the Head took up her stand. A slender, very fair girl rose from her seat at the end of one of the seats, which stood to one side of the dais, and gave out the number of the hymn. Clem had seen that Carola was supplied with a copy of the School's own hymnbook, so that young lady was able to join with the others in singing "Lord, behold us with Thy blessing." As her voice rose, sweet and clear, and amazingly powerful for a girl of fourteen, two or three people in front turned to stare, and the mistress at the piano also turned her head with startled look to gaze at the ranks of singing girls.

The parable of the talents came next; and then they knelt while Miss Annersley read the collect for the day and the "Lighten our darkness" before they all joined in in repeating "Our Father," and—for the little ones—"Gentle Jesus." The blessing followed and then they all stood up.

"Sit down, girls," Miss Annersley commanded; and they sat down on the long forms and waited for a moment or two until the door at the top of the room opened again, this time to admit a stream of girls who went quietly to take their places beside the others on the forms. Two or three mistresses joined those on the dais, and a tall, white-haired lady with an amazingly young face went to the reading-desk. Carola knew this must be the other Head and looked at her with interest.

When everyone was in her place, Miss Annersley spoke

announced. She scanned the pegs again. "It's most unlikely you'd be in a junior Splash, and this is the only one there was any room in. Let's see. Oh, *luck*! Here's one vacant! You snaffle it and we can see Miss Dene about a label for you later. Hang up your coat and cap and wait till I come. I'm at the other side." She hurried off to her own peg, leaving Carola to do as she was told, but was quickly back.

"Now then, it's just on supper-time and I'm ravenous, and I guess you are even more so. There's the gong! Come on!"

She took Carola's arm and pulled her out into the corridor where they joined a long stream of girls of all sorts and sizes on the way to the big dining-room where Clem seated her beside herself, and after Grace, jumped up and went to the buttery hatch to come back with two plates of cottage pie, steaming and savoury and very welcome to Carola, who suddenly felt famished.

"Wire in!" Clem commanded as she set the noble plateful before the new girl. "You look starved!"

"Oh, I *am*!" Carola said fervently. "Thanks fearfully much, Clem."

Clem sat down with a grin, and proceeded to tackle her own while carrying on half a dozen conversations with as many people, who all seemed to want to know what she had done during the holidays. The silent Carola, steadily eating her way through her share, noted that everyone seemed to like Clem, who kept a watchful eye on her and saw to it that she had all she needed, but was too busy to say much to her. The girl on her other side, who had been saluted as "Lalla," made a few friendly remarks; but on the whole Carola felt herself very much one alone. She was the only new girl at this table and, from what she heard, she gathered that there would be only a few of them this term. However, all things considered, she got through supper very well. The brisk walk through the fresh January air had roused her thoroughly, and she felt decidedly better when she had finished her meal, which was topped off with a plateful of junket and bottled plums. But after supper came Prayers; and after that, dismissal to the dormitories; and now her troubles began in real earnest.

"Are you Protestant or Catholic?" Clem demanded as, supper over, they marched along to the school hall.

Carola stared at her. "I'm Church of England," she said. "Why?"

course I've read them. Is she really your aunt? You lucky soul!"

"Well, actually she isn't," Mary-Lou replied honestly, if reluctantly. "Only, she and Mother are pals, so she said I was to call her Auntie. Two of her triplets are at school, you know——"

"You're talking too much," Clem interrupted. "I always did say your tongue was hung in the middle and waggled at both ends. Anyhow, we're nearly there, so you'd better put a lid on it, Mary-Lou, and go to your own form. See you later." She gave Mary-Lou a shove and that young chatterbox departed after making a weird and wonderful grimace at her.

The ferry had reached port and the mistresses were calling the girls into line. The gangplanks rattled down with a great clanking of chains and such part of the School as was on board marched off and through the little turnstile on to the high-road which, as Clem informed the new girl, wound right across the island.

It was not really a long walk—about a mile—and the girls were glad of the chance to stretch their legs which were cramped after the long journey in the motor coaches. They chattered gaily among themselves as they wound up the road which ran between high hedges. Before long they were turning in at big gates and going up a drive walled on either side by a high holly hedge. A dark mass loomed up at the farther end and then a sudden stream of light poured down the drive as someone opened the front door.

"Welcome back, girls!" said a deep, very musical voice; and as the girls replied, Carola realised that here was one of the Heads.

They marched in, depositing their cases in a deep pile in a corner of the wide hall and then were sent to the cloakrooms.

"I expect you'll be in our Splashery," Clem told Carola. "Come away and we'll find your peg and locker."

Carola meekly followed her new friend into the long, narrow room with pegs round the walls, and peg-stands set down the middle, and Clem began a hasty search for her name—something that naughty Carola knew would be quite unavailing, but she didn't see what she could do about it at present. Presently Clem turned to the new girl looking blank.

"Someone's slipped up. Your name's not here," she

Carola looked round. The speaker was a sturdy twelve-year-old, with two fair pigtails bobbing about her shoulders. She looked up at the new girl with dancing blue eyes, and grinned companionably. "Hope you'll like us," she remarked. "We're a pretty good school, if I do say it. What's your name? Clem did say it, but I wasn't really listening, so I didn't catch it."

"Mary-Lou, you hush up!" retorted Clem herself who was close at hand. "I never knew a kid with as much cheek. You've enough for fifty your size."

Mary-Lou remained unperturbed. "I was only being polite. I'll tell her my name first, if you like. I'm Mary-Lou Trelawney," she turned to the new girl. "You know that this ginger creature is Clem Barrass, and this," drawing forward a slight, dainty girl of her own age, "is my other great pal, Verity-Anne Carey. Now tell us your name."

"I'm Carola Johnstone," Carola replied rather dazedly. She knew so little of other girls that Mary-Lou's unruffled calm rather stumped her.

"Really? Then you're jolly lucky!" Mary-Lou informed her.

"Lucky?" Carola stared at her. "Why? How do you mean, lucky?"

"Having a name like that, of course. There's not another Carola in the place, though we've dozens of Annes and Pamelas and Elizabeths and things like that. How d'you spell it, by the way?"

"C-a-r-o-l-a," Carola spelt for her, and Mary-Lou considered it.

"But isn't that 'Carōla'?" she asked at last.

"Rather not! It's Carola, without any accent anywhere," the owner of the name told her.

"Well, I'm glad to know. If you hadn't told me I'd have thought it was spelt like the Christmas carollers," Mary-Lou explained. She gave a sudden deep chuckle. "I say, Auntie Jo will be all over it! She's always on the look-out for new names for her books. She's a writer, you know. Her name's Josephine M. Bettany—at least her writing name is. Of course, really, she's Mrs. Maynard now. Have you read any of hers—*Tessa in Tyrol*, or *The Rose Patrol in the Alps*, or any of those?"

By this time, Carola knew where she was. Biddy O'Ryan had told her all about Jo Maynard, and she was a Josephine Bettany fan and owned most of the books. "Of

eight this morning and I seem to have been going ever since—especially since I left Southampton after seeing the liner off."

"And it's a good bit after six now! Oh, poor you!" the girl in front sympathised with her. "Well, it's early bed for everyone tonight. Keep going for a while longer and then you can do all the sleeping you want till seven tomorrow morning."

Somehow or other, Carola contrived to keep awake now, and when they finally reached the ferry-landing at Carnbach and tumbled out of the buses, the fresh breeze from the sea swept the sleepiness from her eyes for the time being. She stared round at all she could see under the light from the arc-lamp. The black water rippling against the landing, reflected back the rays, and tied up to the posts were two broad-beamed ferryboats, clearly waiting for them. They were lined up in pairs and each girl took charge of her own case as her name was called when it came from the boot. Suddenly, Miss Slater paused in her calling.

"Carola Johnstone!" she read. "How is this, Carola? I thought I had called your name already?"

"I have two cases, Miss Slater," Carola said, going red under the startled eyes of the girls about her.

"But the instructions distinctly say that each girl must bring only a night-case with her—no more. Everything else should have been put into your trunk."

"I—I haven't brought a trunk," Carola faltered. "It's all in the cases."

Miss Slater raised her eyebrows; but Miss Burn interfered. "Oh, well, Carola can explain when we get to the Big House. Take the thing, Carola, and let's get on. We shall be here all night at this rate! Here you are!"

Carola took the case; no more was said; and presently the last girl was on board, the gangplanks were wound up, and the ferries swung clear of the landing-stage and set their course for the island. From the chatter of the girls, Carola discovered that this was the first time most of them had been on the water after dark. She joined the excited crowd thronging round the sides to watch the reflections from their own lights as the lumbering ferry steadily ploughed her way through the tranquil water. She sniffed the salt air with appreciation and felt quite wide awake.

"Ooh! Doesn't it look *wizard*!" said a small, clear voice close to her.

I've seen them in the shop windows, though. Was she really at the Chalet School?"

"Rather!" Half a dozen voices chimed in on this.

"Well, I wonder why——" she suddenly stopped.

"Yes?" Clem prompted her. "You wonder why—what?"

"Oh, nothing. Tell me about Lavender. What a jolly name!"

Clem shot her a quick glance and then decided to change the subject. "Oh, Lavender just hated school at first. She'd travelled just about everywhere since she was a tiny kid, and she didn't like school in the least."

"Well, that's not me," Carola said with decision. "I'm only longing for it. I'm sick of trains and planes and boats. It'll be a rest to settle down somewhere for a few months and not be for ever on the move."

"Oh, I see," said Clem, clearly not seeing at all. She added politely, "I hope you aren't too awfully tired with today's journey?"

"It'll soon be over now, though, won't it? I'm awfully sleepy, but I think I can keep awake a while longer. Have we very far to go?"

"Oh, not so terribly far," Clem told her. "Look here, if you're sleepy, change places with me and tuck your mack under your head. I'll wake you when we get near Carnbach—if I know it in time," she added with a giggle.

"Why won't you know it?" Carola asked when the change had been made and she was sitting next the window, while Clem expertly rolled up her raincoat and tucked it between her head and the side of the coach.

"Well, you see, this is only the third term we've been at St. Briavel's, and before, it's always been daylight when we arrived; but now it's dark and I may not recognise my landmarks," Clem explained. "Are you all O.K.? Then you tuck down and have a nap. We'll probably see the lights, anyhow."

Carola was thankful to do as she was told. She did not exactly sleep, for she was conscious of a murmuring all the time; but she certainly dozed, and when Clem woke her fully with a gentle shake and the news that they were running along the coast-road, she sat up, yawning widely.

"Feel better?" Clem asked. "Have you been travelling far today?"

"It feels like hundreds of miles. We set off at half-past

They moved over to the last of the coaches where the pretty young mistress was standing, and clambered in, Clem taking care to see that Carola sat beside her. Other girls followed them, and when the coach was full Miss Burn climbed in and settled down at the back, and they rolled away.

They were soon out of the town and running through the valleys where here and there they saw lights from farmhouses and cottages far up the hillside. The girls chattered eagerly among themselves and Carola sat silently listening to them and trying to suppress yawns. She was very tired, not only with the journey, but also with the mixture of emotions she had felt through the day, and she was beginning to feel terribly hungry. Presently Clem, who seemed to live somewhere in the Hebrides and have artist parents, turned to her politely.

"This your first time at school, Carola?"

"No; not quite," Carola replied. "I went to a Kinder when I was little. Then Dad got a job in Equatorial Africa and I couldn't go with them, of course——"

"Why ever not?" demanded someone sitting in front who had turned round to listen when the new girl began to speak.

"Because it isn't the right sort of climate for English children—too hot," Carola informed her.

"Oh, I see. Why didn't you go to school in England, though?"

"Well, you see, I've been living with Dad's cousin and she liked travelling about and took me with her. Now she's gone to Jamaica, so I'm coming to school, as I didn't want to go."

"Oh, I see. Won't you be rather bored after going about like that, though?"

Carola shook her head decidedly. "Not me! I'm sick of it!"

She was interrupted by a screech from the girl in front. "I say, you people, I've just thought of it! She's exactly like Lavender Leigh!"

Carola stared. "Lavender Leigh?"

"Don't you know the 'Lavender Laughs' series? Well, Lavender Leigh who was at school till the end of last summer term was 'Lavender.' Oh, you ought to read them. They're *wizard*!"

Carola shook her head. "I've never read them. I think

armed with a list of the pupils they had to meet. The younger lady smiled at her sympathetically.

"New, and very tired, aren't you?" she said. "What a horrid situation for you! She turned to her companion. "Found her, Miss Slater?"

Miss Slater, busy with her list, shook her head. "Not a Carola in the list—unless this queer scrawl at the bottom is it. It might by anything! Rosalie must have been in a mighty hurry at the end and just scribbled it in anyhow. You *are* for the Chalet School, aren't you?" she added doubtfully to Carola. "What's happened to your beret badge?"

"I—I didn't get one," Carola stammered, blushing violently.

"Didn't? Oh, those posts!" She groaned loudly. "Well, it must be all right, and we can see you get your badges at school tomorrow. Now, let me see. Annis Lovel! Come here, dear."

Annis Lovel, a sturdy, dark-eyed girl with a short mop of thick black curls, detached herself from the group of girls with whom she had been chattering excitedly and came up, saying, "Yes, Miss Slater?"

"This is Carola Johnstone—isn't that what you said?—a new girl. Take charge of her, will you? And you people stop gossiping and get into your coach or we'll be here all night."

"Yes, Miss Slater." Annis turned to Carola. "Come along, and I'll show you what to do. How old are you?"

"Fourteen," Carola said, staring. She had never expected to be asked her age so soon.

"Good enough. Here you are—Clem Barrass!" She caught a red-haired girl of about Carola's own age, who was chattering eagerly with two or three others. "Clem, I want you to look after Carola Johnstone. This is her. Take her along with your crowd, will you?"

"O.K.," Clem nodded. "Come on, Carola."

Carola went, and Clem, with an arm through hers, took her back to the group, and introduced them. "Here's a new girl, you folk—Carola Johnstone. This is Jean Ackroyd, Carola, and Anne Whitney and Gillian Moggeridge. We're all in the same form."

The others said, "Hello!" and then Jean added in a rather different tone, "There's Miss Burn signalling to us to get a move on. Come on! We're to go in her coach."

puffs and sandwiches in the café and even found time to rush into a bookshop and invest in a book.

At the station a kindly porter, seeing the schoolgirl in difficulties with her cases, book, handbag, and parcels, came to help her. He found her a corner-seat, swung up the cases on the rack, and left her extremely pleased with herself. She took a packet of chocolate out of her handbag and settled down to enjoy it and *Because of Vivien*.

So far, so good; but at Cardiff she had the first of her real difficulties. She had never been in the big station and she lost her way and nearly lost her train into the bargain. However, she caught it by the skin of her teeth and then found that she had somehow lost the remainder of her food. She faced a long journey with nothing more substantial than what was left of her chocolate and a bag of boiled sweets.

Well, it couldn't be helped now. She had caught the train and that was something. Miss O'Ryan had told her that the last coaches for Carnbach left Swansea after this train arrived there, and if she had lost it, she would have been stranded overnight.

There were no Chalet School girls in her carriage, for they travelled in specially labelled compartments, and in the circumstances Carola had decided it would be better to keep clear of them until she was as near the School as possible. She had put on her brown coat and beret and hoped that in the darkness and on the motor coaches she would pass muster as a new girl.

At long last they arrived at Swansea. Outside the station three big coaches were drawn up, and already the girls were climbing in. She noticed that they added their cases to a pile at one side, so she did the same, and then advanced rather timidly towards the second bus where girls were filing in under the eyes of two mistresses. A third one was already in the first bus, settling various people in their seats. Not very sure what to do, Carola went up to the two ladies still outside.

"Please," she said in a tired voice, "I'm Carola Johnstone. I couldn't get into the proper carriage because I nearly missed the train."

The elder of the two ladies promptly pulled out a list and scanned it, much to Carola's horror. It had never dawned on her that mistresses on escort duty would be watching what was going on with interested eyes and clinging to her cases like grim death.

Presently, the bugle rang out again. Gangways were cleared; hawsers were cast off; gaily-coloured streamers were flung from those on deck to those on the wharf; and with great hooting, the liner swung slowly and majestically round, headed by her guardian tugs, and set her course for the open sea. The crowds struck up "Auld Lang Syne," and the great vessel moved forward to the sound of a great wave of melody. Carola watched her, wondering secretly if she would manage to get safely through the dock gates. She saw a little party of a woman and two girls standing waving violently. Tears poured down the face of the middle-aged woman, and the two girls kept mopping their eyes. She slipped forward, and when, the liner now well away, they turned to leave, she tagged on behind them. The dock officials seeing her there, made no demur, and she passed through and out on to the road with triumph in her heart. She had accomplished the first part of her plan in safety.

From the tales she had coaxed out of Miss O'Ryan at Penny Rest, Carola had learned that the Chalet School was on St. Briavel's, a tiny island off the coast of South Wales. It was reached from Carnbach, a small port, and she had heard that the girls went to Swansea by train and were met there by motor coaches which took the shortest way through the mountains. Her plan was to find her way to the shopping centre of Southampton, get lunch somewhere, and then make for the station, buying food for the journey on the way. She and Cousin Maud had reached the city the day before, and while that lady had taken an hour's rest on her bed at their hotel in the afternoon, Carola had slipped out and made inquiries about trains, so that she knew what she must do. Once she had reached the School, she reckoned that they must keep her, at any rate until someone in authority had been contacted, for the house at Boncombe was closed, and she had no relations in England.

The first part of her plan was easily carried out, for a bus arrived just then, and took her and her cases to the shopping centre, where she found a café and had a meal. That finished, she found a taxi and drove to the station, where she was just in time to catch a train for Cardiff where she had been told she must change. She had bought jam

cramming it with everything she was likely to find useful at school. She had rejected her own old ones, routing out one of her cousin's which was twice as large, and the trunk which had gone to the hold marked "Not wanted on the voyage" contained little but summer clothes. Everything else was in the cases. She had taken the precaution of fastening straps round them, for really they were so crammed she was afraid they might burst if she trusted to locks only.

"I wonder," the naughty girl muttered to herself as she stood to one side, watching her cousin talking animatedly to her friends, "if it would be safe for me to get off now? She's awfully keen on these people, and I don't believe she'd notice if I did slip away."

She eyed her cases doubtfully. They were very heavy, and she simply must have them with her. Carola felt sure that she would need everything in them at school. She fully intended writing to her parents once she was settled there, and getting their permission to stay on; but it would be some weeks before she could hear. Of her cousin's feelings when she discovered that her charge had vanished, Carola never troubled. It is doubtful if she even thought of that side of it.

At that moment Cousin Maud turned for a minute from her friends and came to the girl. "It's time we were going on board, Carola. Pick up your cases, child. You know our cabin, so take them there and begin unpacking until I come to you. I won't be long and we may be separated in the crowd—why, Mrs. Barnett, are *you* coming, too? Quite a gathering of the clans, isn't it?" She beamed at a tall, pretty woman who had just come up.

Mrs. Barnett gave an exclamation. "Miss Curry! Well, isn't the world small? Are you coming to Jamaica? What fun! I've just been seeing my young monkey off to her school; and I suppose you've been doing the same by your small cousin? Oh, there goes the bugle. We'd better make a move, I expect."

Carola picked up her cases and moved forward—exactly six steps. Then a sudden rush of the crowd separated her from Cousin Maud and she slid back to the outskirts of the throng, while Miss Curry moved forward, gaily chatting with her friends and quite satisfied that Carola would go straight to their cabin and she would find her there presently. Carola, however, was now behind a pile of cases,

rested and kept out of draughts and damp, she might be alive this moment, poor little soul!"

Biddy looked very serious as she followed Jo upstairs to the pretty bedroom at the top of the house. Biddy had picked up her case as they passed through the hall, and when they had reached their goal she dropped it with a sigh of relief. "This looks good! You're right, Joey: I'm very tired. I'll sleep well in that bed."

She was in bed when Jo came up twenty minutes later with hot milk. She found her guest half-asleep, though she roused up enough to sip the milk and say good-night before she sank back on her pillow, and was literally drowned in sleep before her hostess had closed the door behind her after tucking her in with a kiss and switching off the light.

Chapter III

ESCAPE!

CAROLA glanced round with a hunted air. Cousin Maud was busy chatting with some old acquaintances she had just met who, so they had informed her, were taking the same cruise as herself. She was still indignant about Miss Bacon. Part of her wrath had descended on the head of Carola, who had never found her so fussy and trying before. Needless to state, it required only this to confirm that young person in her decision not to sail. After the first she had wavered a little; now she was determined. Go to Jamaica she would *not*!

During the sixteen days which had elapsed since New Year's Day, Carola had laid her plans carefully. She had some money—four or five pounds—for her father had sent her a cheque to buy her own Christmas present, and Cousin Maud had cashed it for her while they were at Penny Rest. Carola had not spent a penny of it, having no need and not seeing anything she particularly wanted. In addition, she had saved her pocket money for some weeks. Money was the thing that least worried her, therefore.

Clothes might have been a difficulty, but Cousin Maud had left her to do all her own packing and the young monkey had made full use of her new expanding suitcase, weirder exploits. "They do happen to me," she admitted. "What about this kid?"

"She told me she was going to beg and beg her cousin to let her come to the School," Biddy stated. "I only hope Miss Curry—that's the name she has on her—will see reason, for that child needs school more than most in my opinion. What's more, she *wants* it more than most. Sure, 'tis the main idea the creature has in her head just now. Of course, after all I told her about the Chalet School, nothing would serve her but that she must go there. Dear knows what will happen!"

"Let's hope this cousin of hers sees sense. It's absurd for a girl of that age being dragged round the world from pillar to post! We had one specimen of that kind of thing in young Lavender, poor kid!"

"Yes; but Lavender liked it. She'd never known anything else—or not to count, anyhow—and she hated school at first. Carola *wants* school, I tell ye. Miss Curry means well enough I dare say," Biddy continued honestly, "but she's not unselfish enough to give up her own fun, so poor Carola has to be a kind of wandering Jew," she concluded with a yawn.

Jo got to her feet. "Time you were in bed. I've put you into Robin's room as she won't be home for a while yet, and school begins in two days' time for you."

"I'm longing to see her again—Daisy, too. What's Rob doing now, by the way? I know Daisy's heart and soul in her doctoring."

"Oh, my dear! Of all things she insisted on taking up social service! We let her try, but she isn't strong enough, and she caught a cold which she couldn't shake off. That's one reason why she's in Switzerland. You know what sort of a heritage she has from her mother, and how anxious we all used to be about her years ago. She's far, far stronger now than anyone ever hoped; but she can't do strenuous things like social service. What she'll do when she comes back—which won't be until that cold is cleared up for keeps—I couldn't tell you. Rob's a darling but she knows her own mind, I can tell you. Mercifully, she's generally open to reason. There's a lot to be said for bringing up children to be obedient, Biddy."

"I agree with you. Mavis was an example of what happens when ye do *not*! If she'd done as she was told and

right up in the bush, so school was a difficulty. I helped out by teaching them, and when Mavis died, Mrs. Grant asked me to stay on until Lydia—that's the baby—was old enough to go away to school with the others. So I stayed. That's all."

"I see. Then Lydia is old enough for boarding school now?"

"Ten last August. She went with the others when they went back. So then I wrote to Miss Annersley and asked her could she find me a job back home, and she wrote and said Mary Burnett was leaving to be married and they would need a history mistress and would I like to come? There was only the one answer to that as ye know yourself. I couldn't leave Burra-Burra until the girls went, and Mrs. Grant wanted me to stay on with her even then."

Jo chuckled. "I'm glad you didn't stay. I filled in last term, but I can't go on, of course. I've got my own job here, with all my family. Besides that, Madge and Jem want us to go out to Canada at Easter with all the kids and stay until they come home—June, some time, they think—and I'd love to go. Now, tell me how you liked Penny Rest."

"Och, Joey, 'tis a real home from home it is. I'd a good time there, I can tell you. I made a new friend there," she added with a gurgle.

Jo gave her a quick look, but Biddy's face was transparently innocent. "Who was it?" she demanded.

"A girl of fourteen—rather a jolly kid. Not pretty in the least, but such a vivid little face, and full of bright ideas. She has the queer mix-up in her life."

"What do you mean about a queer mix-up?" Jo asked.

"Well, her parents are on the West coast of Africa, so they can't have her with them, and she's in charge of a cousin who likes to globe-trot. Carola told me it was fun at first, but she hates it now, never having a home, or going to school like other girls. Sure, she nearly had the facet off me for stories about our School." Again came that low chuckle as Biddy added sweetly, "I told her all about *you*!"

"Didn't tell her any of your own evil doings, I suppose?" Jo snapped.

"I did so! But sure, Joey, there's never a one of us has had so many queer adventures as you have. 'Tis a fly-paper for adventures you are!"

Jo chuckled in her turn as she remembered some of her

woman sitting in a big chair with a tiny baby on each arm. "Jo! That's Madame! But—are ye telling me those are *hers*?"

"I am indeed—twin sons, so David has brothers at long last. The only snag," Jo went on ruefully, "is that he's nearly old enough to be their father—sixteen in May!—so they won't be much of pals for him. Still he's very thrilled about them. The girls, of course, nearly went crackers when we told them. One's Kevin and the other's Kester—the old English form of Christopher." She stopped to laugh. "Madge is so bucked with herself for having caught up with Mollie and me! I say it's her own fault for having such enormous intervals between babies. *We* were much more reasonable."

"Yours aren't so close as all that," Biddy argued. "You went and had triplets as a beginning; but there's three years between them and Stephen, and isn't Michael three years younger than Charles?"

"That's a lot closer than Madge's crowd, anyway. Fifteen and a half years between David and this pair, and only three girls between. I admit there's not quite two years between David and Sybil, but she was four and a half when Josette arrived, and Josette was nearly five when Ailie came along. There's a book of snaps as well, but you can see that later. I want to hear *your* news now I've told you our biggest piece. First of all, what about Australia? How did you like it?"

"Quite good in spots. I'd never want to live there—it wouldn't suit me as a home at all, at all. Still, I've enjoyed me four years."

"I've never said anything about it to you before, Biddy," Jo said gravely as she refilled Biddy's cup, "but we all thought you played up splendidly when you offered to go back with that poor child and see her safely home. Only—why on earth did you stay so long?"

Biddy looked thoughtful. "Sure, I couldn't do anything else. She—well, she sort of clung to me. She'd loved Oxford so, and I was the only bit of it left to her. We all knew it couldn't be for long—she was too ill for that, though she did revive for a while once we got her home and she lived for fifteen months, which was more than Dr. Jem gave her when he saw us off on the boat. Her folk begged me to stay with her till the end and I'll never be sorry I did. Then there were three quite little ones and their place was

Jo poured out and then looked expectantly at the guest over the rim of her cup.

"I'm disappointed about one thing," Biddy announced as she sat back in her chair. "I wanted to see your family."

"You'll see them soon enough," Jo told her cheerfully.

"Oh, I know; but I wanted to see them *now*!" Biddy lamented. "D'you happen to remember that Charles was just a baby that no one thought would live when I went to Australia? And I've never seen Michael *at all*. How old are they all now?"

"The girls were nine last November, and Stephen will be six next month. Charles is five in June, and Michael two in July. Anyhow, you're all wrong about Charles," she added. "*I* was never really afraid for him. Oh, I know there was a great fuss made when he arrived so suddenly and was such a miserable specimen; but I *knew* he'd made a go of it all right, misery or not. Can't tell you why, but I knew all right."

"No one would have thought so from the way ye carried on about him."

Jo laughed. "He was so tiny and looked so frail that I felt I had to give him the greatest care; but underneath it all I knew we should pull him through, and we have! Actually, we've had nothing like the worry over him that we've had with Margot. However, we're hoping that that is over, too. See here, Biddy!" She made a long arm, and pulled open a bureau drawer from which she took a sheaf of photographs. "These were part of my Christmas present from Canada." She handed them over.

Biddy looked at them—beautifully tinted photographs, one each of a little girl, and one of the three together. "Well, no mistake who this is," she said. "That's Margot with the wicked twinkle in her eye. Yes, Joey; you're right. There oughtn't to be any need to worry over *that* any more. Now—Jo Maynard! Ye're niver telling me this is Josette!"

In her excitement she became richly Irish, and Jo laughed. "A bit of a change, isn't it? Yes; that's Josette. And that one Ailie, the youngest of Madge's girls. She's not nearly so pretty as the other two but she has a dear little face of her own, don't you think? Now," she drew a fifth photo from its envelope with a flourish, "here's the pick of the bunch. What do you think of *that*?"

Biddy gaped at the portrait of a graceful dark-eyed

Carnbach, so to speak. It's really quite convenient, for I *didn't* want to part with the girls full term just yet. They aren't much more than babies, after all. As it is, I can see them quite often and they come home for two or three week-ends in the term."

Biddy had sat up alertly. "But this *is* all news to me! Why wasn't I told of it before?" she demanded. "*When* did all this happen?"

"But you *were*—told, I mean. It happened last Easter, and Daisy wrote you sheets and sheets about it. Do you mean to say you've never had it?"

"I have *not!* Ye could have knocked me down with a feather when I got your letter saying you were here. I couldn't think what had happened."

"Well, all I know is that Daisy spent the whole of one Sunday with my typewriter, giving you the gen. She produced about fifteen sheets of my thin typing paper, with the whole story. You'll have to thrash it out with her when she comes home again—there's the gong! Supper's ready. Come along; or do you want to wash first?"

"I'll wash."

Jo led the way. "There's the dining-room. And here's the cloakroom. You wash and brush-up and then come along. I'll go and begin on the serving."

Biddy was in the dining-room within five minutes, and sitting down to a smoking plateful of goulash which she ate hungrily. "Oh, but it's nice to be eating the good old Austrian dishes again!" she said as she passed her plate for a second helping.

"You won't get too many of them, I'm afraid," Jo told her. "We can't get the stuff to make them, though Anna does her best. She's made apfeltorte specially for you, so leave a *little* room!"

"The nice creature she is! But I'm hungry, I can tell ye!" Biddy fell to in a way that proved the truth of her remarks, and found plenty of room for a lavish helping of Anna's apfeltorte after.

"We'll take our coffee into the drawing-room," Jo decided when she had finished. "Then I want all *your* news. I've talked myself nearly hoarse and I should think you were fairly well up-to-date by this."

Biddy laughed and picked up the coffee-tray to carry it into the drawing-room. They settled themselves by the fire,

far as possible and even Michael will have some faint recollection of him. The vet says he ought to be good for two or three years yet."

She pulled Biddy over to a chair, and then sat down herself. "Let me look at you, Bridget Honora O'Ryan. Have you altered at all?"

"Older, maybe," Biddy retorted.

Jo chuckled. "Not even that." Her black eyes dwelt thoughtfully on the pretty face with its gloriously blue eyes under their long lashes—real Irish eyes, "put in with a smutty finger"—and the mass of waving black hair. Biddy had the Irish oval face and softly pink and white colouring. Her mouth was generous, and when she smiled she showed a row of white teeth that would have gained her a fortune as a toothpaste advertisement.

"Well?" Biddy demanded, flushing under the steady gaze.

"Not changed a scrap. Biddy, it's fine having you here. I only wish it could have been for Christmas, but we'd fixed up to go to the Quadrant—that's Dick's place—weeks before I had your letter. I'd have taken you with us, but you couldn't have got another creature in with a shoehorn. Six Bettany kids, five of my own, Robin, Daisy and Primula, and four grown-ups, never to mention my own Anna, and Mollie's nurse and Nurse's two nieces! You add that up, my lamb, and see for yourself!"

"Five of your own?" Biddy gasped. "Where's the sixth, then? You've *six* of your own, Jo Maynard!"

"Six it is; but Margot is with Madge and Jem in Canada. I'll tell you about that in a minute. I've heaps of news for you."

"And the first you can tell me is why you are here at all, at all. What's happened to Plas Gwyn?"

"Oh, my dear! It very nearly wasn't! Half the foundations were going and it was only a miracle that it hadn't collapsed on our heads. Jack had us all out in short order, and luckily this house belongs to a friend of his who has let it to us for as long as we want it. They've had to renew a good half of the foundations, so we're doing some work that needed doing, now half the place is in pieces, and we're likely to be here some time. You'd hear that the School had to move because of the drains? They're at St. Briavel's—that's an island just across the road from

now and then thumping the floor with his tail when she spoke to him.

"You know, Rufus," she said gravely, "I am so wondering if Biddy has changed much. And do you think she'll see any change in me? Four years is a long time."

Rufus banged the floor with his tail and then got up stiffly. He had heard the creak of the gate. So had Jo.

She made a wild leap for the door and wrenched it open to run to the front door, Rufus at her side, his tail going like a flail. The front door was yanked open before the newcomer had fairly reached it, and the light from the hall-lamp lit up Jo standing with arms wide open, exclaiming with joy in every note of her voice: "Biddy!"

"Joey! 'Tis yourself, acushla!" came the equally joyful reply in the soft tones of southern Ireland as the visitor tossed her case down and hurled herself on her hostess, hugging her ecstatically.

Rufus forgot his years and his rheumatism and bounced round the pair woofing excitedly as if he were a good ten years younger; and when Biddy O'Ryan had recovered her senses a little, she dropped on her knees beside him and submitted to having her face thoroughly swiped with his tongue as she flung her arms round his neck, calling him love-names in creamiest Kerry brogue.

"Where's your luggage?" Jo demanded, interrupting this touching meeting and looking round severely.

Biddy looked up at her and laughed. "At the station. Sure, there wasn't a taxi to be had for love or money, so I just grabbed me case and left me cabin trunk to be called for tomorrow. The rest's gone straight to the School. I've all I need here, really. 'Tisn't as if I was staying for a real visit."

Jo led the way into the drawing-room, and Biddy, having dumped her case down in the hall and dropped her cap and coat on top, followed her.

"Joey, how do you do it? Rufus is *old* and yet he looks almost in his prime." She turned to him again, to lay her hand on the great head nuzzling joyfully against her. "Ah, acushla, machree! So you haven't forgotten Biddy, even after all this time?"

Jo laughed back at her. "Is it likely? Rufus, bless him, is as loyal as they come. Oh, we take the very greatest care of him, and except for rheumatism, he's amazingly well. I'm so very glad. I wanted the children to grow up with him as

Chapter II

ENTER BIDDY!

JO MAYNARD sat by the drawing-room fire darning stockings. It was a job she loathed with her whole soul; but when you have a long family of youngsters, never to speak of a husband who could only be described as "hard on his socks," you have to see to it sometimes. Jo was expecting a visitor—a visitor whom she had not seen for the last four years—and was wildly excited over it inside, so she had determined that darning was the most subduing occupation she could find and, anyhow, it had to be done!

Tall and slim was Jo, with black eyes that could dance with mischief or soften to pools of darkness in a pale, delicately-featured face under a broad fringe of black hair. Despite her long family and many responsibilities, she looked amazingly girlish, and everyone who knew her could have told you that there were times when she seemed very little removed from the most beloved Head Girl the Chalet School had ever known.

She was alone for once save for Rosa in the kitchen. The entire family had spent Christmas at the Quadrant, the queer old house where her brother Dick Bettany lived with *his* long family, and Jo had been persuaded to leave the children in her sister-in-law's charge when she came home to look after her husband. Today he was away at the big Sanatorium up in the Welsh mountains, where he held an important post. Her adopted sister, Robin Humphries, had left the week before to go to Switzerland for winter sports with one Zephyr Burthill, a friend of hers; and the other two members of the family, Daisy and Primula Venables, who were "nieces-by-marriage" to quote Jo, were staying with friends outside Armiford near their old home. Anna, her faithful maid, had gone to Plas Gwyn, which was undergoing severely necessary repairs, in order to see to several odd jobs there, so the only other member of the family was Rufus, Jo's big St. Bernard, who never left her for long these days, for he was a very old dog, nearly eighteen now. He was lying on the rug at her feet, every

and make your bed, and be down here by ten to nine at latest."

Carola departed, thankful to have got out of the trouble so easily, and when Cousin Maud, still frowning, came bundling down the stairs, she found the girl waiting for her, looking the picture of a neat, trim schoolgirl. They left the house, and when they were walking briskly to the station Miss Curry informed her young cousin that, among other things, she was to have a new suitcase.

"Oh, may I have an expanding one, please?" Carola begged.

"That is what I intend to buy for you," Cousin Maud told her. "They are much the best for long voyages, as they hold so much. You will do your own packing, of course. With this happening, I shall be far too busy to do more than give you occasional oversight. When you begin to pack, please put everything you are likely to need during the voyage in this new case and the bigger one of your other two. Then your trunk can go to the hold and we need have no further trouble with it till we reach Kingstown."

"Yes," Carola said meekly.

Cousin Maud went on talking, but, sad to say, Carola heard not one word of her discourse. She was far too much occupied in rejoicing over the extending suitcase to think of anything else. Really, it did seem as if the luck were coming her way for the moment.

Thanks to Miss Bacon's falling out, Cousin Maud had far too much to think about to worry further over Carola, and that young lady contrived to possess herself of a brown coat and beret and a brown velveteen frock without any comments from her guardian. Brown, it should be noted, was one of the Chalet School colours, according to Miss O'Ryan. She also turned down her cousin's suggestion of a green raincoat in favour of a brown one; and though she could hardly ask for a brown tunic, she felt when they returned home that, on the whole, she would not show up too badly so far as school colours were concerned. Carola went to bed that night thoroughly satisfied with herself and the world.

Maud had some excuse for being indignant. All the same, her purpose of not going to Jamaica was strengthened. She felt that she must apologise for her rudeness, now that her first fury of disappointment was over; but she could do that with a clear conscience. Only, if Cousin Maud really thought she would give in as easily as all that, she had another think coming to her!

Carola woke at seven, and remembered that she had to dress for a trip to London. With a groan, she tumbled out of bed and made for the bathroom where she speedily attended to washing.

The gong sounded as she went downstairs, prepared to eat humble-pie with what grace she might.

Much to her surprise, Cousin Maud seemed scarcely to listen to her very halting apology.

"I'm sorry I was so rude to you yesterday, Cousin Maud."

Miss Curry hardly glanced up from the letter she was holding to say, "Then that finishes it. Sit down, Carola, and begin on your porridge. We haven't any too much time."

Presently, Cousin Maud put the letter aside and started on her own breakfast. She looked thoroughly vexed and worried, and Carola, having emptied her plate, and received a helping of bacon and sausage, ventured to ask what was wrong.

"I am very much annoyed," Cousin Maud said, pouring out her coffee. "Miss Bacon, whom I had engaged for your governess, now writes to say that she has had a cycling accident and broken her leg, so will be unable to accompany us. At this late date I do not see how I am to find you another governess before we sail, so we must just go without. It really is most annoying!"

Carola said nothing, though inwardly she was chuckling. She had been wondering how on earth she was to slip away from her new governess. If there was only Cousin Maud to consider, she might be able to manage it. She applied herself to her bacon and Cousin Maud drank her coffee in a frowning silence which lasted until her young cousin, having finished her breakfast, asked to be excused to go and make her bed.

"Yes—run along," the lady said absently. "Be as quick as you can. We are going by the nine-fifteen train and it's twenty-past eight already, so there is no time for delay. Go

"However, if you are prepared to beg my pardon when we meet at breakfast, we will say no more, and I will forgive you. But I must impress on you that I will listen to no more talk of school—of *any* school. I cannot be expected to rearrange my whole programme just to suit you, and as I have promised to look after you I must take you with me. Please believe that, as you are behaving at present, this is no pleasure to me, but rather an unpleasant duty. If, however, you make up your mind to accept what must be, and to try to be pleasant and accommodating, that should end. Your parents are returning home next year and they can then decide whether or not to give in to you and let you go to school—personally, I can see no need for it. You have had good governesses, and the lady I have engaged for this trip is better than any you have had before. I considered you when I fixed on a person much nearer your own age than usual; and I expect you to consider me and try to make yourself rather more agreeable in future than you have been lately.

"Now this is the last time I intend to discuss the matter with you. We go to Southampton today fortnight and sail for Jamaica on the Wednesday. I will listen to no arguments on the subject, so please make up your mind to that and do not attempt to produce any.

"If you show yourself properly penitent tomorrow, I will, as I said, let the matter drop, so long as you behave properly to me and let me see no more such outrageous exhibitions of childish rage as you gave me this afternoon. I was shocked to think that you could act like that!

"I shall be taking you to London to buy some clothes tomorrow, so come down prepared to set off as soon as possible after breakfast.

"I have no more to say, so I will close. I am putting this on the supper-tray I shall leave at your door; and *remember* that in the morning I shall hope to see you a very different girl from the one who left me in such a fit of temper a few hours ago.

"Your affectionate cousin,
MAUD CURRY."

Carola read the last word. Then she sat up in bed, and tore the paper across and across. She threw the pieces on to the floor, turned off the lamp, and lay down, seething with anger. However, she had to admit to herself that Cousin

see sense. Go to Jamaica she would not! She couldn't quite see how she was going to avoid it, and she had only fourteen days in which to lay her plans, so she mustn't waste a moment.

At this point she fell asleep again, and when she woke up the street-lamp was out, and a waning Christmas moon was sailing serenely across the deep blue of the skies. Carola felt hungry by this time. Once she was properly awake, she got up, huddled on her dressing-gown and bedroom slippers, padded quietly across the floor, switching on the light on her way, and unlocked and opened the door softly. It was as well that she paused to look up and down the passage in case anyone else should be stirring. If she had not, she must have walked right on top of a tray left at the door. With an exclamation she stooped and picked it up.

Feeling rather guilty, Carola lifted the napkin laid over it. There was a well-filled plate of bread-and-butter and another holding a banana and an apple. A glass of milk and a slice of currant loaf completed it. Under the glass was a note. Carola decided to eat her supper and then read the note.

The plates and glass were all empty in less than ten minutes. Carola carried the tray over to the little table in one of the windows and dumped it down. Then she refilled her bottle at the hot tap as it was little more than lukewarm by this time. She straightened the bed and beat up the pillows. Finally, when she could find no further excuse for delaying any longer, she climbed back into bed, having switched off the centre light, and switched on her bedside lamp and opened the note—very reluctantly, it must be confessed.

'Dear Carola," she read, "I hope that by the morning you will have come to your senses again and be ready to apologise to me for your most uncalled-for rudeness of this afternoon. A girl of your age ought to be ashamed to speak so improperly to an elder person—especially one who is your guardian and in the place of your parents. Unless you reform very soon, I am afraid your father and mother will be deeply disappointed in you when they return to England. I will say nothing about my own feelings, though I think you should know that I am very deeply hurt by your ingratitude for all I am doing for you.

Switzerland, and the Gower coast in South Wales, with only the shortest possible intervals between each visit. Having promised her cousin to be responsible for his girl, she insisted on keeping that girl under her own eye, travelling a governess who could also be useful to herself. Christmas had been spent at a delightful guest-house in Cornwall, where Carola had struck up a great friendship with a Miss O'Ryan, rather to Miss Curry's relief, since Miss O'Ryan had been quite willing to have Carola with her, and it had freed the elder lady so that she could indulge in her twin passions, bridge and gossip.

Miss Curry had made a few inquiries, and found that the Irish girl was a graduate of Oxford who was returning to her own old school as history mistress when the Easter term began, having hitherto been in Australia. Evidently she had told Carola the most enticing tales about the school, for ever since they had come home that young person had worried and teased to be allowed to go to this school instead of accompanying her father's cousin on the trip to Jamaica which had been arranged for some months. Miss Curry had treated the idea as a passing whim at first. Then as the girl became more and more urgent, she had grown annoyed and wished that she had never permitted the friendship. It had ended in today's outburst, when it must be admitted that Carola had behaved about as badly as possible before she had fled to the refuge of her own room to cry so heart-brokenly.

Lying in the lamplight, Carola had to own to herself that if Cousin Maud were angry, she had every reason for it. "All the same," she thought sullenly, "she might listen to me. Who wants to be for ever on the go? It's all very well for her, but I'm sick and tired of it. I'm getting all behind in lessons, too. I'm sure Dad and Mother wouldn't want that to happen. But how can you do lessons decently when you never have the same person to teach you for longer than six months and you're always moving about, anyhow? I ought to be at school like other girls. I've never played hockey nor cricket and I've no friends of my own age—not a single one! I just haven't had a chance to make friends." Her eyes brimmed over again with tears of self-pity as she thought this, and she gulped for a moment. Then she drove them back, for she had no time for crying now. She had resolved firmly that she was going to do something about school since Cousin Maud either could not or would not

Jamaica. But she, Maud Curry, knew her duty too well to be turned from her purpose by a naughty, ungrateful child of fourteen. She had promised her cousin Andrew and his wife, before they left for him to take up his post in West Equatorial Africa, that she would look after Carola; and no amount of tantrums and temper on that young lady's part should make her break her word.

Meantime, Carola cried till she could cry no more. For a long time after the tears were dried, she lay, still shaking and gulping, for the storm had been a violent one. Her face felt stiff with tears and her head was aching. She lay still, and presently, worn out with the force of her emotions, she fell asleep.

When she woke up, it was to find that night had come and the room was in darkness, the only light being from the street-lamp at the gate. Her head was better, but her eyes were sore and she was stiff and chilly, since to lie and sleep outside your bed on New Year's Day is hardly a warming process. She got up, switched on her light, and pulled the curtains over the windows. Then she went to the toilet-basin and turned on the taps and bathed her face till it felt more comfortable. That done, she looked at the clock on the mantelpiece. Seven o'clock! She must have been asleep for hours. She might as well undress and go straight to bed. Carola had no wish to go downstairs to meet a righteously indignant Cousin Maud over the supper table. She was still much too upset to feel hungry, and if she woke up during the night she could always slip down to the kitchen and get some bread-and-butter and milk.

To think was to do where she was concerned, and ten minutes later she was curled up in bed, her hot-water bottle filled at the hot-water tap and hugged close to her, and she was gradually losing the shivery feeling with which she had awakened. She had switched off the light again and opened the curtains so that the lamplight could shine into her room, and she lay watching it, thinking of her one deep desire, to go to school, and especially to that school of schools— anyhow, that was how Miss O'Ryan had described it—the Chalet School.

Cousin Maud kept on her pretty house in a small seaside town on the south coast as a *pied-à-terre*, to which she returned at intervals varying from two to six months. She herself had a passion for travelling, and during the past year she had taken Carola to Dublin, Edinburgh,

Chapter I

CAROLA PLEADS IN VAIN

"CERTAINLY *NOT*! You ought to be ashamed of yourself for behaving like this! Now let me hear no more about it, please, Carola. You will come with me to Jamaica as I have settled. I have engaged a very good governess for you—one who is comparatively young, so that she will also be a companion for you. The berths are booked, and all arrangements made, so that's the end of it, I hope."

"But, Cousin Maud——"

"Did you hear what I said? I want to hear no more talk about the affair. You are a very lucky girl to have such chances as you have. I wonder how many other girls of your age have seen as much of the world as you?"

"And I'm *sick* of it!" Carola flared out. "I'm sick—*sick*—*sick* of perpetually travelling about! I want to go to school like other girls, and have the fun of games with them, and proper lessons—not footy little lectures from a governess—and everything! I want to go to the *Chalet School*——"

"I thought I said I wished to hear no more about that?"

"I can't help what you said—you're *always* saying! I tell you I won't go! You'll have to carry me aboard the beastly liner, if you get me that far! I won't stir a step by myself! I—oh, I hate you!"

Realising that tears were very near, Carola made for the door. She rushed out of the room and upstairs to her own bedroom, regardless of her cousin's stern: "Carola! Come back at once and shut the door after you!", slammed and locked the bedroom door after her, and then casting herself full-length on the bed, howled like a small child.

Cousin Maud got up and shut the sitting-room door herself before she went to sit down and try to recover the self-possession Carola's outburst had so rudely—in more senses than one—disturbed. Really, the child was abominably impertinent, not to speak of being utterly ungrateful. She didn't deserve the treat of a trip to

Carola Storms the Chalet School was
first published in the U.K. in a single volume
in hardback in 1951 by W. & R. Chambers
Ltd., London and Edinburgh, and in Armada
in 1968 by Fontana Paperbacks.

© All rights reserved.

3
Carola Storms the Chalet School

before saying good-bye, he sought Joey out. "Mein Fräulein," he said abruptly, "I can never thank you for your so-beautiful thought. But the prayers of my church will follow you always. May God bless you!"

Joey looked at him. "When we have so much," she said slowly, "isn't it only fair that we should share all we can with those who have so little? Isn't that the message of Christmas, mein Vater?"

He smiled. "Ah, yes! But how many think of it thus?"

"Ah, but we are taught to do so," said Jo gravely. "I must go, Vater Stefan; they are calling me. Auf wiedersehn. Fröliches Weihnachtsfest!"

She ran off, scarcely waiting for his farewell, and was at once surrounded by a throng of girls, all begging her to come back next term, and go on teaching them.

"Not likely!" said Joey calmly. "My book is accepted, and I've got to start a new one—Well, of course, I shall! Think I'm going to stop short now? Oh, I'll come down to see you—often. But as a regular thing, I really have finished with school now.—There's Jem calling me: I must go! Good-bye, everyone, and a happy Christmas to you all!"

She wriggled free, raced to the car, and sprang in. Dr Jem started her, and, waving her hand, her eyes not so clear as they might have been, Joey drove away from the Chalet School.

my glasses need cleaning!" And he took them off and polished them.

"A tale that can never be stale nor too often told," rejoined Vater Stefan, a deep glow in his eyes. "I wish my children might have seen this. They could never forget then the Gift which Christmas brought to the world."

Joey, still in her flowing robes, was standing near when he said this. Her eyes suddenly lit up. She turned, and moved away to where Miss Annersley and Miss Wilson were standing speaking to Stacie Benson's uncle and aunt, who had come from Devonshire to escort her to their house for the holidays—the first time she would see England after nearly two years. The Stacie who had left them had vanished, and the girl who was going back was one they would be delighted to have with them.

Jo spoke to them prettily, and then contrived to draw the two mistresses away to a corner, where the Robin, still in her loose white gown, presently joined them. For a few minutes they talked together earnestly. Then the Robin slipped across the room to where Vater Stefan was standing, and put her hand in his.

"If you please, will you come?" she said shyly. "Miss Annersley and Miss Wilson and Joey want you."

Greatly wondering, the young priest let her lead him to them.

As they went, he looked down into the lovely little face at his elbow, and smiled. The Robin smiled back, and squeezed his fingers.

"It is Joey's thought," she told him eagerly, "but Miss Annersley and Miss Wilson say yes. It cannot be at Christmas, for everyone will be at home then. But when we come back—*then!*"

Wondering what she was talking about, Vater Stefan halted before the group in the corner. Then—he could scarcely believe his ears. For in addition to all their previous kindness, they were offering that when the girls returned from their holidays, a hall in his district should be hired, and this beautiful little play should be given there for the benefit of his poor people.

It was as much as Vater Stefan could do to stammer out his thanks. It was so unexpected; and he knew what it would mean, this spot of colour and loveliness, in the grey lives of those among whom he so faithfully laboured.

Later on, he recalled the Robin's mysterious words, and

She ceased, and the curtains closed, while the choir sang the old Swedish carol "Congaudeat turba fidelium." As they finished, the Glockenspiel chimed in once more with joyous pealing, and once more the stage was shown. This was the hillside at Bethlehem, with the "shepherds abiding in the fields, keeping watch over their flocks by night." To one side, and poised above them, were a throng of angels, clustered together. This part of the stage was flooded with rosy and amber light, while the rest was in shadow, so that the eye was swiftly led to the angelic choir. For a few minutes the audience saw it in silence. Then it was blotted from their sight by the curtains.

But almost at once, they were swung back to show the Three Kings—Melchior, Caspar, and Balthasar—bearing their gifts of mystic meaning, while above them swung a great silver star. Slowly they came forward, one after another raising the gifts to show what they had. Melchior swung chains of gold; Caspar swung a censer; Balthasar raised a white flask.

Then, even as they turned to go on their way, the curtains came down, and when they were lifted, it was on the Stable in Bethlehem.

Angels clustered round the central group, in which St Joseph—Thora Helgersen—stood protectingly behind the Madonna—Louise Redfield.

For the last time the curtains fell, to rise on the same place. But now the angels crowded to the back, while at the feet of the Madonna, who stood holding the Bambino, were the shepherds and the kings. The various characters from the other scenes were grouped at the sides, and at either end of the wooden trough, which was in the centre, with St Joseph still behind it, stood the Spirits, only the Spirit of the Bells standing beside St Joseph.

Almost simultaneously with this, the Glockenspiel rang out in a very ecstasy of joyous music. The orchestra chimed in; the music changed; and the sound of the glorious old Latin hymn "Adeste Fideles" rang through the hitherto silent hall. The audience joined in singing it, the curtains fell and the play was ended.

"The most beautiful thing of its kind I have ever seen," said old Mr Wilmot, who had come to take Polly home to England for the holidays. "I—upon my word,

tives were brought in, heavily chained. They knelt down
at the king's feet and begged for mercy. He frowned, and
refused it. They had been his enemies, and they must
suffer for it. Suddenly, the bells rang out again, and the
Spirit of Love floated in, clad in long, rose-coloured
draperies. Hers was a very short carol—only two verses,
for this was Stacie's first public appearance. But she sang
it very clearly and sweetly. The king's attitude slowly
changed as she sang, and he made a gesture, whereat the
guards flung off the chairs from the captives, and they
were free.

Down came the curtains, and while the choir sang the
Welsh carol "O, deued pob cristion," which may be translated, "All poor men and humble," there was a deep
hush on the audience.

Then the curtains parted again, to show the room in
the bell-tower, the Spirit of the Bells standing in the
centre, the little bell-sprites about her, while the Spirits of
the Christmas Rose, the Snow, Holly, and Love knelt
before her.

Joey spoke, softly but very clearly, and with deep
feeling.

> "Now ye have heard the stories of the Bells.
> Now do ye know that when their music swells
> It bears a message unto every heart;
> It reaches through the world to every part.
> And that ye ne'er forget the tale they sing,
> That they their joy and peace to you may bring,
> Look now upon the scene that, long years past,
> Was shown to man amidst the winter's blast.
> We have them still—the Cave, the Manger Bed;
> And still the silent stars shine overhead.
> Down to the earth, drifted on sleeping wings,
> The herald angel still his message brings
> Of love and peace, goodwill from man to man.
> See but the scenes, and then, forget who can!
> While o'er the earth those joyous anthems steal,
> And in the tower the Bells of Christmas peal,
> Here is a King, a wanderer poor, a Child,
> An Artisan, a Mother, humble, mild.
> Oh, Bells of Christmas, ring—ring out all strife,
> And sing to us of Him Who gives us life!"

Evadne, the Spirit of the Christmas Rose, entered, surrounded by a throng of smaller Roses. They filled the stage, passing to and fro, and hiding the poor family as they moved. Evadne, standing well forward, sang the legend of the Christmas Rose, which tells us how, at the first Christmas, a little beggar-girl wanted to enter and offer a gift to the Babe of Bethlehem, but had nothing, until the Archangel Gabriel appeared to her, and showed her a great bank of white flowers, the first Christmas roses to grow on earth, and bade her take those to Him, for God had given them to her.

Evadne's song finished; the little Roses swung back; the bells rang out a merry peal in a changed room. The chilly blue lights had become warm amber; the poor people were neatly and warmly clad; food stood on the table; and in one corner was a Christmas tree, all lit up, round which the children gathered joyously.

Again the curtains fell, and again the choir sang—an old Angevin carol, known to the French as "Quoi ma voisine?"

They rose this time on a darkened stage, to which people presently came limping, as if they had walked a long way. They carried bundles, and staves, and big lanterns, for they were gipsies, and were tramping to find a site for their camp. They told of the long journey over the wintry roads; the sharpness of the bitter wind; the chill of the snow. They were so tired, so cold, so hungry. And then the Spirit of the Holly danced in, all in green and scarlet, and bade them camp where they were, for this was the place chosen for them to keep their Christmas. Yvette had a charming mezzo-soprano voice, and she sang her little song very sweetly. The people sat down. Some of them produced sticks for the fire, and electric torches switched on under scarlet paper gave a fine glow, while the light was changed from blue and green to crimson. At once the bells rang forth, and the scene was hidden, while the choir sang the Czech carol "Hajej nynjej," or, as it has been translated, "Little Jesus, sweetly sleep."

The fourth scene was a king's court, with courtiers, jester, and dancing-girls all complete. A great number of the girls appeared in this scene, and in their gay dresses they made a brilliant picture. It was plain that the king had returned from some great victory, for presently cap-

Robin. Maids were busied about the room and the little maid in the bed. The lady—Anne Seymour—left the wheel, and came to bend over the child, and ask if she could give her anything. The child said there was nothing she wanted. She was only waiting to hear the Christmas Bells that would speak of the Birth of Christ.

"I know I shall be well when I hear that," she said.

The maids clustered round, one offering to tell a tale; another to sing; the third proffering her cup. The child put them all aside. She was listening for the bells. Suddenly, a strain of soft music stole out. Gradually, the restless people on the stage fell asleep. Then, through the curtains, drifted a form clad all in white, frosting on gown and hair, and a crown of silver on her head. It was the Spirit of the Snow. The sick child sat up and held out her arms. But Snow shook her head. She had brought a gift; and standing there, she sang the carol of the snow—again verses of Madge's set by Mr Denny. Cornelia had a charming voice, and she sang very tenderly the little carol with its soft chorus of "Lullay lullay." The bells chimed in with her singing—this was an effect in every one of the solos—and the sick child slipped back against her pillows and fell asleep. Suddenly, the bells rang out in a soft peal. The grown-ups started awake. Their first thought was for the child. They bent over her; the mother's glad voice spoke the message.

"She sleeps at last! The bells have sung her to sleep, and now she will recover! And this is Christmas Day!"

At once the curtains fell. The School choir sang behind the scenes the pretty old English carol "On Christmas Day in the Morning."

Again the curtains swung back, this time on a miserable garret, cold and cheerless. Three ragged children were there, bare-foot and unkempt; and a white-faced woman who wept because it would be Christmas Day to-morrow, and they could have no share in it. Even, they might be without a roof, for if the landlord should come for the rent, they had no money to pay him.

The children tried to comfort her; but she refused their comfort. Then the youngest said, "But we can share the bells, liebe Mutter, for they belong to everyone!"

The next one cried, "Hark! I hear the bells now! Christ is born!" And at once came the faint chiming of the bells. Another voice sounded, singing with them; and played by Herr Laubach, came the sound of twelve strokes, and on the last one, the black curtains at the back of the stage parted, and a tall, slim figure in flowing draperies of gold appeared—Jo.

She advanced amidst an intense silence, and then, to the lovely air played by the strings and wood-wind of the orchestra, she sang a carol which was new to everyone. Madge had written it, and Mr. Denny had composed the music. Softly Jo's lovely voice began; but as she reached the last verse, it swelled up and out, filling the great hall:

> "Ring out, ring out, oh, Christmas bells
> Ring out your tale of joy and mirth.
> Bid man forget his fruitless strife
> This night—the night of Jesus' Birth.
> This one night of the year, oh, world,
> Bid strife depart, dissensions end.
> Oh, world, give love from man to man,
> And with the bells your anthems blend!"

Then came the chorus:

> "Ring out, sweet bells, oh bells of gold
> That sing of Love that cannot cease!
> Join in, ye bells of silver mould,
> Your tale of Christ's eternal peace!"

Softly chanting, "Ring out—ring out—ring out!" the Spirit stood in the centre, and on the last sweet note, the music from the Glockenspiel rang out gaily, and down from the golden mouths of the bells tumbled sprites clad in gold and silver, who caught hands, and danced gaily round Jo.

At length, the music ceased, and the little spirits fell back in a tableau, while the Spirit of the Bells spoke to them, bidding them, one by one, speak of the place to which their music had brought a special message. The violins whispered soft notes on the last word, and the curtains fell.

The choir broke into another carol, the very old German "In dulci jubilo," which ended just as the curtains were raised, to show a richly furnished bedchamber of the fourteenth century. A lady clad in robes of the same era sat at the spinning-wheel, and in the bed lay a child—the

CHAPTER XVIII

THE CHRISTMAS PLAY

THE days fled past so quickly that it seemed to the girls as if they had just begun to rehearse the play, when the dress rehearsal was over, and the actual performance itself was on them.

On the day of it, Vater Stefan came up to Briesau to meet his benefactors. What they had expected, none of the girls were very sure, but it was certainly not what they saw. He was quite a young man, dark and slight, with smooth black hair, and a pair of magnificent grey eyes, which glowed as he thanked them for their goodness to his people.

"Be very sure that the dear God will bless you all this Christmas," he said, as he tried to show them his gratitude.

Then the gong sounded for Mittagessen, and Miss Annersley bore him off to the Staff table, while the girls formed into long files and marched into the Speisesaal.

Once the meal was over, they had to disappear, for all had to dress. Vater Stefan went off with the doctors who had come down, to have a quiet pipe and chat in the library until it was time to go into Hall. They found him, like most Benedictines, a highly educated, cultured man, who, though he often longed for the peace of his monastery, where he might study and know privacy, was quite content to labour among his poor people in obedience to his Abbot.

"And what a fröliches Weihnachtsfest they will have this year!" he said joyously.

"Are you people here?" asked Miss Nalder, peering round the door. "You must come now, for the doors are opening, and we want Vater Stefan to have a good seat."

The hall was filled to its fullest capacity, and the little orchestra, composed of various members of the Staff, began to play the Bach Christmas music. Presently the music ended, and the curtains were drawn to show a chilly-looking room, with ten great golden bells swinging a little above the stage. Suddenly, from the Glockenspiel,

313

He nodded. "Yes! But Madge is right, Joey. You mustn't waste your money over us."

So it was decided. Jo finally provided new fountain-pens all round, and bought a new book she herself had been wanting; but the greater part of the cheque when it came—and when it had been duly cashed—went to Vater Stefan in Innsbruck to provide a summer outing for the children of his parish. It was very thrilling; but, as a matter of fact, Jo was far more thrilled when the following October brought out to the Sonnalpe six copies of her own book, beautifully illustrated, with a gay paper jacket which was warranted to attract any school-girl.

That, however, was almost a year ahead. At present, Jo, after an evening of wild hilarity, retired to bed with the promise that on the morrow she would be permitted to see Mademoiselle for five minutes.

It was scarcely a social call, that visit, for the visitor was very nervous, and all she did was to grin at the Head, say "Hello! Hope you're all right!" and then slip out.

But when she returned to the School, she was able to tell the girls that Mademoiselle, though very thin and white and weak, was still their Mademoiselle.

After that, she had to announce her own news, whereat the School went rampant, and if she had given away all the copies that were promptly demanded, she would soon have become bankrupt. She finally got them away from the subject by demanding to know what had been done about the play while she was absent, and in the excitement of telling her, they forgot other things for the time being.

The rest of the term was divided between lessons, rehearsals, and work for the big boxes they were filling for Vater Stefan, and which rejoiced his heart exceedingly when he opened them. They were crammed full of toys, clothes, and everything the Chalet School could think of that children might need and they supply. Other gifts rained down on the young priest as well, for the colony at the Sonnalpe had heard of what was going on, and insisted on bearing their part.

Finally, Cornelia's father sent a cheque to provide firing for the winter for as many families as possible. And Mr Lannis, not to be outdone by his friend, added a further sum to give them other comforts. So that, all things considered, one parish in Innsbruck had cause to bless the Chalet School that Christmas.

Joey laughed a little. "I'd forgotten about them. I suppose it's never having seen them. I always feel as though you were my sort of mother, you know. You've brought me up, after all."

Madge Russell, with a thought for the long-dead parents, nodded. "I know. But—don't forget them, Joey. They would have been so proud of you."

"Yes; but it's scarcely the same as if I'd known them. Oh, I don't forget them, of course. Only—they're rather—strangers."

"Who are?" asked Dr Jem, coming into the room at that moment. "Hello—post! Anything for me, dear?"

"Over there on the table. But never mind about them for the moment, Jem. Just listen to Joey's news!"

Jem turned to his young sister-in-law. "What is it, Joey?"

For reply, Joey thrust the letter into his hands. "Read that, Jem!—Oh, Madge! I simply *can't* believe it's true!"

After a sharp glance at her excited face, the doctor read the letter through. Then he dropped it, picked up the tall, slim girl, and kissed her heartily. "Well done, Joey! This is splendid news! I'm as proud of you as I can be; and as for Dick, I'm going to send him out a new hat of extra large size, for I'm certain he'll need it!"

"Isn't it gorgeous?" Joey clung to him. "Oh, Jem, I'm so thrilled!" And then the reaction came, and she burst into tears.

She was soon all right again, however, and able to settle down and discuss the news quietly.

"What will you do with your money when you get it?" asked Jem.

"I'm going to buy presents for you and Madge and Dick and Mollie. And I'm going to buy something for myself for a memento. And the rest I want to send to Vater Stefan for his poor children.—You don't mind, do you, Madge? I have so much, and I'd like to feel I could do something like that with it. It's my *first* earnings, you know."

They both knew what she meant, and they agreed. "Only little things for us, though, Joey," said Madge. "We'd love to have something in remembrance of to-day, and of course, we'll have the book. But don't spend much on our things. And I think it's a very good idea to send your first-fruits to Vater Stefan.—Don't you, Jem?"

maths mistress of the School and her husband. The last of the batch, a typewritten envelope, the young lady had tossed aside as uninteresting. But when she had finally concluded all the letters from friends, she took it up with some curiosity.

"Who on earth's sending me typewritten letters?"

"Open it, and then you'll see," suggested Madge, without looking up from her own mail.

Jo turned it over, glanced incuriously at the monogram on the back, and then slit it open. A typewritten sheet dropped out, and she unfolded it, wondering what it could be. Two seconds later, Madge was startled into a violent jump by a wild yell from her sister.

"*Joey!* What on earth is the matter?" she demanded. Then she dropped the letter she was holding, and sprang to the girl's side. "Jo! What's wrong? Tell me this instant!"

Jo raised dazed black eyes to her face. *Oh, Madge! Oh, Madge!*"

"Joey, what *is* it? Tell me at once before I shake you!"

"Oh, Madge!" Joey was stammering in her excitement. "It—it's from those people I sent 'Cecily Holds the Fort' to. Madge! They *like* it—they say so! They say their reader has reported favourably on it! And they offer me thirty-five pounds for the copyright! Think of it, Madge! *Thirty-five pounds!*"

Madge plucked the all-important letter from Jo's fingers, and read it for herself. It was brief, businesslike, but it brought joy to her, for it meant that her sister had set her foot on the first rung of the ladder. Whither it might lead her, no one knew. But Madge felt that no other such letter could ever give her quite the same thrill.

As for Jo, she seemed positively awe-stricken. At first she could only sit in a dazed silence, holding her letter, which she had grabbed back at the first possible opportunity, and looking—as Madge declared later on when she was retailing the whole story to Jem—as if she had been offered the Crown of Britain and a huge fortune at one and the same time. Presently the words came bubbling up as Jo felt her sister's kiss of congratulation. "Madge! My first book! I'm a real authoress!"

"I know! Oh, Joey-baba! How proud I am of you! Oh, how I wish Mother and Father had been alive to-day to know about it!"

guess what came next? That wretched child hadn't used saffron at all. She'd taken the *sulphur* tin, and flavoured her cakes with *that*! Matey blames herself for not giving Joyce the tin with her own hands; but as we all told Joyce, if she couldn't tell the difference between saffron and sulphur by this time, she ought to be ashamed of herself!

"Poor old Joyce! She won't be allowed to forget this in a hurry! I'm going to give her home-made sweets for Christmas, and they shall be in a sulphur-yellow box—they shall, if I have to make it myself!—*and* I shall write 'Sulphur Delights' across the lid!"

Madge Russell laughed till the tears ran down her cheeks at this latest exploit of the girls. She could well imagine the smell there must have been when that sulphur began to warm up! As for Jo's threatened gift to Joyce, she put a stopper on that. Joyce was a touchy young person, and she would certainly flare up over such a joke. Jo groaned derisively at the mention of Joyce's temper, but said no more about the matter. Not that the idea was wasted. Cornelia and Evadne had evolved it on their own, and the result was that among her Christmas gifts, Joyce received a lemon-yellow box containing fondants and marzipan, all bright yellow in hue, while across the bottom of the box was written, "In memory of the latest recipe for cakes."

However, this was much later on, and we return to our story. The post came just then, and Mrs Russell distributed the letters at once. At the moment, Jo took her share of the letters, Miss Annersley having handed them back to the postman with the intimation that Miss Bettany was at "Die Rosen," and he had brought them up with the rest. There was one from Frieda Mensch, full of news of the latest addition to the family. Another came from lovely Marie von Eschenau, who had formed part of the quartette which had ruled the School so wisely for a year. Jo sat and chuckled over this, for Marie was to be married after Christmas, and the letter contained a full account of her trousseau, as well as describing the bridesmaids' dresses. Jo was to be chief bridesmaid, and Frieda and Simone Lecoutier (Mademoiselle Lepâttre's young cousin, now at the Sorbonne in Paris) would be the other two; so the letter was full of interest to Joey. Next came a long letter from New Zealand, where lived the former

I wished she'd keep the lab door shut. But it got worse and worse. I never smelt anything more awful in my life!

"Frau Mieders wasn't in the kitchens just then, as she'd been called away to the telephone; and the Fifths were busy in the Speisesaal, and didn't notice anything—or so they say.

"Anyhow, it got so bad—really suffocating, you know—that I went out to see what on earth was happening. By that time, Frau Mieders had got through with her telephoning, and she was making a bee-line for the kitchens. She got there ahead of me (for by that time, I knew it didn't come from the lab), and I was scooting for there as hard as I could go.

"We got there, and I give you my word that those kitchens smelt as though the devil himself had come to pay us a visit! Half the staff had got there, too; and Nally was opening the oven-doors, quite regardless of the fact that she was making most of the cakes into flat failures! She came to the little oven at last, and when she opened *that* door, we were all nearly knocked over! She raked out the patty-pans, and the stink was worse than ever. Joyce landed into the middle of it, and gasped when she saw her cakes bedewing the floor—literally. They weren't cooked enough to be 'set' through. Oh, what a mess there was!

"Finally, Bill and Nally grabbed up the lot, and chucked them out into the snow. Someone opened the doors and windows—we preferred to be frozen, rather than suffocated—and the smell faded away.

"The next thing was to find out what had happened. Joyce vowed that she'd put in nothing but what the recipe had said, and it must be the German saffron. Then Bill had an inspiration. She took Joyce by the shoulder, and marched her upstairs to find out from Matey what it was the kid *had* used, while Frau Mieders began closing doors and windows, and the Fifths bewailed their spoiled cakes. Naturally, letting in the cold like that chilled the ovens, and most of those cakes gave it up and sat down flat!

As far as I can gather—I had to go back to my babes then, for they were making row enough to raise the roof by that time—Matey unlocked the cupboard, produced the saffron tin, and opened it. Joyce looked inside, and said it wasn't the one she had used—Madge Russell! If you giggle like that, you'll choke!—I suppose you can

one made gingerbread; someone made torte; someone made madeleines—oh, a variety of things.

"Joyce decided to try her hand at Cornish saffron cakes. She had the recipe in a kind of odds-and-ends book she keeps, and as she hadn't expected to want it, she had to go upstairs to fetch it. As it happened, the kitchen saffron was finished, so Frau Mieders told her to get some from Matey, who, it appears, keeps it for her own nefarious purposes.

Joyce got the book, and then hunted up Matey, who was quite amiable, and took her along to the medicine cupboard to get it. Just as she'd unlocked the door, Cyrilla Maurús came along, looking pretty ghastly. She'd slipped with a handful of test-tubes, and cut herself pretty badly. Matey only stopped to tell Joyce to get the stuff from the third tin on the right-hand side of the cupboard, and bring it back when she'd finished with it. Then she marched Cyrilla off to the bathroom, and left Joyce to herself.

"Joyce wasn't sure—in the excitement over Cyrilla—just *what* Matey had said. She opened the tins to make sure, for it was fearfully dark—you know what Monday was like!—and Matey's writing isn't the easiest in the world to read. However, she found it at last, and went off with it, after closing the doors, of course. Matey came along just then for lint and bandages, and *she* only glanced at what Joyce had taken, and then let her go.

"Joyce says she mixed her cakes very carefully—she's quite good at cookery, you know, and likes it—and finally had them ready for the oven. It struck her that the saffron looked rather brighter than usual—almost canary-colour, in fact. But she put that down to its being a German product, and thought no more about it. Hers were the last to go in, as she had been rather a long time getting what she wanted, and by the time she had finished, it was time to lay the tables for Mittagessen.

"Frau Mieders had given her the little oven at the far side, so that the cakes shouldn't be interfered with by the others looking in to see how theirs were doing, and it was just as well.

"I was teaching the Third—German Dictat, if you want to know—when the most *awful* smell began to creep in. We simply couldn't think what it was. I decided that Bill must be giving the Sixth some extra niffy experiment, and

you'd seen her as I first saw her, poor little scarecrow, you'd have had every reason to feel shocked."

"But she's such a length!" said Jo protestingly. "She looks far more like six than four."

"She's just half an inch taller than Rix," said Madge. "You don't notice it so much in him because he's so sturdy. You needn't worry, Joe. Jem says that Peg will be all right before long. She's sleeping well—and you saw what her appetite is like for yourself!"

"Yes; she's certainly improved there," agreed Jo.

"And now, tell me all the news," said her sister. "How do you like teaching? How is that child, Polly Heriot, getting on? Has Biddy O'Ryan told any more banshee yarns this term? And is the Quintette as wicked as ever?"

Jo sighed in an elderly fashion. "The Quintette is sobering down," she said. "Even Corney and Evvy are becoming responsible beings. Oh, Joyce Linton has been distinguishing herself, by the way. Such a joke!"

"What has Joyce been doing?" asked Madge sharply.

"Oh, nothing outrageous. You needn't get so windy. It was only an accident. But it *was* funny—about the one funny thing that's happened this term!" And Jo chuckled infectiously as she thought of it.

"Oh, Jo! Do get on with the story! I could shake you when you sit and chuckle like that!"

Jo slipped further down in her chair, her long legs stretched before her in a most unladylike attitude. "All right; keep cool, my lamb! I'm going to tell you all about it."

She pulled down her skirt, and then began. "You know about Corney's exploit with the garlic when we first began cookery? Well, ever since then, everyone's been almost painfully careful in cooking.

"On Monday, Five A and B had their cookery lesson, and after they had prepared Mittagessen, Frau Mieders, by way of being affable, said they might make cakes for Kaffee—any kind of cakes they liked. They were to do them by themselves, and she wasn't going to interfere at all. She would stay there with them—it was Corney who told me this, by the way—and she would knit. If they were really stuck, they could ask her, but they were to try to do without her if they could.

"So they began. Corney says that she made jumbles; but they got badly singed, so we never saw them. Some-

Miss Denny nodded. "Right! What about solos?"

"Jo, Corney, Evvy, Yvette, and Stacie. They all go to Mr Denny for singing, so he'll arrange them as he chooses."

"What exactly am I?" asked Joey, who had been sitting quietly in a corner, as befitted the youngest and newest member of the Staff.

"You are the Spirit of the Bells," returned Miss Annersley. "The play is called 'The Bells Of Christmas.' Corney is the Spirit of the Snow; Evvy, the Spirit of the Christmas Rose; Yvette will be the Spirit of the Holly; and Stacie the Spirit of Love. You people have very little apart from your singing, so that you will not have much to learn."

Everyone departed, and work began for the day. That afternoon Miss Annersley kept her word. She held Assembly, read out the play to the excited girls; dictated the parts; and before long, the School was hard at work on it.

News from the Sonnalpe continued to be excellent. Mademoiselle would not be able to resume her duties till after Easter, but if she went on as she was doing, the doctors had every hope that she would be able to do so then. "Die Rosen" was at last declared free from infection, and Jo went up to spend a joyous week-end there as soon as possible.

She was amazed at the difference she saw in her nephews and nieces. Sybil had produced two teeth; little Jack was crawling all over; Primula Mary was blooming like a rose in the crystalline, bracing atmosphere, and looked, as Jo said, pounds better. But those who had been ill were most changed. David, Bride, and Rix were as sturdy as ever, and had all grown. But Peggy looked almost another child. She had lost all her dainty chubbiness, and was very tall and thin.

"Madge," said Jo later on, when the children had gone to bed, and the two were together in the salon, "I'd no idea Peggy had been so ill. It gave me a horrid shock when I saw her."

Madge Russell, slight, dark, with the beauty born of a sweet nature in her delicate face, looked into the big eyes fixed on hers. "Jem wouldn't have you told, Joey; but we came very near to losing Peggy during those two or three days she was so ill. However, she's all right now, and she'll soon be plump again. She's much better already. If

CHAPTER XVII

JOEY UNFOLDS A TALE

THE news from the Sonnalpe continued to be good. Very slowly, but very surely, Mademoiselle came back from the Gates of Death, and ten days after the operation was performed, Dr Jem rang up the School to say that, humanly speaking, she was out of danger now.

The School received the news with a certain soberness. Mademoiselle's illness had been so sudden, and her danger so grave, that not even the good news of her recovery could make them wildly hilarious. They had always known that they respected and admired her; but many of them had not realised how they loved her till it seemed possible that they must lose her. So, though there were rejoicings, they were tinged with a certain gravity.

"This won't do," said Miss Annersley to the assembled Staff the day after the news came. "I know the girls have had a bad fright; but it's time they had got over it. Mademoiselle herself would be the first to say so. We don't want the term clouded. I'm going to call Assembly, and dictate the parts for the Christmas play."

"A good idea," agreed Miss Wilson. "In any case, it's high time rehearsals began. We haven't too much time left, and we don't want this year's play to be a frost when we've always done so well before."

"Agreed!" said Miss Nalder. "What time will you hold Assembly?"

"At half-past fourteen. It's snowing again, so they can't go out. I'll give out the parts, and they can have the time for learning them.—Grace," she smiled at Miss Nalder as she spoke, "if you'd like your dancers, I'll send them to you. They won't have any speaking parts, so you can begin on them at once."

"What about the singing classes?" asked Miss Wilson.

"Too bad for Mr Denny to come out," said the senior mistress quickly.—"But, Sarah," she turned to Miss Denny, "you might tell your brother, and ask him if he has the carols chosen. He can begin on them at the next singing lesson."

304

No more was said. The Staff parted for what was left of the night, looking very grave. Miss Annersley fulfilled her promise to the kitchen staff, telling them that the operation was successfully over. She said nothing more, bidding them get off to bed as quickly and quietly as they could. Then she went slowly upstairs to the pretty room where Joey was kneeling by her window, staring out at the black lake in its frame of driven whiteness. As the mistress entered, switching on the light, she turned her head sharply.

"Don't!" she said. "Put that out—I can't bear it just now!"

Miss Annersley obeyed, and then came to sit down on the broad window-seat by her side. Jo lifted heavy eyes to her face. "What else?" she asked.

"Nothing—at present," said Miss Annersley gently. "The heart is very weak; but they hope." She turned and gazed out on the frozen lake for a moment, to give Jo a chance to steady herself. Then she spoke. "Joey, you must go to bed and try to sleep. There will be work for you to-morrow, and you cannot hope to work well if you are tired out. Mademoiselle will have the best of care; and the future lies with God. Remember that, child, and try to trust Him. Now, good-night." She took the white-faced girl in her arms, and kissed her—and from Miss Annersley, that meant much. Jo clung to her for a moment. Then she struggled to her feet.

"Right!" she said curtly. "I'll get to bed. Good-night, Miss Annersley. Thanks for being such a brick to me!"

Miss Annersley left her, and went on to Mademoiselle Lachenais, for she knew the merry little Frenchwoman was devoted to the Head. Mademoiselle had had the long, tiring walk, in addition to anxiety and grief, and the senior mistress felt just a little worried about her.

But little Mademoiselle was quite calm. "I shall compose myself to sleep," she said quietly. "That is the best thing I can do. Bonne nuit, ma chère Hilda. Dormez bien!"

"Bonne nuit, ma Jeanne," replied Miss Annersley. "May there be better news in the morning."

Then, mindful of her own advice to Jo, she went to bed too, and did her best to sleep.

am thankful to say, and looking forward to going home on Thursday."

"Is that when they are coming for her?" asked Jo idly. She knew the answer already; but anything was better than sitting thinking.

Miss Wilson nodded. "Yes; her brother comes for her then, and will take her away at once. Don't let her know anything, girls, for if we can keep it from her, we must. Otherwise, she may try to insist on remaining, and Dr Jem says she *must* have the rest."

"Better not go near her, then," said Jo gloomily. "*I* shan't! I should give it away in a moment if I did."

Silence fell again, and held until the clock chimed for twenty-three hours. Then came the sound of swift feet, and "Matey," who had gone to the study for something, entered. There was that about her which told them that she brought news at last; but for a moment she seemed unable to speak. Then she managed it.

"It's over!" she said, a queer croak in her voice. "The operation has been a success!"

"Then go to bed at once, girls," said Miss Annersley, rising quickly, and checking the demonstrations of delight that would have broken forth if she had not spoken. "No noise, please, or you may wake the others. We shall have fresh news in the morning, I expect. Good-night, all of you!"

"Bill" and Miss Nalder promptly shepherded off their own eight, while the members of Ste Thérèse's departed quietly but joyfully. Jo, last to go, shook her head. Living so close to the Sonnalpe, she realised, as the rest did not, that the success of the operation did not mean that all was well. Miss Annersley saw her, and resolved to let her know whatever else had been said before she slept.

"What else, Matey?" asked Miss Leslie when the Staff were alone at last.

"The operation is a success, as I told you. But the heart is very weak—they are giving injections already—and—" Matron paused, and cleared her throat.

"And—what?" asked Miss Norman, who had come over from St Agnes' when she had seen her little flock to bed.

"They are not sure how she will stand the shock—well, they are doing all they can, and we can only hope and pray for the best."

bring Abendessen for Mademoiselle. Perhaps she will eat it here among us."

"Indeed, I should prefer that," said Mademoiselle.

"Can't I get your slippers?" suggested Jo, rising. "Where are they? Tell me, and I'll bring them. Your feet must be tired in those great boots!"

Mademoiselle smiled. "They are not light, certainly," she agreed. "I should be grateful for my slippers. They are on the little shelf below the window in my room. A thousand thanks, my Jo!"

Jo hurried off, and presently returned with the dainty slippers so characteristic of the little lady, who slipped them on with a sigh of relief, while Evadne removed socks and boots to the kitchen. Then Elsie appeared with the tray, on which was a dainty little supper, and two of the maids followed her with huge trays, laden with bowls of milky coffee for the girls.

Miss Annersley looked her surprise at this, whereupon Trudi explained that Maria thought the young ladies would be glad of a hot drink while they waited for news.

"It is most thoughtful of Maria," said Miss Annersley. "Please tell her, Trudi, that we are very grateful. And say that when any news comes through, I will myself bring it to the kitchen."

Having handed round their trays, Trudi and Gretchen bobbed their curtseys, and went out, and once more the girls settled down to that seemingly endless waiting.

"Oh, will they *never* ring up?" wailed Anne Seymour, when the clock struck for twenty-two hours, and there was still no sign from the Sonnalpe. "It must be *hours* since they began!"

"Not yet three; and they said it would take longer than that," said Mademoiselle Lachenais.

The sound of hurrying feet in the corridor made them all jump with frightened anticipation; but it was only Miss Wilson, come to report that Miss Stewart, who still knew nothing of the shadow which hung over the School, was asleep. "Is there any news?" she added anxiously.

"None," said Miss Annersley.

"Doesn't Miss Stewart really know yet?" asked Evadne.

"Bill" shook her head. "No; the doctors say that we are not to tell her till—till we know one way or the other. So she has gone to sleep quite happily. She is much better, I

attack on history for the morrow; the rest of the Staff either struggled with work, or else joined the silent girls in the common-room, and tried to keep them from dwelling too much on what threatened. They were soon joined by the others, who found all attempt at work fruitless while their minds were occupied with other things.

Mademoiselle Lachenais had gone up with the ambulance, so that the Head might feel that she had a compatriot with her, and she returned about twenty-one hours, white with grief and fatigue, but very composed. She brought no later news. Mademoiselle Lepâttre had stood the journey as well as they could hope. She had been semi-conscious most of the time. They had taken her straight to the Sanatorium, where she had been prepared for the operation at once, and they had just wheeled her into the theatre when Mademoiselle Lachenais set out to return to Briesau.

"Did you see anyone who knew anything?" asked Jo fearfully.

Mademoiselle shook her head. "But no, my Jo. How could I? All thought was for our dear Mademoiselle. I could not disturb them by asking unnecessary questions. Dr Jem will see that someone rings us up when it is over; but that is all."

"They're an awful time about it," said Miss Leslie restlessly. "How long is it since they took her away—five, six hours? It must be something like that."

"They were not quick in going," Mademoiselle reminded her. "The ambulance had to drive slowly. I came down by the direct path."

"Yes; how on earth did you do it?" demanded Jo, thankful for something to distract her thoughts.

Mademoiselle Lachenais held up one foot. "I wore my nailed boots, of course, and I had my alpenstock. Also, there are many stars and a young moon, so that I was well able to see. And I am an Alpinist, as you know. It was not difficult, and that way I could come by myself. To have come down by the coach-road, someone must have driven me; or else I must have waited for the train, and I knew that I might be needed here."

"It was good of you, Mademoiselle," said Miss Annersley quietly, but with deep gratitude in her voice. "But you must be very weary after such a climb.—Elsie, go and

We can only buck up as hard as we can. It—we can't think of *us* at present."

Cornelia's shoulders heaved a moment with a heavy sob. Then she straightened herself. "Guess that's all it amounts to," she said, squaring her jaw. "You're bully good, Joey! I'll play up, too!"

Wise for once, Jo said no more, but left her to herself, and went back along the corridor, where she met Yvette Mercier, who told her that Miss Annersley wanted her in the study. Jo nodded, and went thither, to find a pale-faced Miss Annersley busy with the time-table.

"Telephone-call from 'Die Rosen,' Joey," she said curtly.

Jo turned to the telephone. "Madge!—what's that?—Just arrived, you say? How has she stood it?—No; I suppose they can't, yet—*What?*—Oh, Madge! That's horribly soon! Will she be able to stand it?—Yes; I suppose it's best to get it over. You'll let us know, won't you.—You know how worried we all are.—Right! We will! Goodbye!" She rang off, and faced Miss Annersley.

"Yes; they are going to operate at once," said that lady gently. "I think we'll have Prayers now, Joey. Everyone has come, I think."

"Babies as well?" asked Jo, as she went to the door.

"Yes; this is something for us as a school. Even the babies shall have their part in it."

Jo hurried away, and presently the sound of feet, moving quietly, came to the study, where the mistress was still struggling with the necessary rearrangement of the time-table. When Miss Annersley entered the common-room, she found her flock standing quietly in their places, every face grave, and a strange hush in the atmosphere.

Miss Annersley did not dwell very much on things. She reminded them that their Head was dangerously ill, and that they could help her with their prayers. Then she began, and if her voice shook a little now and then, only the elder girls noticed it.

Prayers over, they were dismissed for Abendessen, and all the younger girls were sent to bed as soon as it was over. The elder girls begged to sit up till news came of how the operation had gone. Miss Annersley agreed, knowing that they were little likely to sleep at present. They could have their sleep out in the morning. She returned to the study and the time-table; Joey made a determined

So the elder girls were told that Mademoiselle's life was in grave danger, and that an operation must be performed immediately. She would not return to the School for many months, and they must not look for it.

"It will be a very difficult and dangerous operation, girls," said Dr Jem heavily, when he told them. "We shall do all we can for her, but the final issue must rest in God's hands. You can help her with your prayers, remember. You shall have regular news of her, for I know how anxious you will be. One other thing: the Staff will be short-handed for the rest of the term. You can help the School by what you *are*. Remember that the little ones will be watching and following your example. That is all; I must go back to Mademoiselle now. Chin up, all of you! Down-heartedness never helped anyone. Courage has often carried a man to what looked like an unattainable goal."

He left them then, and they went to their own places, very subdued.

Cornelia knelt down by her bed, and buried her head against the plumeau. She was perfectly still, and if anyone had asked her, she would have said that her mind was a blank. A motherless girl, she had had most of her mothering from the two Heads of the School; and in the very nature of things, much of it had come from Mademoiselle. Cornelia had been a firebrand when she came; but the influence of the School had taught her many things, and she knew that she owed Mademoiselle a heavy debt.

Jo, coming to ask her about the Fifth-Form work, found her there, and stopped short, feeling intrusive. But Cornelia had heard the light step, and she lifted to the elder girl a deathly-white face, in which her great blue eyes seemed brighter and more enormous than ever.

"Joey," she said.

Joey went in, dropping the cubicle-curtains behind her, and sat down on the bed. She laid a slender hand on the square shoulders. "Poor old woman!" she said, her beautiful eyes soft and misty.

Cornelia squirmed till she was kneeling against the elder girl, an arm flung round her waist.

"She's been all the mother I've ever had," she said in muffled tones. "She and Madame between them. I—I guess I feel kind of bad about this!"

Jo smoothed the fair curls that just reached Cornelia's shoulders. "I know. But you heard what Jem said, Corney.

no likelihood of it before nightfall, if then. The girls were told to wrap up well, take their skates, and go up to the Seespitz end of the lake for the morning. They were safe enough there, and it would get them out of the way. Stacie and the Robin might not skate, so they and Jo set off to walk round the lake to Buchau and back, and Miss Edwards went with them.

It had been hoped that the girls on the ice would be too much absorbed in their sport to notice the "Die Rosen" car when it came. Unhappily for this plan, someone looked round as the car drove over the crisp snow and recognised Dr Jem at the wheel. There were shouts of welcome at sight of him, and two or three girls came to the edge of the lake, Cornelia and Suzanne among them. They saw the nurse sitting at his side, and Gottfried and another of the Sonnalpe doctors behind.

"Something is wrong," said Suzanne instantly. She stared at Cornelia. "Corney! It is Mademoiselle! She is more ill than they have told us, and that is why we have not seen her at all this holiday."

They had been enjoying themselves, but this finished it. They hurried to take off their skates, and raced back to School with anxious faces.

It was long before they got satisfaction from anyone. Indeed, it was not till "Matey," arriving even sooner than anyone had dared to expect, had heard all the news, that they were told anything beyond the fact that Mademoiselle had been taken suddenly worse. *She* promptly declared that the girls had a right to know a certain amount. For Mademoiselle was gravely ill, and already they had phoned for an ambulance to be sent from the Sonnalpe, whither she must be removed.

The doctors declared that they had no idea how she had managed to keep up as long as she had done. She must have suffered more or less continual pain all the term.

"The girls must know," decreed Matron. "They all love Mademoiselle, and if—*if* anything were to happen, they would never forgive us for not warning them. Of course, the babies need only be told that she is very ill but I think the older ones should know how serious it is. I don't believe in trying to shield girls from all sorrow and trouble. We want to make strong, helpful women of them —not spineless jellyfish!"

as she surveyed it from the window of the Yellow Dormitory.

"Are onyxes black?" asked Cornelia. "Say, guess you're some of a poet, aren't you?"

Polly flushed, suspecting teasing, though nothing was further from Cornelia's mind at the moment. I'm no such thing! But Aunt Mariana had an onyx brooch she always wore, and it was shiny black as the lake is now, and it reminded me."

"Polly, is your case ready?" asked "Matey," coming in. "Hurry up, then, and take it over to your own House. We want you people out of the way as soon as possible. Be quick, now! We've trouble enough without your adding to it!" Then she went out again.

At the reminder, Polly flushed again, shoved her possessions into her case, shut it, and went off to St Clare's, very thoughtful and silent.

Trouble had come to the Chalet School indeed.

That morning, Matron Gould, going to see how Mademoiselle Lepâttre was, had found her lying unconscious in her room. Matron had flown for Miss Annersley, and between them they had got her back to bed. They managed to bring her round, but the slightest movement brought back faintness, and, thoroughly alarmed, Matron had rung up the Sonnalpe, and begged that one of the doctors might come down as soon as possible. She also rang up the hotel at Kufstein, where Matron Lloyd was spending the holiday, and asked her to return as soon as she could. Matron Gould was only young, and she was frightened at Mademoiselle's condition.

Meanwhile, Miss Annersley had gone over to St Clare's for Nurse, who came at a run when she heard what had happened. It was a tremendous relief to hear that "Matey" said she was coming by the next train, and would be at Spärtz at noon. They were to make arrangements to meet her there, and she hoped to be at the Chalet as soon as possible.

From the Sonnalpe came the news that Dr Jem and Gottfried Mensch would both come down at once, and one of them would go on to Spärtz to meet "Matey." So, having done all they could, Miss Annersley left Matron Gould with the patient, and went to the girls.

It was a fine day, grey, and bitingly cold, for the frost had the land in an iron grip. But there was no snow, and

296

"If *that* won't teach her to stop doing mad things, I don't know what will," said Miss Edwards, when she had calmed down again.

"She deserves it," said Miss Annersley. "Give it to her, by all means, Gwyneth. Perhaps it will make her think twice another time before she rushes out into the bitter cold without enough on her."

Matron chuckled. "And it's all for her good, too. It shall be done!"

And done it was. Protest she never so wildly, Jo found that she had to submit to having her chest and back rubbed with "Matey's" patent embrocation, *and* swallow a generous dose of the hated cod-liver oil into the bargain. She stopped her protests when she found that Matron Gould was as determined as ever "Matey" could be. Besides, the Robin was sitting up in bed, eyeing her with astonishment. Jo choked down the horrid stuff before that look, and then collapsed on her pillow.

"Go away, Matron! I hate you! If there were a society for the suppression of cruelty to girls, I'd report you to it!"

Matron gurgled aggravatingly, and left the room. However, she returned shortly with two very big and comforting bull's-eyes, one of which she gave to Jo, and the other to the Robin.

"That will finish the warming process," she said as she took her departure. "Good-night, both of you. I'm going to switch off the light now, and there is to be no more talking."

Jo sat up. "Good-night, Matron. All is forgiven between us!" she said dramatically; then dropped on her pillow with a sigh of contentment. Bed was so soft—so warm. And she did love peppermint!

CHAPTER XVI

A FRESH CALAMITY

THE School came back on the Tuesday night to find that the Tiernthal was veiled with snow, the lake black with ice.

"It looks like an onyx set in crystal," said Polly idly,

legend in the School to the effect that when she was really roused, she could beat "Bill" at her own game, and she was obviously roused now. The girls melted out of sight with startling rapidity, and Jo scuttled away to the staff-room, shaking in her shoes.

It took the entire Staff, the cook, and Eitel, Jockel's immediate overlord, to make the lad see sense. He had known nothing about the morning's "sculping," for he had had permission to set off early to go and see his mother and the new baby-brother who had arrived three days before. The place chosen for the statues had been where two of Eitel's lanes met. Poor Jockel, coming by the one from the far gate, had suddenly come upon those hard-frozen images, and in the shock, his scanty wits had deserted him. The light had been streaming over them from the uncurtained staircase window, and, as Miss Annersley herself acknowledged, they had a most ghostly look.

At long last they reduced the lad to something approaching his normal state, and then Miss Annersley left the kitchen regions for the staff-room, where she read the penitent Jo such a lecture on taking insufficient care of herself as sobered that young lady for the rest of the evening.

It was nearly time for Abendessen before the School had finally calmed down, and, all things considered, Miss Annersley decided that once that was over, the best thing would be to send everyone to bed. They had had a late night yesterday; and what with the morning's hard work, and the evening's alarms and excursions, the girls ought to be tired out. It would be the wisest thing for Jo, who could not behave madly with impunity. Two years before, she had nearly died from pneumonia, and Miss Annersley had no desire to have that experience repeated.

"Bed—and hot bottles—and warm milk all round," she told her colleagues. "And you might rub Jo's chest, Matron. It's wiser to take no risks."

"I quite agree," said Matron briskly. She paused, mischief in her eyes. "And what about a dose of cod-liver oil, Hilda? Jo can't monkey with colds."

The Staff rocked with delighted laughter as they pictured Jo's disgust when she was faced with the nauseous draught.

her, with the exception of the little ones, who clung round big Thora, so that she had to stay where she was. She also put out a hand and grasped the Robin as she galloped past her.

Headed by Joey, the others reached the side-door where the mistresses were congregated, to find them surrounding one Jockel, a youth who helped in the gardens and attended to the cricket-pitches and tennis-lawns in season. Miss Wilson had always declared that he was slightly "wanting." At first the bewildered Staff were under the impression that "slightly" had become "altogether." He could only grovel there, mouthing at the ladies, and clutching the skirts of Miss Annersley, who happened to be nearest.

"Jockel, cease this nonsense!" she said authoritatively in German. "What does all this mean?"

"The devils—the beautiful white devils!" howled Jockel, crossing himself rapidly. "They rose round me as I entered the snow-lane, mein Fräulein. I have barely escaped with my life!"

"*Rubbish!*" said Miss Annersley trenchantly. "What do you mean?—Bring him in, some of you, while I go and see what has upset him."

She was forestalled by Joey, who rushed out, regardless of the fact that she was bare-headed and coatless.

"It's our statues!" proclaimed Jo, standing a little way down the lane. "He hadn't seen them before, and—well, I suppose they *are* rather alarming if you come on them suddenly."

"Jo! Are you mad?" cried Annersley. "Come in at once!"

Suddenly realising how she was clad, Jo obeyed meekly, and the mistress, having seen for herself that the statues were almost certainly the cause for Jockel's extraordinary outburst, followed her in, and shut the door.

"Go to the staff-room, Jo, and wait for me there," she said grimly. "You girls, go back to the common-room at once."

Miss Annersley was generally regarded as the gentlest member of the Staff. Miss Wilson was renowned for her biting tongue, and Miss Stewart had a peppery Scots temper, while even merry little Mademoiselle Lachenais could be roused to fury on occasion. But Miss Annersley was an equable person as a rule. However, there was a

Meanwhile, the maids were bringing in the big urn of coffee, and the pretty baskets laden with cakes and twists of fancy bread, and the girls gathered round with merry talk and laughter. They were inclined to be drowsy, however, for the hard work of the morning, allied to the warmth of the room and the quiet afternoon they had spent, made them sleepy. Indeed, the four babies *had* slept during the afternoon. From outside came an occasional sharp "cr-r-rack!" as some heavily laden branch gave way beneath the weight of frozen snow.

Joey nodded her head. "Skating on Monday with any luck! It must be freezing hard now. The windows will be all ice-ferns and flowers in the morning."

"D'you think the lake will bear by Monday?" asked Cornelia. "Those springs, you know—"

"It'll bear all right at the Seespitz end. It's shallow enough there. I don't say it'll bear all over. The frost will have to carry on for much longer than that before it is."

"Why?" asked Polly curiously.

"Don't ask me. I only know that the springs do make a big difference, and no matter how hard or how long it freezes, there are certain parts of the lake that are never safe."

"Jo, do you think we might ask to go to the Dripping Rock to-morrow for our walk?" asked Yvette suddenly. "It must be wonderful now."

"Good idea! It'll be fresh to Polly, and Robin hasn't seen it for years—nicht wahr?"

The Robin shook her black curls. "Not since I have been at the Annexe. I am so seldom down in the winter. Oh, I do hope Miss Annersley will say yes!"

They were talking idly in this strain, when a sudden wild yell from outside startled them all to their feet, making Jo upset her newly filled cup. As the hot liquid soaked through her skirt, she added to the shrieks that still resounded.

"What is it, then?" gasped Yvette, in her own language.

"Guess it's someone being murdered," announced Cornelia, tearing to the window to drag back the curtains and see if she could see anything.

The rest flocked after her, all except Jo, who suddenly tossed into a corner the handkerchief with which she was trying to scrub her skirt dry, and made for the door. Turning to see what she was doing, the rest rushed after

was his profile Greek, for his nose was a decided pug!

Thora's six had a pretty representation of Flora, and had been sensible enough to portray her lying among flowers. It is true Jo asked what "those funny-looking lumps of snow about her are?" But at least none of her head dropped away.

Cornelia, nothing if not ambitious, had aimed at the Goddess of Liberty, and the less said the better about the maledictions uttered against the lady as they struggled with her torch and her rays of light. In the end, they had to leave out these important parts, and then, as Yvette pointed out, she might have been anything.

The Staff had produced a young knight asleep with his hands clasping his sword. They had meant to give him a helmet, but no one could decide how the helmet should go, so they left it off, and gave him a deep fringe instead. The girls cheered this loudly, and the Staff felt rewarded for their hard work.

By this time, it was time for Mittagessen, and they all went in with glowing cheeks and tremendous appetites. They had intended going out after the meal, and snowballing the statues; but when Miss Annersley poked a head out to see what it was like, she found a decided change had taken place. The air was bitter, and it was plain that it was freezing hard. The girls had had a strenuous morning, and some of them were looking sleepy. Besides, yellowish clouds were beginning to float across the horizon, sure harbingers of more snow. So she told them they must content themselves indoors for the rest of the day, and they settled down contentedly enough with books, letters, jigsaws, sewing, painting—and always chatter. No one thought any more about those somewhat ghostly figures left to freeze solid.

Meanwhile, the cold intensified, and the statues grew harder. When Jo went to draw the curtains before Kaffee und Kuchen, she gave an exclamation of delight, for the snowy scene was glittering and sparkling under the warm light flowing from the windows, and the whole landscape looked as if it were covered with brilliants.

"If this goes on, we shall get skating shortly," she said. "Topping fun!"

"I can't skate," said Polly sadly. "There never was any ice where we lived—not enough for skating, anyway."

"Oh, you'll soon pick it up," said Jo cheerfully.

could find, despite the protests made by Maria, the Ste Thérèse's cook.

"We'd better not try to make arms sticking out, I suppose?" said Thora doubtfully. "The snow does not stick well, and they would drop off, I am afraid."

"I'd advise lying-down positions," said Miss Edwards, pausing in her task of flattening the snow her colleagues brought her.

"We're going to do an upright one," said Jo. "We needn't have arms flying all over the place."

"*We're* doing Plato," said Margia, with an air. "Ought he to have a book, Joey?"

"Talk sense! You know quite well they only had scrolls in those days. If that's all you know, I'd advise you to choose something you *do* know," said Jo, staggering under the heaped-up dish she held.

Margia sniffed. "And I'd advise *you* to leave most of the modelling to the others. I'm sure Herr Laubach would say so."

There was a roar of laughter at this. Herr Laubach and Joey had had many a passage-of-arms, for drawing was decidedly *not* her gift. The finale had come about a year before, when she had set out to see how trying she could be, and he, losing his temper, had flung paper, pencils and rubber at her head. As a result, Jo had been removed from all art classes and put on to extra maths, for it was felt that the irritable art-master must be protected against any further loss of dignity. As Jo hated maths, she got only what she deserved, as everyone had rubbed well in, so she flushed now, but said nothing further.

At length, everyone decided that the snow-piles were large enough to begin modelling. And very tantalising they found it. Just as you got a really classical nose shaped, it either sank in the middle, or the end turned snub, or it fell off altogether. Those who had not been wise enough to keep to simple lines, soon found their mistake. Arms were worse than noses, and hands were simply dreadful.

At Jo's suggestion, her group had made a statue of little Ste Thérèse of Lisieux, with her hands folded on her breast. The severe lines of the Carmelite habit were much easier than a Greek chiton, for they fell to the feet.

Margia's group had also managed quite well with "Plato's" flowing robes. But his beard had been simply dreadful, and the scroll had had to be given up. Nor

However, when bedroom work was finished, they were all told to put on their winter-weather clothes, for they were to go out for a couple of hours.

"No chance of a walk," said Miss Annersley. "We don't want to have to dig you out of the drifts. But Eitel has swept some paths for you, and it is going to freeze, so you can run along. Only keep moving."

Thrilling over the novelty of it, Polly got into climbing-breeches, nailed boots, pull-over, leather jacket that zipped up to her chin, and crossed-over woollen shawl. She wriggled her head into a close-fitting cap that covered her ears, and her hands into mitts, and was ready. There was no sun, and the sky gave no signs of its coming, so the girls were not expected to wear snow-glasses.

"But if the sun *should* come, then you must all fly," said Miss Annersley. "We don't want any cases of snow-blindness."

"What's that?" asked Polly of Jo, as they went along the passage.

"Horrid!" said Jo, who had had a taste of it. "Everything goes red and swimmy. So mind you scoot if the sun does come."

Outside, the girls found themselves walking between walls of snow that were well over the heads of all but the tallest. However, it was outside, and that was all that mattered. They ran races, tossed snowballs, and generally enjoyed themselves. Then Jo had an inspiration.

"Let's make figures in snow," she proposed.

"Snowmen?" shrieked Amy and the Robin. "Oh, yes!"

"As it happens, I didn't mean anything so commonplace," said Jo with dignity. "We'll choose some sort of statue and try to make it. If we pack the snow hard and then cut it out, we ought to be able to manage all right."

The noise they made over this brilliant idea brought the Staff out to see who was being murdered, and they joined in at once.

"Let's make up groups of so many, and each take one statue and see who can do best," proposed Miss Norman.

No sooner said than done. Four groups of the girls and one of the Staff set to work at once. First they built up huge piles of snow, pressing it down to make it more solid. All the shovels in the toolhouse and the kitchens were commandeered; and Jo, unable to get one of these useful implements, went off with the biggest bowl she

"Oh, rats!" said Jo hastily. "Hello—Subject and Object? Good! Come along!" And she led the way to the circle they were forming, while Matron took the sleepy Juniors off to bed.

She returned half-an-hour later to find the entire party arguing as to whether Cyrano de Bergerac had had a handkerchief or not, this having been Jo's idea when she and Polly had gone out. Jo, who was the Object, had stoutly maintained that she was vegetable, and many and varied had been the guesses, till at length they had had to give it up. She had then proclaimed what she was, and stuck to it, saying, that, as in those days there was no artificial silk, it must be linen, and that was a vegetable all right.

Miss Norman vowed that Cyrano would certainly never have such a thing, and the camp was divided. Asked for her opinion, Matron declared that she knew nothing about the gentleman, whereupon at least six people tried to enlighten her at once, in the midst of which the clock struck the hour, and Miss Annersley promptly put an end to the babel by ruling that the party was over.

CHAPTER XV

STATUES—AND A SEQUEL

NEXT morning, they woke to find the storm at an end for the time being, and the land covered with great drifts of white snow, while the clear, grey-blue sky betokened a fine day.

Polly, gazing out at it from the common-room window, heaved a sigh of delight. "I never even imagined snow could look so lovely! D'you think they'll let us go out in it?"

"I expect so," said Stacie Benson, joining her. "It wants frost, though, to make it right for walking. We shouldn't get far in this!"

"Why not?"

"It's so powdery, we should sink at once. And some of those drifts would be above our heads if we went through them," said Stacie thoughtfully.

"Oh, Miss Annersley! Don't *you* rub it in! I feel aged as it is," said Jo with a sigh.

Miss Annersley smiled. "A sure sign of how young you really are. Well, it's over now. Hurry up with your supper, and then we'll present the prizes."

"How did you come to have them?" asked Jo.

"Miss Edwards went down to Innsbruck this morning," said Miss Annersley.

"In all that snow?"

"Eigen took her. He knows every inch of the way."

"Oh, I see. How topping of her to go!"

Miss Annersley left them after that, and when they finally reached the common-room, dancing was still going on. Miss Norman clapped her hands when she saw them, the music stopped, and everyone looked round.

"Prizes, now! said Miss Annersley. "Sit down, all of you."

Miss Norman and Miss Edwards carried the table from behind the screen, and set it in the middle of the floor. The senior mistress took up her position behind it, and Mademoiselle Lachenais read out the list. The Robin won first prize for the prettiest dress, and Polly, as a Skating Girl, received second. The most original went to Margia Stevens, and Suzanne Mercier. Cornelia won the funniest, with Biddy O'Ryan (as a Snowball) the second. Then came a surprise.

"Most applicable, Yvette Mercier, and Thora Helgersen," read Mademoiselle Lachenais.

The ex-Nun came up blushing and delighted, to receive the fountain-pen she had won; and big Thora was delighted, too, with her little brooch. The four "babies" had boxes of sweets, and Jo got a book she had long coveted for being "most helpful."

"Oh, I'm glad you've got something, Joey," said Stacie Benson when it was over, and the girls were dancing again. "You practically made the dresses for Robin and me, and you hadn't any time left for yourself."

"I'm glad to get this," said Jo, with a pat for André Maurois' latest novel. "But it was a surprise. That Indian get-up couldn't have won me anything. You couldn't have anything much simpler."

"That's just what I'm saying," said Stacie. "You gave all your time and ideas to us. It's only fair you should have something."

Stay with her, Jo, while I get the scissors."

The Robin obediently choked back her tears, and Jo, looking like the Tragic Muse, stayed with her. Matron returned in a few minutes with her scissors, and was as good as her word. With the greatest care, she snipped at the obstinate curls, and at length the poor little angel was free from her nimbus without much damage.

"Now come and wash your face," said Matron. "You certainly can't go to take the first prize for the prettiest dress looking like that!"

"Have I won that?" asked the Robin doubtfully.

"Yes; yours was by far the prettiest. We decided on it at once," said kind Matron.

The Robin cheered up. "I didn't expect that.—Joey, do you hear? Is it not nice?"

Joey's face cleared. "Ever so nice, my Robin."

"And who has won the others?" asked the Robin, as they went to the bathroom.

"You'll see when you've had your supper," said Matron. "Make haste, both of you."

Jo hastily washed her hands, and then pinned up her straying locks, by which time the Robin looked her usual self, though her top curls had gone. Indeed, when they got downstairs to the Speisesaal, Amy Stevens voiced the views of the others when she said, "Why, you look just the same!"

"What did you expect?" demanded Jo.

Amy giggled. "Corney said Robin would have to be shaved and wear a wig," she said.

"Corney's got a lurid imagination," commented Matron, as she sat down to her jelly. "All we had to do was to cut the hair round the edge of the halo. Now run along, all of you, and leave us to get our supper."

The girls trooped off to the common-room to dance again, and the three left went on with their meal.

"All the same, it was a senseless thing to do, Jo, and I can't think why you did it," said Miss Annersley. "You might have known that the enamel would stick."

"It said on the tin it was quick-drying," protested Jo. "It said it would harden in two hours, and I did the halo before Mittagessen to give it a chance."

"I can't help what it said. You've seen the result for yourself," said Miss Annersley severely. "I do wish you'd try to grow up now!"

trappings and change into the ordinary brown velvet frocks of evening wear. The prizes had already been allotted, Miss Annersley told them, and they would be more comfortable in their usual garb. They raced off upstairs, and changed hurriedly, and were soon down again, consuming sandwiches, jellies, creams, fruits, sweets, lemonade, and coffee, as if they hadn't had a meal all day.

"Where are Joey and the Robin?" asked Mademoiselle Lachenais, suddenly pausing in the act of helping Amy Stevens to lemon sponge.

Everyone looked round. Neither was to be seen.

"Joey must have sewn herself or the Robin into the dress, and is having to cut free," suggested Margia.

It seemed the likeliest solution of the problem, and would have been accepted; but at that moment Joey herself appeared at the door of the Speisesaal, desperation in her face.

"Matron!" she said. "For goodness' sake come and help me! The enamel on the Robin's halo can't have been quite dry. The heat must have melted it a little, and now it's stuck."

"*What?*" exclaimed Matron, while the rest sat, stunned to silence by this happening.

"I can't get it off," repeated Joey. "I've tried and tried, but I can't move it without pulling her hair out by the roots. For pity's sake, come and see what *you* can do!"

With an indescribable expression, Matron got to her feet and followed the agitated Jo from the room. Just as she shut the door, Cornelia's clarion tones could be heard pronouncing on the catastrophe: "Gee! Well, I guess at that rate they'll have to *shave* the Robin to get rid of it! —Miss Annersley, what will they do till they can get her a wig?"

Do what she would, Matron could not get that obstinate halo removed from the Robin's head. It stuck firmly, and gave way before neither hot water, turpentine, nor anything else she could suggest.

"There's no help for it; we must cut it away," she said at length, when the Robin had been reduced to tears, and Jo was in the depths of despair. "What possessed you to use enamel at all, Jo, I can't think! Now don't cry, Robin. I'll get my embroidery scissors, and cut as carefully as I can. Miss Annersley will keep back some supper for us, so you won't miss anything but a little dancing.

hooting outside, and an abnormally tall figure rushed on them, waving batlike wings. One or two of the little ones shrieked, and rushed to hide their faces in the nearest big person. But Margia recognised the movements of the Ghost which had swooped down on them, and cried out, "Corney Flower! I know it is!"

The next moment, they were thronging round her, demanding to know how she had managed it. For reply, the figure squirmed a minute, an opening appeared somewhere about the middle of the lengthy figure, and Cornelia's square-jawed face with twinkling blue eyes grinned out at them.

"How have you done it?" demanded Margia.

"Hockey-stick strapped to my back and head. My wings? Oh, badminton racquets, of course. It's a bit confining, but I guess I can stand it for an hour or so."

"We shall all be ready to change by that time," sighed the nun. "I feel as if I were cooked already!"

"Here come Joe and Stacie and the Robin," said her sister Suzanne. "They are the last, so we can now begin."

All eyes were turned to the door, through which a tall Indian lady in white sari appeared, followed by an Arab chieftain, and an angel with great curving wings, sandalled feet, and glistening silver halo laid on the thick black curls. The Robin looked a picture, as everyone agreed, and the other two were quite effective. Jo had "scrounged" all the bangles and bead-strings she could, and the result was that whenever she moved, she jingled musically.

"'Tis a nose-ring you ought to have," said Biddy O'Ryan.

"Not likely!" retorted Jo, "I've got ear-rings—Mademoiselle lent me a pair—and the screws hurt, but I'm so afraid of losing them, I daren't slacken them."

"You'll soon get accustomed to them," said Miss Norman soothingly. "The first dance is a waltz. Will you have it with me, Joey? Matron is going to play."

The Arch-Druid sat down at the piano, and the floor was soon filled with merry girls, as the lilting notes of Strauss's "Morgenblätter" went rippling through the room. The Angel, the Butterfly and the Ghost found it somewhat difficult—wings and a hockey-stick are not the best adornments when dancing—but they managed, and enjoyed themselves enormously.

Abendessen found them all thankful to cast aside their

ones of crimson paper. The furniture was all set back against the wall, and the rugs were rolled up and carried off to the nearest form-room. When at length the work was completed, the common-room had been transformed.

"Most effective!" said Miss Edwards, when it was all done.

"Most," agreed Matron Gould. "But do you know the time?"

They glanced hastily at their watches, and then fled with little shrieks of horror, for they had barely twenty minutes in which to change and be ready to welcome their guests.

They were all in time, all looking very festive in their unwonted attire. Miss Annersley was garbed as a Roman Matron, with her hair banded with white tape. Matron Gould, who stood five feet ten in her stockings, had elected to appear as an Arch-Druid, with a Welsh harp slung across her shoulders. Miss Norman was a Scots fisher-lass, with upturned skirt, and the pillow-case folded and tied under her chin. Miss Edwards was a geisha, and as she was very small and dark, she looked very well.

But Mademoiselle Lachenais had outdone them all, for she was attired as a Normandy peasant, with the pillow-case turned into a charming cap, goffered and wired to make it stand up. Her vivacious little dark face stood the dead white admirably, and Miss Norman cried, "Why, Jeanne, I'd no idea you were so pretty!" which brought a most becoming blush to Mademoiselle's cheeks.

The next moment, there was a tap at the door, and their first guests appeared—Thora, Margia, and Amy. Thora had transformed herself into a Norwegian peasant-girl; Amy was a white butterfly, with wings made of sheets of tissue-paper, wired to the right shape; Margia herself wore flowing robes, a wreath of white-paper leaves round her brown curls, and a sheet of paper in one hand, on which was inscribed "The Republic."

"Plato!" gasped Miss Annersley. "Well, upon my word!"

"Not bad, is it?" said Margia complacently. "Who's this coming?"

A ballet-dancer, her skirts held out by means of canes and wire, tripped in, accompanied by a nun, who was already complaining that she felt as if she were being boiled alive. Then others appeared, and great had been the ingenuity the girls showed. Suddenly, there was a loud

"Aha! That, as Hamlet so neatly says, is the question. Wait and see, my child."

"What are you being, Polly?" asked Jo, as she handed her cup to Thora.

Polly chuckled. "I'll give you your own answer: wait and see."

"Impertinent infant! I ought to rise and ker*rush* you, but I can't be bothered. Lights ho, someone! I can't see the way to my own mouth!"

Dorothy Brentham obligingly rose to the situation, and the much-needed lights were switched on. Polly and Yvette ran to draw the curtains, and the big room took on an air of cosy comfort.

"That's better!" sighed Jo. "Thanks, Thora. Well, if you'll all excuse me, I'll go and finish.—Coming Robin?"

"But yes, Joey!" The Robin jumped up from her stool, and the pair left the room. Margia, who still had a good deal to do at her own costume, though Amy's was finished, ran off, too. One by one the others followed, and when Miss Annersley presently peeped in, the room was empty. She nodded to someone behind the door, and beckoned.

"All right; they've gone! Come along, Jeanne, and you other four! It's no use hoping for Joey's help. She declares that she means to be a girl for the week-end.—Bring those draperies, Ivy, and you fetch that screen, Dorothy."

Miss Norman appeared, laden with crimson curtains, and Miss Edwards followed her, dragging a tall screen after her. Mademoiselle Lachenais and Matron Gould came last, bearing between them a table which was covered with sundry parcels.

"Where shall we put it, Hilda?" asked the latter anxiously.

Miss Annersley looked round. "In that corner, I think," she said, gesticulating. "We'll set the screen before it, and hang up a notice to keep the girls off."

They bore the table to the corner, and Miss Edwards staggered after them with her screen, while Miss Norman, having dropped her draperies on a near-by settee, hurried from the room, to return with one of the maids helping her to carry a tall, library ladder.

The Staff then became busy. They tacked up the curtains round the wall, and draped against them long paper chains and sprays of artificial flowers. Miss Norman took off the ordinary light-shades, and substituted home-made

beyond the palisade. Ordinarily, those in charge might have found it difficult to keep the girls amused. But thanks to the latest idea for a party, nobody even asked for amusement.

"When does the party begin?" asked Yvette Mercier of Miss Annersley during Mittagessen.

The senior mistress looked at Jo. "Didn't you put the time on the invitation, Jo?"

"Mercy! I believe I forgot all about it!" cried Jo. "Sorry, everyone, I'll go and rectify that as soon as I've finished."

She finished her Kalbsbraten (stuffed roast veal), and then asked permission to go to the common-room for a few minutes. Miss Annersley nodded her head and laughed, and Jo fled to enter the hours of the party, returning to find the others busy with Apfel-torte.

"All serene," she said, as she took her seat again. "You'll all see when you're finished."

They swarmed round the board as soon as they were freed, to find that the party would take place from nineteen to twenty-two hours, whereat some of the smaller folk clapped their hands. Late hours were almost unknown at the Chalet School.

"What about Abendessen?" demanded Margia of Jo, who had elected to desert the Staff.

"Not till twenty hours," returned Jo. "It's part of the party—sorry, everyone! That was not meant for a pun!"

"Thank goodness!" Margia heaved a sigh of relief. "Then I may be able to finish in time!"

"I *have* finished," said Cornelia with a self-satisfied smirk.

"Corney Flower! You *haven't*!"

"'Have, though. I finished early this afternoon, and I've been reading for ages."

"Then you must be nothing but safety-pins."

"It's sewn—every it of it," said Cornelia indignantly.

"The age of miracles is still with us," said Jo lazily. "Corney Flower has made a frock in about three hours, and hasn't safety-pinned it! Better send the news to the daily papers!"

"What about your own?" demanded Stacie. "I don't see where you've got time to make yours, for you've been busy with Robin and me all day. What are you going to do?"

want any more, you must come and ask me. I shall be in the linen-room from ten till eleven in case anyone should require another. Now get on with your work as quickly as possible."

She left them to go on to the next dormitory, and they hurried to finish their beds and tidying. Once that was ended, they all departed to the common-room to discuss dresses, and there the Staff found them when they came in for Prayers.

Prayers over, the girls gathered round the mistresses for a few minutes, talking eagerly.

"Mademoiselle," cried Cornelia, "are you folks going to dress up too?"

"Mais certainement," replied Mademoiselle, laughing. "Is it that you wish to keep all the fun to yourselves?"

"Listen, you people," said Miss Annersley, "we are offering prizes for the prettiest costume, for the most outstanding costume, and for the funniest. Now we are going to leave you to it. We have our own dresses to make. Come along, everybody!" And she swept off her colleagues, while the girls were still gasping.

"Well!" cried Cornelia, the ever-ready, as the door closed on the Staff, "I guess this is going to need some right smart thinking. I'm off to the Fifth to think it out by myself. So-long, everybody!"

Most of the elder girls followed her example, and Jo Bettany, sitting in the library sewing, with the Robin beside her, was startled when the door was opened, and Margia Stevens, accompanied by her young sister, came in with a hunted expression, which changed to one of disgust as she saw the room already occupied.

"You here!' she exclaimed. "There simply isn't a solitary place in the house where you can be decently alone!"

"Sorry I can't go to my own room," said Jo amiably. "It's too near Mademoiselle. And besides that, something's gone wrong with the stove, and till Eitel can put it right, Matron says it's much too cold for me. Besides, Robin couldn't sit there, and I've got her dress to do, as well as my own. Why don't you try Vater Bär's music-room?"

"Good idea! So I will.—Come on, Amy!" And Margia vanished.

It continued to snow throughout the day, the snow whirling down so dizzily that it was impossible to catch even a glimpse of the lake, which lay barely four feet

"Guess you're the one to do the explaining," said Cornelia. "It's your stunt—I know that all right."

"Clever child!" said Jo aggravatingly.

"What's it mean, Jo?" asked Margia, pushing back the thick curls that were always tumbling into her eyes.

"Exactly what it says, my child." Then Jo condescended to explain. "You manufacture some sort of fancy costume from two sheets and a pillowcase, and there are prizes for costumes. You've got all day to do it in, and there certainly won't be any going out while this storm lasts, so it'll occupy your time nicely. There goes the gong for Frühstück, and if you're all as hungry as I am, you're not sorry. Come along, all of you. And when it's over, don't forget to R.S.V.P. to the invite!" And Jo walked off to the Speisesaal, chuckling to herself over their stunned faces.

The imperative sound of the gong sent them after her, but for once there was little conversation at Frühstück. Everyone was much too busy wondering what sort of a costume she could evolve from two sheets and a pillowcase to want to talk. Some of the very tinies were thoroughly perplexed, but Miss Edwards and Miss Norman, their own special mistresses, who were also spending the week-end at the School though they were not on duty, promised to help them.

"Can we *cut* the sheets?" asked Cornelia suddenly, between two mouthfuls of roll and jam.

"*Cut* your sheets, Cornelia? Most certainly *not*!" cried Miss Annersley. "Please, all of you, understand once and for all that your sheets and pillowcases are to remain intact. You may safety-pin them, or stitch them lightly; but there is to be no cutting."

There was silence again after this, and when grace had been said, they all went off to make their beds and tidy their cubicles, still exercising their brains to find costumes that could be made of sheets and pillowcases without cutting the materials.

"But I say!" exclaimed Dorothy Brentham suddenly, "if we're going to use them for dresses, what's the use of making our beds now?"

"You're all going to have clean ones for the dresses, of course," said Matron Gould, appearing at that moment laden with sheets, while Jo followed with pillowcases. "Here you are—two each, and one pillowcase. If you

AMUSEMENTS AND RECREATION!

COMPETITIONS! DANCING! SINGSONG!

R.S.V.P. to members of the Staff-room.

Those present read this striking notice, and then turned and looked at each other. Margia was the first to speak.

"What," she demanded of the assembled circle, "*is* a sheets-and-pillowcase party?"

"Is it zat we have to bring our sheets and pillowcases wiz us?" suggested Suzanne, who, despite several years at an English school, had never yet mastered the English "th."

"Yes; but what under the canopy do we *do* with them?" asked Cornelia, still staring at the invitation.

Dorothy Brentham, who had now joined the group, had a suggestion to make: "P'raps we're going to make up beds on the floor like a kind of camp—"

"It says 'dancing,'" Cornelia reminded her. "Oh, here's Thora! P'raps *she* knows!—Grüss Got, Thora! Come and see this, and tell us what you think it means."

The big Norwegian returned Cornelia's greeting with a laughing "Grüss Gott!" and then came to the notice-board, and read the notice it bore.

"What on earth is a sheets-and-pillowcase party?" asked Cornelia. "D'you know, Thora?"

Thora shook her head. "I never heard of one before. I cannot think what it can be. It is Jo's idea, of course. Our best plan is to catch her, and ask what it means."

Polly Heriot skipped out of the room on the word to seek Jo, and met her just outside the door, the Robin clinging to her arm, and looking up at her with merry laughter. Polly eagerly grabbed Jo's free arm, and exclaimed, "Jo! Do come and tell us what a sheets-and-pillowcase party is, for we've no idea!"

Jo grinned. "Haven't you? How fearfully dull you must all be! All right; I'm coming—In you go, Robinette, and don't get into any draughts, whatever you do."

The Robin chuckled as she danced into the room, to be seized on by Amy Stevens, and borne off to the notice-board to inspect the cause of all the excitement. Jo was promptly besieged by the rest, all demanding to know what it meant.

They're jolly decent, really. But don't you remember, Corney, that morning when Maynie had the Seniors, and Charlie us Middles, and we went for a walk, and got caught coming back? I believe the Seniors got it worse than we did, for they weren't anywhere near home when it came on. But I had quite enough of it as it was. It was a few days before we took that walk when the lake-path gave way, and we all had to climb up to Mechthau and go over the shoulder of the mountain and down the Pass to get home. *Now* do you remember?"

Cornelia did. "Guess I do. That awful ass Elaine Gilling rowed with Mary," she said reminiscently. "And that other creature, Vera Smithers, was there. Yes; it was some storm."

"As bad as this—really?" asked Polly, pausing in the act of pulling on a stocking.

"Every bit—if not worse," said Margia promptly. "You don't know what it's like when it starts to snow here. You wait till the end of this term. You'll know all about it then."

Polly thought she knew a little already after seeing that mad dervish-dance of snowflakes outside. However, she said no more, but went on with her dressing. When the bell rang, they all raced downstairs in a hurry.

"We must have wasted a fearful lot of time at the window," said Margia to Cornelia. "I didn't think we were standing there so long.—Did you, Corney?"

Cornelia shook her head. "Guess 'twas longer than we thought," she said.

Suzanne Mercier was in advance of them, and while they were only just at the foot of the stairs, she had gone on, and into the common-room. Now they heard her exclaim, "Mon Dieu! Qu'est-se qu'il y a?"

At once they tore after her, to find her gazing at a huge sheet of drawing-paper which covered the notice-board. It had a border of rabbits in various attitudes—Mademoiselle Lachenais was very clever at sketching animals—and inside the border was written:

INVITATION

The pleasure of the company of all girls left at school for half-term is requested to-night at

A GRAND SHEETS-AND-PILLOWCASE PARTY

half-term, so there was a rush to the two window-cubicles. Margia, in her hurry, contrived to trip over Biddy O'Ryan, and the pair of them came down with a crash, Biddy giving vent to a howl as she went.

"Ow, Margia Stevens! 'Tis yourself's the heavy gerrl! Be getting off me hair, will yez, now?"

Margia picked herself up in a hurry. "Well, I haven't killed you," she said soothingly. "Shut up, Biddy! You'll disturb Mademoiselle if you squall like that! Get up, now, and don't lie there, howling like a banshee!—O-oh! I *say!*" For by this time she was in Cornelia's cubicle, and gazing out of the window at the falling snow, which was coming down as if it never meant to leave off.

"Just into November and the snows have come! Oh, well; it's no earlier than last year, after all."

"It's come earlier than this before now," remarked Cornelia, as she turned to find her dressing-gown.

"But—but isn't it *awful?*" gasped Polly from the other cubicle. "I never even imagined snow like this! I wouldn't like to be out in it!"

"Nor should I," said Dorothy Brentham, with a shake of her head of yellow curls.

"I *have* been out when it was as bad as this," said Margia, beginning to stroll back to her own abode. "D'you remember, Corney?"

Cornelia, who had left the window and was now hunting for her stockings beneath the bed, replied in a muffled voice, "No; I don't. When was it?"

"Corney! Of course you do! Don't you remember that first term the Saints came here?"

"Who are the Saints?" demanded Polly.

"Oh, goodness! Don't you know that yet? It's St Scholastika's, at the other side of the lake. They came two years ago, and we did *not* love them at first."

"Jolly good reason why," said Cornelia, wriggling out from beneath the bed.—"Here, you folk, vamoose! I want to get dressed, and I guess you'd better be thinking about it yourselves. It must be mighty late if the light's anything to go by."

They went, reluctantly, and when everyone was busy, Polly lifted up her voice again. "Why didn't you like the Saints, Margia?"

"Oh, we just didn't fit in," said Margia hurriedly. "We had one or two rows; but it all came right in the end.

kiss the rosy face. "Your guardian angel watch over you all night long!"

"Good-night, Joey, *dearest* Joey!" said the Robin, with a hug.

Jo tucked in the blankets more securely, and then went to the window to make sure that the draught-board was in. As she opened the curtains she uttered an exclamation.

"What is it, Joey?" asked the Robin sleepily.

"Snow, Robinette! It's coming down in cart-loads! With any luck we shall get a snow-fight to-morrow, to say nothing of other joys! Now you go to sleep, mein Blümchen. I'll be coming presently. I know Miss Annersley means us all to get to bed in decent time to-night. Schlaf' wohl!" And with a final kiss, Jo went off downstairs to announce the joyful news that the snow had come.

CHAPTER XIV

A "DIFFERENT" PARTY

EXCITEMENT had made the girls drowsy, and it was nearly eight o'clock before they woke the next morning. As there were so few of them, they were sleeping in four dormitories. Polly had been put into the Yellow Dormitory, along with Cornelia Flower and Margia Stevens, who slept there normally; the others being Suzanne Mercier, Biddy O'Ryan, Kitty Burnett, Stacie Benson, Dorothy Brentham. Cornelia and Margia had their own cubicles, and the others were distributed round the dormitory.

"What's the weather doing?" demanded Margia from her cubicle near the door as she sat up with a shiver. "Urrh! Isn't it cold?"

There was the sound of clothes being thrown back, and then a bump told that Cornelia was out of bed and pulling back the window-curtain. She uttered a cry of surprise.

"Say, girls! It's snowing—snowing fit to beat the band! Just come and look!"

Rules were always more or less in abeyance during

to see it! Irma was telling me all sorts of fairy-tales about it being like dust."

Jo shouted. "What a simile! I'm surprised at Irma! Oh, it's powdery, all right, and absolutely dry. But to liken anything so sparkling and lovely as snow to *dust* . . ." Words apparently failed her at this point, and Polly laughed.

"Well, anyhow, they all say it just brushes off you, and doesn't wet you. *I've* never seen any snow like that," observed young Doubtful. "I'm looking to see if it's likely to come. It'll be something out of the common when it does, if all their yarns are true! What do you think, Joey? Will it be along soon?"

Joey peered out into the gathering gloom. "It doesn't look impossible," she conceded. "In fact, it wouldn't surprise me in the least if it snowed before midnight. I don't think it's likely to come much before then, though. You come along and meet the Robin, Polly. The snow won't come any sooner for you sitting there, trying to mesmerise it!"

This was true, besides being sensible, so Polly left her post at the window, where she had been beginning to feel a little chilly, and went with Joey to meet the Robin. Both of them were bidden sit down and help, for the puzzle contained eight hundred pieces, and the two little girls were beginning to be afraid that it was beyond them.

The only breaks came when Joey and the Robin were called to bid the doctor good-bye when he left, and Kaffee und Kuchen. Otherwise, they continued with their pleasing occupation until Abendessen came, and after Abendessen it was the Robin's bedtime, for, even at half-term, there might be no slackening of the régime under which she was being brought up. Her pretty Polish mother had died of tuberculosis, and, along with that mother's dark beauty, the Robin had inherited her fragile constitution. So early hours, plenty of milk and fresh air, and very little excitement were hers.

When Joey called her, she went off blithely, full of glee because she was to sleep with her adored "big sister," who attended to all the details of her toilet, heard her prayers, and then tucked her up in the small bed set beside her own.

"Gute Nacht, mein Engelkind," she said, bending to

in ear-phones. But the ends will stick out when I do it that way, do what I will. It touches my shoulders now, though, and I'm hoping that by Easter, at least, I'll be able to plait it."

"Won't it be funny—to see you with tidy hair!" The Robin gave a gurgle.

"Don't be impertinent, you monkey! Come along now; Mademoiselle will want to see you before we go to the others."

Hand in hand they went to the study, where they found Mademoiselle and Dr Jem chatting together. The Head kissed and petted the Robin for a minute or two, and then released her, saying, "Take her to the others, my Jo. You must bring her up to see me every morning while she stays, for your so-strict brother tells me I must not be with you girls at all this week-end."

"Certainly not," said the doctor. "You are to have a complete rest, Thérèse, or you'll never last the term out."

The Robin obediently kissed Mademoiselle, and went off with Joey to the common-room, where the twenty-three girls left behind were all seated round the tables or at the windows, busy with various amusements.

There were shouts of welcome when the pair appeared, for most of the girls knew the Robin, who had been at the Chalet School before the Annexe had been opened, and had been everybody's darling.

Amy Stevens, Margia's younger sister, had been at the Annexe until this term, when she had been pronounced strong enough to return to the larger school, and she and the Robin were great chums, though there was more than two years between them in age. They met joyfully, and presently were seated together on the floor over a big jigsaw which Amy had been trying to make, while the rest of the girls returned to their own interests.

Seeing that the Robin was happily occupied, Joey glanced round, and then crossed the room to the wide window-seat where Polly Heriot was curled up by herself, looking out at the grey lake and sky.

"What on earth are you looking at?" she asked curiously. "It's appallingly bleak out there, and there's nothing to see. Thank goodness we shall have lights presently! This grey monotony gives me the jim-jams!"

"I was only wondering if it would snow soon," explained Polly, moving in order to make room for her. "I'm dying

"And the babies?"

"Growing amain! You'll see them as soon as it's safe for you to come up. Jackie's a big boy now—got seven teeth, and very fit and bonny. Sybil will be crawling all over before long. And Primula Mary has kept well, and is much stronger."

Jo nodded her satisfaction at this last statement. Primula Mary, Mrs Venables' youngest child, had been almost tragically frail when she had been brought to the mountains in the early summer, and there had been real reason to fear for her. Evidently she was responding well to the sparkling mountain air and the strict régime her doctor uncle was using for her.

"Mademoiselle is in the study," was all she said. "You go to her while I take the Robin to get her things off. The house is warm, and she oughtn't to stay bundled up like this in it."

"Quite right," he said, as he turned aside to the study. "Here's her case, Joey. See that she puts on her blazer when she's untied."

Joey took the small suitcase, and led the Robin away, while he went into the study to see the Head.

"Is everyone here, at Ste Thérèse's?" asked the Robin, as she hung up her brown beret on a peg and let Joey unbutton her coat.

"Everyone who is staying. The rest went off well over an hour ago. Let me look at you, mein Blümchen. What rosy cheeks! You look as if life at the Annexe agreed with you!"

"It *is* fun. But I would rather be here with you," said the Robin, as she wriggled into her blazer, and then stood back to let Joey look at her.

"Not growing very much yet, are you," said Jo, surveying the small, slim person before her. "You're not going to take after Uncle Ted in that respect, anyhow. And you've still got your pretty curls, thank goodness! I was terrified lest Madge would let them grow long. I suppose you must, some day. But we'll wait for it, I hope. You wouldn't be the same with long hair."

The Robin chuckled. "But you are growing yours, Joey. How neat it looks! How do you do it?"

Jo turned solemnly round to let her see and admire the neat arrangement of clasps and pins that kept her long-short locks tidy. "This is only till it's long enough to wear

patriot. But she now confided to Jo that when Mademoiselle did not require her, she meant to join the holiday party.

"Good!" said Jo. "We'll have a really good time this half-term, even though we can't go to the Sonnalpe. I say, Mademoiselle! I've got an idea or two! We must have a pow-wow."

"A pow-wow?" Mademoiselle Lachenais looked puzzled. "What, then, is that?"

"A conference, if you like it better—I say! Is that voices I hear outside?"

Mademoiselle Lachenais glanced out of the window of the staff-room, where they were. "Yes; it is our good Dr Jem and the Robin—but, *Joey!*"

For with a wild "Yoicks! Tally-ho!" Jo was out of her chair, and away downstairs to greet the little adopted sister she loved so dearly.

She reached the door just as the tall, fair doctor came to the step, his arm round the shoulders of the Robin. Joey wasted no time on him. With a hasty, "Hello, Jem! How are you?" she was at the Robin's side, clasping the child closely, and kissing her fondly.

"Oh, Robin, my Robin! How long it is since I've seen you!"

The Robin's arms were round her neck. "Joey—Joey! I have so longed for thee! It is six weeks—but *six weeks* since I have seen thee!" In her excitement, she forgot her English, and lapsed into the tenderer French.

"Now, then, you two, when you've quite finished enacting the fond reunion scene, you'd better come in out of the cold," interrupted Dr Russell. "How are you, Joey? Teaching not too much for you? Not overdoing it, are you?"

Jo laughed, released the Robin, and lifted her face for his kiss. "Do I look like it? How's everyone at 'Die Rosen'? Oh, Jem, you don't know how I'm longing to get back to you all! I've never been homesick in my life, but I've come uncommonly near it this term."

"Yes; it's been a trying time all round," he agreed, as he drew them into the house and shut the door. "However, we seem to be getting to the end of it at last, thank goodness! The measles cases are all out of quarantine, except David, who finishes the day after tomorrow. Rix is much better, too, though he still whoops on occasion."

Johansen. "The lake freezes, Polly, and people skate across instead of walking round. And in January, they light great bonfires round the lake on one day, and people come from all the villages round to skate and make merry—"

"Only we are not permitted to join in, for it is often rough," added Jeanne le Cadoulec.

"No; but we skate on our own when it's over," put in Kitty Burnett. "Jolly good fun, too!"

"Oh, you will love the snow here, Pollee!" Irma assured her.

"I'll believe that when I see it," said Polly sceptically. "Anyway, it looks more like rain than snow at present."

"Oh, no! There aren't any clouds to speak of," said Kitty confidently. "I think it'll be fine to-day."

She proved to be right. The wind fell towards noon, and a queer hush prevailed. But no rain came, and no snow either. Fourteen hours saw all those who were going away for half-term assembled in Hall at Ste Thérèse's; and after the Staff had seen that they were warmly wrapped up, and had everything they were likely to need, they said good-bye, and set off.

Miss Wilson and Miss Nalder took charge of one party, for they were spending the week-end at Innsbruck themselves. Miss Leslie and "Matey" had the people who were going to Salzburg or Kufstein. Matron Venables took charge of the few who were going up to the Sonnalpe.

All told, it was a big clearance, and, when the last had gone, the twenty-three girls left behind felt rather lost in the big buildings. They were to be at Ste Thérèse's, though Miss Stewart would still stay in the sanatorium at St Clare's, with Nurse. They hoped that she would be well enough to travel by Thursday of next week, when a doctor brother was coming to take her to her home in distant Herefordshire.

Miss Annersley would be in charge, and would have some help from Miss Norman and Miss Edwards, who had elected to stay behind this time. Little Mademoiselle Lachenais was also to be at school, mainly to keep Mademoiselle Lepâttre company, for Dr. Jem had ordained that she must remain in her own room and have nothing to do with the girls. He hoped that this rest would enable her to continue with her work till the end of term, when she hoped to go home to Paris. Mademoiselle Lachenais had at once declared that she would attend to her com-

and let you have the rest, and I'll give it to you when you come back."

Maria laughed as she looked at the notes Joey had given her. "There is far more here than is needed, Jo. I shall have some to return you when I come back."

"Indeed, you won't—get chocolates with it if there's any over. Yes, Maria; I mean it. I've plenty, goodness knows! I'm on an allowance now, you know, and so far I've spent next to nothing."

Maria gave way, and then ran off to put the precious parcel into her case before she locked it, while Joey went on to the staff-room.

Over at St. Clare's, the girls were thronging round the stove waiting for the gong to summon them to Frühstück.

"Oh, how cold it is;" shivered Polly, when she came down to the common-room.

"It'll be colder than this," said Violet Allison, who was following her. "Wait till the snow comes! Then you really *will* find it cold."

"But so pretty," put in Stacie Benson, better again, and without the pinched look she had worn the previous week. "Jo always calls it 'Christmas-card Land' then."

"Does it snow much here?" asked Polly innocently.

A chorus of laughter greeted this. "Snow much! I just guess it *does*!" said Mary Shaw decisively. "You just wait!"

"Urrh! How horrid!" Polly shivered again. "I hate snow—all wet and messy! And then people walk about in it, and it turns to mud and looks horrid!"

"But no, Pollee!" said Irma Ancokzky. "How can you mean? The snow is like powder. Then we play snow-balls, and build forts to defend, and sledge and ski, and so many jollee things!"

Polly stared. "Is this true, or are you having me?" she asked doubtfully.

"But have you not heard of the winter sports in the Alps?" cried Irma.

"Yes; but that's Switzerland."

"And here, also. What mountains do you think ours are? There are winter sports at Innsbruck, and many people come from England for them. So it is here, only no one comes—"

"Except for the Carnival on the lake," put in Thelma

away. So the scaramouche is going to finish her term with you? Good for her!"

"Indeed, Jo is the dearest girl," said Mademoiselle quietly. "I only wish we might keep her here always. Her influence is excellent."

"Oh, come! That wouldn't do! We want Jo ourselves, you know. With all those babies in the nursery, Madge will need her sometimes."

"I know that. And I know she would not consent. But I cannot help wishing it."

"Aren't you feeling right again?" His voice came quickly. "Look here, Thérèse, I'm going to insist on a thorough overhaul when I bring the Robin down on Thursday. I'm inclined to think you need a change of medicine."

Mademoiselle would have protested, but he had guessed that and rang off on the final word. Though he had said nothing to her, he was beginning to think that there was something seriously wrong. The Head of the School sighed, and then laughed a little sadly before she went to seek Joey and tell her of the arrangements for half-term.

Thursday came, a grey day, but quite fine. It was very cold, and the girls were thankful for their blazers. The stoves in the rooms were all glowing brightly, so that if it was cold out-of-doors, it was warm enough within.

Jo woke early, danced a noiseless fandango when she saw the weather, and then hurried into her clothes. When she was all ready to go downstairs, she turned to her table—since she had still half-an-hour left—and became very busy. The result of her work was a neat square parcel carefully tied up, and sealing-waxed within an inch of its life, which she later entrusted to Maria Marani, who was going home to Innsbruck, with certain instructions, and some money.

"You won't forget, and you *will* be careful, Maria, won't you?" she said.

Maria nodded, her little dark face glowing with eagerness, for Joey had entrusted her with an important secret. "I will be most careful, Jo, and indeed I know what to do, for I have been with Papa when he has registered his parcels."

"I don't know what it'll cost," continued Jo, "but if I haven't given you enough, ask your father to be a dear

knew that you were prepared to finish the term with us, she would consent. But are you prepared to do it? Remember, it will have to be for the whole five weeks left."

"I know; but I'd be a pig if I didn't after you've been so jolly decent to me!" Jo was forgetting her grown-up dignity, and using school-girl speech in her earnestness. "Madge thinks so, too. We've just been discussing it, and she all but said I must. If you'll have me, I'm willing to have a shot, anyhow."

Mademoiselle put her arm round the girl, and drew her close and kissed her. "Thank you, Joey. It will be a great relief to me, and it will mean that as soon as Miss Stewart is fit to travel, we can send her home to rest and recuperate. Then, in all probability she will be strong and well next term.

"Right you are! I'll do it," said Jo with decision.

"Thank you, ma chérie. And I have a plan for you, too. If Dr Jem will agree, how would you like to have the Robin here for half-term? She could share your room, and you would be together for the whole week-end, which will be a long one. You see, we break up on Thursday this term and will not begin work again until the Wednesday morning, as Miss Stewart and I have both been on the sick-list. Would you like it?"

"Oh, Mademoiselle! If she only could! Do you think Jem would agree? She's getting stronger every day, now; and she's been so well, ever since last year. Of course," Joey's face clouded a little, "if the rain comes again, he certainly *won't* agree."

"I will ring him up this afternoon and ask him," promised Mademoiselle. "Now, dear child, the bell is ringing for Prayers."

Jem, after Mademoiselle had explained the state of things to him, said that, provided the weather was good, there was no reason why the Robin should not come down for the holiday, and he undertook to "manage" Juliet Carrick, once a pupil of the Chalet School, and now Head of the Annexe, so that she would agree to letting the little girl come down on the Thursday afternoon instead of waiting till the Friday morning, when the Annexe would begin its own half-term.

"I'll tell her that Thursday suits me better than Friday," he said. "As it happens, it will. We have an important consultation on Friday, and I might be late in getting

"If I may. You know, I could wring young Rix's neck for spoiling our half-term like this," continued Rix's young aunt, as she lifted the receiver and began dialling the number. "There's poor Robin as well; *her* half-term's spoilt—to say nothing of Stacie, and Daisy, and the Lintons. I haven't seen Robin since term began."

Mademoiselle smiled. "That is hard for you both. I must go, Joey. I will see you later, mon enfant."

"Yes, Mademoiselle—Oh, hello! Is that you, Madge? This is Jo."

Mademoiselle left the room, and Jo sat down to hear the last report of the "Die Rosen" family.

She rang off, and hung up the receiver, just as Mademoiselle re-entered the room. Mademoiselle had gone very thin, and there were shadows and dips in her face, which had lost its old, healthy colouring. She moved languidly, which was something new to Mademoiselle, who had always gone about her duties briskly, though she had never been of the bustling kind.

When she sat down, the girl went over and knelt down beside her. "Mademoiselle, aren't you fit *yet*?"

Mademoiselle looked down into the soft, black eyes lifted to hers. "Perhaps I am not so well yet, Joey. I do not grow younger, my child, and these attacks of malaise are trying."

"Are you worried about Miss Stewart?"

"Yes; I am a little. She has been quite ill, and the doctors tell me that she ought to attempt no more work this term. I have tried to persuade her to go home till after Christmas, but she refuses, as she fears lest her absence should make too much extra work for us."

Jo said nothing for a moment. Then: "But it needn't— or not much. If I stayed on till the end of term, it would really make very little difference, wouldn't it?" she asked slowly.

Mademoiselle looked at her. "I did not think you enjoyed teaching so much."

"Oh, it isn't that. But you've all been so good to me, I'd like to help you if I could—and Madge says it's no more than I *ought*," she added honestly. "If I stuck it till the end of term, don't you think you could tell Miss Stewart that we could manage all right; then she might go."

"It might just make the difference, Jo. I think if she

and the rest were getting ready for bed that night. "She's always so on the spot! If we'd only known beforehand, we could have warned Alixe—Yes; I know you *did* have a shot, Hilda, but it didn't come to much, did it?

"Jo's a regular Johnny-on-the-spot," grumbled Mary Shaw. "*Anne* wouldn't have found it out—not so soon, anyway. Why was Jo taking prep? It was Anne's turn, and she ought to have been there."

"They were all doing extra science with Bill," said Dorothy Brentham. "Didn't you folk know?"

"Guess not. Alixe wouldn't have played the giddy goat if we *had*!"

What more they might have said about Jo will never be known, for at that moment "Bill" herself appeared to remind them that silence-bell had been rung five minutes ago, and to award a conduct-mark to all those who had spoken after it had gone, which put a most effectual stop to any further conversation among them.

What Jo herself said in the privacy of the staff-room, where she had been retailing for the benefit of the rest the story of the evening's happenings, was, "Middles don't improve a little bit. Goodness knows *we* were bad enough; but some of these imps beat us hollow!"

CHAPTER XIII

HALF-TERM BEGINS

HALF-TERM came at the beginning of November. The rain poured down early in the week, but cleared up later, though the weather remained cold and grey. As many as possible of the girls went home, but some had to stay at school, among them, the "Die Rosen" people.

On the Monday of that week, Joey Bettany made her way to the study to ring up her sister, and make inquiries about all the invalids. Mademoiselle was there, busy with her usual heavy mail, and she smiled sympathetically when the girl entered.

"You wish to telephone, my Jo?" she queried.

that had been *inside* the room. Jo could not understand how Alixe had contrived to work hers when she had been outside all the time.

"Where were you standing?" she asked with real curiosity.

Alixe pointed: "Under that ventilator there. We found out the other day, that if anyone talks beneath it, the sounds are just as if they are in the middle of this room. I thought it would be a joke to use this thing outside it one night during prep. I did not know that you would be here instead of Anne," she finished in injured tones.

Joey nearly collapsed at this, but she managed to keep a tight grip on herself, and only looked very stern and judicial. "I see. Well, you have brought your own punishment on yourself. You can go and tell Matron that you've got your feet wet, and I have sent you to her because I think it better for you to go to bed at once in case you should catch a cold."

Alixe began to protest wildly at this, for so far she had done no preparation.

Her protests availed her nothing. Joey marched her off, delivered her over to Matron with the suggestion that it might be as well to take *all* due precautions, since both slippers and stockings were soaking wet, and left her to her fate.

And fate proved bitterly hard.

Alixe's mother was up at the Sonnalpe, where she was being kept under observation. Matron Venables knew this, having met pretty Frau von Elsen, and she was running no risks with Miss Alixe. That young lady was ordered into a hot mustard-bath, and when it was over, she was popped into a warm bed, her chest rubbed with camphorated oil, and a dose of nauseating cod-liver oil added to complete the prevention. Finally, she was tucked up, and left, with strict orders not to put her arms out from under the blankets.

As for the others, Jo sent off all the practising people without more ado; made certain inquiries, which resulted in four more conspirators being condemned to copy out sundry poems in their best handwriting on Saturday evening (when the rest would be dancing and playing games); and wound up by treating them all to a lecture, which left them remarkably subdued for the time being.

"That's the worst of Jo!" sighed Enid Southern, as she

Sigrid went even redder, and looked at her slipper-toes. "I forgot. I am very sorry."

"Well, you can come to me at the end of prep for twelve lines of repetition. Perhaps that will help you to remember," said Jo sarcastically. "And what about you, Alixe? Have *you* been trying to get your music-case from behind the piano, too?"

"Oh, but *no*!" said Alixe with great fervour, though she had winced at the edge in Jo's tones.

"Then what *have* you been doing?"

"Just practising—and I had to put my music in the locker."

"*That* didn't take you all this time. What else? Come here."

Alixe came, her saintly expression a little less in evidence as she did so.

"Hold up your foot," said Jo sternly. "Show me your slipper-sole."

Alixe no longer looked like a young saint in embryo. She was merely a very naughty little girl who had been caught out. She extended one foot reluctantly, and Jo saw, as she had suspected, that the sole of her slipper was soaking.

"So it *was* you?" she said thoughtfully, as Alixe put her foot down again.

The culprit said nothing. She had not bargained for Jo's being quite so sharp, though she knew, from past experience, that very little escaped that young lady. It was a nuisance that the weather had changed. The day before had been beautifully fine, and all to-day it had been quite dry, if somewhat grey. But with nightfall there had come up a heavy mist which had soaked everything. Besides that, Jo's quick eyes had seen a trace of gravel on the floor by the door.

"What have you been doing?" she demanded.

"It—it was only a joke," muttered Alixe sulkily, still in her own tongue.

"A very foolish joke, and one that might have startled someone very badly. How did you manage it?"

For reply, Alixe produced from her pocket one of those balloon creatures which, when blown up and then released, let out the air with unearthly screeches. Once, in the dim and distant past, Elsie Carr had brought in a similar thing to prep, and had got into serious trouble over it. But

send them here," she said. "In any case, their practice-time is over by now. Who is due at the pianos next?"

Five hands were raised. They all belonged to people who were more or less possessed of good characters.

"You five may go," said Jo, dismissing them. "Hurry up, and don't waste your time."

"May—may I not rise early to-morrow and do my practice then, please, Joey?" queried Inga shyly.

"Oh, nonsense, Inga! You aren't frightened by a silly trick, are you?"

"It—it is such a very horrid noise," said Inga shakily.

"I know it is. But it's most likely Alixe up to monkey-tricks of some kind," said Jo soothingly. "However," she added, with an eye to Inga's white face, "if you'd rather wait a little, you may. What about the rest of you?"

"It's only someone trying to be funny," said Kitty, scorn in her voice. "*I'm* not going to funk it. Besides, it's my lesson to-morrow."

"But I do not like it either," put in Emmie in her own tongue. "Please, Joey, I would rather wait, if you do not mind."

"Very well, Emmie, though I must say I think you and Inga are very silly little girls.—What about you, Faith and Thelma?"

Faith and Thelma elected to go to their practice, probably moved to this decision by the fact that they, like Kitty, had lessons on the morrow. Emmie and Inga sat down again, and the people who had just come in took their seats. Two minutes later, Ruth and Violet entered, bringing Alixe and Sigrid with them. Sigrid looked startled, and Alixe wore her most seraphic air—which Jo promptly recognised as a bad sign. That the expression changed to one of shock when she saw the ex-head girl of the School at the mistress's desk, settled this latter young lady's mind.

"Well, and what have you people been doing?" Jo asked in chilly tones. "You were supposed to be here ten minutes ago."

"Please, Jo, my music-case slipped behind the piano, and I could not get it out until Violet and Ruth came to help me," explained Sigrid, with a blush.

"I thought you people weren't supposed to put your cases on top of the pianos?" said Jo.

sitting still, she got up and went the rounds. Half-way through the business, the noise came again, and Mary Shand, a nervy child from Louisiana, squeaked with horror. Biddy O'Ryan also gave a little gasp.

"Don't be silly," said Jo bracingly. "Someone is playing tricks—I know that. And I know another thing: you will all sit like that until whoever is responsible for it owns up."

"But, Jo! We don't know, honestly!" protested Ruth Wynyard. "And I haven't touched either my history or geometry yet."

"I can't help that. *Someone* knows what it's all about, and the innocent must suffer with the guilty, unless the guilty choose to confess and have done with it," said Jo, with her most inexorable expression.

The door opened, and three girls came in—Dorothy Brentham, a tomboyish person from Five B, Joyce Linton, and Renée Lecoutier, Mademoiselle Lepâttre's young cousin.

"Where have you all been?" demanded Jo.

"Only practising," replied Joyce, opening her eyes at the tone.

"Any others to come from practising?" continued Jo.

"Yes—Alixe von Elsen and Sigrid Bjornessen," replied Violet Allison, one of the Senior Middles, after a quick glance round.

"Alixe and Sigrid—H'm!" Jo thought over the pair in her own mind. She knew Sigrid for a somewhat colourless little person, very law-abiding, and not likely to have had anything to do with this. Alixe was a different matter. To look at her, you would have said that butter wouldn't melt in her mouth. She was very fair, with a misleadingly saintly expression, which got saintlier as she became more wicked. Her voice was soft and shy, and she said outrageous things in a gentle manner, which made people frequently pass over her remarks till they had had time to consider them. In Alixe's case, still waters were apt to run very deep indeed.

Not by the widest stretch of imagination could Jo picture Sigrid having taken part in this disturbance. Alixe was quite capable of it. What was more, Miss Alixe's own particular circle were glancing at each other, and this time the elder girl was able to read deep meaning into their glances.

"Violet, you and Ruth may go and find those two and

with a rich Kerry brogue, when Jo asked her what she wanted.

"Bring it out here, then—and speak decent English," added Jo. "You can when it suits you."

Biddy meekly trotted out with her French grammar, and Jo patiently explained what had to be done. Biddy listened with exemplary gravity, said she understood, and returned to her seat. Incidentally, her French was returned next day, with horrified ejaculations from little Mademoiselle Lachenais.

There was peace again after that, till Mary Shaw, a small American who was famed for the fertility of her wits, proclaimed that she could not understand the poetry Jo had given them to learn for repetition. Jo called her out, elucidated her difficulties with a somewhat tart remark to the effect that, if she kept her brains for her work instead of thinking of various evil deeds, it would be better for her, and then sent her back to her seat.

An almost oppressive silence settled down on the room after that, though Jo was too much absorbed in her work to notice it. Suddenly, there came the most hair-raising sound, apparently from the middle of the room. Jo jumped violently, and one or two of the more nervous girls who were not in the secret, shrieked.

But though Jo might jump when startled, she had plenty of common-sense, and she guessed at once that this was merely a new effort on the part of the Middles to liven things up a little.

"Who made that noise?" she demanded sharply.

No answer; but one or two people giggled, and Beryl Lester, a highly strung child in the Fourth, burst into tears, wailing, "Please, Jo, it wasn't me! I never did it!"

"I didn't for a moment imagine you did, Beryl," said Jo. "Stop that babyish crying, please.—Well?" This last being addressed to the room at large.

There was a dead silence. No one would confess to being the author of the sound, and even as she waited for an answer, it came again. Two or three more nervy people started. Joey decided that this must *cease*!

"All of you put down whatever you have in your hands, and sit back with your arms folded behind you," she said.

Everyone obeyed. With Jo Bettany looking like that, they felt it to be the wisest course. When they were all

she retreated to inquire after the patient and then went to her room to gather up her books before she went off to St Clare's, where she was due to take preparation.

No one at St Clare's had heard of what had been happening at Ste Thérèse's, and Jo had no intention of enlightening them. She called them to order and, spreading out the Second Form's history exercise-books on the desk, settled down to some correcting. Sharp as she generally was, she had failed to notice the looks of dismay exchanged between two or three of the Middles when she entered, and beyond asking who was practising now, she took little further notice of them, once the room was quiet.

At first, all went well. The girls settled to their work, and there was comparative silence for the first half-hour. Then Enid Southern, an imp of twelve, put up her hand.

"Yes?" said Jo. "What is it, Enid?"

"Please, Jo, I can't do my algebra. I don't understand it."

"Bring it out here, then," said Jo, pushing aside her books, and removing the red ink to a place of safety. She had no fears that she could not cope with Enid's mathematics, for that young lady had only just begun algebra, and though Jo's own work had been the despair of Miss Leslie, she knew that she could deal with the elementary rules well enough.

Enid brought out her work, and Jo carefully explained simple multiplication to her, Enid listening with perhaps half an ear. When she said she understood, she was sent back to her seat, and Jo prepared to go on with her work.

Hilda Bhaer made the next interruption. "Please, Jo, my throat feels dry. May I go and get a drink?"

"Very well. But don't be away longer than three minutes," said Jo, glancing at her watch.

Hilda saw her, and retreated with a very downcast face. She dared not stay longer than the three minutes, and the thing she had meant to do would certainly take longer than that. Jo was evidently on the war-path, so she waited in the corridor till she thought the time was up, and then returned, with a shake of her head at one or two other people, who promptly looked very chapfallen.

Biddy O'Ryan held up her hand ten minutes later. "'Tis meself doesn't know what to do wid this at all," she said,

there with her eyes shut, and her face white." And she shuddered.

Jo measured the distance with her eye, and shuddered too. "She might easily have been killed! What other mad things did she do?"

After severe questioning, she discovered that Cornelia's "race" had been begun from the chair near the door. From there, she had jumped to a small table—the investigator discovered that an accident had nearly happened then, for the table was a light one, and it had rocked dangerously under the shock—and had then taken a wild leap to the nearest window-seat, on which she had fallen on all-fours. From there, it had been child's play to run along the shelf, which they had cleared of the photographs and ornaments it normally held, and so, to the second window-seat.

Her next feat had been to leap to the settee, along which she had strolled, and then, making a long leg, had stretched up to the top of the porcelain stove, which was kept going both day and night at this time of year. She had tried to get back to the settee when the heat struck up through the thin sole of her dancing-sandal, had overbalanced, and crashed down.

"You must all have been mad!" said Jo finally. "Corney might have been killed. As it is, she's had a nasty knock, and the table is badly damaged."

"Do—do you think Corney's—likely to be real sick?" asked Evadne shakily.

"I couldn't say. She looked to me as if she had slight concussion. I didn't like that dazed look in her eyes," said Jo gravely. She meant to frighten them, for, as she said later on, there was no saying what pranks they might play next if they weren't stopped now. Apart from that, while going round the room without touching the floor was all very well in the gymnasium, with Miss Nalder there to see that it was properly done and the mattresses in position, the same feat in the common-room, with no precautions whatsoever, was a very different matter.

Evadne bit her lips and turned away. Ilonka turned a face of absolute horror on the elder girl; and Irma and Giovanna burst into tears. The rest of the throng looked very sober. Jo had convinced them that they had come very near a tragedy.

As for Jo herself, having scared them all thoroughly,

on earth she was doing to fall? She must have come down with an awful crash to get a bang like that—to say nothing of the noise she made."

Evadne shuffled uncomfortably from one foot to the other.

"Go on," said Jo inflexibly. "I can guess that you imps have been up to something wicked, and what it is, I mean to know before any of us are very much older. So the sooner you cough it up, the better for us all!"

"We-ell," drawled Evadne at length, "Corney was just trying to go round the room without touching the floor, just as we do at gym, you know."

"What?"

"Well, you know how we do it—swinging from the ropes and the rib-stalls. We thought we'd try it here, with the furniture, and the window-sills, and so on. If you touched the floor at all, you'd be disqualified."

"Disqualified? What on earth do you mean?"

Prodded on by Jo's questions, Evadne finally informed her that five girls had volunteered to try it, and the one who did it in the shortest time would be proclaimed winner.

"And how many of you have done it?" asked Jo with real curiosity.

"None of us. Corney was the first, because it was her idea," said Evadne. "We others were to come after in alphabetical order."

"I see. And who were the others, if you've no objection to telling me?"

"Me, of course—"

"Of course," agreed Jo. "Who else was in it?"

"Lonny—and Irma—and Giovanna. That was all."

"And quite enough, too. I'm glad the rest had more sense than you five seem to have! How did Corney happen to fall, by the way?"

"It was when she was climbing from the settee to the top of the stove," explained Ilonka, pushing back her long brown plaits as she spoke. "She had one foot on the stove, and she found it was very hot—too hot to stand there. She cried out, and tried to get back to the settee. I suppose the stretch was too far, for she slipped and fell backwards on that table, and they both went. I suppose that was really what made the crash. We were too frightened to notice properly. Corney looked so terrible lying

and piles of books they must to the shops. I did hope I'd know something definite about it this term."

"Never mind! You've had an experience that will probably be very useful to you later on," said Matron soothingly. "By the way, when do they expect you back at 'Die Rosen'?"

"Barring accidents, a fortnight after half-term. That will give Miss Stewart and Mademoiselle time to pull themselves together, and I shan't be needed then, so I can go with a free mind. The girls are all saying there'll be little more than three weeks left of the term, and I might as well stay and see it out; but—Mercy! What's that?"

"That" was a crash which sounded as though someone had dropped a bomb through the roof. Matron dropped the clean towels she had been carrying and scurried off, followed at top speed by Jo, both sure that, at the very least, some part of the house must have collapsed.

Guided by the sound of excited voices, they reached the common-room, where they found at least half the house standing round one girl, who was getting up from the floor with a rather dazed expression in her eyes, and a rapidly rising bump on her forehead.

"Well, Cornelia," said Matron, "what have you been doing this time?"

At the sound of her voice, the throng parted, and she advanced on the unlucky Cornelia, who had managed to gain her feet.

"What have you been doing?" repeated Matron, as she examined the lump. "We heard the crash in Jo's room, and I thought that at least the roof had fallen in. Here; you must have this attended to at once.—Give her a 'queen's chair,' two of you. She looks shaky."

Cornelia did look shaky—but no more so than her boon companion and usual accomplice in evil, Evadne Lannis. Jo, running her eye rapidly over the scared-looking crowd, saw her white face, and as soon as the patient had been borne away by Gillian Linton and Cyrilla Maurús, beckoned to her, and demanded to know what they had all been doing.

"Corney—fell," said Evadne, who seemed, for once, to be completely deprived of her self-possession. "I say, Joey! She looked real bad. She'll be all right, won't she?"

"I don't know," said Jo truthfully. "And as for 'fell,' I gathered that much myself. What I want to know is, what

precious book as circumstances would permit. "Cecily Holds the Fort" was the pride of her heart at the moment. She had taken Matron's advice, and her characters were neither diabolically bad nor angelically good, but just normal girls of the type she met every day. She had expunged the one or two most startling adventures of her heroine, after Polly's exploit, and Matron, who had insisted that she should be privileged to read it, was of the private opinion that it would most certainly find a publisher somewhere. Jo had a crisp, racy style of her own, and she could tell a story well. Cecily was remarkably well drawn; and as for the science mistress, Matron gurgled over *her* most reprehensively, for Jo had reproduced "Bill" to the life.

"Well, you're getting on with it," Matron said on the night of Frieda's return home. "How much more have you left to do?"

"Oh, about seven chapters," said Jo. "I don't know when you'll get the rest to read, for I certainly shan't get at it again before Saturday. Now that Frieda has had to go home, I've offered to take over her classes where they don't clash with my own. However, I'll have the whole of Saturday after Guides, and that ought to see me through at least two more, and with luck I'll get the rest done next week. Then it'll have to be packed off, and after that, I'll have to wait and hope for the best, I suppose."

"Where are you sending it?" asked Matron curiously.

Jo mentioned the name of a well-known firm, and Matron nodded. "I know them. They publish a good many books for children. I should think 'Cecily' will have quite a good chance with them. Well, I must go now. I've got all the household linen from the laundry to go through." She turned, and went to the door. Arrived there, she swung round, facing Jo squarely. "You've been a brick through all this trouble, Jo," she said bluntly. "The Staff would have managed somehow, I suppose; but your taking on all this teaching has helped them tremendously."

"I dare say!" quoth Jo sceptically. "Anyone who likes it can have the job for all of me! I wasn't born to be a teacher, Matey. And I don't mind telling *you* that I hoped to have had that book off before this. As it is, I doubt if I shall hear anything of it till next year. Publishers must be frantically busy about Christmas, sending off all the piles

before that wonderful machine, and when the gong rang for Abendessen, she had her first chapter typed out.

CHAPTER XII

LIVENING THINGS UP A LITTLE

FOR the next week or so, things went on quietly. Mademoiselle recovered more or less—chiefly less— from her indisposition, and came into school to take Prayers and see to organisation. But she was not permitted to teach. The doctors from the Sonnalpe forbade it most positively. Miss Stewart, who had had a very sharp attack, was still far from well, and was kept in the little sanatorium which lay at the far end of St Clare's, divided from the workaday part of the School. News from 'Die Rosen' continued to be much the same. Whooping-cough had not spread beyond Master Rix, fortunately; but he was having an unpleasant time of it, and his Aunt Madge reported that he was very fretful and tiresome.

Frieda Mensch came up from Innsbruck to spend a few days, and she was promptly pressed into service by the Staff, taking French and German among the Juniors, who were thrilled at being taught by Frieda. Unfortunately, she had only been there four days when Frau Mensch wrote to beg her to come home. Frau Mensch's sister had slipped on the stairs and sprained her ankle badly. So Frieda had to pack up and return to Innsbruck, which she did with a good deal of reluctance.

Meanwhile, Polly, having decided to shelve adventures for the present, had struck up a tremendous friendship with Joyce Linton, who was rather more than a year older than herself. In this way, she came under the influence of Joyce's sister, Gillian, who was noted throughout the School for her quiet common-sense. She was not likely to encourage Polly in any wild fancies, and Joyce was also on her best behaviour, so the folk in authority allowed themselves to breathe freely.

As for Jo, she plunged as deeply into the typing of her

"The wonder is he didn't catch you," said Mollie.

"He very nearly did one morning. I had to nip into that cupboard where he hangs his things, and I thought he was never going.—By the way, have you two had Kaffee und Kuchen?"

"You're rather late with your hospitalities, aren't you?" demanded Dick. "Of course we have—had it in Spärtz before we came on up here."

"Are you staying the night?" Joey had forgotten the illness at the Chalet.

"No, Joey," said her sister-in-law gently. "We couldn't be doing that with Miss Stewart and Mademoiselle ill. We've got a car outside, and we're driving round to the coach-road. So we must be going now. We've seen Margot and Daisie and Stacie. We left you to the last. Come and kiss me good-bye, Joey."

Jo raised dismayed eyes. "Going already? But Mollie! You'll be away another three years! Can't you possibly stay, just for to-night?"

"No, we can't," said her brother curtly. "As you say, we'll be away for three years, and—well, we're leaving the kiddies behind."

"I'd forgotten that," said Jo remorsefully. "Oh, Dick, I wish you weren't in India! It's so gorgeous having you and Mollie with us, and India is so far away!"

"Rot!" he said, somewhat roughly. He cut the farewells short. He knew his wife too well to risk a storm of tears, and it seemed to Jo that they had barely come before they had gone, and she was left to go back to the salon to collect her newest treasure and cart it back up to her room. There she disposed of it on the table very breathlessly, and then examined it, and slipping in a sheet of paper, typed the title-page of her new book.

CECILY HOLDS THE FORT

BY

JOSEPHINE M. BETTANY

It did look nice! The only thing that would look nicer would be the title-page of the printed book. Joey forgot all about history, her form, and everything else. She sat down with one of the mercurial changes which were so characteristic of her Irish temperament. "Listen, mavourneen. Madge told us about the book you're writing, and Dick and I wanted to give you a really decent present, for it'll have to be birthday and Christmas in one, since we're not likely to reach Bombay before Christmas Day. So we went to Innsbruck to get it for you, and there it is—by the settee yonder, in that case."

With a whoop, Joey was on the case pointed out and unlocking the clasps. A moment later, and she uttered a wild shriek of joy, for there lay one of the desires of her heart—a portable typewriter!

"Neat but not gaudy," said her brother, with a grin. "Also a delicate hint that a few more letters would be acceptable, and this gives you no excuse for not writing. Do you like it?"

Like it? Jo was far too overcome to tell him what she really felt. But her flushed face and sparkling eyes spoke for her, and satisfied the generous donors. They had provided paper, ribbons, rubber, dusters, and everything they could think of.

"You dears!" she cried ecstatically. "What a gorgeous present!"

"It'll save Jem's temper, anyhow," said his brother-in-law, submitting to being hugged vehemently. "I can just imagine what he'd feel like if he happened to want to use his typewriter and found you lugged it off to your own room!"

"Yes," said Jo calmly. "I was going to use that as a good reason why he and Madge should give me a portable for Christmas. However, I needn't now.—Mollie, as soon as I've done the copy of 'Cecily' to send away, I'll type you one, too, and send it to India, so that you don't have to wait for it to be publshed—if it ever is!—before you read it."

"But don't you think that'll get you out of sending us a copy when it *is* published, Miss!" said her brother severely. "You needn't think we intend to be fobbed off with a typewritten copy. By the way, can you use the thing?"

Joey nodded. "Oh yes! I used to get up early in the summer and sneak down to the office and practise on Jem's. He wondered why on earth he was using so much typing-paper," she added, with her most impish grin.

took her turn in the embraces. "Joey, mavourneen, we've come to say good-bye to you."

"*What?*" Jo stared. "Say goodbye? But I thought you had another three weeks before you had to move?"

"So we have," said Dick, as they all sat down. "The bother is that, as you know, we want to take the overland route to Port Said, for the Mediterranean seems to be suffering from the jimjams, if all one hears is true, and Mollie still remains the world's worst sailor. All this wretched rain and the gales we are having seem to be putting the railway out of action temporarily, so we feel we'd better get off and not risk missing the boat. We've been spending the last two days in Innsbruck, saying farewell to all we know, and we're taking you on the way back, for we're off on Thursday, and there won't be time to get down again, I'm afraid."

"And if there was, d'you think I'm leaving my babies a minute I don't have to?" demanded his wife.

"Yes—where is Jack?" asked Joey looking all round, ratther as if she expected to find her youngest nephew adorning a shelf or the picture rail. "What have you done with him?"

"He's at 'Die Rosen,' of course. You don't imagine we were going to let a ten months' baby in for a succession of Kaffeeklatschen, do you?" queried Dick, suddenly graver.

Mollie turned to her young sister-in-law and said, with a choke in her voice, "Sure, Joey you may as well know first as last. Jack is staying here. We aren't taking him back with us."

"But—I thought you'd decided as he was so young another three years or so wouldn't hurt him," said Joey in bewildered tones.

"True for you. We did so. But Jem says he's doing so well here 'twould be a pity to risk upsetting him by taking him back there again. And then—well, there's to be another litttle brother or sister for them at the end of next April, and Jackie would be just the age when he was one person's work. So, as Madge, bless her, said she'd be a mother to him, the same as she is to the rest, we decided it would be best to leave him where he is," said Mollie.

Dick hurriedly changed the subject. "Now, then, Moll! Where've you put that little case?"

"Och, yes! Your birthday gift, Joey!" cried Mollie,

from the study. But I doubt if any publisher will ever take it."

"Don't be pessimistic, Jo! After all, you can but try!"

"Well I mean to. But you know the saying, 'Happy is he who expecteth nothing, for he won't be disappointed.' I've made up my mind not to break my heart if it is turned down all round.—Then I *may* borrow the typewriter, Miss Annersley?"

"Of course. I don't think you'd better take it out of the study; but no one is likely to be there in the evenings, which is when you want to use it, I suppose?"

"Yes; that's what I'd thought of doing," agreed Jo. "I really must coax Jem and Madge to give me one for Christmas. I shall need it if I'm to go on with this sort of thing."

Miss Annersley nodded. "Yes; that's true.—Come in! Yes, Gredel? What is it?"

"The Herr Bettany and Frau Bettany wish to see Fräulein Bettany," said Gredel, a stolid Tyrolean peasant, of whom Cornelia Flower had once said that if you tied jumping-crackers to her skirts and let them all off at once, she would never turn a hair.

Up jumped Jo, and away went her red ink—she had been correcting the Fourth Form tests. Luckily the ink was in a safety-pot, so no harm was done; but Miss Annersley felt that she had done the right thing in forbidding Jo to set much written work to her forms.

"Dick and Mollie here?" cried the authoress of the accident.—"Sorry, Miss Annersley! Luckily, it can't spill! —Where are they, Gredel?"

"Sie sind im Salon, mein Fräulein," replied Gredel.

"Excuse me, *please*, Miss Annersley," begged Joey, making for the door. "I simply *must* see what they want! I hope there's nothing wrong at the Sonnalpe!"

The last part of her speech came from a distance as she fled down the corridor, took the stairs in about four bounds, and entered the salon, out of breath and untidy.

"Well, you imp," said her brother severely, as he kissed her, "we heard you coming! What's all this rigmarole Miss Wilson has been unloading on to us? You teaching history?"

"Sure, Dick, be quiet, will you, and give the poor creature a chance to speak!" protested his wife, as she

"Nothing for the first two periods, as you are taking the Sixths. I have Five B for the third hour, though; and Four B for the fourth."

"And the afternoon?"

"Miss Stewart has 'private coaching' written across it, and a lot of initials," said Jo, puckering her brows over the time-table.

"Let me see!" Miss Annersley took the sheet and studied it thoughtfully. "Yes—that's Gillian Linton and Louise Redfield. They are doing your own special period—the Napoleonic era. You could manage that quite well, couldn't you? I'd advise you to find out exactly what they are doing, and put in an hour's reading unless you happen to have it at your finger-ends. But as you have the whole of the first half of the morning free, that should be no trouble."

"No-o," said Jo.

"This second period is Stacie Benson, Joyce Linton, and Irma Ancokzky. I happen to know that they are having special coaching on the Wars of the Holy League. Do you think you could take it on?"

Jo nodded. "Rather! I've been reading it up lately, and I really do know something about it. So I'll take them, too, shall I?"

"Yes, please, Joey. I would take them myself, but I have one of Mademoiselle's French translation coachings then, and that mustn't go. I know that Gillian and Louise, at least, could be trusted to work on alone—possibly, even the other three. But if you *can* take them on, it would be a blessing. And, while I think of it, I'd rather you set them all as little written work as possible."

"Would you?" asked Jo doubtfully. "You know, even slackers do more at written work than at learning, as a rule."

"Oh, I know that, but I think you'll find plenty to do without giving yourself piles of essays and exercises to correct. Finally, there is your own special work. I don't know how far you are on with that book of yours, Jo, but we are all expecting great things from it, and you must get on with it. Just think what a glorious finish it would be to the term if we could announce that a publisher had accepted it!"

"That's not too likely," said Jo. "Oh, it's finished now, and I meant to ask if I might borrow the typewriter

With another heartfelt sigh, Joey got up, and retired to the staff-room over at Ste Thérèse's, whither came presently Thelma Johansen, Kitty Burnett, and Bette Schmaltz, the respective heads of the three top forms of Middle School. Jeanne le Cadoulec of Five B arrived a little later. They all brought copies of their text-books; and the two elder girls had note-books with the notes Miss Stewart had dictated to them as well. They left these with Joey, after explaining what they had been doing lately, and then departed to their own work.

Jo looked at the heap before her, clutched her head, much to the detriment of her hair, and groaned loudly. "Oh, what a fearful business!"

"Nonsense!" laughed Miss Leslie, the only other occupant of the staff-room at the time. "It'll do you good, my child—teach you to feel a little sympathy for your former instructresses!"

"They're all at different stages," groaned Jo, turning over the pile of books before her. "And every form uses a different text-book. If only they were all at the same period, it wouldn't be so bad—or if it were only history of *one* country. History of Europe is such an all-embracing subject!"

"It's not as bad as all that," said Miss Leslie, taking pity on her, and coming over to see what was happening.

A few kindly words and helpful hints born of experience soon put Jo at her ease, and in a few minutes Miss Leslie retired to her table, and Jo set to work to evolve a test which later made a good many people groan when they saw it. She managed very well next day, for the Third Form still regarded her rather in the light of the head-girl she had been, and were on their best behaviour. Four A were still at the mark-hunting age and too keen to make nuisances of themselves. Jo enjoyed the lesson with the younger girls. she went to the staff-room after morning school feeling quite pleased with herself.

"What about this afternoon?" she asked anxiously. "There doesn't seem to be any work down."

"Miss Stewart was on walk duty," said Miss Annersley, "but," with a glance at the streaming panes, "I'm afraid walks are definitely off. The Middles will do prep instead, with you to supervise, and have the evening free. You can do your own work then, Joey. What have you to-morrow?"

the snows can't be delayed much longer."

"If it comes on top of this it won't be snow—it'll be mud," said Miss Wilson pessimistically.

"If the rain would only cease, that wind would soon dry up things," declared Miss Nalder. "Don't worry, Nell! We never get much in the way of mud here."

"Well," said Miss Annersley, "to revert to the earlier subject of our conversation. I'll send the head-girl of each form to you with their text-books and notes, Joey, and you can see what they've been doing with Miss Stewart. And that reminds me. They must try not to call you by your baptismal name while you are teaching them. You will be a member of the Staff for the time being, and they must treat you as such."

Joey nearly dropped her coffee-cup at this. "Oh, Miss Annersley! You surely don't want them to call me 'Miss Bettany'? I stopped even Polly doing it—it makes me feel such an awful ass!"

The Staff chuckled. This was Jo all over.

Miss Annersley considered the point for a moment or two. "It's a difficult proposition, Jo. Well, so long as they behave with you as they would with any other member of the Staff, I'll let it go, as you are so much against it. But if they start taking liberties with 'Jo,' it will have to be 'Miss Bettany,' I'm afraid, whatever it makes you feel."

"Besides, you've got to be it some day soon," added Miss Leslie. "You aren't a baby any longer now, you know."

"Oh, I don't mind outsiders," acknowledged Jo. "It's the School doing it that I object to. Why, Thora, and Anne, and Luigia, and the rest were in form with me last term. I simply couldn't expect them to 'Miss Bettany' me all over the place—and I should hate it, too," she added with decision.

"Well, we'll leave it at that," said Miss Annersley, rising. "Any more coffee, anyone? No? Then ring the bell, someone, to have all this cleared away. "I must get back to my own quarters. The bell should be ringing for prep, shortly.—Joey, where will you be?"

"In the staff-room, I suppose," said Joey with a groan. "I'd better not go back to my own room, in case I get buried in 'Cecily.' Which table do I bag, please?"

"You'd better have Miss Stewart's," said Miss Wilson. "Don't sling the ink over it—that's all we ask of you."

the next day or two. In the meantime, it was hoped that the girls would be very quiet, so as not to disturb her. That was all. She sent them off to their form-rooms after that, where they settled to work, rather overawed.

Mademoiselle remained very poorly for the rest of the week, and Miss Stewart, who had not been looking well, went down with a severe attack of laryngitis on the following Monday.

"There's no help for it, Jo," said Miss Annersley, as the Staff, with Joey, were having their Kaffee und Kuchen. "You'll have to take history for the entire Middle School. Polly Heriot must just do without your private lessons, and manage as well as she can in form with the others. I can take on Senior history myself, and Miss Carey has had all the Juniors since she came; so it might be worse. If you'll take on the Middles, I think we can manage. But I can't do more than the Seniors. Neither Miss Wilson nor Miss Nalder could give us help in that subject, and Miss Leslie says she can't. We seem to have a painfully mathematically-minded Staff! Can you undertake Third, the two Fourths, and Five B? It should be only for a week or two."

"I can manage all right if I haven't to worry over Polly's coaching," said Jo sturdily. "I don't know that I'd care to tackle either of the Sixths or Five A," she added, with a laugh. "After all, some of the Sixths were in the same form with me only last term. How is Miss Stewart, by the way?"

"Very poorly indeed," said Miss Wilson. "It is a sharp attack, and she can neither swallow nor speak at present. She's worrying, too, about the work, as Mademoiselle is *hors de combat* as well; and that's not good for her."

"You can tell her not to worry since Joey and I can see to the work between us," said Miss Annersley sympathetically. "Besides, Matey has rung up the Sonnalpe, and I expect someone from there this evening."

"It's a sweet night if he's coming by the mountain-path," said Jo. "Just listen to that!" And they heard the rising wind drive the heavy rain against the closed jalousies. "If this goes on, we'll be having a second flood. I don't remember such a wet autumn in all the years I've lived here!"

"Don't worry! It can't go on much longer," said Miss Leslie. "We are very nearly into November now; so

As for Jo, she sat down that afternoon to review her own book, and with a stern hand she remorselessly removed any pranks that might be supposed to incite brainless Juniors to imitation.

"Matey was quite right," she thought, as she consigned the last sheet to the wastepaper-basket. "What a horrible responsibility it is to write for the young!"

CHAPTER XI

TROUBLE FOR THE CHALET SCHOOL

IT is certain that Polly would have heard much more from the School about her latest exploit if it had not been for what happened next. As it was, she had to endure a good deal of "ragging" from her own clan for the next two or three days. But then something occurred which put all thoughts of the alarm-bell out of their heads. Mademoiselle fell ill.

It was a rare thing indeed for the Head of the School to be ill. She rarely even suffered from a head-cold. So when, one morning, Miss Annersley not only took Frühstück, but also read Prayers, the girls were thoroughly startled. They knew that Mademoiselle had not gone to the Sonnalpe, for four people had been sent to her at nineteen hours the night before to explain—if they could!—why they had spent a good part of preparation in playing at noughts-and-crosses instead of going on with their work. Renée Lecoutier, Elma Conroy, Emmie Linders, and Gretchen Braun had reported on their return to St Clare's that Mademoiselle had been "at her most severe," and had given them such a lecture on wasting their time as they had never had from her before. Therefore, when Miss Annersley, as senior mistress, went to the reading-desk on the hall platform at Prayers, they wondered what could have happened.

They were to know soon enough. When Prayers were over Miss Annersley told everyone that Mademoiselle had been ill all night, and would certainly not be in school for

their hands, thanks to that ceiling coming down, without *you* adding to their troubles."

"That was why," murmured Polly.

"What?"

Polly explained. "You see, I'd thought of doing it ages ago only it didn't seem possible to get from St Clare's to Ste Thérèse's without waking anyone. And when we were sent over here, and I was put right up at the top, next door to the bell-rope, it—it seemed an opportunity."

"I see!" Joe mused over this for a few minutes. "Well, you've made a howling ass of yourself. And if your idea was to make yourself popular, you've gone the wrong way about it. You've made Mademoiselle look a fool before the valley; you've upset two or three people, including Stacie, pretty badly; and you've hauled us all out of bed on a freezing night for no good reason. If you think that sort of thing amuses us here, you're vastly mistaken, and so you'll find out before you're much older. Well, I've nothing more to say to you.—Wait a moment! Yes, I have! You can give my compliments to whoever is junior librarian, and ask her to give you *Stalky and Co.*, by Kipling, and you can read it—every word of it. And you can just read, mark, learn, and inwardly digest what the Three have to say about old Prout. Now I'm going to tell this extraordinary rigmarole of yours to Mademoiselle. You'd better sit down till she comes to you, when she'll probably give you her own opinion of your conduct." Joey rose and left the room, leaving a completely deflated Polly behind her.

Nor was she much cheered up by the subsequent interview with Mademoiselle, who told her that she had expected better things of a girl of her age. She was to read the book Joey had recommended, and she was to take all her possessions downstairs to the observation-room, which opened out of Matron's.

That was all; but it was quite enough. It was a very crushed young person who crept from the room, and went, as Joey had commanded, to ask meekly if Arda van der Windt would give her *Stalky and Co.*

Nor did it end there. Many of the girls were decidedly cross at being hauled out of bed for nothing, and they told Polly plainly what they thought of her. Finally the immortal Trio's views on the subject of "Popularity Prout" completed her demoralisation.

hanging down, shifted from one foot to the other, and felt supremely silly.

It was left to Mademoiselle to win the trick. Rising, she said, still in that grave, rather impassive voice, "You will stay here till you are given permission to go, Pollee." And she left the room, closing the door quietly.

Polly stared after her wide-eyed. Was this to be her punishment—imprisonment in the study? And must she remain standing all the time, or might she venture to sit down? She wasn't sure, and she didn't quite dare to take it for granted; so when Joey Bettany entered the room, her face very grave (though her eyes danced with a wicked light), the prisoner was still standing where the Head had left her.

Joey strolled across the room to the swing-chair before the big desk and sat herself down. "Now then, come here and tell me what all this means," she ordered calmly.

It was very much what Mademoiselle had said; but Joey was a different sort of person. She wasn't so far from her own school-days that she wouldn't understand, and Polly felt this. She crossed the room till she was standing by the desk, and facing Jo.

"It—it was the—school-stories," she faltered.

"School-stories?" exclaimed Joey, a slight flush coming over her face. She knew the type of book which had inspired Polly, but she still couldn't understand exactly what the child meant, and she fully intended to do so before she had finished. "What in the world had school-stories to do with your doing such a mad thing?" she asked.

Polly flushed. Somehow, now that it was all over and she was facing the music, what she had done didn't seem either so funny or so clever as she had thought. "It—those girls—they—did things like that," she got out.

Jo shaped her lips to a silent whistle of surprise. "Do you really mean to say that just because the heroines of your favourite form of literature do insane things, you feel you've got to copy them to keep your end up?" She exclaimed. "I didn't think a sensible kid like you could be so idiotic on occasion!"

As this was exactly what Polly had felt, she said nothing; but she felt quite as idiotic as Jo had called her.

"What possessed you to do it last night of all nights, anyhow?" pursued Joey. "I should have thought you would have realised that the Staff had quite enough on

Thankful for the respite, Polly fled, and by the time the Head put in an appearance, she had recovered her self-control.

Mademoiselle sat down by the stove. "Now, my child, please begin at the beginning, and tell me this little history," she said.

"I—er—rang the bell for—for a joke," stammered Polly.

"But—*Why?*"

You couldn't exactly tell your head-mistress that all your favourite book-heroines were always doing such things—and getting away with it as a rule, so Polly was tongue-tied.

Mademoiselle looked gravely at her. "I must know the reason for this so foolish piece of mischief, Pollee. It was a very stupid and wrong thing to do. Apart from the fact that you roused the whole valley—and I am willing to believe that, since you are new, you did not know that our alarm-bell is also meant for everyone in Briesau—you disturbed the entire School, including Stacie Benson, who has been suffering with her back for a few days, and several of the girls who are inclined to be nervous. This was very thoughtless and unkind of you, and I wish to know why you did it?"

"I—I didn't know about Stacie's back," began Polly. Then she stopped. She *had* known. Matron and "Bill" had both said something about it, but she had been so excited over her own plans that she had thought no more of it. Being truthful by instinct as well as training, she corrected herself at once. "Yes; I *did* know; but I never thought of it at all. But I didn't know it would wake up the whole valley, Mademoiselle; truthfully, I didn't."

"Yes; I felt sure of that," said Mademoiselle. "But why did you *do* it, Pollee?"

"I—I don't know."

"But, my child, you must have had a reason."

Polly fidgeted with her fingers, which she had interlaced behind her back. This interview wasn't following the approved lines at all. If Mademoiselle had given her a sharp scolding and ended up with a still sharper punishment, Polly could have understood that. But this serious talk spiked her guns. Mademoiselle, having no clue to the mystery, sat back and looked at her; and Polly, her head

was what generally gave her away. Joey Bettany had once declared that when Alixe looked extra angelic, she had inevitably been up to something very much the other way.

"What is it? What is she saying?" whispered Polly anxiously to Cornelia Flower, who was sitting next her.

"Asking who rang the alarm-bell, of course," said Cornelia. "Hi! What are you up to now?"

Her question was left unanswered, for Polly had jumped up from her seat, and was making her way, terrified but determined, to where the justly incensed Head of the Chalet School was standing.

"Pollee!" exclaimed the amazed lady. "What then have you to say?"

Luckily, she spoke in English, for by this time all Polly knew was that she must own up at once, and she certainly had no wits left for any language but her own.

"Please, Mademoiselle, it was me," stammered the culprit.

"*You!*" Mademoiselle sounded as if she could scarcely believe her ears.

"Yes, please." Polly was terrified, but determined. In her beloved books, either the heroine came in for a tremendous "wigging," or else the Head was unable to stop laughing.

Mademoiselle did neither of these things. She looked at Polly with such a startled face, that Polly, nervy already, could only keep herself from laughing by beginning to repeat in her mind the multiplication-table. The result was funnier than anything she had anticipated.

"Pollee, my child, do you understand what you are saying?" Mademoiselle asked.

And Polly answered swiftly, "Yes, Mademoiselle. Seven nines are sixty-three." Which certainly gave Mademoiselle some reason for wondering if she were quite normal!

Luckily, Miss Annersley recognised the signs. Indeed, twenty-odd years ago, when she herself had been a very naughty Middle—who *would* have thought it of Miss Annersley—she had often been reduced to the same expedient herself.

"I think, Mademoiselle," she said in her soft voice, "that Polly is speaking the truth, but that she is a little—upset."

Mademoiselle nodded. "Go to the study," she said slowly. "Wait there till I come to you."

looked heavy-eyed and white, and Gillian Linton, who had gone in to lessons but had been forced to plead a headache half-way through the morning. These two greeted the new-comer with languid interest, and Polly sat down, wondering when she could see Mademoiselle and confess what she had done.

That didn't happen till after Mittagessen. Everyone was down by that time except Stacie. Matron declared she had better remain in bed for the next few days. Her back had been aching on and off for three days now, as she duly confessed, but she hated to seem complaining, so had said nothing about it.

"Well, Stacie," said Matron in the end, "I think you have been exceedingly foolish. I know that Dr Jem told you that you must be careful for a long time to come; and to go on with an aching back was certainly not being careful. Now you have to stay where you are for the rest of the week, whereas, if you had only told Matron Venables when it began, a few hours of lying down might have made all the difference.

"It was only that I didn't want to be a nuisance," began Stacie.

"I dare say; but you're much more of a nuisance now! Now don't begin to cry," for Stacie's grey eyes were filling, "for *that* will only upset you, and it won't improve matters. I'll shake up your pillows, and move you—there!—and you must try to sleep again. But the next time your back aches, just have the sense to go straight to Matron and tell her. What do you think she's here for, if not to look after you people?" And with this, "Matey," whose bark was always a good deal worse than her bite, tucked in the weary girl with a gentle hand, and then left her.

Meanwhile, in the Speisesaal, where Mittagessen had just finished, Mademoiselle was standing, looking very serious.

"Last night, the alarm-bell was rung," she said gravely in French, which happened to be the language for the day. "It could not have rung of itself, and no outsider could have done it. Therefore, I wish to know if you girls know anything about it." She glanced across to where Alixe von Elsen was sitting, for Alixe had a reputation that made the mistresses pitch on her at once as the most likely person to cause trouble. But for once, Alixe was looking just a very normal little girl, and not a plaster-saint, which

"Just after half-past eleven. Don't worry! You aren't the only one, by a long way. Joey Bettany was still asleep when I looked in on her ten minutes ago; and Cornelia Flower was just rousing. Be as quiet as you can, though. Stacie is in the window-cubicle, and though she's awake, she is feeling rather washed-out, what with the pain in her back, and the shock of last night's affair."

Polly roused up finally at that. "*Oh!* I'd forgotten all about it!" she exclaimed.

Matron hushed her. "I told you to be quiet. Stacie has had some breakfast, and I'm hoping she may get to sleep again. That's her best medicine at present. Now lie still till you've had something to eat, and then you can get up if you like. You seem all right—quite cool, and quite refreshed now."

With that, she withdrew, and Polly was left to face the fact that there would certainly be inquiries about the night's affair, and that equally certainly she need not hope to get off scot-free. The only thing that worried her was what would her punishment be? No one would take a lenient view of such wrong-doing as hers. And—*what* had Matey said about Stacie? Was she really ill? Polly knew Stacie's story, for Cornelia Flower had told her about it. Oh! Just supposing all the excitement of last night should have upset her so badly that she had to lie still on her back again for months and months!

The bare idea upset Polly so much, that the tears came, but she choked them back resolutely. The thing was done and couldn't be undone. Crying wouldn't help matters.

Fortunately for her, the door opened, and Gredel came in, bearing a tray with a plate of bread-and-butter and a glass of milk. She smiled at Polly as she brought her tray to the bedside; but she had very little English, and Polly's command of German was almost nil. She sat up and took the tray with a shy, "Danke sehr!" and Gredel went off again to her other work.

After drinking her milk and eating her bread-and-butter, Polly got up, and when Matron came back a little later, she found her fully dressed. Stacie, when Matron peeped through her curtains, was sleeping quietly again. Matron sent Polly down to the common-room (since it was no use sending her into school for half-an-hour or so), and then went to see if Jo was still asleep.

In the common-room Polly found Alixe von Elsen, who

and when "Matey" made her rounds to discover what casualties the exploit of the night had brought, she found the child sleeping so heavily, and looking so weary, that she considerately left her to have her sleep out. Consequently, it was well on for noon before Polly woke to the new day and the consequences of her own idiotic behaviour.

CHAPTER X

CONSEQUENCES

MADEMOISELLE had very little to say at Prayers next morning. For one thing, several of the girls were still in bed, "Matey" having decided to let them "have their sleep out."

"I have brought a list of those who must stay where they are till they wake of themselves, so I have asked that no bells shall be rung," she had said to Mademoiselle early that morning. "Some of these people were worn out before they finally dropped off this morning; and in any case Stacie Benson must stay where she is for the next day or two. We don't want her thrown back again for want of a little care."

Mademoiselle quite agreed with this dictum, so she merely nodded, and the girls were left. Polly was sleeping soundly now and it was not until Matron peeped in again at about half-past eleven that she stirred.

Then, just as the kindly domestic tyrant of the School was about to withdraw, Polly rolled over on to her back and opened her eyes.

"Well," said Matron briskly, coming into the cubicle, "I hope you've had a long enough sleep! How do you feel this morning?"

"All right, thank you," said Polly, bewildered.

"Ready for breakfast? Then I'll send you something. It won't be much, for Mittagessen will be ready in another hour-and-a-half; but some milk and bread-and-butter won't hurt you."

"Thank you, Matron," said Polly, still rather fogged, since she was not yet properly awake. "What time is it, please?"

funny sights. For some people wore their coats with bedroom-slippers; others had on dressing-gowns and Wellingtons; Mademoiselle Lachenais appeared in a slumbernet, with her face thickly smeared with cold cream; Matron had tied on her apron over her dressing-gown.

It was quite clear that there was no fire, so they were all marched back to the houses, by which time the men of the valley were beginning to thunder at the doors of the Chalet, demanding to know why the alarm had been rung. Nobody knew, so nobody could tell them. The only thing to do was to tell them that nothing was wrong—an accident must have occurred. They were asked to let everyone living in the valley know as soon as possible.

Meanwhile, the Staff had their hands full, trying to get their excited charges quieted and in bed again. Matron bade the maids of the various houses prepare jorums of hot milk, and then set about dosing every person within her own jurisdiction with cinnamon and quinine as a precaution against cold. Matron Venables of St Clare's and Matron Gould of St Agnes' took the same measures, and various people spoke their minds plainly about "the ass who thought it *funny* to ring the alarm!" to quote Joey.

By the time hot milk and the nostrums of the three matrons had been choked down, most people were sound asleep again. Only Stacie Benson, whose back was aching worse than ever as a result of the excitement, and Polly Heriot, who was beginning to feel thoroughly frightened at what she had done, were awake when Mademoiselle came to the Green Dormitory in the course of her rounds. She spoke a few words of sympathy to Stacie, telling her not to trouble, but to sleep if she could. Then she went into the cubicle by the door. There she found a very wide-awake Polly, who looked at her with big, scared eyes, afraid of what she might be going to say. But Mademoiselle had no idea that the author of the alarm was lying before her, and she only tucked the child in, bidding her go to sleep and forget all about it. Then she went out, switching off the light, and Polly was left to make what she could of the night.

And that was very little. Matron came in to attend to Stacie three or four times, and though she was almost noiseless in her movements, Polly's conscience was so active that she scarcely slept at all and woke at the least sound. It was six o'clock before she finally slept properly, and hopped out of bed as speedily and silently as she could. She drew aside her cubicle curtain, and fumbled cautiously for the door-handle. She found it at last, and opened the door. Polly slipped out, and then stood still. The guidelight at one end of the corridor shed a faint glow over everything, and the full moon, peeping in through the windows at either end, lit up the narrow passage. It was all very still and rather eerie, but Polly was plucky enough, and once she had got her bearings, she made straight for the bell-ropes.

They were looped up, out of the way, but Polly was tall and also agile. she made an upward spring, clutched at the bight of the rope, and brought the end down, setting the bell pealing as she did so. In all her life, Polly had never heard such a noise as that bell made! It clanged out sonorously as if it meant to rouse the whole valley—*as, indeed, it did!*

What no one had explained to Polly was that when the bell was established, it had been arranged that it should be a signal not merely to the School, but to the whole of Briesau. The result of its sudden call through the still night over the sleeping valley can be better imagined than described! The good people of Briesau, wakened violently by that clangour, at once imagined that something direful had happened—perhaps the stream flooding.

Whatever it was, it must be something bad, and they all tumbled out of bed, and made haste to rush to their doors to find out what was happening. The men flung on such clothes as they had doffed for the night, and rushed off to the Chalet. The women hastened out to see that cattle and poultry were safe, and got the stoves going. Some went down to the stream, but it was obvious that nothing was wrong there. It was full after all the rain, but not more full than usual at this time of year. Plainly, it wasn't a flood. Sadly puzzled, they returned to their homes, to wake up to the fact that the bell had ceased ringing almost as soon as it had begun. What *could* this mean?

Meanwhile, at the School, there was turmoil. Rudely wakened from their sleep, the girls tumbled out of bed, some of them screaming, others rushing to look for the fire which, they imagined, must have broken out. The Staff hurriedly called them to order, saw that they were wrapped up, and marched them downstairs, and out into the playing-field, where the moon looked down on a good many

She hurried upstairs with the rest, and undressed in silence. They had been warned to make as little noise as possible, as Matron hoped Stacie would sleep soon and wake better in the morning. But Stacie herself was very wide awake when they reached the dormitory, and only too anxious to talk to take her mind off her own discomfort.

"How silent you are, Pollee," said Suzanne Mercier, as she stood in the middle of the room, brushing out her long, thick hair. "Are you, then, not well?"

"I am quite well, thank you," said Polly politely. "Only, I'm thinking."

"It must be something very heavy!" said Stacie, with a forlorn attempt at a laugh. "You might tell us, Polly."

"I beg your pardon, but it is private—at present," said Polly.

"Oh—sorry! I couldn't know, of course," apologised Stacie.

"It's all right," said Polly. She laid down her hair-brush, and presented herself to Suzanne to have her thick hair plaited for the night. Under her great-aunt's régime a maid had always attended to her flowing locks, and even now, if left to herself, she was apt to get it fearfully tangled. Suzanne was good-natured, and had undertaken to help with her mane of hair. She plaited it into two loose pigtails, tied the ends, and dismissed Polly to bed.

Gillian appeared shortly after to put out the lights, and see that they were all right. She went the rounds; tucked them all in; told Stacie that if her back was worse during the night to be sure to call her; and then switched off the lights, and went back to the common-room for another hour of free time.

Polly had fully intended to lie awake, but Nature was too strong for her, and by nine o'clock she was sound asleep, and slept through Gillian's coming to bed, and the murmured conversation she had with Stacie and Matron when the latter arrived to see how her patient was. Stacie's back still ached, but the hours of quiet and darkness were beginning to have a little effect, and by the time the last of the Staff had retired to her room, and the house was in darkness, she too was sleeping quietly.

It was with a sudden jerk that Polly finally awoke, shortly after midnight. At first, she couldn't understand why she should feel so excited. Then she remembered,

"I'm afraid this means spending to-morrow lying flat, Stacie. You are a silly girl, you know.—Well, Polly?"

"Please, Matron, this is Stacie's case. Miss Wilson told me to bring it to you," said Polly meekly.

"Oh, very well. Set it down in the corner there, and then you can go upstairs to the Green Dormitory, where you are to sleep. Gillian Linton is there to show you your cubicle. Now run along, for I've so much on my hands, I don't know where to begin."

Polly nodded to Stacie, and departed to find Gillian Linton in the dormitory. Gillian welcomed her, showed her which cubicle she was to occupy, helped her to unpack her case, and then suggested that Polly should find her way downstairs to the common-room.

"The gong will sound for Abendessen soon," she said. "It must be nearly nineteen hours, now. You go down, and the rest will come along presently."

Polly went downstairs, thrilling with the knowledge that she had been given the cubicle nearest the door. It should be easy for her to slip out, give the bell-rope a few good hard tugs, and get back without being discovered. She calculated that in the first excitement of being waked so unexpectedly, no one would notice whether she were there at the beginning or not. That her plan was likely to upset a good many people, among them Stacie (who was certainly not fit for such a shock), never occurred to her.

For the rest of the evening she was very quiet—so much so, that Jo, thinking there must be something wrong, came over and sat down to chatter to her till bedtime, which came at the usual early hour for the six Middles who were visiting.

Polly had very little to say, and Jo finally tired of trying to carry on a one-sided conversation, and went off to dance with Gillian, who was feeling rather worried about her unexpected responsibility. Four of the St Clare folk were billeted in the Green Dormitory, the other two being in the Yellow, so Gillian would certainly have to keep her eyes open, for among her four were included Alixe von Elsen, one of the naughtiest girls that ever wore the Chalet School uniform, though to look at she was a little saint; and Stacie, who had gone to bed, tired out with the pain in her back.

For once, Polly had nothing to say when bedtime came.

pain which reminded her that, though she was permitted to be in school again, she must take no liberties.

Suzanne noticed her fatigue. "But go on, Stacie chérie. I will bring your case and put away your books," she said gently.

"Will you, Suzanne? Thank you so much. My back really has been a nuisance to-day," said Stacie gratefully. She left the room slowly, and while the others shuffled their books together, Suzanne dealt quickly and efficiently with her friend's as well as her own. Then she hurried off after the rest, to find Matron, Miss Wilson, and Miss Nalder all busy in the Wheatfield Dormitory, while its ordinary occupants waited by the door with their cases.

"Here are your things, Stacie," said Miss Wilson, bringing them out. "Put them into your case, and then trot off to Ste Thérèse's. Wait a moment," she added, as her eye was caught by the flush in the girl's cheeks and the black shadows beneath her eyes. "Has your back been troubling you?"

"Just a little," said Stacie truthfully.

"Then leave your case here, and go straight to Matron. —Polly, you can take Stacie's things with your own. Go to Matron's room when you have packed, and she'll tell you where to put them."

"Yes, Miss Wilson," said Polly in subdued tones. She dared speak in no other, for inwardly she was seething with excitement. Never had she imagined that things would go so well for her plan! It must come off tonight, of course, for she guessed that those in authority would see to it that one of the unused dormitories at the top of St Clare's would be made ready for them next day.

Miss Wilson got Polly's things together, and brought them to her. "There you are! Pack as quickly as you can, and get off. Whatever else you want, you must get tomorrow after Frühstück. You have everything you'll need for the night."

Polly quickly packed her possessions, caught up Stacie's case, and set off to Ste Thérèse's, and upstairs again to Matron's room, where she found that lady busy settling Stacie on a narrow sofa, a pillow under the aching shoulders and a light rug thrown over her.

"You should have told Matron Venables your back was troubling you," she was saying, as Polly came in.

"The ceiling fallen down? But however could it do that?" cried Joyce Linton.

"No one knows. But I heard Bill say that it was the last done, and the men had been obliged to hurry with it, and it was—was—scamped work, I think she said. At least it is down, and everything is white with plaster. No one knows what to do with those who sleep there, for none of the beds in the upstairs dormitories is aired or made up, and there is not time to-night. Also, Kitty Burnett is in San. with influenza, and Nurse says that no one is to be with her," explained Alixe.

"P'raps they'll let us share beds for once," suggested Mary Shand, who was an inmate of the said dormitory.

"Talk sense!" retorted Joyce crushingly. "You know as well as I do that our beds wouldn't hold us comfortably. Those that shared would have to spend the night clinging to the bed like grim death."

"It's much more likely they send us over to Ste Thérèse's," said Stacie, as she leaned back in her invalid-chair with a sigh. "Some of the Seniors are away for the week-end, so their beds will be vacant. Elsie and Evvy have gone up to the Sonnalpe to stay with Elsie's people, I know. And some of the others went down to Innsbruck because they have to go to the dentist's, and Mademoiselle thought they'd better go this afternoon and stay overnight, now the trains have stopped running."

"*Girls!* Is this how you behave when you are left alone for a few minutes?" Miss Stewart came into the room and surveyed them all. "You ought to be ashamed of yourselves! Sit down at once, and go on with your work. The following girls will put their books away, and come with me: Stacie Benson—Polly Heriot—Suzanne Mercier—Alixe von Elsen—Biddy O'Ryan—Klara Melnarti. Be quick, you six, and don't waste any time." She left the room, and shut the door behind her.

"Coo!" murmured Joyce. "What's gone wrong with Charlie?" Then she buried her head in her books, for the door opened again as Miss Stewart looked in to say, "Bring your attaché-cases with you if they are down here."

Stacie got up wearily, for her back had been aching off and on all day. Though she was practically well, there was a weakness which would last during all her growing years, and now and then she had these attacks of dull

difficult to have to turn round and work all your sums by quite new rules when the old ones are always tugging at your memory.

She struggled with it sadly, and finally set her exercise-book aside, thankful that she had got some sort of answer to every one of the five sums. French was easy to her, but geography was not; and with the knowledge of Anne's sarcastic tongue, she dared not waste any more time.

And then Fate suddenly came to her aid. Breaking through the quiet of the preparation-room, came the sound of a dull *Thud*! followed by several lesser ones. The girls looked up eagerly, glad of an excuse to do so. Even Anne stopped for a moment in her task of explaining to Biddy O'Ryan the mysteries of H.C.F.'s, and raised her head with a startled air.

"Anne, what do you think that was?" asked Joyce Linton.

"Something fallen down—perhaps one of the pictures next door," said Anne. "It can't be anything very much. Go on with your work, all of you.—Biddy, pay attention to me!"

Nothing more was said. The Middles obediently returned to their work, and Biddy, with a backward fling to one of the long pigtails that kept falling over her shoulders, fixed her attention once more on the troublesome arithmetic.

Twenty minutes later, the door opened, and St Clare's matron entered. The girls rose to their feet, but Mrs Venables nodded to them to sit down again and go on with their work before she called to Anne to come with her, saying that Miss Wilson wished to speak to her. Anne sent Biddy back to her seat, with strict injunctions to use her brains and be careful, and then followed the tiny lady from the room.

Five minutes later, Alixe von Elsen, one of the wilder spirits among the Middles, returned from her practising, and there was that in her face as she entered which made every girl sit up, while a subdued chorus demanded to know what had happened.

"The ceiling of the Wheatfield Dormitory has fallen down, and the beds are all in a most terrible mess, and no one can sleep there tonight," announced Alixe with satisfaction.

brooded over it, wondering and wondering how she could manage to carry it out. It would be very difficult to do it at night, for she was over at St Clare's, and, try how she would, she could *not* see how she was to get downstairs, through the covered-in passage, and up to the top landing of Ste Thérèse's, without waking someone during her peregrinations.

Most girls would have given it up; but Polly, coming late to school, and with most of her ideas based on the stories with which she had crammed her brain during the past year or so, had no mind to give it up. What is more, she determined to keep it to herself—which was a pity, for if she had taken any of her friends into her confidence, they would have given her some information which would have effectually stopped her. But many of Polly's books had described how the new girl came to the school, and, either by an act of heroism, or by saving the school at games, or else by her mischievous pranks, became the leader of the school. Polly had enough sense to know that acts of heroism don't turn up for the asking. Games were out of the question at present, for the heavy rains had turned the playing-fields—both at the Chalet and at its friendly rival's St Scholastika's—into a species of morass. There remained, therefore, the mischievous prank idea.

It seemed to Polly that if she could ring that bell, and bring them all out, they would be so thrilled by the daring of the act that she would become a real live school heroine. "Just like in *Pat, the Pride of the School*," she thought, with a recollection of the heroine of one of her favourite tales.

Polly then turned her attention once more to the problem of how to get from St Clare's to Ste Thérèse's in order to ring the bell. She was so absorbed that she never noticed that Anne Seymour, who was taking preparation for the Middles, cast more than one glance at her, and therefore she jumped violently when her name was called.

"Polly Heriot! Have you finished your prep?"

"Er—no-o," stammered Polly, with a sudden remembrance of French, geography, and arithmetic not touched.

"Then do you mind getting on and not dreaming?"

"Yes, Anne," murmured Polly. She looked at the problem she had been trying to work out according to Miss Leslie's directions, and heaved a deep sigh. It is very

and we were all pushed out in doublequick time, because everything was so dry, and the grass had caught fire," added Evyy. "Wasn't it fearful when the hail came, though? I was right away from the house, and by the time I got back, I was all bruises."

"What gorgeous fun!" sighed Polly. "Do you think such a thing is likely to happen again?"

"Oh, you never can tell," said Jo airily. "We're not likely to have such a fearful flood again, for they deepened the bed of the stream in the summer, and built up the banks with concrete—as you can see for yourself."

"And anyway, there's the big ditch to drain off the water all round us. That's why it was dug," added Cornelia.

"Oh, I *wish* it hadn't!" cried the sensation-seeking Polly. "I'd just love to be in a flood!"

"I guess that would depend on where you were while it was going on," retorted Cornelia, with a thought for her friend, Stacie Benson, who, nearly two years before, had been caught in a cleft in the mountains by another, though lesser, torrent, and who had paid for it by injuring her spine so that this was only her second term at the School. Cornelia thought that even Polly wouldn't care to be in a flood like that.

"You don't know what you're talking about," said Jo. "A flood's a pretty ghastly thing, my child. Hello! There's the bell for the end of Break. We must adjourn this happy meeting."

She turned, and led the way to the School, the others following; and in the usual turmoil of lessons, books and all their other ploys, no one gave another thought to the conversation—except Polly herself. She was wild with envy of those who had experienced the two adventures mentioned, and only wished that a similar affair might fall to her lot.

"It wouldn't be so bad if the alarm-bell was rung for a false alarm," she thought as she promenaded by the side of her partner, Klara Melnarti, when they took their daily walk round the lake. "What a joke it would be to ring it and have everyone out of bed in the middle of the night! Just like the school-stories, too! I wonder—"

However, at this moment, Klara claimed her attention, and her thinking had to end for the time being. Only for the time being, however. Once she had got the idea, Polly

Evadne grinned. "Yes; that's so. But it never rises above its shores, and that, I guess, is what Polly meant."

"Well, I did," agreed Polly. "But if the lake doesn't overflow, what makes the floods?"

Elsie waved a dramatic hand towards the place where the mountain-stream flowed into the lake from the great Tiernjoch which overshadowed the whole valley. "*That* does! We've had one flood since I came here; and there was one before. You'll have to get Evvy to tell you about that, though, for I hadn't come then."

"Really, Evvy?" Polly sounded excited. "Do tell me about it!"

"Not much to tell," said Evadne. "It was our first spring here, and happened during the thaws. The stream got choked higher up, and when the barrier gave, the water simply came down like—like a wall. We'd all gone to bed, and the first thing we knew, it was swooshing all round like mad. Wasn't there a mess when it went down, though!"

"What did they do?" asked Polly eagerly. "What a gorgeous adventure! I wish something like that would happen this term!"

"Something like what?" demanded a fresh voice, as Jo Bettany, accompanied by two or three of the Seniors, sauntered up to them. "What are you people talking about?"

"The flood we had that first spring we were here," explained Evadne.

Jo laughed. "Wasn't it a thrill! D'you remember how Madame and the Staff got the wind up early in the day, and we had to clear all the lower rooms?"

"Rather!" said Margia Stevens. "I say, Jo! D'you remember Plato and Sally were with us, and how Plato hauled us all out on to the stairs and made us sing when the worst was past?"

"I do! And we had hot cocoa and biscuits in our dormies before that."

"And the next two days, when the waters had gone down, we had lessons up there, too," added Paula von Rothenfels.

"True for you. The Seniors helped to clear up, but we were out of all the fun!" sighed Jo.

"And the next year, there was that awful thunder-storm in the summer term when the thunder-bolt fell in the field,

Polly had certainly had no right to help herself to his book, still it hadn't turned out badly; so she heard no more of it from anyone. All the same, as Evadne truly remarked, she had succeeded in creating a fine sensation that night, for no one had ever suspected that Herr Laubach could take an interest in anything apart from his classes.

Perhaps the most benefited of all was poor, dreary Frau Laubach, who found her days becoming unexpectedly brighter when she had puzzles to occupy her. Joey also made opportunities to call and see her whenever she was in Innsbruck, and further insisted that Frieda Mensch should also go at least once a week. The new interests cheered her so considerably, that she became quite a different woman. Jeanne le Cadoulec, brought down by Joey, showed her how to make simple stitches in pillow-lace, till finally she was able to weave great lengths of pretty lace, which found a ready sale. Then Frau Laubach's joy was complete. Altogether, Polly's sensation proved to be quite a success.

CHAPTER IX

THE RESULT OF TOO MANY SCHOOL-STORIES

"EVVY, what is that bell up there for?"

Evadne Lannis turned round from Cornelia and Elsie, with whom she was strolling round the playing-fields, to look up at the little tower which crowned Ste Thérèse's, and held a large bell swung by a rope.

"Oh, that's the Ste Thérèse bell," she said casually.

"Yes; but when is it rung? I mean, it doesn't call us to lessons or anything like that," persisted Polly, who was the questioner. "What use is it?"

"It's the alarm-bell," said Elsie Carr, joining in the discussion. "If there should be a flood or a fire, that bell's rung, and we have to get to safety as hard as we can go."

"A flood!" gasped Polly. "Do you mean that the lake sometimes overflows?"

"Nonsense!" said Evadne. "Of course it doesn't!"

"It can soak the path with its waves, though, in a gale," Elsie reminded her. "It did last spring, you remember."

Fräulein, I have a sick wife who must always lie on her couch. She finds the day long and dreary, and this would be a new entertainment for her."

"But if you'd let me, I'd love to cut puzzles for her," said Jo, pulling herself together.

"Another time, perhaps. But this time, I have asked it of you."

Jo was silent. The idea of using her hobby otherwise than to give pleasure had never dawned on her before. But she could see the drawing-master's point. What is more, she saw something in his eyes that she had never seen before. She finally gave in. "I shall be very pleased to do as you ask me, Herr Laubach. But you must allow me to add another for Frau Laubach as—as a love-gift."

He nodded, and turned abruptly away to ask Elsie Carr what she was going, to find fault with some details of her work, and to push her unceremoniously from her seat, and show her what he meant. Then he passed on to Jeanne le Cadoulec, and from her to someone else, till he had gone all the rounds. Finally, he came back to the mirror. He sat down in Polly's chair, painted a buttercup and daisy for her, giving her rapid instructions all the time, and finally rose.

"When you wish to borrow my books," he said, speaking very slowly that she might understand, "please come and ask.—And, young ladies," he turned to the others, "this is an excellent thing. If my knowledge can give you any assistance, please ask for it. Now I will wish you Gut' Abend, and go to my hotel." He bowed to them, and then departed, leaving them all gasping with the shock.

Once he had gone, Gillian danced a Highland Fling in a corner of the room. "That's Polly you've got to thank for that!" she said, when she had finished. "I'd no idea he could be such an old duck!"

Jo was silent. She was recalling the look in the drawing-master's eyes when he had spoken of his invalid wife. "I'll give him that puzzle I've got upstairs to-morrow," she decided. "He can't leave before it's light, and I doubt if he will before Frühstück. I can run round to the hotel with it, and ask them to give it to him. Poor soul! It must be ghastly to have to be away from her most of the week, and know that she's dull and bored most of the time."

Herr Laubach kept his word, and thereafter took a deep interest in the Hobbies Club. So it was felt that, although

"Zen vy 'ave you sooch shockeeng vork to me shown? You can like zis paint, and you ze most terrible vork me show. Vy, I ask?"

Polly was gravelled. She had no idea what he meant. To tell the truth, she only understood half of what he was saying, for his broken English and queer accent were almost beyond her. Moreover, as he became more excited, he also became more incoherent, so she could only say, "Yes," and hope she was saying it at the right places.

Herr Laubach poured questions on her, and finally Gillian had to take a hand. In the course of the talk, she explained to him about the Hobbies Club, and he promptly demanded to be taken to it. With his book tucked under one arm, and the mirror in his other hand, he marched the girls off to the common-room, where the little company certainly created a sensation when they arrived. Elsie Carr started so violently that she made a bad smear of violet beside the pansies she was painting on a tall jar. Joey stopped her machine so suddenly that she snapped her saw-blade. Anne Seymour pulled at her leather so violently that she puckered it; and Jeane le Cadoulec got her lace bobbins twisted, and evolved a new and original quirk in her lace-pattern.

The master looked round at them. "And so this is how you young ladies occupy your spare time?" he remarked. "Ah, Fräulein Joey. What do you do?"

"Jigsaw puzzles," said Jo briefly, for she was too much startled to think of anything else to say.

He came and examined her machine; questioned her about it, insisted on seeing how she worked; and then he amazed her by asking if she took orders.

"No," said Jo, still amazed into curtness.

"But I request that you will take mine, at least," he said. "Will you make for me two puzzles? And accept money at the usual cost?"

"I can't take money for a hobby," said Joey. "I'll cut the puzzles if you like."

He glanced at her. "You could use it to buy other materials for your work which, I know, you make for your bazaar," he remarked. "But if you are too proud to accept money for an order, I am too proud to accept as a gift that which I *ordered* as a customer."

"Oh," said Jo slowly.

"And I wish those puzzles," he continued. "See, mein

All this time, she had been holding the damaged book. Now the drawing-master took it from her, and going to the mistress's table, laid it down, and examined the injuries carefully. With his long, sensitive fingers, he smoothed out the crumpled pages, but they didn't look very much better. His eyes gleamed with anger as he saw them. He swung round on Polly, who nearly shrank back again.

"See vat you 'ave done!" he growled. "I mooch desire you to punish! Naughty child! Vv 'ave you my so-beautiful book take and him destroyed."

"I—I'm sorry," faltered Polly, "but I was looking at it one day, and I saw that lovely wreath, and—and it w-was just what I w-wanted for my m-mirror, and I didn't know I-I m-mustn't."

He glanced from her to the coloured plate, his heavy brows knitted. "You say you 'ave zis wreath copied? And for a mirror? Go; bring me your mirror, zat I may for myself see if you ze truth have spoken."

"I never tell lies!" said Polly haughtily, her fear suddenly going at this insult.

"So! Vell, ve vill see. Go and ze mirror her bring."

Polly stalked off, her cheeks burning at the thought that she was being disbelieved. She entered the common-room furiously, and Joey looked up. "Hello! What an age you've been? Get it safely put away?"

"No! That pig of a Herr Laubach caught Gillian and me after I'd fallen down with it, and he's sent me for the mirror because he doesn't believe I'm drawing the wreath!" Polly seized her mirror, and was off again before Joey could pull her up for her unparliamentary language.

Straight into the little class-room she burst, and thrust her work at Herr Laubach, crying, "Here it is! And Gillian can tell you that it is all my own work!"

He grunted, and took the thing. He examined the carefully drawn wreath, at first in silence; then with an exclamation. Polly had just begun to tint the daisies when Joey had interfered, so there was not much done. But what she had painted was done with a steady, self-assured stroke, and showed nothing of the stippling he had so girded at in her class sketches.

"You 'ave zis yourself getan?" he grunted at length.

"Certainly!" Polly's head couldn't go any higher, but her grey eyes were flashing.

order to make with Mademoiselle some arrangements about classes, and was just going off to the Adalbert Hotel, where he was to spend the night. Naturally, seeing the two girls standing there, horror in both their faces and attitudes, he came to inquire what was wrong. Equally naturally, he took it all in at a glance, and only consideration for the wan-looking lady he had just left kept him from a vociferous outburst of wrath then and there.

He looked round, and his suppressed anger was dreadfully apparent to the terrified Polly, who tried to get behind Gillian and make herself as small as possible. Then he swung across the hall, opened a door and motioned the pair into the room, where he switched on the lights. It was that same room in which Polly had her extra coaching with Joey, and it seemed to her that though on those occasions it was a very pleasant, bright little place, now it was heavy with gloom.

Herr Laubach followed them in, and shut the door behind him. Then he faced on them. "Now," he said in his own language, his voice shaking with fury, "I will know what all this means?" He pointed to the tome which Gillian still held.

Polly took a step forward. "It—it wasn't Gillian," she said shakily. "It was me."

But Gillian interfered. "Herr Laubach," she said, speaking German "Polly is new, and she thought she might borrow books from the shelves. She took this one to copy *this* design." She held it out that he might see. "She was taking it back, and tripped, and fell with the book. But I know she is very sorry, and wishes to beg your pardon."

"Now if there *was* a girl in this school who should not have dared such an impudence to commit, I should have chosen this one," returned Herr Laubach, pointing to the shrinking Polly. "But to take without leave my so-precious book! To fall down with it and crush the pages like this!"

Understanding only that he was angry, Polly was unable to say anything; but Gillian was quick to defend her. She said afterwards that Polly's need must have given her own German a good "shove-on," for she had had no idea she could be so fluent.

"Polly doesn't understand German yet, I'm afraid, Herr Laubach " Gillian said apologetically. "But she really is sorry, and if there is anything she can do to repair the damage she has done, she will do it."

As it was, however, she said nothing about it, and the woeful result was that, never heeding where she was going, Miss Polly tripped over a mat in the corridor, and fell headlong, the book beneath her. She was not hurt, but the book *was*. Polly was a well-grown person for fourteen, and beneath her weight, several pages, including the precious illustration at which she had been looking, were badly crumpled.

Too horrified to cry out, she stood with the book in her hands, looking at it with eyes that seemed ready to fall out of her head. What to say or do, she did not know. She only knew that there was going to be trouble for her—and bad trouble, too.

She was still wondering what she should do, when there came the sound of quick, light steps behind her, and then a voice said, "Why Polly! Why are you blocking up the corridor like this?"

She turned to meet the sapphire-blue eyes of Gillian Linton; and something in them caused her to hold out the book as well as she could, half-sobbing, "Look—look what I've done!"

Gillian snatched the volume from her hands—nearly dropping it, incidentally, for it was exceedingly heavy— and surveyed the damage with horrified face.

"Polly! What in the world were you going to do with this?"

"I took it to get the design," said Polly with a gasp. "I—I didn't know. Oh, Gillian, will Herr Laubach be very cross with me?"

"Cross? He'll be raving!" ejaculated Gillian. "Why, he scarcely lets *me* look at it when he's there to turn over the pages. Oh, Polly, what possessed you to do such a thing?"

"I thought we could always take those books on the shelf. And I never meant to fall. Oh, Gillian! Whatever will he do?"

Gillian looked at the crumpled pages again. They were badly bent, and Herr Laubach would certainly be furious. At the best of times he was peppery; so what he would be like over such an accident as this, Gillian could not imagine.

And then, the very worst thing that could have happened—or so it seemed to the two girls—burst on them. A door further along the corridor opened, and Herr Laubach himself appeared! He had stayed up at Briesau in

are hundreds of designs, I should think, and this one is so pretty, and very simple. See; I've drawn it already!" And she exhibited the back of the mirror to show the simple, pretty wreath she had drawn there.

"You'd better put Miss Wilmot's initials in the centre," suggested Jo. "Hasn't Herr Laubach got a book on lettering somewhere? Ask him; I feel sure he has. But, I say! you *must* be improving in your drawing!"

"He hasn't ragged me the last two lessons," admitted Polly, as she laid down the mirror, and ran off to get the book.

When she came back, somewhat breathless—for it was a veritable tome—the others were all busy with their own work, even Jo being fathoms deep in an extra large jigsaw. Polly laid the book on the table she was using, found her place, and settled down happily with paints and brushes to reproduce the colouring.

Jo chanced to look up presently, and her eyes widened as she saw what the book was. "Polly Heriot! You don't mean to say that Herr Laubach has lent you *that?*" she exclaimed.

Polly flushed slightly. "Not exactly," she said.

Jo got up and came over to her. "How do you mean— 'not exactly'?"

"Well, it was on the shelf, and I thought we could borrow anything from there, so I took it. Isn't it all right?" asked Polly in some alarm.

"Of course it isn't! It's all wrong! Do you really suppose that Herr Laubach intended all and sundry to borrow a book like that? Why, it must be a really valuable affair with those coloured plates. Take it back, Polly, before any harm comes to it. And don't borrow from those shelves again without permission. Otherwise, Herr Laubach may have something to say."

Polly got up reluctantly, and closed the book. Then she suddenly opened it again. "I must just see how the colours go for my mirror!" she pleaded.

Jo removed her painting-water, and then said, "Now trot off with it. You've looked at it quite long enough."

Polly went off reluctantly, still gazing earnestly at the plate which showed her design. Jo, engaged in putting back the painting-water, never saw her.

"If I had," she said later, "I'd have told the little ass to shut the book up. Then it might never have happened."

weather permitted—and the various out-of-school ploys wherewith the Chalet girls occupied themselves, a quite important one being the Hobbies Club, where they met together once a week to compare notes and pursue various handicrafts. Joey, for example, cut jigsaws with a treadle-machine. Elsie Carr had taken up painting on china. Gillian Linton went in for leather-work, and her younger sister, Joyce, showed a decided gift for chip-carving. For two hours on one night in the week, the girls used the big common-room for their collections and crafts, the one stipulation being that they should clear up the mess before they went to bed.

Polly had no hobby. The only handcraft her great-aunts had approved was sewing. Let loose among all sorts of interesting things, she had no idea what to choose, though everyone was generous with suggestions and advice. Many of them offered to start her in any collection she liked to choose; but Polly was a canny young person, and she decided to wait a little before deciding. Meanwhile, after a survey of the various handcrafts, she made up her mind to go in for painting on wood. In spite of Herr Laubach's judgment, she was really quite artistic, and once she had realised that the delicate, finicking brushwork adored of Miss Smithson was no use here, she did very well. She began with small boxes and trays of white wood, and took a keen delight in the unnatural-looking posies with which she adorned them. By the time she had provided three pretty boxes of various kinds, all beautifully decorated, she had a wild craze for her work, and her one grief was that Hobbies Club couldn't be held every night.

One evening, about a week after Rix Bettany's latest outbreak, Polly came down to the common-room, armed with paints, brushes, and a hand-mirror which she proposed to paint as a Christmas gift for Miss Wilmot.

"What will you put on it?" asked Joey.

"Daisies and buttercups," said Polly promptly. "I got the design out of that book that Herr Laubach keeps in the art cupboard."

"Which book is that?" demanded Gillian Linton, who had overheard the conversation.

"I forget the name of it. Anyway, it's German, and I'm not sure that I could pronounce it, even if I remembered it. But it's about designs and how to use them. I've got it in my desk in Five B. I'm just going to fetch it. There

"Mischief, I suppose," said Rix's aunt cheerfully. "Joey, I must ring off now. Call you to-morrow."

"All right! Good-bye! Give my love to everyone!" Joey hung up the receiver, and turned to Mademoiselle who had just come in, and knew all about it.

"I should like to box Rix's ears!" she wailed. "Madge won't let me go near the Sonnalpe till this is over, I know. Whooping-cough was one of the things I *did* manage to miss when I was small, and I know she won't take the smallest risk of it now."

"I do not blame her for that. Whooping-cough is so much worse when one is grown up. Now I must go to see Matron before Prayers. And you?"

"Oh, I shall go and write the last chapter—or as much of it as I can manage before twelve o'clock. Then I'll put the thing away for a few days before I correct it. If this wretched weather would only clear, we might get some hockey."

"Perhaps it will," said Mademoiselle soothingly. "You have done well to finish your book so soon, chérie. I shall look forward to reading it."

Jo laughed. "It's not a very big book. But it's the first I've ever accomplished, so that's something." Then she went off to wind up the tale of Cecily's exploits, which she managed to do just before the School clock chimed twelve.

CHAPTER VIII

POLLY CREATES A SENSATION

POLLY HERIOT was enjoying school. After the dull years in a schoolroom all to herself, with only an elderly governess for companion, she found lessons in company with eighteen or twenty other girls and a succession of mistresses quite a thrill. The work she did by herself with Jo was another joy, for Jo, whatever her shortcomings as a teacher, did not include dullness among them. All things considered, therefore, Polly was having a good time.

Apart from lessons, there were games—when the

"It's only for two or three weeks, anyhow," she said cheerfully.

"That's all you know!" came back Mrs Russell's voice, accompanied by a half-rueful laugh.

"Madge Russell, what do you mean?"

"Only that Rix has a cough which Jem says sounds uncommonly like whooping-cough. He's not sure yet, and we're keeping Master Rix in strict quarantine. But he certainly has a distinct tendency to whoop, and if that's the case, you're likely to have to stay down much longer than either of us bargained for, my child."

"But how on earth has he managed to get whooping-cough when he's been in quarantine for measles?"

"That's what *we* wanted to know. It seems that Master Rix has struck up a friendship with another small boy whose people are out here with his mother—and the pair have been hobnobbing over the palings for the last three days, if not more."

"But what was he doing out?"

"Oh, well, he's never been really ill, and the weather has been so lovely—what's taken you, Jo? Why are you mooing at me like that?"

"Only the weather," said Jo with another unearthly groan. "It's been pouring cats and dogs here!"

"Poor you! It's been glorious here. I did notice that the clouds were down, but I didn't bother about it. We've had wonderful sunshine—a real Indian summer. Rix being really quite well in himself, he's been wrapped up and allowed to be in the garden for a couple of hours every day lately, so he met Alan Lindsay—probably exchanged illnesses with him too. Jack Maynard was attending Alan for whooping cough, and as far as we can gather, the pair of them have been breathing heavily on each other during the past few days. They're both safely penned up again now, and fortunately they're the sturdiest little pair of ruffians you could find anywhere."

"And the others?"

"Oh, never near it. Peggy's been too weak for visitors, and the other invalids are still strictly quarantined. But this means that you and the Robin and Primula Mary and Stacie can't come near us for weeks to come."

"Well, I could just shake young Rix for this! Bother him! Why must he go chumming up with a whooping kid at this stage of the proceedings?"

At Mittagessen, those of the Staff sitting near her asked, with some curiosity, how she had got on.

"Oh, all right, I think," said Jo casually.

"I'm thinking of asking you to take two or three other girls for German coaching, Joey," said Miss Denny, who was responsible for all modern languages but French. "Joyce Linton is still appallingly shaky over grammar, though she can chatter well enough on occasion. And Mary Shaw and Enid Sothern could do with extra work, too. Will you take them on?"

"But they couldn't work with Polly," objected Jo. "She knows next to nothing about it, and is just at the 'have-you-the-book-of-my-father?' stage."

"I know that. But you could take them another time. There are three afternoons in the week when they don't have games, and if you could take them for an hour or so then, it would help both them and me enormously."

Jo looked blue; but Mademoiselle Lepâttre nodded encouragingly at her. "Why not, ma petite? You could do it, and you would find the work very interesting, I assure you."

"It wasn't exactly my idea of life," murmured Jo.

"All the same, Joey, those three more hours a week wouldn't hurt you," put in Miss Annersley in her gentle voice. "As Miss Denny says, it would do those children a world of good."

"Anyway, I shan't be here more than a month or so," Jo pointed out.

"Even so, that would do quite an amount for those three," said Miss Denny cheerfully. "Miss Norman can't take on any extra coaching this term, she has so many new children at St Agnes', and her time is fully occupied. And I have piano lessons every afternoon, or I would take them myself."

"Jo will consider the matter and discuss it with me—eh, Joey?" said Mademoiselle. "We will have Kaffee und Kuchen together this afternoon, in the study, my Jo, and talk about it then."

Whatever happened during that talk, Mademoiselle won the day for Miss Denny, and when Jo rang up the Sonnalpe next morning, it was to inform her startled sister that she had agreed to take over the other three for German.

Elsie tossed over the soap. "Teaching?" she said incredulously, ignoring Jo's last sentence. "Teaching what? Hadn't you better try a bigger bait while you are about it, my dear?"

"Oh, I'm not pulling your leg," said Joey, setting to work. "I really have been teaching."

"*Jo-seph-ine Bet-tany!*"

"Well, private coaching really," amended Joey. "I've had that new child, Polly Heriot, for history and German."

"Joey! What a priceless idea!" Elsie collapsed on a boot-locker in fits of laughter.

"What's there so priceless about it?" demanded Jo, slightly nettled. "Do you think I don't know enough?"

"No; you know enough to teach *us* in those two subjects, I should think. But it seems so weird for you to be *teaching* when it isn't so fearfully long since you were merely being *taught*," explained Elsie, rising from her uncomfortable seat on the lockers.

"What's the kid like to teach?" asked Margia, emerging from the towel with which she had been scrubbing her face dry. "Amy says she's the rummiest mixture in form. Some things she knows awfully well. Others she never even seems to have heard of. And I believe Bonny Leslie regularly has hysterics over her arithmetic, so it must be awful! Bonny's a calm sort of soul as a rule."

"She's bright enough," said Jo, rinsing her hands. "The trouble is that she seems to have been taught along the same lines as her own great-grandmother. Antiquated isn't the word for some of her ideas!"

"Anything like Stacie Benson when *she* first came?" demanded Elsie, pausing in the act of tying the ribbon that kept her bushy curls off her face.

"Oh, good gracious, no! Stacie wasn't antiquated—anything but! Polly is. However, she'll soon pick up different ideas, let's hope.—I say! There goes the gong! Come on, or we shall be late!" And Jo dropped her towel, and led the race from the splasheries till she came to the common-room, where she parted with the other two, remembering suddenly that she had been told at Frühstück that for the future her place would be with the Staff.

"I suppose I should have used the Staff splashery, too," she thought as she made her way rather more decorously to the Staff-room. "What a horrid bore! Still, I'd better remember, or Mademoiselle will have things to say."

However, that's besides the point. In the meantime, we might try a little German for a change."

"I hate German," grumbled her pupil. "I don't see why we should have to learn such a sickening language."

"German is one of the chief languages in this School," was Jo's chill retort; "and I suppose you don't want to go dumb every third day here—for that's what will happen if you don't learn it. Besides, you don't suppose the Staff would put up with that, do you? I can just see Bill's face if you refused to answer her because she was speaking to you in German!"

Polly gave it up after that. She had a very wholesome awe of "Bill," and the thought of what her house-mistress would be like if she had to deal with a suddenly-dumb pupil was more than enough to quell any ideas of rebellion on the part of the new girl. She listened quietly, which relieved her new governess. By the time the bell rang for the end of morning school, she had learned at least a little of the new language.

"You haven't done so badly for the first morning," said Joey. "You come to me at noon to-morrow. We'll tackle essay-writing, so you need only bring along your scribbler and a pencil, for that's all you'll require."

"Yes, Miss Bettany," said Polly.

"Jo, if you please," returned that young lady with a grin. "I'm not three months away—or, at least, not much more—from my own schooldays, and 'Miss Bettany' from people like you makes me feel nervous; so don't do it again. You'd better trot now, or you'll be late for Mittagessen."

Polly, with a startled glance at her new wrist-watch, fled on the word. She had not been at the Chalet School all this time without learning that punctuality was considered one of the most important of the minor virtues. Jo watched her out of sight, and then, habit swaying her, went off to the Sixth-Form splashery to make herself presentable.

Margia Stevens and Elsie Carr were there for the same purpose, and they looked round as Jo entered.

"Hello, Joey!" said Margia. "What have you been doing with yourself all this morning?"

"Teaching," said Jo serenely. "Buck up with that soap, Elsie. I don't want to be late for Mittagessen, and there doesn't seem to be any more here."

the poor, and orphans, for there weren't any workhouses in those days."

Polly sat with wide eyes. "I say! I'd no idea they did all that!" she exclaimed. "I thought they just enjoyed themselves and were lazy."

"Was it likely? Of course, just before the Clunic Reformation, a number of the monasteries had fallen on evil days, and many of the monks were idle, I suppose. That was just why the Reformation started. But you don't suppose men were accepted into monasteries, and fed and clothed and generally looked after till they died, for nothing, do you?"

"Didn't they pay board or something?"

"I believe some of them brought money with them. But some of them were quite poor men. Now is it likely that they would be encouraged to sit down and do nothing?" demanded Jo.

"I—I suppose not," agreed Polly, who was assimilating some new and totally unexpected ideas.

"Well, then, use your common-sense. And put down that Reformation. You can illustrate it by a picture of a Benedictine monk later on, if you like. I've got some somewhere."

Polly bent her head over the chart and printed in the words. The rest of the lesson passed quickly, and by the time Jo decreed that they had done enough history for one morning, Polly had something down in each column.

"You can read up about those events when you have time," said Jo. "And see what you can do about illustrations. It's a pity you can't draw—not that I can myself. But if you *could* have put in some jolly little original pictures, it would have made it much more thrilling."

"Miss Smithson said I could sketch quite prettily," said Polly defensively. "It's only Herr Laubach who says I'm bad. He does get so worked up about my work."

Jo grinned reminiscently. "He can do that without even an excuse," she said feelingly. "But if you sketch 'prettily,' my child, it's no wonder! 'Pretty' work is like a red rag to a bull with him."

"I don't see why," protested Polly.

"Well, he's all for the modern methods, you know. I've never seen your drawings, but I should imagine you put in piles of detail instead of taking 'a broad view,' which is his mania—that, and seeing purple in every blessed thing.

"France!" said that young lady. "Find the pages. Here you are!"

Polly glanced through the pages, and then turned eyes of dismay on her teacher. "There doesn't seem to be a thing," she said.

"Nothing fearfully exciting in the way of battles and so on. But this time was the time of the Cluniac Reformation."

"What was that? I've never heard of it."

Jo sat back. "I suppose you've heard of St Benedict who founded the Benedictine Order of monks? Well, that happened a few centuries before this, and in the interval, the monks had fallen away from St Benedict's Rule. The Cluniac Reformation was begun at the Abbey of Cluny, to bring them back, and generally improve matters. Naturally, they got away rather from St Benedict's original idea, but they did a great deal of good, and tightened up things. That was important, for until the Renaissance brought in the Greek learning, and the printing-press made books cheap, it was only the monks who kept alive any learning at all in the world. So it mattered very much that they should not be ignorant, nor idle, nor wicked. If they had been, goodness knows what would have happened, for the nobles couldn't even write their own names as a rule; and the secular clergy were generally too busy to spend the time copying old manuscripts and sending them round."

Polly pulled down her lips at the corners. "Oh?"

"Well, what did you expect?" demanded Jo reasonably. "If a priest had the care of a parish on his shoulders, he had about as much as he could do to look after it. But the monks were different. They lived in monasteries to sing God's praises in choir at regular hours of the day and night; to pray for those who either couldn't or wouldn't pray for themselves. And as they had a certain amount of spare time on their hands after that, and St Benedict's Rule said that they must work as well as pray and praise, they spent a lot of their time in copying out the works of people like St Jerome, and—and Irenæus. Of course, some of them had to do field-work; and others helped to build the glorious abbey churches. And then," went on the teacher, warming to her subject, "if anyone did want to learn, there were only the monasteries where he could go. And they were the doctors, too. And they looked after

column. See—here's the Holy Roman Empire. This is France. Here you have Spain. England's this column; and so on. It's awfully useful, for it does help you to keep things in their proper places. Then, if you like to put in pictures to illustrate any of the events, you can do so. Can you draw, by the way?"

"Herr Laubach doesn't think so," said Polly sadly. "He gets cross about everything I do."

Jo grinned. "I see. Well, do the best you can. And you can always cut out pictures—if they're small enough, of course—and paste them on so long as you do it neatly. D'you think you understand?"

"Yes, I think so. Anyhow, it looks very interesting," said Polly, whose earlier experience of history had included "learning" a chapter out of a very dull history-book, and being questioned on it by Miss Smithson, who never permitted her pupil to do any of the questioning. This had been boring to Polly, who was full of curiosity about certain things. For instance, what would have happened if Wat Tyler had never been killed? Supposing the Roundheads had captured Charles II during his wanderings, would they have executed him as they did his father? Like most girls of her age and mentality, Polly was a Cavalier in feeling, and had shocked her prim governess by calling Oliver Cromwell "that horrid man."

Jo left her little time for thinking. Opening her history, she said, "Well, we'd better see what we can find to fill those columns; they look emptyish at present."

Polly opened her book too, and glanced rather helplessly at the first page. She really had no idea what to look for, though she was greatly thrilled at the prospect. Joey guessed it, and came to her help.

"Look here; the first event of the time is the death of the Emperor, Otto III. He died in 1002, and was succeeded by Henry II."

"But I thought Henry II's dates were 1154 to 1189," objected Polly.

"I mean the *Emperor* Henry II," explained Joey. "We aren't bothering with English history at the moment, though we must put in the events in their proper column, of course. Put your dates down in the right place, and then print in Otto's death."

Polly did as she was told, and then sat back, looking expectantly at Joey.

polished. If you balance yourself on the edge of a chair standing on a floor like ice, it is apt to slide from under you. Polly had such an experience, disappearing incontinently under the table, while the chair, under the impetus of her fall, shot to the other side of the room. Joey jumped up in some alarm, and hauled her to her feet, inquiring anxiously if she was hurt.

"No-o-o, thank you, I think not," said Polly, rather bewildered by the shock.

"But how on earth did you *do* it?" asked Jo.

"I—I don't know. It just—happened."

"Well, if you're sure you're not hurt—you *are* sure, aren't you?—bring that chair back, and we'll begin again."

Polly brought the chair, still rather mystified as to what had really happened, and this time sat on it firmly, determined that if it should go off again, it should take her with it.

"Miss Stewart says you've done no European history," began Joey again.

"No," said Polly shyly.

"Have you done any Greek or Roman history?"

"Yes; Mr Bryant, our curate, taught me lots when I went to him for Latin."

"Oh, good! Then I needn't waste any time over that. Suppose we begin with the Middle Ages? It's a very interesting period, all sorts of things happened then, and all sorts of famous people lived then. I suppose you've heard of Roland, and Charlemagne, and all those people?"

Polly nodded. "Yes; I've read about them. There were lots of books about them in the library at home, and I read all I could, until the aunts stopped me."

"Very well, then!" Jo spoke briskly. "We'll just start with France and the others at the beginning of the eleventh century. See here!" She produced an enormous sheet of cartridge-paper which she spread out on the table showing Polly that it was divided into columns, each of which was headed with the name of a different country, with the exception of the first, which was for dates.

"What is it?" asked Polly curiously.

"It's a history-chart—at least, it's *going* to be. I got Anne Seymour to do it for me. Look here; we put down a date *here*—1000 to 1050, for example, and then we put down the different things that were happening in the different countries during that time, each in its proper

CHAPTER VII

JOEY EMBARKS ON A NEW CAREER

IT was not without some qualms that Joey picked up her *Histoire de l'Europe* at twenty-five minutes past eleven the next morning, and made her way downstairs to a small class-room that was generally used for private coaching. She would not have turned a hair if she had been asked to take on an entire form; but to face one girl, and have her all to herself for an hour and a half, required some doing. Besides, though no one would have believed it, and she would never have admitted it herself, Joey felt shy. She never minded meeting people, and her propensity for butting in on perfect strangers had brought her some queer experiences in her time. But this was entirely different.

Meanwhile, sitting with Five A who were reading *Voyage autour de mon Jardin*, Polly herself was feeling even worse. She had taken a great fancy to the tall, slim girl who had looked after her so competently that first day they had met. But since then Jo had spent each week-end at Innsbruck by special command of Matron; and during the week she had been too busy to be much at St Clare's. Moreover, Polly had heard all sorts of stories about her from her fellow-Middles, who were tending to make a tradition of their late head girl.

The eleven-thirty bell rang, and while the rest of Five A streamed away to the science lecture-room for a hard-working hour or so with "Bill," Polly armed herself with history text-book, scribbler, and pen, and made her way to the class-room, wondering what was going to happen.

Joey, seated at the mistress's table, looked up with a rather forced grin as her pupil entered. "Hullo, Polly! I thought you'd be coming along presently. Fetch yourself a chair, and come along and sit down."

Polly meekly laid down her books, brought the chair, and sat down on its extreme edge.

"I think," went on the new teacher, "that Miss Stewart said—Help! What *are* you doing?"

Now the floors of the Chalet School were kept well

210

Jo flushed at this reminder. "I couldn't teach maths if you paid me!" she retorted, leaving the question of drawing alone.

"We all know that," agreed Miss Wilson. "What we want to know is, will you take on Polly?"

"Oh, I'll do it if you really think I *can*. I'll do my best, anyhow."

"Of course you can do it," said Miss Stewart decidedly. "And Polly is a nice child, and won't try to play you up as some of those other young imps might."

"What exactly does it entail?" asked Jo.

"Well, lessons in European history, and a period for essay-writing," said Miss Annersley. "And Miss Wilson would be very grateful if you could give her one period in map-reading. And Miss Denny wouldn't be sorry if you gave her a couple of half-hours in German."

"All right," said Joey. "I'll take it on. My book is nearly finished, anyhow, and I've heard you should always let a book lie fallow for a week or two before you start correcting it. Anyhow, now that those wretched imps, David and Bride, have started measles, I might as well do something for my board and lodging, seeing that I shall be down here for another month at least."

"And there's something more, Joey," added Miss Annersley. "If you are going to write school-stories, you ought to have some idea of school-life from *our* point of view. At present, you have next to none. We aren't always teaching or on our best behaviour, you know. If you can learn something about the Staff side of a school, it will be all to the good."

Joey went beetroot-red at this public acknowledgment of her future work, but she knew that Miss Annersley was right, and that this was an exceptional opportunity for her to learn about a side of the School of which she knew very little. She murmured her thanks for the hint, and then, having settled with Miss Annersley, Miss Wilson, and Miss Stewart about the text-books she should use, she said good-night, and went back to her room and "Cecily." She was gratified to find that the little break in the work had freshened her up and cleared her brain; and she was enabled to finish the last chapter but one before she went to bed that night.

Lannis in the corridor, and sending her to seek Jo and tell her she was wanted in the staff-room.

"In the staff-room? What on earth for?" demanded Jo when she heard the messenger.

"*I* don't know,' returned Evadne. "Teddy simply said to tell you they wanted you to go to them pronto."

"Oh, drat and drabbit it!" said Jo fervently. "I'd better go, I suppose. But I do wish people would leave me alone when I'm busy!"

"I guess you had, if you don't want the peach of a row," said Evadne, referring to the first part of her sentence.

Jo sighed and marched off, racking her brains for light on the wherefore of this unexpected summons.

She was welcomed by the Staff, who offered her a chair and the box of sweets with which they had been regaling themselves. When she was comfortably settled, Miss Annersley unfolded the latest scheme to her, reducing her to breathlessness.

"Will you do it, Joey?" asked Miss Wilson.

"But—but—you surely don't mean you expect *me* to teach the kid?" gasped Jo, regardless of her language. "Why, she's only four years younger than me!"

"My dear girl, to Polly you are grown up—especially as your hair is—up, shall we say?" said Miss Annersley.

Joey clutched her head, and found that little tails were sticking out all round the funny little knobs she wore over her ears. "Oh, bother my hair! For two pins I'd have it cut off again to-morrow!" she vowed.

"Nonsense!" said Miss Annersley, coming to the rescue, and removing the pins to twist up the shaggy ends and re-pin them neatly. "Your hair grows very quickly, Jo, and it will be long enough to keep tidy by Christmas. Until then, try parting it into two tails and drawing them across each other at the back, and fastening them there. I think that might do it. Shall I come and show you at bedtime?"

"I wish you would," said Jo. "I'll be thankful for anything that will make me look less like a gollywog!"

"But what about Polly?" asked Miss Leslie. "Will you take her on, Joey? They are your own subjects—we don't ask you to teach her maths—or drawing," she added with a twinkle, for a year before this Jo had had such a fuss with the short-tempered drawing-master, Herr Laubach, that she had been removed from his classes.

very well," said Miss Annersley. "Peggy's had a bad dose, but she seems to be making progress now. Primula Mary is safe, thank goodness, and so are the babies. But Jo will have to stay here for at least another month, and she ought to have made quite an impression on Polly by that time."

"Another *month*! Why, that will bring it to past half-term!" cried Miss Wilson. "Are you sure, Hilda?"

"Certain! Madame says she's taking no chances with Joey—*or* Primula Mary."

"No; that poor baby is still very frail, isn't she?" said Miss Wilson, looking serious. "That's the Queensland climate, I suppose?"

"Evidently. I've heard that North Queensland is worse than India."

"How is Mrs Venables managing at St Clares'?" asked Miss Edwards.

"Very well. She has the girls well in hand, and they like her. For one thing, she is tactful. For another, she never says anything she doesn't mean. And she *does* consult other and more experienced people and doesn't try to promulgate new orders off her own bat," returned Miss Wilson.

"Oh, Mrs Venables has had a long family of her own. There were three little boys, besides Daisy and Primula," said Miss Annersley.

Dorothy Edwards raised her eyebrows. "Really? I'd no idea of that."

Miss Annersley nodded. "Yes; they died of the awful climate. Poor little soul; no wonder she clings to Daisy and Primula Mary."

"Well, this isn't sending for Jo and telling her what we want her to do,' broke in Miss Wilson.

"But what about Joe's book?" asked Miss Leslie.

"Jo won't mind helping us," said Miss Annersley confidently. "And besides that, Matey doesn't want her to sit too closely at it. You know what Jo is when she does anything. Dorothy, do see if you can find a child somewhere, and send her to fetch Jo."

Dorothy Edwards got up, smiling. "All right. And I'm going straight back to St Agnes', or the good people there will be wondering if I've been kidnapped. Good-night, everyone!" She took her departure, catching Evadne

decidedly. "Jo's ideas of maths are wild and woolly in the extreme."

"I wasn't thinking of maths," returned Miss Annersley. "But Jo could certainly coach Polly in history, which is her own subject; geography, in which you've always said she was good, Nell; and essay-writing. Apparently, the child's French and Latin can take care of themselves; but her German is enough to make one tear one's hair—so Sally Denny told me yesterday. Now Jo is good at languages, so she could give us a helping hand there. As for maths—where's Dorothy Edwards?—Dolly, could you give her a couple of periods a week?"

Miss Edwards shook her head. "Can't be done, my dear! I'm sorry, but I haven't a moment to call my own this term."

"Oh, I'll take her for maths if you like," said little Miss Nalder, the physical training mistress. I used to be rather good at school.—Kits, will you put me up to the latest dodges?"

"Like a shot! A couple of evenings will soon settle that." Miss Leslie turned to Miss Wilson, laughing. "Nell, get up and propose that vote of thanks at once. The problem of educating—*what's* the child's hair-raising name?—Hildegard Mariana Sempronia—"

"Sophonisba," corrected Miss Annersley with a smile.

"What a name! Well, anyhow, the problem of how to get on with her education has been very neatly solved, it seems to me."

"Thank goodness for that!" ejaculated Miss Wilson. "Ladies, I rise to propose a vote of thanks to Miss Hilda Mary Annersley for being so clever. All agreed? Then please show in the usual manner."

The Staff broke into an outburst of applause, while Miss Annersley somewhat witheringly requested them not to be so silly. "You might be Middles!" she concluded.

The applause died down, and then Miss Leslie suggested that it would be well to send for Joey and break the news to her.

"I simply must see her face when you tell her the glad tidings!" she said. "How long is she likely to stay down? The twins must be nearly finished by this time; but haven't the other children begun?"

"Madame rang up this morning to say that, with the exception of poor little Peggy, *all* the invalids were doing

"She knows all the dear old stories—Canute and the Waves, Alfred and the Cakes, and all the rest of it. As for anything outside of *English* history, Europe and the rest of the world might never have existed, so far as she's concerned!"

"Well, she's a problem," repeated Miss Wilson. "She's in Five B, but in most things she's scarcely fit for the Fourth.—Jeanne!" She stretched out and poked Mademoiselle Lachenais in the back. "Wake up! Never mind that stuff you're reading! What have you to say about her French?"

"But, Nell!" expostulated jolly little Mademoiselle Lachenais as she regarded a blot of red ink the poke had caused her to drop on Gillian Linton's translation. "What, then, have I done?"

"Been deaf to the pearls of wisdom I'm pouring at your feet," said Miss Wilson. "Oh, never mind the ink! Mop it up—here's my blotchy! What I want to know is your opinion of Polly Heriot's French."

"Oh, but excellent!" exclaimed Mademoiselle. "She speaks prettily, and very fluently, and her knowledge of the grammar is good. She tells me that her aunts had a maid who was Parisienne, and they insisted that the child should converse with her every day. She must have been an educated woman, for Polly uses certain expressions that are quaint and old-fashioned, certainly, but always the purest of French."

"And Latin?" queried Miss Annersley, who was listening intently.

"That, also, is good. She can work with Five A, and— and 'keep her end up,' as you say. She had special lessons with Monsieur le Curé, whom she begged to teach her when she had lessons in her catechism from him."

"*Oh!*" groaned Miss Wilson. "What on earth are we to do with such anomaly?"

"I have an idea," said Miss Annersley.

With one accord, they turned and looked at her.

"What is it?" demanded Miss Wilson. "If you can solve this problem for us, Hilda, I shall immediately propose a vote of thanks to you."

Miss Annersley laughed. "What nonsense! All the same, don't you think it might be a good idea to turn Jo Bettany loose on her?"

"Not for maths, if you please!" said Miss Leslie

only her shyness that kept her from trying to find or fulfil all the adventures with which she had stuffed her mind. Fortunately the girls were usually too busy with their own concerns to trouble about imaginary adventures, though there *had* been a time—as Joey and her compeers could have told the new girl—when they had tried to copy as many of the customs of school-stories as they could.

In the meantime, while Polly was settling down and assimilating the ideas of the School as rapidly as she could, she was also presenting a problem to the Staff.

"Polly Heriot is a bright child," declared Miss Wilson one evening when Polly had been there about a month. "But oh my goodness! Her prior education leaves a good deal to be desired!" She surveyed the young lady's botany exercise with a rueful smile.

"What's wrong with it, Nell?" asked Miss Annersley, leaning across from her own table to examine it. "It looks neat enough."

"That's as may be. The trouble is that it's at least fifty years behind the times!" retorted Miss Wilson. "Just look at those *niggling* little sketches!"

"Oh, she's out of date," agreed the English mistress. "Her essays aren't essays at all—they're good little 'compositions,' all nicely spelled, written, punctuated, and paragraphed, and without an original idea in them. Polly Heriot is an original young person when she isn't trying to express herself on paper."

"Her arithmetic is enough to turn anyone's hair white!" groaned Miss Leslie from the other side of the room. "Oh, beautifully neat, and set down with ruled lines and carefully formed figures. But I'd give a bookful of all this meticulous working for one untidy page of to-day's methods!"

"She's a problem!" commented Miss Wilson, as she scribbled a brief remark at the bottom of Polly's work and took up Joyce Linton's. According to Kits, she doesn't even know how to do arithmetic. Her science is conspicuous by its absence; botany, mid-Victorian; geography, the limit—have I shown you the centipedes she draws for mountain ranges?—What's her history like, Con?"

"Oh, matches with the rest. Just what you'd expect—fearfully biased stuff, and no idea of standing back and taking a good, general view of things," said Miss Stewart.

sheet, and she knew that it would finish somewhere in the neighbourhood of forty thousand words. But it would be a *book*, even if it never found a publisher, and if she could write one, she could write another. Already her brain was teeming with ideas, but she had enough common-sense to set them aside until her present work was done.

And then something happened which held her up appreciably—something of which she had never dreamed. All the same, her book did not suffer in the long-run, though Joey was certain at first that it would. The chances are that "Cecily Holds the Fort" would never have been the book it was; might never have seen more of the light of day than what was in Joey's own room; might never have been read by anyone but the two for whom it was intended, had it not been for that hindrance.

CHAPTER VI

THE PROBLEM OF POLLY

CONTRARY to the expectations of some people, Polly Heriot had soon settled down at school, and proved herself to be a law-abiding young person on the whole. After her years with an elderly governess, this coming amongst a horde of cheerful young people, who saw nothing wonderful in school but took life very much as it came, was a revelation.

Since her aunts' deaths, Polly had been able to satisfy *one* longing. Mr Wilmot had, as she truly said, been generous enough with her allowance, and Polly had indulged in an orgy of school-stories. She had read at least fifty during the months before her illness; and when her guardian had asked during her convalescence what she wanted, she had begged for more. Mr Wilmot was only too anxious to do what he could, so he had sent an order to a famous firm to send down a dozen or so of their latest, and Polly had revelled in them.

Naturally, they had helped to colour her ideas of school, and when she found herself at the Chalet School, it was

"I know they were gorgeous chapters," she wailed to her sister on the telephone after Frühstück. "Isn't it like the thing? I might have written a book worth writing, just as Robert Louis Stevenson did with *Dr Jekyll and Mr Hyde*. Now, it'll just be an ordinary school-tale—if it ever reaches completion."

"Don't you dare show your face here again if it doesn't!" threatened Madge. "Do as Miss Stewart says, Jo. Give it a rest for a day or two, and then come back to it. Or you might borrow Mademoiselle's typewriter and begin copying what you have done. Take a carbon, and send it to me. I *need* cheering up now, I can tell you!"

"Poor old thing! Those infants *would* wait to the limit of the quarantine! Well, at least they're not badly ill, so that's something. Hello! Evvy's screeching for me—I must fly. Bye-bye, and love to the entire family." She hung up.

Jo had the sense to take her sister's advice. She borrowed Mademoiselle's typewriter, purchased some carbon-sheets from the stock-cupboard, as well as a packet of typing-paper, and set to work to copy as far as she had gone. Needless to state, she kept making alterations as she went, and, as she was no expert on the typewriter, she made heavy work of it at first. The long sitting in the one position made her shoulders ache, and many a sheet had to be thrown away because she had either jumbled letters, or spelt words so wrongly, that no amount of correction would suffice. But after five days of hard work, it was done, and she found that she could go on quite well. The chapter she had torn up almost wrote itself, and when that was done, another idea came to her, and she made haste to get it down on paper before it slipped from her.

After that, she steamed ahead, and the book grew daily, till one fine day she realised that she had only two chapters to write.

"And I've done it myself," she murmured as she turned over the closely written sheets. "Goodness knows I've *begun* piles in my time; but this is the first I've ever *finished*. Won't Madge be thrilled! I must get on with it, and then I can go over it, and correct, and so on. And then I can finish the typing. That oughtn't to take too long if I only stick in at it."

She glanced through it. It was not a really long book. Joey religiously counted the number of words on every

"But that's marvellous!" cried little Mademoiselle Lachenais, coming up with a box of French chocolates. "I make you my felicitations, my Jo! Soon it will be finished. And then, perhaps, we are to see it, n'est-ce pas?"

"Thank you, Mademoiselle—Oh, I don't know," said Jo; "it's only meant for the babies, you know. You wouldn't enjoy it."

"Of course we should!" said Miss Stewart. "How many of your own wicked deeds are you immortalising, Jo?"

"None," returned Jo solemnly. "There are plenty of other people's to use." She suddenly chuckled.

"Such as?" demanded Miss Leslie.

"*If* it's ever finished, and *if* it's ever published, I'll present one copy to the Staff, and then you can all read it in turn," said Jo.

"Joey! How mean of you! You know quite well that I'm leaving at Easter," protested Miss Leslie. "You'll have to send me a copy for myself—and autograph it, too. Are you dedicating it to us? You ought to! You certainly owe us something for all the grey hairs you've caused."

Jo surveyed her brown head thoughtfully. "Can't say I see any on *your* head, Miss Leslie. D'you use dye, by any chance?"

"*Jo!*" protested the maligned mistress. "I won't put up with such impertinence, even if you *are* emancipated now. For two pins I'd set you down to a page of quadratic problems!"

Jo scuttled to the door of the staff-room. "Not if I know it! I love you, as you well know, but I loathe all your works. Whatever you are going to do when you are married, I can't think! You can't do the housekeeping bills by quadratics, you know."

"Indeed, I shall manage very well," returned Miss Leslie, flushing pink. "Go your way, you evil damsel! Go and get on with your great work. You make hay while the sun shines, my child. You never know when you may be prevented from doing any more."

Amidst a general chorus of laughter, Jo took her departure, and, since no one seemed to want her, she retired to bed, greatly refreshed by her encounter with the mistresses. She was tired, and fell asleep as soon as she had switched off the light, and dreamed at least six chapters of "Cecily," all of which vanished from her when she woke next morning, much to her disgust.

on all-fours and gathering up the fragments, which did not sweeten her temper. "*Drat* the thing! I've a jolly good mind to send the rest after it and giving up writing—at any rate until I'm older."

However, Jo had a strain of doggedness in her which prevented such drastic measures. But she flung the finished sheets into her case, shoved it under her bed, and went down to Abendessen in a thoroughly bad temper.

"What's wrong with you?" demanded Cornelia after the meal was ended. "You look as though you'd lost a dollar and found a dime. Guess you've got a pain in your temper."

"Don't be silly and impertinent," said Jo coldly. "You are getting too old for such childish rudeness, Cornelia."

She moved away, leaving Cornelia staring after her with wide eyes and dropping jaw. "*Say!*" gasped that young lady when she had recovered from the shock of her full name. "I guess Joey Bettany's going bats!"

"What on earth's the matter with *you*?" demanded Elsie Carr to whom this was addressed.

"Jo's mad about something," said Cornelia. "She needn't work it off on me, though."

"Oh, rats!" said Elsie impatiently. "Come on! Aren't you going to have this waltz with me?"

Cornelia put an arm round her partner, and they whirled out into the centre of the floor. But for once the young American was almost silent as she danced. She had known Joey in all sorts of moods, but this one was a shock to her.

Meanwhile, Joey had retired to the staff-room, where she found several of the Staff relaxing, and gossiping comfortably among themselves.

"Well, Joey," said Miss Leslie cheerfully, "are you bored that you are honouring us with your presence?"

"Oh, I thought I'd drift along and see how you all were," said Joey. "Haven't seen anything of most of you for ages."

"That's what comes of being absorbed," said Miss Wilson. "How's the book going?"

"Stuck for the moment."

"I believe most writers get to that stage sooner or later," observed pretty Miss Stewart, the history mistress. "Never mind, Jo. Give it a rest for a day or two, and then go back to it. How far have you got, by the way?"

"Nine chapters done," said Jo.

"Oh, it's coming on," said Jo lightly.

"When am I to see it?"

Jo went red. "Oh—give me a chance to finish it first!" she said.

Miss Annersley chuckled. "Well, don't, I implore you, mix your metaphors or split your infinitives," she said.

"As if I would!" said Jo scornfully.

There was a twinkle in Miss Annersley's eyes as she said, "I seem to remember an essay given to me in which the writer said, 'Like a rosebud opening to the dawn, the maiden sailed across the grass, casting light by her very presence.' Do you remember, Joey?"

Joey had the grace to blush again as she replied, "It wasn't an essay—it was a fairy-story. And I was only about fourteen when I did that, anyhow."

"Well, be careful now."

"And I never did split my infinitives. I hate the sound of it too much, and always did."

"No; I don't believe you did," admitted Miss Annersley. "How many of us are you caricaturing, Joey? Let us down lightly, won't you?"

With a guilty consciousness that she *had* used Miss Wilson, at any rate, for one character, Jo looked hastily round for a loophole of escape, and found it in the face of the clock that adorned the end of the corridor. "Mercy! Look at the time—I must fly! 'Scuse me, please, Miss Annersley!" she ejaculated; and fled, leaving Miss Annersley laughing whole-heartedly at her discomfiture.

"All the same," said the English mistress to Miss Wilson as they put away their books together, "I feel positive that Miss Joey *has* portrayed some of us. Well, it may be good for us to 'see oorsel's as ithers see us.' I wonder whom she has victimised?"

Now, whether it was the result of Miss Annersley's teasing, or whether she had tired herself, when Joey sat down to work again, she found her fount of inspiration dry. She wrote five or six sheets—a whole chapter—and when she read it over, it struck her that she had never read such rubbish in her life. The prank she had meant to be so funny was merely silly; and Cecily and her companions spoke and behaved like a set of puppets.

Joey heaved a sigh, tore the pages across and across, and tossed them into the wastepaper-basket—or rather, she tried to, and missed, so had the pleasure of going down

thing of the kind. With recollections of a certain fatal "experiment" of Evadne's, Jo provided a similar sensation for St. Michael's High School, when Cecily nearly wrecked the laboratory in consequence of carelessness. Further memories helped her to add a few more pranks to her heroine's record. At the same time, the book contained nothing that might not have happened at the best regulated of schools, though it must be admitted that most schools do not have quite such a spate of happenings all at once.

Then came a morning when, reading all she had done to date, Jo made the discovery that she had mixed up two of the prefects, and, consequently, must either re-write one of the early chapters, or the five succeeding ones.

"Oh, bother—bother—bother!" she groaned when she found this out. "That's what comes of being too lazy to make out lists. Well, I'd better do it now and save trouble for the future. Then I suppose I'll have to re-write that blessed chapter. Where's my note-book?"

Making out the list occupied her for the greater part of the morning, for having begun it, she found it so fascinating, that she finally made out the roll for the whole school, staff as well as girls. Then she put ticks by the side of all those who had appeared in the story so far.

"There goes the bell for cocoa!" she thought as she capped her pen on accomplishing this. "I'll get on with that chapter after. But this is a sickening bore! I thought I'd have got nearly the whole of the next one done before Mittagessen."

She glanced at herself in the mirror, caught up two or three hairpins to secure straying "ends"—Miss Wilson vowed that Jo's head in these days was a very good imitation of a porcupine!—and went off to seek cocoa and biscuits, feeling that she really hadn't done so badly after all.

Cocoa and biscuits over, she retired once more to struggle with the chapter that must be altered, and, by dint of strenuous work, got it all but finished before the warning gong sent her flying to wash her hands before Mittagessen.

"How's the great work going, Joey?" asked Miss Annersley, the English mistress, as she met the girl on the stairs. "Remember, you've been *my* pupil for three years or more, and I expect you to do credit to me."

was seized on by at least half-a-dozen people who all wanted to know the latest news of Frieda.

Next day, as soon as School Prayers were over, Joey dashed upstairs again to her room, and settled down—with different people, this time. She felt that she could not use Malvina and Co. in another book, so she had to evolve a completely fresh set of characters, and was soon so engrossed in her work, that she never noticed that a car drove up to the door, though she was at her open window, just above it. Nor did she hear the voices in the garden, nor the steps that came along the corridor past her room. Indeed, it was not until she came down to Mittagessen with a few extra hairpins in her hair, flushed cheeks, and very bright eyes, that she realised that the Chalet School had just received another pupil, and that Polly Heriot had arrived.

CHAPTER V

JOEY—THE AUTHORESS

JOEY duly settled down to her new attempt on a school-story, which presently was in full swing. She could not call this heroine Malvina. That had been sacred to her first shot. After much thinking, she decided on Cecily, and thereafter got on swimmingly. Warned by Matron's diatribe on the subject, she contrived to keep Cecily merely an ordinary school-girl, who led quite an ordinary life at school. She was making it a day-school, for though the past five years or so of her life had been spent at a boarding-school, she had had four years at the girls' high school at Taverton in Devonshire, where the early part of her existence had been spent.

For a fortnight, she revelled in her work. With a wicked grin curving her lips, she introduced a science mistress, who bore a remarkable resemblance to Miss Wilson, who held that post at the Chalet. Jo was fond enough of "Bill," but that did not prevent her from using two or three of that lady's idiosyncrasies in the portrait of Miss Travers, with whom Cecily was frequently at war. Jo was not of a scientific turn herself, and Cecily was made to hate any-

As she read on, the colour burned in her usually pale cheeks, for, coming to her story freshly after nearly a week of not seeing it, she could grasp how absurdly unreal most of her characters and many of her situations were. Jo had always prided herself on her sense of humour, but it struck her rather forcibly as she turned the last page that it must have been completely in abeyance for once when she wrote those seven chapters.

"Of all the idiots!" she said aloud as she tossed the sheets down on the table. "No wonder Matey advised me to burn it! Straight into the incinerator it goes. I'm thankful only Matey saw it—and *she* must have thought me weak-minded!"

She jumped to her feet, the book clutched in her hand, and raced from the room, down the stairs into the garden, and to the place where Otto, head-gardener on the Chalet estate, was burning rubbish in the incinerator. He looked up with a friendly smile and a salute as Jo appeared.

"Grüss Gott, Fräulein Joey! You have had a happy time with Fräulein Frieda, nicht wahr?"

"Grüss Gott, Otto! Yes, it was very pleasant," said Joey. "Have you a decent fire there? May I see, please?"

He obligingly moved to one side, and she peered in. The fire was quite hot enough for her purpose, and with a firm hand she rammed down the sheets, watching till they caught fire. Then, with a nod to Otto who had been watching her performance wonderingly, she turned and left the place, feeling rather as if she were a mother who had just sacrificed her first-born to Moloch. After all, it *had* been her first serious attempt to write a book; and even now, though she could see that much of what she had written had been rubbish, still, it had been *hers*.

She went back upstairs rather more decorously than she had descended, for it was not quite time for Kaffee und Kuchen, and sat down at her table. She planted her elbows on the table, and set her chin on her doubled-up fists, scowling into vacancy with the intensity of her thought. Then she sat back.

"I'll begin again," she vowed. "I know I can tell a story, and I mean to do it. I can't begin to-night, but I shall to-morrow morning. And what's more, I'll jolly well *succeed* this time!"

The gong sounded just then, so she deferred hurling defiance at the Fates, and went off downstairs, where she it was to find that the Chalet School had yet another girl on its roll.

"I liked the girl," Joey said when Matron had finished retailing the story. "I thought she seemed quite a nice kiddy, if a bit of an ass. And, you know, Matey, she must have been bored to tears with her life! First those old great-aunts—who should have been pilloried for loading her up with such a baptismal name! Thank Heaven I'm plain Josephine Mary!—and then two aged people without much go in them! All that's been wrong with the poor kid is that she's wanted a few friends of her own age. She'll be all right once she's settled down and got into our ways. I must say the old lawyer-man sounds a duck from all you say; but you can't expect people as old as that, especially who seem to have lived in Sleepy Hollow all their lives, to understand a modern school-girl. I don't suppose for an instant that she'll do anything so mad as running away from here—she seems far too keen on school for that, from what she said to me."

"Well, I hope so," said Matron. "And if she's been brought up as you say, I hope she'll settle down quickly."

"She's not a bit pretty," said Jo thoughtfully, "though she has glorious hair and nice eyes. But she has an honest face, and I really was sorry for her—she sounded so utterly forlorn."

"Oh, I expect she's an average enough girl," agreed Matron. "As you may remember, Jo, I told you a few days ago that most people are. By the way you may have your paper again. But remember: you are not to write all day when you begin again. The mornings, if you like; but in the afternoons, you must go for walks, or play hockey or netball. And you can work while the girls are at preparation in the evenings. So much won't hurt you. But I must insist on your taking things a little less strenuously."

Jo grinned. "Right you are! I really will keep calm about it. And now, Matey, if you'll excuse me, I think I'll go upstairs and get my unpacking out of the way."

"Run along," said Matron amiably.

And, whistling gaily, Jo went off upstairs to unpack her case, and then to take "Malvina" from the drawer, and settle down at her table to read it with as unbiased a mind as she could.

Polly produced a somewhat grimy handkerchief, and scrubbed her eyes fiercely. "I—I'm glad it wasn't me made Miss Wilmot ill," she said, with a lack of grammar that would have called down rebuke on her head at any other time. "And I *am* sorry I ran away—truthfully I am."

"But why did you not tell us you wanted more amusement than we arranged for you?" he asked, taking the slim hands in his and looking keenly into the tear-wet eyes. "I would have taken you about more if I had thought of it. But it is going to be all right, Polly. I have been asking this good lady to accept you as a pupil in her school, and if her partner will consent, I am in hopes that it may be arranged. You would like that, would you not?"

Polly got to her feet, looking bewildered. It was the dream of her life come true, but just at the moment, she felt that she must go back with her guardian and make what amends she could for having called that white, weary look into his face. She could find no words for her thoughts, so just stood silent clinging to his hands.

"I think, monsieur," said Mademoiselle gently, "that Polly feels that she owes it to you to return with you, and show you that her grief for having—er—so discommoded you is real."

"Is that it, hey?" he asked. "Well, she must come back with me for a day or two, of course. She will have her—er—garments to pack, and, perhaps to get some new ones. But if you and your partner, madam, can see your way clear to taking her as a pupil of your school, I will see to it that she is here—shall we say next Thursday? In the meantime, permit me to give you my bankers' address, and also those of our vicar and doctor, that you may write to them."

Thinking it better to settle business matters without the help of Miss Polly, Mademoiselle sent her back to St Clare's to get ready for Mittagessen, and then rang up the Sonnalpe. Mrs. Russell considered that they should certainly give Polly a trial. Probably this freak of hers in running away was the sort of thing to occur only once in her life.

"And even if it weren't, we've had other girls do it, and they've turned out all right in the end, my dear Thérèse," she finished laughingly. "Take the child, by all means. I like the sound of her."

And so it was that when Joey returned from her visit,

see plainly that it must have been dull in the extreme for her to travel with an elderly man and woman. We are, I fear, many years from our own youth. But—but I am fond of Polly, madam; and so is my sister. We are anxious to do our best for her, only I sometimes doubt if we can know what *is* best. Two old people—living very quietly in a sleepy little country town—I fear we have forgotten that times have changed, and the progress there has been. But here, with you, I feel sure that she would be happy and well cared for, and learn lessons we are too old to teach her."

Mademoiselle was deeply touched by this speech, though she said very little. Finally, she had rung, and sent for Polly, who came with a semi-defiant air which vanished as she saw the old man leaning back in his chair. She ran to him, and dropped on her knees by his side.

"Guardian! Have you been ill? Oh, I'm so sorry! It was all my fault—little *pig* that I've been! I never thought you'd worry about me—honestly, I didn't! Oh, please, please forgive me, and don't look like that, and I'll come back whenever you like—*now*, and take any punishment you like without a word!"

This little outburst of feeling was what had really settled it. Sitting back, Mademoiselle decided that the child might be headstrong, but she had a good heart. That she was absolutely sincere in what she said was plain to see. Her lips were quivering as she searched her guardian's worn, pale face with anxious grey eyes, and there was no pretence about her.

Mr Wilmot put out his hand and took the pointed chin in it. "Why, Polly, my love, are those tears? No, you mustn't cry. I am only a little tired. I fear I am getting an old man, Polly—an old man, now. And then my poor sister was so ill, and that troubled me."

Polly broke down and sobbed. "Oh, is it my fault? What a *beast* I have been! But I never meant—"

"Come, Polly! You mustn't cry, child. And as for Jane's illness, that was the result of eating éclairs for her tea, though I warned her they would upset her. It had nothing to do with you. Indeed, she does not know that you ran away. I—er—told her that I had a little business to transact in Innsbruck, and you would be with me,—not quite the truth, I fear, but I did not wish to disturb her."

am an old bachelor, and this is the first child with whom I have had anything to do. Were it the engrossing of a lease, or the drawing up of a will, I could do it with my eyes shut. But to choose a school for a girl is quite another matter."

"You must write to several schools for prospectuses, and then, with your sister Miss Wilmot, go and inspect those you approve," said Mademoiselle.

He shook his head ruefully. "I fear my dear Jane would scarcely know how to decide. She is older than I by some years, and what was correct in her girlhood must be out-of-date nowadays.—But I was forgetting. Of course! You have a school here! You have rescued the child from unknown dangers, and looked after her. Could she not come here without more ado?"

The thought deepened in Mademoiselle's face. "We are very full, monsieur. I am not sure that we could make room this term for even one more. And, apart from that, would you not prefer to have her near you in England?"

"For holidays, my dear madam, it might be more convenient, I admit. But I feel sure that if you would consent to accept her as a pupil, it would be an easy matter to arrange for an escort for her on such occasions. Come now, I am greatly taken—yes, greatly taken with all I have seen of your establishment"—he had seen only the front hall and Mademoiselle's study!—"and I feel sure that the influences at work here would be the very best possible thing for the child. There need be no difficulty about the financial side of it. I can give you bank references and any others you might desire. Polly will not be poor when she comes of age—far from it. And I am her trustee as well as her guardian."

Mademoiselle noted how tired and frail he looked after all the worry of the past two days; she felt her heart softening, though she was by no means certain that she wanted such a head-strong young person as Polly. "I am not the sole owner of the Chalet School," she said slowly. "I have a partner, and she must be consulted."

"But of course, my dear madam! By all means! But I trust you will put the whole matter before her in as favourable a light as possible. I know the poor child's foolish action must make you take a very dark view of her character. But I can assure you that until Thursday, her behaviour had never caused us any anxiety. And I can

Fortunately, Polly's wire had come just as he was about to seek a detective, and it was followed very shortly by Mademoiselle's; and the news that the child was safe in a school had soothed him a little. At the same time, such anxiety for a man of seventy-three—Polly had over-estimated his age—had not been a good thing, and he had succumbed to a severe headache which made it impossible for him to leave Garmisch until the afternoon of Saturday.

He reached Innsbruck only to find that the last train to Spärtz had gone, except one at eighteen hours which would get to the little town too late to enable him to catch the last train up to Seespitz, the station at the head of the Tiernsee. He was in no fit condition to undertake the long walk up the mountain-side, so he had gone to the Tiroler Hof for the night, and consoled himself as best he might with the knowledge that at least his ward was in the hands of those who would look after her.

He had caught the first available train to Spärtz next morning, and arrived at the School about noon, at which hour Miss Polly was out for a walk with the other girls from St Clare's House.

Mademoiselle had interviewed him, and had talked to him very gravely about his young ward, for she had succeeded the previous evening in extracting from her further details of her life.

"You are very good, madam, very good," he had said, "but what am I to do? I am well aware that old people like myself and my sister are not fitting guardians for a bright young girl, but I could scarcely refuse our dear and life-long friends, the Misses Heriot. Come! You are the head-mistress of a school. You must have had considerable experience of young people. What do you advise me to do? I am anxious to do my best for her. She is a dear child, if somewhat headstrong, and should make a fine woman if she is only trained aright. The trouble is how to arrange for such training." And he shook his head.

"She ought to go to school," said Mademoiselle thoughtfully. "She needs the discipline she would have there both from the staff and from the other girls. Could you not send her to a good English school? She would be able to spend her vacations with you, and I feel sure that she would answer well to such training."

"Quite possibly, my dear madam. But the point is that I do not know how to set about finding such a school. I

watchful eye on her. Incidentally, Mademoiselle gently suggested that it would be wiser if Polly handed her wallet over, keeping just the few schillings that all the girls had, and Polly was so enamoured of the new life to which she was being introduced, that she did as she was told like a lamb, and never suspected that one reason for the suggestion was to deprive her of the means of running away again!

It was now past sixteen o'clock, and Kaffee und Kuchen would be in full swing in the girls' common-room at St Clare's, so Mademoiselle sent the two girls along there at once. Then, after phoning her wire to Spärtz with injunctions that it must be sent off at once, she turned to the private telephone to the Sonnalpe to tell the people at "Die Rosen' of Joey's latest exploit.

CHAPTER IV

MR WILMOT ARRIVES

AS Matron insisted on Jo's keeping to her original plan of spending the week-end at Innsbruck, that young lady knew nothing about subsequent events until she got back to Briesau on the Tuesday.

Mademoiselle's wire had brought old Mr Wilmot to the Tiernsee post-haste on the Sunday. As it turned out, no one had missed Miss Polly until the Friday, owing to old Miss Wilmot having fallen ill on the Thursday with a severe bilious attack. Mr Wilmot had told their chambermaid to look after the child, but his German was shaky and the girl was sulking under notice to leave. She had chosen to pay no attention to his orders till the Friday morning, when she had discovered, to her horror, that the young lady's bed had not been slept in.

Mr Wilmot had, by that time, gone off to seek a doctor for his sister, who was really quite ill, and the girl had not dared to mention her discovery to the manageress of the hotel, so no one but herself knew anything about it till noon, when she had finally come to him and, with many sniffles, told her news. For some hours thereafter, he had been nearly frantic with worry.

thing of any of the party again. Then I came, and mother died. There was no one left but father's two old aunts, and they took me. They chose my names, too. I had to be Hildegard because that was mother's name, and one of the aunts was Mariana, and the other was Sophonisba, so they just gave me the lot. They meant to call me Hildegard, I believe. But when I was little, I couldn't say it, and I called myself Polly somehow, and it stuck—though they didn't exactly like it. So I've been Polly ever since."

"I don't blame you," said Jo with decision. "Well, Polly, I'm going to take you to our headmistress, Mademoiselle Lepâttre, and you must explain things to her. Oh, you needn't look scared. She's a perfect dear, and most awfully understanding. You'll stay at the School until she can hear from your guardians, and then she'll talk to them. You'll have to go in to lessons, I expect, with the rest. You won't mind that, I suppose?"

"Mind it? It's the one thing I've wanted all my life!" said Polly fervently. "That—and to have my hair cut off." She gave an impatient toss to the thick, untidy pigtail that dangled down her back to her waist.

"I don't think I'd have it cut if I were you," said Jo thoughtfully. "The fashion's going out. And anyway, your hair is lovely. I should think it looks gorgeous when it's loose."

"It's a sickening nuisance to keep tidy," grumbled its owner ungratefully. "And as for lovely, it's *red*!"

"Yes; but a deep chestnutty red. You be thankful it isn't ginger," advised Jo. "You might have something to growl about then."

By this time, they had reached the front-door of the School, and Mademoiselle, amazement in her eyes, was in the hall as they entered. Jo went briskly forward to explain matters.

It was a full hour before the Head of the School had got all the information she thought she should have, for Polly suddenly turned shy, and it was with difficulty that they dragged "yes" and "no" out of her. But at length the whole story came out, and on Jo's assuring her that Polly's wire had been duly sent, Mademoiselle decided to send a fuller one on her own account. In the meanwhile she made up her mind to place Miss Polly at St Clare's, where the house-mistress, Miss Wilson, science and geography mistress of the School, could be trusted to keep a

measles! In fact, my dear, if it's *school* you want, you've come to the right shop! I'm staying at my own old school—the Chalet School. You must have passed it to get here. Didn't you notice three houses linked up by covered passages inside a high palisading?"

The girl looked up, interest in her face. "Of course I did! Do you mean to say there's a school here? What a gorgeous place for it! I wonder—" She paused, scribbled her telegram, signed it with four initials, and handed it over to Frau Pfeiffen with some money. "Can you make it out? And is that right, please? I don't understand your money yet."

Jo gasped again, for the wallet-case was simply bulging with notes of high value, and this child handled it as carelessly as if all she possessed were worth a few schillings. Then she glanced at the form and noted the initials.

"Oughtn't you to sign your surname?" she asked. "Will they know who that's from?"

The girl nodded. "They'll know all right. There couldn't be another person with a collection like that! But I'll stick in 'Heriot' if you like." She took back the form and added the name. Then she got her chocolate, and followed Jo from the tiny shop, leaving good Frau Pfeiffen consumed with curiosity to know what all this meant.

"What is your baptismal name?" asked Jo as the stranger fell into step with her.

"Hildegard—Mariana—Sophonisba—Heriot," said its owner, with a pause between each word to give it due effect.

"*What?*" Jo was startled out of her manners.

"Yes—all of it. Of course, I don't use it. Well, would *you*?"

"Not if I could help it," Jo assured her. "But if you *don't* use it, what *do* you use?"

"Polly—nice, and short, and not sentimental."

Jo nodded approval. "Yes; I like that—though I don't see how you get it. And it's not so ordinary these days as Mollie, for instance. And I hope you don't mind me saying so, but what on earth possessed your people to give you such a mouthful as that?"

"They hadn't anything to do with it," explained Polly, who seemed considerably cheered up now. "You see, father died before I was born—at least, he went with an expedition up the Amazon, and nobody ever heard any-

nounced it with the "Sch" hard instead of soft as the people round Tiernsee always do—"and then I walked back round the lake and came on here."

"And do you mean to say that your guardians haven't any idea where you are?" gasped Jo, wild visions of a panic-stricken old pair whirling through her brain.

"No. But I'm going to send them a card now, and I did tell them in my note that I should be all right. My head's screwed on pretty tightly, you know."

The girl said all this in the same, dreary, matter-of-fact tones that she had used all along. There was no idea of boasting. Jo grasped this. She also grasped the fact that this Mr. Wilmot and his sister must have been enduring agonies of anxiety about their charge, so she laid an imperative hand on the girl's arm.

"My dear, you simply can't just send them a card! You must wire, of course. They must be nearly crazy with worry about you. Give me their address, and I'll send it for you at once."

The girl looked at her with a little amazement. "Oh, I've plenty of money. I can send a wire myself—thanks, all the same."

"Then send it, for goodness' sake!" urged Jo.

"Oh, they won't be worrying about me. They're pretty placid. That was what I found so trying. They just go on the same way, day in and day out, and I'd had more than enough of it with my aunts! *They* wouldn't even let me go to the most seminaryish kind of school. I had to have a governess. Aunt Mariana thought schools were not the proper place for girls like me, and Aunt Sophonisba backed her up."

"Well, I can't help that," persisted Jo, who was nearly breathless over the names of the aunts. "If you think your guardians aren't almost off their heads with anxiety over you, that's where you make a big mistake. They aren't going to do anything *but* worry about a school-girl running loose over Europe, however aged or placid they may be. Here's the form. Fill it in, and Frau Pfeiffen will phone it down to Spärtz. And then, I think you'd better come back with me for the present."

"Won't your people object?" asked the girl, beginning to lose a little of her indifference.

"Not they!" returned Jo airily. "However, I'm not at home at present—I can't go home—the babies have

187

"Guten Tag meine Fräulein," said Frau Pfeiffen briskly. "Was ist es?"

"Oh, dear!" said the girl disconsolately. "Don't you speak English, either?"

"Oh, yes; she does," said Joey cheerfully, butting in in her own inimitable way. "And I can translate for you if it's anything out of the ordinary. What is it you want?"

The gloomy face lightened a little. "Oh, will you? Thank you so much. It's simply awful being surrounded with people who don't speak a word of your own language! I want some stamps, and picture-postcards—oh, and a bar of chocolate."

Frau Pfeiffen smiled reassuringly. "All zose I have, meine Fräulein. "Is it ze pictures of ze lake you wish?"

"Oh, I don't know," said the girl listlessly. "Anything will do. It's only to let them know where I am."

"Do you mean," demanded Jo, "that you're here alone?"

The girl looked up from the views through which she was glancing. "Yes. What about it?"

"But—why?" asked Jo. "I mean, people of your age generally have fathers and mothers running round after them."

"Well, I haven't—never had any. They died before I was born, more or less."

"But you must have *some*one," argued Jo. "I never knew my parents, either. My brother and sister brought me up. And we had a guardian too, of course."

"Oh? Well, my great-aunts brought *me* up. Only now they're both dead and my guardians are an awful, snuffy old lawyer and his prim maiden sister—both eightyish, I should think! I got influenza very badly, and when I was better, the doctor ordered me to the mountains for a change. It would have been fun with someone of my own age; but they only have ideas from before the Flood, and I got so dull and bored with it all, that yesterday, when they were asleep at our hotel at Garmisch—or whatever they call the place—I just packed a bag, and left a note saying I was sick of everything, and left. I've heaps of money—I will say for Mr Wilmot that he isn't mean!— so I rang up the Tiroler Hof in Innsbruck before I left, and told them to reserve me a room. They stared rather when they saw me, though." Here she indulged in a faint grin. "This morning, I came up here in that funny little mountain-train. I took the boat to Scholastika"—she pro-

tired. She went along slowly, her eyes on the lovely lake, which was a deep purple-blue. Underfoot, the grass on which she was walking was a rich green. The chestnuts and plane-trees were golden and russet. Very few flowers remained in the meadow-land, but those there were held up their heads bravely. Jo revelled in the autumn beauty, and pulled off her hat to let the little breeze cool her head.

Presently, her thoughts went back to her book. Since she had listened to Matron's diatribe on the subject, she was able to see more clearly.

"What an ass I've been!" she thought as she turned over in her mind the various characters. "Malvina *was* too sweet to live! And not even Thekla—and she was expelled!—ever was as bad as Rosetta! I wonder," and she grinned suddenly to herself, "that Matey didn't point out that no school would have kept such a girl for two minutes! I think she must have said everything else! Thank goodness she came along in time to save me from making an abject idiot of myself!"

Here she was halted by Herr Braun, proprietor of the "Kron Prince Karl," the biggest hotel in Briesau, and had to answer his inquiries about her family.

When he finally left her, she went on making good resolutions as she went to the great Hotel Post, where was also the only shop in the district. "I'll only work in the mornings," she decided to herself, "and perhaps a little in the evenings. And I simply must put in some practice at my singing. Plato will go off the deep end next week if I don't. And if Madge gets to hear of it, there'll be trouble!"

By this time she had reached the Post, and she strolled into the little shop situated beneath the hotel entrance. Her face bore a wide smile for the post-mistress, who knew her well, having seen her grow up from a wicked Middle to her present stage. Frau Pfeiffen was a merry-faced young woman, who spoke English quite well, though she and Jo conversed in German. That young woman got her stamps and oranges—Matron proposed to dose some unlucky wights with castor-oil that night—and invested in chocolate on her own account. Then, after a brief conversation which included the giving of the latest news from "Die Rosen"—Frau Pfeiffen knew them all—she turned to go. But just then, a slender girl of about fourteen came in, and stood looking forlornly round.

Apply that to your people, and you ought to write something that some kind publisher may accept."

"D'you really think so?" queried Jo, half-rapturous, half-doubtful.

"Shouldn't say so if I didn't. And now, I'm going to confiscate your paper, pen, and ink till after the week-end, and you can put on your blazer and go and do some errands for me at the Post. I want stamps, and oranges, and one or two other items. Get ready, and I'll bring the money." And gathering up the bundle of foolscap, the new pen, and the fat bottle of ink, Matron stalked off. She turned back at the door, however, to add, "And while I think of it, you'd better ring up the Mariahilfe and tell them you'll be down for the week-end after all. You ought to be ashamed of yourself for disappointing Frieda as you did!"

Jo had nothing to say for herself. She had felt conscience-stricken at the time when she had rung up Frieda Mensch to tell her that she couldn't possibly get down to Innsbruck for the week-end as had been arranged. Now Matron was going off with her tools, and she had no means of getting any more paper in Briesau. She might as well go.

Having settled Jo, Matron finally departed, and when she came back, it was to find the table cleared of its litter, and the room looking orderly for once. Not that Jo had followed her advice and torn up the book. She could not quite bring herself to do that—yet. But Malvina and all her clan were tucked away under Jo's blouses in the bottom drawer of the bureau.

"You can go to St. Clare's for Kaffee und Kuchen when you get back," said Matron as she followed the tall girl downstairs. "The girls are complaining that they haven't seen anything of you there this week, and that you might as well be at the Sonnalpe and have done with it."

"All right, Matey," said Jo submissively.

When she had gone, Matron shut the front-door on her with a grim smile. "Some of that book was quite good," she thought, "but some of it was rank bad! Jo has it in her to do good work—but not if she tries to work herself to death. However, I've put my foot down, and I don't *think* she'll disobey me."

Once she was out in the fresh crisp air of a late September afternoon, Jo realised that her head had been aching dully for the past two days, and that she felt very

Jo refused to answer this, but her scarlet cheeks were reply enough.

Matron went on. "If you want to publish, Jo, take my advice, and keep your characters as close to life as possible. No one is ever without *some* redeeming point. It would be a sad look-out for us if it were not so! And, in any case, no child of fourteen ever was the abandoned little wretch you've made your Rosetta. According to you, she's not only a liar, but she cheats, steals, makes mischief, and is apparently without either morals or manners. Do you *want* the Robin and Daisy to think such girls exist— now *do* you?"

"No-o-o," said Jo, very low and ashamedly.

"And then, Malvina! Such a plaster saint of a girl would aggravate anyone into thinking, 'Well, she asks for her troubles, and she jolly well deserves them!'" Matron smiled as she brought out the slang. Then she added the jam to the powder. "You've managed Flavia and that head-girl of yours very well. I can see them; they're real people. But Malvina and Rosetta never lived outside the pages of the sort of school-story with which *we* used to be bored when I was a girl—and rather worse than some, at that!"

"I—I *was* beginning to think that perhaps Rosetta was a little overdrawn," confessed Jo, nevertheless feeling her self-respect returning at Matron's approval of two of her characters.

"Overdrawn? I should think she is! And just remember this, Jo. Your gift was given you to help your fellow-men, not to hinder them. You won't help if you give them people so bad that they're either comic or irritating. I don't see why you shouldn't write school-stories—and publish them, too. But tear up this rubbish, and begin again."

"Oh, Matey! I've put in hours of work on it!" pleaded Jo clasping her manuscript as if it were a baby.

"The worse for you, then. This won't *do*! Begin again, my child, and just remember the old rhyme:

'There is so much good in the worst of us,
And so much bad in the best of us,
That it ill behoves any of us
To talk about the rest of us.'

The pink in Jo's cheeks deepened to crimson. "It—it's only a story I'm writing," she said guiltily.

"May I see it?" Matron stretched out her hand.

She was not exactly the reader the girl would have chosen but Jo was not yet sufficiently emancipated from school to refuse her. She handed over a bundle, neatly clipped together at one side, and Matron dropped into the nearest chair, and plunged into the story, skimming the sheets rapidly. Jo watched her with misgivings. She knew that, whatever happened, she would get the truth and nothing but the truth—and the truth might not be palatable.

What it was to be, she soon found out. Matron, having glanced through the final sheet, laid the bundle down, a queer smile hovering round the corners of her mouth. "So *this* is why you've been so tiresome these last few days!" she said.

Fully awake now, Joey began to protest. "Oh, Matey! I'm sure I haven't been tiresome! I've kept the thing up here, and I haven't talked about it to a single person— not one! You're the very first to see it."

"I'm glad to hear that," said Matron composedly.

"Why?" demanded Jo defiantly.

"Because in a few weeks' time you would hate to think that anyone else *had* seen it."

"I'm sure I shouldn't! Anyhow, it's only meant for the Robin and Daisy Venables!"

"Then you ought to be ashamed of yourself for giving them such ideas!"

Joey gasped. "*What* ideas?"

"Such ideas about girls. Did you ever, in all your life, meet anyone as bad as that Rosetta Fernandez creature you've written about? Now don't answer me yet. Take a minute or two and think about it."

Accustomed to knuckle down to Matron, Jo did as she was bidden.

"Well?" demanded the School tyrant when she judged that the girl had had sufficient time for reflection.

"Well—er—no; not quite. But that's only to make the story."

"Do you want to write rubbish—or something that a publisher *may*—I only say 'may,' mind you—be induced to accept?"

heroine to be in the habit of smuggling sweets into school and eating them in bed): had sent her flying for the doctor on her bicycle when the Head had a stroke (thus undoubedly saving that lady's life): had caused her to be the means of saving the honour of the form in an interform tennis-match; and was now engaged in causing her to be enmeshed in yet another plot of the wicked Rosetta (which sought to prove her a user of cribs).

This was the point at which Joey began to wonder about her villainess, for even the worst girl she had ever known had been an angel of light compared with this creation of hers.

"I wonder if she's *too* bad?" she thought anxiously as she read over the last chapter she had written.

She was to be left in no doubt. Just as she finished—shortly after fifteen o'clock (three, by English time)—there came a brisk, imperative knock at the door, followed by the person of "Matey."

Matron Lloyd had been at the Chalet School for nearly six years, and during that time she had come to know Jo and all her clan pretty thoroughly. When, therefore, she observed how peaky the girl was looking, how she seemed to be always wool-gathering, and what a poor appetite she had, she determined to act.

Joey heard the knock and absently responded, "Come in!" She had no idea that the dogs of war were about to be let loose on her.

The door opened, and in walked Matron, looking fresh and crisp in her clean uniform. "Now, Jo," she said briskly, "listen to me a moment, if you please. I want to know why you ate nothing at Mittagessen?"

Jo turned dreamy eyes on her. "Mittagessen?" she repeated vaguely. "Oh, am I late? I'm awfully sorry, Matey."

Matron took her by the shoulders and shook her. "For pity's sake, Jo, wake up! It's nearly time for Kaffee und Kuchen. Mittagessen was over more than two hours ago. Give me your wrist."

Jo stretched out a slim hand, the colour flushing her cheeks faintly. Matron took her pulse, then demanded to see the girl's tongue. Thereafter she turned an eagle eye on the closely written sheets of foolscap that littered the table.

"What's all this?" she demanded.

the baby should be baptized Malvina. However, the idea had been laughed to scorn. She had had no chance of choosing for any of her brother's children, since, by the time the news of their arrival came, the baptisms were over. But now she had a free hand, and she made up her mind that her heroine should be Malvina—Malvina Featherstone. Malvina's friend was to be Flavia Meredith —Joey scorned plain names, as most very young writers do—and the villainess was Rosetta Fernandez. Having got so far, Jo took up her new pen, filled it, and wrote "Chapter I" at the head of her paper.

"What on earth can I call my book?" she ruminated when she had done that.

Nibbling the end of her pen, she revolved sundry titles in her mind, finally hitting on "Malvina Wins Through," which would not tie her down too much, and had an attractive sound. She took another sheet, scribbled the title in the middle, and then, casting it aside, set to work to introduce Malvina, Flavia, and Rosetta, and sundry other folk as well, to her public-to-be.

By the time Friday afternoon had ended she had done seven chapters and her story was well on its way. Malvina proved to be a most alluring person, with all the virtues that were ever known. Rosetta was certainly one of the most unpleasant little wretches that ever came to life in the brain of an authoress. Privately, Jo was beginning to feel uneasy about her. Surely no girl ever lived who was capable of such wickedness! And Flavia was a delightful creature—and the only one of the three at all true to life, though Jo had not yet grasped this fact.

In short, Jo was completely wrapped up in her own creation, and, consequently, became trying to live with. She was so abstracted that half the time she never listened to what was said to her. The girls declared that Joey wasn't half as much fun as she had been last term, and if this were the result of her giving up lessons, the sooner she came back to them the better!

The only time when she really did wake up to everyday life was after Frühstück, when she rang up the Sonnalpe each morning, and had a short conversation with her sister. Once her mind was relieved for the day, Joey retired to her room and her work, and became the complete authoress. She had already rescued Malvina from one wicked plot of Rosetta's (which aimed at proving the

"Certainly not!" gasped Jo with horror. "I'll join the others, of course. I'm not so sure," she added laughingly as she held the door open for Mademoiselle, "that I mayn't get bored with things and come back to lessons if the Staff will have me."

"Come by all means," said Mademoiselle, wicked laughter in her eyes. "I believe Six A have algebra this morning with Miss Leslie, and your algebra was never your strongest point, my Jo, so come by all means!"

Jo had no more to say. Mathematics was her weakest subject. She hated it in its every form, and only the term before, Miss Leslie, the mathematics mistress, had vowed that the one thing that worried her was Jo Bettany's ideas on the subject. Whatever classes Jo might attend, she was firmly resolved to keep clear of Miss Leslie and all her works—in school-time, at any rate. Out of school, it was very different.

She went upstairs to begin on her book in good earnest.

"But oh, those twins!" she thought as she opened her door. "They've certainly done it for us this time!"

CHAPTER III

JOEY'S NEW DISCOVERY

JOEY, being Joey, never did anything by halves. Having decided to try her hand at writing a school-story, she settled down to it in earnest. She found it difficult to evolve a plot to suit her. Several ideas she cast aside as having been "done to death." Others were too elaborate, and she had sense enough to know that she was too inexperienced to untangle anything too highly involved.

"Besides, I don't believe people of Robin's and Daisy's ages like things that are all muddled up," she thought. "And I must try to keep the number of characters down, or kids will get mixed trying to sort them out."

Finally, she decided to write down events as they occurred to her, and let the story tell itself. That being settled, came the pleasing task of selecting names for her characters, and she revelled in it. When her small niece Sybil had been born, Jo had been very anxious that

"So are we all. Now I must ring off. I can hear Sybil howling for me. Ring me up at this time to-morrow, Joey, and I'll give you the latest news."

"Right-ho! Give the family my love, and say I hope that Peggy will be all right soon. Good-bye, old thing!" And Joey rang off.

She left the telephone, and went to look out of the window at the flower-garden where asters, late-blooming roses, and dahlias were making all things gay. She dropped down on the broad window-seat, and gave herself up to her thoughts.

"What awful luck this is! Here I thought I'd finished with school, and now the twins have let me down like this! Wait till I get hold of them! One thing," and her face grew very tender, "the Robin is safely out of it. I think I really couldn't have obeyed Madge if *she* had been in any danger."

Her splendid eyes grew misty at the thought.

With the memory of the exquisite little face, framed in its short thick crop of black curls, floating before her mind, Jo felt suddenly sick at the thought of how nearly the Robin had been exposed to infection. It was, perhaps, as well that Mademoiselle came in at that moment, having secured the books she wanted.

"It's no good, Mademoiselle," said the girl, looking up at her with a smile. "They won't have me there at any price. Can you put up with me for a week or two? I shall probably go down to Innsbruck at the week-end, if you don't mind. Frieda asked me, and Madge said I could always go there whenever I liked. So may I write and tell them to expect me?"

"But yes, dear child; certainly," said Mademoiselle. "And have you any news of the little patients now?"

"Rix seems to be more cross than ill," said Rix's aunt. "Peggy is pretty bad, I'm afraid."

"Well, my Jo, it is almost time for Prayers, so I must go. Will you sit here? Or do you prefer your own room? There is a steady table there if you wish to write. Au revoir; I shall see you at Mittagessen."

"Thank you, Mademoiselle," said Joey. "And if it's all right, I think I'll go to my own room."

"Do not forget that you must come down at eleven for cocoa and biscuits in the prefects' room. Or would you prefer that I send it up to you?"

how many unfortunate children they may not have infected! The rash only came out this morning, or we might have guessed sooner. Luckily, they've both been so poorly, that they haven't been so very much with the other children. And Primula Mary is at the Annexe for the week-end, and is well out of it."

"Thank goodness for that!" ejaculated Jo. "How is Mollie taking it?"

"As calmly as Mollie takes most things. She says that all children have to have it, and they might as well get it over before they go to school. Jem tells her that's false logic, and there should be no need for children to get anything if they're properly looked after."

"Is he worried about Peggy?"

"He doesn't like the temp. But the rash is out; and she's got a tough little constitution. Don't worry about her, Joey. Those twins are a sturdy pair, you know. They haven't ailed since teething. The babies are the real worry, since Primula Mary is out of it. Jackie was in contact with the twins throughout the journey, and I don't see how he can possibly escape it. I don't want the worry with Sybil either—especially when she's beginning with her teeth."

"I see. But look here, Madge; I'm sure I'd better come back. I don't see how ever you are going to manage with all the babes and me not there."

"I can manage very well. I *forbid* you to come here, Jo, till I give you leave. Understand that!" Madge's voice had taken a sharp tone, and Jo knew better than to argue the point any further. Besides, she was well aware that her brother-in-law would most certainly back up his wife; and though they were exceedingly fond of each other, there was one side of his character that inspired Jo with wholesome awe.

"All right," she said meekly. "If they can keep me here, I'll stay. If they can't, I'll go to Frieda for a few days. They asked me when I was down on Saturday. Don't worry about me, Madge. I'll be good!" Then her voice changed as she asked anxiously, "What about my Robin?"

"Quite safe, so don't worry. She had gone back to the Annexe before Dick and his family came back. As far as measles infection is concerned there's nothing to worry over. She's never been near it."

"Oh, Madge, I'm so thankful for that!"

and nephews all about my wicked deeds. I'll never count myself as anything but a Chalet School girl."

"Well, shall we say that you are no longer under my jurisdiction? That will meet the case, I think. But you are wondering why I bade you come. The reason is, my Jo, that Peggy and Rix have caught measles, and our dear Madame does not wish you to return to 'Die Rosen' until all fear of infection is over."

"Oh, what nonsense!" cried Jo. "As if I'd leave Madge and Mollie with all those babes and measles! Of course I'm going at once! The sooner the better!"

She jumped up, and was making for the door, when Mademoiselle's voice called her back. "And your sister's message, my dear Jo?"

Jo turned irresolutely. "Madge knows I'll go up at once. In any case, she's got Sybil to think of. She won't be able to do much herself as long as Baby's depending on her."

"Dr Jem has brought in Nurse Martin to see to the children," said Mademoiselle. "And he has forbidden your sister and Mrs Bettany to go near them. But the point is, Jo, that our dear Madame wishes you to ring her up now that she may speak with you herself, and tell you of her wishes. I will return presently, but I must seek some books from the library." She left the room, closing the door, and Jo marched over to the telephone, and got the private line to "Die Rosen."

Her sister's voice answered her. "Is that you, Joey?"

"Yes; it's me. Look here, Madge, what is all this rot about my staying down here? I've *had* measles. You can't get it twice."

"Oh yes, you can, my child. I've had it twice myself. In any case, we don't want any more invalids than we can help. Peggy is pretty bad, poor kiddy; and Rix is the limit! He's fretful and tiresome, and is inclined to lead everyone a dance. Luckily, he's rather scared of Nurse— or so she says—so he's behaved a little better since she arrived. But Peg is running a very high temperature."

"Poor little Peg! What about the other babies, Madge?"

"Quite all right so far. It couldn't show itself so early, anyway."

"When did it begin?"

"Jem says Rix and Peggy must have had it on them when they left Ireland. It's pretty awful! Goodness knows

"Look here! I think you'd better let Jo speak to me herself. Otherwise, she'll be coming off up here as fast as her feet can carry her, and I don't want her. I simply can't do with her!"

"Very well, mignonne. I will say nothing until Frühstück is ended. Then I will bring Jo here and say that you wish her to telephone you, and she will obey you as always."

"That's all very well," sighed Madge Russell. "But Jo is grown up now, ridiculous as it seems, and I'm not her mother—only her sister. But I won't have her here— that's flat! If she does come up, she'll simply have the pleasure of walking straight back again. Mercifully, Jem will back me up, and she *is* afraid of annoying him. He can be nasty with her when he likes, fond as he is of her."

The gong rang just then, and Mademoiselle rang off with an admonition not to worry, and hastened away. She had no time to think things out. She must go to the Speisesaal, where the girls would be awaiting her. During Frühstück she might be able to think of some way in which she could help; but it was going to be difficult.

When the meal ended, and as Jo was about to follow the Seniors from the room, the Head touched her on the arm. "Jo, please go to the study; I wish to speak with you a minute."

Jo was no longer a school-girl, but she was still very near her school-days, and the request made her search her mind uneasily for any misdemeanours as she went along the corridor to the head's room.

"It's perfectly asinine of me!" she thought as she stood by the desk, waiting for Mademoiselle. "I'm not even at school now; and if I was, I never got into trouble quite so early in the term as this—not even in my worst days as a Middle."

At this point in her reflections Mademoiselle came in quietly. Jo heard her, and started guiltily, the warm colour flooding her clear skin. The Head realised her frame of mind, and laughed softly. "Ah, no, my dear, Jo," she said as she motioned the girl to a seat. "I have not bid you come here for a scolding. You are no longer a Chalet girl."

"Oh yes, I am!" said Jo quickly, as she sat down. "I'll never be anything else, Mademoiselle. Even when I'm an old lady with white hair, telling all my great-great-nieces but she got up, and went along to the night-nursery. Peggy was very poorly, and her temp. was soaring. Mollie got frightened, and came for me. Luckily, Sybil has never been near the twins, for I was afraid of Rix's cold. Jackie has been kept from them, too, since they arrived. But David and Bride have been with them all right."

"Oh, ma petite! I am grieved to hear that! And the little Primula Mary?"

"Mercifully, she'd gone to bed before they came on Thursday, and when we saw Rix's cold, we kept her right away from the nursery."

"Good," said Mademoiselle, with a thought for the new matron's fragile younger child. "But why not isolate David and Bride, too?"

"Well, Primula was sleeping in her mother's room, and we hadn't moved her to the night-nursery. But the other two were there to start with, and we honestly didn't think anything of it till next day, when they'd all slept in the same room."

"And when did you discover what the sickness actually is?"

"Just about an hour ago."

"Oh, Marguérite chérie!" Mademoiselle's horror sounded in her tragic tones. "What an affair!"

"Yes—isn't it? Jem has sent for Nurse—*our* dear woman, you know—and he says Jo must not come back. Grown-ups always take measles badly, it seems. So that's the position. The thing is, can you keep her? If not, she can go to Gisela."

"We shall be delighted to have her," said Mademoiselle. "But tell me, Marguérite, are the twins seriously ill?"

"Peggy has a high temp. which is alarming. Rix is mainly crochety and whiney. But isn't it appalling? David and Bride are certain to get it; and we can't be *sure* about Jackie."

"I am so sorry," said Mademoiselle. "Still, how thankful you must be that the little Primula is likely to escape."

"More than thankful," Madge Russell's voice assured her.

Mademoiselle nodded. She knew, only too well, that Primula Venables was exceedingly delicate, with very little strength to fight any illness.

"Thérèse, are you still there?"

"But yes, chérie. What is it?"

be wrong, for the people at "Die Rosen" were usually too busy in the early morning to trouble with telephone calls.

"'Ello!" she called. "Qui va là?"

Back came an agitated voice. "Oh, Thérèse! Is that you? This is Madge Russell!"

"Marguérite chérie! But what, then, is wrong?" asked Mademoiselle anxiously.

"What *isn't* wrong, you mean! Can you possibly keep Joey for the next few weeks?"

Mademoiselle raised her eyebrows. "But certainly, ma chère. But what, then, has chanced?"

"It's measles!" said the agitated voice. "Jo's had it, of course; but there's no point in risking her getting it again."

"No," agreed Mademoiselle, though inwardly she was wildly deciding to quarantine Jo the first moment she could. "But how has this come? Jo has said nothing to me; and, indeed, I thought all the children were well."

"So they were. But Dick and Mollie and the babes came back from Ireland on Thursday—luckily *after* Jo, Daisy, Stacie, and the Robin had gone off to school! Rix had taken cold on the journey, they thought, and he was very tiresome and fretful. I just thought it was natural tiredness, especially when Dick calmly informed me that they'd come straight through from Paris—and with all those youngsters, if you please!"

"Yes—yes!" said Mademoiselle impatiently. "But I am desirous to know all about this illness."

"Oh, you needn't worry about infection," returned Madge Russell with a rueful laugh. "Dick and his family have been away nearly five weeks, and those children must have got it in Ireland—probably from their young cousins there. We haven't heard yet."

Mademoiselle heaved a heartfelt sigh of relief. "I am thankful to hear that, ma petite. I do not wish to start the term with measles in the School."

"No need to fear it—from here, anyhow."

"No. Then tell me the rest of cette petite histoire."

"Well, no one bothered very much about Rix's cold. Even when Peggy seemed weepy, we didn't trouble. But early this morning, Rosa came to summon Mollie to Peggy, who had been very sick and seemed feverish. Poor Mollie had been up half the night with Jackie, who is teething, and takes care everyone shall know it. Jem wasn't in, of course—he never *is* when he's specially wanted!—

"An excellent idea, Joey," said Miss Annersley, who was pouring out coffee for the rest of them. "All the babies have always loved your stories, and it will be good practice for you before you start on that historical novel you intend to do some time."

Jo reddened. "That may never happen. However, I'm going to have a go at this. And I might as well be *in* the atmosphere when I begin.—Thanks, Mademoiselle. I'll love to stay."

"Then that is settled," said Mademoiselle. "But if you go into Innsbruck to-morrow morning, my Jo, I will give you a list of various goods I wish sent up as soon as possible."

"Oh, rather! I'll run round to the Mariahilfe and dig Frieda out, and we can shop together. They'll give me Mittagessen, and then I can get the afternoon train back. I'll be careful not to miss it, so you may expect to see me some time about sixteen or so."

Miss Wilson, the science and geography mistress, got to her feet. "You might do some shopping for me as well, Jo. It's only a list to leave at the bookshop. But ask them to get them through as soon as possible, will you?"

Jo nodded, and then she looked round the rest of the Staff. "Anything I can do for anyone else?"

Nobody seemed to want anything, so, as it was getting late, the meeting broke up, and Jo returned to the pretty guest-room next door to Mademoiselle's.

On the morrow, she set off by the early train to Innsbruck, the nearest big town, where she fulfilled her programme to the letter. In due course she arrived back at the Tiernsee, with a new fountain-pen, a bottle of ink, a ream of foolscap, and three of Miss Wilson's books which happened to be in stock.

It was not a pleasant day, being foggy and cold. Jo reported on her errands, and then departed to her own room, where the stove had been lighted. There she settled down to make a start on her book by scribbling down a list of all the monkey-tricks she and her set had played in the joyous days when they were Middles.

Early on the Monday morning, Mademoiselle was sitting in her study, glancing over the work for the day, when the telephone-bell rang. The switch-board indicated that it was the private wire from "Die Rosen," and she hastened to plug in, wondering, as she did so, what could

the room rang with a mixture of tongues. Jo, equally at home in English, French, or German, and with a working knowledge of Italian (not to mention snippets of other tongues), was kept busy telling the girls about their beloved ex-Head, and the small nephews and nieces who lived in "Die Rosen," the big chalet on the Sonnalpe, where the Russells had their home. At other tables, various people attended to the wants of the new girls, and exchanged notes on how the holidays had been spent. The Juniors would be marched over to their own house once the meal was ended; but the Middles and Seniors would all dance in the big common-room of Ste Thérèse's, and on the morrow, the three divisions of the School would take their meal in their own Speisesaal. Just for to-night, however, they were all squeezed together.

Abendessen over, the girls, along with such of the Staff as were not otherwise employed, enjoyed themselves thoroughly for an hour or so. Then came Prayers, and the girls departed bedwards, convinced that, despite the fact that the Chalet School had lost some of its best and most popular members at the end of the previous term, this one was going to be very jolly after all.

CHAPTER II

THE TWINS DO IT

JO's original idea had been to stay for one night at the School, and return to the Sonnalpe next day. Her brother, Dick Bettany (who was in the Woods and Forests department of the Indian Civil Service), with his wife and children, would then have returned from Ireland, where they had been spending a month of his furlough with some of his wife's people. However, Jo was easily persuaded to extend her visit to the Monday.

"It might be as well," she said when the question was discussed in the staff-room. "I'm going to have a shot at a school-story for the babes, you know. Margot"—she smiled at little Mrs Venables who was with them—"thinks it would be a good idea, since I *ought* to know something about school. Daisy would love it; and so would my Robin."

not yet capable of the more highly specialised work required from the top form of the School, and had been wondering if it would mean a very big Fifth Form this year. Now, here they were, Sixth Form—B, it is true; but it meant different work, and a slightly different status in the School.

Evadne Lannis and her chum, Ilonka Barkocz, hugged themselves with glee at the thought. Only Cornelia Flower looked slightly dismayed. She with Evadne, Ilonka, Elsie Carr, and Margia Stevens, had formed what was known throughout the School as "the Quintette." They had all known that Elsie and Margia would be prefects, and therefore Sixth Form. But Evadne and Ilonka were a shock.

"Guess I wish I'd dug in a bit harder sooner!" she thought gloomily.

Evadne, guessing her thoughts, kicked her gently. It was true that they would be separated during school-hours, but Corney must not forget that out of them they would be together. Mademoiselle might have left Cornelia over at St Clare's; but she had relented, and Cornelia would share the Yellow Dormitory with their own set, as well as two or three others who were very friendly with them. Cornelia guessed what she meant, and being a cheerful young person as a general rule, brightened up a little.

Then Miss Annersley read the names of the four who would act as Senior Middles over at St Clare's, but there was no surprise here. Eustacia Benson, Yvette Mercier, Irma Ancokzky, and Jeanne le Cadoulec were all known to be steady people, quite capable of the work.

This final ceremony over, the Staff departed, leaving Jo behind, and at once the gong sounded for Abendessen, as the last meal of the day was called.

"Come and sit with us, Jo!" cried Louise eagerly.

"No; come to us!" implored half-a-dozen voices.

Jo grinned amiably. "How do you know I'm not going to sit at the Staff table?" she inquired.

"You aren't, are you?" asked Anne doubtfully. "You'll find it rather dull if you do that, Joey."

"Keep calm, my child! I'm sitting at my own old table, of course—there goes the second gong! Come along, everyone, or we shall hear sweet nothings about punctuality being the politeness of princes."

In more or less good order, they marched to the Speisesaal where Abendessen awaited them, and presently

her to follow worthily in the steps of those who have preceded her—Gisela Marani, Juliet Carrick, Grizel Cochrane, Gertrud Steinbrücke, Mary Burnett, and Jo Bettany. These girls have left us a tradition that I am sure Louise will do her best to continue. The other prefects are Anne Seymour, Elsie Carr, Margia Stevens, Arda van der Windt, Luigia Meracini, Thora Helgersen (who leaves us after this term, to go home and keep house for her father), Gillian Linton, Paula von Rothenfels, and Cyrilla Maurús.

"And remember, my children, that the time is coming when some of you will hear your own names read out in such a list. If you do not now learn to co-operate with the prefects, you cannot expect that those who will then be in your present places will help you. Some girls forget this when they try to rebel against prefectorial authority. It is, as the old proverb says, 'to make a rod to beat their own backs.' As you are now, so will those be that follow you.

"Now, that is all, I think. We all wish you a very happy term, full of good work and good play. But before we part, I wll ask Miss Annersley to read out your names and forms. To-day, you may speak your own languages, but to-morrow we have our English day; Friday is French day; and on Monday we speak German. New girls are permitted licence for the next fortnight. After that, they must do their best to keep the rule."

She sat down then, turning with a smile to the senior mistress, who rose amidst the clapping of the girls, and stood smiling down at them. She was a slender, graceful woman, with glossy brown hair, a pleasant face, and keen blue eyes. She was famed for her gentleness; but report said that when she was really roused, she had the most stinging tongue on the Staff. Presently she indicated that, in her opinion, the applause might cease, and the girls were quiet at once; for, with the exception of the prefects no one had any idea what her place would be for this year.

From the seven-year-olds in the Kindergarten, right up through the Second Form to Middle School, and so, from Five B to Six A she went; and as she read out, "Form Six B," and gave the names of the twelve damsels who made up that form, there were audible gasps of delight, for no one had expected this. Many of the girls knew they were

"I welcome all who have come new to the School, and wish them the happiness that most of our girls find here. I feel sure that they will soon have friends and enjoy our life. And now, I must speak of other matters." She paused, and the girls sat wondering what was to come.

After a moment, she went on: "As this is the term when we spend so much time over our Hobbies Club, I have wondered if, perhaps, some of you would wish to extend your usual Christmas gifts to the children of our own Tiernthal, and send some boxes to Innsbruck? I have heard of a poor parish there, where many of the children scarcely know that Christmas comes at all. Not for them the sweet gifts and happiness you girls know! Not for them the merriment and rejoicings that form so large a part of our Christmas festival!

"The parish priest, Vater Stefan, tells me that he tries to arrange for Christmas Mittagessen for the most destitute, but cannot hope to feed all. As for gifts, he finds that out of the question. How would you so-happy girls, who all have your shoes or tables filled on Christmas Day, like to help him, and make gifts for these little children who lack even the necessities of life? I have said nothing of this to Vater Stefan, for it seemed to me that if you did it, you would wish to give him a happy surprise. But could you not makes toys for the little ones at your meetings? Frau Mieders tells me that if any wish to make garments to send, or knit stockings, or hoods, she would teach you how to do it in your needlework classes. Would you not like to think that perhaps *one* child is warmer and happier at Christmas time for *your* efforts?

"For remember; if you do it, it must be of your own free will, and in your own free time. Nor must our children up here suffer. We shall have our usual play at the end of term to provide funds for their festival, however. So, if you desire to help these other poor little ones, you may go to Frau Mieders, who has undertaken to be responsible for all, and give her your name, and she will help you to choose what you shall do.

"Now we must turn to other things. We have to welcome our new matron of St Clare's, Mrs Venables, whom some of you already know. Also, Miss Carey has come to St Agnes' to help with the little ones.

"Finally, there are our new prefects to name. Our head-girl is Louise Redfield, and I know we can all trust

(known to the entire School as "Matey," and feared wholesomely, and beloved by all) and her tall young colleague Matron Gould from St Agnes'.

They knew something of the new matron's story. She was the sister of Dr Russell, and had been left a widow. Her elder girl, Daisy, was new at St Agnes' this term, and she had another little girl, Primula Mary, who (as she was still a mere baby) was up at "Die Rosen" with her Uncle Jem and Aunt Madge.

But interest in Matron Venables lasted a bare moment. For, last of the procession, came a tall slim girl, with thick black hair pinned up over her ears, soft black eyes just now dancing with a wicked light, and a clever sensitive face. As the girls recognised their late head-girl, a perfect yell of delight arose.

"Joey Bettany—Joey come back to teach!"

Above the cheers, Joyce's clear voice was to be heard: "Told you so, Corney Flower! I just wish I'd made you bet on it!"

Jo went darkly red with embarrassment, and several members of the Staff choked audibly, adding to her discomfort. She had persuaded them to let her enter in this dramatic manner, though they had warned her what she might expect. But she had insisted that the girls would never be so silly, and rushed on her doom with fatal readiness. Now, even as she made haste to drop into a chair behind the mistresses and hide herself, she was wishing that she had not made *quite* so spectacular an entrance.

Mademoiselle stood on the dais, her plain, kind face beaming at the excitement of the girls, who suddenly realised where they were and what they were doing, and sat down in a hurry with mingled feelings. Then, as the noise died away, she took a step forward, and began to speak. "Welcome back to School, everyone," she said in the French that was one of the three staple languages of the School. "I am glad indeed to see you all so well and happy after your holidays. But I am sorry to have to tell you that Joey has *not* come back to teach, but only to greet you all, and wish you a happy term."

A groan sounded here and there, but for the most part the girls only showed their disappointment by their faces. Mademoiselle smiled at them again, and went on with her speech.

the Head, Mademoiselle Lepâttre, and the Staff, and even the new girls were drawn in as much as possible.

"Do you know," said Joyce Linton, Gillian's younger sister, turning to her own friend, Cornelia Flower, "I could have sworn I saw Jo Bettany in the distance this afternoon."

"Guess you were dreaming with your eyes shut, then," said Cornelia with great decision. "Jo's not here—more's the pity! She's up at the Sonnalpe—helping to put the babies to bed, I shouldn't wonder. You'll be saying next you've seen Simone, or Marie, or Frieda!"

"Talk sense! Simone's in Paris, and Marie in Vienna, and Frieda—well, I'm not sure where Frieda is, but she isn't here! But Jo—I'm not so sure. It was just her height, and the way she moves."

"If Jo were down here, we'd have seen her before this," said Cornelia positively. "You don't think Dr Jem would let her come down *after* Kaffee und Kuchen, do you? And she certainly hasn't been here this afternoon, because we've been about the place almost all the time, and someone would have been sure to see her and shriek."

"What is that, Corney?" asked Ilonka Barkocz, one of their circle, leaning across Joyce to speak to Cornelia.

"Joyce is going batty, I guess," returned Cornelia with a snort of contempt. "Says she saw Jo round here this afternoon."

"I only wish it might be true!" sighed Ilonka. "The School will be so different with all those older girls gone. Oh, I know that Louise and the others will do their best; but they seem so *young* after Jo, and Marie, and Frieda, and the rest."

Just then were heard the sound of footsteps coming along the corridor, and the merry chatter all over Hall ceased as the girls rose to their feet to greet the mistresses.

They came by the door near the dais, Mademoiselle Lepâttre leading, and the rest following. They were a bright, happy-looking set in their dainty evening frocks, and one or two of them were exceedingly pretty—notably, Miss Stewart, the history mistress, and little Miss Nalder who was responsible for the gymnastics and games.

Behind them came the matrons of the three houses, walking abreast, clad in trim nurse's uniform. The girls looked with interest at the new matron of St Clare's—a tiny woman in lilac, walking between Matron Lloyd

CHAPTER I

A SURPRISE FOR THE CHALET SCHOOL

THE girls of the Chalet School were all in their places for the assembly with which School always began on the first night of the term. There were now more than a hundred and fifty girls, thirty-five of whom belonged to St Agnes', the Junior house; while the rest were distributed between St Clare's, as the Middle house was called, and Ste Thérèse's, the original school, where the Seniors lived, and all form-rooms were.

The Chalet School had been started by Madge Bettany, now Mrs. Russell, wife of the doctor who was head of the sanatorium at the Sonnalpe, a broad shelf up in the mountains on the opposite side of the Tiernsee, near which lake the School was situated. For the four terms before this Jo Bettany had been head-girl. But Jo's schooldays had ended with the end of the summer term, and she was to be followed by Louise Redfield, a charming girl from one of the southern states of America. Louise felt rather diffident as to her ability to take Jo's place; but those who had appointed her felt no doubt. She was seated in the head-girl's chair, next to her own chum, Anne Seymour. On her other side was Paula von Rothenfels from Hungary, another of the prefects. The remainder of the prefects were Thora Helgersen, a big Norwegian, who would leave at Christmas; Luigia Meracini, a dreamy Italian; Margia Stevens, the School musical genius; Elsie Carr, a pretty English girl; Arda van der Windt, from Holland; Cyrilla Maurús, a compatriot of Paula's; and Gillian Linton, another English girl. Gillian had only come at the beginning of the year, but had shown herself so reliable and steady that she was gladly included by those who had the appointment of the prefects.

These ten people sat on one side of the dais which filled the top of the room, the Staff seats facing theirs. The rest of the School was packed into the long forms before the dais, only the Juniors being accommodated with cushions on the floor directly in front of the girls of Five A. The room rang with the sound of gay chatter and soft laughter as the girls waited for the arrival of

Jo Returns to the Chalet School was
first published in the U.K. in a single volume
in hardback in 1936 by W. & R. Chambers
Ltd., London and Edinburgh. This revised
edition was first published in Armada in 1970
by Fontana Paperbacks.

© W. & R. Chambers 1936.

2
Jo Returns to the Chalet School

The first guests began to arrive shortly after this, and the afternoon was full and very busy.

Dick and his wife and babies were there, of course, and so were Gisela and her husband. Wanda and Friedel had come from Partenkirchen for two days, so as not to miss this event; and all the old friends were there, as well as some new ones, among whom was Herr von der Witt, highly delighted with everything and everybody.

The girls gave a concert in the garden, and sang some of the lovely old madrigals that Mr Denny revelled in. Margia and Grizel both played, and Frieda enchanted everyone by her lovely harp solo. Joey sang two folk-songs, and, of course, they showed some of the folk-dances, and Herr von der Witt was actually heard to say that it was a very pretty sight. As his two ideas in life were fresh air and geology, they all felt that this was a great compliment.

Then *Kaffee* was served, the girls acting as waitresses, and after that people began to make a move homewards. In the playing-fields, the girls clustered together for a last speech from their head girl.

Grizel looked round them all. "You are dears," she began uncertainly. Then she stopped. She felt that if she went on she would break down.

Joey guessed what she was feeling, and sprang into the breech. "Three cheers for Grizel, one of the best head girls the school has ever had!" she yelled at the top of her voice. They were given with a vim that made those of the guests who still remained literally jump, and sent Grizel flying to a place of refuge before she should disgrace herself in front of them all by crying.

Jo found her later, looking rather red about the eyes, but very happy. "Good for you, old thing!" she said.

Grizel looked round at the lovely lake with the huge mountains towering all round it; the flower-garden, quiet now that all the guests were gone; the chalet, where she had spent four happy years; finally at the girl who had stood by her through so much. "It's been a good time, Joey," she said. "All my life I shall remember how much I owe you, and Madame, and the Chalet School."

them would be going home with parents at the end of the afternoon, and all had much to say about holidays.

"Be sure you let us have your Florence address, Grizel," said Gertrud in the prefects' dormitory. "You must write to us every week, and let us know what you are doing."

"And you must all write to *me*," said the head girl as she rapidly put a gloss on her short curls. "I shall be coming to Innsbruck for Bernhilda's wedding in December, you know, so I shall hope to see most of you then."

"And we will all come here for Madame's birthday next year," added Rosalie, who was going home to England, where her father had obtained a living in Kent. "We couldn't miss *that*!"

"Rather not!"

"Even Miss Carthew is coming for that, if she possibly can," put in Mary, who was looking forward to being head girl next term, and was wondering if she would ever be so good as any one of the four who had preceded her.

Grizel threw down her brushes and proceeded to wriggle into her frock. "Hurry up, you people," she said, as she emerged and began shaking its folds into place. "We mustn't be late."

They made haste, and presently they were all out in the flower-garden, where most of the middles were already. Madge Russell, looking at them as they wandered about, sighed to herself. This term's outgoings would be large, and many of her own girls would have left them. The school would go on flourishing, she felt sure. They were firmly established, and she knew that the vacant places were already more than filled, for the fame of the school was spreading. But after this it would not be *her* school, as it had been. Perhaps it was as well, for her hands were full as it was, and would probably grow fuller as the years went on. Joey would have only another year at the school, for she was to go to Belsornia when she was seventeen, as lady-in-waiting to the princess. Her education would be continued there by masters and governesses with Elisaveta, but she would cease to be a schoolgirl. After that, no one knew what the future held for her. Madge hoped that her writing gifts would bring her something. That was all she would think of at present. She finished her dressing, and went down to join her girls, looking scarcely older than they did, in her dainty white frock and big shady hat.

much time to spare. Grizel took her place as head of the junior table for the last time, and Jo went off to her own seat, where her beloved friend the little Crown Princess of Belsornia was waiting for her. Princess Elisaveta had gone to Vienna for Wanda's wedding, and then had come back to the school for the last week of the term, to wait for her dear Jo, who was to spend the summer holidays with her. She had come in to lessons, and had lived with the girls, just as she had done two terms ago when she had been one of themselves, and had delighted them all by vowing that it was a relief to be at school again. "Hurry up, Joey!" she said now. "We've got to dress yet, you know."

"I should think so," retorted Jo, with a glance at the crumpled frock the princess was wearing. "You look as if you had been to bed in that cotton thing you've got on!"

"Well, you look as if you'd been washing the floors in yours!" returned the princess.

"More potatoes, please, Simone."

Mrs Russell, in her old place at the head of the staff table, glanced down the room with a smile. "How excited they all are! Just listen to Evadne screeching!"

"A good many of the others are doing their best to rival her," laughed Miss Maynard. "It must sound like a parrot-house to anyone passing!"

"Oh well, it's the end of term," said Miss Carthew tolerantly. "You've got to allow for that."

"Oh, *I* don't mind," Miss Maynard assured her. "I'm so thrilled about going home that I don't really mind what they do to-day."

"I also," put in Mademoiselle. "I know that our girls will never forget that they are of the Chalet School, and must not disgrace it, so I do not trouble if they are excited."

'Yes; even Cornelia seems to have learned that lesson," agreed Miss Maynard, with a glance to where that young person was sitting, much thinner than she had been, and still rather pale, but evidently very happy, and thoroughly one of them.

"I think we've all finished," said Miss Wilson at that moment.

Madge Russell nodded, and said grace. Then the girls were dismissed to their rooms to change into their prettiest frocks and make themselves as dainty as possible. There was a great deal of chatter as they changed, for many of

down with her small son to join them in the chalet Dick had taken for three months, and the girls had revelled in having their beloved Madame so near. Peggy and Rix were delightful small people, full of original sin; Baby Bridget proved to be "the *image* of Dick!" to quote Joey; and little David was declared to beat them all by every girl in the school.

After that eventful night when they had rescued Cornelia the term had gone on fairly evenly. Cornelia had had a sharp attack of rheumatic fever as the result of lying in a damp place for many hours, but she was a tough little mortal, and had come through all right. The next event of importance had been Gisela's wedding, which had taken place in Innsbruck. The entire school had gone down for it, and had had a remarkably good time. Then, on his mother's birthday David's christening feast had been the treat for this holiday. Finally, Wanda and Herr Hauptmann Friedel von Glück had been wedded a week ago, and were now enjoying their honeymoon at Partenkirchen in the Mittelwald.

The big event of the term, however, was the opening up of the caves, which proved to be wonderful beyond expectation. Herr von der Witt had found that the passage led right down to the first, which had the most marvellous stalactite formations, and thence to three others. In the last one were discovered relics of what must have formerly been a great city. Pavements and fragments of walls, all encrusted with lime, were there; excavations were going on, and more was being found every day. Jo was wildly excited about it all, for it proved that the legend of the lake's origin was no legend, but a statement of fact. Experts who had come to see the place agreed that the lake must have risen quite suddenly and overwhelmed the city, though not, perhaps, quite as awfully as the old story said.

"It's been a full term," said Jo, when they at last turned away from the pram and strolled on to the chalet. "What with one thing and another, I think it's been the fullest we've ever had."

"We've managed to crowd a good deal in," agreed Grizel. "I say! There's the bell for *Mittagessen*! Come on!"

They hurried in to take their places at table, for there was to be a garden-party that afternoon, and no one had

Then Herr Braun approached them, and with a "Pardon, *gnädiges Fräulein*!" picked up Joey in his arms, and strode off in the wake of the doctor, leaving Herr August to treat Grizel in precisely similar manner. The rest trooped after them, and they were carried in safety up the passage, and across the bush-grown turf till they came to the road where the path leads to the Tiern Pass, where they found three motors awaiting them. They were all bundled in, and then they set off. It was daylight by this time, and the sun was shining when Joey and Grizel, after a good meal, were finally tucked up in bed in their cubicles, and left to sleep off the effects of their latest escapade.

CHAPTER XXIII

"THREE CHEERS FOR GRIZEL!"

"I HATE end of term when it's the summer term!" Thus Joey, viciously.

Grizel Cochrane, to whom she was speaking, looked at her seriously. "It's worse when it's your last term, Jo! And don't say anything to make it worse, my lamb! I will *not* make a sentimental ass of myself, but I can't answer for the consequences if you rub things in."

Jo cleared her throat. "Righto!—Oh, there's Rosa with David! Come on and see him!"

She turned and raced across the grass to where Rosa Pfeiffen was wheeling Master David Russell along in his white pram. Joey came up panting, for the day was hot, and hung over the pram, and made cooing noises to her small nephew, who lay looking at her with bland indifference, though when she slipped a finger into his dimpled paw he gripped tightly. "Isn't he a darling?" said his adoring aunt.

"Jolly little chap," replied Grizel, peeping at him over her shoulder. "He's going to be awfully like Madame, Joey."

"Yes; isn't he? I think he's very like young Rix, too," replied Jo. Her brother had brought his family to the Tiern See three weeks ago, and the entire school had gone in for a course of baby-worship. Mrs Russell had come

He caught her to him. "Jo! Thank God—thank God! No; she doesn't know!"

"We're all here," went on Joey, "only Cornelia has hurt her head. Herr Friedel has tied it up."

Jem set her down and hurried across to the little group. Then Joey found herself seized by a weeping Mademoiselle, who kissed her over and over again—rather to the young lady's disgust—and called her *"Chéri—ma mie —ma bien-aimeé!"* till unsentimental Jo simply didn't know where to look. It was Grizel's turn after that, and while Miss Maynard helped the doctor to bandage Cornelia rather more scientifically than Herr von Glück had done it, the two girls were passed round among the company, and made to tell their story. Then the big man grabbed Joey—"Just as if I was a pick-pocket!" grumbled Miss Jo later on—and demanded whether they knew where was the road to the other caves.

"Friedel knows," returned the young lady, dropping all formalities. "You'd better ask *him!*"

"What! Young Friedel *here?*" roared the big man. He let Jo go, and the next minute she saw him pouncing on Wanda's betrothed, and pouring out a perfect flood of questions. By this time Dr Jem had finished his work, and Miss Maynard was rolling Cornelia in a big shawl she had brought with her.

"Come," said the doctor, lifting up the bundle. "We must get back now."

"But I will stay!" roared the big man. "I am assured that we have the way, and I doubt not but that we shall make some marvellous discoveries! Here!" he turned to the men with the ropes and pickaxes, who had been standing to one side looking on. "Come, you! We go forward now! Do not wait for me, Herr Doktor! Take that imp of a child home, and those others, too. You may look for me some time on the morrow!"

With that he plunged down the path where Friedel had found Cornelia, the men following him, and was soon lost to sight. Jem laughed as he turned to the other entrance. "I suppose we must leave him to his discoveries. These children should be got to bed as soon as possible, and if I know Herr Professor von der Witt, no power on earth would turn him back now when he knows that the caves *must* be near!"

So *that* was who it was!

"So am I," said Grizel. Then she added softly, "He has fallen asleep to wake with God."

They lay there quietly, and presently both fell asleep. Friedel found them like that when he came back to the salt cave, carrying Cornelia, who was now in a heavy stupor. He did not wake them, but he laid the other girl down beside them, and proceeded to bind up the nasty cut on her forehead, after scraping some salt from one of the pillars and rubbing it in. It was spartan treatment, but the best antiseptic he had at hand. The smarting of the salt on the open wound brought Cornelia to her senses, and she sat up with a low cry which awakened the other two. "Oh, where are we?" she wailed. "What has happened? And oh, my head does hurt so!"

"It's all right, old thing," said Jo soothingly. "You're quite safe, and we're here with you. You must have banged your head a bit."

"But the madman!" cried Cornelia. "Oh, he'll come and kill us all!"

Friedel pointed to the still figure with his handkerchief over its face. "He will never hurt anyone again," he said gently. "He is dead." Then he stripped off his coat and gave it to Grizel. "Her clothes are damp—that is a wet place. Undress her, and put that on her. Then I will wrap her up in one of the skins, and we must get her home as quickly as possible."

He moved over to the other side of the cave, out of sight, and they undressed her, and wrapped her in the coat. Grizel took off her own frock, and put that on her, too. Then they called to him, and he came and rolled her in one of the deer-skins. Just as he was about to lift her, they heard the tread of many feet and the sound of voices. Lights showed at the entrance from the passage, and a throng of people poured into the cave. Mademoiselle was there, and Miss Maynard and Miss Durrant. Good Herr Braun from the Kron Prinz Karl, Dr Jem, Herr August, and—Joey rubbed her eyes in amazement, but it really was—Herr Anserl, looking more like a shaggy bear than ever, with his long hair all tangled and untidy. There was also a big man who seemed to be vaguely familiar, and two or three others, who were armed with ropes and pickaxes. But she heeded none of them. Like a flash she had run across the floor, and was in her brother-in-law's arms. "Jem! Is Madge all right? She doesn't know?"

A long silence followed. Then Jo suddenly turned towards the elder girl. "Death—is just falling asleep to wake with God;" she said softly.

"I know, Joey. It's just the memory of Madame's words that is helping me now."

Then they turned and faced what might be coming, calm with that thought.

Suddenly a call of "Come!" sounded through the passage. They started to their feet and bolted along to the glow. Suddenly they came on the great salt cave which had so filled Cornelia with wonder some hours since. The torches "Herr Arnolfi" had lit were beginning to die, but there was still enough light for them to see the glistening crystals, and Jo uttered an exclamation of admiration. In the centre of the cave, before a huge pillar, Herr von Glück was kneeling beside a dark heap. He seemed to be laying something white over part of it. Even as they looked he crossed himself and bent his head. A horrible fear that it was Cornelia, and that she was dead, came to Jo, and she swayed against Grizel, who caught her. "No, Joey! It's too big!" cried the elder girl. "It must be the lunatic."

Friedel von Glück, his brief prayer for the repose of the poor lost soul ended, rose to his feet. "It is safe now," he said gravely. "He died in my arms just before I called you. He says that the girl ran down the path that leads to the other caves—she is somewhere down there, and I am going to find her. Will you be afraid to stay here while I seek for her? I will not be long. He said he thought he heard her stumble, but he fell himself, and broke his leg in falling, or he would have gone to her. He struck his own head, and the double shock is what has killed him. He was very old, and I gather that his heart was not right. His senses had come back at the last, and he was able to tell me so much. Will you stay here, dear children, while I bring the other little one? You might say a prayer for the repose of his soul."

Grizel nodded. "Yes; we will stay. Go quickly and get Cornelia, please. Come, Joey; we will go over there to those skins, and wait." She led Joey to the heap of deerskins on which Cornelia had lain, and made her lie down. Herr von Glück saw that they were all right, and went off on his final quest. Grizel held Joey close.

"Poor old thing!" said the younger girl. "I am glad he is dead, Grizel!"

"Thank goodness!" thought Grizel. "But what a little ass!"

The path had been going downhill for some time, but now they found that it took a sharp turn upwards, and went on at a fairly steep gradient. Both girls were tired and the young captain was weary, too, for he had been out nearly all day hunting for the missing child. Their progress was slow, and Grizel, glancing round, was horrified at Jo's white face. They did not dare to pause, however. None of them could help thinking of the maniac who had tried to kidnap the Robin those few short months ago.

Suddenly Herr von Glück gave vent to a low exclamation and stopped. The girls stopped too, and crowded up to him. "There is a light ahead," he said, pointing.

They looked. Yes; it was true. A faint glow straight ahead of them told them that the first part of their journey was at an end. Rapidly the captain gave them their orders. They were to follow him till he said "Stop!" Then they were to stay where they were till they heard him call "Come!" If he called "Run!" they were to turn and run as quickly as they could till they came to the crossroads. There they were to turn to the right, extinguishing their torches, and go a little way down. If he did not come soon after that, they were to listen for sounds, and, if all was quiet, to go back and follow the string till they got outside, where they were to go straight back to meet the search-party he felt sure would be hastening after them even now, and warn them that there was danger from the madman. He made them repeat his orders, and then led them on for another ten minutes. Then, short and sharp, came the order to stop. They stopped instantly, and he went on, while they crouched down by the wall, fearful of some unseen danger.

Jo was praying to herself very softly, but Grizel heard her. "Our Father Who art in Heaven, oh save us all from danger, and bring us safe back to the chalet!"

The elder girl bent her head. "Joey, let's say the 'Lighten our darkness,'" she whispered.

Jo began at once, and the murmured sound of the words strengthened them. When they had finished Grizel put her arm round Jo, and held her close. "I've *tried*!" she said. "You'll tell Madame, Joey."

"Yes," said Jo, "but I don't think there'll be any need, Grizel."

saal, and Grizel had grabbed up some of the *Butterbrod* which Friedel had left from his hasty meal.

It was an easy journey till they came to the cross-roads, but there they paused. Which way would the girl have taken? The two Guides hunted round for some sign, and Grizel uttered a sigh of relief when she found a small piece of apple-peeling, which Cornelia had dropped as she walked. "Here it is! This is the way she has gone!" she cried.

Friedel von Glück was at her side at once. "You will pardon that I lead the way, *mein Fräulein*? It is *necessary*!"

Grizel stared at him, but she squeezed herself against the wall and let him pass her. Then it suddenly struck her that he feared lest the lunatic might be there with Cornelia, and, recognising her as the saviour of the Robin, harm her. Meekly she followed him, insisting on Jo keeping behind her.

"It's—horribly dark!" said the latter impressionable young lady, with a shudder. "Don't get too far ahead, Grizel."

"All right, old thing," replied Grizel gently. "Grab my coat, and we'll keep together."

At this point the young captain stopped and demanded another ball of string. Grizel produced it, and rapidly knotted the two ends together with a reef-knot. Then they went on.

"We're going downhill," said Joey in low tones presently.

"I know," murmured the head girl in reply. "I'm certain now that Margia was right, and this *is* the way to the caves. I only hope we've enough string to last us!"

"Pardon that I ask that you do not talk," said their leader, stopping and turning round. "We cannot know how sound will carry in this place."

There was common sense in what he said, and they were silent as they went on. Presently they came to the place where Cornelia had lain down to rest, and here they had proof of the fact that she was here, for on the ground was her torch, just as it had fallen from her relaxed grip when she had gone to sleep. Friedel von Glück picked it up and examined it. Her name was on a narrow band of silver round it, so there was no more doubt.

CHAPTER XXI

RESCUE

HOW long she lay there unconscious, Cornelia never knew. She came to herself with a splitting headache, to find that she was very damp, and in a thick darkness that frightened her. She tried to get up, but her legs gave way under her, and her head throbbed so sickeningly that she was thankful to lie back again. She wondered, half-dazedly, how long she would have to lie there before help came. She never doubted but that help would come, sooner or later. She guessed that the school would be frantic about her being lost, and she had a hazy recollection of the fact that Rufus had helped to track the Robin. He would help to find her, and then she would be taken back to the Chalet School. Once there, she would honestly behave herself, and be as good as she knew how.

"I'd just despise to be anything else!" she thought. "Oh, I wish my head would stop aching for a bit! How cold and damp it is! There must be a fog!"

By this time she was half-delirious, and had no idea that she was talking aloud. It never crossed her mind to wonder why "Herr Arnolfi" hadn't come on her. She had forgotten all about him. By and by she fell into an uneasy slumber, in which she tossed and moaned, talking at intervals in rapid undertones.

It was a mercy for her that help was very near. At the moment when she had been making her effort to escape, Grizel, Joey, and Friedel von Glück were entering the cleft in the mountain-side, and the young man was fastening one end of the first of the enormous balls of string which they had brought to a bush just outside. All three had torches, and all three had spare batteries with them. Friedel carried a tiny flask of brandy in one pocket and some bandages in the other, though the girls knew nothing of these. Time enough to tell them when they were needed, he thought. Joey had stuffed her pockets full of ripe gooseberries, which she had snatched from a dish in the Speise-

and, running his fingers across the strings, sounded a shower of silvery notes which the echoes took up, returning them in an elfin chorus of beauty which would have enchanted the child had she heard it under other circumstances. As it was, she had to clench her hands and set her teeth to keep herself from springing up and screaming.

The old man paid no heed to her. He lifted up his voice, and howled—no other word will describe the sounds he made!—a song about a beautiful lady and her true knight up to the vaulted roof. It was terrible; and the mocking echoes made it far worse. When he had finished it he started another, and he went on singing—or howling —for nearly two hours. After that he advanced once more to the throne, picked up the girl, and, carrying her over to the heap of deer-skins on which she had wakened, laid her down.

"My little princess looks weary and must sleep," he said, covering her over very gently; but there was a strength in his hands which the terrified girl sensed rather than felt. She dared not dispute him. She lay submissively still, and when he had attended to the torches, and replaced with fresh ones those which were flickering to their death, he went and lay down himself before an opening which she rightly guessed to be the entrance from the passage. He was asleep in a minute, and his snores resounded through the cave.

Cornelia waited a full half-hour. Then she got up cautiously, slipped off her shoes, and, carrying them in her hand, went towards another opening she had noticed when she had been wandering round the cave before. She had just reached it, when she suddenly heard a wild yell of rage, and, looking back she saw him leaping across the floor to her. With a scream of uncontrollable terror she rushed through the entrance, and made off down a path which felt damp to her feet. She tore on, expecting every minute to feel his claw-like grasp on her shoulder. Suddenly, she crashed into something with stunning force. A blaze of stars followed; then thick darkness, and she knew no more.

"The gracious lady must be careful," he said reproachfully. "You shiver, my little princess. Are you cold? Permit that I wrap this round you."

He picked up one of the skins, and drew it round her shoulders; then stooping, he picked her up, and carried her to the other side of the place, where two pillars rose on each side of a mound, forming a kind of fantastic throne, on which he placed her.

How it was Cornelia managed to keep her senses was something no one was ever able to understand. Jo declared after it was all over that she would have died if it had been she. However, she *did* keep them, and, when he brought some bread and a handful of berries, she even managed to control herself sufficiently to take them and eat them. He brought her a wooden cup full of water, and she drank it thankfully. When her meal was over she felt better, and rose from her seat, anxious to explore.

She had been right in coming here, so far as the caves were concerned—she recognised that. Margia had been quite correct when she had guessed the cleft to be the entrance. Cornelia looked round her in wonder at the white, gleaming walls. What could it be? She thought it looked like diamonds. Wondering, she scraped her finger over the nearest pillar, and then took it to her lips. Salt! It was salt!

She knew of the great salt-mines in the Salzburg district at Hall, nearer to Innsbruck. It was evident that this was a kind of off-shoot from them, and, if that was so, then these caves would be of even more value to the people than Joey had imagined. She wondered where her strange host was, and glanced round. He had stolen on noiseless feet to a nearby pillar, and was standing there, watching her with a child-like smile of benevolence.

"I wish to go farther," she said in halting German, forcing her lips to utter the words.

He shook his head. "But no, gracious lady. That may not be. This is your home, little princess, and here you must dwell till the queen come to you. But have no fear! I, Sigismund Arnolfi, will guard you, and keep all harm from you. Does the gracious lady will that I sing for her?"

Terrified lest she should rouse his anger, Cornelia agreed, and the strange creature took her hand in a claw-like grasp, and led her back to the throne, on which he seated her. Then from some niche he took down a zither,

Joey, go and dress at once, and put on thick shoes. You also, Fräulein Grizel.—Fräulein Marani," he turned to Gisela, "you must find me some brandy. We may need it!"

The girls hurried off to do his bidding, and an hour later found the three who formed the vanguard of this wild expedition creeping along the mountain, hunting for the cleft.

Could poor terrified Cornelia have known how near they were, things would have been better. Unfortunately, she had no idea that help was coming, and it seemed to her as if she was alone—abandoned to the tender mercies of a maniac.

When she had awakened, shortly after five in the afternoon, it had been to find herself in a gigantic hollow place, full of pillars that glittered in the light cast by rude torches which someone had lit and placed in holes here and there. The shape was nearly circular, and for a moment Cornelia lay and wondered if she were dreaming. She seemed to have got into some fairies' palace. Then, there was a movement near her, and, looking round, she repressed a scream with difficulty, for coming towards her was the man she recognised as being the lunatic of Grizel's and Joey's story of the Robin's rescue. He came softly, smiling at her, and with a strange light in his crazy blue eyes which scared her. "The gracious lady has slept long," he said in his soft, mumbling patois. "Almost I thought her under a spell, and would not open her eyes for a century. What does the gracious lady will that I, her servant, shall do for her?"

With a mighty effort Cornelia pulled herself together, and stood up. "Take me back," she said.

He shook his head with a cunning smile. "Nay, gracious lady. That may not be. They who come here are prisoners of the Kobolds and other fairy-folk. Anything but that!"

He had raised his voice as he spoke, and it boomed through the great pillared cave, echoing and re-echoing weirdly among the pillars. He came nearer as he spoke, and stretched out his hand to her. Cornelia shrank back against the pillar under which she had been lying. In her movement, she tripped over the deer-skins which had formed her bed, and reeled, and would have fallen had not the maniac caught her, and set her gently on her feet again.

to think of *where* Cornelia could have gone. The rest just mooned about—to quote Mary Burnett—and did nothing.

The great fear in everyone's heart was that the child might have got herself into difficulties on one of the mountain slopes, and might be lying, even now, hurt and helpless. Their main consolation was that she could not have fallen into the lake, since she had been going in the opposite direction. At nine o'clock the middles were sent to bed, and the seniors were made to follow at half-past. Only Grizel sat with the old girls, her face white with anxiety, while the staff still searched through the nearby pine-woods, even Mademoiselle having gone with them.

Herr von Glück was with the five girls in the study, having just come back from a fruitless hunt through the woods across the little stream. He was tired and hungry, and Grizel had gone to the kitchen to get Luise to bring *Kaffee und Butterbrod* for him. She had just returned with her laden tray when there came the sound of bare feet running down the stairs, and then Joey, clad only in her pyjamas, and with her hair standing on end, burst into the room. She paid no heed to anyone but Grizel, on whom she flung herself. "Grizel! I believe I know where she's gone! It's the caves! Don't you remember all the questions she's asked about them? Well, I believe she's gone off to try to find them on her own! Come on! I'm going to fetch her out!"

"Oh *no*, Joey!" It was Gisela who spoke, springing to her feet, and nearly overturning the tray the captain now held. "You must not! Think of what Madame would say!"

"I'm going," repeated Jo, her jaw set square. "I *am* thinking of Madame! If she knew about this, it would be enough to kill her. Grizel and I are the only two who know exactly where that entrance is, and, if we go, we can get there without wasting any time. She must be brought back before Madge has to hear about it, and I'm *going*!"

Herr von Glück set down the tray, and spoke with determination. "I will come with you, Fräulein Joey. What you say is right.—Listen, Wanda." He turned to his betrothed. "I will take Fräulein Joey and Fräulein Grizel with me now, and we will set off at once. You must tell the others, and bid them follow us. We will take string, so that we may leave a guiding cord for them to follow, and so that we may not lose our way when we are returning. Fräulein

over her. She had no knowledge of being carried for some two miles thus, and then being laid down on a heap of deerskins, while the strange being who had found her hung over her, and talked to himself in queer gutturals.

It was, in point of fact, nearly five o'clock when she awakened, and by that time the whole valley had been roused, and was out searching for her. Dr Jem had been summoned from the Sonnalpe, and had come down to hear that she had vanished. She had not gone *downwards*, for she had not been seen on any of the trains. Equally, no one had met her on the mountain path leading to Spärtz. The only clue they had to go on was that she had bought apples at one of the cottages on the way to Lauterbach; but that she had not gone on to the great Tiern Pass was proved, for a party of German students came that way, and they all agreed that they had seen nothing of a little girl with fair bobbed hair, a blue cotton frock, and a short brown coat.

"Can she have tried to go up the Tiernjoch?" questioned Grizel of Jo.

"Goodness knows," was Jo's gloomy response. "I don't *think* so, though. She's not keen on climbing—you know the fuss she made about going up to the Bärenbad alpe."

Grizel flashed a quick glance at her. "Dr Jem won't tell Madame yet, Joey," she said.

"My goodness! I hope not!" returned Jo vigorously. "It would make her ill if she knew!"

Mademoiselle came up to them at this moment—a distraught Mademoiselle, with her hair untidy, and her face white. "Come, *mes enfants*. You must come and eat. Going without food will help no one!"

The two turned and followed her in from the garden where they had been talking. There was wisdom in her words, as they knew. They sat down at the table and ate their bread and butter, and drank their milk in silence, which even the talkative middles didn't break. Once, towards the end of the meal, Marie turned to her next-door neighbour, Deira. "It's almost as if the Kobolds had carried her off," she said seriously.

"Ah, then, hold your tongue, will you?" said Deira in answer, and Marie obeyed.

When they had finished, the girls wandered out again, and roamed restlessly about the grounds. The younger middles clustered together in the flower-garden, and tried

hill. It was quite dry underfoot, and as she went, the roof, which had been low at first, seemed to rise. There was no sound to be heard save the ring of her own feet on the hard ground, and many children would have been terrified. Not so Cornelia! She had made up her mind that she was going to discover those caves and discover them she would. Of what dangers might be ahead of her, she never even thought.

When she had been walking a long time—or so it seemed—she came to a kind of cross-roads. This was the first check she had received, and she looked in dismay as she wondered which way she ought to take. She was tired now, for she had been up all night, and her legs were aching. With a little sigh, she sank down on the ground, and stared dismally round her. What should she do?

As if in answer to her question, one of the apples in her coat pocket rolled out, and trundled off on the path that led to the left as if setting forth on a journey on its own account.

"I'll go that way," decided Cornelia, getting on to her weary feet again. "Of course, they said that the caves were probably under the lake, so this must be the path. But I wonder where the others go."

She stooped down, picked up the apple, which had come to rest against a hump in the ground, and walked on, munching as she went. She was dreadfully tired and only her indomitable will kept her going. Suddenly she tripped up over an unexpected depression in the earth, and fell headlong. She was not hurt, but she felt that she simply could not drag herself one step farther. She *must* rest a little before she went on!

She stretched herself out, sighing for very relief, and switched off her torch. The air was fairly fresh here, and she had sense enough to realise that she must not waste light. The thick darkness which descended on her dismayed her a little, but she argued that she didn't need a light to rest by. Then weariness did its work, and before she had grasped anything she was asleep.

For long hours she lay there, slumbering as peacefully as if she were in her own bed. She never heard light, stealthy steps coming along the passage, nor saw the flare of a rude torch of pinewood and resin. Neither did she feel herself lifted up in strong arms, and borne on steadily, while a cracked voice murmured exclamations of wonder

woods and took no notice of it, as Matron certainly would have done.

Cornelia waited till she heard the last door shut, keeping herself awake by sitting up in bed; and when she thought she had given everyone sufficient length of time to fall asleep, she got up, dressed herself with the utmost quietness, and climbed out of the window on to the balcony. From there it was an easy matter for her to drop to the ground, and then she set off at her best pace, making for the cleft in the rock of which the girls had spoken that afternoon; while Frieda, who had been disturbed by the sound of her drop, sat up and looked round her wonderingly. However, Frieda could not see through the curtains; she decided that it must have been a dream, and lay down again, and was soon fast asleep. Cornelia was not missed till *Frühstück* next morning, and by that time she was safely at the cleft, and making her way in, undeterred by any fears, though, had she known what was before her, she would have turned tail, and never stopped running until she was safely back at school.

CHAPTER XX

IN THE CAVES

IT was almost eight o'clock when Cornelia reached the cleft of which Jo and Grizel had spoken. She recognised it at once—long, and narrow, and almost under the mountain. She was hungry, so she sat down and ate one of the apples she had bought at a chalet on her way. Then, throwing away the core, and cleansing her fingers by the simple method of licking them, she felt in her pocket to see that the two new batteries she had put there were all right, switched on her torch, and squeezed her way in.

She found herself in a dark, narrow passage, which went on as far as she could see. Walking warily, for she had no desire to tread on any snakes, and one *might* have made its home here, she went slowly along, her torch casting its bright light on the ground in front. For a long way the passage went fairly straight, then it suddenly took a sharp turn to the left, and she found that she was going down-

Right below here, you know, and along nearly to where the river turns to enter the valley. I can't tell you exactly, but that's the direction. It is a long, narrow cleft. I don't think we'd have noticed it if we hadn't seen that awful old man and the Robin." She glanced round to make sure that none of the juniors were anywhere near, but they had gone off on some business of their own, and there were only the seniors and the middles round them. "You cut across that grass-land, and turn round to the left. It's right under the mountain, really. They say, you know, that that old lunatic has come back. Herr August told us at Marie's wedding."

"Only he called him a demon," added Jo. "They all think he comes from hell, I believe, and I know they think he was going to carry off the Robin to hell!"

The return of the juniors from their expedition put an end to the tale, and they all moved off in other directions. But *one* young person had heard all she wanted, and it would not be Cornelia's fault if she did not get ahead of them in finding the caves. "And that'll be one in the eye for Joey and that pig Grizel!" she thought complacently to herself. Her greatest difficulty would be in getting away. She must manage it through the night, if she could. Fortune favoured her for once. Matron, who had been looking rather white and poorly, now owned to a head-ache, which increased so that when they got home she was only fit for bed.

"You must go at once," said Miss Maynard. "As for Cornelia—I'm sure you don't want a tiresome child next door to you to-night—she can go over to Le Petit Chalet for the night. I'll tell her to get her things."

When Miss Maynard made up her mind to a thing it was generally done quickly. On this occasion Cornelia found herself bundled off to Le Petit Chalet, along with three or four other middles, who had had to turn out to make room for the four old girls. Her joy when she found that she was given a window cubicle was great. She had managed to secrete her electric torch, and she went to bed with unusual serenity. One of her minor grievances against the school lay in the fact that she was not allowed to sit up as long as she chose, and she generally made a fuss about this. To-night, however, she went off as quietly as the others, and unsuspicious Mademoiselle was under the impression that she was tired by the long day in the

that he was nice; and while Wanda and Grizel went on ahead with Paula and the other two English girls, she and Marie escorted him over the meadowland and through the dark pines, chattering away all the time. The newly arrived pair received quite a little ovation when they reached the picnic ground, and then everyone sat down to milk and cakes, while Wanda heard all the school news, and he was presented to various people of whom he had heard.

Cornelia, standing with Evadne, was introduced as "one of our American girls—this is the other." She was on her best behaviour for once, and her best behaviour was very charming. She soon induced the young man to talk of the caves, though he really knew little more than Marie, and the rest listened with deep interest.

"It would be topping if the entrance really could be discovered," said Mary, when he had finished.

"I think we've found it," said Jo quickly. Then she told them what she and Margia had discussed at Marie's wedding.

"It seems likely," he said, when she had finished. "As you say, the very fact that the peasants fear the spot would help to keep it secret through all these years. If it is so, then it is to you two that they will owe it. Herr Professor von der Witt is coming soon to see if he can find them. He is interested in the question, for he is a great geologist, as you may have heard."

"I do hope he finds the caves, and that they can be used for sight-seeing. But how will he manage? I'm certain none of the men round here will go near the place, even if they weren't all busy all the time," said Jo eagerly.

"He is bringing a party with him," said Herr von Glück. "I think he spoke of coming this week-end. We must bring him to see you—if Mademoiselle will permit," he bowed to Mademoiselle as he spoke; "then you and Fräulein Grizel can show him where your cleft is. That would save him a great deal of work, if it is really the entrance to the caves!"

"I'm sure it is," said Margia. "It's the only possible place."

"Could you show me whereabouts it is from here, Fräulein Grizel?" asked the captain.

Grizel got up from the log on which she had been sitting, and turned to the north. "It's over there, somewhere.

and we don't want to hurry if we can help it. Go and join the others, Evadne and Cornelia."

It must be admitted that Grizel's tones were rather dictatorial, but she really felt out of patience with them. Cornelia, at any rate, had no right to ask to go. The head girl considered that she had done very well to be let off her punishment as it was.

Evadne turned away, with a growled "Guess I want to see Wanda as much as anyone!" Then she made off to join Frieda and Simone, who were looking for last year's pine-cones.

Cornelia sat down on a nearby stump, a gloomy frown on her face, and glared after the departing girls. She hated Grizel at that moment. She could have gone off if she liked then, for no one was watching her, but she had got it into her head that Herr von Glück might be able to tell her more about the caves than Marie knew.

"Silly kid!" commented Grizel, looking back and seeing her.—"Come on, you folk! It's a good way to walk in this heat."

They strolled along, glad of the shade in the pines. When they reached the edge of the forest they would have to cross the open pasture-land, and the sun was blazing down. The great limestone crags of the mountains glared white beneath its rays, and the Tiern See was blue as a piece of lapis-lazuli. No breath of wind stirred its calm surface, and it was so still that their own voices sounded louder than usual.

"Ouf! It's hot!" panted Mary, who was scarlet with the heat. "If it's like this in May, what will it be like in June?"

"Well, June's nearly here," said Rosalie, who still contrived to keep cool and fresh. "Next Sunday will be the first. Oh, look! Isn't that the boat setting off from Seespitz? We'd better hurry a little."

"Heaps of time," said Grizel easily. "It's got to go to Buchau first, and it doesn't hurry itself."

Still, they broke into a trot, and managed to get to the landing just as the graceful little white steamer neared the moorings. Five minutes later they were welcoming Wanda and her fiancé. Herr Hauptmann Friedel von Glück was a tall, dark young man, with a pleasant face and a merry laugh, and it was obvious that he adored his lovely Wanda, who looked more like a fairy-tale princess than ever in her white frock and big shady hat. Jo made up her mind

"People who live in glass houses shouldn't throw stones. That's your fifth, anyhow! And Evadne is outdoing all of us!"

"Well, you aren't a bad second," laughed Miss Durrant, who was sitting near enough to hear them. "More milk, Robin?"

The Robin nodded her head—her mouth was too full for speech. The mistress attended to her wants, and then turned to see that Cornelia, who was sitting on the other side of her, had all she required.

Strictly speaking, Cornelia should not have been there, but it was not in Mademoiselle's heart to deprive her of the fête, and she had told her that the rest of her punishment should be remitted. We do not wish that our old girls should have to see one of our present girls so punished, my child," the good lady had said gently. "So we will forgive you now, and you will try to do better, will you not?"

Cornelia had muttered something which might have been a promise to this effect. Mademoiselle hoped it was, and accepted it as such, so the young lady was out of durance vile and with the others once more. Her own friends still looked rather askance at her. They were a sinful crowd, but they had never aspired to the things she did, and, had they known what was at the back of her mind all the time, they would assuredly have cut her. After *Mittagessen* was over, and the baskets were repacked, the girls sauntered off in twos and threes to gather flowers, hunt for early wild strawberries, and chatter about school affairs. The three old girls stayed with the staff, talking; and Grizel, Joey, Rosalie, Mary, and Marie von Eschenau prepared to walk down to the boat-landing.

"Where's Paula?" demanded Joey just before they set off. "Oughtn't she to come too? Wanda's her cousin."

"She's over there with Cornelia and Evadne," said Mary, pointing. "Run and bring her, Joey, old thing."

Jo went off, and presently returned with the trio.

"Here, we don't want the entire crowd," protested Grizel. "You two run off and find the others. Paula may come if she likes; but not you, Evadne, nor you, Cornelia."

"Why not?" demanded Cornelia. "I want to see her."

"You'll see her when they get here. Now don't start making a fuss about it. Come along, you people. It's hot,

the gate which led to the mountain slopes. The middles had taken the food baskets; the seniors carried the big cans of milk; and the juniors bore long loaves of bread, which they would cut up when they began to eat. Everyone was responsible for her own mug, and the chalet was shut up for the day, Luise and Hansi going home for a short while.

"We've turned the people out of the Green dormy," said Grizel, who was walking with Bette, "and you people are to have your own old beds. Wanda is going into the Blue dormy where she was, Bianca being sent over to Le Petit Chalet. We shall be a full-house this week-end! It's hard luck Juliet couldn't come, isn't it?"

"I am sorry she isn't here," agreed Gisela. "I am very fond of Juliet. And now, my Grizel, how does it go with you this term? Is all well?"

Grizel shook her head. "I can't exactly say that, Gisela. D'you see that fair, fat child walking with Evadne?"

Gisela looked in the direction she was indicating, and nodded. "Yes; what is wrong with her, Grizel?"

"She's the limit!" said Grizel. "Honestly, Gisela, she's hopeless. What do you think of this?" and she plunged into an account of Cornelia's last activities.

Gisela listened in startled silence. "But what a senseless thing to do!" she exclaimed.

"Yes! I was pretty bad in the old days, but I never did a mad thing like that," said Grizel. "And she's so untruthful too!"

"Ah, well, *that* you never were," said Gisela. "You were full of mischief, Grizel, but we all knew that we could rely on your word."

"Hi, there, you people! Don't you want any *Mittagessen*?" Mary Burnett hailed them at this moment, and they found that the others had settled on a little clearing and were already laying the cloth, and setting out the eatables. They made haste to join them, and presently they were all sitting round, and eating as if they hadn't seen food before that day.

"It's funny how much more one can eat out of doors than in," sighed Jo, as she began on her seventh sandwich.

'Yes; I notice you generally eat enough for three when we picnic," observed Margia.

After that there was little talk of work. The old girls were welcomed vociferously, and escorted back to the chalet, where they were regaled on cakes and lemonade, while everybody talked at once, and tried to tell them all that had happened during the term.

"And Madame, Joey?" said Gisela, when she could get in a word edgeways. "Maria told us when she wrote. How is she?"

"Topping!" said Jo. "Just wait till you see David. Imagine it, Gisela, I have two nephews and two nieces! Isn't it priceless?"

Gisela looked at her with a smile. "It must be very pleasant. I am glad for you, Joey."

A wild shriek from Marie at this moment startled all of them.

"Marie! What has happened?" demanded Grizel. "Anything stung you?"

"No! But oh, Grizel! Just think! Kurt, my eldest brother, is betrothed!"

"What? Who to?" exclaimed Jo, with a great lack of grammar.

Grizel's eyes fell on Bernhilda's fair face, rosy with blushes. "Why, it's Bernhilda!" she cried.

"Bernie! *You*?" gasped Jo. "I say! How splendid!"

Poor shy Bernhilda scarcely knew which way to look as they all crowded round her, asking questions and discussing the latest excitement at the top of their voices.

"So *that's* what you were driving at the other night, Frieda," said Margia, when they had calmed down a little. "I say! Aren't we growing up? Three of us engaged, and two going to be married soon! When are you going to do anything like that, Bette?"

Bette laughed, and shook her pretty head. "You must wait, Margia."

The arrival of the staff made fresh pandemonium, for everyone wanted to tell them the news. When they understood it, they wished Bernhilda every happiness, and she was the centre of attraction till Mademoiselle, having pity on her discomfort, suggested a move to the pine-woods where they were to picnic. "Some of you may go to meet Wanda and Herr von Glück by the three o'clock boat," she said. "And now, who will carry the baskets?"

They all made for the house to load themselves up, and presently they were straggling across the playing-field to

Rosalie's as steady as old Time! We ought to have a very decent four this term!"

Then the bell rang for *Abendessen*, and they went in to struggle for a place at the Splasheries, and make themselves tidy.

CHAPTER XIX

CORNELIA TAKES HER CHANCE

ON the Friday Wanda von Eschenau and her betrothed arrived at three o'clock in the afternoon. Gisela, Bernhilda, and Bette had come up in the morning, and Stephanie from Lauterbach had walked to school in time for prayers. There were lessons for half the morning, then all work was at an end. A message had been sent down to Herr Anserl to say that the girls would not be having music lessons that afternoon, and Grizel, at any rate, had heaved a deep sigh of relief. "Thank goodness! I've scarcely looked at my Bach, and what I know about those Scriabin preludes would go into a nutshell! I must get up early and have a go at them to-morrow, for he'll expect them to be almost perfect by Tuesday."

Jo, whose music was of a very negligible quality, and who had patient Mademoiselle for a teacher, grinned. "If you mean those awful caterwauling things I heard you struggling with last night, I'm not surprised! There's neither tune nor meaning in them!"

"Oh yes, there is!" said Margia, who had learnt two of the preludes. "It's only because Grizel doesn't know them yet."

"The first one is a brute," declared Grizel. "Groups of three against groups of five! And he knows I hate contrary rhythms!"

"I wanted to do that one badly," said Margia wistfully, "but he wouldn't hear of it."

At this point in the conversation Evadne had dashed up to shriek excitedly that the boat was leaving Buchau at the other side, and there was a wild stampede to get hats and make for the Briesau landing, where they all stood waiting till the little lake steamer would come in.

"We've been in some tight places, you and I," pursued Jo. "That makes us more than just ordinary friends, Griselda, my lamb."

"I'm glad you look on it like that, Jo. Oh, I'll come if I can! I don't often yarn, but you know how much I owe Madame and the Chalet School! It's been home to me these last four years."

"It can be home to you still," said Jo. "There's Evadne on the yell for us! What does she want *now*?"

Evadne came racing over the grass to them, shrieking their names as she came. "Gri-zel—Joey! Come on and play tennis! Rosalie's bagged the end court, and we're waiting!"

The two ran, glad on the whole for this interruption. Neither of them was in the habit of discussing her feelings, and both felt a little awkward about it, now that it was over. A fast set of tennis was just the thing they wanted.

It was also the thing they got. Rosalie was a steady player, and Evadne was brilliant on occasion, with a service which could be untakeable at times. Grizel was promising to be more than average, and Jo played a good average game, with odd flashes of inspiration and an uncanny gift for placing her balls, which made her a difficult opponent when she used it, as she did this evening.

The set finished, leaving Rosalie and Evadne as the victors with a score of nine-seven to their credit. Every point had been hotly contested, and the winners had only just got their two games.

"We're jolly good, aren't we?" said Jo most immodestly, as they walked together to the games-shed to put away the balls. "That last service of yours was a brute, Evvy! I couldn't do a thing with it!"

"No one ever called you conceited, did they?" teased Rosalie.

Jo laughed. "I didn't mean it *quite* like that! But you must own that we aren't bad for school-girls, anyhow!"

"You'd be a good deal better if you'd only think what you were doing *all* the time instead of only occasionally," Grizel told her severely. "You can play decently when you try, but half the time you simply make wild swipes at the ball, and send it into the net or out of the court."

Jo did not look very much disturbed at this stricture, but she said, "Well, anyhow, *you* are awfully good, and

Jo! If only Juliet could come, we should be all here at once, for Stephanie would come too. And as so many of us are leaving this term, I don't suppose we'll get another opportunity to be all together again."

They trooped off to the flower-garden, where the staff were taking their ease in deck-chairs, and Jo proffered her request.

"I am glad you like the idea," said Mademoiselle, smiling. "I have already written to our dear girls, and they are all coming, so Friday, Saturday, and Sunday we will make a little fête."

Jo swung off her hat, and waved it above her head. "Three cheers for Mademoiselle!" she cried. "Come along, all of you!"

They cheered with a vim. Then, seeing that the staff probably wanted their free time to themselves, Grizel herded the noisy group away, and they went discussing the unexpected holiday in all its aspects. "It won't be quite like old times, though," said Grizel with a sigh to Jo, when they were alone a little later on. "Madame will not be with us."

Jo followed the direction of her gaze towards the Sonnalpe, and nodded. "No; but you can tell her all about it when you go up for the week-end."

Grizel looked at her curiously. "Jo! Don't you mind our going without you?"

Jo shook her head sturdily. "Of course I don't. I've had a week with her—or five days, anyway. Of course, I haven't seen much of her; but I've been there, anyway. And I shall see lots of her later on!"

"And I shan't," sighed Grizel. "I'm dreading Florence, Joey. I feel as if I should never come back, once I get there!"

"That's rot," said Jo. "You might as well say that when I go to Belsornia to be with Elisavita *I* shall never come back! But I jolly well *shall*! I'll always come in the hols—and so must you!"

"It's different for you, Jo. You're sisters; I'm only a friend!"

Jo's black eyes grew soft. "You've been a good friend, Grizel. We'll want you, and you must come. Think of all we've done together."

Grizel turned away once more, and looked up at the beautiful mountain on the other side of the lake.

"That's like Madame," said Mary. "She is the fairest person I've ever met, I think."

"We've some news for you—guess what?" chimed in Margia.

"Yes; make her guess!" laughed Rosalie. "Come along, Jo."

Jo thought hard, screwing up her mouth and frowning deeply the while. "Someone else is engaged," she hazarded.

"No! Not that! And who is there, anyway?"

"Well, Bette might."

"At seventeen and a half? Talk sense, Joey!"

"There's Bernhilda."

"No: Bernhilda is not betrothed *yet*!" said Frieda, nodding her head as if she could tell secrets if she only would.

Jo was on her in a flash. "Do you mean she's going to? Who to?"

But Frieda only shook her head, and refused to state, in spite of all their eager entreaties.

"Well, they've put the trains on early, as it's such glorious weather."

"I don't think much of your guessing capacities!" said Grizel scornfully. "The trains *were* put on on Monday, but it won't make a lot of difference to us just now."

"Someone's coming to see us, then?"

"Ah, now you're getting at it. Yes; guess who."

"Elisaveta?" asked Jo excitedly, her mind going to this dear friend of hers.

"Elisaveta may be coming, but no one has told us of it," said Marie von Eschenau. "No; it's Wanda and Friedel."

"Marie! You little horror!" cried Rosalie. "You shouldn't have told!"

"Oh well, I was going to say them next," said Jo easily. "How topping! When are they coming, Marie?"

"On Friday. Tante Sofie is coming with them, and Wanda is to stay here, but Friedel is to go to the Kron Prinz Karl. They are coming for three days while Tante Sofie visits her cousins in Innsbruck, and then they will go back with her."

"Gorgeous! It will be nice to have Wanda again! Perhaps Gisela and Bernhilda could come too, and Bette as well! Then it would be almost like old times again! What do you think, Grizel?"

"Let's go and ask Mademoiselle. It's a splendid idea,

seven o'clock she put in the last stitch, and that part of her punishment was over.

Miss Durrant came for her then, and made her wash her face and hands, brush her hair, and come for a walk along the lake-side. "You have had no exercise to-day," she said quietly, "and that will not do. Get your hat; the sun is still hot."

Cornelia did as she was told in sulky silence, but, as Miss Durrant had no idea of talking to her, her silence fell rather flat. She was out for an hour; then she was brought back, and sent to bed in the sick-room, which was the only one of the rooms to be without a balcony, so there was no possible escape from it, for it opened into Matron's room, and that lady was popularly reported to sleep with one ear open.

Joey came back on the next day, and was promptly assailed by several people all wanting to know how "Madame" was; what the baby was like; and when they were going to see them both. She was willing to chatter now, but she still had that curiously older air. "Madge is splendid," she said, "and the baby's a dear! He's got the duckiest little hands and feet you ever saw, and heaps of soft, black hair."

"What are they going to call him?" asked Grizel.

"David, after my father," said Jo. "And James too, of course."

"David James Russell," said Simone, trying it over to see how it sounded. "I think it is veree nice, Joey."

"Oh, so do I!" put in Evadne eagerly. "What will they call him for short?"

"David, of course. Madge objects to Dave, which was what Dr Maynard suggested. All the same," added the baby's aunt with a chuckle, "I bet he'll be Davy before very long!"

"But that is a pretty name too," said the Robin, who had been listening. "Joey, when are Grizel and I to see him? I do so want to see a very *little* baby!"

"The week after next," said Jo. "You and Grizel are to go up for the week-end, and I'm coming for the Sunday."

"But why not for the whole time with us?" objected Grizel.

"Madge says it wouldn't be fair. I've just had a week with her, and she thinks I ought not to have any more than just a day till half-term now."

Stevens to send Mademoiselle to her. "And at *once*!" she concluded. Then she turned back to where Cornelia was lying. "We'll see what Mademoiselle has to say to this, miss! Of all the outrageous things to do! You deserve a good sound whipping!"

And this is exactly what Mademoiselle thought when she surveyed the beds.

A long lecture, the confiscation of her pocket-money for three weeks, gating to grounds, and five French fables to be learned and repeated to the irate Head of the school were among her punishment. But what she felt far more was Matron's decree that she should take all the beds and the bedding, put everything outside in the garden to dry, and, when it was ready, remake all the beds. The mattresses were to be hung over the balcony; the clothes to be carried downstairs, and spread out on the playing-field. Finally, the mattresses were to be put into fresh covers, and Cornelia was to do it.

It took her all day, and Matron saw to it that she had nothing but dry bread and milk till it *was* done. What made this one of the sharpest parts of her punishment was that fact that Herr Marani came up from Innsbruck for a short visit, and brought with him a big basket of his wife's cakes for them.

Sitting on the floor of the dormitory, stitching at one of the hated covers, Cornelia shed bitter tears as she heard the others making merry over the cakes which they had with their *Kaffee* out-of-doors, as they usually did when the day was hot. She heard the Robin's exclamation of, "Me, I love Herr Marani!" followed by Maria's, "Mamma has made these cakes even better than usual!" and she looked with loathing at the plate of dry bread and the big cup of milk which Luise had brought up for her.

Her first idea was to go on a hunger strike, and refuse to eat what they had given her, but Matron's contemptuous "Well, it won't hurt you to fast for once!" put an end to *that*. With tears dripping saltily down her face, she swallowed the hated meal, and then turned again to her task. She would have rebelled against it if she had dared, but she knew that if she did Matron would keep her word, which was that she should have no play at all till it was done, and that she should also do the other beds which would be changed at the week-end. So she kept on, and by came *Kaffee und Kuchen,* and after that tennis or cricket. *Abendessen* was at seven, and when it was over, they were free till bedtime. Work was considerably lightened too, so that the short preparation periods might be sufficient, and all practice had to be done before *Frühstück,* which was at a quarter to eight.

Under these circumstances Cornelia found that it was not going to be easy to get away. This upset her so badly that she became a perfect nuisance in lessons—fidgeting, not attending, and answering the mistresses with so much impertinence when called to order that it was scarcely surprising that she found herself in the black books of the entire staff. Finally, she came into violent collision with Miss Maynard, and was marched off to bed—the only punishment she appeared to mind—and there left to come to her senses.

It would have been a good opportunity for slipping off if Matron had not been working in the room across the passage, and there could be no question of her climbing down from the balcony, for the Lower Fourth's form-room was immediately beneath the dormitory, and they would have seen her. Since getting away was out of the question, the young lady proceeded to revenge herself for her punishment by getting the sponges of the seven other people who slept in the same dormitory, soaking them thoroughly, and placing them in the exact centres of their owners' beds. Then she retired to her own, and lay looking again—for it was becoming a characteristic pose with her—as if butter wouldn't melt in her mouth.

Her suspicions aroused by the silence in the Yellow dormitory—the last time Cornelia had been sent to bed she had sung all the songs she knew at the top of her voice—Matron came in to see if all was right. So far as she could judge there was nothing wrong—except Cornelia's expression. *That* was too good to be true! Matron looked round the room sharply. Then her eye was caught by a spot of wet on Paula von Rothenfels's counterpane. She made a dive, threw back the clothes, and displayed a nicely soaked bed. Five minutes later all the beds had been taken to pieces, and there were the wet sponges. They had been there for half an hour, so the beds were thoroughly damp.

Just at that moment the bell rang for break, and Matron, popping her head out of the window, called to Margia

that horrid Jo!" She didn't say so to Marie, who would have been up in arms at once at the merest suggestion of it. All she *did* say was, "What a funny idea!"

"But I think it is a very good one," said Marie in her soft, pretty voice. "The people here are so poor, and such a sight would mean a great deal to them. So I hope Jo and Grizel find the caves, for that would be a very nice thing to be able to say that it was they who had done it; though I know they do not think of it that way."

Cornelia said nothing, and as the bell rang just then, summoning them to *Kaffee und Kuchen*, she had a good excuse for making no answer. But to herself she thought, "Oh, *will* they? I know better!"

CHAPTER XVIII

JOEY RETURNS

CORNELIA fully intended to carry out her great scheme as soon as possible, but various events occurred which made it impossible. To begin with, she was watched carefully by Matron and the prefects. Matron's opinion of the young lady was that she was a little demon, and goodness knew what she would do if left to herself. The prefects' impression was that there was more in her than met the eye. Grizel, who had herself been a nuisance in the early days of the school, was aware that the American child was quite likely to break out sooner or later, so warned the others to be careful.

Time was fully planned out at the school, and, though the girls had a certain amount of freedom, there was also a good deal of supervision—more so than in many English boarding-schools. Besides, in the summer term there was always more to do, and the girls devoted a great deal of their time to games. These were compulsory, and had to be played in the evenings, as the afternoons in summer were very hot as a rule. Work began at half-past eight, and went on till a quarter to one. This included preparation periods. After *Mittagessen* there was an hour's rest, when they went to their cubicles and lay down. After that they had singing, sewing, hand-work, or music-lessons. Then

They must have gone away after this, for Cornelia heard no more, but what she *had* heard had roused every bad feeling in her. She literally squirmed as she lay there thinking, thinking what she could do. Suddenly she sat up, rubbing her fair hair out of her eyes. "The caves!" she said aloud. "That's how I can get back at them!"

Till that moment she had never given another thought to the caves since Thursday, which had been so eventful. Now they came rushing back to her memory. She knew no more than she had heard on that day, but she had realised then that they were of enormous importance to Jo. She had said something about the school having discovered them. Well, if she, Cornelia, were to go and find out the way herself, it wouldn't be the school, because she meant to write to her father and ask him to take her away at the end of the term. If she coaxed hard enough, she felt sure he would! Then, if she had to go and look for them, it would give the people in charge a nice fright when she wasn't to be found. It was a *lovely* plan!

She was so pleased with herself that she actually lay still, and when Matron came upstairs an hour later to tell her to get up and dress, she found the girl sound asleep. It took some shaking to waken her, but Matron accomplished it at last, and bade her hurry up and come downstairs. "And just try and keep your hands to yourself for the future!" she concluded.

Cornelia got up meekly, and dressed herself and came downstairs, looking, so Margia said, as if butter wouldn't melt in her mouth. Inwardly she was hugging herself with glee over her plan. She was very subdued for the rest of the day, and Matron, watching her, congratulated herself on having found a method of subduing a most unsubduable child. But all the time she was watching her opportunity, and, late in the afternoon, she managed to catch Marie von Eschenau alone, and asked her to come for a stroll.

Marie was a very nice child, but she was by no means clever. She felt sorry for Cornelia, who had had such a bad morning of it, so she agreed, and by the time they came in, Cornelia knew as much as she did about those caves. She also knew just why Jo Bettany was so keen on finding them. Cornelia had never spent a winter here, so she was unable to appreciate the reason behind Jo's idea, and it struck the American child as "rather mad, but just like

denly deprived of the American girl, and was still wondering, since Matron had given her no explanation.

To Mademoiselle, Matron had simply said that Cornelia was behaving very badly at table, and she had sent her to bed as punishment. Mademoiselle, her thoughts elsewhere, had scarcely listened, and merely replied that it was all right.

The greater part of the school was, of course, Roman Catholic, so only a very few were present in the big schoolroom for the service they had there, and inquiries as to Cornelia's whereabouts were only answered by Grizel's statement that Matron knew about it. When service was over the girls once more went into the garden. Most of them got chairs and books, and read quietly till the others came home. But Mary Burnett, Margia and Amy Stevens, and Signa Johansen elected to bring cushions, and sit under the great lime-tree that grew near the sick-room window. On the still air their voices floated up and, even as Grizel herself had done long since, she heard their opinion of her stated in clear unvarnished terms.

"I don't like Cornelia," said Amy, apparently *à propos* of nothing; for Margia answered, "Who on earth asked you to? And what makes you drag *her* up so suddenly?"

"Well, I was wondering where she was," explained Amy. "No one's seen her since Matey hauled her out from *Frühstück*."

"She's no loss," declared Mary. "She's an absolute little brute. Evadne's a monkey, but she's straight enough!"

"Cornelia tells lies," observed Amy slowly.

"She cheats," added Margia, who had already had one battle with Cornelia over the question.

"It's a jolly good thing she's not a Guide! She'd let us down wholesale!"

"Perhaps it's Guides she needs," suggested Mary. "After all, Margia, that's what Guides are *for*—to help people to play straight."

Grizel's voice was to be heard at this juncture calling Mary, so she evidently went, for Cornelia heard no more. However, Signa had something to say on the subject. "Is it because Cornelia is American and not English zat she does not play zee game?"

"Rats!" said Margia. "That's got nothing to do with it! Evvy's American, and she's as straight as a die! No; it's just general nastiness."

"Mademoiselle, will you excuse Cornelia?" she said, rising.

"Certainly, Matron," said Mademoiselle, who at the distant staff-table had seen nothing. "Go with Matron, Cornelia.—Simone, why do you weep?"

Simone pulled herself together, and murmured something unintelligible to anyone. Seeing that she appeared to be all right, Mademoiselle ceased her inquiries. She knew her young cousin to be given to tears on all occasions, and came to the conclusion that the child was missing Joey. That Matron's abstraction of Cornelia had anything to do with it never struck her at the time.

Meanwhile the new girl was marched off by Matron, and up to sick-room, where she was ordered to undress and go to bed.

"Why?" she demanded.

"You know well enough why," retorted Matron. "If you really don't, you can spend your time between now and *Mittagessen* in finding out! For sheer unpleasant, cowardly tricks, Cornelia Flower, you beat everything. A good whipping is what you deserve!"

Cornelia dared say no more. Matron was a martinet, and—well, that pinch bestowed on Simone would have an unpleasant sound if it were retailed to Mademoiselle. She undressed herself sulkily and got into bed, while Matron closed the jalousies after opening the slats to let the air in.

"There you stay till one o'clock," she said grimly, when she had seen Cornelia between the sheets. "If ever I catch you at such a nasty thing again, miss, I'll take you straight to Mademoiselle! And don't you dare to stir till I give you permission!"

With that she marched out, closing the door behind her, and leaving a thoroughly rebellious Cornelia to toss about and listen to the gay voices of the others as they wandered about the grounds in the interval before they went to church. She would have set Matron at defiance if she had dared. But even Cornelia the rebel drew the line at that. They were all rather in awe of Matron, and she was no exception to the rule. So she stayed there all through the pleasant, sunny hours, thinking how she could revenge herself on Jo, Matron, Frieda, Simone, and Grizel, whom she quite unfairly included in her vendetta, since that young lady had had no idea as to why she had been sud-

Her curly crop somehow made her look older than the floating curls had done, and the mistress realised that the girl was growing up almost as fast as Joey. "Things may turn out differently, Grizel," she said gently. "In two years' time you will be twenty. Other things may have come into your life by that time—you might not want to come back."

"Do you mean I might want to marry?" asked Grizel. "I don't think so, Miss Carthew. I can't imagine it anyway."

"Not now; and it's as well not to worry about it till it comes—if it does. But if it does, Grizel, it's one of the ends for which God made woman. Never forget that. Madame loved her school. She still loves it. But I think she would tell you that she is happier now than she ever thought she could be."

She changed the subject after that, but Grizel referred to it when they went in at the summons of the bell for *Frühstück*. "I will remember, Miss Carthew," she said. "Thanks for what you said just now."

They went in to find Cornelia and Frieda in the middle of a battle royal—a rare thing for quiet Frieda, who lived up to the meaning of her name on most occasions, and had earned for herself the title of "Peacemaker".

Frieda wouldn't, and Cornelia scarcely dared say what was wrong, so Grizel had to content herself with administering a conduct mark apiece to them, and sending them into *Frühstück* with the remark that they ought to be ashamed.

"I'm not!' said Cornelia defiantly.

"Then you ought!" snapped Frieda, so surprisingly, that Grizel nearly sent her to Matron to have her temperature taken. It was so unlike Frieda.

Cornelia contented herself by pulling a face at her adversary, and Grizel thought it wiser to take no further notice.

"Cornelia's a perfect little brute," she thought, as she ate her rolls and honey. "Just like what I used to be.— Mercy, Simone! What *is* the matter?" For Simone had suddenly dissolved into tears.

Matron, who was sitting at the next table, took matters in hand at once. She had been glancing across, wondering what made the head girl so grave, and she had caught sight of Cornelia administering a sharp nip to her next-door neighbour.

"Jo seems different since Thursday," she said to the mistress as they turned to go back.

Miss Carthew glanced at her. "Yes; she is beginning to grow up a little. But you needn't regret it, Grizel. We shall need some of our elder middles to grow up, for so many of you big girls are leaving this term."

Grizel nodded. "I know," she said. "Gertrud, Luigia, Lisa, Eva, Dorota, and me. Rosalie may go too, if her people come home, as they were saying. That leaves very few of our original girls indeed. Jo will be sixteen next term, though it hasn't seemed possible till this last day or two. I think she will make a splendid senior, don't you?"

"Yes," said Miss Carthew. "She has been very young for her age, of course; but this has made her older."

"Well, can you wonder? She adores Madame. We all do that, of course; but with Jo it's something much bigger."

"Someone else has grown tremendously this year, Grizel," said Miss Carthew, as she passed through the gate the head girl held open for her. "You have been a splendid head girl, dear. I don't know who will follow in your steps, but, whoever she is, she will have her work cut out to keep up with you four."

Grizel coloured. "Thank you, Miss Carthew," she said simply. "I *have* tried."

"And succeeded." The mistress laid her arm round the slender shoulders of the girl at her side. "I am only sorry I shall not be here next term to see how the school goes on when you, the last of the original 'big' girls, have left."

Grizel sighed. "That's the worst of getting fond of a place! You have to leave it. But after all, Miss Carthew, you are going because you are getting married. I've got to go because my people say so. Well, I've had four gorgeous years, and after all—I'm almost eighteen now; week after next I shall be—I suppose I've had my fair share of school-life. But I wish it wasn't coming to an end. I'd give worlds if I could think I might come back here to teach! But I never shall. I wouldn't teach music for anything on this earth, and father won't let me have a physical training. He won't even let me go to the Royal Holloway College to read maths. I did think he would agree to that, but he won't. It's to be two years in Florence, and then home, I suppose!"

Miss Carthew looked down at the pretty face at her shoulder. She was a very tall woman, and Grizel was small.

your hat," he said. "Put on strong shoes, and come at once."

Miss Maynard, who was standing near, turned white. "Jack! What is it?" she asked.

"Mrs Russell has a little son, born this morning, and she wants Jo," he said brusquely. Jo was off like a shot, and was back in almost less time than it takes to tell. They set out for the Sonnalpe, leaving a startled school behind them, and all thought of the caves passed completely out of the minds of everyone for the next twenty-four hours. It was not till a flushed and, wonderful to relate, tearful Jo reappeared on the scenes that they settled down to tranquillity again.

She had very little to say, but she assured them that the baby was a darling, and Madge was all right—now. She was to go up again on Sunday, and stay for a few days, and they hoped that Grizel and the Robin would be able to go up two weeks later. That was all she would say, and she remained uncannily reserved and taciturn for her. When Cornelia referred to the caves, she shook her off. "Bother the old caves! I don't care a toss for them! Go away and leave me alone!"

Cornelia went; but the patched-up peace was at an end as far as she was concerned. She would take jolly good care to get her own back somehow!

CHAPTER XVII

REBELLION

ON the Sunday, Jo departed for the Sonnalpe, accompanied by Miss Maynard, who wanted to see her brother, and bearing a message from the school to her sister, as well as a big armful of flowers from the garden, which the girls had all joined in gathering. Grizel, the Robin and Miss Carthew escorted them to the landing where the Chalet School boat was moored, and saw them off, Miss Carthew calling after them that they were to stay as long as they wanted, since everything would go well in their absence, while Grizel waved her hand silently.